PASQUALE'S ANGEL

PASQUALE'S ANGEL

Paul J. McAuley

An AvoNova Book

William Morrow and Company, Inc.
New York

AVON BOOKS
A division of
The Hearst Corporation
1350 Avenue of the Americas
New York, New York 10019

Library of Congress Cataloging in Publication Data:
McAuley, Paul J.
  Pasquale's angel / Paul J. McAuley.
    p. cm.
"An AvoNova book."
1. Rosso Fiorentino, 1494–1540—Fiction. 2. Painters—Italy—Fiction. I. Title.
PS3563.C332P37 1995   94-43615
813'.54—dc20   CIP

First Morrow/AvoNova Printing: June 1995

To V

Salai, I want to make peace with you,
not war. No more war, I give in.

LEONARDO DA VINCI,
from his notebooks

PART ONE

———— ❦ ————

The Feast
of Saint Luke

I

Morning, just after dawn. The sky, for once clear of the murk spewed by foundries and manufactories, the rich blue of the very best four-florins-to-the-ounce ultramarine. Men ambling to work along the Street of Dyers, leather-aproned, long gloves slung around their necks, hair brushed back and tucked under leather caps. Clogs clattering on flagstones, cheerful shouts, the rattle of shutters raised as the little workshops opened up and down the street. Apprentices hanging skeins of colored wool on hooks over workshop doors: reds, blues, yellows, vibrant in the crisp slanting light against flaking sienna walls. Then a hollow rapid panting as someone started up the Hero's engine which by an intricate system of pulleys and belts turned the paddles of the dyers' vats and drove the Archimedes' screw that raised water from the river. A puff, a breath, a little cloud of vapor rising above the buckled terracotta roofs, the panting settling to a slow steady throb.

Pasquale, who had drunk too much the night before, groaned awake as the engine's steady pounding shuddered through the floor, the truckle bed, his own spine. Last year, when things had been going badly— the scandal over the commission for the hospital of Santa Maria Nuova, and business, never more than a trickle, suddenly drying up—Pasquale's master, the painter Giovanni Battista Rosso, had rented rooms on the second floor of a tall narrow house at the eastern end of the Street of Dyers. Although one room was only a closet, and the second, where Pasquale slept, was not much more than a passage with a bed in it, the main room was airy and light, and had a pleasant aspect over the gardens of the Franciscan friars of Santa Croce. On winter mornings, Pasquale had lain late in bed and watched the swarming shadows made on the ceiling of the narrow room by the lanterns of the dyers' workmen as they passed by in the cold dark street below, and in spring he had turned his bed to face the opposite window so that he could watch the trembling dance of light and shadow cast through the leaves of the trees in the garden. But all that summer he had been woken at first light by the Hero's engine, and now its vibration mingled with the queasy throb of his hangover as he groped for and failed to find his cigarettes.

Too much wine last night, wine and beer, a great swilling indeed, and then he'd taken a turn at watch over the body of Bernardo, he and three others all armed with pistols in case corpsemasters discovered its hiding-place, all of them drinking thick black wine sweet as honey, waving the weapons about and as likely to shoot each other in drunken jest as any corpsemaster. Poor Bernardo white and still, his face seeming rapt in the light of the forest of candles burning at the head of his coffin, the two silver florins that shut his eyes glinting, more money than he'd ever had in his short life. Twelve years old, the youngest pupil of Jacopo Pontormo, Bernardo had been knocked down by a *vaporetto* that morning, his chest crushed by its iron-rimmed wheel, and his life with it. Altogether a bad omen, for he was killed on the seventeenth of October, the eve of the feast of Saint Luke, the patron saint of the confraternity of the artists of the city.

Other noises rising, floating through the open window. Automatic cannon signaling the opening of the city gates, their sounds arriving one after the other according to the law of propagation of waves through air, first near and loud, then farther and fainter. The clatter of a velocipede's wooden wheels over cobbles, its rider cheerfully whistling. Women, calling across the narrow street to each other, the small change at the start of the day. Then the bells of the churches, far and near, ringing out for the first mass. The slow heavy tolling of Santa Croce itself mixed with the beat of the dyers' Hero's engine and seemed to rise and fall as the two rhythms pulsed in and out of phase.

Pasquale made a last futile swipe for his cigarettes, groaned and sat up, and discovered himself fully clothed. He had a distinct impression that a surgeon had bled him dry in the night. Rosso's Barbary ape sat on the wide windowsill at the foot of the bed, looking down at him with liquid brown eyes as it idly picked at calcined plaster with its long flexible toes. When it saw that Pasquale was awake it snatched the blanket from his bed and fled through the window, screeching at the fine joke it had played.

A moment later a human cry floated up. Pasquale thrust his head out of the window to see what was going on. The window overlooked the green gardens of Santa Croce, and the young friar who had charge of the gardens was running up and down the wide white gravel path below, shaking an empty sack like a flag. "You keep that creature of yours inside!" the friar shouted.

Pasquale looked either side of the window: the ape had disappeared. He called down, "He *is* inside. You should be inside too, brother. You should be at your devotions, not waking up innocent people."

The friar said, "I tell you, he was after my grapes!" He was red in the face, a fat young man with greasy black hair that stuck out all around his tonsure. He added, "As for innocence, no man is innocent, except in the eyes of God. Especially you: your profane and drunken songs woke me last night."

"Well, pray for me then," Pasquale said, and withdrew his head. He couldn't even remember getting home, let alone singing.

The friar was still shouting, his voice breaking in anger the way that fat men's voices often do. I'll see to your grapes, Pasquale resolved, as he lit a cigarette with trembling fingers. The first puff was the test: the trick was not to inhale too deeply. Pasquale sipped cool green smoke cautiously, then more deeply when it seemed that he would not lose the contents of his stomach. He sat on his rumpled bed and as he finished the cigarette thought about angels, and Bernardo's sweet dead face. Bernardo's family would try and smuggle their son's body out of the city today, taking it back to Pratolino, beyond the jurisdiction of the corpsemasters.

Pasquale poured water into a basin and splashed his face. Combing his wet springy hair back from his forehead with his fingers, he went into the main room of the studio and found his master already at work.

Rosso and Pasquale had whitewashed the walls and floor of the big airy room just two weeks ago, and even at this early hour it glowed with pure light. The ape was curled up in the brocade chair, the blanket wrapped around itself, snoring contentedly, hardly stirring when Pasquale wandered in and Rosso laughed long and hard at his pupil's bedraggled state.

Rosso was working by the big window that overlooked the street. Its shutters were flung wide. He was using a feather to brush away charcoal from the lines of the underdrawing on the canvas that, sized, primed with oil, lead white and glue, had been standing against one wall for more than three weeks and was now propped on the worktable. He was barefoot and wore only his green work-apron, girdled loosely at his waist and falling to just above his knees. A tall pale-skinned man, with a shock of red hair stiff as porcupine quills, a sharp-bladed nose, and a pale-lipped mobile mouth. There was a smudge of charcoal on his forehead.

Pasquale picked a big goose-quill from the bundle on the worktable and lent a hand. Rosso said, "How are we this morning? Did Ferdinand wake you up as I asked him? And what was the good friar shouting about?"

Ferdinand was the Barbary ape, named for the late unlamented King of Spain.

"He waited until I was awake before he took the blanket. And he did it because he likes my smell, not because of anything you told him. You couldn't get him to drink a glass of water by asking if you chained him for a hundred days in the Araby Desert. As for the friar, he has a jealous soul. Do you like grapes, by the way? I've an idea to make our friend shout so loud he'll burst."

"You'd have Ferdinand steal those grapes? You

persuade him to do it, and I'll believe you can talk to him with your fingers."

Pasquale switched away the charcoal dust that had accumulated at the bottom of the canvas. The lines of the underdrawing had to be all but erased, or else they would show through, or even worse, tint, the oils.

"Master, why are you doing this now? Shouldn't you be dressed?"

"Why, I only just this minute got undressed."

"Out with your bumboy, I suppose."

"That," Rosso said, "is none of your business. Besides, just because you couldn't sweet-talk Pelashil into giving you more of that poison, there's no need to take it out on *me*."

"Pelashil? Did I try?" Pasquale did remember talking to her, never quite an argument, he more and more insistent about wanting to try the híkuri again, and she telling him that a drunken man would only be bewildered by the visions it gave, but she had come up and given him a kiss later, in front of everyone, and told him to come and see her when he was in his senses. Pasquale groaned, half in pleasure, half with guilt. Pelashil was the servant of Piero di Cosimo, a Savage brought back from the friendly shores of the New World and widely held to be his common-law wife. She was twice Pasquale's age, dark and heavy-haunched, but Pasquale was attracted by the challenge of keeping her attention long enough to make her smile. She had no time for small talk, and if conversation bored her she would turn away. Her silences were long, not so much sulky as self-absorbed; her sudden, flashing smile was all too rare. Strangely, what Pasquale took seriously, the euphoric híkuri dream, the sense of diving deep into the weave of the world, Pelashil maintained was nothing more than entertainment. She wouldn't even listen when he tried to tell her what he'd seen after he'd chewed the shriveled, nauseatingly bitter gray-green button she had fed him in her hot, brightly decorated little room.

Rosso, who understood his pupil, laughed and made the sign of a cuckold's horns on his forehead. "For shame, Pasqualino! You take advantage of a poor crazy old man."

"Perhaps I want to follow in his footsteps, and see for myself the New World. We could go, master, you and I. We could make a fresh start over."

Rosso said, "I'll not hold you to your contract if you want to leave. God knows you've learned all you will from me. Go if you want, but don't break an old man's heart and steal his servant. Old men need the warmth of women."

"Think of the light, master, and think that a man can live like a king for the rent you pay for this place."

"A king of Savages? What kind of honor is that?"

"I know you will tell me you have your reputation here," Pasquale said. "I'm sorry to have mentioned it. You should get dressed for the procession."

"We have plenty of time before the procession." Rosso stepped back and looked critically at the underdrawing. It was the deposition of Christ, looking down the length of His dramatically foreshortened body as He was tenderly cradled by His disciples. "Surely this can wait."

"I have to finish it in two weeks, or I'll be fined. That's what the contract stipulates."

"You've been fined before. And we have to finish the wall for that light-show."

Rosso had agreed to paint patterns on a newly plastered wall as part of an artificer's scheme to amaze

and entertain the Pope. Years ago, the spectacles celebrating the visit of a foreign prince would have been
entirely provided by artists; now, they were reduced
to assisting in the devices and designs of the artificers.

"We will paint the wall tomorrow. I can't afford to
break that contract, and neither can I afford to break
this one. We're close to asking Saint Mark for half
his cloak. Listen, if Signor di Piombino likes the picture, he may offer his private chapel to us. How
would you like that, Pasqualino? Perhaps I would be
able to engage new pupils."

"You'll have to find a new bed, then. Mine is too
narrow for two, and has a groove in it so deep I dream
I'm buried alive."

"It has to be narrow to fit in the room. Ah," Rosso
said with sudden exasperation, "what's the point of
new pupils anyway!" His mood had swung around
as it so often did these days. Pasquale knew his master was not recovered from the business with the director of the hospital, who had seen devils in the
sketch of a commissioned painting where saints
should have been, and loudly proclaimed how he had
been tricked to any who would listen. Rosso said,
"Maybe I'll let you do the whole chapel, Pasqualino.
But I feel like painting this, at least. It's time it was
finished. And there's that panel you've been working
on. When are you going to make a start on it? As for
this, don't worry, it'll be a piece of piss to do. We'll
start by shading it across, right side brighter than the
left. I sold one of your prints, by the way."

Pasquale had found some of yesterday's bread.
Chewing hard, he said, "Which one?"

"You know, the kind the women buy, the kind for
which they never quite dare ask outright. She was a
pretty woman, Pasquale, and blushed all over, I

swear, as she tried to make me understand what she
wanted. Put some oil on that bread, although how
you can eat after all you've drunk . . . you won't
spew, I hope."

Pasquale had made a number of studies for that
kind of print—they were called stiffeners, in the
trade. He had found a model in one of Mother Lucia's
girls, a compliant whore who would pose for pennies,
and hold the same pose for an hour or more without
complaint. He said, "Which one exactly? How much
did you get?"

"An early one," Rosso said carelessly. "Very virile,
with cocks running rampant through it."

"That? It was pirated this spring."

"Yes, and the copy has improved on your original—the passage with the arms of the man holding
the bladder and cock on a pole is much freer. Still,
our blushing customer wanted a print of the original,
which is a compliment of kinds, I suppose."

"Well, I'll do another." Pasquale wiped oil from his
hands on a bit of cloth and picked up the blackened
goose-quill. "Are you really going to use this underdrawing, or are you going to start over again?"

"Oh, I think this has promise. Although I don't
like the positioning of the two figures lifting the legs.
Maybe I'll move them back a little."

"It will spoil the lines of their arms, surely. Besides, if you lift a heavy weight, your arms are close
to your sides, so they must be close to the body."

"Here's my pupil, telling his master what he's
about."

"What about my fee for the print?"

"As for that, it is already spent. Don't look at me
like that, Pasqualino. One must pay rent."

"Yesterday you said the rent could wait."

"I didn't mean for the studio," Rosso said and winked.

"Which bumboy was it last night? The Prussian with the scar?" .

Rosso shrugged.

"He's a thief."

"You don't understand a thing, Pasqualino. Let an old man find love where he can. Is it your hangover making you mean?"

Rosso was twenty-four, only six years older than Pasquale.

Pasquale scratched the ape around the ears. The animal stirred, and sighed happily. Pasquale said, "We should get ready for the procession."

"We have hours yet."

"We have promised to collect the banners from Master Andrea. Master . . . do you think he'll be there?"

"It would be very rude of him not to be."

Raphael. They didn't need to name him. His name was on everyone's lips in the three days since he had arrived from Rome in advance of his master Pope Leo X.

Rosso added, "In any case, I must dress appropriately, and I haven't quite decided . . ."

"In that case I think I'll have plenty of time to try and teach the ape something."

They arrived late, of course. Rosso was famous for being late. Instead of dressing he lounged about in his work-apron, moodily staring at the cartoon, then started sketching Pasquale in red chalk while Pasquale tried to teach the ape to climb down a rope— not as easy as it seemed, for Barbary apes are not great climbers, and certainly not of ropes. Rosso was still in his odd changeable mood too, reluctant to

leave and yet restless. By the time he had thrown on
some clothes, he and Pasquale had to run through
the streets to reach Andrea del Sarto's studio, and
still they were late.

Master Andrea was in a bate because of some business with his new wife. His pupils hung around the
front of the studio, where rolled processional banners
leaned against the wall. Their master's angry voice
rose and fell from an open window above. Cheerful
with holiday spirit, in their best clothes, the pupils
passed a fat marijuana cigarette back and forth and
munched on the plump juicy Colombano grapes Pasquale and Rosso had brought with them, and laughed
at the story Pasquale had to tell. He had a rope burn
to prove it; at one point on its way down the ape had
panicked and had nearly jerked the rope from his
hands. By and by more painters and pupils drifted
along—this street housed a dozen studios, mixed
amongst the workshops of goldsmiths and stonemasons. Someone had brought a flask of wine, and
it too was passed around.

Master Andrea came out at last, a portly man
dressed in black velvet, with a belt of braided gold
thread. His face was mottled, and his hands trembling as he smoothed back his long hair: he looked
like an angry bee, shot out of its hole to see off in-
truders. He was in fact a kindly man, and a good
teacher—Rosso had been his pupil, so that in a way
Pasquale was his pupil, too—but he was prone to
rages, and his new wife, young and pretty, provoked
him to fantastic jealousies.

Rosso put his arm around his former master, talking with him as the group made their way to the
Piazza della Signoria while Pasquale, a banner-pole
on his shoulder, followed amongst the other pupils.
He felt frumpy, still in the clothes he had worn the

day before—he really didn't have anything better to wear, things being what they were, but if he had not been so drunk, he would have taken off his doublet and hose and tunic and laid them under the mattress before going to bed. At least he had thought to scrub his face and hands, and anoint his palms with a rose-water receipt of Rosso's. He had brushed his curly hair until it shone, and Rosso had put a circlet in it, and called Pasquale his little prince of Savages, just to annoy.

The party gathered other painters and their assistants and pupils as it went through the streets, and by the time it reached to the Piazza della Signoria there were half a hundred. The same number was already waiting in front of the Loggia, chief amongst them Michelangelo Buonarroti, towering over all by sheer force of personality, clad in a white tunic so long it was almost a robe—to hide his knock-knees, Rosso said, adding that, even so, had he possessed a thunderbolt, he would have made a passable Zeus.

Raphael and his entourage were not there.

The hired band struck up with shawm, sackbut and *viole da braccio.* Banners were unfurled, bright with gold and ultramarine, like flowers suddenly blooming in one corner of the stony fastness of the piazza. Following the example of the other pupils, Pasquale socketed the pole of his banner in the cusp of the leather harness he had put on; even so, his shoulders soon started to ache as wind tugged the heavy banner to and fro.

Not many of the passersby took notice. The importance of the confraternity had dwindled, and they seemed a small, insignificant group, dwarfed by the big stage that workmen were hammering together in front of the Palazzo, in preparation for the Pope's imminent arrival.

The hammering didn't even stop as the blessing was read from the steps of the Loggia. What with that, and barked orders as companies of city militia drilled across the square's vast chessboard, and the noise of the signal-tower atop the Palazzo della Signoria as its arms clattered and weaved in a kinetic ballet, the frail voice of the old Secretary to the Ten could scarcely be heard as he pronounced the annual blessing. The priest shook holy water towards the assembled painters even as the Secretary was led off by his attendants at what seemed an undignified speed. The priest muttered a prayer, sketched a cross in the air, and that was that.

The procession set off, gathering itself into a ragged line as people jostled for position. Gradually, they wound out of the piazza, through the shadow of the Great Tower. Square, studded with narrow windows and balconies, and machicolations and platforms clinging to its smooth stone as swallow-nests cling to a barn, the tower reared so high into the sky that it forever seemed to be toppling as clouds moved behind it. It nailed down the northwestern corner of the colleges and laboratories and apothecaria and surgeries and dissecting-rooms and workshops of the new university which had replaced an entire neighborhood of crooked streets where once goldsmiths had worked, an interlocking complex of red roofs and white colonnades and terraces all overlooked by its architect, the Great Engineer himself, who in his Great Tower brooded hundreds of *braccia* above the common herd, perhaps even now watching the procession of the Confraternity of Artists creeping like a line of ants at the base of his eyrie as they turned towards the Ponte Vecchio. They had to march in single file, a heavy traffic of carts and carriages and *vaporetti* thundering past, before they turned to strike out along the wide promenade beside the river.

Pasquale, holding up the pole of a banner painted with the likeness of Saint Luke, benign and white-bearded, and painting one of his portraits of the Blessed Virgin (there were three, now at Rome, Loreto and Bologna), kept an eye on the river as he marched. He loved to watch the ships go by: the small barges which were the work-horses of the river-transport system; the paddle-wheel ferries; the big ocean-going *maonas*; and, on occasion, a warship on some mission that had taken it far from the naval yards of Livorno, prowling with its screw drive like a sleek leopard amongst domestic cats.

Sunlight fell through a rift in the clouds. The banners glowed; the musicians beat louder and everyone picked up his step. Pasquale's heart was lifted at last, and he forgot his headache and his uneasy stomach, where bread and oil made an unwelcome weight, forgot the ache in his arms from holding up the heavy banner. Gulls, which followed the Grand Canal inland, were flakes of white skirling above the river-channels. Cries, far cries. He could dream of taking sloe-eyed brown-skinned Pelashil back to her native land: the New World, where white, stepped pyramids gleamed bright as salt amongst palm-trees, and every kind of fruit was there ready to fall into your hand if only you reached out for it, and flocks of parrots flew like arrows from the bows of an army.

The river was divided into channels, and the channel nearest the shore ran with strange colors that mixed and mingled in feathery curls—dye-works and chemical manufactories poured out mingling streams which unlike pigments did not mix to muddy brown but formed strange new combinations, chemical reactions fluttering across surface in exquisite patterns as if the water had been stirred to

life. Along the full flood of the raceway channel, water-mills sat in chained lines strung out from the
piers of bridges, their water-wheels thumping and
churning, their machineries sending up a chattering
roar. Most drove looms, trying to compete with the
modern automatic machineries of the manufactories
on the far bank. At night some went freemartin, cutting the mooring of their rivals, trying to jockey upstream to get advantage of a stronger current.
Sometimes you could hear pistol-shots carrying
across the water. The journalist and playwright Niccolò Machiavegli had once made a famous remark
that war was simply commercial competition carried to extremes: and so here.

At the Ponte alla Grazie the procession turned
away from the river, plunging into a warren of narrow streets between tenement buildings faced with
soft gray *pietra serena*, stained with black streaks by
polluted rain and crumbling away through the action
of the tainted air and smokes poured forth by the
manufactories. At street level, workshops and *bot-
tegas* had opened their shutters for the day's business, and their workers came out to cheer the
procession as it went past. They especially cheered
Michelangelo, who marched with steadfast dignity
at the head of the procession, his white garments
shining amongst the blacks and browns of the other
masters. Florentines loved their successful sons,
most especially if they were prodigals. Even better,
Michelangelo had returned because of a furious argument with the Pope over the tomb of the Pope's
predecessor. He was seen as having upheld the honor
of Florence over the wishes of her old enemy: not for
nothing was his most famous work the statue of the
giant-killer, David.

So at last the procession reached the homely

church of Sant'Ambrogio, in the neighborhood where most painters worked. In the years before the Confraternity had broken with the Company of Saint Luke and its physicians and apothecaries, who in truth had long bankrolled their impoverished artist brothers, the service had been held amongst the marble and bronze of the church of Sant'Egidio, in the hospital of Santa Maria Nuova. No more.

A fine rain had started. The drums beat on as the procession filed through the narrow door into the homely little church, with its plaster walls and shadows up amongst the rafters, and the noise of the reciprocal engines in the manufactory across the street.

Raphael was not there, either.

2

The mass was almost over when Raphael finally arrived. He swept in at the head of a gaggle of assistants and pupils, and the bustle at the door of the little church turned everyone's heads. The idlers at the back, who had talked all through the service in the casual way of Florentines, the church being simply another public place that, except for its altars and chapels, was as secular as any other, stopped talking and gaped and nudged each other. The masters and pupils in the congregation glanced back, every one of them—with the exception of Michelangelo, who sat stiffly at the far end of the front row of seats in exactly the same pose he had held throughout the mass (and in which pose Pasquale had surreptitiously sketched him), not deigning to look back at his rival and yield him the satisfaction of recognition. Even the priest paused for a moment, before continuing with his blessing of the host amidst the ringing of many small bells. As Raphael and his followers doffed their raincapes to reveal fashionably black machine-cut tunics, doublets and leggings, the six-piece orchestra wheezed into the *Agnus Dei,* the aging castrato coming in half a beat late, and almost everyone in the congregation began to whisper to everyone else.

Rosso nudged Pasquale and said in a stage whisper, "God's second favorite son blesses us."

Pasquale couldn't help looking around to stare at the great painter. Raphael sat at ease amongst his assistants, some of whom would be masters in their own right if they had not chosen to serve Raphael. As who would not? Raphael earned more than any artist in either Rome or the Florentine Republic, and so more than any in all of Europe and the New World. Like Michelangelo, Raphael had taken the New Age to heart. In the age of the individual, he had become his own man. He took commissions as he chose, and his own fame made the rich, both the old money and the new, fiercely contest in bidding for his work, while the poor decorated their houses with shadow-engraved reproductions of his work. No other artist had that kind of cachet. Michelangelo did as he pleased, and usually fell out with his clients as a result, but only Raphael made sure that his clients got what they wanted while painting as he chose.

"He's come back to his roots to make sure they're as bad as he remembers," Rosso said.

"He has paid his florin," Pasquale said, meaning that Raphael had the right to celebrate mass with the Florentine Confraternity of Artists on the day of their patron saint because he had signed his name in the Red Book and paid his fee. Because Pasquale had been eager to catch a glimpse of Raphael, now he felt that he must defend him.

"About the only one here," Rosso said, which was almost true. The Red Book of the Confraternity recorded more debtors to Saint Luke than creditors, for few bothered to pay a whole florin to become a recognized master in a guild whose best days were gone, while those like Raphael Sanzio of Urbino or Michelangelo Buonarroti didn't need a confraternity to promote their interests. Pasquale had heard Master Andrea grumble, as the procession had filed through the church door, that they were less than the rat-catchers' guild now, that once upon a time the whole street on which this little church of Sant'Ambrogio stood had been crowded with a joyful procession, all come out to see a single painting leave the studio of Cimabue, and where now was that ardor?

But the processional banners were still bright, for all that their finery was patched and faded, older than the century. And even in this little church there was evidence aplenty of the Golden Age, when image had sung straight to God. There was a flaking fresco of the Annunciation over the first altar, and, in better condition, a beautiful fresco over the second altar of the Madonna on her heavenly throne, with Saint John the Baptist and Saint Bartholomew. This theme was repeated over the third altar, where this time the Virgin was portrayed in her glory with an array of saints. The gold-leaf of the frescos shimmered in the candlelight, giving the illusion that the church was larger than it really was, as a lake glimmering through trees will seem like a sea.

Pasquale had contrived to sit as close as he could to the best work in the church. It was in a niche between the third and second altars, a little roundel of the Annunciation painted by Lippi in the Golden Age before the rise of the artificers. For most of the mass, which was a full ceremony paid by subscription from every master, debtor and creditor alike (Rosso had grumbled mightily over this imposition), Pasquale had gazed at this little window into another world, a world of clear colors and clean lines. The grave acceptance of the Madonna at her window, her face and demeanor expressing the fourth of the fifth of the Laudable Conditions of the Blessed Virgin, namely *Humiliatio*; the golden line from the dove of the Holy Spirit to her womb; and the angel Gabriel kneeling in the garden amongst spring flowers. Most of all the angel. Pasquale was collecting angels. Except for his wings (which despite the gold tracery were clearly modeled on the wings of a pigeon; Pasquale had seen another of Fra Lippi's Annunciations where the angel had the Argus-eyed wings of a peacock), this one could have been any youth from some great house in the time of Lorenzo the Unlucky. He was fourteen or fifteen, pale-skinned, with a long, wondering face and blue long-lashed eyes, and was dressed in the sumptuous costume of those courtly days. Stripped of his superficial exoticism he could have been a deacon or a page-boy. What held Pasquale's attention, what he had twice tried to fix on a scrap of paper, was the angel's expression. It was raptly attentive, filled with sorrowing knowledge at the burden which the Holy Child must bear, but also with joy at this compact between Heaven and Earth at last made flesh.

Or that at least was how you were supposed to read it, Pasquale thought. But how could you capture the true feelings of a creature both greater than man (for he stood closer to God than any but the most blessed of the saints) and lesser (for despite his command of legions of lesser angels, Gabriel was in the end no more than a messenger, a go-between who carried the Word from God to man but was not the Word, only its vessel: angels did not choose to serve, for not to serve was to fall)? It was something he had been trying to work out ever since the conception for his masterwork had fallen on him. Piero di Cosimo, who Pasquale liked to think was his secret master, had in a rare moment of lucidity told him to paint truly if he was to paint at all, but how could you paint the truth of something beyond ordinary human comprehension? How could you paint the face of an angel?

Fra Lippi's solution to this question had been to portray his angel as a beautiful courtier; it was the solution of most painters of the Golden Age. And most painters in Florence, at one time or another, had painted at least one Annunciation, a popular theme because the feast-days of both the Annunciation and the New Year fell on the same day, the twenty-fifth of March. But the Golden Age was gone, as fragmented by the devices of the artificers as reality itself. The New Age had arrived, and demanded genius or nothing. In his youth, Raphael had painted angels as idealizations of idealizations, not the best or most beautiful courtier but the ideal courtier of Castiglione's imaginary conversations. It was said that when Raphael painted he caught not just the hues of his model's face, but the very thoughts and personality. But he had not painted an angel since his apprenticeship, except in his depiction of the flight of Saint Peter from prison, and that in shadow. If the greatest painter in the world shied from the task, how could Pasquale meet his self-imposed challenge?

For while Pasquale had his vision and the ruinously expensive little panel he had prepared with great care, he had not made a brush-stroke towards realizing it. He had glimpsed or thought he had glimpsed more than mere beauty or even the ideal of beauty, but did not know how to begin to express what he had been vouchsafed. He only knew that to fail in this was to fail himself, and believed that if he could only talk with Raphael, the great painter would understand.

Poor drug-crazed Piero di Cosimo, with his talk of creatures from worlds that interleaved this, understood more than most, but for all his adventures in the far shores of the New World, his way of seeing was that of the Old World; he had not entirely escaped his training. And as for Rosso, Pasquale had barely mentioned the subject of his painting to his master, let alone his vision. Rosso was a master of the technical problem, of perspective and plastic space, of the swift decisions needed to paint tempera panels and the bold revisions that the new Dutch and Prussian formulae for oil paints made possible, but while he was a good man and a generous master, he was also increasingly bitter with his lot, and more conservative than he liked to admit. Artists were artisans first and last, was his constant motto.

Bells rang for the elevation of the host; following the masters of the Confraternity (Rosso, who had forgotten to go to confession, had to stay behind), Pasquale and the other pupils lined up at the rail to take the sip of blood-red wine, the thin coin of the wafer of transubstantiated flesh. As Pasquale rose, with the wafer dissolving on his tongue, sweetening the ferruginous taste of the wine, he saw that Raphael was kneeling humbly at the end of the line, democratic amongst his school, as if he were only an ordinary man.

The communion over, the prayers for the celebrants said and the dismissal intoned, people began to drift towards the back of the church, mixing with the layabouts and with the ordinary citizens who were waiting for the regular midday mass, which would begin as soon as this one was finished. The pupils were gathering up the banners. When he had

wound up his own, Pasquale asked one of Master Andrea's pupils to carry it back for him. He had seen
Raphael walking down the aisle, conversing with a
few of the masters.

The pupil, a cheerful fellow by the name of Andrea
Squazella, said, "God sees the sparrow fall, so Raphael might look on you, I suppose. But he'll only see
a sparrow."

"I would be more than that, I hope."

"I know of your ambition, but as for your talent . . ." As Raphael passed by, Andrea grabbed Pasquale and said with mock alarm, "Steady, don't faint.
He's only a man."

Raphael was of ordinary height, with a mild white
face and curly black shoulder-length hair. His black
tunic, doublet and hose were of the finest Dutch
cloth, cut expensively on the cross. He was gesturing
to underline some point. His fingers were as slim as
a woman's, and so long that it seemed that they had
an extra joint.

Pasquale breathed out when the little group had
passed. "Only a man," he said.

"There goes someone with a different opinion,"
Andrea said. "Master Michelangelo thinks your
Raphael is definitely something lower than a man.
A louse perhaps."

Michelangelo was making his way up the far side
of the church, craggy head held high, followed by two
of his assistants. He looked like a warship beating
out of port ahead of a storm, escorted by a couple of
sloops.

"My master says that Raphael stole his ideas," Andrea said to Pasquale. "Raphael was secretly shown
the Sistine Chapel after Michelangelo quit his work
there, and as a result he immediately repainted the
prophet Isaiah that he had been working on so that

it seemed to be a collaboration, although not one Michelangelo knew about. Your Raphael is something of an improver rather than an improviser."

"If you mean that his inspiration begins where that of others ends, then mine begins with his," Pasquale said, and Andrea laughed and said he was shameless.

"I'm desperate. How can I talk with him?"

"Tell him you like his work," Andrea said sensibly. "Or better still, let my master introduce you. Go on, Pasquale! If you don't stand near him you'll have to shout, and one simply doesn't do that. Even in a Florentine church."

Andrea was from Urbino, and considered all Florentines boorish, most especially in the way they chattered openly during mass, even on high days.

By now, the party with Raphael in its center was almost at the door. Someone stepped inside just as Pasquale hurried up, and it was as if a breeze had blown aside a screen of leaves, for the people around Raphael parted and moved back, leaving him to confront the newcomer.

He was a portly, middle-aged man, dressed in a fashion more suitable to someone twenty years younger: a short gray cape spotted with sooty raindrops, and a white loosely laced shirt; an exaggerated doublet, fantastically puffed and slashed, of the kind favored by Prussian students; parti-colored hose. His hectic face still held more than a trace of the beautiful youth he had once been, in his profile and the sulky downturn of his full mouth. His curly hair was still thick; extravagantly arranged, it fell to his shoulders.

Pasquale knew him at once: Giacomo Caprotti, nicknamed Salai, the Milanese catamite of the Great Engineer. He also saw that the man was drunk. He stepped back, but still Salai shouldered into him.

"Don't you know to mind your step," Salai said, "when your betters pass by?"

Pasquale retorted, "I'm sorry, signor, but I fail to recognize the high opinion you have of yourself."

He would have said more, but one of Raphael's assistants, Giulio Romano, a burly middle-aged man, caught Salai's arm. He turned him aside and said in a whisper, "Not here. This is not the place."

Salai shrugged him off and straightened his sleeves. "Only too true, but I missed you at the tower and would pay my respects, if I am allowed."

Romano threw up his hands.

Salai turned back to the others and said with a slurred eloquence, "A million apologies for having missed your little party. I went to the wrong place, which is to say where you used to hold your feast-day mass, when you meant something in Florence. How I searched to find this small church—charming in its way, I'm sure, but obscure. Actually, I'm not sorry at all, I'm only here to represent my master. He paid his money long ago, before he took up his real calling and left off daubs." Salai faced up to Raphael. He couldn't quite keep his eyes focused. He said, "So, painter. For once the dog goes before its master, eh? I compliment you on your choice of dress, Signor Raphael, and those of your hangers-on. Somehow, in these circumstances, mourning appears appropriate. You funny little artists have had your day, even you, Signor Raphael. We'll soon outshine you all in capturing the real light of the world."

Another of the assistants said, "If you bring a message from *your* master, speak it now. Master Raphael is too busy to trifle with the likes of you."

"Some love-affair no doubt. An affair of the heart,

such as we read of in the broadsheets. Well, I'm not one to stand in the way of love."

Raphael laughed. He said, "You weren't sent at all, were you?"

Salai grinned broadly, as if enormously enjoying the fact that his bluff had been called. "Well, if it comes to it, no."

The second assistant said, "Lorenzo de' Medici was murdered in a church, I recall."

"Be quiet," Giulio Romano said.

Salai touched the pommel of the French rapier slung from his silver brocade belt. "Signor, I can step outside if it makes you feel easier. I'll even wait while you arm yourself."

There was a moment of tense silence, for Salai was well known for his swordswork. The assistant turned red and looked away.

"Go now," Romano said. "Go away, Salai. Not here. Not now."

Raphael said, with a benign smile, "You have your audience, Signor Salai. Speak your piece."

Salai bowed. "I hope I need not speak, Signor—no, *Master* Raphael. That's the point. We are soon to be blessed by the first of the Medicis to step within the walls of Florence since the Republic was founded. A pity if that dainty footfall were to be lost in the outcry of scandal."

"I'm not afraid, Salai. Certainly not of any small mischief you can manage to whip up."

Salai winked and laid a finger alongside his nose in a coarse parody of intimacy. "And the honor of a certain lady . . . ?"

"That's old gossip," Raphael said, even as the second assistant pushed forward, hand on the dagger thrust in his belt.

Salai danced back, suddenly not drunk at all,

coarse cunning and a kind of eagerness printed on his face. "That olive-sticker won't do you much good, friend. I suggest you use it to clean your fingernails—they really shouldn't match the rest of your costume."

Romano laid a hand on his fellow's shoulder. The others of Raphael's party, emboldened by this move, started to jeer and stamp. A few of the Confraternity, Master Andrea amongst them, were shouting out too, crying shame, shame on the honor of Florence, that one of her citizens should insult one of her guests. Salai looked at them, then bowed, mockingly low, before turning and marching out through the door.

Several of the older masters started to apologize to Raphael; off to the side, Rosso was talking animatedly with Giulio Romano. Pasquale tried to push forward, but Raphael's followers had closed around their master, and they moved as one body through the high doors of the church into the gloomy, rainy afternoon. When Pasquale dared follow, Master Andrea turned and said, not unkindly, "He's here until the Pope leaves, Pasquale. You'll have a chance to talk, I'm sure, but not now, eh?"

Pasquale caught his sleeve. "What did Salai mean, when he raised up the matter of the honor of a lady?"

"You know the kind of mischief the Great Engineer's catamite likes to stir up," Master Andrea said vaguely. "Women are the root of all evil, some say. Or would say, if they were allowed . . ." He set his four-cornered cap squarely on his grizzled head, shook out the wide sleeves of his tunic, and hurried after the receding party. A couple of pigeons detonated into flight from his path: angel-wings.

Pasquale watched the pigeons a while, getting soaked in the gentle, polluted rain, until Rosso came out of the church. Pasquale saw his master's white, anxious face, and said, "Shouldn't you go with them, master? The dinner in honor of Raphael—"

"Let the old men go and make pictures with their food," Rosso said. "I think we both need a drink."

3

The bar which Pasquale and Rosso favored was a low dive frequented by a sometimes explosive mixture of artists' pupils, journalists and Swiss mercenaries. The landlord, a fat bullet-headed Prussian Swiss, had the habit of taking swigs from the drinks he served, and kept a hound the size of a small horse which, when it wasn't flopped in front of the fireplace, wandered amongst the crowd trying to cadge titbits. The Swiss scrutinized each person as they came in, and if the new arrival was a passerby he didn't like the look of, or a regular he'd argued with, he set up a tremendous volley of oaths and insults until the unfortunate man was driven out. Otherwise he jollied his regulars along, attempted clumsy practical jokes that usually backfired, and created a little world outside the world. Surprisingly, there were few fights. If the Swiss couldn't handle troublemakers he set his dog on them, and needed no other weapon.

The scandal of Salai's confrontation with Raphael was already the talk of the bar. Pasquale regaled two

separate audiences with his account, accepting
drinks from his eager listeners. He was hoping to see
Piero di Cosimo, but the old man wasn't here. Increasingly, he retreated from noise, living more and
more inside his own head. He'd spend hours gazing
at patterns rain made on a window, or paint spattered
on his filthy floor.

Pasquale had taken him food a few days before, but
Piero had refused to let him in, speaking only
through the crack in the half-opened door. He was,
he told Pasquale, engaged on an important work. He
spoke as if asleep, paying attention to something
only he could see.

Pasquale said, "One day the stuff you take, the híkuri, will kill you. You cannot live entirely in
dreams."

"There's more than one world, Pasquale. You've
glimpsed it once or twice, but you don't understand
it yet. You must, if you're to be any kind of painter."

"I have yet to master this world. Let me in, just for
a moment. Look, I have bread and fish."

Piero ignored this. He said wistfully, "If only I'd
had you for my pupil. Together—what voyages, eh,
Pasquale? Come back in a few days. In a week."

Pasquale tried not to sound exasperated. "If you
don't eat, you'll die."

"You sound like Pelashil," Piero said. "No. She has
the sense not to disturb me. She understands."

"I would understand, if you would let me. I need
to be able to see . . ."

"Your angel. Yes. But you're not a real person, not
yet. Don't bother me any more, Pasquale. I need to
dream now."

It occurred to Pasquale now, in the crowded noisy
bar, that it was because of that conversation he had
drunkenly persisted in asking Pelashil for more of

the híkuri, the simple which Piero had brought back from the New World. He looked around for Pelashil, who usually worked in the bar every night, but couldn't see her. He hadn't seen her all evening, and for a moment wondered, because he was young and self-centered, if she had left in disgust at his behavior, never to return.

A group of loud and foul-mouthed Swiss cavalrymen had colonized Piero's usual corner. The *condottiere* who had hired them was sprawled in the straight-backed chair Piero favored, elaborating with vivid obscenity why he would never be fucked up the arse or fuck anyone up the arse either, Florence or not, while the rent-boy who sat in his lap pretended to be fascinated. "I mean, I like my dick sucked as well as any man, and I don't care if it's a woman or a man or a baby who thinks my come is her mother's milk does the sucking. One of the best fucks I ever had was with an old granny that had lost all her teeth. But only Turks and Florentines fuck each other in the shit-hole, am I right or am I right?"

The *condottiere* had a lean pockmarked face, with a mustache waxed to elaborate points. His fist twined a handful of the rent-boy's hair; the boy winced and blew him a kiss, half-mocking, half-placatory. The *condottiere* glared around the room, little eyes glistening under beetling brows, perhaps hoping that someone would contradict him. No one did, for as the broadsheets never tired of pointing out, the citizens of Florence were intimidated by the foreign soldiers they employed. A little shameful silence hung in the room before the man laughed and called for more wine.

It was Pelashil who served him. Pasquale's heart turned when he saw her. After she'd refilled the *condottiere's* pitcher he called to her, and she sauntered over. Pelashil of the insolent eyes, black as sloe-berries in a face the color of fall leaves, broad-hipped in a ragged brocade gown, its sleeves ripped away to leave her muscular arms bare. Pasquale had slept with her once, last winter, and ever since had not been able to decide if it had been her choice or his.

"I was in my cups last night," Pasquale said. "You're not still angry, I hope."

Pelashil stepped back when he tried to embrace her. "Why do men always think only about them-selves?"

"You're angry! What did I say? Don't I have the right to know?"

Rosso, who had been drinking steadily, stirred and said, "You offered to take her away, Pasqualino. Back across the sea to where the sand is white and the sea is blue and the women go naked."

"That's what you'd like to think," Pelashil said, "but it isn't anything like my home. Besides, I sup-pose you'd rather think of naked boys." She caught Pasquale's hand. "The old man is ill again. You must go and see him," and she went off to fetch more wine, dodging the groping of a drunken soldier.

Pasquale sat back down and drank more wine and thought again of Piero's vague talk, and then of the way that, after he had eaten híkuri, separate mo-ments had folded into a continuous sheaf, and of the blurring of pigeon-wings in rainy light. Angels and time . . . was their time the same time as men en-dured, moment to moment? Some notion, vast yet as fabulously fragile as a frost-flower, seemed to be creeping across his brain, threatening to fade to nought if he stared at it too hard. He thought that perhaps Piero would know what this revelation meant. Perhaps Piero would feed him another dried leaf of híkuri. He should go and see the old man, yes, but not yet. Not just yet. He needed courage to face the dilapidated claustrophobia of Piero's room.

Giambattista Gellia, a hothead leftist as famous for being a shoemaker turned tract-writer as for anything he wrote, was pushing through the crowd. The journalist, Niccolò Machiavegli, had just come in, and Gellia was pulling him towards Pasquale's table, saying loudly, "Niccolò, you must listen to this. Someone who was there, at the root of the scandal."

"Often you need distance for the truth to emerge," Niccolò Machiavegli protested with a laugh. "Besides, I have already written my piece and left it to be set. In fact, I have to go back soon to check it over. Give me the peace of a drink uninterrupted by business, Gellia. Revolution may be your life, but journalism is only my profession."

"This young man saw it all—or so he says."

"It's true," Pasquale said.

"And I see you have profited well from your luck," the journalist said, and smiled as the others around the table laughed at Pasquale's expense.

"It's true!" Pasquale insisted.

Niccolò Machiavegli smiled gently. "I don't need words, my friend."

Rosso said, "He's right. You don't need words, Pasqualino."

Pasquale said, "What about a picture?"

"It is a rich irony that in all of that congregation of artists, no one thought to sketch the confrontation," Niccolò Machiavegli said, gaining another laugh.

Rosso stood up, gripping the edge of the table. He had drunk more than Pasquale. "It's a private matter," he said.

"But it happened in a public place," Gellia said.

Pasquale dug his elbow into Rosso's hip and said in a fierce whisper, "We need the money, master."

"You do what you will, Pasqualino," Rosso said wearily. One of his black moods had suddenly descended upon him. "Do it with my blessing. I suppose it will all come out soon enough."

Gellia stepped out of the way as Rosso plunged into the crowd, moving towards the door. Pasquale said, because they really did need the money, "I will show you that I was there. You must forgive my master. What happened was a . . . shameful thing." He drew out the scrap of paper on which he had been scribbling during the first part of the mass, dipped the corner of his tunic in wine and would have wiped away the drawing he'd already made when Niccolò Machiavegli caught his hand.

The journalist said, "Allow me to look," and held the paper to his eyes, moving his gaze back and forth across it as if it were a text. He was slight yet straight-backed, with the clever, boyish face of a monastery librarian. His prominent cheekbones were shadowed with stubble, and his hair, receding around a widow's peak above a high forehead, was clipped short. He said, "I see Michelangelo Buonarroti brooding on which mortal to dispatch with a well-chosen thunderbolt. You did this?"

"He's the best of us," Pasquale said.

"If you will, come with me—no, don't drink up, you'll need a steady hand and eye, and certainly not an inflamed memory."

It had stopped raining, and a yellow vapor was thickening the air. It smelled of wood-smoke and sulfur, and burned in Pasquale's nose, made his eyes itch. Although the six o'clock cannonade that signaled the closing of the city's gates had not yet sounded, the vapor had already brought on the night.

People stumbled through it with their faces muffled; two artificers passed arm in arm, faces masked with pig-snouted leather hoods.

"The artificers poison the air, and then must invent themselves a means to breathe it," Niccolò Machiavegli said. "A pity only a few can afford their cure."

It was one of the smogs that plagued Florence when the wind didn't blow and the smokes of the artificers settled like a heavy blanket along the course of the Arno. The journalist coughed heavily, covering his mouth with his fist, and then apologized. He had once been locked up in the dungeons of the Bargello, he said, and had suffered fluxations of the lungs ever since.

"But that was before I had taken up the pen in the cause of truth instead of the cause of the state. As for truth, now you are away from your fellows you can tell me truly whether you saw all."

"I was as close to Raphael as I am to you," Pasquale said, which was not accurate enough to satisfy an artificer, but would serve as commonplace truth.

"And you can remember it well enough to draw it?"

"I train my memory, Signor Machiavegli, especially for faces and gestures. If I can't draw it I can at least remember it."

"Good enough. And please, I am Niccolò. Signor Machiavegli was another person, in another time."

A dozen years ago, Machiavegli had been one of the most powerful men in Florence: as Secretary to the Ten he had been privy to most of the secrets of the Republic, and had been a prime mover in much of its foreign policy. But then the old government had been overthrown after the surprise attack by the Spanish navy on the dockyards at Livorno. Half the

Florentine fleet had been burned at its moorings, and a regiment of the Spanish army had burned and sacked its way to the walls of Florence before the Florentines had rallied and overwhelmed it. Gonfalonier-for-life Piero Soderini had committed suicide, and Machiavegli had fallen into disgrace. Despite his frequent republican proclamations, and despite the fact that his own family had been killed and his property destroyed by the Spanish raiders, his enemies put it about that he had always been a Medici sympathizer. In the chaos following the attack it was rumored that he might form the nucleus of a movement to bring the Medicis back into power for the first time since the short but cruel and disastrous reign of Giuliano de' Medici, who thirty years earlier had prosecuted a campaign of terror that had gone far beyond the summary execution of the assassins and their immediate families after the murder of his elder brother and his own lucky escape from a papal-inspired conspiracy. Even while Rome waged war on Florence, and after Rome's defeat by the devices of the Great Engineer, Giuliano had purged every great family as God had purged the Egyptians to secure the escape of the Israelites. It was a brutal time that was still not forgiven.

Thrown out of office, Niccolò Machiavegli had refused to swear an oath of loyalty to the new government, and for his pains—or pride—had suffered for two years in the dungeons of the Palazzo del Bargello. When he had finally been released, with no charges ever brought, he had become one of the new breed of journalists who worked for one or another of the *stationarii* competing to bring out daily broadsheets that proffered a mixture of sensationalism and scandal. After the fall of the old government, the artificers' faction packed the councils of the Eight and the

Ten and the Thirteen. Taking advantage of their creed that nothing truthful should be hidden—although taking care never to write anything that would contradict the government's particular version of the truth—Niccolò Machiavegli had blazed a career as a political commentator.

He worked for a *stationarius* who used as offices the shop where once Vespasiano da Bisticci had worked, an irony since this most distinguished of publishers had retired to his country estate rather than introduce the new-fangled printing-presses which had driven copyists out of business. Some said that this coincidence was an indication that Machiavegli was bankrolled by the Medicis, for Cosimo de' Medici had once been Bisticci's best customer, ordering a library of two hundred volumes which forty-five scribes had completed within a record two years. Florentines liked nothing better than to gossip, and much gossip was founded on association or coincidence with events long past, for Florentines were also acutely aware of, and acutely proud of, their city's colorful and turbulent history. Men might struggle against fate, but they could not defeat the past.

Even at this late hour, lights burned along the length of the broadsheet's offices. Half a dozen men were lounging inside, sharing a meal of pasta and black bread and wine at one of the writing-tables. A blue haze of cigarette smoke drifted in the air above their heads. A couple of printer's devils slept in a kind of nest of rags under the gleaming frame of the spring-driven press. Bales of paper were stacked in the back, and printed sheets hung from lines like drying washing. Candles backed with reflector mirrors burned here and there, and one of the new acetylene lamps depended on a chain from the ceiling. It threw out a bright yellow light and permeated the stale used air of the room with a garlicky stink.

Machiavegli was greeted with cheerful cynicism by his fellows. The publisher of the broadsheet, Pietro Aretino, was an ambitious man half Machiavegli's age, stocky and running to fat, with a full beard and black hair greased straight back from his forehead. "An eyewitness, eh?" he said, when Machiavegli introduced Pasquale. He was puffing on a green cigar that gave off dense white smoke as poisonous as the smog outside. He peered at Pasquale with kind yet shrewd eyes. "Well, my friend, we only print the truth here, isn't that right, boys?"

The men around him laughed. The oldest, his bald pate fringed with fine silver hair, said, "Do the public care so much for a squabble amongst artists?"

"There's a deal more to it than that," Niccolò Machiavegli said. He had poured a measure of a yellow-green liquor in a tumbler of water; now he drained this cloudy mixture with a shudder that was half eagerness, half disgust.

"Steady, Niccolò," Aretino said.

"It's good for my nerves," Niccolò said, as he commenced to mix another drink. "Now, as to this squabble, it is the visible symptom of something that underlies the whole state. The Spanish pox begins with an innocent-looking sore, not even painful, as I understand. I hope you realize that I'm not speaking from experience," he added, to laughter. "But the unfortunate who finds the shepherd's golden coin on the end of his cock ignores it at his peril. I often think we're like doctors, advising the best way of living, drawing off excess humors. This little incident seems a trifle, I know, but it's diagnostic."

Aretino blew out a long riffle of smoke. "The public only cares about what we want them to care about. As long as we print it, it is news. If we print it big enough, it's big news. Remember the war in Egypt? Well, there wasn't a war until we reported it, and then the Signoria had to send in a squadron."

"There would have been a war anyway," Niccolò said mildly. Somehow, he had finished his second drink, and half-finished a third.

"But not the same war!" Aretino said. "You are too humble, Niccolò. You should enjoy your power."

"I know well enough where use of power can lead," Niccolò Machiavegli said.

"Without risks there can be no gain."

Aretino rolled his cigar from one side of his mouth to the other with epicurean relish. Candlelight was blankly reflected in his eyes. He looked like the devil, Pasquale thought. On a night like this it was easy to imagine that these few cynical men really could manipulate the world with their words, as they so clearly believed.

The elder journalist said, "But what makes this petty squabble significant, Niccolò? What's the disease?"

"Please read my report, Girolamo. It's so late that I fear if I told you it over, I might contradict myself."

Aretino said, "It's the old against the new, the artificers against the artists, the Medici Pope against our dear Republic. Our question should be, which side are we on? Who are the angels here?"

"Whoever God favors," one of the others said.

"That's fine," Aretino retorted, "but we can't wait on Heaven's judgment, which is often slow and passing strange."

"This is hardly news," the elder journalist said. "Anyone with eyes knows the Pope is coming in two days' time. Anyone with ears knows that this embassy could bury the ashes of the long war between

Florence and Rome. Rome once tried to destroy the Medicis by assassination and war, and now a Medici is Pope, and comes to treat with the same artificers whose devices saved the government of Giuliano de' Medici. A silly little squabble is a slender peg on which to hang something so weighty as a conspiracy to hide the truth from the citizens."

Niccolò said, "It's well known that Raphael is an outrider for the Pope. All artists have eyes, eh, young man? And Raphael has the best of them all, to spy out the mood of the city. There's also the matter of the wife of a certain important citizen, a woman with a personal interest in the arts—" here all the men smiled, and even Machiavegli looked amused "—but we'd best not mention her name here, well known thought it is."

Pasquale, wondering just who this woman was, said boldly, "The catamite Salai threatened to reveal her name, if Master Raphael would not keep his peace."

"An idle threat," Aretino said, "since your Master Raphael's amorous exploits are amongst the most widely publicized in Christendom. Many husbands are eager to be cuckolded by that young genius, it seems, although I fear they mistake Raphael's cock for his paintbrush, and believe that their wives are made more valuable by his amorous strokes just as pigment turns to gold when he wields his brush."

"Perhaps he should sign his women as well as his works," one of the younger journalists suggested.

"There is a feeling," Niccolò Machiavegli told Pasquale, "that the Great Engineer has already made arrangements with the Pope, and that Raphael is the conduit for this commerce. Naturally, this would not be in the interests of Florence, for our empire is founded on the fruits of the Great Engineer's genius.

There is also the matter of the Spanish navy, at present on maneuver off Corsica under the command of Cortés himself."

"Cortés the killer," one of the journalists said.

"Cortés of the burnt arse," Aretino said. "Greek fire saw to his fleet when he tried to invade the New World, and will again."

"The Spanish have ironclads now," the eldest journalist said, "and they have not lost their lust for gold and converts. Having rid their own land of the Moorish caliphate, they would take their Holy War to every corner of the New World. Imagine what would have happened if it had been Cortés, instead of Amerigo Vespucci, who first made treaty with Motecuhzoma!"

Pasquale said, "And what of Salai in all this?"

"Salai feels himself threatened by Raphael, no doubt," Niccolò said, "and hence the blustering attack that you witnessed. The Great Engineer has a penchant for pretty boys, and Salai has long lost his bloom."

"The bloom of the grape has replaced the bloom of his manhood," one of the other journalists said.

"Raphael is a man whose taste runs only to women," Aretino said. "And the Great Engineer is an old man who eats leaves like a peasant, and he probably hasn't managed to get it up since he erected his tower. But Salai lives by his cock, and so he'll die by it too, one of these days. If he doesn't have the Spanish pox, then no one deserves it."

"They say the Great Engineer has it," the elder journalist said. "They say he's crazy. I've heard that he keeps birds in his apartments. They fly free there."

Aretino said, "That's less fantastic than the story that he has reanimated a corpse. Or rather, a patch-

work man sewn from the pieces of a number of ca-
davers. Even I do not believe that story, boys! As
for birds, well, every man must have a hobby, eh?
There's no harm in birds."

"Unless you think you are one, and not a man,"
the elder journalist said. "They say he crouches on
his bed-rail and caws like a rook, and flaps his elbows
all the while."

One of the younger journalists sniggered and said,
"I have it from a whore that one of the leading members of the Ten of Liberty and Peace likes to have in
half a dozen wenches at a time and strut around naked with a feather up his arse, crowing like a
rooster."

Machiavegli said with a smile, "If we believed all
we heard, then, to give but one example, every man
and woman in Florence would have died of the Spanish pox a dozen times over. Sex isn't the issue here,
despite its universal popularity. The issue is alli-
ances. Salai's the wild card who may force all to reveal their hands too soon. I do not believe that
Raphael is here to seduce the Great Engineer—it
would be too public a seduction. But if Raphael has
come to bring the Pope's terms to the Signoria, so
that they may have their reply ready when the Pope
arrives, then such a secret embassy would be embarrassing to the government if it were revealed. After
all, their motto is that democracy lives only by discussion and honest debate. That's why this incident
is so important, and why we must run it as hard as
we can, especially as not one of our rivals has
thought to cover it at all."

"It's the exclusivity that interests me," Aretino
said. "Here's something that combines sex and
honor and high matters of state, and we have it and
no one else does. That means money, boys."

"And that means you'll run it," the elder journalist said, stiffly rising from his tall three-legged stool. "I'll see what we can cut."

Aretino stubbed out his cigar, suddenly all business. "Everything else, if we have to. Gerino, kick those two young devils awake and have them break apart the type. We'll need a two-column space fifty lines deep, and I'd like it as near to the top as possible. Leon, write up a hundred-word piece on Signor Salai, nothing gratuitous, but with enough exaggeration to flatter him and serve our purpose. He's the villain of the piece, but a dupe too. As for you, young master painter, what do you know about copperplate engraving?"

Pasquale took a deep breath. His head was still packed with the fumes of all the wine he had drunk and the marijuana cigarette he had smoked: everything seemed slightly blurred and inflated. He said, as steadily as he could, "I've practiced it."

"Good. There's a desk over there. Jacopino—drag it under the lamp, and turn up the gas, too. This young man will need good light to work by. Fetch— what will you want?"

Pasquale drew another breath. "Paper of course, with as fine a surface as possible, and tracing-paper and stylus to prick a transfer for the outline. A good pen. Signor Aretino, I have practice of woodcuts, would that not be cheaper? Holly-wood is almost as good as copper."

"But I have no holly-wood, and I have a liking for copper plates because they can make very many reproductions. There will be hundreds of this edition produced. Let the last be as sharp as the first. How quickly can you do this?"

"Well, perhaps three or four hours to get it right."

"You've an hour," Aretino said, and clapped Pasquale on the back and left him standing there.

The youngest of the journalists helped Pasquale drag the desk under the hissing circlet of gas, showed him how to turn the key that regulated the drip of water onto the white rocks in the fuel-pan; as more water trickled in there was a palpable hiss and the yellow flames blossomed, starkly lighting the white sheet of paper, and throwing shadows across the room.

Pasquale lit a cigarette and shaped the scene in his mind, used his hands to block out the spaces on the paper. Space, Rosso had taught him, was the primary consideration in composition. The relationships of figures in the volume of space which contained them must draw the eye in the correct sequence, or else all was chaos. Salai at the left, then, foregrounded by Raphael who, in three-quarters profile, slightly turned from view, was the center of the picture. Raphael's followers ranged around him in a half-circle, and the masters behind them, made half-size because they were not important. Detail only for Raphael and Salai, generic postures and expressions of shame and horror for the others. To depict shame, draw a figure with its fingers covering its eyes; for horror, bent fists and shaking arms.

When Pasquale had sketched in the outlines of the two main figures he worked in the background frieze of watchers, most prominent amongst them Giulio Romano, holding Salai in check, and the assistant who had feebly threatened Salai now transfigured into a loyal and fierce servant ready to defend his master to the death, hand on dagger, face defiant. Then Salai himself, his eyes narrowed, his grin crooked, and his posture crooked too, twisted left to right. Raphael the proud upright center, the column supporting the weight of the little picture, steadfast while others shrank from Salai's bitter attack.

Pasquale worked his cramped fingers, then laid the drawing on the block of soft copper and bent to prick first the outlines of the figures, then the necessary details. Once this was done he commenced to incise the main lines, working with the rapid decisiveness and delicacy that Rosso had taught him so well. Then work in the detail, dot and dash and cross-hatch, shade and highlight.

He worked in a fever, hardly aware of what was happening around him except when he paused to work his cramping fingers, straighten his stiffening back, and light another cigarette. The printer's devils were firing up the little stove that drove the rocking springs of the printing-press. Bands of interleaved alloys creaked and groaned, stretching away from the heat to work the screw mechanism that wound the big barrel-spring, contracting back down to be heated again. The elder journalist was stooped over a tray of type, measuring lines with a marked stick. Aretino was quietly talking with Niccolò Machiavegli, puffing at a cigar which he also used to punctuate his sentences.

Their talk fell through Pasquale's fever. Niccolò was expounding a theory of power, suggesting that every society, to be stable, must in its construction emulate the Egyptian pyramid, broad at base and crowned at apex. Italy's troubles, Niccolò explained, were caused by diffusion of power, so that the ruthless could exploit the masses. States ruled by absolute decree could always conquer those ruled by democracy, for decision by one strong man was always more rapid and more flexible than decision by committee, where what emerges is not the best action but compromise. Aretino laughed and said this was all very well, but Italians would always destroy their rulers in the end, for the needs of the family always outweighed the needs of the state. Somehow Pasquale became lost in this talk, and didn't realize for a few minutes that he had sat back from his work not to rest but because it was finished.

Aretino wanted a test print at once, and insisted that the block was fitted into the press. One of the boys set the ratchet levers with a practiced hand and released the brake on the barrel-spring. With a rattle of leaf-springs and caged ball-bearings, the carrier shot back to grab a leaf of paper as the ink-roller ran over the surface of the plate, ran back to scrape off excess ink as the paper was deposited. The loom of the press fell with a rattle of counterweights, sprang back up.

The boy nimbly caught up the paper, and there, beneath the broadsheet's device, between close columns of ornate small type, was the picture Pasquale had made, shiny with wet black ink.

As Aretino took the broadsheet and held it to the light, the door of the printing-shop was flung open. Everyone turned; the man who had burst in caught the door frame, panting as if at the end of a bitter race. Wisps of smog curled around him.

"Speak up, man," Aretino said.

The man caught his breath. "Murder! Murder at the Palazzo Taddei!"

Someone else said, "Fuck. That's where Raphael is staying."

Aretino set down the broadsheet and took his cigar from his mouth. "Boys," he said soberly, "I do believe we have us a story."

4

The Palazzo Taddei was a four-square building with an imposing frontage of blocks of untrimmed golden sandstone. Windowless, it loomed out of the smoggy darkness of the Via de Ginori like a fortress wall. It was eight o'clock, but even at this late hour, when most honest citizens should have been abed, a small crowd was gathered at the Palazzo's great round gate. Niccolò and Pasquale had to use their elbows and knees to push through to the front.

Niccolò had a word with the sergeant in command of the unit of city militia which kept a space before the gate, handing over a cigar with a smile. The sergeant shook Niccolò's hand and spoke into the brass trumpet of a speaking-tube beside the gate. With a sudden arthritic creaking the dozen wooden leaves of the gate began to draw back into their sockets. A ragged opening widened into a circle. One of the upper leaves stuck, like the last tooth in an old man's jaw, and although a servant appeared and gave a hearty shove to try and force it, Niccolò and Pasquale had to duck under it as the sergeant waved them through.

Pasquale turned to watch as the gate closed up with a rattle of chained weights that in falling recompressed the spring mechanism, regaining all the energy used to open the gate except that lost through heat or noise. Successful merchants like Taddei were in love with such devices, which signified status in the way that sponsoring an altarpiece or a fresco had once done. There were tall mirrors of beaten silver on either side of the door, and Pasquale looked himself up and down before hurrying to catch up with Niccolò Machiavegli, crossing the marble floor of the sumptuous entrance hall and following the journalist through an open door into the loggia that ran around the four sides of the central garden.

The Palazzo was built in the new fashion of architecture inspired by the excavations of the Roman city of Herculaneum. Acetylene lamps on slim iron columns cast a yellow pallor that made the grass and clipped bushes of the formal garden look like their own black shadows. A scaly stone fish gushed water into the central pool, and a mechanical songbird twittered in a gilded cage, turning its head back and forth, back and forth. Its eyes were pinpoint rubies, its feathers fretted gold-leaf. A signal-tower rose above the garden; it was built into a corner of the loggia, the curve of its smooth stone wall gleaming white against the night sky. Niccolò looked up at the signal-tower for a long minute. Pasquale looked too, but saw nothing except a lighted window round as a ship's porthole, and the green and red lamps burning at the end of the long T-shaped signal-vane.

Niccolò hailed another civil guard, this one with an officer's short red cape. "The captain of the precinct station," he told Pasquale after he had had a brief word with the man. "You would expect no less than that in a case like this. He tells me it happened up in the signal-tower. He will let us through, as long as Signor Taddei is agreeable."

Pasquale said, feeling a kind of sick eagerness, "Was it Raphael that was killed?"

Niccolò took a pull from a leather flask, screwing the cap back on with deliberation. He was quite drunk, Pasquale realized: he had been drinking steadily ever since they had entered the office of the broadsheet. As a man plodding through a blizzard will choose his steps with care, so Niccolò said, "Oh no, of course it wasn't Raphael. No, it was one of his followers. A fellow by the name of Giulio Romano."

Pasquale remembered the man who had challenged Salai. He said, "He defended Raphael against the Great Engineer's catamite, as I showed in my picture. If someone wanted to strike terror and despair into the heart of Raphael, then killing his best assistant could not do it better. And if Salai did this, then he would choose the man who stood against him."

"We do not know that it was Salai who did this," Niccolò said, smiling.

"Call over the captain," Pasquale said, "I'll tell him what I think, at least."

Niccolò took Pasquale's elbow and said quietly, "You are here to record the scene, if we can but see it. In a case like this . . . it would be better if you kept your own counsel."

"I don't want to accuse anyone," Pasquale said with a sudden indignation that surprised himself, "but I want the truth of what I saw to be known."

Niccolò said, "Signor Aretino has given me leave to rewrite my account: all of the front page is mine. Ours, I should say. Do you realize what that means, young Pasquale? Well no, I don't suppose you do. But believe me that it *is* important, and it is important that enough of what I write is new, not retold common knowledge. I have had enough of that. If you tell me your story first, and to the guard the next day, where's the harm? The man is dead, and if Salai killed him it is not very likely that he will flee, for that would confirm his guilt. And if he does flee the city militia will capture him in short order. Listen, Pasquale. You are in deep water here, and do not know it. I admire your desire for justice, but think: would you die if it would save a thousand men?"

"That depends."

"If they were your fellow citizens?"

"Well, perhaps."

"Ah. And if your death would save only five hundred? Or seventy? Or ten? And if you would still lay down your life for ten men, what good would it do you when you were cold and dead and they were in the tavern drinking to you, and eating *arista*? What good is laying down your life for the common good when you can't enjoy the taste of pork and rosemary—or anything?"

"Perhaps my children will enjoy it."

"A good answer, but I don't think you have any children."

"Well, none that I know about."

Niccolò laughed. "And if you die now, you never will, and so you will be killing them. Listen: if you want to lay down your life for others, then confront your enemy in mortal combat and let him kill you, for then at least you will have saved one life: his."

"I have no enemies."

"You think not? Perhaps you don't. Then why lay down your life?"

Pasquale said, although he knew how weak it sounded, "I only want to tell the truth."

Niccolò laughed. "If you are to indulge in the vice of honesty, I hope you can afford its price."

"What's wrong with the truth?" Pasquale thought that Niccolò's love of argument would make him steal another's soul simply for the joy of it.

"Your truth is very different from that which the killer of Giulio Romano believes. You see it as murder; he as survival, perhaps, or a task which will put bread in the mouths of his children." Niccolò uncapped his flask and took another drink, shuddering with exaggerated satisfaction. "Ah. I'm an old man, and the night air settles easily in my bones."

"It seems so matter-of-fact. Like accounts. Bloodless."

Niccolò made a vague gesture, and dropped the cap of his flask. As he stopped awkwardly, he said, "Morality is not a guessing-game. There are laws, checks and balances. Where is that cap?"

Pasquale picked it up for Niccolò, who took a while screwing it back on. "I'm tired," Niccolò said, as if the matter were over. "Now I must talk with Signor Taddei."

Pasquale followed the journalist through the formal garden. A stout man in a heavy embroidered robe, a Turkish cap set squarely on his tousled thinning hair, had appeared at the edge of the loggia. This was the master of the Palazzo, the merchant Taddei, who explained calmly that the household had been preparing for bed when a terrible scream had been heard. His servants had rushed about in a panic until someone had noticed a light burning in the signal-tower, and that was where the corpse had been found, although they had to break down the door to reach it: the murderer had locked the door after him.

Niccolò listened to the merchant without interruption, and now he paused as if in thought before asking if the house had been locked up at that time.

"Of course," Taddei said, "although it saddens me to say so. These are the times of enlightenment, yet even within the city walls we must protect ourselves from vagabonds and thieves. The Swiss mercenaries who are here to protect us cause more deaths of innocent citizens than the Spanish pox, it sometimes seems."

"And of course you had your guests to protect."

"Master Raphael is attempting to calm his followers. If not for him, they would all have rushed incontinently into the night, in pursuit of the murderer."

"Master Raphael is a sensible man," Niccolò said. "Has any of the guard looked along the walls of your house? No one could have left by the doors, if they were locked, so perhaps our murderer left by a window. And if so, then there will be marks where he landed, for he would have to jump from one of the upper stories, there being no windows at ground level."

Taddei said, "I will ask the captain to order it done, if it has not been done already. But the murderer must have had a key to the signal-tower, for that is always locked at night if I have no messages to send, and expect to receive none. If he had a key to the tower, then he could also have a key to one of the doors to the outside."

"A good point," Niccolò said. "Thank you for your time, signor. Is it possible that we might see the infamous scene now?"

"Of course, if the captain will allow it."

"With your permission. One more thing. Did you send any signals tonight, or receive any?"

"No, none. As I said, the tower was locked. When the murder was discovered, one of my servants went

for the militia straight away. Their quarters are at
the end of this street."

Niccolò considered this for a moment. "There may
be a simple solution to the puzzle," he said at last,
"but I must see the tower before I can reach any firm
conclusion. Come on, Pasquale."

They walked across the garden to the other side of
the loggia, where two or three of the militia, in white
waistcoats and red and white parti-colored hose,
clustered at a door. Niccolò said, "What do you
think, Pasquale?"

"It could be a servant who did it—he may have a
key to the tower, and would certainly know where
one is kept. If no keys are missing, well, he could
have replaced it in the confusion before someone
thought to see if it were missing. And a servant
would not need to escape. Or it could be one of Raphael's other assistants, or one of his pupils. But that
would not explain why the murder was done where
it was, in a high place in a strange house."

"Bravo, Pasquale! Your thoughts mirror mine."

"Why didn't you say any of this to Signor Taddei?"

"It would insult him to imply that one of his servants would kill a guest. When asking questions of
a man, you must never slight his honor, even though
that means you must come upon the truth by a
crooked path. Slight a man's honor, and he will tell
you nothing more. Flatter him, and by and by he will
reveal more than he ever intended."

One of the militia, a slim boy hardly older than
Pasquale, let them through to the wooden stairway
that wound widdershins inside the signal-tower. It
was so narrow that Pasquale had to follow on Niccolò's heels. Niccolò stopped halfway up and banged
the flimsy rail back and forth, then went on at a
quick pace. Near the top he turned to Pasquale and

said, "Have you ever seen a dead man?"

"Certainly."

"One killed violently?"

"This past winter I attended the dissection classes at the New University, to learn how a man is put together for my painting. I've no fear of tripes."

"Bravely said. But remember that dead men do not bleed. I fear there will be a lot of blood. And then there is the matter of the bowels, which loosen at the moment of death. You didn't press your study in summer because of the smell, eh? Do not worry if you grow faint, or even are ill, Pasquale. It is no disgrace."

With two militia guards as well as the red-caped captain in the tower's little wooden cabin, it would have been crowded even if they had not had to keep to the sides, because Giulio Romano's body was laid on the raised round platform in the center. Someone had already tracked through the sticky pool of blood around poor Romano's head, adding footprints to the spatters and streaks that spangled the polished ash planks of the floor. The air was thick with a slaughterhouse reek; it coated Pasquale's mouth. There was paper everywhere, torn into scraps the largest of which were no bigger than a man's hand, and broken black glass in a heap by the little round window.

Despite Niccolò's warning, Pasquale did not feel faint; rather he was filled with an eager curiosity. He wanted to see what the journalist would do and ask, and besides, he had never before been in a signal-tower. The corpse bore little resemblance to the lively fellow who had stayed Salai's hand in the church only that morning. Rather, it resembled a badly modeled mannequin dressed in expensive black and curled around itself, remote from the affairs of men. Nothing done to me, it seemed to im-

ply, can be worse than that which was done to me
before my death. Furrows had been ripped from the
flesh of its face down to the bone of the jaw, and there
was a deep ragged wound in its throat, packed with
a kind of clotted black jelly.

The wooden cabin was no bigger than the private
cabin of a ship, brightly lit by a hissing acetylene
lamp that hung from the apex of the domed roof. The
corpse lay on a round platform lifted waist-high
above the walkway that ran around it. This little
platform was where the signaler would stand, using
his spyglass to watch, through the windows let into
the domed roof at each compass point, one or another of the local repeater arms, or the big multiple-
route complex on top of the Great Tower. Directly
opposite the door was the counterbalanced arm
which operated the tower's small signal-vane. There
was a brass speaking-tube beside it, and a slate
washed milky white, and a ball of chalk on a string.
One of the small round windows hung open, and
through it Pasquale glimpsed lights burning red and
green at the top and bottom of the signal-vane.

Niccolò greeted the captain again, took out a little
notepad and a sharp sliver of black lead, and asked if
the corpse lay just as it had been found. Pasquale
remembered what he was here for, and took paper
and chalk from his scrip, although he was not yet
ready to start sketching.

The captain said, in answer to Niccolò's question,
"Not at all. It was jammed up against the door; you
can see where blood pooled. We had the devil of a job
getting in even after the door was unlocked, and then
laid him out there so the surgeon could look at him."

Niccolò bent to inspect the door. He peered at the
lock, then stooped further and ran a finger along the
lower edge before standing. "He was dead when he

was found. That's what the servant said."

The captain was a tall man with a cap of black hair and a neatly trimmed beard around the line of his square jaw; he looked like a Roman centurion. Pasquale had his likeness in a dozen nerveless lines. The captain said, "Quite dead. His throat was torn out; there must have been a race between suffocation and blood loss to finish him off, the poor devil."

Niccolò paced around the edge of the walkway, circling the cabin once, twice. While the captain and the guards watched the journalist, Pasquale started to sketch the corpse, its huddled arms and legs, the torn throat tipped back, the face set in a remote expression Pasquale had never seen on any living face. His head felt very clear as he worked. He was beginning to understand that death was not simply a loss of vitality, but a profound change. It was something he would never forget, and it made him fear death less. You did not suffer after death. There was nothing left to suffer.

Niccolò reached through the open window, drew in his hand and showed the captain the blood smeared on his fingertips. The captain said, "There's blood all over. As if the poor devil staggered around in a mad frenzy before dying, perhaps even while his murderer tore the place apart—you see, of course, the paper everywhere. The signaler keeps a log of all messages sent or received, apparently—that's where most of the paper came from. Whoever killed Romano will be covered in blood, like as not. That's why I don't think it was anyone in the palace. We had them all lined up as soon as we could, and that was not twenty minutes after the alarm was raised. No trace of blood on any of them, and no one could have washed so quickly and so thoroughly. And no mark of a struggle on any of them either, no

with its helical screws revolving slowly the other way, the boat sank back down.

Pasquale, who had the quickest eye, caught it before it reached the floor. It was as light as a feather: in fact, the sparring which gave it rigidity was made of the shafts of a bird's primary feathers. A pigeon. Angels, pigeon-wings too small to sustain them. Artificers. "Artificers," Pasquale said. "Artificers and angels."

The captain said to Niccolò, "There's talk amongst the artificers of machines that can row the air as lightly as a peasant's coracle crosses the Arno's flood. You don't think—"

Niccolò said, "With your permission, Pasquale," and lifted up the little flying toy, peered at it with his dark eyes—pigeon's eyes, Pasquale thought, pink-rimmed and rheumy with years of drink, but still sharp.

Niccolò handed the little flying boat back to Pasquale and said, "We need invoke no fantastical explanation until all mundane possibilities are exhausted. Only then do we begin to search for the footprints of angels. This is only a toy, popular in Rome. I have seen others like it." He cocked his head as footsteps were heard mounting the wooden stairway. "Here is our missing key, in more ways than one."

The signaler was a boy at least five years younger than Pasquale, with a tonsured cap of blond hair and a fringe of fine blond hairs along his acne-speckled jaw. He was dressed in the four-pocketed ankle-length brown tunic of his order, cinched with a broad leather belt from which depended a leather pouch and a small rosewood cross. The Order of Signalers was a congregation of the Dominicans which, although secular rather than monastic, was nevertheless under strict religious rule.

The captain asked the boy pleasantly enough if he would use his key on the lock of the cabin's door, and from the way the boy looked from one man to the other Pasquale knew that his nerve was already gone. The boy signaler straightened his back and said, his voice reedy but steady, "Sir, Signor Romano bribed me to use this tower. I ask that you put me in the hands of the masters of my order."

"Not just yet," the captain said. "There's a man dead here. He's the one who bought the key from you?"

The boy gave a small tight nod. Sweat stood out on his forehead.

The captain said sharply, "Did he explain his purpose? Speak, boy! He's dead, and won't complain."

"Just, just that he wanted to make a private rendezvous."

"Not to send a message?"

"I would not have allowed him to use the apparatus, sir."

Niccolò said, "All messages sent from here would be passed through the Great Tower."

The signaler, eager to please, said, "We call it the mains trunk. It handles all traffic routed across the city, and is the relay for the land-lines south and north."

Niccolò told the captain, "The Order of Signalers are very thorough record-keepers. If Romano managed to send a signal, then you will find a record of it. No doubt it will be some simple, apparently honest and trivial message, but it will be code for something else. Signor Romano would have sent it himself because this lad refused. He would have sent it in plain talk, which is easy enough to master—

even I have knowledge of it. Anyone who practices a simple signal beforehand could send it with sufficient skill to deceive those receiving it into believing it had been sent by the proper person, which is to say our signaler lad here. Not so, boy?"

"He didn't say he wanted to use the apparatus, sir. As I said, I wouldn't have allowed that."

"But letting him borrow your key gave you a clear conscience, eh?" the captain said. "And now there's a man dead. Think on that, signaler. You'll spend the night in our lock-up before we hand you over to the tender mercies of your order."

When the signaler had been marched away, Pasquale asked what would happen to him.

"The Order of Signalers deal with their own more rigorously than we would," the captain said. "They must, to enforce and protect their scrupulous code. If the signalers were believed corrupt, who would trust a message to them?"

Niccolò said, "I can add little more to my tale, Captain. I hope you find it satisfactory."

"Your reputation is upheld, Niccolò," the captain said. "If you could tell me the content of the message, and who received it, then we would have the whole of it, I think."

"There are still many questions to answer, the least of which is the content of the message. I am more concerned with the motivation of the man who sent it. Was he a spy? And if so, did his master, Raphael, know of it or even order it?"

"Unfortunately, Raphael and his crew have diplomatic status, and so cannot be questioned, let alone arrested," the captain said. "Certainly, they will be kept under strict observation from now on, but that is not my duty. I am only a poor precinct captain who must try and catch a murderer. As to who that was, and why he murdered Romano, I am afraid your tale, satisfactory though it may be from a narrative point of view, is lacking in an ending."

"I can't tell you much about your man," Niccolò said. "Except that he is unskilled in killing, and perhaps not even armed. There is no sign of use of a blade, for there are no clean rents in Signor Romano's clothing or on his face or neck, and neither are there cuts on the palms of his hands of the kind which you would expect to find in an unarmed man trying to defend himself, or an armed man defending himself at the last from a superior opponent. A man will grasp at the blade in a last vain attempt to save his life even though it cuts him to the bone. There are no such cuts, but instead wounds made by nails and possibly teeth, and bruises in the pattern of a strong grip. Romano was bludgeoned to death in a hot fury, I would guess, by someone far stronger than he, even in his last desperate throes; even a woman may call up unguessed reserves of strength when pressed to the point of dying, and we must imagine Romano possessed of such strength, yet still he was overcome. Our murderer is a strong man then, perhaps of uncertain temper. And this man was not an accomplice to whatever Romano was up to, for if he entered with Romano, who locked the door behind him to ensure he would not be disturbed, he would have known of a key and taken it. So we must assume that he climbed in through the window and fled the same way—and I have shown you the marks of his escape, the blood that he left on the sill of the window. So while Romano's murderer is a strong man, he is also small or slender enough to enter through that small window."

"In my experience," the captain remarked, "a thief may enter through any aperture large enough to accommodate his head. Certain thieves employ young children, who can wriggle through a chink you would swear would bar entrance even to a snake. And I must say that with all my experience in housebreaking I have never known any who could scale a tower such as this without equipment. Signor Taddei is a wealthy man, and employed builders who fit blocks of stone almost as closely as those in the ancient villas of Herculaneum."

"You have visited that unfortunate city? You're a lucky man."

"My wife's family has a farm close by; they grow grapes on the slopes of Vesuvius."

"If I must bow to your knowledge of housebreakers and of Roman ruins, and indeed of architecture, I do know something of mountaineering, and would judge that it is not impossible for a skilled mountain-climber to scale what we Tuscans, who find hill-walking troubling, would assay impossible. I also note that Romano has coarse hairs caught in his fingernails; not the hairs of a man, but perhaps of the coat or collar of a coat that his murderer was wearing. In winter, and on unseasonably cold nights such as this, the Prussians and Swiss take to wearing overcoats with fur-trimmed collars. Perhaps you might start your inquiries amongst the ranks of Florence's mercenary army. A slim strong ruffian, from one of the rural cantons rather than Zurich or Geneva, and with recent deep scratches on his face or hands; there are shreds of skin along with the hairs under the victim's fingernails."

The captain said, "The Pope employs Swiss soldiers, as well as Florence. These are deep waters, Niccolò. You write this up, and I don't know what kind of trouble it might lead to. You will, I think, need the permission of the Signoria itself, and meanwhile, I must take your notebook, and the sketches of your young assistant there."

Niccolò sighed. "Of course I'll cooperate. We always do, Captain. Facts, not sensationalism."

The captain said, "That's why you were allowed here. I trust you to keep to the facts, Niccolò."

"I hoped to flatter myself that it was for my forensic skills that I was allowed to witness this terrible scene."

"I am always grateful for your opinions, Niccolò. You know that. And I will report your opinions, but the matter will soon be out of my hands, I am afraid. Now, your notes and sketches, if you please, and I will see that you are safely escorted from the palace."

The street outside the gate of the Palazzo was empty. The foul smog and unseasonable cold had defeated the crowd's thirst for sensationalism. Niccolò walked quickly to the corner, where he fumbled out his flask. He drank everything he had, and wiped his mouth with the back of his hand.

Pasquale lit a cigarette and said, "You might have left me some."

"My thirst admits no generosity," Niccolò said. He was shivering, hunched in on himself with his hands thrust between his thighs.

Pasquale took the journalist's arm, and they started down the street towards the publisher's office. He said, "What will you do now the militia have stopped your story?"

Niccolò laughed. His voice was congested. "It would take more than confiscation of my notes to stop me writing up what I've seen."

"But the captain—"

"He followed the form of the law to protect himself. He has my notes, and your sketches, and can tell his superiors that he tried his best to stop me. But he knows I will write the story anyway, and I know that you can draw the scene from memory. You have already shown how well your memory serves your art. And you have the little flying device."

"I put it in my scrip. Do you think the toy is important?"

"It isn't a toy. That's just a story I told the captain, so he would not wish to keep it. Instead, you must guard it, Pasquale. Will you do that for me?"

"Of course. But why—"

"Ah, but I'm weary, young Pasquale! Turn down here. There's a drinking-den that stays open all hours, if you don't mind vagabonds and whores."

It was a low dive in a cellar lit only by a small brazier in the center of the straw-strewn earth floor. A dozen people sat on crude smoke-blackened benches around this rude hearth, drinking new rough red wine they dipped from a common dish. Rats rustled in the dark corners. The slattern who kept the den threw stones at any which ventured near the warmth of the brazier.

Niccolò thawed after a couple of drafts of wine. "I haven't sustained such a passage of thought since my interrogation," he said. "I had forgotten how brainwork tires you."

"Is it all true, what you said?"

"Some of it, certainly. Although I'm not entirely sure about the motives which the captain ascribes to the murderer."

Pasquale said, "Perhaps the murder has nothing to do with Romano. Perhaps he merely surprised a thief or spy rifling through the messages."

"Then we must believe that Romano chose to use the tower illicitly at the same time this thief broke into it. I do not say that it is impossible, but it is highly unlikely. We can only consider the unlikely when the probable has been ruled out, and the impossible when nothing else is left."

"But there must be a conspiracy. There must! Surely it is no coincidence that an assistant of Raphael was murdered on the eve of the Pope's visit!"

Niccolò smiled indulgently at this outburst. Pasquale drained his cup and dipped more wine from the common dish—if he was to pay for this, he would get his rightful share. When he sat down again, Niccolò told him, "We are only at the beginning, Pasquale. I can assure you that I crave the thrill of the hunt—there is no finer way to keep away boredom than to solve a puzzle like this—but I must make sure I am following the right quarry."

"What of the little flying device? I've never seen anything like it."

"It may be everything, or nothing. I do not yet know. A man will carry all sorts of odds and ends with him, especially artists. What do you have in your scrip, Pasquale? Apart from the coin you'll need to pay for this vigorous wine? I will guess that there will be charcoal and goose-quills, and a little knife for sharpening the quills, scraps of paper for sketching, some English lead, a bit of bread for rubbing out lines. A block of lampblack, and a dished stone for mixing the ink. Those set you apart as an artist. But I'll wager you also have bits and pieces which set you apart as an individual, and have nothing at all to do with your profession. So perhaps with Giulio Romano. We find a little toy, and if we are not careful it takes on a significance out of proportion to its worth, and we are astray, gone from the path direct, chasing imagined shadows. Yes, it may be important, but it may also mean nothing."

Pasquale said, "In a painting, everything can be riddled for meaning. Things resonate because they have been used before, and because there is a story or a tradition behind each gesture, each flower. I saw that little toy flutter up and I thought of angels . . ."

Pasquale wanted, but did not dare, to speak of his vision, the painting that glowed in his mind, still obscure yet slowly growing clearer, as an object hidden in mist grows clearer as the viewer advances towards it. No, it was not at all like the way Niccolò had worked, piecing together a brief history of violence from its scattered aftermath. He was suddenly gripped with an ache to begin painting at once, but knew that if he did it would be a botched beginning that would set him back days, weeks, months. Whole sight, or none at all.

The cellar was dank, but the brazier's fire warmed Pasquale through, and its smoke was better than the sharp chemical stench of the artificers' smog that still clung to his tunic. On the other side of the brazier, a skinny weasel-faced fellow in rags was slowly inserting his arm in a fat whore's massive pendulous bosom, as if he hoped eventually to climb all the way into this maternal cleft. The other customers mostly nodded, befuddled by rough wine, transfixed by the glowing brands in the brazier and their own unguessable thoughts.

After a while, the old white-haired man sitting beside Pasquale spoke up. A livid sheet of scar tissue stretched across the left side of his face, drawing down his eye and the corner of his mouth. He laid a finger alongside this scar and said in a thick Milanese accent, "You're wondering where I got this, young fellow. Let me tell you I got it when I was building the waterway to the sea. The artificers used Chinese powder to blow through the solid rock at Seraville,

and one of the explosions threw burning fragments
amongst the tents where we workers was living. A
lot didn't get away from the fire, because it touched
off a store of powder, but I was fortunate, you might
say. More men were killed that night than in the
Egyptian War, but I escaped with only a scar. All
those factories there now, using the power of the water we channeled to make their goods . . . but what
did I get out of it but a pension and a face to curdle
milk? They say the artificers have freed men to be
themselves, but their machines make men like me
less than beasts, working to their pace until we can
work no more, and when we have outgrown our use
we are thrown aside."

The old man shifted a cud of tobacco from one
cheek to the other, and spat a long liquid stream towards the brazier. Leaning forward to look past Pasquale, he said, "I know you, Signor Machiavegli. I
seen you here before, and heard you talk, too. I know
you'd agree with me."

Niccolò was cheerful and alert once more, Pasquale saw. The wine had done its work, its fire driving away his dolor as a torch will drive away mist.

"We've always been free to be ourselves, in our
heads, signor," Niccolò said. "But only a few can ever
free themselves from the physical lot of the many. It
can be proven mathematically that the work ex-
pended to produce material wealth can never enrich
but a fraction of the population that must labor. Indeed, it is best for the Republic if it remains rich yet
its citizens remain poor, for individual wealth en-
genders sloth. Think of Rome, which for four hundred years after it was built harbored the greatest
poverty, yet those years were also the last happy
times of the republic. Think of Aemilius Paulus, who
with his triumph over Perseus brought much wealth

to Rome, yet remained poor himself. Like conquest, work should not make a man rich, but keep him in active, not idle, poverty."

"Now, forgive me, Signor Machiavegli, but you sound like one of those Savonarolistas," the old man said. "I can't say that I hold with them."

"I've had good cause to favor the followers of that grim prophet," Niccolò said, "but I thank God I've enough sense never to have done so."

Pasquale said, "All this talk. What good is talk." He was dismayed to realize that he was drunker than he had believed.

A figure sitting in the shadows beyond the play of the firelight stirred. It was an immensely fat, completely bald man, wrapped in a much-darned woolen cape. "The last days are here, journalist. A beast sits on the throne of Saint Peter, and will soon die. The false towers erected by the pride and vanity of the artificers will be overthrown. Put that in your paper."

"It is well known that words and not bombs are my weapons." Niccolò drank off his wine and turned his cup over, shaking the last drops over the straw between his boots. "Pay the host, Pasquale, and we will be off. We must put our story to bed before we can think of bed ourselves."

5

Pasquale returned to the studio at cock-crow. He was tired yet a long way from sleep. As he worked through the night on an engraving of the murder scene in the signal-tower of the Palazzo Taddei, Signor Aretino had treated him to several cups of thick bitter coffee, the new and expensive drink imported from the Egyptian Protectorate. Aretino had said that it cured all ills, and most particularly sleep. He was right in the last; although Pasquale was bone-tired, he felt a frail peculiar lucidity, as if he had just woken from a strange and wonderful dream.

The artificers' smog was lifting. In the veiled airy distance, beyond the swayback red-tiled roofs of the modest old houses along the narrow street, the traceries of lamps that limned the bulk of the Great Tower were fading into a watery dawn. Green and red signal-lights winked and glittered. Little arms swung to and fro on one pinnacle at the tower's top. Flocks of messages on the wing, as invisible as angels.

The city was waking with the light. Housewives

were rattling open cane shutters of first- and second-floor windows and throwing slops towards the street's central gutter—the artificers' new drainage scheme had not yet reached this part of the city—and talking to one another across the width of the street like swallows chattering in the eaves of a barn. The bells for the first mass were tolling, here and there, far and near, a communion of bells across the roofs of the city. The high chimneys of the sleepless manufactories on the other side of the Arno were sending plumes of smoke high into the dawn air, each kinked at the same height by the westerly wind which had blown away the smog. The rumble of their engines and looms was faint and regular, the monotonous heartbeat of the city's trade.

Pasquale stopped a baker's boy in mid-cry and bought a length of hot bread, its crust crunchily char-coaled. Two silver florins, payment for his night's labors, nestled in his scrip, along with the flying toy, which Niccolò Machiavegli had charged him to keep safe, and a crisp folded copy of that day's edition of the broadsheet, his two engravings anchored amongst the columns of Niccolò Machiavegli's rhythmic, urgent prose. He felt at one with the city, as if he were a part of a great intricate mechanism poised an instant from happiness. He even welcomed the company of a scrawny yellow cur that joined him on his way home and trotted at his heels until it suddenly remembered some business of its own and loped off down an alley.

The door of the studio was open at the top of the stairs; a light burned inside. Rosso was already at work. He was grinding blue pigment, seated astride the smoothing-block, his loose, color-stained apron girdled at his waist, sleeves rolled back from his freckled forearms as he worked grainy vinegared copper back and forth across the surface of the block, reducing granules to fine powder with brisk strokes, pushing the powder into a pannier already half-full with skyey color.

Pasquale felt a surge of guilt and affection at the sight of his master at this humble task. He hurried in, apologizing, but Rosso brushed aside his excuses.

"You do as you must," he said. There were smudges of blue on his forehead and cheeks; his fingers were dyed blue to the knuckles. It seemed that he had been working all night; at the worktable by the window, sections of his painting had been blocked in with washes shading to a deep, almost black umber, limning the volume which framed the figures.

Pasquale showed his master the two florins, and then the broadsheet, which Rosso took to the window and looked at for a long time. "Poor Giulio," he said, at last. "No one knows who killed him?"

Pasquale started to tell his master about Niccolò Machiavegli's investigations, while Rosso stared out of the window in a distracted way. A blade of light fell between the shutters, illuminating precisely one half of his face. When Pasquale had finished, Rosso said, "I have it in me, Pasquale, to be a great painter. That fool of a hospital director—he knew nothing, nothing! They knew about painting here in Florence, once upon a time, but no more. It is all artificers and their devices, and trade, and talk of an empire to rival that of ancient Rome. But without art it is hollow, Pasquale. It is nothing."

So it was back to the business of the misunderstanding over the cartoon—the devilish-looking saints Rosso had sketched as a misfired joke, the director's outrage at seeming sacrilege. Rosso turned from the window and added, "That fool of a monk shouted up to me a few minutes before you came in. He was asking if we had rats."

"He must take a census of his grapes every day."

"You will look to Ferdinand," Rosso said sharply. "He's caused enough trouble, and I need no more distractions while I'm working. I tied him to your bed, Pasquale, so don't go untying him."

He had Pasquale write up the two florins in the workshop's leather-bound account book, weighed the coins in his hand and then handed one to Pasquale. They were equals, he said, they had been so for some time. He could teach Pasquale no more, and soon enough Pasquale should make his own way in the world.

"Master, I'll never stop learning from you."

"That's kind," Rosso said, with a vague sadness, although he smiled. "In better times, if things were different . . . More and more, it is not what we can do, but we have done, Pasquale. We are fading into history."

"You know that isn't true, master," Pasquale said, and suddenly yawned.

"Get some sleep. A few hours. We have work to do today for that crazy artificer."

Pasquale fell asleep as soon as he lay down on his bed, hardly noticing that the Barbary ape was tied by a length of rope to the frame. He awoke to the sound of the ape screaming, and sat up and saw that it was gone. It had slipped the loop of rope around its leg. Men were shouting, too, Rosso in the next room, and the monk in the garden below. Pasquale sprang to the window and saw the ape cowering in a corner and chattering and screaming as the monk tried to dislodge it with a pole, and all the while Rosso hurled curses on them both.

Pasquale cut the rope from the bed-frame with his

knife and flung an end towards the ape. It saw its chance and swarmed up the grape trellis using hands and feet. As the trellis started to collapse under its weight the ape managed to grab the rope—and almost pulled Pasquale out of the window. The monk flung aside his pole and dodged backward as vines and trellis collapsed around him.

The ape climbed to safety, leaping across the sill and landing on the floor. Suddenly, Rosso was in the room, belaboring the ape about head and shoulders with a broom. Pasquale got between them, shouting that Rosso should stop, please, it was over. Rosso's face cleared, and he flung aside the broom and buried his face in his hands. The ape jumped onto the bed and threw the blankets around its head.

Pasquale didn't know whether to comfort master or ape. The monk was shouting up from the garden, using words no man of God should know, let alone voice, shouting that he would call on the Officers of Night and Monasteries.

"Pray for us, brother," Pasquale shouted back. "Show some Christian charity." He banged the shutters closed and turned to Rosso, who had calmed himself.

When Pasquale started to apologize, for after all he had taught the ape to clamber up and down the rope, and to steal grapes, Rosso said simply and flatly that it wasn't his fault at all. "It is the nature of the beast, Pasquale. I got it as a joke, you know, and here it is still, a burden around my neck like the old man of the sea, or a demon."

"Do you think he'll call on the magistrates?"

Rosso pressed the heels of his palms against his eyes. "Oh, no doubt he will. He has a narrow selfish soul. Remember that Dante reserved a circle of Hell for those pillar-saints who retreated from the world to enrich their own spirituality, as a miser hoards his coins. Monks are just the same, in my opinion."

The ape, hearing their voices, took the blanket down from its face, and they both had to laugh to see it looking at them like an old woman peering around a fold of her shawl.

Rosso sighed. "There is still much to prepare for today's work."

Pasquale helped Rosso grind the rest of the pigments they would need for their commission. The blue salt made by placing copper over vinegar, the new white lead pigment, red from crushed beetles, bright yellow sulfide of mercury. Each was suspended in egg-yolks thinned with water and vinegar (which turned the blue green), or in size (which kept the blue blue), mixed in the big wooden buckets reserved for fresco work.

The commission was simple enough. They were to paint a fresco of primary colors in sinuous shapes on the wall of a bank in the Piazza della Signoria. The Pope, entering the piazza in the shadow of the Great Tower, would be confronted with this fresco, somehow changed by artificer's trickery into a marvel. Or so the artificer promised: so far he had told the painters nothing about how the trick would be done, being a man who delighted in secrecy. Still, a commission was a commission, and the artificer paid well, and in advance.

The façade of the bank had been given its first layer of plaster and the outline of the design had been drawn on it in charcoal under Rosso's supervision two days before. Newfangled scaffolding had been erected, based on modular units jointed like the legs of an insect, with a regularity quite unlike the forest of props which underpinned the irregular wooden planking of traditional scaffolding. The artificer was waiting for Pasquale and Rosso when they arrived shortly after noon, with the little gang of laborers who carried their pigments and brushes and buckets and sponges and the rest.

The artificer was a plump young man with a round, shining, olive-skinned face, watery blue eyes and a neatly trimmed beard. He was dressed in the usual artificer's uniform of a many-pocketed leather tunic, loose black Turkish trousers and shiny black leather boots with iron toe-caps and buckles at the knees. His name was Benozzo Berni; he was a distant relative of the great satirist.

Berni had been commissioned by the bank to create this spectacle, and was consumed with a high nervousness that he might, through some fault of omission, fail and be destroyed. He had already raised a great fuss because of the delay caused by the celebration of the Feast of Saint Luke, and now made a great deal of the fact that his apparatus was already in place. This was a device a little like a catapult, except that instead of a ballista cradle it held an array of acetylene lanterns, and a series of lenses and mirrors through which the light would be projected. It sat in front of the scaffolding like a skeletal goggle-eyed frog. Just how this device would combine with the big amorphous shapes of the fresco was, Berni said, still a secret.

"You will see on the day. That is, if we are finished."

Berni did not treat Rosso as a skilled craftsman hired to carry out a task as best he might, but rather as a laborer, and insisted that he and his assistants, two beardless boys younger than Pasquale by at least five years, check every line of Rosso's translation of the outline pattern onto the wall, using little brass sighting instruments hinged on a semicircular scale.

The pattern was not complicated, and it only took an hour more to go over the charcoal lines with brushes loaded with red ocher, and then to brush away the charcoal to leave only the red ocher outline, the *sinopia*.

Rosso and Berni then fell into an argument over the best way to proceed. Rosso insisted that he should work as he had always worked, from one area to the next, from top to bottom, but the artificer wanted each color done in order because there must be no tonal variation, something he deemed impossible if different patches of the same color were painted at different times. Rosso, slighted by this implication, pointed out over and over, his voice rising each time, that his skill would ensure that different patches of plaster could be painted to exactly the same hue, and at last Berni threw up his hands and stalked off, quivering, to light a cigar.

"We'll start at the top, as we always work," Rosso told Pasquale. If he was still upset by the behavior of his ape, this small victory had done something to restore his self-esteem. "The fool needed convincing that otherwise drips would fall on finished work. We use the blue first, on the dry plaster. I've had them overplaster the *arriccio* for the blue yesterday, to save time. Let's hope they've done it properly. It's getting dark, and Berni promises light from his machinery, but I don't know, Pasquale, I have never worked with artificial light."

Pasquale and Rosso worked with tacit agreement, quickly finishing the areas of blue, then supervising the laborers who mixed and applied the plaster to the remaining areas of the *sinopia*. The trick was to make sure that the plaster was thin enough to dry quickly to the right consistency, yet had enough tooth to take the pigment. They worked area by area, painting on pigments diluted in lime-water with quick sweeps of the largest hog's-hair brushes once the plaster was at the right stage of drying. Halfway through the work, with daylight fast fading, the artificer had the big acetylene lamps of his apparatus lit, and its mirrors and lenses adjusted to cast diffused yellowish light across the face of the building, so that now Pasquale and Rosso had to work with the angular shadows of the scaffold-framing and their own shadows thrown across the face of the fresco.

"This isn't painting, but a race," Rosso grumbled.

Pasquale said, "So now we're house-painters, master." In fact, he was happy enough because of the sheer physical pleasure of slopping on pigment.

"We will work as best we can, as we have always worked," Rosso said. "We are still craftsmen, first and last, no matter what the work."

Pasquale had worked on enough frescos to know about the problems. Rough walls had to be made smooth by applying a thick coat of rough plaster, *arriccio,* either directly to the brick or stone, or to thin mats of reed laid over it to protect the work from moisture, the greatest enemy of fresco. That was an art in itself: the *arriccio* had to be smooth, but not so smooth that it lacked the roughness necessary for the adhesion of the final layer of plaster, and its consistency had to be carefully controlled. The point of dryness at which you applied the paint affected not only the resulting color, but also the life of the fresco: too damp, and the paint would sink too deeply and thinly into the plaster; too dry, it would not take properly, and flake. Blue pigments, mixed in size, could only be applied to dry plaster, and had to be patched and replaced every thirty years or so. For that reason, the fresco was divided into small areas by the *sinopia,* a quick sketch or a finished detailed drawing covered in turn with one more layer of plaster, the *intonaco*, put on in patches: small patches where detailed work was needed, as in a face or a hand; larger areas where little detail was required, such as the background drapery or landscape.

If this had been a proper fresco, they would have worked one patch at a time, one day to one patch. Here, with two dozen patches of similar size but irregular shape, each washed with just one primary color, they could work at speed, laying relatively dry plaster on three patches one after the other, so that by the time they had plastered the third the first would be ready for painting.

Even with the help of the laborers, who mixed plaster and paint to specified dilutions and carried the trowels and buckets to and fro, Rosso and Pasquale were hard-pressed. There was no time to think. Pasquale was absorbed in the task at hand: the sweep of the smoothing trowel over a freshly applied patch of plaster; the slap of the big coarse-haired brush over the grainy, absorbent wall. The sky bruised beyond the glare of the artificer's lanterns. Moths kept blundering into Pasquale's face, attracted to the light as to a candle-flame; his bare arms, scaled with spots of dry paint, were itchy with mosquito-bites. Pasquale hardly noticed, and was so caught up with his work that he had to be told to stop by Rosso when at last they were finished.

6

Pasquale was watching the laborers dismantle the oddly jointed scaffolding when Niccolò Machiavegli found him. He was sitting on an overturned crate, eating black bread and salt cod with one hand, making quick notes about the workers' postures with the other; a flask of coarse red wine was at his feet. The taste of coppery pigments and dry plaster-dust mixed with the salt tang of his food. His arms quivered with exhaustion. One of the workmen, a yellow-haired Prussian, had a perfect unmarred physique, and Pasquale resolved to try and get the fellow's name: perhaps he'd pose for a few pence.

Rosso was talking with the artificer beside the light-throwing device. The ape, Ferdinand, leaned against its master's leg, pleased to be freed from the chain which had tethered it to the foot of the scaffolding during the work. The artificer's assistants were wrestling with the lenses of the device, thick greenish glasses in copper rings on jointed armatures which they moved this way and that in response to their master's fussy orders. Circles of light moved on the painted wall; shadows thrown by the scaffolding rearticulated themselves, drew up in new configurations. The lamps made a steady roaring.

Niccolò Machiavegli walked through the glare of the lamps, and Pasquale jumped up when he recognized him, happy to see the journalist. Perhaps he had solved the mystery already.

"I'll take some of that wine," Niccolò said mildly, and while he drank Pasquale asked about his investigations.

"Do you remember that I believed that poor Giulio Romano had sent a message before he was murdered?"

Pasquale lit a cigarette and blew out smoke with a luxurious voluptuousness. "You found out what it was? The captain of the militia was going to make inquiries."

"There was no message. The captain had the relevant logs searched. Nothing."

"Then Romano must have used the tower for some other purpose."

"And yet he had lit the signal-lamps, Pasquale. Why would he do that if not to send a message?"

"Perhaps that was the signal." Pasquale thought of the little toy tucked away in his scrip.

Niccolò smiled. "That is just what I think. Perhaps Romano was not sending a signal to the relay-tower, but to someone close by the Palazzo. Perhaps a signal that it was safe to enter by a prepared way. Perhaps Romano was not a spy, but a turncoat within Raphael's circle. Or perhaps he had business of his own. Or perhaps he was tricked by the murderer, which means that someone wanted him dead—or wanted to hurt Raphael by killing his best assistant."

"Well, we can't know that Romano was a traitor. The man is dead. God must judge him."

"The captain has charged me with a task, Pasquale. I'd have you help me, if you would. I would interview Raphael himself, for the captain cannot. Raphael has the Pope's embassy, after all. Will you come? You needn't say a word, but use your sharp eyes, your artist's sensibility."

"I'll do it gladly." Pasquale would do anything to meet Raphael. How jealous the other pupils would be!

"We have one call to make before we visit Raphael," Niccolò said. "I have made a list of the enemies of Raphael, and this is the second name on the list. Michelangelo Buonarroti."

"Surely not!" Pasquale said, with a mixture of scandalized affront and prurient interest.

"It's well known that they are bitter rivals. Michelangelo claims that Raphael has stolen his ideas."

"They say that's what caused Michelangelo to quarrel with the Pope. But I do not think Michelangelo would kill one of Raphael's assistants because of it."

Niccolò said, "Certainly, to do so in Florence would be very foolish, but anger can make a fool of anyone."

"He really will talk with you?"

"On this hour."

"And if Michelangelo is only the second fiercest enemy of Raphael, who is the first?"

"Why, the husband Raphael has cuckolded, of course. Unfortunately, as he is one of the optimates who currently rule this city, and who was among those who had me imprisoned on trumped-up charges, I can hardly put him to the question, much as I would like."

Pasquale said, "Am I allowed to know who he is?"

"If it is necessary . . . but it is not yet necessary.

There's one more thing," Niccolò Machiavegli said, his mild face bent to look straight into Pasquale's. "I have received what I may suppose is a death threat, a broken knife in a package. Of course, it may mean nothing. We journalists are often threatened, and this arrived long after the broadsheet was distributed. I would take it more to heart if it had arrived before the broadsheet went on the streets." He raised the flask to his lips and tipped back his head. "Ah. This is terrible stuff, Pasquale. Surely Signor Aretino paid you properly?"

"More than enough. Signor Machiavegli—"

"Niccolò. I'm no landowner. Not any more. The Spanish took that away."

"Niccolò . . . Do you really think Raphael is involved in a plot against our city?"

"There's no evidence for that. I'm not going to put him to the question, Pasquale. I'm just going to ask him about his poor assistant, who was so brutally murdered. This is no official investigation, you see. There can be none, for Raphael is under embassy from the Pope. He cannot be prosecuted, or arraigned, or even accused. To do so would be to yield the moral high ground to our enemy. That this is not official, in fact, is just why we are allowed to proceed. There is to be no scandal, no rumor. You understand?"

"Completely."

"Then if you are finished here, say farewell to your master. We have only a little time."

Despite Niccolò's haste, Pasquale persuaded him to make a detour to the studio, where Pasquale changed from his work-clothes to his best black serge jerkin, a doublet with deep slashes lined with expensive red silk offcuts, and red hose. He washed his face and hands, carefully brushed his curls and pinned a soft velvet cap to the back of his head, Niccolò by now pacing up and down with impatience, then splashed his palms with fresh rose-water and rubbed dried lavender flowers between them, patted the fragrance under his jaw, on the sides of his neck.

"How do I look?"

"You'll make some lucky man a fine bride," Niccolò said.

"I'm visiting the two greatest artists of the age— of course I must look my best. Just one more thing." Pasquale found the lily he had made from scraps of gold-foil, and pinned it to his breast. "There," he said, "now Raphael will know my allegiance," and wondered why Niccolò laughed. He added, "Should I take my sword, do you think?" It was a short, sweetly tempered Flemish blade with a pommel he had reworked with gold-leaf and red leather.

Niccolò's smile was both amused and sardonic. "We are petitioners. As such, we persuade with a keen edge to our intelligence, not our swords. Put down your sword, Pasquale, and follow me."

Michelangelo owned a large property on the Via Ghibellina, three houses side by side. He had his workshop in the middle one, which had a large stable he had converted to a studio by raising its roof to the height of three stories. One half of this big room was screened off; behind the screen, as Pasquale well knew, was the half-finished heroic statue commemorating the victory of the Florentine navy at the Battle of Potonchán, when the Great Engineer's underwater vessels had sunk half the Spanish fleet bent on invading the empire of the Mexica, and his Greek fire had destroyed most of the rest. Michelangelo had been working on this monument, fitfully, for the last ten years. He would allow no one to see

it, not even members of the Signoria, which had
sponsored it, and his enemies said that he would
never finish it.

Two apprentices, in long smocks and paper hats,
were working on a small block of pure white stone
under a flaring crown of acetylene lights. The ringing
taps of metal on stone echoed in the high space as
they made the preliminary passes to free the shape
trapped in the stone. The smell of fresh stone-dust
sharpened the air. A trestle-table was littered with
their tools: pointed punches, flat chisels and toothed
and clawed chisels, battered mallets of different
sizes, files, a bow drill. Tubs of abrasives—emery,
pumice and straw—stood beneath the table. Above
all this, like the skeleton of one of the fabulous an-
tediluvian dragons, towered the steam-winch which
maneuvered large blocks of stone in and out of the
studio.

Michelangelo took Niccolò and Pasquale into his
office, a small shed tacked to the side of the studio,
its walls scaled with perspective drawings. He had
them sit on low stools, handed them glasses of bitter
artichoke liqueur, and smiled when Niccolò, who
immediately drained his glass, said that it was good
of him to agree to this interview.

"I've nothing to hide. I was working here last
night, at first with my assistants, and later on my
own, but that was very late. Several friends were
here—I can give you their names if you require it."

"That's very kind, but I'm sure it won't be necessary."

Michelangelo said, "I'm sorry for Giulio Romano's
death—he could have been a first-rate artist if he had
not chosen to live in his master's shadow. But I never
had a quarrel with him. Do have more of this liqueur,
Signor Machiavegli. It is the only thing about Rome

that I miss. Do you know, by the way, of the Fraternity of Saint John the Beheaded?"

"That, like your excellent liqueur, is also of Rome. I believe its brothers comfort condemned prisoners."

"Exactly. I was a member of it, you understand. We believed that some good could be found even in the worst of humanity, just as I found my David in stone that had been hacked and botched by Simone da Fiesole (perhaps you have heard of him, Pasquale), a crime, in my opinion, as bad as murder. Through my involvement in the Fraternity, I know all about justice, signor, and the rewards of murder. I have a good business, as you see. I would not give it up for anything, and certainly not for Raphael."

"Perhaps," Niccolò said, "you know of someone who may have quarreled with Signor Romano."

"I don't keep up with the gossip in Rome," Michelangelo said dismissively. He was a lean, sinewy man with excessively broad shoulders, and a keen gaze beneath a craggy brow furrowed by seven deep lines. He leaned forward, his head alertly cocked, gripping the edge of his stool with his powerful hands. His fingers were nicked and scarred, and one nail was blackened by a fresh bruise. They drummed the edge of the stool to the rhythm of his assistants' work on the stone.

"Old grudges are often the most deadly," Niccolò said.

Michelangelo laughed. "That's true enough. Everyone thinks I have a quarrel with Raphael, but anyone who fights with a good-for-nothing gains nothing. My opinion of Raphael is well known, I won't deny it, but I have better things to do with my time than campaign against his reputation. The light in the public square will reveal that for what it is, by and by."

Niccolò said, "I believe you once said that no one who follows others can ever get in front of them."

"Oh, exactly. Those who can't do good work on their own account can hardly make good use of what others have done. My quarrel is not with Raphael, but with those who don't see him for what he is. As for Giulio Romano, no one had reason to dislike him, unless there was some quarrel between assistants. The way Raphael runs his business, it wouldn't surprise me. He is so careless he must appoint a man to manage his affairs. So long as he wants to be rich, he'll remain poor."

"I'm certain that whoever killed Romano was known to him, but that it was not someone of Raphael's immediate circle."

"I'd question his assistants closely, Signor Machiavegli—you are going to interview them?"

"Tonight, as you probably know."

"And you, Pasquale? Are you going to give Signor Machiavegli the benefit of your advice?"

"I'll help him if I can," Pasquale said, pleased and embarrassed by Michelangelo's attention.

"Then I hope you're a strong swimmer," Michelangelo said. "Your master, Rosso, helped gild my David when he was the assistant of Andrea del Sarto. I trust you're as diligent a pupil as was he."

Michelangelo excused himself and had a brief but earnest conversation with his assistants, then returned and poured another round of artichoke liqueur, and affably exchanged political gossip with Niccolò for a few minutes, before gently making it clear that he had much work to do before the next day, when he was leaving for the quarries at Serevezza.

Niccolò Machiavegli did not seem disappointed by this interview, although Pasquale felt that it had been a waste of time—they had learned nothing that they did not already know.

"On the contrary. We know that Michelangelo still fiercely resents Raphael, and we also know that he will leave the city for the next few days."

"A polite withdrawal, so that he will not need to meet the Pope," Pasquale said. "That's been known about for weeks."

"Without doubt. But if anything happens while Michelangelo is away, then we will know he is innocent."

"He could hire ruffians to do his work."

"Perhaps," Niccolò said cheerfully. "But did you not observe how he treated his assistants? He could scarcely bear to let them work unobserved, and dashed out to check their work as soon as he was able. A man like that, a master of his trade, would not trust others to complete his work for him. I've made a long study of the behavior of men, Pasquale, and Michelangelo is one who will never delegate important work. Now let us hope our interview with Raphael goes as well."

There was no crowd of onlookers outside the Palazzo Taddei, and only a single militia guard remained. The man waved Niccolò and Pasquale past with a smile. The gate irised open, and as before one segment stuck; Niccolò gave it a rap, as if for luck, as he and Pasquale ducked beneath it. The major-domo of the Palazzo, splendid in a crimson uniform trimmed with gold, his air grave and faintly disapproving, led them to the half-dozen rooms of the top floor which had been allotted to Raphael and his followers.

The chambers, lit by candles as scattered as stars, casting more shadows than light, had a rich disordered look, like an encampment of gypsies endowed not only with fabulous wealth but also a ravishing artistic sensibility. The stone walls were swagged with drapery or covered with Flemish tapestries. Canopied beds were in disarray, clothes scattered across them, trays of half-finished meals set on their rumpled sheets. In one room, a naked young man slept face-down on a couch, his buttocks pale crescents in the half-light; in the next, black hunting-dogs sprawled on rushes before a cavernous, empty fireplace; in a third, two men at a chessboard hardly looked up as Niccolò and Pasquale were led past by the major-domo.

Raphael lay on an immense bed in the last of the rooms, propped up on a heap of bolsters. He wore a white chemise loosely tied across his smooth-skinned chest, black hose with an obscenely large codpiece, red felt boots. A young woman slept beside him, her hair unbound and her shoulders bare, the coverlet carelessly cast over her.

A gray-haired man sat on a stool by the bed; three more of Raphael's followers sat at the fireplace, close to a roaring blaze. One of them, a fat man with sweat standing on his jowly face, loudly and jovially told the major-domo that they would have to start chopping at the furniture if more wood wasn't brought. The major-domo bowed and said without demur that he would see what could be done, then announced Pasquale and Niccolò and bowed and withdrew, more like a polite host than a servant doing his duty.

Raphael sat up straighter, stroking the hair of the woman beside him when she stirred in her sleep. He welcomed Niccolò as an old friend, looked askance at Pasquale. Pasquale stared back at him boldly, although he was beginning to sweat in the close heat of the room.

"My assistant," Niccolò said.

The gray-haired man whispered something in Raphael's ear; the artist nodded. "He's the pupil of Giovanni Rosso," Raphael said, staring directly at Pasquale. His eyes were heavy-lidded and half-closed; his eyebrows made a straight black line across the bridge of his proud nose. Threads of gold were wound in the mop of his long black curly hair. In a few more years, Pasquale thought, he would be fat: you could see it in the way his neck made a fleshy bulge to meet his chin as he lounged amongst the bolsters like a sultan; in the thickening of his wrists. The thought did not lessen Pasquale's awe—here was the richest painter in the world, painter to princes and popes. He looked around, hoping to see sketches, cartoons, perhaps a half-finished canvas propped on a chair. There was nothing of the kind.

Niccolò said, "Pasquale has been good enough to help me. He was here last night. Perhaps you saw the drawings in the broadsheet that illustrated my article."

Pasquale said with dismay, "They are nothing."

Raphael flicked his fingers, as if at a fly. He wore rings on every finger, heavy gold rings studded with rubies and emeralds. "I don't read the broadsheets. I do see that Florentine painters still dress with their customary flair. Is that paint in your hair, or a new tint?"

Pasquale blushed and said, "For your honor, sir, I would have preferred to have had enough leisure to remove all traces of my day's work, but the matter is urgent, although Master Niccolò is too polite to tell you."

The gray-haired man whispered in Raphael's ear again. Raphael said, "Painting a backdrop for an artificer's light-show isn't really working, but I suppose you must take what you get."

The fat man by the fire said with jovial malice, "There's the motto that made Florence the center of the artistic world. How often I heard it, so that I never wished to hear it again."

A second man said, "We have enemies here, Signor Machiavegli. Michelangelo Buonarroti in particular. He is consumed in a fury of jealousy since he lost the Pope's patronage. We have been subject to his false accusations, his crazy assertions that he invented every technique in the history of painting. He is a dangerous man."

Raphael said, "We do not fear Michelangelo. But he can be troublesome, and he has many friends."

"Many friends amongst the so-called artists," the second man said.

Niccolò said, smoothing things over, "I have suffered enough false accusation to understand your caution, but let me assure you that we are here as servants of no one, except truth. You all know me. You all know I cleave to no faction, take no side."

This seemed to satisfy Raphael. He clapped his hands and loudly called for wine, then winked at Niccolò. "I assume one of Signor Taddei's vintages will be acceptable."

"You're very kind."

"Taddei is a good friend to me, Niccolò. What's happened is distressing enough. That it should happen in the house of my friend makes it worse. I'll help you if I can, if in turn you'll be frank with me. Is there a chance that his murderer will be found by the city militia?"

"I don't think so."

Raphael said to the gray-haired man, "I told you!

They care nothing for us. We are amongst enemies here, and there is danger on every side."

The gray-haired man said, "We mustn't speak of that."

"No," Raphael said, "no, I suppose not. All in good time, eh?"

A sleepy-eyed boy half Pasquale's age brought in a gold tray bearing a flask of wine and half a dozen gold beakers. He poured wine, handed round the beakers, smiling when Pasquale gasped at the solid weight of his beaker, its buttery smoothness. It was pure gold, worth a year's profit. The wine gave off a rich, heady aroma.

Raphael drank his wine down in a gulp, held out his beaker to be refilled. He said languidly, "What do you think, Niccolò? Be truthful. You know I respect your opinions. Who murdered my friend?"

"In truth, I have yet to form an opinion, except that I am certain that the murderer does not live in this house."

The fat man by the fire said, "Which leaves only two hundred thousand of my fellow Florentines, every one of them with a knife in his purse and murder in his heart."

"Be quiet!" Raphael thumped the bed. Wine slopped from his beaker and stained the coverlet. The woman beside him stirred, but did not wake. "Be quiet," Raphael said again, softly. "Giovanni, you're a fine painter, most especially of animals, but right now you don't see the nose in the middle of your face. I loved Giulio best of all of you, and he is dead. I want to find who killed him, but more important than that, I want all of us to get home safely. We are the focus of some terrible conspiracy, our enemies are everywhere . . . but it is nothing that we cannot overcome, eh? A day, two days, and Papa Leone will be here. Meanwhile we must be vigilant. You all know how much my fame has cost me. For every admirer there are two who say I am only derivative, that I am only a reflection of Perugino, or that I stole from Michelangelo. I, whose ideas have been stolen more often than any other, whose works are copied and printed in every country without my permission . . . !" He took a breath, clearly struggling to master his emotions. "Niccolò, what would you know?"

Niccolò waited until he had everyone's attention. "In my experience," he said quietly, "the best way to understand how a man came to be killed is to work backward from the moment of his death. That is, to know what he said and what he did, and what was said to him, and by whom. To know who hated him, and who loved him, to know his enemies and his friends. I'd talk with you and your disciples, if I may, about all that befell Giulio Romano after his arrival in Florence. That, to start with."

"You ask a lot," Raphael said.

"Forgive me, but I ask only because I know what your friend meant to you."

"Only that? You don't know how much you must work, to earn one-tenth part of what Giulio meant to me." Raphael inclined his head to listen to the gray-haired man's discreet whisper. "All I ask," Raphael said, "is that your assistant waits outside while you put us to the question, Niccolò."

Pasquale's anger flared. He said, "Romans are very fond of secrets, it seems. If I speak plainly, forgive me, but I can't help it, being a mere Florentine."

The gray-haired man said mildly, "Myself, I am from Venice. As to secrets, I have heard that Florentines love secrets above all else, particularly those of other people."

"Excuse me, signor," Pasquale said, "but we haven't been introduced. If you are from Venice, why then you must love secrets more than any Roman, and certainly more than anyone in Florence. Your city is a city of secrets."

"Lorenzo is my agent," Raphael said. "I trust his opinion. Please, young man, as a favor, wait outside. Baverio," he said, to the boy who had brought in the wine, "look after the friend of my friend."

"It's all right," Niccolò told Pasquale, adding in a whisper, "I'll tell all after."

"And have them send up more wood," the fat man said, as the boy servant led Pasquale away. "Florentine air is bad enough; but I'd forgotten that Florentine cold is worse."

"They don't mean any harm," the boy, Baverio, told Pasquale as they left the room. "My master is convinced that his mission here has put him in mortal danger, and his assistants are all convinced that they will be cut down one by one. We are painters, not soldiers or ambassadors."

"Then you do have a mission," Pasquale said. "We thought as much."

Baverio looked unhappy—a pout, a toss of his shoulder. "Please, I'm not skilled in these games. Here, sit, I'll fetch wine, we'll talk. I want to help." They were in the room where the black hunting-dogs dozed in the cold fireplace. Pasquale sat on a carved stool, let the dogs smell his hands and rumpled their folded ears. His father had owned two such dogs; their soft mouths could bring back shot songbirds without hurting a feather. His anger was gone. He was simply tired.

Baverio brought a flask of wine and a round of hard cheese; Pasquale sliced off a hunk of cheese and chewed and sipped alternately. Baverio watched

him. He wore a velvet tunic striped in dark green and
black, elaborately buckled breeches of the same material, and black stockings. A gold circlet rested on
the mop of his springy brown hair.

Pasquale remembered the circlet Rosso had placed
on his own head—but Baverio's was real gold. He
told the boy that he looked more like a princeling
than a servant, and asked if he too was a painter.

"I draw a little, but not well enough."

"Anyone who is properly taught can draw well
enough. Surely, with a master such as yours—"

"Then perhaps I lack ambition. It is enough to
serve my master as best I can."

"You said you wanted to help. Perhaps you can tell
me . . . do you know why Giulio Romano was in the
tower?"

Baverio shook his head. "I was helping my master
at his bedside toilet when we heard the screams. We
rushed out, all of us, and that was when we realized
Giulio was not amongst us. But as to how he came
to be in the tower, and what message he was sending . . ."

Pasquale took a risk, calculating that one disclo-
sure might be worth another. "Giulio Romano sent
no message, but perhaps he sent a signal, simply by
lighting the lamps on the signal-vanes. A signal to
someone outside the Palazzo, someone waiting to
come in, or wanting to know that it was safe to come
in."

Baverio said with some agitation, "You must not
think that Giulio would betray my master! He was
my master's best friend, a master in his own right
who for love pure and simple used his talent to help
my master complete his commissions. Listen, Pasquale, if Giulio was killed by someone outside the
Palazzo, as Signor Machiavegli implied, then why

was Giulio signaling that it was safe to enter? And if that person had entered on Giulio's signal, why did he make his way to the tower and kill Giulio and then escape?"

"I think that's why Niccolò wants to ask his questions. It's like the cartoon for a painting. We have the lines, as it were, but none of the details. I don't think Giulio meant to harm your master or any of his friends, Baverio, but perhaps he was mistaken in his choice of allies on whatever business he was about."

"That is my master's burden," Baverio said. "Take more wine, against the cold if not for your stomach's sake."

"It's very good."

"Then you must thank Signor Taddei." Baverio grew serious, leaning forward and fixing his eyes on Pasquale's face, and enveloping Pasquale in a cloud of musky perfume from the silk pomander hung at his breast. "I said that I want to help, and it was not an idle boast. While the others were trying to break down the door of the tower, and then trying to find a key, I went to look for Giulio. I do not know what I was thinking of, except that it seemed to me that he might have returned to his bed. It seemed that if I could find him there, then all would be well, all would be as it had been."

"I understand."

"He wasn't there, of course. He slept in the room adjacent to my master's, in the same bed as me. I knew his satchel was still there, hidden under the bolster, and I looked in it. I don't know why. I am ashamed of having done it, and haven't told anyone, not even my master. Especially not Raphael."

"I won't tell anyone, Baverio, not even Niccolò."

"It was the wrong thing to do," Baverio said, "but

it may have been the right thing to do, too. I found something there, and have it still. I heard the guards coming, you see, and thrust it into my scrip. Here."

Baverio drew out a square of shiny glass. Pasquale thought at first it was a small blackened hand-mirror, but the black coating was too friable, and he could scrape off a curl of the stuff with his thumbnail. He sniffed: a piercing chemical reek.

Baverio said, "It was wrapped in black silk, and when I drew it out it changed from gray to black, I swear this. There was also a box of stiff black-painted leather. On one side of the box was a kind of sliding cap, covering a little hole. But the guards took that away, with the rest of Giulio's luggage."

"An artificer's toy of some kind," Pasquale said. "There was glass like this, broken in a heap, in the signal-tower. And there was this, too." He drew out the little flying toy from his own scrip. "Here, look. Your friend's dead hand was clutching this. These are common in Rome?"

Baverio took it between his fingertips, turned it around and handed it back. "I've never seen one before."

"I thought perhaps some artificer in Rome might have made them."

"Your own Great Engineer is the greatest artificer of them all. Perhaps he would know."

"I'm pleased to hear that there is someone of the embassy from Rome who sees some good in Florence."

Baverio said, "I saw your Great Engineer only yesterday. We had an audience with him, and he spoke alone with my master for an hour. He will attend the feast in honor of the Pope, my master says."

"Then it will be the first time in twenty years that he has left his Great Tower. He awaits the new

Flood, that will sweep away the wickedness of the world and leave only the pure in heart behind. He has written pamphlets on this—some say that is why he invented the movable-type printing-press. But I'm not the Pope, Baverio. I can't ask him about these things."

"Then ask some other artificer." Baverio cocked his head. "My master calls." He handed the flying toy and the blackened glass to Pasquale. "These things were important to Giulio, Pasquale. You keep them. Find out what they mean."

7

As they were led out by the impassive major-domo, Pasquale asked Niccolò what he had learned, but Niccolò Machiavegli shook his head and whispered, "Not here."

Outside, as the sections of the round door ratcheted shut behind them, Niccolò told Pasquale that they would wait and watch from the other side of the street. They sheltered in a doorway, watching the Palazzo's gate through traffic rattling past. This was a main thoroughfare, busy with carts and carriages, velocipedes and *vaporetti* in the last hour before the city gates closed. The city was filling with people from nearby towns and villages who had come to see the Pope. Acetylene lamps shed a weary simulacrum of daylight.

Pasquale asked, "Who do you expect to arrive?"

"We are waiting for someone to leave. I believe that not only Giulio Romano is involved. We will wait and see who leaves, and then we will know who it is. And we will follow him, for he will lead us to those who plot with him."

"Everyone sees plots everywhere."

Niccolò took a little nip from his leather flask. "When I was Secretary . . ."

"Is this the time for drinking?"

"There were plots everywhere, back then. There are always plots."

Pasquale felt a pang of sympathy. "Those memories must be painful, Niccolò."

"All memory is painful. We remember what was, and in remembering inevitably think what could have been. It is the nature of men never to be content with their lot, no matter that they are rich or poor. The beggar may curse the optimate in his carriage as it goes by, thinking that there goes a man without worry, but that same optimate may look out and see a free man in rags, without the responsibilities of power. By Christ's balls, it is cold out here." Niccolò blew on his hands. Stray light from a distant lamp made his stubble-shadowed cheeks look blue, his dark eyes black.

Pasquale lit a cigarette, and offered another—his last—to Niccolò.

Niccolò smiled his sadly pensive smile. "That's one vice I don't have."

"Unlike drink, it is a simple pleasure that will not kill you." Pasquale instantly regretted his moralistic tone. "You talked with Raphael, and now you seem unhappy."

"In wine I escape from my past, forget what has happened to me and what I fear might happen, and think only of the moment. A problem like this, Pasquale, is nearly as good as wine. One needs problems, to keep back the past, and boredom. There! Look there, Pasquale!"

Pasquale saw a paired spark, red and green, high

above the tiled roof of the Palazzo. The sparks moved away from each other, then back again.

"The signaler has been dismissed, yet someone uses the tower," Niccolò said, with a certain satisfaction. "Unless of course Signor Taddei is a part of this conspiracy."

"Can you read the lamps? What was the message?"

"I can read plain-talk, if it is transmitted at a slow enough rate. But that was no message, just a simple swing of the signal-arms. Now we will wait and see what has been summoned."

"What did Raphael tell you?"

Niccolò said, "Raphael has much to protect. He is a careful man, friend of princes . . . and of course of popes. In such company you learn circumspection should you wish to survive. You cannot behave like our own Michelangelo."

"He talked of plots. He dismissed me because he feared I was part of a plot." Pasquale remembered the little square of black glass in his scrip, nestled next to the flying toy. He knew that he should tell Niccolò about what Baverio had said, but did not know how to begin.

Niccolò said, "There are always plots, in the circles in which Raphael's ambition has thrust him. Such men can trust nothing and no one. It was not a personal thing, Pasquale. It is just business."

"I know that, but thank you."

They smiled.

Niccolò said, "It is my understanding of human nature that men are evil-ready. Since the Fall they must struggle against their nature to achieve goodness, because their nature tends to evil. Think of the single virtue of goodness, and the army against which she stands: ambition and ingratitude, cruelty and envy, luxury and sloth. In particular, sloth. We are all drunkards at heart, and curse the drunkard not out of hate but jealousy. If we were brave enough, we too would roll in the gutter with him."

"Niccolò, are you talking about men in general, or men in particular?"

"Oh, I feel it in myself," Niccolò said, and took a long pull on his flask.

There was a silence. There was less traffic now. Passersby hardly spared a glance for Pasquale and Niccolò: after all, they were doing no more than lounging and watching the world go by, a popular sport in Florence. They watched the guard walk to and fro in the circle of lamplight by the closed maw of the gate in the Palazzo's forbidding wall. Once, he stopped and bent over a flare of light, then sucked on his lighted pipe and blew out a long riffle of smoke, flicked away the spent match.

Niccolò, watching its arc, remarked, "Lucifer falls."

"More and more I find myself thinking of an angel . . ."

"Lucifer Morningstar was the prince of angels, the most beautiful until the instant of his rebellion. I've always wondered which wounded God more, Man's Fall, or that of His chief lieutenant."

"Well, He sent His son to redeem us."

"Perhaps our redemption is only the first step towards the redemption of Lucifer. But that is not a thought you must repeat, Pasquale. Even in excommunicated Florence, it may be enough to send you to the stake as a heretic, as they tried to burn Savonarola. You cannot count on a thunderstorm saving you. But what angel are you thinking of, Pasquale?"

"The archangel Michael, who drove Adam and Eve out of paradise."

"Never a popular theme, I must admit. You know,

I have always found it odd that the Fall does not have a feast-day. Perhaps then there would be a tradition for you to follow. Although I suppose you have seen the painting by Masaccio."

"In the Cappella Brancacci, yes. I admit there is a certain despair conveyed in the attitude of the figures of Adam and Eve, but they are somewhat crudely rendered—poor Adam will never straighten his leg, which is curved inward. I have also seen Mantegna's allegory in which Pallas expels the vices from the garden of virtue. But I am interested in the angel himself. I wish to paint only him, yet in such a way that the viewer at once knows what is happening."

"They would know that by his burning sword."

"Then perhaps I would omit the sword, too. I want to make something new . . ." Pasquale was embarrassed. Ordinarily he enjoyed talking over the problem he had set himself, yet this was no tavern brag about a commission, but a personal truth. He confessed, "I do not yet know how to begin."

Niccolò said, "I suppose that, like writing, the beginning is always the hardest part of a painting. Ah, here now. What is this?"

A carriage had pulled up at the gate of the Palazzo. It was one of the new designs. Pulled by a single horse, its black body was taller than it was long, an enlarged upright coffin set between two large wheels. The driver leaned down from his high seat to have a word with the guard, and then the leaves of the circular door grated back, and a man stepped out.

It was the fat assistant, the painter of animals, Giovanni Francesco.

He clambered into the carriage, and at once it started off. As soon as it had driven past their doorway, Niccolò rushed out into the street, waving at a *vaporetto* with an empty load-bed. He shouted to the driver that if he could follow the carriage there was good money in it, and waved Pasquale over.

"Show this good fellow your purse."

"Niccolò—"

"Hurry! We'll lose him."

The driver, a gnarled ruffian with a sacking hood cast over his head, seemed convinced by the florin that shone amongst the little slew of clipped pennies, but told them they'd have to ride in the back and started up his machine even as they clambered aboard.

The little *vaporetto* trundled down the Via de Ginori and swung around the symmetric church in the Piazza San Giovanni, which shone a pure white in crossed beams of light thrown from lensed lamps burning at its base. The *vaporetto*'s boiler, fired with soft Prussian coal, sang a dreary unvarying note; its exhaust waved a vast smut-laden plume of steam in the night air like a banner. Pasquale and Niccolò clung to the rail of the load-bed, jounced and buffeted as the unsprung wheels rattled over bricks and Roman paving-flags. They jolted down the Via Romana, tangled in traffic going east and west across the Mercato Vecchio where carriages, carts and *vaporetti* threaded around each other in a clangor of bells and hooting of steam-whistles, and the shouts and curses of the drivers.

Niccolò leaned out and shouted to their driver to go as fast as he could, and the man said sharply, "That's just what I'm doing, signor. Don't think I don't know my own business."

"Of course not, my dear fellow."

"Any more than this and the gears will strip. The new models have gears rimmed with beaten iron, you see, but this is one of the first made, nothing but wood in her drive-train. And besides, the road will do for her axle-trees."

"A horse, my dear fellow, would go faster. I'm minded to find one."

"You do that if you want, but I'm your man that will take you where you want to go without delay. I still have sight of your carriage, don't worry. Looks like he's heading for the river."

"We can't run all that way," Pasquale said.

Niccolò told the driver, "Your cursed smoke-stack hides my view. I trust you to follow correctly."

"I'm your man," the driver said again. "There he goes, see, straight down the Via Calimara. Don't you worry, he's going to cross the river at the Ponte Vecchio."

"If I could see him, I'd be a great deal happier," Niccolò said.

Pasquale leaned out and, sighting around plumes of steam, glimpsed the high profile of the black carriage only a little way ahead of them. The driver's guess was right. They entered a queue of traffic that was slowly making its way past the little shops that lined both sides of the bridge. Lamps strung high above the roadway cast a cold glare; the doorways of the shops, most of them butchers' or tanners', threw patterns of warmer yellow light. Frescos on their stone façades were faded under soot and grime. People were threading amongst the slow-moving single line of traffic, offering food or drink or machine-made trinkets to the drivers and passengers. Once, the line of traffic stalled entirely, and the driver of the *vaporetto* took the opportunity to stoke his vehicle's boiler. Pasquale leaned out again and saw the top of the black carriage half a dozen vehicles in front and told Niccolò.

"He'll turn left at the end of the bridge," Niccolò shouted at the driver, who nodded.

There was a gap in the buildings at the middle of the bridge. As the *vaporetto* passed, Pasquale could look down at the central channel of the Arno's tamed braided flow. Far off, a great two-masted ship, lights burning on every spar, was making its way upstream towards the new docks across from Sardinia. It was the *Our Lady of the Flowers,* towed by a wood-burning tug with churning paddles, at the end of its long voyage from the New Florentine Republic of the Friendly Isles. Pedestrians had stopped to watch her approach out of the darkness. Pasquale felt a great stirring in his breast. Then the *vaporetto* edged forward with a hiss of steam and he saw her no more.

At the end of the bridge, the carriage turned left, just as Niccolò had predicted. "He would hardly be going to the Palazzo Pitti," the journalist said, "and there's little enough up-river but the shanty slums of manufactory workers and the manufactories themselves. If our man was going there, he would have stopped at the bridge and walked, so as not to draw attention to himself."

The carriage turned left again, onto a dark dusty road which, with cypress-trees on either side, climbed the side of the valley towards the southern city wall. Crickets made their chorus; a full moon stood low at the head of the valley, made red by the fumes of the manufactories. The *vaporetto* followed the carriage at a respectful distance, its boiler laboring.

At last the carriage drew up at a gate leading to the extensive walled grounds of a large villa. A crest of a lion rampant was set in the arch over the barred gate. The driver of the *vaporetto* drove on without slowing, and at the last moment Pasquale managed to get Niccolò to crouch down. Fat Giovanni Francesco was leaning at the window of the carriage, talking to a uniformed guard.

"For the sake of Christ, we must keep out of sight," Pasquale said to Niccolò, who tried to stand up again. "If they see us, the game is up."

"I want to see what he is doing."

"Going to the villa, I should think. Stay down!"

"You must learn never to assume anything," Niccolò said, but he stayed where he was.

As soon as they were safely out of sight, Pasquale told the driver of the *vaporetto* to stop and turn around. Niccolò jumped down, and told Pasquale to give all his small coins to the driver. "Wait here for us," he told the driver, "and you may exchange that money for the florin we have."

"I'm your man, signor."

"See that you are. Come, Pasquale."

They walked back down the road in cricket-filled moonlight. On one side were the walled gardens of the villa; on the other, a grove of wide-spaced olive-trees where the wooden bells of goats grazing in the moonlight made a random clattering. Pasquale protested mildly that Niccolò was very free with money that wasn't his.

"I was responsible for your commission, if you remember. I know that even if you spend that florin, you'll have one left over."

"And to think that I started out with two this morning," Pasquale said, remembering his act of generosity when he had given both florins to Rosso, remembering how glad he had been to receive one back. But he could not have seen how things would have fallen out, and besides, there would be a little money from the fee for painting the fresco for the artificer.

Niccolò said, "You'll earn more from this. This is just the beginning. A story like this, in episodes, will keep the populace buying the broadsheet for days. They would rather waste their time reading idle gossip and speculation than Plato or Ariosto, and I am in no position to deny their wishes. Well, but do you know whose villa this is?"

"He's a Venetian, by the crest over his gate." Pasquale was thinking that he'd earn little enough from this: there were no dramatic images to be had from sneaking up on a walled house at night, even by moonlight. Or rather, if there were such images, he would be in no position to draw them.

"That's very good," Niccolò said with approval. "In fact it is the villa of Paolo Giustiniani, a writer and mystic, a nobleman of Venice, and a disciple of Marsilio Ficino. You know of that last gentleman?"

"I know that he was a magician."

"He was a priest and philosopher first, but his studies led him to the black arts, and astrology. And into trouble with Rome. He took his magicks entirely too seriously."

Pasquale took Niccolò's arm, halting him. "We can't just walk up to the gates," he said. "Giovanni Francesco will know at once that we followed him. I'm not certain that we weren't seen as we went past. You were standing as plain as the Gonfalonier in a procession."

"They would have thought us honest laborers on their way home from a hard day's toil."

"Laborers don't ride *vaporetti*, Niccolò. And even if you might pass for one, no laborer has ever dressed like me. If we want to learn what is going on, I think it will be best if we skirt around the wall, and climb it well away from any lights."

It was not, of course, as easy as that. Wild thorn-bushes grew in the ditch at the base of the high rough-dressed stone wall. Niccolò's cloak kept catching in their canes or amongst tufts of rank grass, and to his vexation Pasquale's best hose was torn in two places. He climbed to the top of the wall easily enough, but then had to haul up Niccolò by main force.

They jumped down, landing amongst dusty laurels. Beyond was a long formal lawn crossed from several directions by gravel paths which met at a big seashell fountain standing in its center. An avenue of cedars bordered one side. The branches of the trees, black in the moonlight, each seemed to float at a different level. This part of the garden was higher than the villa, so that Pasquale could see, beyond its tiled roof, the nighttime city spread in the valley below. The largest buildings caught the light of the rising moon—the golden dome of the Duomo, the Great Tower and the smaller tower of the Palazzo della Signoria beside it, the towers of churches, the private *palazzi*. A scattering of small lights limned the main streets, while the green and red lamps of signal-towers made a radial pattern converging on the Great Tower's constellation.

"We must beware," Niccolò said in a hoarse whisper. "I hear that Paolo Giustiniani is accomplished in his arts."

"Surely a rational man has nothing to fear from magicians."

"Magicians have kept pace with the artificers. They are science's black reflection, and should not be underestimated. Or better, magic is science's shadow, for surely where light is cast there must also be shadow."

"Not if the light is directly above the object, or if the light comes from all directions equally."

Niccolò said with asperity, "I should not suppose that I could argue optics with an artist. It was merely a figure. Come now. We will learn little here but how diligently the gardeners attend to their labors."

"Not diligently enough outside the wall. My clothes are ruined. If I had foreseen this, I would have left them behind, and brought my sword instead."

"I'm not unprepared," Niccolò said. "Keep close to me, and do as I say."

They started towards the house, keeping to the shadows beneath the cedars. Pasquale fumbled in his scrip and drew out the square of black glass. He said simply, "While you were talking to Raphael I was given this."

Niccolò held the glass up to the moonlight, sniffed it, then scraped its friable coating with a fingernail, which he put in his mouth. "It may be nothing, or it may be something."

"It was in Giulio Romano's possession," Pasquale said, and explained about the box that Raphael's boy servant Baverio had also found.

"Then it may well be something. I think you may have learned more than I, Pasquale. You must keep it safe, together with the flying toy."

"Venice is in alliance with the Pope, isn't she?"

"Yes, but Paolo Giustiniani is an unlikely representative. He was forced to flee Venice in disgrace after an incident involving a virgin and, I believe, a black cockerel."

"Perhaps he wishes to return to favor."

"Perhaps. Or perhaps Giovanni Francesco is also a practitioner of the black arts. Or perhaps they are simply friends, who enjoy each other's company. Speculation can be useful, but it is always better to learn. Quietly now, Pasquale, and carefully. There may be traps, and there will certainly be guards."

The single-story villa was built of white-painted stone, with a roof of red, ridged tiles, and a square tower at one corner. Lights blazed from every one of its tall arched windows, and Pasquale and Niccolò slipped from one to the other until they came upon one which looked into a room where fat Giovanni Francesco stood. His back was turned to the window as he faced an older man who sprawled carelessly in a high-backed throne-like gilded chair. Dressed in a black robe, with a square black cap on his long straight gray hair, he rested a fist under his chin as he listened to Francesco expound some argument.

The window was closed to keep out the night's chill—a fire burned in the grate of the room's fireplace—and Pasquale could only hear the murmur of Francesco's words, not their sense. Beside him, Niccolò took out a short hollow wooden rod. It had a kind of trumpet at one end, to which he applied his ear after setting the other end against the glass. "A trick I learned from a physician," he whispered. "One must master all of the arts and sciences, to be a good citizen. Keep watch, Pasquale."

They squatted there for several minutes, Niccolò listening through his hollow rod, Pasquale dividing his attention between the dark garden and the lighted room. Then the voices of the two men inside rose, and Pasquale heard Giovanni Francesco shout something about pictures. He brandished a small wooden frame that held a picture done on glass.

The gray-haired man, without doubt Paolo Giustiniani, rose from his high-backed chair and snatched at the picture. Francesco stepped back from Giustiniani's advance, then bowed and handed it over.

Black-robed Giustiniani, his face showing a cold contempt, listened to what Francesco had to say, then threw the picture into the flames. Francesco waved his hands and protested in his high, slightly hoarse fat man's voice that as there was another made at the same time, it would be well to keep to the agreement, and Giustiniani said, in a loud clear voice that made the glass in the window shiver, "I've no more need of our agreement!" He snatched his cap from his head and pressed it to his face, and dashed something to the black and white tiles of the floor.

Brown vapor boiled up, and Francesco stumbled back, choking, as the other man made for a door, slamming it shut behind him. The room was dim with brown fumes. Francesco was on his knees, then on his belly. The fire guttered, sending out black smoke to mix with the deadly vapor.

Niccolò threw off his cloak, wound it around his left arm and smashed in the window with his elbow. Vapor poured out, a vile acrid stink worse than any artificer's smog. Pasquale pulled Niccolò out of the way and said, "Francesco is surely dead." He was frightened that the noise of the breaking glass would alert the guards.

"Perhaps," Niccolò said, "but the worst has blown out—look, the fire burns again."

He knocked out the rest of the glass and clambered over the window's low sill. Pasquale took a deep breath and followed.

At once his throat started to burn, and his eyes stung and filled with tears so that he could hardly see. Groping together, he and Niccolò turned Francesco's heavy body over, but it was clear from his bulging eyes and the froth on his blue lips that he was dead. Pasquale remembered the picture and managed to snatch the charred frame from the rekindling fire. The effort was almost fatal. His whole chest was filled with a burning pain; his mouth and nose flooded with watery mucus.

Then Niccolò got his bony shoulder under Pasquale's arm and helped him to the window. They tumbled through it together, and Pasquale promptly vomited as cold fresh air strong as heart of wine hit his face.

He still had the charred picture-frame in his hand.

Niccolò got him to his feet, and together they made a stumbling run for the shadows beneath the avenue of cedar-trees. Pasquale's throat was parched, and a band of iron had tightened around his brow, but with every step he felt his strength return as the magician's poisonous smoke was purged from his lungs.

Just as they reached the trees they heard the clamor of several voices raised in alarm. Pasquale threw himself flat and Niccolò dropped beside him. The grass was wet with cold dew. "I am too old for this," Niccolò groaned.

Pasquale pointed to the three men silhouetted in the light from the broken window. He said, "They'll think that Francesco brought friends with him. There, see!"

The three guards, each carrying a lit torch, set off in different directions. Somewhere else a dog barked.

Two more figures broke out of the shadows at the corner of the villa and sprinted across the lawn towards the high wall. A cloak flapped around the taller of the two as he ran with clean strides; the other ran bent almost double, with a curious loping gait. The guards saw these two and shouted and gave chase, their torches hairy stars streaming sparks.

"Francesco had friends after all," Pasquale said, astonished.

Niccolò said, "We will go towards the gate."

"It is already guarded!"

"Perhaps the guard is one of those giving chase."

Shouts, and then a single pistol-shot. Niccolò said, "One thing is clear. We cannot stay a moment longer."

They turned the corner of the villa, ran down the wide graveled path towards the gate. The path divided around a statue of a griffin sitting on its haunches, one front paw supporting a shield. As Pasquale ran past it, ahead of Niccolò, he felt something tug at his ankles. He stumbled, caught himself on hands and knees.

Above him, the statue of the griffin stirred. It shook at every joint, then reared up on its hind legs. Pasquale crouched beneath it in terror and amazement. The shield fell with a wooden clatter. Steam burst from the griffin's mouth and it made a tremendous grinding roar as its head turned to and fro. Its eyes were red lamps. All down the long path to the gate great flares burst into flame, hissing and sizzling and throwing up thick smoke that glowed whitely in the moonlight. Somewhere distant a brazen gong clanged and clanged.

Then Niccolò was pulling at Pasquale, shouting that it was only a mechanical device, a festival trick. Pasquale got to his feet, feeling foolish. The griffin's movements were already subsiding. Niccolò was right; it was a mechanical device of the sort constructed by artists or artificers as centerpieces for those great public spectacles so loved by Florentines. No magic—or not yet.

Niccolò flourished a pistol, an odd weapon with a kind of notched wheel over its stock. "Have a brave heart," he said. His face was alive: Pasquale realized that this was what he lived for, desperate moments where courage and luck determined whether you lived or died.

They ran on, and as they neared the gate its guard took a wild shot at them. Niccolò fired back as he ran, fired and fired again without reloading, the wheel of the pistol ratcheting around with each shot. The guard fled through the open gate, and a moment later Pasquale and Niccolò gained the dusty country road and saw the *vaporetto* jolting towards them at top speed, fast as a galloping horse, and wreathed in vast plumes of steam.

They waved at it, and had to jump aside as it slewed to a halt, wheels spinning in the road's soft rutted dirt. The driver shouted that they must climb in and released the brake at the same moment, so that Pasquale had to jump onto the load-bed and haul Niccolò after him, his arms almost starting from his sockets with the effort.

There were pistol-shots as the *vaporetto* banged down the steep road. Something burst overhead, a bright glare that grew and grew until it outshone the full moon. By this floating magical light Pasquale saw that a carriage, perhaps the same one that had delivered poor Francesco to the magician's lair, was chasing them at full tilt. Niccolò saw it too, and calmly told the driver to go faster. When the man started to argue, Pasquale took the florin from his scrip and held it over the driver's shoulder. Without looking, the driver reached up and plucked the coin like a grape. The *vaporetto* leapt forward, throwing Pasquale and Niccolò backward onto the load-bed's rough planking.

Niccolò rolled over on his belly, making a kind of choked laughter. "Did you see how that guard ran? I would have killed him if I could. I shot to kill. My blood was up."

"From your talk it still is," Pasquale said, feeling his bruises. He tried to sit up and a great jolt as the *vaporetto* shot over a hummock in the ill-made road knocked him back down again. He swore and said, "We still aren't free yet."

"I have my pistol. The self-loading wheel does little for its accuracy, but rapid fire is certainly discouraging to those who face it. Did you see the guard? He ran like a Spaniard."

"This isn't a war."

"Any kind of combat makes beasts of men. They revert to their base nature."

"You may have another chance to enjoy your base nature very soon," Pasquale said, squinting past the tattered clouds of the *vaporetto*'s exhaust into the night behind them. The black carriage had fallen far behind, for its horse could not keep up with the *vaporetto*'s breakneck downhill speed, but he was certain that it would not give up the chase.

The slope of the road flattened out, houses crowding now on either side, and the *vaporetto* began to slow. The driver shouted that water in the boiler was low, that he would have to stop soon and refill it.

"Go on as best you can," Niccolò told him.

"If the tubes boil empty over the burners, they'll blow," the driver said. "There's an end to it."

Pasquale said, "I think you will need your pistol, Niccolò. They are gaining on us."

As he spoke, crossbow-quarrels flew out of the darkness with shocking suddenness. Most missed the *vaporetto*, but two thumped into the load-bed and promptly began to give off acrid white smoke. Pasquale wrestled one from the plank in which it had embedded itself. Its shaft was almost too hot to hold, and its point was hollow and fretted with slots from which the smoke poured. Pasquale threw the quarrel over the side, but burned his hand when he tried to pull out the second. Then more quarrels whistled past and he ducked down. One thumped into the splintered planks a hand's breadth from his face, burying itself up to its flight feathers; an ordinary quarrel, but still deadly. The new crossbows fired quarrels with such force that even a glancing blow could kill a man.

Niccolò clutched one of the posts of the load-bed, waving his pistol. The shaft of the smoking quarrel that was still embedded in the load-bed suddenly started to burn. In a moment, bright blue flames spread across the tarred planks. Niccolò steadied his pistol with both hands and fired back at the carriage, laughing wildly all the while, so that Pasquale feared he had lost his reason.

The *vaporetto* made a sharp right turn onto the Borgo San Jacopo and was suddenly amongst a crowd of workers. Workmen flung themselves to either side as the *vaporetto* plowed into their midst. They were the *ciompi*, the shift-workers of the sleepless manufactories. They were dressed in shabby patched tunics girdled with rope, shod in wooden clogs, and wore shapeless felt hats on their heads to keep off the night's cold. Many were shaven-headed, a result of a scheme of the artificers to eliminate lice. They shouted and jeered as the *vaporetto* sped past. The carriage was very close now; Pasquale could see the driver standing on his bench, his arm rising and falling as he whipped the horse on.

The driver of the *vaporetto* looked over his shoulder, his face white and his eyes reflecting the flames leaping up from the load-bed. He uttered a wordless cry and threw himself from his bench into the crowd. The *vaporetto*, rudderless, slewed and slowed, and ran into the wall of one of the houses that fronted the river. Its boiler-tubes split open and vented live steam; the burner-pan broke loose and spilled burning coals that set fire to the undercarriage.

Pasquale jumped down at once, but Niccolò stayed defiantly atop the burning vehicle. He emptied his pistol at the carriage, which had pulled to a halt, its terrified horse rearing in its traces. Here was a picture for the broadsheet, Niccolò raving and firing his pistol through flames, the crowd backing away, the black carriage and its plunging black horse. It burned itself in Pasquale's brain.

Then Niccolò threw away his pistol and jumped down. Pasquale grabbed him and they ran. *Ciompi* parted before them like the Red Sea before the Israelites. More shots from the carriage. Pasquale saw a man in a hemp jerkin struck in the teeth by a pistol-ball; he collapsed spouting blood from his ruined mouth.

Niccolò was out of breath, and Pasquale had to haul him along by main force. He was after all an old man of fifty, and for all his wiry frame not fit to run this race. Suddenly, he staggered and swore and clutched at his thigh. Blood welled over his hand. "I'm hit!" he shouted, and seemed strangely exhilarated.

Pasquale hauled him on, daring to look back and seeing the carriage stranded amongst the angry mob. The Ponte Vecchio was ahead. Its angle-tower loomed over the heads of the crowd. Pasquale and Niccolò limped on, dodging through streams of *ciompi* shuffling wearily towards their shanty-town hovels at shift's end, or marching in resignation towards that night's work. From a viewpoint high above Florence, from the top of the Great Tower perhaps, there were no individuals visible in the gaslit crowd. Two men escaping with their lives were less disturbance than a pebble thrown in the river. Along the Borgo San Jacopo, there was a commotion around a burning *vaporetto*, and a carriage was surrounded by an angry mob, which suddenly drew back as the carriage was enveloped in a spurt of flame and colored smokes, which blew away to reveal it empty. But this was only a temporary disturbance. All disturbances in the calm unfolding of the city's routines were temporary, no more than an incalculably minute faltering, as of a speck of grit caught and crushed in a gear-train, in its remorseless mechanisms.

PART TWO

---◦◦◦---

As Above,
So Below

I

The caravan of carriages which carried His Holiness Pope Leo X, lately Giovanni di Bicci de' Medici, his advisers and attendants, his page-boys and cooks, his dwarfs and jesters, including his favorite, Father Marioano, his physicians and his Muslim rackmaster and bodyguard, and cardinals Sanseverino Farnese, Luigi de' Rossi, Lorenzo Pucci, Lorenzo Cibò and Giulio de' Medici, and their own lesser entourages of servants, moved in a great cloud of dust visible for many miles as it toiled past the little villages of Pozzalatico and Galluzzo. A squadron of the Swiss men-at-arms marched at the rear, their burnished chestplates, helmets, pike-heads and halberds glittering like a river in the clear fall sunlight; a pipe and drum band of fully fifty men in scarlet and white uniforms marched ahead.

Rumors of the procession's approach flew ahead of it as birds fly ahead of a forest fire. The chain of signal-towers along the Siena road passed messages back and forth in a continual flutter of semaphore arms. As the procession reached the brow of the last hill before the valley of the Arno, it began to pick up a tail of private citizens who had ridden out on horseback or private carriage or *vaporetto*, adding to the official escort of city militia that flanked the papal procession as it rattled down the long dust-white road, banners flying and drummers beating a frenzied marching-beat even though their hands were blistered and bleeding.

It was noon when the procession at last reached the great open space before the Roman Gate in the city walls. Here it stopped, and with a flurry of attendants the Pope climbed down from his carriage. He wore a dazzling white silk rochet embroidered with heavy gold thread, white gloves of fine kid, embroidered with pearls, and white silk slippers. He was a heavy man, with a coarse face and bulging shortsighted eyes, rolls of fat at his neck and a generous paunch. A jeweled tiara was pinned to his vigorous black hair. He looked bothered by the fussing of his attendants, although he bore it with stoicism, and did not neglect to wave to the crowd gathered at the gate.

A mounting-block was brought, and the Pope was helped onto it. He drew out a little brass spyglass and stood for a few minutes looking at the city in the valley, spread either side of the channeled river beneath its own umber haze. He turned this way and that, taking in the bristling defenses of the rebuilt walls: the organ cannon, rocket-launching tubes, ballista, broad cannon, and from each tower the diamond shapes of tethered man-kites flying high in the brisk wind. He focused on the Great Tower rising out of a tumble of red-tiled roofs and dominating the square crenellated tower of the Palazzo della Signoria, the great gilded dome of the Duomo beyond, topped by its shining gold ball and cross. The smokes rising from the manufactories along the river, the angular maze of docks packed like a pincushion with clustered masts of ships, the complex geometry of the sluices and channels and gates that tamed the flow of the Arno: the Pope looked at them all.

Perhaps he was thinking of the cruel assassination of his father in the Duomo, at the hands of the Pazzi conspirators, or of the uprising against the tyranny of his uncle which until now had banished every one of his family from the Republic. At any rate, tears rolled down his florid cheeks as he put away the spyglass and submitted to the indignity of being hauled onto the side-saddle of a fine white Arab stallion. Although he was a passionate huntsman he was a poor rider, and suffered from anal fistulas that made sitting in a hard narrow hunting-saddle agony after only a few minutes.

Still, he was smiling as the procession ponderously got under way again, and became a pageant that slowly rolled through the great gate and along the Via Maggio.

Crowds lined the wide street, ten deep. The Pope ceaselessly signed his benediction with plump hands cased in pearl-trimmed white leather gloves. Half watched in silence, remembering the heavy yoke of Giuliano de' Medici's rule when, bent on revenge for the assassination of his brother, Lorenzo, he had purged half the city's merchant families and robbed the rest to repay his debts, or remembering the words of Savonarola's famous sermon which had started the brief but bloody civil war in which the Medicis had been overthrown. Savonarolistas in the pay of the King of Spain had been busy defacing walls with slogans culled from their exiled leader's published works, and workmen were still busy washing them away as the procession moved past. The other half of the crowd, drunk with faith or wine, or both, cheered and waved pennants and shouted out their approval.

Palle! Palle! Papa Leone! Palle! Palle!

The Pope rode slowly, with two pages leading his white stallion by its gold-encrusted bridle. Eight Florentine citizens of noble birth held over his head hoops of moire silk cunningly locked together to form a canopy in the shape of a butterfly's wings. Despite this shade, the heat of the day soon turned the Pope's heavy face an alarming tinge of purple. Now and again he would halt to admire the banners and decorations that hung from every building, or watch the staging of brief tableaux. In one, a child dressed as an angel announced the birth of Christ to a young woman dressed as the Virgin, and burning halos swung above both their heads while a mechanical dove fluttered down and emitted a ray of dazzling light that struck a mirror stitched into the woman's dress above her womb. In another, an actor in the burnished silver armor of Saint Michael fought a copper-scaled mechanical serpent, piercing it through its mouth so that it gushed realistic blood from every orifice. There was a brief pageant in which Cristoforo Colombo stepped from his boat through waves represented by twisting blue cloths, to be greeted by actors naked but for loincloths and with feather head-dresses and skins stained red with tobacco juice, the noble Savages of the Friendly Isles of the New World. Further on, Amerigo Vespucci was received by King Motecuhzoma II of the Mexican Empire, who was seated on a small white, stepped pyramid amidst a cornucopia of maize, hog plums, guavas, pitahayas, avocados, sweet potatoes and manioc set on gold and silver plates.

The Pope only glanced at this last tableau before

jogging his horse forward. Rome supported the contention of Spain that the Savages of the New World, from the innocent Indians of the Friendly Isles to the proud bloodthirsty Mexican and Mayan empires, must be conquered in the name of Christ, and that Florentines were endangering their souls by consorting with Savages and accepting them as equals.

At each halt the Pope's huge escort stopped too; by now it was stretched so far down the street that by the time the tail had halted the head was setting off again. At each halt the drummers drummed and the pipers blew shrill trills; chamberlains threw coins into the crowd from bulging moneybags; the men-at-arms marched smartly on the spot, their faces luminous with sweat; and cardinals leaned out of their coaches and craned forward to see what now had caught His Holiness's attention, for later they would have to remark on every feature of the procession. Firecrackers and colored smokes made the soldiers uneasy. On the rooftops, sharpshooters armed with the latest long-barreled rifles stood against the sky, watching for any trouble.

So the Pope gradually made his way down the Via Maggio and across the bridge of Santa Trinità, riding slowly beneath a triumphal arch of canvas and wood painted by the workshop of Raphael and erected only that day by over two hundred men. Fully five hours after he had mounted his horse at the great gate, Pope Leo X finally entered the Piazza della Signoria to a tremendous clangor of bells and thunder of cannon that set every bird in Florence on the wing.

The welcoming shouts were louder and more numerous there, for the more favored citizens had been drinking sweet white wine from gilded barrels, and there were trestle-tables groaning with food under awnings pitched along the sides of the square. Spectators leaned out of every window of every building, and the confraternities raised up their standards and banners so that a flock of strange hieratic images of saints seemed to bend their attention towards the Pope as his horse was led slowly across the square. Patterns of colored light revolved across the plastered front of the First Republic Bank, swarming in the gathering dusk.

The councillors of the Signoria and other officials sat on a canopied stage, with the miraculous statue of the Madonna, brought from Impruneta and arrayed in cloth of gold, raised on a platform behind them. The pair of pages led the Pope's horse to them and men rushed forward and assembled a kind of platform around the horse so that the Pope could step from the side-saddle directly onto the stage. The Gonfalonier, bareheaded, in black silk robes slashed with scarlet, stepped forward and knelt at the feet of the Pope and kissed the tasseled tips of His Holiness's white slippers while priests shook bells and swung censers which poured forth sweet sandalwood smoke and aspersed everyone in range with holy water.

The Pope raised up the Gonfalonier and kissed him ceremonially, his hands either side of the Gonfalonier's face as if he were his most beloved son. The crowd cheered wildly.

And in the middle of the square, with a rattle of gears barely disguised by a fanfare, the two halves of the huge cosmic egg swung open in front of a great white curtain. Along the edge of the bottom half of the egg were windows engraved with the signs of the zodiac and illuminated by lamps. There was a sudden flare of light as the lensed lamps of the sun in the center of the engine were ignited and, to strange stately music played by a host of mechanical devices, actors, costumed according to poetic descriptions of the planets and standing on gold discs, rotated slowly and smoothly in their orbits.

The Pope took in this spectacle with a bemused short-sighted gaze. The crowd cheered the cunning of the workshops of the Great Engineer.

There was more. Lights blazed down from the Great Tower itself. Brighter than the setting sun, the shafts of light seemed solid as they slanted above the heads of the crowd. Images rose and melted on the white screen behind the cosmic egg, suddenly coalescing into an angel that suddenly moved in jerky steps. Half the crowd screamed, the rest gasped. The Pope, suddenly unnoticed in the midst of this miracle, touched his pectoral cross.

The angel smiled and bowed and briefly closed its great white wings. When they opened again, a vision of a detailed landscape was revealed, an artificer's Utopia in which every river was regulated and channeled, every city was symmetrical, and great machines rowed the air.

And then the vision faded. A great murmur went up from the crowd, and fireworks shot up from all around the circumference of the cosmic egg, cascading tails of sparks like comets and bursting high above in showers of gold and silver. A thousand white doves were released to whir high into the air above the heads of the cheering crowds, and from within the cosmic egg stellar divinities arrayed in silver, their faces and hands painted gold, rose up on pillars and stepped down onto the stage to greet the Pope.

2

Pasquale saw the fireworks from the tall double window of Niccolò Machiavegli's room. He was sitting at the writing-table, sketching poses and attitudes of angels, particularly concentrating on the relationship between wings and arms and body. The window over-looked a narrow dark courtyard, and Pasquale could hardly see what he was doing. The sky, bruise-colored above the clutter of terracotta roofs, seemed to soak up the last light, but he was reluctant to light the thick candle on the desk.

He bent close over the sheet of heavy paper, the back of some official document from the last century, quickly and minutely hatching the folds of the sleeve of the gown of an angel that hung in mid-air with feet together, arms flung wide. Shadows and light in the folds of the gown blending without lines. Soft cloth contrasting with the long primary feathers of wings taller than the figure they framed. He saw the form of the angel clearly. A furious light was burning behind it, and behind the light was a great wild parkland threaded with white paths and populated by animals of every kind, including the great dragons which had not survived the Flood, all of them fleeing the light, the fire of God's wrath. All this: but he still couldn't see the angel's face. Papers littered the writing-table, loosely stacked or bound with ribbons, along with a bundle of goose-feather pens, ink-pots, a tray of sand, a tilting writing-stand. Beside the desk was a rack of a hundred or more books, some calf-bound octavo volumes, the rest the cheap paper-covered editions from the new printing-houses. Works ancient and modern. Ariosto's *Orlando Furioso* in three volumes, Terence's *Andria*, Cicero's *The Republic*, Dante, Livy, Plato, Plutarch, Tacitus. And Koppernigk's *De Revolutionibus Orbium Celestium*, Guicciardini's *On the Paths of Light and Microcosmonium*, Leonardo's *Treatise on the Replication of Motion*. And two by two, Niccolò's own plays, *Belfagor, The Ass, Mandragola, The Temptation of Saint Anthony*, a thick sheaf of polemical brochures and pamphlets. More unchained books than Pasquale had ever seen in any one place.

As for the rest of the room, there was a black patent stove with a pair of spoon-shaped chairs flanking it, pictures in gilt frames crowding the walls, prominent amongst them blotchy oil-portraits of Niccolò's dead wife and children, a *cassone* with a cracked front panel, and a truckle bed on which Niccolò Machiavegli slept amongst dusty cushions, breathing through his open mouth. The bandage tied above the knee of his left leg was spotted with dried blood. An empty bottle of wine lay on its side on the carpet. Niccolò had deadened the pain of his wounded leg with wine and cloudy absinthe, drinking with an increasing desperation, until finally he had slept.

Pasquale too had slept through most of the day,

curled on one of the old Moorish carpets that lapped the splintered wooden floor. He had had no sleep for almost two days, and was exhausted by the night's escapades. By the time he had cleaned and bandaged Niccolò's wound, a deep bloody groove in the flesh above the back of the knee, and examined the glass in its charred frame that he had saved from the fire, the sky had started to lighten and the automatic cannon had fired to announce the opening of the city gates, and the bells of the churches were ringing for the first mass.

Pasquale draped his best black serge jerkin, stained with sweat and smoke as it was, over a chair and slept, and was woken after a few hours by Niccolò's housekeeper, Signora Ambrogini. This was a small fierce old woman, no more than four feet tall, her back bent by years of labor, still dressed in widow's weeds, layer on layer of black, for a husband who had been dead ten years. She looked after all the rooms in the rambling building where Niccolò had his lodgings, off a court backing onto the Via del Corso, midway between the Piazza della Signoria and the Duomo. She was feared and loved by the bachelor scholars and itinerant writers and musicians and artificers who lodged there, chastened by her scorn at their lackadaisical absentmindedness and cosseted by her fierce stern loyalty.

She burst into Niccolò's room in the early afternoon, gave a faint scream when she saw Pasquale sleeping curled up on the carpet by the writing-table, and then a louder scream on seeing Niccolò's wounded leg, propped up on cushions on the truckle bed.

Alarm gave way to a kind of angry mothering. Signora Ambrogini banged to and fro, ordered Pasquale to boil up some water on the stove, told Niccolò, who was still dazed with drink, to pull down his leggings. She bathed the wound and neatly bandaged it, looking sideways at Pasquale as if to blame him for the suffering of her tenant.

Niccolò bore this stoically and with good humor; he was used to her ways. "We had a little adventure," he said, and smiled when she scolded him.

Signora Ambrogini threw up her hands. "A man of your age! You shouldn't take up with young ruffians like this," she added, darting a fierce black look at Pasquale. Her eyes were bright and black in a face folded with deep wrinkles. White hairs coarse as wire sprouted from her chin.

"I know I've learnt my lesson," Niccolò said. He was eyeing a half-finished bottle of wine that stood on the writing-table, but did not dare ask for it. Signora Ambrogini disapproved of his drinking. He added, "But I think it was profitable, all the same."

"Gallivanting shamelessly!" Signora Ambrogini cried, and rolled her eyes with dramatic pathos. "And now you will miss the arrival of the Pope, and so will I, by the time I have finished with you. Oh! What a time of it you give me, Signor Machiavegli."

"Now you know you would never go and see the procession," Niccolò told her with fond patience, "because of the crowds. And as for me, there will be plenty of journalists there. All of the journalists in Florence, I shouldn't wonder. My contribution won't be missed."

The old woman bent to tie the bandage around Niccolò's leg. "And I suppose this young blade is another of your journalist friends. You, young man, you should be about your work, not lurking here bothering my tenants."

Pasquale protested that he was an artist, but the old woman refused to believe him. She tied the bandage tightly and neatly, and Niccolò leaned back when she had finished and sighed and told her she was a miracle-worker, and he would truly believe it if she could fetch them some broth.

"That young fellow is strong enough to fetch his own broth," Signora Ambrogini said sharply.

"He is helping me," Niccolò said. "Helping me on a truly important project. And he really is an artist, a good one too, an apprentice of Giovanni Rosso."

"Can't say I know the name," the old woman said with a sniff, but went off to fetch some broth all the same.

"She means well," Niccolò said, leaning back on his pillows. "For the sake of God, Pasquale, pass me the bottle, there on the table."

"How is your leg?"

Niccolò drank straight from the bottle, and used his sleeve to mop spilled wine from his chin. "I'll try it later, but now I feel like resting. Pasquale, you still have that glass?"

"Of course."

"Let me see it again."

Mounted in a wooden frame that was flaking with black char, the glass had been cracked by the heat of the fire, and the picture printed or drawn upon it was so browned by heat that only a segment was visible. In fact, the picture seemed altogether darker than it had when Pasquale had rescued it, as if the medium on which it had been made was undergoing a transformation. Still, it was possible to make out figures, muffled in robes and hoods, stiffly modeled yet depicted with exquisite meticulous care, that stood behind a kind of altar on which a naked woman lay, drawn in such a way that it was impossible to tell if she was supposed to be dead or alive. Giustiniani, his hood thrown back from his hawkish face, stood with a sword, its blade softly blurred, raised above his head.

"A black mass," Pasquale said.

"Blackmail," Niccolò said.

"What did you hear, at the window?"

"I heard the name of Salai, and I heard Francesco threatening Giustiniani in a feeble but quite desperate manner. It occurs to me that Francesco has evidence that Giustiniani is performing rites such as that shown here, and is blackmailing him to provide a service."

"What service would that be?"

Niccolò became animated. "What indeed, Pasquale! And why blackmail? Magicians like Giustiniani are always in need of money, and someone like Francesco would have money enough, I should think."

"Unless it is some task so terrible even someone like Giustiniani would hesitate to perform it."

"That's the obvious explanation, although—forgive me, Pasquale—it smacks of the plot of some cheap melodrama. Perhaps Giustiniani has already performed the task, and Francesco was trying to threaten him to keep quiet. There may be a connection with Salai, and with Romano's murder. I must think hard about this," Niccolò said, and drained the rest of the wine. "Fetch my little flask, and pour a tumbler of water from the pitcher there."

"That stuff will send you crazy, and then kill you, Niccolò. I know what it is. It has wormwood in it."

"Seven parts to a hundred parts water is the correct measure. Please, Pasquale, I do not need to be lectured about this! I need to think!"

"You shouldn't excite yourself. You're wounded."

Niccolò shook his head. "There's still much to discover. This is deeper and trickier than I first thought.

Perhaps the scandal of the age lies around us!"

"I'll do it just the once," Pasquale said reluctantly.

"Seven parts to a hundred," Niccolò said, watching closely as Pasquale poured the yellow-green liquid dropwise. He took the glass from Pasquale and drank the cloudy stuff straight down, then lay back, his eyes closed, his thumb and forefinger pinching the bridge of his nose.

Pasquale sat and watched Niccolò. Presently he heard footsteps on the stair outside the door, and set the picture of the black mass face-down on the writing-table just as Signora Ambrogini returned. She carried a tray bearing two bowls of soup and a hunk of dry bread. Niccolò said to the housekeeper, without opening his eyes, "Why, what would I do without you, Signora Ambrogini?"

"Drink yourself into the gutter, I shouldn't wonder," Signora Ambrogini said, departing after another fierce look at Pasquale.

Niccolò said that reminded him, and burrowed under his bed, coming up with a bottle of wine. He drew the cork with his teeth, drank off a good draft. He met Pasquale's look, and said, "For medicinal purposes only. Besides, it's the last."

Pasquale drank a glass with the soup, but it was thin and bitter stuff, and he was happy enough to let Niccolò drink the rest. Niccolò hardly touched his soup and later slept again, and Pasquale sat at the table in the fading light and studied first the darkened picture, and then the little flying device. Try as he might, he could make no connection between the two, and set them aside and sketched first the sleeping journalist and then Signora Ambrogini, calling up her likeness by remembering her characteristic glare at him, half turned away, quick and cross. That was how he had taught himself to remember faces, not by individual details, but by an attitude or expression which called up the whole memory. He sketched the scene moments after the *vaporetto* had crashed, mostly from imagination, and finally turned to drawing angels, losing himself in the work until fireworks burst in the darkening sky and Niccolò woke.

The journalist's wounded leg had stiffened. He hobbled around the room, cursing under his breath, then collapsed on the bed. Pasquale said that he should rest, but Niccolò was determined to get out. There were questions to be asked, he said. There had been two murders, and it would not stop there.

"You don't have to come with me, Pasquale. You have done enough, risked enough. These are deep dangerous waters in which we have dipped, and I must needs go deeper. Now, I have some idea of what might lurk there, for I have charted these waters before, but you're an artist. Your world is light, the surface of things. Go home."

"I'll go with you," Pasquale said, with passion. "I'm no innocent."

He had surprised Niccolò at least as much as he had surprised himself. The journalist rasped the black stubble on his chin with his thumb. Eventually he said, "I'm tired, it is true. I would not object to help, if such help was offered for a good reason."

"Well, if it is reason that you need, you still owe me the money I flung at the driver last night."

Niccolò laughed. "And in the end that fare was hardly enough for the man's trouble, eh?"

"I want to know what this is about. I've never before been involved in plots. It's more exciting than etching portraits of the Pope, which is what we'll be doing next week to earn our bread." He was thinking of the bare cold rooms he shared with Rosso, the grind of poverty. If he could regain the florins paid to him he could at least afford most of the materials for his painting. And when that was done he would not need to search for money. He scolded himself for believing this so fervently and foolishly, for hope is foolish, given the hard ways of the world, yet he could not help his hope.

"I forget how young you are," Niccolò said, looking shrewdly at Pasquale. "Help me around the room a few times to loosen this stiffness in my leg. There will be a good deal of walking to be done before this is finished."

But before Pasquale could help Niccolò to his feet, there was a knock at the door and Signora Ambrogini burst in, saying that there was a lady who wished to see him.

Niccolò sat up, suddenly alert. "A woman? Who is it?"

"Not a woman, but a lady," Signora Ambrogini said firmly. "She would not give her name."

"Well, send her up, send her up. If she wishes to speak to me I can hardly refuse."

"With your room in the state it is! Really, Signor Machiavegli, you can hardly receive a lady here. It isn't proper."

"If she is desperate enough to wish to see me, she will not be concerned with my circumstances. Please, Signora Ambrogini, do not keep her waiting."

"I am thinking," Signora Ambrogini said with great dignity, "of my reputation."

"Your reputation will shine forth, signora. Now please, my guest if you will."

She was indeed a lady. Pasquale recognized her at once, for she was Lisa Giocondo, the wife of the Secretary of the Ten of War. He would have whistled with pleasure, if Niccolò had not shot him a sharp look.

Niccolò settled his guest in the best chair in the room, taking her heavy velvet cloak and handing it to Pasquale. In the last light that fell through the window, her indigo gown, of the finest silk trimmed with Flemish lace, set off her white shoulders and black hair, which was thickened with swatches of black silk. She wore a net veil held by a circlet of gold, which softened the contors of her face. As Pasquale lit candles, he glanced sidelong at this face: Signora Giocondo did not have the beauty of an angel—her nose was perhaps a little too long, and one of her dark eyes was slightly higher than the other, and besides, she was a mature woman with fine lines at the corners of her eyes, while the beauty of angels was the beauty of youth—but she had a solemn radiant grace that seemed to light her oval, paleskinned face from within. Her perfume, a sweetened musk, filled the room.

She was as direct about her business as her gaze. She folded her hands and said that she would not be here except for a certain unfortunate event at the Palazzo Taddei, and could not stay long for her husband would soon expect her at his side at the service which the Pope would hold in the Duomo. She hoped that Signor Machiavegli would forgive her candor, but she must speak to clear her husband's name.

"I hope that you will forgive my candor in turn," Niccolò said, clearly enjoying himself, "but while I have yet to form an opinion of your husband one way or the other, it is certain that it is in his power to commission a death should he have need of it."

"My husband is indeed a very powerful man."

"I'm not likely to forget that," Niccolò said.

Lisa Giocondo said with resolve, "Signor Machiavegli, I know that we can never be friends, for my husband has the office which you once enjoyed, but perhaps we can at least not be enemies. I would help you in your investigations, and hope that in your heart there is a measure of Christian charity that will respond to my plight."

"Let me assure you, signora, that I am pursuing not a vendetta, but the truth. It's truth that interests me."

"In that we can agree."

"Then if I may ask a few questions."

Lisa Giocondo looked up at Pasquale, who at the moment, with a piercing thrill, understood that she was the lover of Raphael. She was here to assure Niccolò that her husband had not had Romano killed for revenge, or as a warning.

Niccolò, who was leaning forward at the edge of his bed with a hungry look, said, "He will be as discreet as I, signora."

Lisa Giocondo said, "If what you ask me can help uncover the truth, then I'll answer as truthfully as I'm able."

"Does your husband know of your friendship with Raphael?"

"He does not approve, but he . . . tolerates it. He is an old man, signor, caught up in the affairs of state, and I am his third wife. Our marriage was never one made from love, although you must believe me that there is love, and since our only child died we have been apart more than I would have wished."

"And his honor, signora. Does he worry about that?"

"He would worry about his position, but that is secure. A man raised up as he is, as you will know, Signor Machiavegli, is subject to many attacks, including rumors about my . . . conduct. He takes them without hurt."

"But there is some truth to these rumors, or you would not be here."

"I am at your mercy, Signor Machiavegli."

Niccolò pinched the bridge of his nose between finger and thumb. It was his characteristic gesture while he was thinking. After a moment he said, "Your husband was instrumental in arranging the Pope's embassy. In fact, he has many contacts in Rome."

"He would not interfere with the affairs of the Republic because of personal matters."

"Not directly, of course. But was Raphael invited by your husband?"

"Why would he do that?"

"Perhaps to arrange that Raphael be humiliated."

"An interesting idea, Signor Machiavegli, but I believe that it was the Pope himself who sent Raphael as an ambassador."

"The Pope himself, and not Giulio de' Medici?"

For the first time, Lisa Giocondo looked perturbed. She said, "I have it from Raphael that it was the Pope himself. I believe him, Signor Machiavegli."

"As is your right, signora. I think, for now, that I have asked enough. I see that you glance out of the window, and worry about the passing of time. Of course you must do your duty to your husband. I would not keep you from him."

Lisa Giocondo rose. She was a tall woman, as tall as Pasquale. She dropped a small bag on the writing-table and said, "You will no doubt incur expenses in your investigations, Signor Machiavegli. I would not wish to see you out of pocket."

Niccolò got to his feet with Pasquale's help, apologizing that he had already been hurt in his investigations, a trifling wound but a nuisance even so. "I had not thought to serve the Republic again, signora.

May I ask, if my inquiries should lead to your husband . . . ?"

"I also am interested in the truth. You will, I trust, keep me informed."

When she had gone, Pasquale could finally whistle. He said, "I hadn't realized the depth of your hate, Niccolò."

Niccolò said, "Francesco del Giocondo is a good silk merchant, a competent secretary, and a bad poet with an inflated opinion of his worth."

"You imitate Michelangelo's opinion of Raphael."

"It is a matter of fact, not opinion. What is your judgment of Signora Giocondo?"

"In the tender soul of a woman there dwells prudence and a courageous spirit."

"Indeed. And a most determined one."

"And generous," Pasquale said, spilling half a dozen florins from the small bag, which was heavy with Signora Giocondo's musky scent.

"We are embarked on a voyage over deep and dangerous waters. Those may help speed our passage. Do you know how our lady became Raphael's mistress?"

"Until now I didn't even know she *was* his mistress. I am only a painter, after all."

Niccolò smiled. "Raphael painted a portrait of her, but not at her husband's commission. It was her lover at the time, Giulio de' Medici, who set Raphael to the task, while our Florentine secretary and his wife were on embassy to Rome."

"So you think that perhaps Giulio de' Medici sent Raphael here, into certain danger?"

"Signora Giocondo certainly believes it may be possible, and more, that perhaps her husband was involved in Romano's murder, although she hopes otherwise."

"Yet what we saw at Giustiniani's villa would suggest that Romano was involved in a plot of his own."

"Or lured into a plot," Niccolò said spryly, "although that would be a very complicated way of performing a simple task."

"You didn't tell her of Giustiniani."

"She did not pay for that. Let her wonder and worry. She may be moved to tell us more, although I doubt it. She has a core of iron. Now, hand me the money, young Pasquale. We will have need of it before the night is out. We will make inquiries, and this will ease our questions."

3

When Pasquale and Niccolò left the apartment
building it had just turned night, with three stars
pricking the patch of blue-black sky between the
roofs above the courtyard. Pasquale tacked his likeness of Signora Ambrogini to her door, saying that
now she would know he was an artist, and Niccolò
dryly remarked that Pasquale shouldn't count on
public opinion.

Dusk usually drove most honest citizens indoors,
but that night the city was embraced by the carnival
begun by the entry of the Pope. Florentines loved car-
nivals and festivals, and any anniversary or occasion
of state was an excuse for celebration and holiday.
The streets were lit as much by the lanterns and
flaming brands carried by parties of costumed men
tramping here and there as by the infrequent acetylene lamps. Groups of youths serenaded favored girls
who sat at their lighted windows. One gang strode
along on stilts that doubled their height. Music and
singing and cheering sounded from near and far, but
Niccolò led Pasquale away from the celebrations,

into the maze of narrow passages and courts behind the imposing façades of the buildings that lined the main streets. Always, Florence's private lives turned inward, hiding from public gaze, breeding vendettas and dark plots behind high walls and narrow barred windows.

Niccolò was still limping badly, leaning on a stick of ashwood tipped with iron at either end, and the way was difficult, over slick flagstones or rutted earth, lit only by infrequent shafts of light leaking from high shuttered windows. Pasquale was nervous, and kept his hand on his knife. This was just the kind of place where people imagined that cutthroats and robbers lurked—although because of that, any robbers would have a poor time of it, and were no doubt lurking elsewhere.

After a little while, Pasquale asked, "Who are we looking for?"

"A certain physician of ill repute. A man who goes by the name of Dr. Pretorious. It is not his real name, of course, and as far as I know he has never been examined for his doctorate, although he has been thrown out of at least a dozen different universities in five different countries. But none of his kind use their real names, in case demons learn them. He was put in jail in Venice for trafficking in dead bodies, although he had some influence that meant he was not put to the question but instead served his sentence on the galleys. There were rumors that he was trying to construct a woman, a new Venus or Bride of the Sea, from parts of corpses, and planned to animate this patchwork construction by substitution of an arcane liquor for blood."

"Another black magician, then? Venice seems to breed them."

"Do you know, Pasquale, I'm not quite sure where

Pretorious was born, but it was certainly never Venice. As for black magic, *he* does not call it that. He calls himself a physician, and it is true he has done some good amongst the *ciompi* shanties, where he holds a clinic and takes whatever people will pay in return for treatment. His clients are in love with him. There were rumors some years ago that he was associated with the disappearance of children, but to his credit the *ciompi* did not believe them."

"And you think he is an associate of this other magician, this Giustiniani."

"Ah, because both have fled the city by the sea, for the same reason! All I can say now is that it is likely that Pretorious may be able to shed some light on the business of Paolo Giustiniani, for they move, if not in the same circles, in circles which intersect. Moreover, Dr. Pretorious is a collector of facts. He hoards them until such time as the right buyer comes along. Meanwhile, Pasquale, we must be vigorous in our examination of the facts *we* have collected, and in the conclusion we draw from them."

"As rigorous as the artificers?"

"Well put," Niccolò said with a smile. "Down here."

The tavern they were seeking was in a dark courtyard bounded on three sides by tall houses, on the fourth by a reeking stream that gurgled throatily in the darkness. Pasquale had to half pull, half lift Niccolò up the steep arch of the bridge which crossed this Stygian waterway.

Just as they reached the far side of the bridge, fireworks burst overhead, and the courtyard began to throb to the solemn tolling of the cathedral bells. The mass in honor of the Pope was over, and he was departing for the feast at the Palazzo della Signoria. By the brief light of star-shells, Pasquale caught a

clear glimpse across the courtyard, and saw a bundle
of twigs crooked over a doorway masked with sacking, and scattered tables where figures hunched over
bowls or flagons. Little lamps, wicks floating in saucers of oil, cast faint reddish lights. Someone was
playing the bagpipes, and doing it badly.

Pasquale said, remembering the dive where he had
taken wine with Niccolò after witnessing the murder scene, "You know many interesting places."

"Not all business is transacted on high, and besides, news always falls from high to low, just as water seeks the lowest place."

"This Dr. Pretorious must have fallen far."

"He doesn't believe so," Niccolò said. "Listen
carefully, Pasquale. Pretorious is as subtle and poisonous as a serpent. Be careful. In particular, be very
careful what you say to him. He'll use any unguarded
remark as a way into your soul."

"You make him sound like the devil."

"He is," Niccolò said, and pushed aside the sacking at the door.

Dr. Pretorious sat at a corner table, playing single-
handed tarot whist. A tall white-haired old man, he
was thin to the point of emaciation, fastidiously
dressed in a russet tunic with puffed sleeves and a
white shirt trimmed with Flemish lace, and seemed
quite oblivious to the dirty straw on the floor, the
mice that scuttled to and fro. Exuding a brittle
charm, he stood and bowed to Niccolò and Pasquale,
and called to the landlord for his very best wine. His
servant, a hulking Savage with a square scarred face
and a helmet of coarse glossy black hair, sat beside
him, a knife as big as an ordinary man's sword laid
across his thighs.

The wine served was as bad as anything Pasquale
had ever tasted, although Niccolò sipped it without

complaint, and Dr. Pretorious seemed to relish it. He said, "I have not seen you for a long time, Niccolò. I had hoped it would be longer."

"You have been quiet, or if not quiet at least careful."

"I've been working," Dr. Pretorious said. His eyes looked black in the flickering light of the rushlamps, like deep caves under the overhang of his craggy brow. "And with great success, too."

"I'm not here to talk about your work, or anything else you've done. In fact, I'd rather not hear about it."

"Oh, don't worry! It is, you might say, the antithesis of my previous research. Instead of subverting death, I attempt to subvert life itself, to short-circuit the Great Chain of Being. I have made mannequins, small as mice, and infused them with a spark of life. How my children dance and sing!" There was a measured silence. The gloating way he said *children* chilled Pasquale's blood. Dr. Pretorious added, "Well, you'll know all about it soon enough. Everyone will."

Niccolò said, "I've come about the business at Paolo Giustiniani's villa."

Dr. Pretorious started to gather together his tarot cards. He had long white fingers, and yellow nails trimmed close and square. He licked his bloodless lips with a tongue as pointed as a lizard's. "Ah, so you were involved. I had heard as much."

"From Giustiniani's men?"

"Perhaps," Dr. Pretorious said carelessly, and folded the cards together and wrapped them in a square of black silk.

"I don't think so. If Giustiniani knew I was involved, then he would have come straight away to my room."

Dr. Pretorious shrugged. "Well, perhaps I heard it somewhere else. At a time like this, there are many stories. You know that my sources are as various as those of the Nile."

"You did not welcome the Pope."

"I have no cause to celebrate. After all, he *is* only the Pope, you know. Not the one we hoped for." Dr. Pretorious looked directly at Pasquale for the first time. "You've brought an artist along, I see."

Pasquale felt a queer compulsion to say something. Light lived deep in Dr. Pretorious's dark eyes, floating and faint. He said, "Who were you hoping for?"

Dr. Pretorious said, "We live in the time before the end times. The Great Year has come and gone, and soon the black pope, the antipope, will rise. Then the Millennium will begin, but it will not be what most fools believe it to be, young man. Tell me, did you see the entry of the Pope into this foul city? Did you see him enter the square in the shadow of that ridiculously high tower of the so-called Great Engineer?"

"I was . . . otherwise engaged."

"Then perhaps I have something you would like to know. I wonder now, what it would be worth."

Niccolò said sharply, "Remember that we have serious business here, Pasquale."

Dr. Pretorious smiled, cruel as a knife. "Ah, this would not of course be a social call. It never is. I suppose that is why you did not introduce your catamite here. From the country, by his accent, although he has taken pains to disguise it. Fiesole I would say, a town well known for its quaint rural ways—they favor goats over women there, I believe."

"Sit!" Niccolò pressed down on Pasquale's shoulder as he started to rise.

Pasquale subsided, anger a thick taste in his mouth. The Savage smiled broadly at him: his front teeth were gone, and his incisors had been sharpened to points and capped with gold. Pasquale returned the big man's yellow gaze, but he had to lock his hands between his thighs to keep himself from shaking.

Niccolò said, "He is here to help me, should I need help."

"Times must be bad for you," Dr. Pretorious said, with a bright smile. "And of course, they'll shortly be worse still for all artists, if the Great Engineer's new invention proves as popular as it deserves. I sympathize."

"I need your help," Niccolò said. "Times are bad enough for that, at least."

"Ah. Well, I wondered when that debt would be called in. What shall we say . . . three questions? I'll need paying, too, of course. My debt to you isn't that great."

Niccolò drank down his wine, and Dr. Pretorious quickly poured him some more. Niccolò drank that too, and said, "You always liked playing games. This will be payment enough." He set the little bag of florins on the table.

Dr. Pretorious breathed deeply through his nose and said, "From a woman—a rich one, too. Well. There are rules you are not even aware of, my friend. Perhaps to you what I do seems a game. It is not. Ask away. You have my attention."

"What interest does Paolo Giustiniani have in the painter Raphael?"

"So you *are* involved in that sordid little business. Fascinating."

"I asked the question."

"Oh, he has no interest, at present."

"If I may say so, that is not a very full answer."

"It is the truth. Aren't you satisfied with that?"

"Perhaps that depends upon the answer to the next question."

"Press on, my friend," Dr. Pretorious said, with a knife-edged smile.

"On what Great Work is Giustiniani engaged?"

"I can tell you what little I know, so it cannot be a full answer."

"You are an honorable man."

"I take this more seriously than you because I know about the consequences of error, dear Niccolò."

"Then tell me what you know. As full an answer as you are able."

"I believe he is either engaged in enlisting into his service a great prince and his army of lesser demons, or invoking one of those who serve the celestial throne."

"These are hardly small matters," Niccolò said. He was sweating, Pasquale saw, a dew gathered just below his receding hairline.

"It depends on how you go about it," Dr. Pretorious said carelessly. "Giustiniani is using the worst kind of necromancy, the kind of thing that hedge-wizards long ago abandoned. I hardly think he'll succeed. He is an amateur, you know. He even uses his real name. Most likely, he'll succeed in consigning himself to Hell. That kind always do."

"And you hope to evade it?"

"Oh, of course," Dr. Pretorious said. His sudden smile was bright and generous—it was then that Pasquale realized that the man was quite insane. There was a chill in the air, as if somewhere nearby a door had opened onto the hyperborean regions, radiating anti-heat.

"There are always ways of avoiding the attention of Hell, for those who know," Dr. Pretorious said. "Of course, my friend, I know that you don't think Hell such a bad place. I've read your play on the matter, where a demon discovers that matrimony is in truth a living hell, and Hell itself is a corner of Heaven ruled not by the Fallen One, but by rich Pluto. Who is rich, of course, because in the end death claims all, and rules not over eternal torment but over a garden where those whose deeds or intellect exclude them from Heaven, the heroes and philosophers, converse. A place that you, foolish Niccolò, perhaps yearn for. Perhaps you should examine your own soul, my friend. Lapses like that are hooks for the claws of demons."

Pasquale was almost hypnotized by Dr. Pretorious's mellifluous voice. The noise of the other patrons of the low tavern had receded, as if Dr. Pretorious had created a world within a world, where each was intimately connected to each by words. Then Niccolò laughed, and the spell was broken.

"You read too much into my fantasies," he said. "Although I am flattered, you shouldn't misunderstand my interest in Hell. If one is to find the way to Paradise, one should first learn the road to Hell, so that it can be avoided. Without temptation, there can be no Fall, and so no redemption."

Dr. Pretorious said sweetly, "We are both seekers after power. That is why we are so alike, you and I."

"Not at all," Niccolò countered. "It is true that we both seek power, but by different roads, and for different ends. You wish only to serve yourself, and none other, and so avoid falling into Hell for beside such as you, the damned would seem pure."

"Spare me the analysis. You have asked two questions. Ask me the third and be done with it."

"No. No, I don't believe I will. I have learned enough for now." Niccolò rose, and for a moment Dr. Pretorious looked up at him with astonishment. "Come, Pasquale," Niccolò said. "We have much work to do, this night."

Dr. Pretorious said, "No! Wait! You have one more question to ask me."

"Perhaps some other time."

Dr. Pretorious swept the table clear of beakers and sprang to his feet. Behind him, the Savage also stood, his head brushing the ceiling. "No!" Dr. Pretorious shouted. "You will not keep any hold over me after this, I swear it! It is done!"

"I have no more questions for now," Niccolò said mildly, and took up his stick. "Come, Pasquale."

Pasquale dared look back only after they had crossed the bridge over the little stream. No one seemed to be following.

Niccolò said, "Don't worry. In his own way, Dr. Pretorious is a man of his word, and while he still owes me the favor of an answer he will not harm us."

"What favor could you possibly do a man like that?"

"I once showed that he could not have done what he was accused of having done. I thought that I was acting on the side of justice, for if the wrong man had been hanged then the real criminal would have remained free to continue his dreadful work. Those were terrible times, and I had to act without foresight. If I had known that the real killer would have evaded justice after all, then perhaps I would not have helped Pretorious. There are many things he has done for which he deserves death. But in hindsight it is easy to judge your actions, less so in the

heat of the moment. You still look troubled, Pasquale."

"I was wondering what new artificer's device he
was alluding to, that he said would greatly impov-
erish all artists."

"You must remember that Dr. Pretorious seeks to
gain power over everyone he meets, Pasquale. It was
probably no more than a snare set to catch your attention. Dismiss it from your thoughts."

Niccolò seemed troubled and exhausted, and they
walked on a way, through dark narrow courts and
passages, with Niccolò's stick tapping in the darkness, before Pasquale asked him what he had learned.

"That this is not as great a matter as it might be.
If Raphael is not involved, then in all likelihood Giulio Romano and Giovanni Francesco were not acting
for him, or acting to protect him, but were acting for
themselves. The little flying device you keep safe,
and the picture you rescued from the fireplace, un-
doubtedly have something to do with the matter, but
I do not think they are ends in themselves."

Pasquale remembered, with a guilty shock, that he
had left both the picture and the device on Niccolò's
writing-table, but thought it best to keep quiet about
this lapse. "Is Giustiniani really a magician? Dr. Pretorious seems to believe no one is, save himself."

"It is true that men of that kind delude themselves
into thinking only they have true powers, but that is
precisely the point. Dr. Pretorious is well placed to
see through any trickery, none better, for he believes
himself to be a true magus—the only true magus. In
the end, men like him deceive no one but themselves."

"Artificers think they know everything, too."

"No, Pasquale. While they do believe that they
have the means to unriddle locked mysteries of the

universe, they share their knowledge because it is discovered by a common system. Men of Dr. Pretorious's kind hoard it, and each one believes that only he understands the operations crucial for the conjuration of power. There's the difference."

Pasquale couldn't help letting his disappointment show. Signora Giocondo's florins lost so quickly. His best clothes ruined. He said, "Then this may not be important after all."

"We are starting from a lower rather than a higher place. We may yet climb far. Don't worry, Pasquale. You'll get your money."

So Niccolò saw through Pasquale, too. He saw through everyone it seemed, even (unlike Dr. Pretorious) himself.

They reached the main thoroughfare, and as they passed under the light of the first of the acetylene lamps Pasquale at last took his hand from his knife. Moments later, between the first lamp and the next, they were attacked.

4

Four men ran out of a passageway on the other side of the road, ran right at Pasquale and Niccolò before they realized that these were not revelers. In an instant, Pasquale was wrestled away from Niccolò. His assailant, breathing heavily and stinking of bad beer, locked an arm around his neck and Pasquale shoved backward, unbalancing the man, and slamming him against a wall. Breath knocked out of him, the man loosened his grip for an instant, and Pasquale stamped on his instep and pulled free.

Then it was knife against knife. The man, a burly bully-boy, grinned when Pasquale drew his knife. He tossed his own from one hand to the other with a streetfighter's ease and taunted Pasquale in a slurred voice, telling him to come on, come and get it, come and get fucked good. They warily circled each other before the man suddenly leapt forward. Pasquale dodged a slashing blow which might otherwise have unseamed his guts, and caught the man's knife-arm with a lucky swipe. The man squealed like a stuck pig and dropped his weapon. Pasquale kicked it away and the drunken fool grinned and ran at him, and Pasquale sank his knife to the hilt in the other's guts. The man gasped and sagged, clutching Pasquale's shoulder with one hand and pawing at his wound with the other. The haft of the knife twisted from Pasquale's grasp and the man fell to his knees, swearing that Pasquale had killed him.

Niccolò had already disabled one ruffian with a blow of his stick; the man curled in the road, sobbing and holding his smashed knee. Niccolò threw the stick at the second and gained enough time to draw his pistol, but the third stepped up behind him and sapped his arm. The second man grabbed the pistol and turned toward Pasquale.

For a moment it seemed that all was lost, but then someone growled and ran out of the darkness, brushing Pasquale aside. It was the giant Savage, Dr. Pretorious's servant. He smashed into the ruffian who brandished Niccolò's pistol, swung him into the air by neck and hip, and threw him against his companion.

For a moment everyone froze, like actors at the end of a tableau. Then the two fallen men picked themselves up and ran down the street, shouting. The man with the smashed knee looked whitely at Dr. Pretorious's servant and picked himself up and hobbled after his companions, gasping with pain.

"My thanks," Niccolò said. He was out of breath. So was Pasquale, whose heart was banging against his ribs.

The Savage fixed Niccolò with a stare and said in a low voice, "My master says that the debt must be discharged." And then he ran into the shadows and was gone, moving with incredible lightness for so big a man.

Pasquale said admiringly, "He showed no fear at all."

"He believes himself dead," Niccolò said. "Dr. Pretorious once told me that the magi of his godforsaken island, when they wish to enslave a man, make from the liver of a certain fish a potion which renders a man so insensible that he is taken for dead by his family, and is duly buried. The magus then digs up the supposed corpse and revives him, and so gains an obedient servant who is without fear. A potion sewn into a pouch is slung at the servant's neck, to mark him as the property of the magus. Such a one is Pretorious's servant, although how he came by him, Pretorious did not say."

The brute wounded by Pasquale's knife started to whimper. He was curled up on the ground, both hands pressed to his belly. Niccolò grasped the man's hair and wrenched his head up and asked him who had paid him, but the man only sobbed that he was killed.

"What shall we do with this fool?" Pasquale asked. He had wounded someone before, but that had only been a trifling scratch in a sudden quick drunken fight over something both he and his opponent had forgotten about in the instant of blood-letting. He knew now that he could, if he willed it, fight to the death. He had it in him. It was both exciting and disturbing. It made his blood sing.

Niccolò said, "We'll find the militia."

"We should leave him to die."

"That's hardly Christian charity. Besides," Niccolò said with a smile, "he may then wish to tell us about himself. Such as who sent him—"

Pasquale stooped and grasped the brute's ears, shook his head from side to side. The man groaned.

"Who sent you! Was it Giustiniani?"

The brute said in a slurred voice, "You've killed me, you motherfucking bastard."

Pasquale tried the question again, but the man would only groan and cry. Niccolò said, "He will talk, if not now, then later." Then he lifted his head and said, "Hush. Someone comes."

They came from the direction in which the other assailants had fled, half a dozen men in carnival motley, masked as griffins and dragons and unicorns. They were led by a giant—no, it was a man on stilts, stamping along with quick adroitness. He wore a white mask which covered his entire face, with triangular eyeholes rimmed in black. He pointed at Pasquale and Niccolò, and began to whirl a slingshot around his head. His troops surged forward with a yell. Pasquale and Niccolò fled just as the first slingshot load whistled past their heads.

It was a glass globe which shattered on the pavingstones, spraying liquid. A fog whirled up, thick and yellow. Pasquale and Niccolò plunged through the vapor, choking on a vile thick scent like burning geraniums. The ruffians gave chase, yelling loudly. One blew a tinny toy trumpet. Niccolò was laboring, leaning heavily on his stick, and Pasquale dragged him along by main force.

Then they reached the Piazza del Duomo and were suddenly amongst crowds. The congregation of the mass celebrated by the Pope, and supporters of the Medici, and revelers who had joined the party for the fun of it. Pasquale pulled Niccolò through the noisy people, glancing back and seeing the stilt-man looming above the crowd's swirling heads, his white masked face looking this way and that. For the moment they were safe, but Pasquale felt suddenly more exposed than he had when being chased, and imagined a masked assassin whirling toward them out of the festive crowd at every turn.

The cathedral reared above the heads of the crowd, its great gold-skinned cupola shining in focused lamplight, its white marble walls shrouded by cloths on which, by artificer sleight of hand, transparent scenes trembled and shook. The white tower of the campanile was lit too, and its Apostolica bell solemnly tolled the hour of ten.

Pasquale supported Niccolò, and they made slow progress through the noisy crowd. "Who are they?" Pasquale said, and realized that he was almost as breathless as Niccolò.

"I would guess that they are Giustiniani's. If Dr. Pretorious knew of our involvement, then so surely must Giustiniani. The devil is after us for what we know, or what he thinks we know."

"We have that picture."

"Which he thinks he destroyed. More likely he knows us as witnesses to the murder of Giovanni Francesco."

"Or as his accomplices."

"Very good, Pasquale!"

"Well, they will know us for certain now, because I left my knife behind, and it has my name on its blade. At least I have lost sight of the stilt-man."

"We have a long way to go this night," Niccolò said. "Confound this crowd. The fools should all be abed."

"A poor thing to say for those who have unwittingly hid us. I would have all the citizens of Florence awake all night, until we are saved."

"It will take more than one night," Niccolò said grimly.

"Then I'll stay with you. I'm marked now anyway. Though I would like to know where we are going."

"Whatever the reason, I am glad of your support, Pasquale. The devil take this crowd! Where we are going, if it is at all possible, is to the Palazzo della Signoria, because that is where Raphael will be dining this night, with the Pope and the first citizens of Florence. We must warn him of what has happened."

The Piazza della Signoria was scarcely less crowded. The people had taken the long platform in front of the Palazzo on which the Pope had been received, and were carousing like Moorish pirates celebrating the capture of a fat merchant vessel. Bands of university students roamed to and fro, roaring the songs of their nations. There was a clash between the Prussian and French nations around the Great Engineer's cosmic engine. The latter seemed to want to tear at the engine which commemorated the great truth discovered by Canon Koppernigk, while the Prussians were defending the honor of their national hero. "Still it moves," they shouted, taunting the French. Beyond this, dancers danced in a circle around Michelangelo's great statue of David. The statue's gilded hair flickered with reflections of the torches they juggled.

Artificers were celebrating, too. Great figures of light rotated over the wall that Pasquale and Rosso had so carefully prepared—was it only yesterday? The artificer, Benozzo Berni, was tending his light-cannon, and greeted Pasquale cheerfully. The big acetylene lamps of his device hissed and roared, their light concentrated through slits onto revolving wheels of painted horn, and big lenses of thick bubbled glass threw the changing patterns vastly magnified onto the painted wall. Light splinteringly refracted from the edges of the lenses threw Berni's shadow a long way across the paving-stones as he came over to Pasquale and Niccolò. The artificer had taken off his many-pocketed tunic and was sweating into his hemp undershirt from the heat of his great lamps. Grinning like a madman, he clapped Pasquale on the back and whirled him around to face the show of lights with a grand expansive gesture.

"Now you see!" he shouted exultantly. "Moving light making its own picture. What do you think of that, painter?"

"Perhaps I am not sophisticated enough, signor, but I see no pictures, only the kinds of patterns a candle-flame may make against a wall."

"That's the point! The light patterns act on the eye itself, and deceive it into making pictures. This is a new way of thinking, you see! The marvel of it is that the machine operates upon you."

"It is certainly a marvel, but perhaps machine thoughts are too difficult for me to understand." Perhaps Piero di Cosimo might appreciate this light-show, Pasquale thought, but it seemed a costly way of reproducing the random patterns found every-where in nature.

Berni laughed. "Have it your own way for now, but you'll come around. We stand at the threshold of a new age. The curtain is hardly raised, and we glimpse only the first flickers of what is beyond, and these are so bright that we can scarcely believe our eyes. But soon we will have to deal with these visions. Machines force new ways of making things, of doing things, and now seeing things. The progression is in-evitable."

"It seems there is no room for the artist," Pasquale said. To his tired mind, Berni seemed a kind of devil, full of restless energy, celebrating change for change's sake.

Berni dashed sweat from his brow with a scorched red rag. "The age of representative art is past. There will be new kinds of artists, painting directly with light, producing fleeting images that linger in the screen of the eye. My kinetoscope draws patterns which the eye seeks to interpret, and then there is the marvel of the Great Engineer's moving pictures as produced by his ipseorama! And tonight he will capture the true likeness of the Pope in light itself. Surely you must agree that the age of interpretation and laborious symbolism is past!"

"As a matter of fact," Pasquale began, "I know nothing of these moving pictures—"

Niccolò had sat on an upturned crate to rest. Now he struggled to his feet and said, "I don't know you, signor, but I hope you will not mind if I ask a question."

"But I know Niccolò Machiavegli!" Berni sketched a bow. "Perhaps your broadsheet might wish to report the new miracles first demonstrated here."

"Perhaps. That isn't for me to say. What I would ask, Signor . . ."

"Benozzo Berni, at your service!"

"Signor Berni, I would ask you if any soldiers have lately entered the Palazzo."

"Why, no. None, since the great procession made its way from the Duomo to the Palazzo for the feast. That's still going on, and I will run my engine until it is over—which means until well past midnight, for I hear more than twenty courses are to be served."

"Then we may not be too late, Pasquale." Niccolò smiled vaguely at Berni. "I'm sorry, signor. Perhaps we will discuss your marvel another time."

"You are witnessing the dawn of a new age, Signor Machiavegli! Just remember that!"

As they crossed the square, taking a long route to avoid the rowdy students, Pasquale said, "What are you expecting to happen?"

"I'm not sure, only that something will. Wait, look! Perhaps we are too late!"

Niccolò pointed up at the Palazzo. It loomed at the eastern corner of the square like a ship. Every window in its bulk was ablaze, even in its square high tower, and flags bearing the Medici emblem of twelve gold balls flew amongst Republican banners showing the Florentine lily. Someone had flung wide a window under the overhang of the castellated top floor and was shouting to a group of soldiers below.

More figures appeared at the window. Two men struggling with a third, who suddenly tipped over the sill. People shouted in the square below. The man plummeted, jerked, swung, kicking and kicking at the end of a cord.

Soldiers were jogging smartly around the corner of the Palazzo toward the main entrance. A bell rang out with a quick urgent jangle. Pasquale and Niccolò chased after the soldiers as best they could. City militia in red and white hose, polished breastplates over white tunics, steel caps on their heads, were trying to block the high narrow door of the Palazzo with their pikes, but with little success; Pasquale and Niccolò were not the only ones who wanted to know what was happening. They pushed in with dozens of others, into the cold echoing cortile.

More soldiers, the Pope's Swiss Guards, were pushing a wedge through the crowd. Men were flung out of the way; an officer barked an order and the soldiers cocked their pikes with a rattle of ratchets and held them forward, fingers on the catch-releases. People scrambled backward, falling over each other; fired at close range, a pike-head could go clean through a man.

Pasquale pulled Niccolò around a pillar just as the Pope appeared. He was bareheaded, in a white cape that fell in generous folds around his bulky body. Servants liveried in black velvet supported him on either side. A flock of red-hatted, scarlet-robed cardinals trailed behind, amongst a rabble of servants. Screams and shouts, a tremendous tramping of boots, soldiers clashing their pikes as they came to attention. The Pope swept past, so close that Pasquale could see the beads of sweat on his blue jowls, and then he was gone, through the narrow door into the night.

Niccolò snagged a councillor at the end of the procession; the man struggled in a moment of panic before he recognized Niccolò and relaxed. "I can't talk to you here!" he said loudly.

Niccolò spoke directly into the man's face with a quiet firm intensity. "You can tell me what happened at least, my friend."

The councillor blurted, "Murder! Murder, Niccolò!"

"Hardly the first time the Palazzo has seen blood shed."

"Blood? No, no, it was poison. Right before the Pope himself. It is a miracle I am here to speak to you; my own glass was almost at my lips when he fell—"

"Who was it?"

"We could all have been murdered! All of us! Any hope of alliance is done for. As for what will happen now—"

Niccolò grasped the lapels of the councillor's heavy fur-trimmed robes. The man goggled at him. His hat was askew; his face was white above his full black beard.

Niccolò said softly and urgently, "Who was it?"

The councillor gathered himself together, shook off Niccolò's grip and straightened his robes and his hat with a kind of distracted dignity. "Niccolò, old friend, please, for the sake of Christ keep clear of this. It is dark dark business, dark and terrible."

"I want only to know who it is that was murdered."

"The painter. The Pope's painter, Raphael. He made a toast to the Pope and drank, and we were about to follow him when he clutched his throat and fell. Horrible, horrible! There, I've already said too much and will say no more. Take care, my friend. Don't even dip a finger in these waters. My advice is to get off the streets at once. Go home. There'll be a terrible reckoning this night—if we're lucky, that will end it. If not—" The councillor had been looking around as he talked. Suddenly he shouted to an officer of the militia, shook off Niccolò's hand and hurried away, two soldiers falling in behind him.

"We must go up there," Niccolò said.

"Then Raphael was involved after all!"

"Perhaps, perhaps." Niccolò looked drawn, suddenly looked every one of his fifty years. "Stay close to me, Pasquale. Help me as you can. I've always tried to see things as they are, not as they ought to be. Christ knows that I will need all of that ability now. If I'm right, this little conspiracy into which we have fallen has spread further than it should. Those in wise council see only a small part of it, and may mistake it for something worse than it is."

Soldiers barred the way to the grand staircase, grim-faced behind their closed visors. Niccolò hailed a clerkly man, who shook his hand and began to repeat the story of poison. "I need to see," Niccolò said. "I believe it less worse than it is."

The clerk said, "They have precipitately hanged the assassin, Niccolò. There's no way to put his corpse to the question, and besides, you're not the man to do it. Go home."

"You're the second person to tell me that. It makes me more determined."

"No one can go up there, Niccolò. I certainly can't, so please, don't ask me."

The soldiers parted to let two or three people up the staircase. Pasquale recognized one and called to him. The boy, Baverio, turned and stared. He was dressed in the same dark green tunic and breeches as before. His face was quite white, as if powdered with chalk, and his eyes were red-rimmed and wet.

Pasquale quickly explained what Niccolò wanted. Baverio shook his head and said, "The man who killed my master is dead, and nothing can hurt my master now."

"Raphael's name must still be defended. Please, Baverio. For the sake of your master's name. You helped me before, and I remember and am grateful. This one more time."

The boy bit his lip. "Yet you have not found out why poor Giulio was killed. And now my master is dead, and Giovanni Francesco has disappeared."

Pasquale could not tell the boy that Francesco too was dead. "It is all a piece, Baverio. We see only a few parts of the picture. We must see the rest to understand it."

"If it will help, then follow me."

The boy, after speaking with his companions, led Pasquale and Niccolò past the soldiers and up the stairs. He explained that Raphael had been struck as if with apoplexy after making a toast at the serving of the fifth course of the feast. The Pope's own physician had rushed to his aid but in vain, except to say that it was poisoned wine.

Baverio said steadily, "Two of my friends rushed

from the room and caught the wine steward, looped a cord around his neck and threw him out of the window. A soldier who ran in at the cry of murder helped them. I was not there, Pasquale, and I should have been. If I had tasted the wine first my master would not be dead." Tears stood in his eyes, and he tipped his head back so that they wouldn't run and spoil his powdered cheeks.

"There's no end to what might have been," Pasquale told the boy. "What's important here is the truth of what has happened."

The feast had been held in the Hall of Victory of the Republic, the big high-ceilinged room at the heart of the Palazzo della Signoria. Two long tables ran down the room, and a third was set across the head of these, beneath the fan of stairs that led up to the balcony. The tables were strewn with dishes and bowls of food, fine fluted glasses, silver spoons and knives. Burning forests of candles filled the room with heat and steady light. Pasquale gaped at the frenzied glory of Michelangelo's gigantic friezes of the war against Rome and her allies, the Battle of Cascina on one wall, the Florentine victory at Anghiari at the other, where the Great Engineer's armored turtles had marched through the enemy lines, and multi-barreled cannon had decimated what was left of their ranks. Then he remembered himself and hurried after Niccolò and Baverio, toward the knot of people gathered at the end table, where the canopied papal throne stood.

Raphael's body lay under a heavy tapestry someone had torn from the wall. Niccolò bent and gently uncovered the face. There was foam on the blue lips; the eyes were closed by silver florins. Niccolò looked up at the men around him and asked who was the physician. When a handsome gray-haired man

stepped forward and bowed and said he had that
honor, Niccolò said, "How quick was this?"

"It was very quick, thank Christ, or there would
be many more dead. It struck at his lungs—you see
here the foam and the cyanosis of the lips—and it
paralyzed his breathing. He was clawing at his
throat, then suffered an apoplectic fit. He would have
known only a little pain before dying."

"A strong poison, then."

"Obviously, signor."

"Administered in the wine?"

"His glass is here. Raphael knocked it over when
he fell, so the wine is spilled, but I have tested the
spill and found poison. A miracle, as I say, that Raphael drank before anyone else."

"He made a toast," Baverio said. "He was a loyal
friend to His Holiness, and it has killed him."

The captain of the Palazzo Guard said, "The wine
steward was responsible for testing for poison. Instead, he must have stirred poison into the wine himself."

"It was not friendship that killed him," Niccolò
said, "nor was it the wine, I think." He peered at the
black stain left by the test on the heavy linen table-
cloth, then took the fallen glass by its foot, sniffed
it, and said, "It is subtle. You have not tested the
glass."

"What need? The wine—"

"If you would, signor. The rim of the glass, but
carefully. Perhaps someone else will fetch the wine
that was served."

The captain of the Guard said, "The wine steward
is already executed."

"Yes," Niccolò said with asperity, "but they did
not fling out his wine with his body. Bring me what
was served here at the high table."

The physician exclaimed, and held up the glass. The poison-specific stain had left its black deposit around the gold band at the rim of the glass.

"Well," Niccolò said, looking pleased. "Here we have it. It is a long time since I have had the honor of attending one of these feasts, but I do seem to recall that new glasses are set out with the serving of each wine. I fear that the wrong man has been accused and tried and executed. It was not the wine that was poisoned, but the glass."

The physician said, "Surely the glass shows a positive trace because it was in contact with the poisoned wine."

"Ah, but not a trace like that, signor. If the glass was contaminated by the wine it held, then the trace would be evenly spread over the inside surface. Here, though, we see the trace is in a distinct ring, a very narrow ring, around the inside. This poison—is it a contact poison, or must it be ingested?"

"It would not pass through the skin unless there was a cut or a wound, if that's what you mean."

"That's precisely what I mean," Niccolò said, his eyes gleaming with excitement. He was possessed by the spirit of inquiry. "Here is how it fell out. The assassin would have known that there would be checks for poison in the kitchen, and by the head stewards, before food or wine was served. So he smeared poison on his finger and wiped his finger around the edge of the glass before setting it before poor Raphael. You can see the break in the ring where Raphael sipped, and took the poison on to his lips. We will haul up the body of the wine steward, and test his fingers for poison. I am sure that it will test negative. Ah, now here is the wine. Have we a clean glass?"

Niccolò poured a generous measure, then downed

it in one. People around him gasped. He smiled. "You see. I am unharmed. The wine was not poisoned—indeed, it would be a mortal sin to pollute this fine vintage. No, it was Raphael's glass that was poisoned, quite deliberately. This is not a general plot against the Pope and the good councillors of the Signoria, but a specific one, to murder poor Raphael."

The captain of the Guard called up four of his men. To jeers from the crowd gathered in the square below, they hauled up the dead weight of the wine steward's body and laid it on the floor beneath the window from which it had been flung. The physician applied his stain to the dead man's fingers while Niccolò hummed tunelessly.

"There's no trace," the physician said at last, creaking up from his knees.

Someone said, "That only proves he did not contaminate himself."

Niccolò said sharply, "You would have him wear gloves? Where are they? Who would have set out the glasses, Captain?"

The man considered this gravely. "No one specific, I would suppose. Any of the servants of the first table."

"Then we will round them up and put them to the test! Pasquale, you can best help by comforting poor Baverio here." Niccolò grasped Pasquale's shoulder and added in a whisper, "Go with him, see what else you can find out. Perhaps Raphael was killed because he knew something." He raised his voice. "Captain, we will not find the assassin by tarrying here."

When they had gone, and when the soldiers had removed the body of the unfortunate wine steward, Pasquale took Baverio in hand and had him sit at the end of one of the tables. Pasquale was hungry, but he couldn't bring himself to touch the fruit and bread piled in baskets of woven gold in the center of the tables, not with Raphael's body still lying there on the floor at the far end of the huge candlelit hall.

As if reading Pasquale's thoughts, Baverio suddenly said, "We came for my master's body."

"The soldiers will be back. Or I can go and look for them now, if you'd like."

Baverio shook his head. "Signor Machiavegli will find who killed him?"

"We'll help you, if you'll let us."

"Is this to do with the glass I gave you?"

"Yes, yes I think so." Pasquale could not put off the moment any longer. "Baverio, we saw Giovanni Francesco murdered. He too was poisoned, by a choking vapor."

Baverio's face was chalk-white, but his voice was steady. "I knew that he was dead. When he did not come back this morning, I knew it, and so did my master. That was why he was determined to speak out."

"If there is something that your master knew, can you tell me what it was?"

"He would only say that it was to do with a secret of your Great Engineer. He believed that Giulio Romano was being blackmailed in some way, which was why poor Giulio took the little devices, the flying toy and the box and its glass, although that last secret is no longer a secret, of course, not after tonight. But he did not know that Giovanni Francesco was also involved." Baverio looked down the length of the candlelit room, to where Raphael's body lay under its tapestry shroud, looked back at Pasquale, his eyes brimming with tears. "My poor master, Pasquale! He cared so much for his assistants!"

"Do you know why Romano was being blackmailed? Was it the usual?"

"The usual?"

"Well," Pasquale said, thinking of Signora Giocondo, "I mean an involvement with a married woman."

"Oh, no! Nothing like that. My master . . . but I won't speak of that."

There was a silence. Pasquale prompted the boy, "And Romano?"

"My master thought that he had been involved in a commission to produce . . . a certain kind of art. You know the kind."

"Stiffeners, you mean. Hardly a matter of honor, I would have thought." Pasquale thought at once of the picture he had rescued from Giustiniani's grate—he supposed that it was a kind of stiffener, if your tastes ran to blasphemy.

"I didn't ever see what it was," Baverio said, "but I know that it was something different, something more real than the usual woodcuts or engravings. My master saw something of it, and said it was a perversion of art in every sense. I think that the glass I gave you was something to do with it."

"How so?"

"It is the great secret that the Great Engineer revealed this night. A way of registering light and shadows. His assistants brought into this room bright lights and a larger version of the box I found amongst Giulio's possessions. All present at the first table, the Pope and my master and members of the Signoria, had to pose stiffly before it. *Taking a picture*, the Great Engineer called it."

Pasquale thought of the glass plate blackened by some chemical process, and then of the picture he'd rescued from the fire, the strange shadowy picture. Shadow art, art of shadows . . . Dr. Pretorious had said that the artificers would put the artists out of business, although this business of simply capturing a likeness of a scene could hardly be the full answer. Even if it could be done, it would be no more than simple reality. There would be no narrative, no grace, none of the dense allusive symbolism by which paintings gave contentment and pleasure and glory to God.

He started to ask Baverio about this, but even as he began to speak a strange dull tremor shook the floor. Knives and glasses jingled along the tables; candle-flames bobbed. As Pasquale and Baverio looked at each other with wild surmise a tremendous clamor was raised somewhere outside the hall. A moment later the captain of the guard ran in with his soldiers at his heels, and shouted that they must leave.

Baverio started to say something about his master's body, that he was here to take it away. His voice rose in panic, and the captain slapped his face and said with a hysteria hardly more controlled than the boy's, "No time for that, you fool. We are under attack. Your master's safe enough lying there—he won't be going anywhere."

Pasquale was hauled to his feet by two soldiers; Baverio by two more. As they were marched toward the door which opened onto the great staircase there was a thunderclap in the balcony that ran above the far end of the room. The windows there blew in with a crash of glass, followed by a tremendous outpouring of smoke.

The captain began to shout about fire, but then the acrid stench of rotting geraniums reached Pasquale. His eyes and nose stung and watered, and he knew at once who was responsible for this.

The soldiers holding Pasquale began to choke. He twisted out of their grip, clapped one hand over nose and mouth, caught Baverio's sleeve with the other, and dragged him through the door.

At the bottom of the staircase, the cortile was filling with the choking orange vapor, and a panicky throng of soldiers and clerks and bystanders were pushing and shoving as they all tried to get out at once. Pasquale kept hold of Baverio's sleeve in the crush as the crowd carried them along—then they were outside, in the cold black torchlit night.

Pasquale, dragging Baverio with him, found shelter in the lee of the ceremonial platform that jutted out from the Palazzo. Half his mind, caught up in the crowd's fear, believed that anything could happen, at any moment; the other half, the rational half, coldly observed, with an epicurean particularity, that it was indeed a kind of magic that could make people suddenly distrust the very skin of things they'd previously thought of as solid and unchangeable. He wondered where Niccolò was.

Overhead, orange smoke was pouring out of windows on the second floor of the Palazzo. The Great Engineer's cosmic engine lay wrecked, its lower half blown apart and on fire from the oil spilled from the smashed lanterns of its central sun. Bodies lay around it, reduced to bloody rags. Some cried out, feebly stirring in pools of their own blood. People ran here and there, soldiers amongst them as panicked as the rest. From the crenellated roof of the Palazzo burning rockets shot down into the square with keening howls and whistles, trailing great tails of sparks, striking paving-stones and bursting with sharp thundercracks or skittering off amongst the legs of the mob. And here and there masked men on stilts strode about, tossing little glass globes that burst into clouds of orange smoke. The very air was alive and inimical, stinging the skin of the face, making eyes and nose water. It was altogether a scene out of one of the paintings of that school of Flemish artists who delighted in depicting the grotesqueries of Hell.

A soldier fired his pike at one of the stilt-men— the pike-head went wide and flew straight across the square and struck Berni's light-cannon, smashing the armature of its lenses. The patterns on the façade of the bank froze around a blurred white web. Another soldier whirled his mace-net around his head and flung it, entangling the legs of one of the stilt-men, who crashed to the paving-stones and erupted in thick jets of vapor that jerked his body this way and that: a cache of gas-bombs, letting go all at once. The mob surged back from this new horror.

Baverio broke from Pasquale's grip and ran across the square in the direction of the Great Engineer's tower, which loomed above the turmoil, its lights as remote as stars. Pasquale screamed after Baverio and ran too, dodging amongst people running in every direction.

A stilt-man stalked forward to intercept him, blowing hard on a toy trumpet. He was unmasked, with a narrow white face and a shock of red hair. Pasquale changed direction, running now not after Baverio but to save himself, running hard toward the narrow passage at the side of the Loggia. The red-headed stilt-man lobbed a gas-bomb that blocked the way. He was laughing wildly, enjoying this sport. Pasquale turned again, and saw, above the heads of the crowd, two more stilt-men swiftly picking their way toward him in one direction, and a coach and pair galloping at full tilt toward him from another. The coach bore the crest of the house of Taddei.

Before Pasquale could make a run toward the coach, the shadows of the pair of stilt-men loomed over him. Pasquale yelled defiantly. The nearest bent toward him—and then arrows sprouted on his chest and he staggered back, blundering into his companion. The coach swung past, its pair of white horses tossing their heads. The carriage door banged open and a man leaned out and caught Pasquale around the waist and drew him in, just as the mortally wounded stilt-man toppled and exploded.

5

The Palazzo Taddei was busy with men coming and going even at the late hour, past midnight, when Pasquale and Baverio arrived. As soon as they climbed down from the carriage, Baverio was taken off in one direction, and a page led Pasquale in another. Pasquale, excited and curious, and certainly in no condition to sleep after his close brush with the stilt-men, followed readily enough. He was taken inside to see Taddei himself, who was holding an audience in the great hall on the first floor of the Palazzo, listening to a report from a sergeant-at-arms of the militia.

Taddei was sitting in a high-backed chair near the cavernous fireplace, his jowly, pugnacious face lit on one side by the crowns of hissing acetylene lamps that hung from the ceiling, on the other by the shuddering light of the fire. He wore a richly brocaded robe, and a turban embroidered with gold thread. His eyes were half closed as he listened to the sergeant's stuttering account of a riot in the workers' quarter across the river. His secretary sat at a table beside him, taking down the sergeant's words. On the other side of the fireplace sat a thin young man clad in black, and a cardinal in scarlet robes and a red skullcap, both listening keenly.

The sleepless manufactories had shut down, it seemed, because the workers, the *ciompi*, had left their labors and were looting and burning their way through the commercial district which served their impoverished quarter. Pasquale realized that the point of the report was the defense by a detachment of the city militia of a warehouse owned by Taddei.

The sergeant concluded, "Those scum will burn their own houses in their rage, but if we are lucky they won't think or wish to turn to the factories or warehouses, or cross the bridges. They know that if they do, they will have to face mercenary troops as well as us, and I do not think that they have the stomach for a real fight."

The cardinal leaned forward. He was a spry handsome man of some forty years, with lank black hair cut in a fringe, a long straight nose, and a heavy-lidded gaze with which he fixed the soldier. A big jeweled cross on a heavy gold chain rested on his chest. "Be assured that they will try the bridges. The Savonarolistas are behind that riot, of that we can be certain."

The sergeant said in a nervous rush, "Begging your pardon, your eminence, but even the Savonarolistas, of which I admit to having seen no sign, would be hard put to lead this many-headed mob. The *ciompi* aren't led at all, not this time. They have no cause, but are rioting for the sake of it, every man for himself, taking what he can and burning the rest. They live like animals, and so they behave."

The cardinal wore rings on every finger of his hands, and he rolled these back and forth on the carved arm of his chair with contained impatience as the sergeant spoke. Now he said, "The Savonarolistas will show their hand soon enough. They have been much abroad recently, amongst your manufactory workers."

"That's true enough," Taddei said. "One was discovered in my weaving-sheds only a month ago. He was disguised as a loom operator, and was preaching sedition amongst the other workers. I had him flogged to the city wall and back, and thrown in jail, and sacked all the workers on that shift. But where there is one, there are others, if not in my warehouses or manufactories, then in those of my less careful friends and associates."

The sergeant said, "Signor Taddei, I ask for your recommendation."

"I'll pay for guards on all my manufactories and warehouses. You know the arrangements, and I know they will be acceptable to you. Go now, Sergeant, you have a long night ahead of you."

"Signor," the sergeant said steadfastly, "if the Savonarolistas are involved, I may be ordered to help guard the bridges."

The young man in black said sarcastically, "If you have to defend the bridges, they won't be attacking the manufactories, will they?" This fellow was hardly older than Pasquale, with a mop of tousled blond hair and a face as keen as a knife-blade, his hollow cheeks hectic with acne. His left hand was tucked beneath the bend of his knee, thumb and forefinger working on the ligament there.

"You'll do your best to make sure that those orders never reach you," Taddei told the sergeant. "I'm sure a man used to being rewarded so well can manage a small task like that."

The sergeant said slowly, "If the worst comes to

the worst, we can always dispose of any messengers, make it look like rebel work . . ."

"I don't want to know about *how* you'll do it," Taddei said with distaste, and turned to his secretary. "Marchetto, you won't write that down. I'll have no part in sedition."

"No visible part," the young man said, with a humorless smile.

"No part," Taddei repeated firmly. "Go to your work, Sergeant. We'll pray for you."

The sergeant saluted and marched out, and Taddei smiled at Pasquale as if he had seen him for the first time. "Come here, boy! Come along. Perhaps you can tell us more of these matters, and enlighten my friend here. This is the boy I told you about," he added, turning to the cardinal.

The cardinal lifted a pair of spectacles, shaped like the handles of scissors, to his eyes. He peered at Pasquale for a long moment. "Ah, the apprentice of Giovanni Rosso. I have a small painting by Rosso's master, Andrea del Sarto. An old-fashioned piece, but it gives me pleasure."

Pasquale said eagerly, "I have learnt many things from my master, and from Piero di Cosimo, too. Perhaps you saw the drawings of the scene of Giulio Romano's murder—those were my own engravings. I am also skilled in all kinds of drawing, especially silverpoint, and in all aspects of the painting of frescos, and of any kind of picture your eminence might require. At this moment I am engaged in the painting of an angel the like of which has never been seen before—"

The cardinal said, "How I wish I was here to discuss painting."

"If it please your eminence, perhaps he would at least accept this token of my skill." Pasquale unfastened the emblem of the Florentine lily which he had pinned to his black serge jerkin—its gold-foil loops were a little crushed by his adventures, but it still shone with a fine buttery luster—and held it out. He wondered if he should kiss the cardinal's ring. He had never met a cardinal before, after all, and knew vaguely that you should kiss the Pope's foot—there had been a small scandal some time ago, when it was discovered that Leo X, when he went hunting, wore thigh-length soft leather boots which made kissing his foot impossible. Certain broadsheets had commented that the Medicis were corrupting the Holy See for their own convenience, just as they had once corrupted the government of Florence.

The cardinal took the little brooch and twirled it between his long white fingers. "If only I could wear this openly," he said, "I would be the happiest man in the world."

Taddei made a gesture, and the page-boy brought a stool. Pasquale sat, and found that he had to look up at the others.

Taddei explained, "This young man has been involved with the inquiries of Niccolò Machiavegli into the murder of Giulio Romano. He was rescued from the Palazzo della Signoria this night, and brought straight here." He said to Pasquale, "I must suppose that you were with Signor Machiavegli, investigating Raphael's murder."

"Well, that's true," Pasquale said. He was not sure just how much he should admit, but that seemed safe enough.

The cardinal said, "I had believed Machiavegli reduced to a petty journalist, a poor enough occupation for a man of his talent. This news heartens us. Do the members of the Signoria relish the thought of having him involved in matters of state once more?"

"I do not believe they are much aware of it," Taddei said. "I engaged Machiavegli myself, for the private matter of investigating the death of poor Giulio Romano. His murder—"

"Yes, yes. I heard all of that sorry tale from Raphael, not an hour before he himself was murdered. I had not believed that Florence was so dangerous. But I did not know that Machiavegli was investigating these matters. A provocative choice," the cardinal said, "and one that pleases us greatly. We have always considered Machiavegli to be supportive of our family."

With a soft sinking shock Pasquale realized who the cardinal was: Giulio de' Medici, the Pope's cousin. He wondered what he had fallen into. Of course, Signor Taddei was a good friend of Raphael's, and so would know the Pope, but Pasquale was beginning to understand that nothing was simple in these circles. As in a painting, where every object is not only itself but also its allegorical meaning, so here each action had a sinister shadow.

Taddei said to Pasquale, "I see that you recognize my illustrious guest. Be assured that he is a friend of Florence."

"I do not doubt that any friend of yours is a friend of Florence, signor," Pasquale said.

Taddei said, "I must also introduce Girolamo Cardano, a mathematician, and more germane to the matter at hand, a scientist of natural magic and my personal astrologer."

The young man in black, Cardano, shifted on his seat with a grimace. He said, "In my opinion, Machiavegli is a summer soldier, a competent playwright, a no more than ordinary poet, and a failed servant of the state. He's not to be trusted. Even his friends say that, for love of this city, he has pissed in many a snow. But then you never take my opinions into account when you act."

"On the contrary, my dear Girolamo," Taddei said, "there's always a good deal of truth in what you say. But the thing of it is that Machiavegli has a fascination with problems and riddles. A problem can possess him and consume his entire attention if it is sufficiently complex, and I believe that this problem has indeed possessed him. He needs no commission from me, now. It has become his life." Taddei's forthright gaze bore down on Pasquale. "Tell us about his investigation, my boy. More to the point, tell us where he is now. My men could not find him, or he would be here with you."

"In truth, signor, I would wish that he was here with us too, for I do not know where he is, and I greatly fear for him. I saw him last at the Palazzo della Signoria. He left with the captain of the Guard to question the servants who had been in attendance when Raphael was assassinated, after he discovered that it was not the wine steward who poisoned Raphael."

Pasquale told of what had fallen out at the Palazzo della Signoria, speaking mostly to Taddei, but with sidelong glances at the cardinal. When he was done, he realized that the page had appeared at his side, holding out a gold tray on which stood a jeweled beaker of wine. He drank gratefully, and at once the rich wine's fumes invaded his head, as if driven by the heat of the fire.

Girolamo Cardano shifted in his chair, with a sudden wince as if he'd been struck. Pasquale saw that his thumb and forefinger had closed, pincer-like, on the soft muscle under his knee, and that this self-chastisement had brought tears to his eyes. The young magician caught him looking and said with a sneer, "Like Machiavegli, I need to be reminded of the failing of my body."

Taddei said, amused, "Niccolò Machiavegli drinks; Girolamo inflicts pain upon himself. He says that otherwise he is overcome by a certain mental anguish. He does not believe in himself, you see, unless he is subject to some small hurt."

Cardano ignored this and said to Pasquale, "You do not tell us why the stilt-men were pursuing you."

"In truth, signor, I do not know why. It seemed to me that the stilt-men were attacking any of the crowd that took their attention."

"He dissembles," Cardano declared. With a languorous flick of his wrist, he pulled a white mask as if from thin air, held it up so that its angles flashed in the light of the fire. He tossed it to Pasquale, who caught it by reflex. It had triangular black-rimmed cut-outs for eyes, and black ribbons to tie it around the wearer's head. The ribbons were stiff with dry blood.

"A Venetian carnival mask, taken from one of the men on stilts," the astrologer said. "What would you have us know of Venetians, painter?"

"Nothing more than what you already seem to know."

Cardano made another languid gesture, and held up a little box. It was covered in black leather, and the astrologer flicked a hinged slide that covered a pinhole opening at one end. Pasquale knew at once what it was: Baverio had described it well.

Signor Taddei said, not unkindly, "We found this amongst poor Giulio Romano's possessions."

"There's something missing," Cardano said. "You have it, I believe."

Pasquale discovered that he was sweating hard, although he felt as if he was bathed in ice. "It was only a piece of glass, covered in some black stuff."

He could see it quite clearly. It lay on a pile of papers on Niccolò's writing-table, with the flying device resting beside it.

"Ah," Cardano said, "exposed, then. If we are to believe you that is."

"You can ask Raphael's page. It was he who entrusted it to me, out of the best of motives. He believed it would help me find Romano's murderer."

"Hardly," Cardano said. "Where is it?"

Pasquale said, "I do not have it." Signor Taddei's uplifted eyebrow compelled him to confess, "I gave it to Niccolò, to Signor Machiavegli. If you please, I would know what it signified."

"Something or nothing," Cardano said. "It depends what image it captured."

Pasquale said, "Then it was a kind of mirror magic."

"More powerful and exact than that," the astrologer said. "This box throws an image on a coated glass plate, which captures it and is blackened to various degrees by various degrees of light. That plate you had may or may not have held an image, but it had not been treated to make it insensitive to light. That's why it turned black when it was exposed. Don't tell me that you are ignorant of the process, painter. You shouldn't be: it will be the end of your profession."

"I have heard of such things," Pasquale said.

Taddei said, "The Great Engineer decided to reveal his invention once he realized that a spy had discovered it. With a masterly stroke, he did so by making a likeness of the Pope and his immediate entourage."

"It is a very slow process," the cardinal said. "How Leo complained! We had to sit still for a full two minutes, and Leo had to rest his head in a brace devised by the Great Engineer, for any movement would blur the image."

Pasquale suddenly understood the true nature of the charred picture in his scrip. It was no drawing, but a true image, a residue of something that had really happened. Giustiniani had posed for it, out of monstrous pride or arrogance, and Francesco had tried to bribe him with a copy. But if this was an invention of the Great Engineer's, how had Raphael's assistants come by it? Had Salai given it to them? And if so, for what purpose?

In answer to these questions, which tumbled one upon the other in Pasquale's brain, Taddei said, "One of these devices was taken from the Great Engineer's workshops. It seems that Romano was a spy."

The cardinal said, "Not for Rome, despite his name. It seems that Giulio Romano had been promised advancement and employment in return for the smallest of favors. He was not a disloyal man, but was beginning to believe that he had labored too long in Raphael's shadow. The court of Spain offered him a position there, if he performed certain tasks. But poor Romano was an innocent, killed once he had learnt what his masters needed to know, or so we believe."

For a moment, Pasquale thought that he was falling into the sudden silence of the long firelit room. He said to Taddei, "And you set us to the task of finding the murderer, knowing this?"

Taddei protested. "I knew nothing until tonight. I learnt it from a message from which arrived only moments before you did. It would seem that whoever has taken Raphael's body wishes to exchange it for you, young man."

"Was this message sent by Giustiniani?"

"It was sent anonymously. It told of Romano's betrayal, and asked that you be delivered to the south side of the Ponte Vecchio at a certain time. Why do you suspect Giustiniani?"

"I saw a man killed at his villa," Pasquale said.

Cardano leaned forward. "That would be the missing man, Giovanni Francesco. It would explain all. It seems that Francesco was an accomplice of Romano, and it may be that he killed Romano to win all the glory for himself. In any event, he was killed in turn because he failed in his task."

Pasquale decided not to tell them about the picture of the black mass, or of the flying device, or of Francesco's attempt at blackmail. It could well be that Francesco was Romano's killer—Romano would certainly have opened the door of the signal-tower to him—but it was unlikely that Francesco could have cleaned himself of Romano's blood in the short time between Romano's dying cry and the search which it immediately started. And even if Francesco was Romano's murderer, why would he have gone to treat with Giustiniani? Surely he would have first tried to win back the box—it was in Taddei's possession, and so within reach—and he would also have taken the flying device from Romano. For the moment, exhausted and more than a little drunk from the heady wine, Pasquale couldn't unriddle it. He wished that he could benefit from Niccolò's sharp, clear insight . . . and with a pang realized that he might never see him again. Giustiniani's men could have killed him in the confusion at the Palazzo della Signoria.

Taddei said, "You had better explain to us, Pasquale, just what happened at Giustiniani's villa."

When Pasquale had finished, omitting any mention of blackmail, there was a silence. Finally the cardinal said, "It pains us to hear how badly things have fallen out here. My cousin was thinking of presenting Raphael with a commission to complete the chapel which Michelangelo has left unfinished for so long."

"There's no doubt that Giustiniani was the broker in Romano's compact with Spain," Taddei said, "and would be still if he could. That is why his men tried to capture this boy. But Raphael's assassination is the kind of devilry the Savonarolistas might use in their clandestine war. Suddenly it appears that we are playing a three-handed game here."

The cardinal said, "Raphael's body must be returned. For all that my family love Florence, my cousin cannot avoid war if he returns to Rome without it."

"Raphael was a guest of this city," Taddei told Pasquale. "That he was murdered is bad enough, although it can be excused as a Savonarolista plot. But that his body was taken and Florence cannot return it . . . There will in truth be war between Rome and Florence if it is not returned. And with the alliance broken, Spain will win all. It is well known that she will not be content with the south of Italy, but would rule all, and our colonies in the New World as well. The Spanish fleet has been standing off the coast this past week, and no doubt will land as soon as the alliance fragments into war. They have been funding the Savonarolistas for so long, and at last the unrest they have sought is coming about."

Pasquale said, "Surely no one will attack Florence. We are defended by the genius of the Great Engineer, whose inventions defeated the armies of Rome and Venice after the assassination of Lorenzo."

The cardinal said, "How ironic that Lorenzo's son may have to make war on Florence because of this sorry affair."

Taddei told Pasquale, "All states are now armed with similar weapons, copied from the originals that Florence has first used, and in many cases improving upon them. All governments have their rocket cannon, their mobile armored shields, their Greek fire and the rest. If the Great Engineer has invented new weapons, then he has kept them secret even from the Signoria."

Cardano said, "He is an old man. It is said that he is crazy, and obsessed with escaping a deluge that will end the world. What Spain hoped to learn I do not know, but in the end two men are dead for an invention which is of no use in war, and which in any case has now been revealed to all the world."

"You know that I saw your Great Engineer today," the cardinal said. "I will say that he seemed to have withdrawn from everything around him. He spoke not at all, and did not once look at the marvel of his cosmic engine, while his assistants worked to capture my cousin's likeness with no word or order from him."

"He has not invented anything for a long time," Cardano said. "As his university has grown, so his own powers of invention have dwindled."

Taddei said, "Nevertheless, this misadventure threatens the very existence of the Republic, and its renewed alliance with Rome."

The cardinal nodded, suddenly grave. Cardano was staring at Pasquale with a dark intensity, his lower lip caught between his teeth.

Taddei said to Pasquale, "Understand that we do this out of dire need."

"It's nothing personal," Cardano added.

There was a crash of armor; a dozen soldiers passed through the arch of the door at the far end of the room, marching in quickstep. Cardano drew a slim

short sword and Pasquale sprang to his feet and lifted
the stool to parry the blow. A second swing knocked
the sword from the astrologer's hand. The weapon
flew the length of the Persian carpet and Pasquale
ran and snatched it up and turned to face the soldiers,
flicking it from point to point to keep them at bay.

For a moment, only the soft sounds of the fire.

Then a corporal made a sweeping movement and
his pincer mace shot forward. Its toothed maw
gripped the top of Pasquale's head and his left shoulder. Pain lived between these points, pure as light.

The corporal twisted his weapon. Stone smashed
into Pasquale's hip, his back. The sword fell from his
hand, ringing on the flagstones. His body was numb.
He was looking up at the white vaults of the ceiling.
At each of the bosses of the ceiling's vaults a gilded
putto, with round cheeks and a rosebud mouth,
smiled down. A shadow fell across Pasquale. Cardano bent and gently pressed a reeking cloth to his
nose and mouth.

6

The vaporous liquid which soaked the cloth did not put Pasquale entirely to sleep. It was as if he were hovering at the border of dreaming and waking, might again be in his truckle bed in the narrow little room of the studio he shared with Rosso and the Barbary ape, nursing the dull pain of a hangover and easing into day. He felt motion, and dreamed, or thought he dreamed, that he was being carried swiftly on the back of a demon eagle, like the magician Gerbert, who had ridden a demon to save himself from the Inquisition and had lived to become Pope Sylvester II. The eagle turned its terrible horned face to him and with a flick of its wings tumbled him from its back. He tried to scream, but no words would come. A great mouth rushed at him, grinding its teeth as it opened and spat him out into night.

When Pasquale woke, it was to the jolting of a carriage. His head seemed cramped by a band of iron; his mouth was thoroughly coated with a foul sweet taste. He was lying on his belly on the carriage floor, slung lengthwise between benches where two soldiers sat. His hands were bound by a thin strong cord, and although his feet were free he did not yet have the energy or will to try and sit up, let alone stand.

The soldiers, as massive from his prone perspective as statues of Roman emperors, wore iron breastplates and helmets with an elongated beak and an upswept crest that broke into horns, the sort of fantastication loved by the Albanian mercenaries who were employed by private merchants to protect their wagon-trains. Taddei was making good his promise, then. Pasquale was being delivered as ransom for Raphael's corpse.

The coach rattled to a stop, and one of the mercenaries leaned out of the window—Pasquale heard the bang as he slid the shutter back, then felt a draft of cold air—and shouted something to the driver. With the cold air, which helped revive Pasquale's strength, came a diffuse sound like the roar of the sea, and a smell of burning.

The coach set off again, and the roar grew louder: men shouting; a random peppering of shots; screams. The carriage stopped again. One of the mercenaries was talking to someone, saying look, look, here was the pass, here was the seal of the Ten. The carriage door swung open, doubling the roar of the mob. A ray of lantern-light shot into the interior. Rough hands dragged Pasquale to a sitting position; just in time, he remembered to close his eyes. Let them think him unconscious.

The first mercenary said, "This is the piece of shit we have to deliver across the river."

"And by tonight," the second mercenary said.

A third, Florentine-accented voice said, "You'll have to do the best you can, but you won't get across this bridge, or any other."

The first mercenary said, "It must be this bridge,

Captain. We have important business at the other end. Here, it says we can ask for your help."

The captain said, "I'm giving you my advice. It is all I have."

"Then keep it," the second mercenary said, "and give us a few men instead."

"You'll need a fucking army to get through that mob," the captain said, "and I can't spare even one man."

"It says—"

"I can read it," the captain said sharply, "which is more than you can. Bring me the man who wrote it and I might listen to you. Instead, I'll tell you what you can do, and that's turn this carriage around and try and get a ferry-boat across the river down by Sardinia. The seal on that piece of paper might possibly impress some poor oarsman."

The second mercenary said, "We report you, when we return. I remember your face."

"You do that. Meanwhile, turn around and get off the bridge. Anyone trying to force a way through that mob will only inflame them further. Try a ferry. If you have no luck with your bit of paper you can always steal the boat. That's what you mercenaries are good at, isn't it?"

Both mercenaries swore at the captain, fluently and inventively, and the man laughed. Then there was a rattle of steel in the distance, a great shout and the captain shouted, "Now you see why you must turn back! Turn back right now!" A cannon boomed out close by and the carriage rolled forward a pace as its horses started.

The carriage door slammed so hard the vehicle rocked. Pasquale allowed himself to be laid back on the floor and risked opening an eye as the two mercenaries argued in their own guttural language. Firelight flickering on the roof of the carriage, a glimpse of heads moving past outside the window. Then the horned helmet of one of the mercenaries blocked the view as the man leaned out of the window and shouted to the driver to get on. The driver must have argued, because the mercenary swore and shouted that they must reach the far end of the bridge, to go, go now, go now at a gallop!

The carriage lurched forward so abruptly Pasquale rolled against the boots of the mercenaries, who kicked him back as one might roll a log, bruising his hips and shoulders. Blows thundered on the sides of the carriage; a window was punched in with a sharp clatter. The carriage rocked as the blows doubled and redoubled; then the carriage gained speed.

Shots, thunderous in the small space. The mercenaries were crouched at either window and firing pistols through them at a rapid rate. Pasquale started to sit up, feeling an airy panic, and one of the soldiers cried out and fell backward, sprawling across him.

Pasquale felt the man's hot blood soaking his tunic. He writhed beneath the dead weight and groped for the man's belt with his bound hands, but could find no knife. Then the weight shifted and the first mercenary lifted him by the hair so that he howled as he was dragged from the carriage into noisy firelit night.

They were on the Ponte Vecchio. It looked like the gateway to Hell. Shops burned in unison on either side, their roofs fallen in, flames leaping high and sparks whirling higher. Broken acetylene lanterns spat hissing geysers of yellow flame. The far end of the bridge was crowded with men, their faces red-lit by fire, their eyes pinprick glints. Some capered on the parapet, or on the roofs of those shops not yet burned. A great ragged chanting came from them, and a rain of small missiles, visible only as they arced down through the firelight. Most passed over the carriage, but some struck the pavement around it, stones smacking with sharp thumps, bottles shattering. A corpse lay a few *braccia* away, and others were scattered up and down the roadway, indistinct bundles in the leaping firelight.

Shots plucked the air overhead—soldiers holding the barricade through which the carriage had driven were returning fire. Pasquale saw a man spin and topple from the parapet into the river below, any sound he might have made in his last fall lost in the howl of the mob.

On either side of the burning bridge, along the bank on either side, buildings burned too, squatting over their inverted reflections.

The mercenary wound his fingers in Pasquale's hair and jerked his head back. The mercenary said, "Your bastard militia shot the driver and Luigi. You try and run and I shoot you. I shoot you dead."

Pasquale's mouth was dry. He rubbed his tongue over his palate until saliva flowed and said, "I think your master wants me alive."

"I was told to deliver you to the other side of this bridge, that's all. Dead or alive makes no difference to me. But I think the soldiers back there want you alive, or they'd use their cannon on us, like they used on the mob to keep them back."

"What would you have me do?"

The mercenary wrenched Pasquale's head again, and started to march him backward. "We're walking back there, and you tell them to guarantee safe passage across the river. Maybe they listen to a fine gentleman like you."

Pasquale couldn't believe the fool, and laughed right in his face. The mercenary lost his temper and knocked Pasquale down. Pasquale saw his chance. He rolled under the carriage, scrambled to his feet on the other side, started to run toward the barricade, the only thing he could think to do, waving his bound hands above his head and shouting that he was kidnapped. Behind him, the howl of the mob doubled: it was surging forward. Little lights blinked and flickered amongst the militia behind the barricade; then the first bullets struck the paving-stones around Pasquale. One grazed the parapet and went whooping away into the darkness over the river.

Pasquale threw himself down and tried to make himself as small as possible. Incendiary quarrels rained down too, and where they struck the coach they started to burn. The mercenary suddenly sat down, clutching his pierced breastplate. Burning quarrels littered the paving-stones; horribly, one had set fire to a corpse, which in a hideous parody of life slowly writhed in the middle of a ball of orange flame and greasy smoke as the heat shriveled its muscles.

A cannon boomed. Its round whistled overhead, skimmed the top of a burning shop and vanished into the darkness beyond. The mob retreated, men trampling their fallen fellows in panic. The two horses harnessed to the carriage stamped forward, eyes rolling, foam running from their mouths as they pulled against the brake.

Pasquale ran toward the carriage, for it was the only shelter on the bridge. With his hands crossed and bound, he couldn't use the grab-rail, but he got a foot in a bracket and kicked up. The driver slumped on the bench; Pasquale got blood on his hands when he untangled the reins from the dead man's grip. He kicked back the brake and flicked the reins across the horses' sweating backs and they promptly charged toward the mob. For an exhilarating moment, it seemed that Pasquale might succeed, but then the carriage smashed into an overturned velocipede which tangled in the spokes of the front wheels. The carriage slewed, its iron-bound wheels dragging rooster-tails of sparks from the paving-stones.

The horses stumbled, mad with panic because they were caught in a narrow corridor between burning buildings. Pasquale tried to haul on the reins, but had no strength left. The carriage slewed toward a burning butcher's shop and Pasquale jumped, rolling over and over.

As he staggered to his feet, two men ran at him from the mob. No, one was an ape. It was the Barbary ape, Ferdinand. It squatted a little way from Pasquale, gazing at him with brown, intelligent eyes. The man who caught hold of the ape's iron collar and grinned down at Pasquale was Giovanni Rosso.

7

As the mob surged forward, striking up their jeering chants again, Rosso squatted and cut the cord which bound Pasquale's wrists. Pain surged into Pasquale's fingers. Skin had been torn from every knuckle, and more pain came when he flexed his hands, fearful that he had broken bones.

He hadn't.

Rosso helped him through the dense-packed swirling mob. Pasquale had once spent a day watching the madmen stagger to and fro amongst the rocks and skinned carcasses of horses and mules at Sardinia, noting and sketching. Those same expressions surged around him now, from incoherent rage to slack-mouthed idiocy. Heat beat on either side from the burning butchers' shops. The smell of roasting meat was sickening. The light shaking above the writhing bodies of the mob was vermilion and cinnabar and gold. Sweat, the stink of smoke reaching back into the throat, the crisp noise of the fires. When the cannon boomed out almost everyone dropped to his knees, then slowly picked himself up and moved forward again.

"They could kill us all with one shot!" Pasquale shouted to his master.

"And smash the bridge, most likely," Rosso shouted back. "No, they're firing to let us know they can, angling shot over into the flood-channel where it's deepest. The time for killing hasn't come, not yet. They need orders for that."

Pasquale's head was swimming, and it didn't seem in the least odd that his master should be here to help him. He asked, "Where are we going?"

"Away from here. Before they do get orders to aim the cannon into the crowd and clear the bridge with chain-shot. Ever seen that? Pairs of small iron shot linked by a chain maybe a span apart. One will cut a man in two. They call them the Great Engineer's balls, because they will never engender a child."

After Pasquale and Rosso reached the far end of the bridge, shouldering past opportunistic hawkers and their customers, they took the steep steps down to the New Walk that had been cantilevered out above the river not five years ago. It was a promenade much in favor with the artificers, who could look on the system of channels by which they had tamed the Arno, on the Great Tower in which the chief of their number lived, and the manufactories which had made them wealthy and powerful.

Rosso stopped, and made one of his grand gestures at the burning bridge a little way downriver. "Don't you love this, Pasqualino? I'll paint such a picture as has never been painted before! Fire and black water and men baying for the blood of men! They have talked about my handling of highlights and shadow—I'll show them the true worth! If I find the right client it'll fetch four hundred florins at least!"

Pasquale had to smile. "Master, only you would think of a commission in the midst of this. Are we to go much further?"

"What's wrong? Hurt your leg? Quite a tumble you took, although you handled it like an acrobat. Ah, Pasqualino, I never understood why you thought it was so wrong to try and better yourself. A man must be on the lookout for any opportunity. The trouble with us Tuscans is that we're too given over to frivolities of this sort, which is why we're afflicted with wretchedness and poverty."

Pasquale began to laugh. It welled up from deep inside and would not stop. He laughed until he had to clutch the railing of the walkway to stay on his feet. The iron rail was hot under his hands.

Rosso said, "Yes, I know how business amuses you. But a little more business and a little less dreaming, Pasqualino, and you would be a rich man. Look upriver! That will be the cloth manufactory of the merchant Taddei burning. See the colors that the dyes lend the flames!"

Pasquale said, "I was with Signor Taddei not an hour ago."

"Of course."

"You know? Master, how do you know?"

Rosso said casually, "I saw the insignia on the side of the carriage, of course."

He called to the ape, Ferdinand, which was swinging idly on the rail. The creature swung down and ambled over, with a sailor's careless rolling gait. It put a hand on its master's thigh and looked up at him with beseeching eyes, and Rosso dropped a grape which it caught between its strong yellow teeth.

"Damn you," Rosso told it affectionately, knuckling its bony brow, "I should feed you something other than grapes. Grapes are your Eve's apples, and how you grin to show that you know it. Wicked wicked *wicked* fallen creature. You should not have taught him to steal, Pasquale. It was his undoing."

Pasquale said, "You are a part of it, master. Tell me it's true or I will go mad!"

Rosso was amused all over again. "Tell me what you think is true, Pasqualino."

"You knew Raphael's assistants. I remember now that you told me so much about them at the feast-day mass, but until now I didn't think about where you had learnt that gossip."

"But surely you know how much I love gossip? Ah, Pasqualino, you have spent so much time with the famous journalist Niccolò Machiavegli that you see conspiracies everywhere, and no doubt Spain at the bottom of all of them."

Pasquale shivered. He said, "Would you have a cigarette, master?"

Rosso handed one over, stuck another in his own mouth, and lit both from his slow-match. Pasquale greedily drew cool smoke deep into his lungs. His hands were shaking so much he had trouble keeping the cigarette pinched between thumb and fingers. The cold night air stung his skinned knuckles. He said, "It was in Niccolò Machiavegli's company that I saw you, although I did not recognize you at the time. It was in the gardens of the villa of the Venetian magician, Giustiniani. I think that you went there with your namesake, Giovanni Francesco. Something had gone wrong with your plans after the murder of Giulio Romano. Perhaps he was the leader? Or something was stolen from him, that you were going to trade with the Venetian for the promise of new positions."

"Something was stolen, perhaps. Or let us say taken by mistake."

It was an admission that set Pasquale's heart racing. He said, "If you mean the box which captures and fixes light, I no longer have it."

"Ah, no. That was always ours. An experimental device, but one soon to become common knowledge. Raphael had been given one to try out—although he tired of it soon enough, and Giulio was able to put it to better use. More rewarding use, let us say for now. He wasn't murdered, Pasqualino, except if you count a ridiculous accident murder. Let us say for now he didn't die at another man's hands."

Rosso's face, lit from one side by the burning bridge, looked amused and cruel and remote. He blew out a riffle of smoke between pursed lips. So Lucifer might look, at a foolish sinner's boasting, for Lucifer's crime was so great that it was beyond the measure of human sin, no matter how black the heart of the sinner—unless the artificers could mount a challenge on Heaven.

Pasquale said, "I suppose that you know how Giulio Romano died, then, but you will not tell me."

"I'm sure you'll work it out if you need to. But really it isn't important. Not poor Giulio's death, I mean, but the way he died." Rosso pushed away from the rail and put an arm around Pasquale, pushed him forward. "We have a little way still to go," he said. "Amuse me as we walk."

"Well then," Pasquale said doggedly. "After Giulio's death you had to try a new tack, perhaps by threatening the Venetian magician. Instead, he murdered Francesco, and you fled with Ferdinand. I saw you both cross the lawn in moonlight. I thought that Ferdinand was a dwarf."

"You're moving in strange circles, Pasqualino."

"Stranger than you think, perhaps."

"Taddei and his tame magician are hardly

strange," Rosso said. "Staid, I would have said, but not strange. Even the Pope employs an astrologer: presumably the powers of the Holy See do not extend to prognostication. Talk on, Pasqualino, you haven't the half of it yet, although I'm impressed that you know even that much."

Pasquale confessed that he knew only a little more, and that by guesswork. "I would suppose that the Venetian had Raphael murdered because he believed that Raphael was a part of your plot, although I must suppose that he was nothing of the kind. And now someone has the corpse of Raphael, and wants me, too. That's why I had to escape, master. Taddei planned to ransom me for Raphael's body."

"That's beside the point. At one time Giustiniani was acting as broker for us, and after the stupid accident which killed Romano he began to pressure us for delivery of what we had promised. Francesco thought that he could return the pressure, and went to parley with Giustiniani. That was against my advice, I should say. I knew that snake Giustiniani would simply laugh at any attempt to blackmail him. He revels in degradation—after all, it is an advertisement of his power. So I earnestly treated with Francesco, and when the poor fool refused to listen I followed him. As did you, and so you know what fell out there, and that I could not save poor Francesco but had to flee for my own life. But now I need not treat with any agent, for I can deal directly with those who can give me what I want, and I them."

They turned off the promenade, and climbed the clanging iron stair, and started across the wide street. Pasquale said, "Where are we going, master?"

"To see some friends of mine. You may be able to help them. And they in turn . . . we will see, eh Pasqualino?"

Rosso led Pasquale along a narrow street that wound up the steep hillside, leaving behind the tall fine houses that looked out across the Arno. The shanty town of the *ciompi* spread across the hillside, a densely packed wave of dark shapes against the dark land. Few lights showed. The paving-stones of the street gave way to mud. There was a sharp smell of burning in the cold night air, cutting through the ripe stench of the open sewer that ran gurgling down the middle of the street.

Pasquale stopped and said, "Would your friends be Spanish, master? If so, I'd rather not go any further."

"Here's fine gratitude, after all my help."

"A million thanks for your help, master, but I don't want to be involved in this."

Rosso laughed. "But you are involved, Pasqualino. Besides, I know things you need to know. For instance, I know where your friend Niccolò Machiavegli is. Don't you want to see him again?"

When Pasquale tried to run, Rosso caught his arm and managed to throw him to the muddy path. Pasquale sprawled in shock. He was stronger than his master, but the fight was gone from him. The ape chattered, plucking anxiously at Pasquale's chest, his torn jerkin, touching his face with hard horny fingers. Pasquale calmed the animal and slowly got to his feet. "That wasn't necessary," he said.

"I know what you're going to say, Pasqualino. That I am a traitor, consorting with enemies of the State. But it really isn't so. Ever since we left the bridge we have been watched, by the way. I have saved your life, because if you had run away they surely would have killed you."

"If you're caught, you'll hang as a traitor. Master, you can't think of this!"

"These are hard days for artists, Pasqualino. We

must find sponsors where we can. It doesn't matter who the sponsors are—it is the art that we can make because of their support that matters. And I am tired, Pasqualino, tired of scraping a living painting pots and carnival masks, and dirty pictures for lecherous merchants and their vapid wives. I know that I have it in me to paint great pictures, and I need a comfortable position to do it. Many of our fraternity have fled to France for support, and even there the artificers are winning, driving out good art with bad reproductions. Spain, though, is still a friend to us. There are so many in its royal family, so many dukes and princes who wish to show themselves a better patron and connoisseur than their neighbor, who wish to glorify themselves through commissioning great paintings. Ah, but I forget that you think that you can work without any kind of sponsorship, and live on air, I suppose."

"Please, master, I'll take no more of your mockery."

Rosso gave no sign of having heard Pasquale. He said mildly, "Look now, look down there on their work. What wonderful catastrophic light! I shall paint such a picture . . ."

They were high above the Arno now. The huddled roofs of the rude dwellings of the *ciompi* spilled downhill toward the river. The Ponte Vecchio still burned, a small and intense line of fire. The river either side of it was a ribbon of molten copper, molten bronze, burning light alive on its sluggish surface. Beyond was the prickly city, the lighted dome of the Duomo, and the towers and spires of the *palazzi* and churches, and the tower of the Great Engineer with its scattering of lighted windows and crown of red and green signal-lamps. Sounds were small and faint, a distant roar punctuated by the sound of cannons.

Pasquale said, "People are dying down there." But it *was* beautiful, in a powerful strange exhilarating way. He saw swarms of sparks flying up from the burning buildings on the bridge, dimming as they rose, like an inversion of the long fall of the rebellious host.

Rosso recognized his pupil's ambivalence and said, "Ah, but we are elevated above that. Catastrophe always compels from a distance, eh Pasqualino? Battles are the finest subjects of painting, when all conflict is resolved into one desperate hour. All life, and all death, in a tightly focused struggle."

"I'll always remember the many fine discussions we had about the theory of art, master. How much further do we have to climb?"

"Why, we're here. That's why we stopped," Rosso said. He stepped up to the plank door of a hovel, said, "I'm sorry, Pasqualino," and flung open the door and pushed Pasquale across the threshold.

8

A man sprang upon Pasquale as soon as he stumbled into the hovel. He was knocked bodily to the ground, and a sack stinking of moldy earth was thrown over his head. He tried to struggle to his feet, but the man knelt on the small of his back and tied his hands together behind his back before lifting him up. Then the sack was jerked from his head, and he saw Niccolò Machiavegli.

The journalist was twisting in the air, his feet a handspan above the dirt floor, hanging by his arms from a rope which passed over the main roof-beam. It was a crude version of the torture employed by the secret police: the *strappado,* the rope. A brutish man hauled on the other end of the rope and lifted Niccolò a little higher.

Niccolò gasped, and Pasquale cried out too. Then a hand was clamped around his mouth and he was shoved down the length of the room.

The one room was all there was to the hovel, under a ceiling slung with bunches of gorse to catch any drips of rain that might seep through the loose slates of the roof. Two men sat on benches drawn up to a poor fire of dry turf and wood-chips that sent up a trickle of sweetish smoke. One wore the dark home-spun robe, girdled with a rope, of a Dominican friar. He was young and plump and shaven-headed, with small features centered on a mild moon-shaped face. The other smiled at Pasquale, and Pasquale's heart turned over with fear, for he knew the man. It was the Great Engineer's one-time catamite, Salai.

Turning on the rope, Niccolò called out, "Be careful, Pasquale!"

Rosso ducked through the door of the hovel, dragging the ape with him. Pasquale twisted from the grip of the ruffian who had bound his hands, and called on his master to put an end to this at once. Rosso twisted the chain of the ape once more around his hand, fed the creature a grape and said without looking up, "I can do nothing for you, Pasquale."

Salai made soft ironic applause.

Niccolò cried out again as he was jerked another hand's breadth above the filthy floor. The brute who hauled him up was bigger than any man Pasquale had ever seen before, with a bristling beard and an eye-patch, and a knife with a curved, notched blade thrust through his belt.

The friar said, "Oh, but you must not cry out yet, Signor Machiavegli. We have not begun."

Salai said, "The roof's not high enough for proper *strappado*, so count yourself lucky, journalist." He winked at Pasquale. "You know how it's done?"

Pasquale did know how it was done. He had once made sketches of the questioning of a Savonarolista, for the newsletter that peddled the Signoria's line. He remembered too the game he had so often played as a child, hanging from a branch of a tree in his father's olive-grove, waiting and waiting as sharp needles dug into his arms and shoulders, and his wrists ached and his fingers burned, until the burden of his body could be borne no more, and then the airy rush of release when he let go, the wonderful feeling of rolling over and over, free, in the fragrant summer-dried grass. And he thought of how it would be with no release, and turned from the sight of Niccolò's torture, ashamed and angry.

Salai said, "I'll tell you how it was once done to me. They haul you up and then the rope is abruptly released. You fall but you do not fall all the way, and the halt almost tears your arms from your sockets. Then they haul you up again. They do it four times before they put you to the question, and by then you're ready to say anything."

Rosso dared take two steps into the room, hauling the ape with him. He said, "You talked, of course."

Niccolò lifted his head and said, "Of course he talked." There was a sheen of sweat over his white face.

Salai laughed. He was quite at ease in the hovel, with its damp smoky air and its dirt floor strewn with filthy rushes, in which black beetles as big as mice rustled. He was as elegantly dressed as always, in a cloak of black Dutch cloth fastened with scarlet cord over a red silk tunic that must have been worth the annual wage of any ten *ciompi,* and which almost but not quite concealed his paunch, and red breeches with a padded codpiece in the Flemish manner, and black hose on his fleshy legs.

He said, "Of course I talked. I squealed like a happy pig. Why not? I told them something like the truth, and even if the names were wrong, they arrested the right number of men. Who because they were innocent protested their innocence even under question, which made their guilt all the more convincing." A silver box was open beside him, from which he took a square of Moorish jelly, dusted with fine sugar. He popped the confection in his mouth and smacked his rosebud lips together. "It is time this farce was put to rest, Perlata," he said to the friar. "The sooner I am out of this flea-ridden pit the better."

Niccolò said, "I agree. For the love of God, let me down. Why do you do this?"

The young friar, Fra Perlata, said, "For the love of God, of course. These matters can't be rushed."

Rosso laughed. "For the love of God!"

Fra Perlata said quietly, "Look in your pupil's purse. See if he has it."

"I've done all you asked me to," Rosso protested. "That and more."

"And you will do this," Fra Perlata said.

Rosso said, "I'm sorry for this, Pasquale," and unbuckled the flap of Pasquale's scrip and poked through its contents. He said, "It isn't here."

"Of course not," Salai said. "You think he'd carry it with him as a keepsake?"

Pasquale told Rosso, "Master, I hardly believe you can watch this. Your need for patronage is truly great. It astounds me." He knew now why Rosso had been so frivolous all the way up the hill; it was how Rosso, who was fundamentally honest, always hid a lie, a misdeed, a betrayal.

Rosso said, "You got mixed up in this of your own free will, Pasqualino. Tell them what they want, and they'll let you and Machiavegli go. I swear it."

"Be careful what you say," Niccolò called, and groaned as the brute jerked him up by another notch.

Salai made an impatient farting noise with his lips. "Enough sentiment. Let's find out what these fools have done with it and we can get on with our business. I'll heat my knife in the fire here and test him myself rather than watch him twist like a spider. It's making me dizzy!"

Fra Perlata said, "Please, Signor Caprotti, have patience. When we have the proof you will have your reward."

He was the center of power in the room, this plump young friar, his fanaticism scarcely disguised by a superficial mildness, like a sword sheathed in kid leather. It was quite clear what he was, for Savonarola himself was a Dominican, dying even now by slow degrees, it was reported, in a Dominican monastery in Seville. It was said that a cancer had taken away Savonarola's voice, that instrument which had once shivered all of Florence to its collective soul, yet even on his deathbed he wrote an endless stream of tracts and letters and sermons and pamphlets about the great time to come, when the pure in heart would be bodily raised up to Heaven, and the sinners would be left to face the war of the Antichrist. Fra Perlata was one of the foot-soldiers in this holy cause.

As for the brute who held Niccolò suspended, and the ruffian who had taken charge of Pasquale, it didn't matter what they were, loyal Savonarolistas or hired muscle. More likely the latter: both had a Prussian rather than Spanish look. They were landsknechts perhaps—there were plenty of those looking for work after Luther had been caught and tried and hanged by the forces of Rome—but whatever they were really didn't matter, because they were there simply to hurt Pasquale and Niccolò until they talked. It was their job.

"All we have to do is tickle these two," Salai said. "Why make such a fuss about it?"

"What is important is the liberation of the Holy

City," Fra Perlata said. "The hour is at hand. We must observe the proper form."

"A few *ciompi* are not God's Holy Army," Salai said with scorn.

"We're not to say how God's will is manifested," the friar said.

"He seems to be moving in mysterious ways," Salai said, popping another sugar-dusted square into his mouth and masticating loudly. "Certainly if he is using this oaf of a painter as his vehicle for returning what's rightly ours, and an ape as the agent of our misfortune. Rosso, what do you say? Should I kill that flea-ridden brute of yours? I mean the ape, of course, not your pupil."

Rosso, who had regained something of his swagger, said, "Forgive it, Lord. It does not know what it has done."

The ape sat on its bottom beside him, arms folded over the top of its head, peeking from beneath the angle of its elbows at Pasquale like a child. Pasquale smiled back at it, remembering how he had taught it to steal the grapes from the choice vines of the garden of the friars of Sante Croce. Ferdinand was an intelligent animal, and would not have forgotten. But he could not make the signs to it because his hands were tied behind his back.

Salai said, "In Prussia they burn dogs whose barking has been judged to cause thunderstorms."

Rosso said, "God save us that we are not in Prussia."

Fra Perlata said to Pasquale, "You know what we want. Where is it?"

"Signor Taddei has it."

"Bad news for you if he has," Salai said.

Fra Perlata said, "Please be quiet. I'll attend to

this." He stood up, dusting the skirt of his robe, and told the brute to raise Niccolò higher.

Niccolò made a terrible sound as he was raised: he didn't sound like a man at all. Pasquale cried out too, then flinched when Fra Perlata put a hand on his shoulder.

The friar said, "Your friend has hung there long enough, don't you think? Much longer and he'll be a cripple for life. He won't ever be able to write again. Help him. Tell us the truth, and be sure you do. We have a man in Signor Taddei's household, and all the worse for your friend if you lie."

Pasquale said, "If you mean the signaler, then he was arrested."

"I know of the signaler, but he was never privy to our cause. How would we have known where you were being taken for ransom, Pasquale, if we had not been told? Now think carefully, and speak the truth."

Pasquale said quickly, "Signor Taddei took the box. He has it. I'm sorry Niccolò, I had to tell them. Forgive me."

Niccolò shook his head from side to side. "No more," he said.

Salai giggled. "Box? You think we'd worry about a trifle like that? It was good for making dirty pictures, but not for waging war."

Fra Perlata said, "Hold, signor! We'll put him to the drop before we question him."

Salai said, "I tell you the drop is not great enough. Peasants do not make their holes well enough to lend them to torture—in fact, I'm surprised that the roof-beam hasn't split in two by now. If you really want to hurt them, then hang on to their legs. It is the weight that does it, you see. We grow heavier in the moment that we stop falling, something the old man once explained to me. Better still, I'll carve a few slices from them, eh? Maybe trim the boy's fingers joint by joint. A painter loves his hands as much as a musician."

Fra Perlata said, "You will put away your knife. We are on God's business here."

Salai said, "This little blade? Why, it isn't really what you'd call a weapon."

Pasquale said, "You'd best kill me, because if it is not the box that you want, I have nothing."

"Oh, but you have," Salai said. "The flying device. You took it from Romano's corpse, in the signal-tower."

Niccolò laughed.

"Be still!" Fra Perlata said, his voice ringing under the low ceiling. The ape Ferdinand looked at him with momentary interest, then yawned, showing a ribbed liver-colored throat behind strong yellow teeth.

Salai said lazily, "Don't threaten me, monk. We're on the same side, and I want to help you. Believe me, I've had experience in these matters, and the *strappado* will not work here. Besides, even if it made them talk, they might not speak the truth. I did not, after all."

Pasquale said, "It's the toy you want? I can take you straight to where I left it!" He could see it, for a moment, on Niccolò Machiavegli's cluttered writing-table, sitting on a pile of manuscript leaves, faintly luminous in the shadowy room.

Niccolò said, "No more, Pasquale. They'll kill us anyway."

Salai smiled and said, "Well done, painter. But no one will believe you until you're put to the test. We must have our fun, after all."

"Leave off this," Rosso said. "Leave it off! I'd know

if he's lying, and I tell you now that he speaks the truth."

Salai turned on him with a snarl. "You know nothing of the kind. Your ape lost us the fucking thing in the first place."

Suddenly, Pasquale knew what had killed Giulio Romano, knew how his body could have been found in a locked room atop a tower climbable by no man. He and Niccolò had been straining after the answer and now it had been placed into his hands and it was worthless, so that he must laugh.

Salai said, "You see how he mocks us! A little blood will let out the truth. Are you afraid of blood, monk?"

"You know that I am trained in medicine. But I will do this the proper way."

"Perhaps you mean the scientific way? Even torture has its artificers. Better the pain of the knife. It is slow, exquisite. Unlike the *strappado*, it does not stop. It works cut by cut, mounting by degrees. He's a pretty enough boy, so perhaps I should cut away one of his ears, piece by piece, eh?"

Niccolò said, "Hold your tongue, Salai." He had to draw his lips back from his teeth to speak, and took little breaths that broke his sentences. "I think you're no more, no more than an idle boaster. Not even a good one. If you want to hurt me, try flaying."

"Let him down," Salai said coldly, "and we'll see. No, monk. We'll try my way first."

Niccolò said, "You don't dare, Salai," but stiffened when Salai laid the blade of his knife flat against his bandaged thigh, where he had been wounded by a pistol-ball.

Rosso said with a trembling edge to his voice, "Tell them what they want, Pasquale. It can't hurt you, and will save your friend."

Pasquale, for a moment the center of attention, felt an odd sense of control. He looked directly at Salai and said, "I've already told you I have the toy, in a safe place. Cut him, and I'll tell you no more."

"But I think you will," Salai said, and jabbed the tip of the knife into the tensed muscle of Niccolò's thigh. "Tell me the truth, painter."

Rosso cried out, "For the love of God, Salai! Let Pasquale speak."

Pasquale bit the inside of his lips to stop himself from crying out too, and the taste of his own warm salt blood filled his mouth. He spat on the straw, and the ruffian cuffed his head.

Niccolò grinned down at Salai: a death's-head grin. "That's the best you can do?"

"Worse, far worse," Salai said, and thrust again, laughing.

"Leave him be!"

"Stay your hand!"

First Rosso, then Fra Perlata, had spoken. Rosso had drawn his knife. The ape dragged against its master's grip, intently watching Pasquale.

Salai laughed again, stepping back so that everyone in the room could see him. He raised the bloody knife and licked its blade, grinning around it.

Niccolò groaned, and said, "Kill me for the truth. You know the boy doesn't lie."

Salai shrugged and raised his knife. Rosso shrieked and the ape wrenched free from his grip and with an odd sideways bound threw itself on the ruffian who held Pasquale. Man and ape went sprawling, and then Niccolò fell as the brute hireling let go of the rope, plucked the ape from his compatriot by an arm and a leg and threw it across the room before it could fasten its teeth on him. The ape jumped up, chattering with rage and flailing straw with its hands and its hand-like feet. Fra Perlata told Rosso to keep it quiet and bent over Niccolò and quickly examined his wounds.

Salai screamed insults at Rosso. His curly hair shook around his mottled jowly face. When he ran out of breath, Fra Perlata said, "You've done enough harm. This isn't one of your games."

Rosso said, "None of this is necessary. None of it."

Salai laughed and said, "I'll kill you, Rosso. I swear it."

Fra Perlata turned and said quietly, "This is God's business. You must all understand what we're about. These are the End Times, bringing distress as bitter as a dish of borage, and change as relentless as a mill grinding out the flour of wisdom. Florence is at the center of Italy through God's plan, as will shortly be revealed. It must be ruled by the Holy Word, or a sword will fall upon it. It must repent while there is still time. It must clothe itself in the white garments of purification, but must not wait, for soon there will be no time for repentance. Do you all understand?"

"You still need me," Salai said. "Don't forget it."

"I forget nothing," the friar said. He told the brute hireling to attend to Niccolò and crossed the room and bent his round face close to Pasquale's. His breath stank of onions. "I forget nothing, and by God's grace I see what I need to see. Look at me straight, boy, and tell me, or we will continue what we have started."

Pasquale saw Niccolò's blood pooling under his wounded leg and gathering around the fingers of his bound hands, which were twisted behind his back. Fra Perlata pinched his cheeks between sharp-nailed fingers, so that Pasquale had to meet his eyes.

Pasquale said, "I have what you need. I can lead you straight to it."

The brute hireling washed Niccolò's wounds with salt water and bound them with cloth torn from his shirt. Fra Perlata inspected this work and told Niccolò that it was God's will if he lived or died now, and then ordered Rosso to quiet the ape. Salai said he knew a quick way, and was told to be quiet in turn. The Savonarolista friar was making the best of it that he could, Pasquale saw, masking his anger with decision and action. Niccolò was bound by the rope from which he had hung, turned four times around his body and tied tight, and then the bonds at his ankles were cut and he and Pasquale were walked outside and down a foul alley to where a horse-drawn carriage waited.

The ride was not long, but every jounce of the carriage hurt Niccolò's leg and drew a stifled cry from him. He lay across one of the carriage's benches: Pasquale sat on the other between Fra Perlata and Salai, who was cleaning his immaculate nails with the tip of his knife, careless of the jolting ride. The two hirelings and Rosso and the ape rode up with the driver. The curtains were drawn across the carriage's windows, so Pasquale could not tell which direction they were taking, but at one point the noise of a mob rose ahead and passed by and subsided behind, and he knew they would not cross the Arno by any bridge.

All too soon he was proved right. The carriage halted and he and Niccolò were bundled out by the hirelings. They were at the edge of the new docks. The brute slung Niccolò across his shoulders like a sack of meal, and Fra Perlata gripped Pasquale's elbow and marched him down a stone slipway to the ferry which rocked on the dark water of the river.

The Savonarolistas had taken it. There was a dead

man on the decking, lying in a pool of his own blood, and the crew was muffled in scarves.

The ferry got under way at once. Steam billowed from the vents of its burner-pipes and with a laborious flexing of the wooden beams the paddle-wheel churned water into a creamy froth. It moved at an angle against the current, driving toward the far end of the complex series of weirs and steps that controlled the flow of the channeled river.

It was bitterly cold. Downstream, beyond the new docks, where the ocean-crossing *maona* loomed above lesser vessels, the waterway ribboned away across the dark floodplain under a sky crowded with crisp bright stars. Upstream, Florence lay under a mantle of smoke: not the fumes of the manufactories, but the smoke of many burnings. Fire still illuminated the arch of the Ponte Vecchio, and fires burned along the bank which the ferry had just quit. Otherwise the city was dark and still, save for the winking of signal-lights. Pasquale heard the bells of the public clock in the tower of the church of Santa Trinità toll the hour of four.

He sat with Niccolò Machiavegli, massaging the journalist's arms. "I had never thought to have to bear the rope again," Niccolò said wryly, "yet I am pleased that I could bear it straightforwardly. A million thanks, Pasquale, I do feel something in my hands again, where you move the blood into them. Blood is the conduit for pain it seems, for it always hurts us to spill it, and now it hurts when it returns to its natural place."

"I wish I could mend the wound that Salai gave you."

"It hurts no worse for his attentions than it did when the ball of the pistol first struck it."

"How did you come there, Niccolò? Did the Savonarolistas kidnap you at the Palazzo?"

"Not at all. It was the work of Giustiniani's men. I knew them by their white masks, and the vapors they used. They put me in a carriage, but it was stopped at a bridge and they were overpowered. I thought I was saved, but I was placed in another carriage and delivered to the attentions of Perlata and Salai."

"Then Giustiniani and the Savonarolistas are at each other's throats, although they work for the same master."

"Giustiniani does not work for Spain, Pasquale, but for what money he can gain by selling the device. The Savonarolistas do it to overthrow the government of Florence and save us all for the love of God. And you, Pasquale?"

"It was in precisely the opposite way. I was betrayed by Signor Taddei, who received an anonymous note asking that I be delivered in exchange for Raphael's body."

"Raphael's body was taken? I wonder for what end?"

"If the body is not returned, then there will be war between Florence and Rome."

"Ah, I see. And Spain will be the victor."

"That's what Signor Taddei said."

"He is a patriot."

Pasquale said bitterly, "He is foremost a business man."

"The two go hand in hand. And what was taken—I won't speak of it here—is wanted by both Giustiniani and the Savonarolistas. One would sell it to Spain, and one would give it."

Pasquale explained what Rosso had told him about Giustiniani's role as agent for the dissident artists, and Niccolò laughed and said that now he understood why what was sought was sought so eagerly by all.

"But there are also the pictures made by the Great Engineer's device, which Giulio Romano used to copy the Great Engineer's notes about his flying toy. It is a device that captures light, Niccolò, and fixes it precisely. The blackened glass I had from Baverio was one such, and the picture I rescued from Giustiniani's fireplace another."

"Do you not remember the signal-tower, Pasquale? Think. What did you see beside the body?"

"The open window."

"Yes. And?"

"Glass, below it."

"Yes. Yet the window was unbroken, and besides, the glass was black."

Pasquale remembered the glass plate that Baverio had given him, blackened from its exposure to light, and understood. The glass had been the remains of pictures of the Great Engineer's notes. Only the model remained. He said, "What will happen to us, Niccolò?"

"The Savonarolistas aren't known for killing without reason. If they are given what they want they may let us go. They believe, after all, that they are working God's will. If they win, then once again it will be as it was during the brief reign of Savonarola. Blessed bands of children will roam the streets of Florence, singing hymns and seeking out every vanity from rouge-pots to paintings, from chessboards to every kind of artificer's device, and throwing stones at those not yet virtuous. There will be fasting and religious pageants and great bonfires of vanities. The Savonarolistas dream of a pure and simple world, Pasquale, in which all men turn entirely to Christ whether they like it or not. Yet their plans are founded on the certainty that God speaks directly to Savonarola, and I am not persuaded of that, for all that many in Florence once believed it."

"Yes, but I do not trust Salai. I would kill him if I could."

"Many have tried, yet he lives. Don't underestimate him, Pasquale."

Fra Perlata was talking to one of the Savonarolistas who had captured the ferry. Pasquale caught a few of their words, brought to him on the bitter wind that blew past the laboring ferry. Something about fire, and the last times, and justice. No doubt that was what the Savonarolistas promised the *ciompi*, Heaven's justice here and now on Earth, but it seemed to Pasquale that even justice in Heaven was a remote possibility, and he said as much to Niccolò.

"It's true that we are enveloped in the laces of sin, but we must always hope, Pasquale. Without hope there is only despair, and with despair, evil. If we are to have God as a friend, we must hope for redemption. The Savonarolistas promise it, but it is not theirs to give. Ah, we are making for the shore now."

The note of the boiling tubes of the ferry's Hero's engine rose in pitch, a keening whistle at the edge of hearing. The paddle-wheel thumped faster, spraying the deck with cold droplets of water. The ferry was coming about, heading into the quieter water along the edge of the river as it made for a landing at the foot of the city wall by the river gate. The head of the dead crewman was rocked back and forth by the vibration. Its eyes glimmered in the moonlight, blind and foolish-looking. Death makes fools of us all, Pasquale thought.

Most of the crew of Savonarolistas had lined up on the landward side of the ferry, muskets and rifles bristling out at the stony barren shore. Pasquale called to the brute hireling, asking if trouble was expected, and the man grinned and drew his thumbnail across his throat.

Rosso pushed away from the rail, where all this time he had leant and watched Florence burn. He said, "We're enemies to our own city now." Beside him, the ape shifted and rattled its chain. It hated water, and was uneasy and subdued on the little ferry.

"You knew what road you were setting on," Pasquale said. "I hope to see your paintings, master, when you have your commissions."

"I do not know if I can paint again," Rosso said. "This is a bitter business, Pasqualino. You should hate me, and I would not blame you. I've been a fool."

Niccolò said, "There is always redemption."

"No talking," one of the masked Savonarolistas said. "You do what we want, now. All of you."

The shore was suddenly visible, and the city wall looming beyond. Signal-lights winked green and red atop the nearest tower. The ferry was aiming into a small cut that ran back into the shore along the line of the wall, laboring against the current. As it neared the mouth of the cut, lights rose up: rockets.

At first Pasquale thought that they were signals from Savonarolistas waiting on the shore. But more and more rose, scrabbling quickly into the night and bursting in showers of white sparks at the tops of their toppling arcs. Pasquale remembered Giustiniani's men sending rockets bursting through the panicky crowd in the Piazza della Signoria. Smoke blew out across the black river, softening the harsh glare released by the exploding rockets. The Savonarolistas started firing into the smoke, and red muzzle-flashes snapped back at them.

The ape, Ferdinand, was sent into a frenzy by the noise, dashing to and fro in the narrow arc permitted by its chain. Rosso made a gesture, throwing up his hand, and at the same time the ape shrugged free of its chain; or no, Rosso had released it. It bounded away toward the foredeck, after the grapes that Rosso had thrown there. The brute hireling and Salai, his sword drawn, closed on it from different directions; the ape dodged both men by scampering up one of the rope stays of the ferry's steam-vent.

Rosso put a hand on either of Pasquale's shoulders, and pushed him overboard.

The shock of the cold water drove away Pasquale's surprise. For a moment he thought he would drown in darkness; he made frantic frog-kicks, straining to free his hands, which were still bound behind his back. Then Rosso appeared beside him and got one arm under his chin. They were drifting away from the ferry, which had reversed its paddle-wheel as it tried to turn from the shore. Stray shots splashed and pattered around Rosso and Pasquale; one hit the water close to Pasquale's face, tugging at the sodden folds of his jerkin as it sank. The ferry's paddle-wheel stopped and the craft began to drift sideways in the current. It was silhouetted against the smoke and light from the shore; then something rushed out across the water, spitting sparks, and smashed into the stern.

Rosso kicked and kicked, dragging Pasquale with him, and in a minute they were staggering up the shingle bank of a little backwater, where a handful of fresh corpses lay face-down in the water, men killed by the fighting on the bridges, washed here by the river's currents.

PART THREE

The Interrupted Measure

I

By the time Pasquale and Rosso had clambered across the jumble of flood-cast boulders and rotten tree-stumps on the river-bank, the exchange of shots between the Savonarolistas and the forces on the shore had ended. The ferry had run aground and was ablaze from end to end, and those Savonarolistas who had not jumped ship and chanced the dubious mercy of their enemies must surely have perished.

Pasquale would have run to try and find Niccolò if Rosso hadn't held him back. "We must save ourselves!" Rosso said desperately.

Filled with loathing and despair, Pasquale wrenched free and said, "He is my friend!" Then he ran at Rosso and knocked him to the gravelly mud, and might have tried to kill him if voices had not sounded close by.

It was a contingent of the city militia, searching for survivors of the ferry wreck. Pasquale and Rosso hid in a pit amongst freshly flayed bodies of horses and mules. By now both were racked by deep shivers, for their soaked clothes were icy cold and not likely to dry in the cold night air. Teeth chattering, they hugged each other for warmth, but both knew that their friendship had died amongst the stink of blood and the yellow grins of the dead animals.

The militia's search was in any case half-hearted. Moonlight turned the tumbled shore into a shadowy maze where a hundred men could have hidden from the searches of a thousand, and it was a cold night and the militia knew better than most that Sardinia was haunted by the shades of those who were disappeared for the convenience of the Signoria and the safety of the city. Besides, they had to pay for their ammunition out of their meager stipends, and there was no point wasting it on any survivors of those who had (they supposed) stolen the ferry. They marched back to their warm guardroom without bothering to search the area properly, and they didn't even report the incident: there was already enough madness that night.

Rosso and Pasquale arose from their grave and made their way along a track winding between white boulders, over a little hill studded with rotted tree-stumps and the broken skeletons of horses and mules. Rib-cages gleamed like ivory staves in the smoky moonlight. Halfway along, a shadow bounded up towards them, making a faint jingling. It was the ape, Ferdinand, its fur soaking wet and raised in little points.

Rosso groaned, and cried out softly that he was cursed to bear this burden until he died. The ape made plaintive little hootings as Pasquale scratched behind its ears, and it seemed almost glad when Rosso took up its chain again. He roughly wrapped its length around his arm and hauled hard upon it, although the ape trotted along docilely enough between the two men, as if they were simply walking to their favorite tavern after a day's work.

But that time was over.

They quickly reached a little gate at the base of a square ballistics tower, beside a channeled stream which ran out beneath the wall. A mill-house stood on the other side of the fast-running stream; chinks of yellow light showed between the big wooden shutters over its first-floor windows. But the gate was shut, of course, and Pasquale and Rosso didn't dare bang on it and demand entry. It was quite clear that the militia were edgy that night, and would need little excuse to shoot a couple of shivering stragglers, so they had no choice but to pick their way around the wall to the nearest road, to await the opening of the Prato Gate at cock-crow. Walking at least kept the blood flowing.

Rosso told Pasquale that he knew that this rescue would never make amends, but it was all he could do. He jerked the ape's chain and said, "Perhaps you can sell the toy, if the Savonarolistas don't find it."

"Perhaps," Pasquale said. He wasn't convinced that Rosso's help was motivated purely by a desire for redemption—anyone able to offer the flying toy to those who wanted it could name his price, although whether he survived the transaction was another matter entirely. As for his former master, Pasquale felt nothing but an empty pity, and that more for himself than for Rosso. He was suddenly cast adrift, rudderless, without a compass.

"It's not just that I can't stomach torture," Rosso said. He was hugging himself as he walked, slapping his chest with crossed arms like a bird with clipped wings trying to take flight.

"Niccolò found it hard enough," Pasquale said, finding in himself an unforgiving streak.

"Of course, of course. I suppose that at the end I

cannot betray my friends, or my city. It's all very well thinking of these things in the abstract, but the actuality is quite different. It may seem I have no principles, but they are there all the same, buried deep."

"Then I suppose that you didn't intend to murder Giulio Romano."

"No, no! That was a foolish accident. And besides, I wasn't even in the tower."

"I thought you might have put the ape up to it in some way," Pasquale remarked, and even in the fading moonlight saw that his shot had gone home, for Rosso stumbled and cursed and walked on a little way before speaking again.

"Well, you guessed the main part of it, anyway. But no one put him up to murder. The ape climbed the signal-tower, it's true, and I did set him to it, but not with the intention of killing poor Giulio. No, that was furthest from my mind, and I had thought the ape ready, for I had already trained it to retrieve grapes from a higher and higher place until it would climb anywhere I asked it. How do you think it so easily learned to steal those grapes from that silly monk?

"We had arranged that Giulio would light the lamps of the signal-tower of Signor Taddei's Palazzo at a certain time. I would signal in turn by briefly revealing a lantern, and then send the ape to collect the prize. We had to resort to such devices because all of Raphael's disciples were being watched closely, as you might imagine. In fact, that was why I was there that night, because Giulio feared losing that which he had taken, and would entrust it to me instead, although I had no means of getting it to where it was supposed to be."

"Then it was Romano who stole the device, and not Salai after all."

"So you don't know everything, Pasqualino. No, Salai told Giulio how to find the device, that is all, for we knew that suspicion would immediately fall upon him, as indeed it did, once the device was found to be missing. Giulio took the device with ease, when he and his master, Raphael, visited the Great Engineer. He also made pictures of the Great Engineer's notes, for they were too convoluted for easy transcription, even if the Great Engineer did not write in mirror image. How Giulio sweated over each long exposure! The ape wore a harness, with a padded pocket for the glass plates."

"I see now how things fell out. That same day, Salai met with Romano at the service for our confraternity. But why would Romano pass the device and the picture plates to you?"

"Quite simple. Our plan was beginning to unravel. He became nervous when the secret police made discreet inquiries of Raphael. He was worried that the apartments would be searched. After all, the device was discovered to be missing after Raphael's party had visited the tower. We had already thought of this, of course, and thought too of a way of transferring the device and picture plates from one hand to the other without even meeting."

"So that was why you were waiting with your ape outside the Signor Taddei's Palazzo."

Rosso sighed. He seemed weary of the convolutions of his tale, yet set on again, like an ox plodding its round at a water-lift. "So indeed. After you left the tavern I collected the ape and went straight-away to Taddei's Palazzo, and there I waited, watching the signal-tower through a glass, with Ferdinand by my side watching as keenly as me. The devil was in him

that night, I swear. When he saw the arms of the
signal-tower move, he straight away climbed the Palazzo's boundary wall and swarmed up the tower,
without waiting for my order. You can imagine my
feelings as I watched him climb, for all of our plans
resided on the actions of that one animal. He climbed
quickly and strongly, swarming up the side of the
tower and disappearing into the open window. As to
what fell out then, I can only guess, although I heard
Giulio's dreadful cry and must guess that the ape believed that Giulio was attacking it when he tried to
take off the harness. Or perhaps Giulio merely made
a gesture which the ape in its excitement believed to
be a threat. However it fell out, they fought, and so
Giulio was killed, and the ape came back down
empty-handed. By then Taddei's household had been
roused by Giulio's cry, and I had to make my escape.
And so it was that you found the little device on
Giulio's body, and took it believing it a toy. And here
we are, in the cold and the dark."

"Not for long," Pasquale said.

They turned the corner of the city wall, and quit
the stony ground of Sardinia for a rough heath that
saddled away in the moonlight. There was a little
wood and beside it a scattering of campfires, like a
constellation fallen to Earth from the cold starry sky,
with the dark shapes of wagons drawn around them.

It was a night camp of travelers who had arrived
too late to enter the city the previous day. There
were mendicants and refugees from the farms hoping
to find work in the city's manufactories, and a train
of wagons, a knight and his entourage, and a merchant's party. Hawkers and whores from the city
moved amongst them, selling food and wine, or ply-
ing the warm commerce. No one slept except the
smallest children, for the camp was alive with ru-

mors of what was happening in the city. Pasquale
and Romano kept their own counsel, for there were
bound to be spies and informers amongst the hundred or more people camped there, and simply said
that they had been assaulted by footpads and thrown
into the river. They had no coin to buy food, and
charity was not immediately forthcoming, but at
Pasquale's goading the ape turned a few summersets
and walked up and down on its hands, flipping stones
with its feet.

This performance brought not money but bowls of
soup and dry black bread, and cigarettes and a flagon
of smooth red wine from the merchant, an elegant
man in a brocaded caped tunic, with rings on every
finger of his white hands. He was not much older
than Pasquale, and took a liking to him, all the more
so when he discovered that Pasquale was a painter,
and where he was from. For an hour they talked
about Fiesole, which the merchant knew well, and
the broken axle-tree which had delayed the merchant's journey, and the paintings which the merchant had inherited from his father, and the murder
of Raphael, which the merchant had heard from a
signaler who had passed on the news.

The sky grew milky as dawn approached. Pasquale
fell asleep and woke to find himself covered in a
blanket stiff with rime. He had slept only an hour,
but now it was light enough to see the city wall
stretching away, prickly with weaponry, and the
roofs and towers beyond it, and many threads of
smoke already rising amongst them.

The camp was stirring about him. People were
hitching horses to wagons, dousing campfires, picking up bundles of possessions and loading them on
carts and travois, heading along the muddy road toward the Prato Gate. The hawkers and prostitutes

were already clustered before its arch, yawning and discussing the night's work.

Pasquale wandered through the disintegrating camp, looking for Rosso, and at last spotted the ape lurking in the shadows of the little wood. It scampered up to him as he approached. It had lost its chain, and was clearly agitated, for it kept dashing ahead of Pasquale and then running back to clutch his leg.

In that way the ape led Pasquale through the little wood. Pasquale was amused, and then annoyed, and at last frightened. In the midst of the wood was a grandfather oak which sent its long limbs twisting out in every direction above the humped, mossy ground. The ape sat down on its bottom and wrapped its arms over its head and rocked back and forth.

Pasquale left it and slowly walked around the oak to where Rosso hung. He had wrapped one end of the chain around one of the heavy lower branches, and the other around his neck. The toes of his leather slippers brushed frost-shriveled grass-stalks as his corpse turned back and forth in the bitter wind which had sprung up with the rising sun. Crows had already found him and pecked out his eyes, and blood redder than his hair streaked his cheeks like the tears of the damned.

2

As Pasquale ran out of the wood, heartsick and horrified, the ape scampering at his heels, there was a distant flourish of trumpets. The city gates were opening.

But by the time Pasquale gained the road he saw that something was wrong. Those who had been waiting to pass through the customs post were being beaten back by squads of city militia. Hawkers dropped their trays and fled; prostitutes picked up their skirts and ran, screaming imprecations. Those too slow to run, or those brave or foolish enough to stand their ground, were knocked aside. The soldiers' staves rose and fell and rose and fell, and there was a glitter of swords.

A squad of cavalry burst out of the deep shadow beneath the arch of the gate, riding at full gallop, scattering militia and onlookers alike. Pasquale saw the merchant's wagon founder as it was driven off the road, its horses screaming horribly as they tumbled into the ditch.

More riders burst forth from the gateway, riding

on either side of a string of coaches whose drivers flogged their teams with long whips. Sharpshooters in cork-lined breastplates and smooth helmets fitting close to their skulls lay on the roofs of the coaches, and more cavalry brought up the rear. This party passed in a thunder of wheels and hooves, and men bawling like beasts, and a great cloud of dust.

Pasquale saw that the middle coach was drawn by a team of white horses, and that it flew the cobalt-blue banner of the Vatican. He had a glimpse of a man's face peering through the thick glass window, a heavy coarse-featured face with unshaven jowls and small, short-sighted eyes. The man looked angry yet resolute, and his fierce stare burned in Pasquale's vision even after the coach had thundered past.

All around Pasquale, people had stopped what they were doing and swept off their hats; some even dropped to their knees, careless of the wheels of the coaches that rattled past less than an arm's length away. Pasquale understood then. The Pope was leaving, fleeing the riots that threatened to tear Florence apart.

Then the carriages and soldiers were gone, leaving only dust blowing in their wake, and a fading rumble. People slowly returned to what they had been doing, moving as if waking from a dream. As they began to pass through the customs post beyond the gate, Pasquale saw that each was stopped and questioned by armed militia.

Rather than risk immediate questioning, Pasquale lent a hand to the merchant and his half-dozen men. They cut the horses free, unloaded the wagon, and dragged it from the ditch by main force. The horses had been thoroughly shaken but were otherwise unhurt, and the merchant's men were efficient. In less than an hour they had mended the traces and hitched up the horses and reloaded the wagon.

Early-morning traffic was moving up and down the road, making a detour around the wagon. The merchant thanked Pasquale, and asked after his friend.

"He had to leave. A matter of honor."

"Yet I see you have his ape."

Pasquale turned and saw Ferdinand sitting a little way off, and groaned. He had forgotten about the ape, yet here it was, and when it saw him looking at him it ambled over and flung its arms around his thighs in a clumsy hug.

"I have nothing for you," Pasquale told it, his heart turning over at the thought of the death of his master.

The merchant looked at Pasquale shrewdly. "I won't ask the how and the why of it, but I see you are in some trouble."

"I won't inconvenience you further, signor, except to ask a small favor."

The merchant, who was a shrewd, kindly man, laughed and said that Pasquale didn't seem to be a dangerous criminal, if criminal he was, and if he wanted only to get past the militia then there was no problem. So it was that Pasquale rode through the gate on the wagon bench beside the merchant and his driver. The little square beyond, usually crowded with wagons, *vaporetti* and horses, and lined with stalls, was almost deserted. As the wagon rolled across the square, Pasquale saw that a frame-gibbet had been hammered together in the middle of the three-way junction on the far side. Half a dozen men, naked but for sacking hoods, hung from it, and each had a sign hung around his neck: *I looted. Look on me and take heed.*

Pasquale started to shake, seeing at once and all

too clearly Rosso staring sightlessly, twisting in the wind. The merchant, misunderstanding, said that this was only night business, then shouted out as Pasquale jumped down from the wagon and ran, the ape pelting after him.

Pasquale was soon deep in the maze of alleys and yards somewhere between Santa Maria Novella and the Duomo. He recognized a fading mural of the Madonna on the wall of a shuttered shop, and walked on in the direction of the lodging-house where Niccolò Machiavegli had his rooms. The ape ambled behind him in such a way that Pasquale had the morbid fancy that somehow the essence of poor dead Rosso had become embedded in his pet, as dogs are supposed to grow to resemble their owners. So the ape, with its swaggering bow-legged walk and way of looking sharply around, imitated Rosso's assertive yet nervous manner.

Signora Ambrogini was not pleased to see Pasquale; even less so to see Ferdinand. "I don't suppose that Signor Machiavegli is with you," she said, peering through the finger-width gap she had opened after many minutes of knocking.

"I wish that he was. Please, signora, I left something in his rooms that I must have."

"He was out all last night," the old woman said. "He may not be as old as me, but neither is he a strapping young brute like you."

"You can come with me," Pasquale said. "It will only take a minute."

"There was someone else here asking after his rooms. I sent him away and told him the militia would be after him."

"When was this?"

"Not long ago. A foreign fellow. I have to set off

for mass, young man. I suppose the churches will still be open."

"I'm sure they are." Pasquale fell to his knees in a dramatic gesture. "Please, signora, I implore you. I'll return the key in a moment."

"Signor Machiavegli keeps strange friends," the old woman said, "but that was a good likeness of me, young man, even if you did make me look years younger than I am."

"That was a mere sketch. My thanks for this favor will be a portrait in oils!"

"Paintings should be of beautiful subjects. I'm old enough that I don't need flattery."

"None was intended, signora."

"You can push the key under my door when you've finished," Signora Ambrogini said. "I haven't missed second mass since twenty years ago, and that was on the day that my husband died. And don't you let that animal in the room."

Pasquale took the long iron key, gabbled his thanks, and ran up the winding stairs, slapping every turn with his palm. The room was as he and Niccolò left it, and the little flying device sat like a little boat on the sea of papers on the writing-desk at the high window.

Just as Pasquale had finished folding a sheet of stiff paper into a box for the little device, and was stowing it away in his scrip, a face appeared at the top of the window. It was upside-down, its shock of red hair swinging back and forth. It was the stilt-man who had led the others in the Piazza della Signoria. The man grinned at Pasquale and then his hand swung sharply down. A pane of glass shattered, and orange smoke blew in.

Pasquale ran, and heard the rest of the window smash to shards behind him. He tumbled down a whole turn of stairs and picked himself up and ran again, Ferdinand at his heels, not stopping to return the key (which he had anyway left in the lock), not stopping until he was streets and streets away, and then stopping only to regain his breath before running again, to the one place left in the whole city where he could be sure of safety.

3

Pasquale had to bang on the door of Piero di Cosimo's house for a full five minutes before it swung open a crack. Pelashil peered sleepily at him. "I must see him," Pasquale said. "Please, you must let me in."

The woman pushed the door wider, leaning back against the wall so that Pasquale had to brush past her as he entered. Her glossy black hair was down over her face, and when she raised a hand to push it back Pasquale glimpsed her small, spiky breasts inside her loose shirt. Ferdinand bounded through the door and scampered down the passageway. Pelashil shut the door and said, "The old man sleeps. You be quiet, Pasquale, and the ape."

"You know Piero likes Ferdinand. Please, I need to speak to him. Well, of course, and to you."

Pelashil smiled slowly. She was not conventionally pretty, but a woman who, when she smiled, was utterly changed, so that a man would do all he could to see that smile again. Despite himself, Pasquale responded to her smile with one of his own. She embraced him quickly, then stepped back, wrinkling her snub nose. Chocolate freckles dusted its bridge. "You stink of the river! And there is mud in your hair. I will wash you. When did you last wash? You are shy of water, and yet you have so much of it. In the desert, we wash with sand."

"I've been in the river, and that's enough water for anyone. I'll tell you about my adventures, but first I must speak with Piero. It's very important."

"You're too young to know anything important. Go to him, if you must."

Piero di Cosimo owned the whole house, but lived and worked in the big drafty room that took up most of the ground floor. Lit only by a series of rigged mirrors that reflected sunlight to every corner, at this early hour everything in the room was in shades of sepia, that pigment drawn from pulpy body of the common cuttlefish. Big canvases leaned against one wall, their painted surfaces turned away from the light; one set on a trestle was roughly covered with a paint-spattered sheet. When he had returned from the New World, Piero had made his money by painting small wooden decorative panels, *spallieri*, to private commissions. His scenes of the life of the Savages of the high deserts had been especially popular in a time when anything to do with the New World was fashionable. But now he painted for no one but himself, and kept everything.

As well as paintings, the studio was cluttered with bits of old furniture, tables with one or more legs broken and lashed together, a broken-backed couch in which Pasquale knew that mice nested, rickety stools, an old *cassone* with a cracked front panel and its top entirely missing. Bits and pieces of machinery too, for Piero was fascinated by the inventions of the artificers, and he scavenged broken machines and tried to repair them or make them into something new. There was an automatic music-player, all the strings in its scallop-shaped iron frame frayed or snapped, and the hammers bent or missing. A tantalus cup. A colonial long rifle with an octagonal barrel fully two *braccia* long. A kind of plush puppet moved by clockwork sat slumped on a bench, legs splayed in front of it, head drooping. A clockwork prognostication engine, its springs broken and its jammed registers permanently showing *Patience Becoming Virtue*. A machine that at a turn of a handle was supposed to mix and grind pigments, but which in Pasquale's experience only spattered clouds of fine tinted dust over the user; an automatic double-entry abacus; an automatic loom broken into pieces and put back together with the idea that pictures could be generated using its punch-cards; a clock driven by complex gearing to equalize the progressively diminishing power of its barrel-spring. The tick of the clock's ratchet escapement was for a moment the loudest thing in the room, and then Piero's pet raven saw the ape and shifted on its perch with a scaly scratching and croaked, "Danger."

Piero was sleeping on a truckle bed in one corner of the room, behind a screen painted with scenes of the happy isles of the New World. Pelashil went to him and shook him by the shoulder until he woke and feebly tried to push her away. She shrugged and cast a smoldering look at Pasquale before departing.

Piero drew the filthy blanket around himself. His vigorous white hair stood up in all directions around his nut-brown wrinkled face, and he scratched and rummaged in this cockade for a full minute before getting up and scuttling to a far corner of the room and making water into a basin on a stand. Moving so as to keep his back half-turned to Pasquale, Piero opened the window and threw the basin's contents out into the wild garden, where vines scrambled unchecked over untrimmed trees, and hedges had grown monstrously shaggy.

Pasquale said, "Master, have I offended you?"

"You've been a bad boy," Piero said, still managing to keep his back half-turned as he scuttled back to his corner and carefully lowered himself onto the bed. He stretched out slowly and clutched the top of the blanket to his neck with his knobbly arthritic hands. He finally looked full at Pasquale and said, "I'm asleep. You're a dream." And with that his head fell onto the greasy clout he used as a pillow and he commenced to breathe deeply and raggedly through his open mouth.

"You've been taking that stuff again," Pasquale said, but there was no reply. He added, "You should eat. Dreams aren't everything."

There was a pan of hard-boiled eggs on the stovetop—Piero economically boiled them up in big batches when he boiled his size or glue—but when Pasquale cracked one it gave off a nauseous sulfur reek, and he saw that its white was tinged coppergreen.

"Pelashil should cook for you," Pasquale said, because this usually roused Piero into an argument about oppression, with Pasquale telling him that he shouldn't have brought her back from the New World if he didn't want her oppressed, and Piero replying that this was precisely the point, elaborating one or another fantastical argument along the lines that slavery is freedom, and freedom slavery. But this time Piero defiantly stayed asleep, or at least maintained the pretense. Pasquale sat down on a broken stool and watched the old man for a while. Perhaps he dozed, for Pelashil was shaking him by the shoulder, and now Piero really was asleep, snoring with his mouth open to show rotten black teeth in pulpy gums.

Pelashil put her finger to her lips and led Pasquale out into the scullery, where a pot-bellied stove radiated heat, and blankets woven with bright geometric shapes covered the flaking calcined walls, so that it was like being in a tent in some far Moorish land, where the sun blazes so hot at midday that the sands of the desert fuse into glass.

Half-dazed with exhaustion, forgetting why he had come here, Pasquale allowed Pelashil to undress him. His clothes were stiff with mud. She washed his body with a damp cloth, and then thrust a bowl of soup into his hands. Burnt crusty bread had been broken into it, so that he could eat it without a spoon. He wanted to know where the ape was, and she shrugged and pointed to the garden; she had let it out. When he tried to get up to see what had become of it, she pressed him back, and with a strange inward smile bowed her head, brushed his chest with her wiry black hair, then moved lower, so that his manhood stirred to the tickling touch and he groaned and drew her to him.

When Pasquale woke, the sliver of sky that showed through the window had darkened, like a scrap of violet cloth caught amongst the tangled branches of the untrimmed trees of Piero's garden. Pelashil was dressing with careless languor, pulling a tarnished white gown over her tawny skin. Pasquale watched her, swoony with tiredness and affection, and asked her where she was going.

"Work," Pelashil said. "He earns nothing, I must."

"Have him sell one of his paintings," Pasquale said. He stood up and punched at the air with his fists. It was so warm that it felt like a solid substance. "If he sold no more than one, he could live as he does for the rest of his life."

Pelashil shook her head. "No! He needs them. He lives there."

"In the paintings?"

"In a place he finds by making the paintings," she said. "He is the first mara'akame of your people, but perhaps not the last. You can learn much from him, Pasquale. I followed him because he is a great mara'akame. He has traveled far along the branches of the Tree of Life."

Pasquale said, "I thought that Piero had enslaved you, to make you follow him, to make you share his bed."

Pelashil made a sound that was half exasperation, half laughter. She started to fasten her dress across her breasts. "When I first knew him he was younger and more virile, but not as advanced in knowledge as he is now. Power takes power."

"You left your people because you wanted to? I always thought . . ."

"That I am his servant? No more than you are the servant of Rosso. Ah, why do you start at the mention of your master's name? What is wrong?"

"I have much to tell you, Pelashil, but I'm not sure if this is the right time."

Pelashil finished fastening her dress, and calmly wrapped a shawl around her shoulders, casting a corner of it over her head. "If I tell you one thing, Pasquale, you must promise not to tell anyone else."

"Of course."

"You're a handsome boy, full of life. You shouldn't stay here in this city. When you took Piero as your secret master, I knew that in your heart you were a traveler like him."

"Pelashil, I may have to leave soon. Will you go with me?"

"I became the servant of a foreign magus because it is the only way a woman of my people can gain real power. Our own mara'akame speak only to other men, although in the past there have been female mara'akame. But although they would not speak to me, they spoke to Piero, and set him on the road to wisdom. He has been walking that road ever since, and I have followed."

"The plant he eats . . . you eat it too?"

"Was it not me who gave it to you? All of my people eat it. Only we know where to find the true peyote, híkuri, and how to gather it, on the pilgrimages to the sacred land."

"I thought it would help my painting, Pelashil. That's why I took it."

"You are still like the rest of your people, Pasquale. You are not in balance. You are ruled by the makers of things, of machines, but they see only half the world. Híkuri reveals the truth behind what we think we see."

Pasquale thought of Piero's experiments with devices discarded by the artificers. He said, "Then Piero wants to understand both."

"He stands in the middle. He is the first mara'akame to do so. Those who follow him will find it easier, and go further. Now listen to me. You must not stay here. You bring trouble."

"I don't know what you mean."

"Men came here. Soldiers of the city. Look for you. He was scared by that. You must leave, to keep him safe. And think about what I told you. I will watch over you, because you are about to take the first step."

And then she was gone, leaving Pasquale to reassemble his clothes from where they had been scattered about the little room. So he was being chased not only by the Savonarolistas, but by the city government too, no doubt put up to it by the merchant Taddei. If they caught him, he would be sent straight away as ransom for Raphael's corpse. And Giustiniani's men would by now have ransacked Niccolò Machiavegli's rooms and be searching for him, for the device he had accidentally acquired. He knew what he must do. It was the only thing he could do. He must return it to its owner.

Piero was standing at a table in the big room, where candles made little islands of unsteady light. His hands spread to take his weight, he leaned over drawings that were scattered like leaves across the table. He had wrapped his blanket around himself in the style of a senator from ancient Rome, leaving one bony shoulder bare, and with his unkempt white beard and elf-locked hair he resembled Saint Jerome in his study, lacking only the traditional attributes of lion and cardinal's hat.

As Pasquale came into the room the raven shifted on its perch and ruffled its wings. Pasquale said, "Are these new pictures, master?"

Piero didn't look up, but slowly shook his head.

"The woman has left soup for you, master. You should eat."

"Cooks grow monstrous fat on the odors of cooking alone," Piero said, "which is as well, for food grows repugnant to them, just as coal is hateful to a Westphalian miner, and he instead burns wood in his grate."

It was no use forcing Piero in these matters. Pasquale said, "If you're not hungry, master, I quite understand."

Piero shook his head again, and said, "The shadows are crowding me from my room. No light, boy, no light. How can poor Piero paint without light?"

Pasquale lighted fat tallow candles, and set them before the scattered mirrors and lenses, so that their light glimmered through the big cold room.

"The light doesn't stay still," Piero complained, when at last Pasquale had finished.

"That's the nature of light, master." Wistfully, Pasquale thought of his angel—there had not been much time for contemplation of late. He cast his mind back to the glimpse he'd had of its glory, a reflection of the glory of its master, which, like the sun, could not be approached or looked at directly. Yet as sunlight dances upon the face of the waters and multiplies its glory in such a way that its raw beauty is made bearable to the human eye, so with an angel, surely, for it would be driven by the glory of its service, made bemused and breathless by its journey from Heaven to Earth. It moved, it would always move: it would be as restless as light on water. Oh, how to paint that! How to paint its face!

"Bring light here," Piero said, and Pasquale carried a candle to the table. He saw that the pictures were delicately penned studies of fantastic animals cavorting or coiled amongst strange rock formations, sheet after sheet of drawings, and no beast like any other or like anything Pasquale had ever seen, even in the sketches made by travelers of devils cavorting in the weird Flemish paintings of Heaven and Hell.

"Are these from the New World, master?"

Piero tapped his forehead. In the candlelight Pasquale saw the skull under the skin of his secret master's face, and knew that Piero did not have long to live. He had traveled far from humanity, and the journey had worn him out before his time.

"From the country of the mind," Piero said. "Cristoforo Columbo was wrong to voyage out toward the edge of the Earth. There are unexplored regions far wider and wilder and stranger than any glimpsed by a scurvied sailor clinging to the topgallant of the royal mast of his vessel, scrying for landfall. The country of the mind lives inside us all, yet most know it not. You do not know it boy, and until you do you won't be able to paint your angel. Has the woman talked to you yet?"

"She gave me one of your plants to eat, master."

"Don't tell me what you saw—it won't have been anything important. Only true masters see the truth. You'll be going away soon. I had hoped that the woman would have had time to initiate you, but perhaps this is better. Anyway, the plants I have are losing their potency after all these years. I envy you, Pasquale. You'll taste fresh híkuri, and I never will again. Have I told you about Pelashil's people, the Wixarika?"

"Several times, master."

"You'll hear it one more time?"

"Of course, master."

So Piero told Pasquale how the híkuri was hunted, using the same words as he had when he had first told his tale. He told of how it took place in the dry season before winter, of how, when the maize was still green but the squash had ripened, a party of Wixarika set out on a pilgrimage lasting twenty days. After two days of preparing costumes, of prayer and cleansing confessions, they took the names of gods and, led by a mara'akame who had taken the name of the god of fire, were led across the dry plain beneath the two sacred mountains, searching for deer-tracks, for without deer there could be no peyote, which appeared in the footsteps of the first deer in the morning of the world. The first of the small gray-green plants was always pierced by an arrow and ringed with offerings; the rest were carefully examined and scrupulously packed away. Piero had taken his first peyote on the first night of his first pilgrimage, and had been led by a spotted cat through a series of images set out like booths in a carnival, and had known upon awakening that he would be a mara'a-kame.

Pasquale had heard this before, told in exactly the same way, but now he understood that everything Piero had told him, and all Pelashil had done, was to initiate him in this truth: that the world of visions was as real as the world of the artificers. He said, "Master, please forgive me. I doubted that you were a good man. I was wrong, and now I am in sore need of your advice."

"I know, I know. They think me stupid, or a fool or a madman, but I'm not. I know why the soldiers came here. Can I see it?"

Pasquale took out the little device. Piero peered at it from every angle, and finally asked, "And does it fly?"

"Master, as always you astound me. How did you know?"

"Because Giovanni Rosso came looking for it, before the soldiers."

"I must return it to its maker. Master, you have talked with the Great Engineer. How can I see him? Will you take me?"

"He understands me more than most. But we have talked but twice. I know him not. Not well enough for your purpose."

"But master, my life is in danger. I am in the middle of a struggle for a prize I would gladly give up, if I could."

"They say the Pope has left, retreated from the fighting in the streets."

"That's true enough. I saw him with my own eyes." Pasquale described the scene at the gate that morning, watching his master's face soften dreamily. Piero was a great supporter of the Medicis: when they had been overthrown he had left Florence too, for the New World. When Pope Leo X had gained Saint Peter's throne, he and Andrea del Sarto had contrived a carnival triumph whose theme was death. At the center of the procession had been the Chariot of Death itself, drawn by black buffaloes painted with white human bones and crosses, on which stood a huge figure of Death armed with a scythe standing triumphant over tombs which opened and issued forth figures draped in black cloth on which were painted the bones of complete skeletons, so that by torchlight they looked like skeletons dancing in service of their dark lord. As death was exile from life, so the triumph symbolized the long exile from which the Medicis would return to their rightful place, and again rule Florence. But they had not returned. Florence in her triumph was still stronger than Rome. It was the last spectacle that Piero had staged, and afterwards he had retreated from the world.

When Pasquale had finished describing the Pope's retreat, there was a silence. At last Piero sighed heavily and said, "I will die with a heavy heart. How I danced not two days ago, Pasquale. How I danced. And now Florence stands alone again."

"This talk of death makes me uncomfortable."

"I envy you, Pasquale. Suppose you are caught and tried and executed—at least you will go to your death in the best of health, watched by thousands who will mark your passing as only the passing of a favored few men is marked. You will march to your death to stirring music, on a fête-day, your every need having been catered for beforehand, and the announcement of your death will have been prominently placed in every broadsheet. How much better than most deaths, those small sullen private struggles. I do not fear death, Pasquale, but I fear the indignity of dying."

Pasquale had to laugh at this fantasy. It was a trick of Piero's, to invert accepted truths and make them seem as exotic as the ceremonies of the Mexica, or any of the lesser nations of Savages.

"You laugh at death," Piero said. "That's good, at least. Well, I'll look after the ape for you. I don't mind that, although it will drive Pelashil mad, no doubt, and leave me entirely on my own. Poor Piero, they'll say, with only an ape to mend his clothes and cook his food, and warm his bed."

Pasquale had forgotten about the ape, and asked where it was.

"Out in the garden, eating the figs from my trees. It is happy there, Pasquale. Leave it be. Sheathe your burning sword, eh? Don't drive it out. It knows no sin."

Pasquale supposed it was true. The ape had killed, but not out of malice and quite without intent or any knowledge of wrong, and so without guilt. Happy ignorance of the unremembering unfallen—how he envied it, remembering his own burden.

"I may never see you again," Piero said. "That has just occurred to me."

"I'll be back, master. I promise."

"I don't mind," Piero said quickly. "I prefer the sound of rain to that of idle conversation. I wish I could teach you more, but perhaps you know enough already. Let learning be your journey."

Pasquale cradled the device, turning its helical screw back and forth with a forefinger. So fragile a toy, on which the fate of empires rested. He said, "I'll be as quiet as a church mouse, master, when I tiptoe back. And I'll wait for a clear day, with no rain. But if you could tell me, please, how to gain an audience with the Great Engineer, I can be gone now, and leave you to your contemplations."

Piero ruffled the raven's feathers with a finger, so that the bird ducked its head in pleasure, regarding its master sideways with a round black eye shiny as a berry. "He loves birds," Piero said. "That's what we talked about, mostly. I told him of the condor, that soars for hours on outstretched wings."

"But how do I gain audience, master? When I return the device I must make sure it is into his hands that it falls. I can make my own small talk, if I need to."

"He's one of the saddest men I know. And one of the loneliest."

"Can I simply walk into his tower? Is it as simple as that?"

"Of course not," Piero said sharply, still stroking his pet. "Don't be a fool. He is more closely guarded than the Pope, for the college of Rome can always elect another pope, but there will only ever be one Great Engineer. But although he is mostly shut up in his tower, his assistants walk here and there about town. There is one who haunts the kind of low taverns that you like, Pasquale. You could try and find him, I suppose. He has a taste for the low life, and for dirty pictures. He is called Nicolas Koppernigk, a poor threadbare sketch of a man, and a notorious miser to boot. You know him?"

Pasquale remembered the cosmic engine, afire in the square. Koppernigk had proved that the Earth went around the sun, which was the center of the universe. Or perhaps the other way around: it was all the same to him as long as the ground was always under his feet. He said, "This Koppernigk. How do I find him?"

"Oh," Piero said vaguely, "one or other of the taverns of the Prussian student nation, I suppose. But first promise to change your clothes, Pasquale. Have you been swimming in the river at this late season?"

4

Rosso's studio was like a battlefield. Everything had been overturned and smashed. Pasquale's clothes, for which he had risked returning, had all been slashed or systematically slit along the seams: the fine silk shirt for which he had paid ten florins; the white, lace-trimmed shirt of best English cloth and its matching white doublet with gold silk sewn inside deep slashes; the ordinary homespun shirts and hose; the big cape he had bought from an Albanian mercenary and lovingly relined; even his work-apron had been cut to ribbons. The heels of his second-best pair of boots had been broken off. A broad leather belt, which he had tooled with intricate patterns after the Moorish style, had somehow been snapped in two, and its brass buckle bent. His truckle bed was now truly broken-backed, and its mattress cut to ribbons.

Pasquale ripped out the remains of the lining from the cloak and wrapped it around himself. The rest, all the clothes he had carefully collected or mended or sewn together himself, were beyond salvage.

The main room of the studio was in as bad a state as Pasquale's few possessions. The workbench had been overturned, the grindstone cracked in two, the door of the little kiln broken off. Pigments had been spilled everywhere, making gaudy arcs and splashes across the floor, and every canvas had been slashed, every frame broken. In the half-light of dusk, Pasquale felt in the back of the kiln, and found the small cloth bag in which Rosso habitually kept the studio's takings. It contained more than he'd hoped for but less than it should, considering the fees for the stiffener and for the broadsheet engravings. Rosso, had he still lived, would have been grievously short with the rent.

Pasquale turned to go, and stumbled over the little panel he had so lovingly prepared. A hole had been kicked in it. He held it and felt nothing, for all that he had spent so much skill and time on preparing it. It was made of best seasoned poplar, glued and then braced, and given an ornate frame that Pasquale had gilded himself. He had sanded the wood and filled every small knothole and crack with sawdust and glue, then coated the panel with one thin and three thick coats of liquid size and covered the size with strips of linen. The next layers, of *gesso grosso*, or chalk mixed in size, had taken two weeks to prepare; each had been allowed to dry for several days and then scraped and sanded smooth before the next was applied. Finally, he had applied coats of *gesso sottile*, the first rubbed on by hand, the others each brushed on before the previous one had dried, eight in all. And after that had been dried in the sun, Pasquale had smoothed and scraped it with spatula and *raffietti* until it was as smooth and burnished as ancient ivory.

All for some thug to put his boot through, in a moment.

As he stood there, Pasquale heard someone coming carelessly up the stairs. A moment later there was a brisk hammering at the door. He found a little knife and unbent its blade between two floorboards and crept to the door, which he had left open.

The monk who looked after the gardens of Santa Croce was fixing a magistrate's notice with nails and a hammer. Pasquale caught the monk's hand on the upswing, jabbed him in the neck with the point of the knife, where fat made two rolls at the collar of his habit, and caught the hammer when it dropped.

"I don't have any time," Pasquale said, "so please tell me straight. Did you see who did this?"

The monk moved his head cautiously, a thumb's width to either side. His eyes were fixed on the notice he had nailed to the door.

Pasquale added, "The noise must have been considerable. You didn't come and complain?"

"I was . . . elsewhere."

"They may have been costumed as militia, or masked. Which was it?"

"I wasn't here!"

The hammer made a very satisfactory noise as it thumped across the floor of the workshop. "No," Pasquale said, "you were at the Offices of Night and Monasteries, to judge by this scrap of paper. What's this about a harness weighted with lead?"

"To stop it climbing. I mean only to look after my garden. It is my duty, and your ape—"

The monk watched, goggle-eyed, as Pasquale slashed the notice to ribbons.

"Pray for me, brother," Pasquale said. "I'd speak more of this, but I have an important appointment with a scholar."

As he hurried down the winding stair, for the last time, he heard the monk shouting that he'd get a new notice restraining master and ape. You can bang on that drum all you like, fellow, Pasquale thought. Two days ago it might have frightened me, but no more.

5

Doctor Nicolas Koppernigk favored the taverns used by students of the Prussian nation, where he held informal tutorials and took wine as his fee, being too parsimonious to buy his own. He had a cautious taste for the low life, so long as it cost him nothing, and preferred the company of students to that of his fellow artificers, of whom he was both jealous and suspicious.

A band of strolling musicians was playing dance music in the square outside in the hope that they would please enough of the tavern's patrons to gain a free meal. Small chance of that, Pasquale thought, who had a poor opinion of students in general, and Prussian students in particular. Students were no more than intellectual vagabonds, flitting from university to university until they found one that would sell them a doctorate; they had no discipline and no craft, and inhabited an airy world of ideas. As for Prussians, they lacked even the ideas, and had no ear for the finer aspects of music, liking only drinking-songs and bombastic marches.

The tavern was noisy and smoky, filled with students shouting at each other across the tables, their faces beast-like in the flickering rushlights. One group was beating its table with beakers and singing a dreary tune in bad Latin:

The British eat shit because it's all they have,
The Italians eat shit because they're dumb,
The French eat shit because the Italians do,
But we eat shit because we are strong loyal
     Prussians,
Ha! Ha! Ha!

Doctor Koppernigk sat in the furthest darkest corner with three swarthy lumpen-faced students who looked at Pasquale with ill grace when he bowed and introduced himself. Koppernigk started up in a kind of befuddled pop-eyed amazement. He was a gaunt man of about fifty, the cheeks of his bony face scraped red, his eyes set close beneath eyebrows that knit together to form a single line that lowered as he regarded Pasquale. He wore a fur-trimmed cap that sat askew his long greasy gray hair, and a long tunic of what might once have been rust-colored fabric, but was now darkened to a blotchy black.

Pasquale sat opposite Koppernigk and called loudly for more wine, and told the scientist that he would be a new pupil.

Koppernigk's suspicious gaze shifted to Pasquale's face, jumped back nervously away. "What trick is this?"

Pasquale lit a cigarette and sucked smoke deep into his lungs. "There is no trick at all, signor. I need your help, and Piero di Cosimo recommended me to you."

"I need no agent, and no pupils for that matter. I'm

a philosopher, signor, no mere teacher."

"And yet you teach," Pasquale said mildly, smiling at the three students and getting more scowls in return. He showed a coin, and asked how much a private lesson would cost.

Koppernigk allowed cautiously, eyeing the coin with a kind of hunger, that three times as much might be sufficient.

"It's yours," Pasquale said, and sat down when Koppernigk had shooed off his lumpen pupils like an old wife scattering chickens.

"Now, signor," Koppernigk said, "you can ask me what you want, although I should warn you that I am notoriously short of answers."

"I must apologize, signor, for driving away your pupils for this night. But in many ways I'm no stranger to you. Ah! Perhaps this wine will help make amends." Pasquale beamed at the greasy drab who had thumped a flask of wine on the table, and gave her a clipped silver coin with a carelessness he certainly did not feel. "Please drink with me at least, good Canon, and hear my entreaty."

Koppernigk poured wine into his beaker with niggardly care. "I'm a canon at Frauenberg Cathedral, it's true, but I haven't been there since I was installed. My mission is temporal, not spiritual. You call me Doctor, Doctor Copernicus, if you don't mind. My Latin is as good as anyone's, and that's the name that is known in all the countries of the world."

"It's because of your renown that I came, signor," Pasquale assured him.

Koppernigk was suddenly suspicious again. "Who sent you? Why did you come to me? I do not advertise my goods like a merchant, no one does who has any pretensions at greatness in the scientific arts. In any case, too many have made too much from my ideas.''

It was as Piero had said; Doctor Koppernigk, having been forced to loose the truths he had uncovered upon the world, had lost control of them, which was an affront to his soul. His caution was the caution of a miser asked to part with some trifling fraction of his fortune. He would hoard his truths, if he could, for otherwise his rivals might gain from them at his expense. He had divined the disposition of the architecture of the universe, but was not clever enough to profit from his discovery, or indeed to defend it except by evolving complicated epicycles to explain what drove the motions of the planets about the sun. His discovery that the Earth and the other planets revolved around the sun had revolutionized the notion of the place of man in the universe, and yet with his epicycles and equants and epicycles upon epicycles he had sought not to topple the old order, but to reconcile it with his findings through a receding infinity of adjustments. He knew well enough that he could not demonstrate those mechanisms, for in truth they did not exist except in the minds of men, and so, although he had shifted the center of the universe, he was frightened that his discovery would be taken from him. He trusted no one, not even himself.

Pasquale explained again that he was here only because of the good canon's reputation, and the advice of Piero di Cosimo.

Koppernigk glared at Pasquale and said, ''You say you know me already? I don't think so. Have you been following me?''

''Oh no. Not at all.''

''I won't have people following me about the city.''

''Quite right. I understand exactly.''

''I called the militia on one fellow only last year.

He denied it of course, and the militia wouldn't believe me, but it was quite true. Charlatans would dearly love to use my name to further their schemes. Astrologers and the like. I am plagued," Koppernigk said, and drained his beaker, "by astrologers and so-called natural scientists, under which disguise so many magicians trade these days. No, if that's what you're after, then you may go now, or I will call the guard."

"Doctor, I am an artist, not an astrologer. I understand from Piero di Cosimo that you have appreciated some of my depictions of the amorous arts. Please, do take more wine. There's plenty more where that came from." The wine wasn't too bad, Pasquale thought, or at least, it was by no means as bad as he had expected, and if it left a coppery taste in the mouth, the heat it generated was genuine enough. He freely poured wine for both of them, and drank deep to show goodwill.

Koppernigk drank in rapid sips, his veiny hands wrapped around the beaker as if he were afraid that someone would take it from him. He said, "If you're an artist I don't suppose you have come to hear about my theory of the ether and the propagation of light. I must ask you again why you are here, signor. Bear in mind my time is limited. You say I have appreciated your work? What was your name again? Firenze? You are named for the city?"

"No, Doctor. My name is Pasquale de Cione Fiesole. The small town, you know, no more than an hour's ride away."

"I know Fiesole, of course. I have been there several times to make my observations. The city smoke you see, obscures the stars, and then again there are the acetylene lamps . . . Have you more of that wine? This is good wine, for Tuscan wine, although Prussian wine is much better. But I should be careful. It will mount to my head."

"Not at all, signor. Wine fortifies the blood, and so feeds the seat of intelligence." Pasquale found that he was grinning at the thought that this crabbed colorless scholar was his only chance of gaining entry to the court of the Great Engineer, and worked his lips to erase his smile. His face felt both hot and numb, as if it had been thrust into a furnace.

"You artists are wrong, of course," Koppernigk said with grave precision. "You cannot represent the world by smearing pigments on a flat plane. It only works because the eye is so easily tricked—but it is not real. As for reality, light itself is the key, and the motion of light, of course, as so recently demonstrated by the Great Engineer. You did see his tableau of living light?"

Pasquale lit another cigarette from the twisted stub of the first. "I regret that I was detained elsewhere. But you have made the very point I wished to raise. There is something I want to learn, Doctor."

Koppernigk suddenly seemed to take fright, as if he had stepped across a line only he could see, into dangers only he could apprehend. "I am nothing but a student in those matters. I can repeat only what is said many times, that is. I have no direct experience, no, none at all."

Pasquale fumbled out the picture he had rescued from the fireplace at Giustiniani's villa. Flakes of silvery stuff were caught in the black cloth he'd wrapped around the glass plate, and the darkening was worse, a lapping rim of shadows encroaching on all but the very center. He laid it on the table and asked Koppernigk his opinion.

Koppernigk planted his elbows on the table and his sharp chin in his cupped hands, and frowned down at the picture, his eyes wrinkling in the way of the short-sighted. Then he realized what it showed and reared backward, looking wildly around at the noisy tavern, the students carousing or singing crude national songs. They were drunk; everyone in the tavern was drunk. Koppernigk sputtered that he really knew nothing of that sort of thing, no, not at all.

"I mean the process. I would learn of the process. This picture is crude, yes."

Koppernigk said with what appeared to be genuine outrage, "It is the vilest kind of devil-worship!"

Pasquale talked quickly, stumbling over his words, explaining that a composition with artistic merit would be another matter, it was not so much the subject as the presentation. As he talked he took out paper and pen and quickly sketched from memory the outline of a tableau he had once created. His hand was shaking and yet seemed as heavy as lead at the same time; he botched the passage of the woman's hair, and had to peer closely to get her hands right. She was couched on pillows, dressed only in a filmy clinging shift, her face dreamy with delight as she stroked her own self with the bent fingers of one hand, and weighed the globes of her breast with another. The commission had made Pasquale less than a florin, although the *stationarius* had reprinted it over and over.

Koppernigk watched him sidelong, as if he suspected a trick. "Well, I recognize that, of course. It is of its kind, I suppose you would say, an interesting piece."

"It was my hand that first drew it, Doctor. But you see how it is, I make a little money, and the printers make much more. This new process, though. This painting with light. If you could tutor me in it, we could together make much money. I'll reward you well for your time—this florin, here, to begin with."

"Anyone can copy out a print," Koppernigk said, "especially one as popular as that one."

"We call them stiffeners in the trade," Pasquale said. "I'll take you to meet the model. Then you'll believe me."

"Perhaps so. Perhaps so. Ah, the wine is finished."

Pasquale bought another flagon. They drank, to the ether, whatever that was, to Florence, to the Great Engineer. Somehow Pasquale and Koppernigk, without transition, were walking along a road, stumbling arm in arm in darkness toward a distant lamp as dim as a star in the solid darkness. The cold air smote Pasquale's face. Wine, he had drunk too much wine. He smiled foolishly. He was in mortal peril, but at least he could still live a little.

Koppernigk was talking and talking, his hold on his store of words loosened by drink. He was talking about the ether, or the concept of the ether, it being as vaporous as the epicycles which Koppernigk evoked to keep the Earth in motion around the sun. It was, it seemed, no medium at all, but a higher state of matter, of vibration.

"Light is no more than matter, raised to this higher state. It is well known that light travels faster than sound, and my theory shows why. And beyond light, there is God Himself. Dear Christ save me!"

Koppernigk slipped on a wad of filth and had not Pasquale held him up would have gone flying into the open drain that ran not at all sweetly in the center of the street. Koppernigk hiccuped and whispered, "I'll say no more because there are enemies all around who would seize on my ideas and misrepresent them. Science is not to be rushed. Those who try will burn themselves out, you mark me. Hush. What do you hear?"

It was the sound of wagon-wheels, muffled in some way, and coming toward them from behind.

Pasquale pushed Koppernigk into a deep arched gateway. The iron gate was locked at this hour, the courtyard beyond dark. Koppernigk made feeble struggles to get free, but Pasquale held him fast, and clapped a hand over his mouth when he started to exclaim indignantly. The muffled noise of the wagon grew closer, closer. Pasquale discovered that he was holding his breath. He knew what the wagon was even before it went past: it was the wagon of the corpsemasters, who roamed the city with a license to take away any corpses they deemed fit for the use of the dissectors and experimenters in the New University. Many said that, such was the demand in these enlightened times, the corpsemasters had taken to stealing corpses from their own wakes, and even to murdering stray citizens caught out alone in the late night.

It was a low long black wagon, drawn by a single horse. The driver and his mate were hunched on the bench, both muffled in high-collared black cloaks, and with black leather masks covering their faces. The horse which drew the wagon was shod in leather boots; the wheels were wrapped with rags. There was a distinctive odor, a strong scent of violets overlying the odor of rotting meat.

Then it was past. Koppernigk made another struggle for freedom, banging against the iron gate so that it rattled. Pasquale could have hit him, but that would have been an end to his chance of entering the Great Tower. When Pasquale released him, the artificer said indignantly, "I know those men."

Pasquale laughed. "I suppose you do."

"I studied anatomy, amongst other sciences, when I was a student. Theirs is an honorable profession, and they are only going about their legal business. Without them, we would not advance in the treatment of illness. There's no need to be afraid, young man. Now where is this accursed place you said you knew? I will see the woman, then I will believe you."

"I have also studied anatomy, but would not like to meet those gentlemen in these circumstances. You'll help me, Doctor. I must insist."

Koppernigk said with drunken dignity, and not much truth, "You needn't threaten me. I am not afraid of threats."

When they reached the lamp at the corner of the street, Pasquale knew where he was, and remembered where they were going. He had promised to show Koppernigk his model, Maddalena, as proof that he was who he said he was. Wine, there is no end to truth in wine, or the trouble truth can get you into.

Then he and Koppernigk were hammering on the door of Mother Lucia's house. A dog set to barking somewhere, and then the door opened and they tumbled inside, almost falling into the soft fat arms of the whoremistress, Mother Lucia herself. Her face was caked with white lead and rouge, but in the soft candlelight she looked, if not girlish, then more like a doll than the old woman she was. Somehow Pasquale was sitting, a cup of wine in his hands, blinking at the bright lamplight in the parlor. A trio of girls, bareshouldered in velvet gowns, their breasts pushed up like soft rounded shelves, giggled together on the other side of the room, which seemed to be slowly sinking through the ground.

"My friend, where . . . ?"

"Why with Maddalena, of course," Mother Lucia said. "Oh, Pasquale, Pasqualino, you are in your cups."

Pasquale said stupidly, "You're a good woman in your way, Mother Lucia. Did I ever tell you that?"

"Business is business, dearie, and you think about doing another nice picture for me and we won't say anything more about it. Brings in business, those pictures. Like now."

"Can't pay you know. Absolutely broke." There was the florin, of course, but he had promised it to Doctor Koppernigk.

"Your friend pays. Don't you worry. Where have you been, Pasquale? Your clothes are covered in mud."

Pasquale, reduced by wine and exhaustion to sentiment, said, "I'm in a lot of trouble, Mother Lucia. You're a good Christian woman to help me. I'll never go to another place from now on."

"A fine compliment, I'm sure," Mother Lucia said, with the air of one who has heard it all before.

"No, no. I mean it! This is a hinge of history, great terrible times. That you should help me, help me now . . ."

"You remember my charity, dearie, next time you take up your pen." The girls in the corner giggled, and Mother Lucia shot them a severe look. She told Pasquale, "That's as far as it goes. Meanwhile, don't drink any more wine. I can't bear to see a man cry."

"If only I could start painting now . . . you're an angel, Lucia. My friend, has he finished?"

"Old men always take a long time," one of the whores said with a sniff.

"A strange sort of cove," Mother Lucia observed, taking a cup from another of her whores with a regal gesture. "Asked me if I did the operation on my girls, you know, the one where a piece of skull is taken out to make them docile. A little hole it is, and a wire is inserted to stir out the devil. I told him this was a straight establishment, and he said it was the other way around, that I was unregulated. Why, I regulate as I please, you know that, Pasqualino. I know his sort, they'd make us all machines fit only for one thing or another, according to their wants."

Pasquale must have dozed, for he woke to the echo of a shriek from somewhere in the house. He jumped up and pushed past the whores, who clutched at him and told him to sit down, to leave it be, and found himself running down a candlelit passage. There was a roaring in his ears. He kept banging into one or the other of the walls. A door burst open and he tumbled inside.

Maddalena was kneeling on a wrecked bed, a sheet pulled up to her chin in bunched fists. Her unbound hair tumbled down to the small of her back. "He did a runner, right out the window," she squealed, and the Moorish servant who'd followed Pasquale nodded grimly and ran back out.

"You better go," Mother Lucia said, out of breath at the doorway. "We'll sort him out."

Pasquale flung open the shutters of the window, but there was only an empty alley below. He leaned into the cold dark air, his head spinning with an excess of wine and high excitement. "Don't hurt him," he said. "I have need of his services."

Mother Lucia said in a splendid rage, "He gives service and cuts and runs—a fine kind of gentleman he must be!" Her bare upper arms, hung with fatty flesh like dewlaps, quivered. "He won't do that again at my establishment. Fine kind of friends you have, Pasquale. There'll be a reckoning over this."

"Two paintings. Three. Big as you like. Where did he go?"

"I heard the corpse-wagon outside," Maddalena said. "Maybe it frightened him."

Pasquale went to the ewer and up-ended it over his head. Gasping and blinking, soaked and more nearly sober, he said, "I think I'll need to use the back way."

Then there was a hammering on the front door.

Maddalena gave a squeak of fear and the sheet fell, exposing her breasts. Mother Lucia said, "You know the back door well enough, I think. Don't be in a hurry to return, Pasquale."

"Never mind," Pasquale said, "they'd follow me that way anyway."

He swung his legs over the sill of the window and let himself down until he was clinging by his fingertips, then dropped and landed sprawling on the half-frozen muck of the alley floor. He picked himself up, ran to the end of the alley, and squinted around the corner.

The corpse-wagon was parked in the street hard by the door of Mother Lucia's establishment. The two black-cloaked corpsemasters were wrestling with Mother Lucia's big Moorish servant; even as Pasquale watched, one of the men produced a sap and knocked the Moor sprawling. Then the two were inside the house and Pasquale heard Mother Lucia's loud indignant voice.

A man's voice, no doubt that of one of the corpsemasters, rode over it. "Where is the thief?"

"He ran," Mother Lucia said. "One of your artificers had one of my girls and ran off without paying. You should pay, as you also work for the New University. And make recompense for wounding my guard!"

"It was the artificer who told us that the man who brought him here tried to rob him. Where's your pimp? He's the thief we're interested in."

Pasquale groaned. Clearly, drink and spent lust had inflamed Koppernigk's suspicions.

"I have no need of pimps. I have," Mother Lucia said with incandescent dignity, "my reputation. Wait! Where are you going?"

A moment later there was the sound of furniture being overturned, and then a window went out in a cascade of glass, followed by the sound of a whistle blowing, the alarm call for the city militia.

Pasquale could run of course, but he doubted that he would get far. Surely if Koppernigk had alerted these two, then he would alert others. And besides, he must still gain an audience with the Great Engineer. There was only one thing for it, only one way to get into the New University without being seen. He jumped on to the back of the wagon, lifted the heavy oiled canvas sheet, and scrambled beneath.

He barely had time to settle himself before he heard the two corpsemasters coming back, pursued by Mother Lucia's vengeful voice. Pasquale lay still in the darkness, up against a cold heavy body. The rough planks were wet with something that was soaking into his hose. There was a creaking as the two men climbed onto the wagon's bench, then a lurch as they started off. In the heavily perfumed darkness beneath the tarpaulin, a corpse's cold hand fell across Pasquale's face. He didn't dare move it; suppose one of the corpsemasters chanced to be looking down at his load? Another corpse, swollen with gases, made liquid farting noises at every jolt. The smell was not as bad as that in the anatomy theater in high summer, on the third day of dissection when nothing is left but a shell of spoiling muscle and fat over yellow bones, but Pasquale did not have a pouch of camphor to hold to his nostrils, and although the strong artificial scent of violets burned his throat and eyes, it did not mask the stench but only cut through it. He turned his head and was able to thrust his nose close to the cleated edge of the canvas sheet, and so draw in fresh cold air. He prayed that these corpses had all died violent or natural deaths, and that he would not catch the flux or the French pox from their black air.

The corpsemasters' voices could be heard over the rumble of the wagon's muffled wheels and the creaking of its wooden frame. One, slow and deep-voiced, was grumbling about the arrogance of artificers. "As if we weren't busy enough, we're bodyguards to the fools to the bargain."

The other said, "He's a stubborn blockhead of an old man who thinks everyone is set on robbing him. No doubt some pimp asked too much for the favor of introducing him to a nice warm whore."

"Well, the pimp ran off too. Or never existed in the first place."

"It doesn't matter. We'll make sure we get that coin he promised us, even if we didn't find the pimp. Did you see the tits on the girl? I'd have liked to stay there for sloppy seconds."

The deep-voiced one laughed. "The way it's going you'll be able to afford her fresh and warm in a day or two."

"The way it's going we'll be out of business by then. War is good for medicine, bad for the likes of us. Any fool can turn his hand to the trade during war."

"Don't you worry," the first said. "Unless they find some way of preserving corpses in summer we'll always have a job. This lot won't keep the theaters going past the New Year. Look at it like this—at least we don't have to go on the hunt."

The second said, "We might have to, even so. Too many hot-blooded young men killing each other, and not enough women."

"Brains is all they want these days. They're not too particular what kind. Brains are all the same."

"Brains are the seat of reason, which may be why you don't find them interesting."

"Now hearts are a different matter. I always have had a soft spot for hearts."

"Hearts or lights, it's all money in the end."

"You have no poetry, Agostino. The heart now, with its four chambers and its valves, is a miracle. Think of the way the blood must flow in the heart, because the valves are so cunningly designed that they open inward or outward according to need. You need an education in these matters, as I've always said."

The second corpsemaster, Agostino, said, "There's still the medical students to think about. Maybe that young whore you were soft on, the one with the tits. I would look the other way if you wanted to enjoy her before we put her over to the cold side."

"My father was in this trade, and his father before him. They didn't have to use the knife."

"I have heard enough about your father, thank you. You turn down here. We'll make this last pick-up and then get back."

The corpse's hand flopped away from Pasquale's face as the wagon turned, fell back again when it drew to a halt. There was a spell of silence, and then the end of the tarpaulin was thrown back and a corpse slung onto the load-bed. The deep-voiced corpsemaster talked with someone about money. The wagon started up again, rolling ponderously along the silent streets, the corpsemasters talking in subdued voices until at last the wagon stopped again and there was a brazen clash of gates.

The corpsemasters exchanged pleasantries with a guard. The wagon rolled forward a short distance before halting again. Then a lurch, and the sensation of falling amidst the pounding of steam machineries and rattling of iron chains. The wagon was inside the New University.

6

T he falling stopped with a thump. Sudden light outlined the edge of the oiled canvas sheet over the load-bed. The wagon rolled forward slowly. Dull echoes, the noise of an engine thumping mindlessly over and over. Pasquale fumbled out his little knife and was about to risk cutting the canvas when the end of the sheet was lifted and flung back.

Pasquale lay still, peeking through the stiff fingers of the dead hand which still lay across his face. Bright lights burned overhead, a ring of acetylene jets depending from a vaulted ceiling painted plain white. It was freezing cold, a cellar deep under the ground. The corpsemasters began to unload the wagon, using an iron hook to pull a corpse to the end of the load-bed, then swinging it away by hair and feet.

Pasquale eased himself up, and saw that beyond the wagon were rows of slabs, most with naked corpses laid on them. The two corpsemasters were busy with the body they had just unloaded. One was taking down details on a scrap of paper while the other made measurements.

Pasquale scrambled up and jumped over the side of the wagon, landing with a clatter on the cold slate floor. The horses snorted and stamped, dragging on the wagon's brake. The two corpsemasters turned and shouted and gave chase. Pasquale dodged amidst bodies laid on slate-topped slabs and ran for the nearest door, slamming it shut on the faces of the corpsemasters.

He was in a small circular closet caged round with a shell of lattice-work iron a hand's breadth away from the rough stone walls. The corpsemasters banged on the door, and the floor shivered and swayed beneath Pasquale's feet. He grabbed at a rope and whooped with surprise as the room rose, carrying him with it.

The room rose a long way, swaying with a small motion, at one point passing a shield of lead that slid around it in a clatter of chains. When the room finally banged to a stop Pasquale did not at first trust himself to let go of the rope, half-convinced that if he did, the room would promptly plunge all the way back down to where it had started. The door, when he pushed it open, let out onto windy night.

The mortuary must have been lodged in the cool deep basements of the Great Tower, for the moving room had delivered him to the tower's very top. He was looking out across the roofs and terraces of the New University toward the river, its channels defined by the lights of the floating water-mills. The dark hills rose beyond, only thinly mantled with lights. Armies gathering out there, an unseen menace heavy in the air, like storm-clouds.

Wind quite blew away the confusion of the wine Pasquale had drunk. He shivered in the tumble of cold air. His hose clung to his legs, clotted with jelly-like corpse blood and worse. He was on a kind of

platform that took up half the roof. A confusion of
lesser towers bearing signal arms rose behind him.
Even as he watched, a set of arms on the tallest structure turned and clapped upward before commencing
their swooping formal dance, sending a message out
to the edge of the world. Their lanterns seemed to
leave traceries of red and green light in the air.

Winding-gear jutted beyond the edge of the parapet, two sets of triple drums angled either side of a
Hero's engine with a tall narrow chimney. The chimney was topped with a kind of cap that spun and clattered in the constant wind. Cables threaded through
pulleys rose into the darkness beyond the parapet.
Pasquale could just make out the precise geometric
shapes that made swooping shadows against the
night clouds. Kites, tethered by thin yet strong copper cables, flying in the constant wind above the
tower top.

Pasquale laid a hand on a cable, felt its thrumming.
Clinging to the cable, he looked down and whooped
with exultation. The bulk of the tower diminished
darkly, tapering down to its base. Pasquale could see
foreshortened lights on the tower that must be windows, and here and there balconies and platforms jutting from its wall like the nests of swifts in the eaves
of houses. Lights defined the shape of the Piazza della
Signoria, and then the maze of streets that webbed
the Palazzo and the floodlit Duomo and a thousand
lesser buildings, the whole night-time city stretched
between the river and the city walls.

Chains clattered behind Pasquale, unwinding from
the drums on top of the shed which housed the moving room. The room was making a fast descent. By
the red and green light of the signal-lanterns Pasquale could see the chains swaying down, far down
the long long shaft, to the flat disc of the room's ceil-

ing, diminished by perspective to the size of a coin. As Pasquale watched, the disc passed through the ring of the lead counterweight and halted for a few moments before starting to rise again in a roar of chains.

Pasquale looked for something that he could jam into the chains, or into the winding-drums, or the chain-drive which turned the winding-drums, driven by some engine far below, but there were only big drums of cable which he could not shift by even a finger's width. He could hide amongst the signal structures, but not from any prolonged search—and even as he thought of it a hatch banged open on the far side of the tower's roof and a man climbed through and began to shine a lantern this way and that.

Pasquale ducked down, crouching at the base of the winch. The moving room banged to a stop. Its door opened and two men rushed out, one dragging a big leashed hound, the other a lantern whose light shot out across the platform. The man searching amongst the signal-towers turned toward his fellow, and his lantern-beam brushed over Pasquale. The dog barked, pulling its master forward, and Pasquale jumped up and caught a kite-cable and swung out into the rush of the wind.

As soon as Pasquale trusted his weight to the cable, the tethered kite swooped down, and Pasquale was at once plunged below the level of the platform. He kicked out as the smooth stone of the tower rushed past, managed to hook a leg over one of the kite's three cables. He hung upside-down by his hands and the crook of a knee, looking up at cloudy night sky and the tower's looming shadow. He could feel the long drop at his back. Strong cold wind plucked and sang in his ears, lashing his hair around his face and numbing his hands, but he was elated rather than scared, believing that he must have seemed to have run into darkness and disappeared like a wraith.

Then the guards looked over the edge of the parapet, and three lantern-beams shot out, crossing and recrossing.

Pasquale started to climb along the cable, and as he did so the kite rose, unreeling its cables and Pasquale with it. The guards hauled at the cable to which Pasquale clung, but their efforts were nothing compared to the smooth power of the wind, and transmitted only the faintest of jerks. One of them called to Pasquale, something to the effect that he shouldn't be a fool, he wouldn't be hurt if he came down, but most of his words were blown away in the wind. The others were bent at the winch's Hero's engine, trying to spark a light in its boiler-pan with a flint.

Pasquale, knees hooked around the cable, hauled himself hand over hand until he was directly beneath the great kite. Its surface, canvas stretched over a frame of ash, shivered and boomed. By the fugitive light of the guards' lantern-beams, Pasquale saw an open harness or frame of wicker like a short sleeveless tunic lashed to the crossbar of the framing. A steering-bar curved beyond it. He climbed on until he was dangling just beyond the harness, at the point where the cable entered a leather collar and split to fan out in a dozen strands which anchored at the kite's blunt nose.

An urgent vibration started in the cable. Pasquale glanced down and saw that the chimney of the Hero's engine was spitting sparks. In a few minutes it would be warm enough to begin to wind in the triple cables, something that couldn't be managed by main force unless, as Pasquale had seen on carnival days when smaller kites were flown from the city walls, twenty men united their strength.

He steadied his grip on the cable and unhooked his legs and slowly turned himself around. It was no more difficult than his tricks with the ape outside the big windows of Rosso's rooms, even though the drop was a hundred times greater—but he must not think of the drop. His hands were almost numb now, and his fingers seemed to be swollen to twice their usual size. He drew his knees to his chest, then kicked backward. For a moment his feet tangled in the harness and he felt a stab of pure panic, because, stretched out as he was, the twisting of the kite's frame could make him lose his grip. He kicked like a frog, and inched backward, hand over hand again, until he felt the harness cradle his hips and his chest.

The guards were shouting at him again. Their lantern-beams shook back and forth on the kite's undersurface. Working with one hand, Pasquale pulled the harness-straps tight, something easier than he'd thought it would be; little teeth in the brass snaps let the leather straps slide one way but not the other. His feet found hooked stirrups, and he finally let go of the cable with one hand. The harness creaked and took his weight and held. He grasped the bar in front of his face with both hands and twisted it hard over, as he had seen the carnival kite-riders do so many times that summer, when he had begun to search for the shadow of the reality of his angel.

The kite slid down the air at once, alarmingly fast. Its right edge rattled, letting air spill into the space caused by the wind blowing over the top of its surface. He knew from his conversations with the boys who rode the brief loops of the carnival kites that they flew because air moved more quickly over the top of the cunningly shaped lifting-surface than beneath. Air lifted the kite as it sought to fill the emptiness so created, for God so loves His creation that He abhors any space that is incomplete, no matter how small, and crams the world with detail upon detail.

Now, with air spilling under its right edge, the kite fell sideways. At the same moment someone declutched the cable-drums and the kite immediately gained a good two hundred *braccia* of cable. It swooped down and down before the engine started to wind in the triple cables.

Pasquale had been aiming for a platform that cantilevered out beneath the last tier of the tower, but he misjudged the liveliness of the kite. The balcony rushed by him and then he was below it and falling away from the tower. He tried to tip to the left, and with air spilling under both edges the kite lost lift entirely.

For a horrifying moment it plunged straight down. The lights of the piazza spun dizzyingly. Then the winch made up the slack and the kite jerked backward with such force that Pasquale's hands were wrenched from the control-bar and his breath was driven from him as the harness crushed his ribs. The cables snagged on the edge of the balcony and the kite swung inward, pivoting on this hinge-point. Pasquale saw a tall stained-glass window rush at him: an angel, a white angel raising a burning sword in triumph over a prostrate serpentine devil. It burst around him in shards of white and red and gold.

7

Fortunately for Pasquale, the guards were quick-witted, and they threw the brakes of the winch as soon as they saw what had happened; otherwise he would have been dragged up with the remains of the kite and smashed into the base of the balcony. Instead, Pasquale found himself caught amongst the burst and twisted lead framework of the window with multicolored glass falling around him, tinkling to the floor of a big, vaulted room. Its wooden skeleton smashed, the kite's lifting-surface folded around him like broken wings. He looked like a crucified angel.

The cross-braces of the kite and the wicker harness had taken the brunt of the blow, but still his breath had been knocked out of him. Cold air howled, fretting the rags of the kite. By the time he remembered the straps that held him and started to fumble with them, guards had burst through a door and were running toward him between long tables strewn with papers and pieces of machinery. The guards all wore steel armor plated to a mirror finish. Wind blew papers into the air like a flock of startled birds.

An old man, with long white hair and a long white beard falling in waves around his shoulders and over his chest, supported by a guard, blinked up at Pasquale. Another man swaggered in, splendid in red velvets.

It was Salai. Like an actor in a pageant, he threw out an arm, pointing at Pasquale. "There, master! You see! There is the traitor!"

Despite his dizzy confusion, Pasquale realized at once who the old man must be. He struggled against the bonds of his harness, waking pain in his arms and back. The guards made noise, finding a ladder, moving a table littered with machine parts and glass fragments away from the window where Pasquale hung.

"Don't listen," Pasquale shouted. "He is the father of lies. Please . . ."

Salai grinned at Pasquale. He *did* look like a fat little devil in his red tunic and doublet and red and black particolored hose. He said to the old man, "I will bring you proof directly, master, and tell you all."

The old man mumbled something to Salai, laying a hand on the plump man's arm. But Pasquale could not hear what he said, for now the ladder banged into position beside his head and two guards started to climb it while others jumped onto the table and started to pry apart the twisted framework of lead strips in which the kite had become entangled.

Salai made a long speech to the old man, whispering into his ear and now and then glancing sidelong at Pasquale with a mischievous malevolence. When Salai was done, the old man started to speak, but Salai laid his hand on the old man's arm and said something to the guard, who helped the old man away.

A guard cut the straps of Pasquale's harness; then others had his legs, his arms and in a minute they had him down. He tried to struggle as Salai went through his scrip, but the guards were all burly beef-fed Swiss: as easy to wrestle bullocks to the ground. Pasquale could only watch as Salai tossed aside his knife and bits of paper and charcoal with a delicate contempt; then he picked out the little flying device in its paper shell.

Salai unwrapped the device and held it up, turned it this way and that so that shadows and highlights ran amongst its intricate paper spirals and the fretted mechanism. "You see," he said to one of the guards. "Mark this well. The boy had it with him."

Then he thrust it into his red velvet tunic and told the guards, "Bring him and follow me."

They lifted Pasquale up, one man to an arm or a leg, and carried him down a winding stair to a small room shaped like the letter D, or a strung bow, with a curved wall of stone on one side, and a wall of cabinets on the other. When the guards set him down Pasquale picked himself up as quickly as possible and faced Salai, who stood just outside the door, two burly guards at his back.

"Full marks for your entrance," Salai said, and made soft mocking applause. "I cannot tell you how convenient this is. I could almost kiss you. My estimation of your abilities has risen, although it seems that I was right all along about your intelligence. I won't ask why you came here, not now. Why, I will not even ask how you gained entrance to the tower, or at least not at once. That pleasure will come later."

"You know very well why I'm here, Salai." Pasquale spoke to the guards as much as Salai. "It was you who stole the device, and when it fell into my hands and I learned just how important it was, I tried to bring it here. I would bring it directly to the Great Engineer. This is the truth!"

"Oh, shout all you want. You see, these are my men, painter." Salai sniffed the air. "There's a certain odor about you. Did you shit your breeches when you came through the window? Speak up: it's nothing to be ashamed of."

"It is nothing but old blood. A smell you should know intimately. How did you escape Giustiniani's ambush, Salai? I know it was Giustiniani—those fireworks had his mark, and one of his men nearly surprised me in Niccolò Machiavegli's room."

"Who said I escaped?"

"You betrayed my master, and you betrayed the Savonarolistas to Giustiniani. Who else?"

"Ah, such spirit. I shall enjoy putting you to the question, painter. I have not forgotten our last session, of course. We'll start directly where we left off, in far better-equipped circumstances. I'll leave you to think that over until it is light, painter, and then we will have you moved to the Bargello, the better to perform my offices of mercy."

"Niccolò Machiavegli, Salai! Does he still live? Does Giustiniani have him, and Raphael's corpse?"

"For now," Salai said, and the door was shut, its wooden lock rattling home.

It did not take Pasquale long to explore the room, using what little light leaked through the grille over the transom. The cabinets proved to be full of skulls, and wax impressions of the brains they had once contained. There were shelf upon shelf of them, all neatly catalogued. The dome of each skull was divided by a grid of fine black lines, and each had a tag wired through the right eye, bearing a label in cramped writing that Pasquale thought at first was code, until he realized that it was mirror writing. *Woman, age 44, palsy. Man, age 22, blind, congenital idiot. Man, age 56, normal. Man, age 35, hanged as thief.* Dust on the shelves suggested that the room had not been used for some time.

There was nothing that could be used as a weapon, and he did not think that he could climb through the narrow window in the center of the curved wall, which in any case was so high above the floor that he could only touch its sill by standing on tiptoe. Besides, even if he did manage to climb out he would simply be on the outside of the tower, high above the ground, and with no kite to bear him.

He sat opposite the door, in the narrow corner made where the cabinets met the curved wall, legs straight in front of him. The aches and bruises he had suffered throbbed. Whenever he closed his eyes he relived the thrill of his flight and his fall, and the amazing moment when he had burst the window. Perhaps he had become the angel he had destroyed: he imagined Salai as a scaly worm writhing beneath his own burning sword. Or perhaps by passing through the image of the angel he had become its reverse: a black angel fallen from the grace of God and doomed only to torment. In any event, the madness that had gripped him seemed to have passed. It had inhabited him ever since he had dived into the river to escape the Savonarolistas, a rising curve of urgent, increasingly uncontrolled action that had left him stranded here, in this little cell high in the Great Tower. Or perhaps he had been infected long before then, when he had first met Niccolò Machiavegli. Perhaps he had taken the old man's obsessions with plot and counterplot too deeply into his own self,

seeing Spanish conspiracies where there was only coincidence. He gripped his ankles and shivered, feeling a lassitude that was not despair but simple
acceptance of his fate steal over him.

8

He was woken by the door's cumbersome toothed lock ratcheting backward. Milky dawn light was leaking through the high window, falling like a blanket around Pasquale, although quite without warmth.

He blinked back sleep as the door opened and a guard stepped through. The man's polished steel armor gleamed in the light of the lantern he carried, reflected fragmented images of the room so brightly that the man's square-jawed clean-shaven face (he was not much older than Pasquale) seemed to float unsupported above a crazy mirror. Behind the guard was the old man Pasquale had seen in the long room. It was the Great Engineer.

Pasquale scrambled to his feet as best he could. His spine seemed to be a column of jagged fused iron, and his every back-muscle ached. The Great Engineer regarded him mildly, stroking his silky white beard with one hand. He wore a pair of blue-lensed spectacles that perched on the end of his nose like a butterfly.

"You had better bring him along," he said at last, as if to the air, and turned away.

The guard took hold of Pasquale's arm just above the elbow, the thumb and forefinger of his steel-mesh gauntlet nipping the muscles as cruelly and irresistibly as pincers. He half led, half dragged Pasquale up the winding stair, across the great hall where the kite still hung at the burst stained-glass window, its tattered fabric flapping idly, and through a small door on the far side, into a round room noisy with clocks.

Clocks of all kinds were ranged around the walls: clocks powered by falling sand; clocks with water-wheel linkwork escapements; and every kind of mechanical clock, with dials of burnished gold and silver, or carved painted wood, or even of glass, behind which candles glowed through holes pricked to represent the constellations. There were day clocks and calendar clocks which showed the feasts of the saints, and even an antiquated weight-driven astrolabe with a revolving drum that dripped mercury as an escapement. And in the center of the room, twice as high as a man, was a great astronomical clock, its weight-driven mechanism visible inside a cage of brass, with a seven-sided drum above. Each face of the drum bore a dial showing the movement of one of the seven heavenly bodies, the Primum Mobile, the moon and the planets, and below the drum, within the brass cage, were ring-dials which showed the hour of the day, and the fixed and movable feasts of the Church, and a dial for the nodes. This device made a loud regular knocking, like a magnified heartbeat, measured and stately against the background of the brisk chatter of the smaller mechanisms.

The Great Engineer stood at the far end of the

room, looking out of a window, like a section of a bubble, or a lens, that reached from floor to ceiling. The guard walked Pasquale across the room, and when Pasquale started to ask why he had been brought here, told him to speak only when spoken to.

"But the device—"

The guard, a blond fellow with a bumpy close-cropped head, a smooth boyish face, and intense icy-blue eyes, said quietly, "My master has few words, but each is chosen with care. You will have to get used to his little ways."

Pasquale was made to sit at a small table inside the lens of the window. Looking out at the waking city stretched far below, he had the dizzy sensation of being housed in the eye of a giant. He was so high, the Great Tower being four times the height of the square tower of the Palazzo della Signoria, that he could see the circle of the city walls on either side of the river. He saw the manufactories strung along the river, with blackened gaps where some had been burnt out, the bridges across the braided river, and, directly below, the seat of government. The Piazza della Signoria, deep in shadow, was still littered with the wrecks of the devices of the artificers. The great statue of David was reduced by Pasquale's elevation to a chip or fleck.

The Great Engineer remarked to the air, "The guard is Salai's, of course, and will straight away send word to his master, wherever he is."

"Whatever are you thinking of, master! Of course I won't," the guard said, and winked at Pasquale. "Master, don't you want to share breakfast with this young hero?"

"Has he time for breakfast? Shouldn't you take him away?"

"It's the least we can do for him," the guard said, winking at Pasquale again. "Salai's men won't check the room until they get orders." He pulled a red cord set in a channel in the wall, apparently without effect.

The Great Engineer turned and left the window without looking at Pasquale, and started to wind up the weight of the tall astronomical clock, using a toothed key as long as a man's arm. He favored his left hand.

The guard said, with the air of a stage-manager prompting a recalcitrant actor, "This is all about the model of the device that went missing, is it not?"

Pasquale said, "I came to bring it back, but Salai took it from me."

"Well of course, I saw it myself. Didn't we see that, master?"

The Great Engineer set down the key and said, "You don't have to humor me, Jacopo. I suppose I must hear how the model fell into this young man's hands."

"Set on your tale," the guard told Pasquale.

While the Great Engineer pottered about his clocks, winding them one by one, Pasquale started to explain what had fallen out, how he had come by the device, the murder of Romano that was not after all a murder, the assassination of Raphael and the theft of his corpse, Niccolò Machiavegli's kidnap, Salai's plotting with the Savonarolistas and his double-edged game with Giustiniani.

"I had intended to bring your device straight back to you, master," Pasquale said, "but my luck did not run far enough for that."

The guard said, "It was a brave try, eh master?"

There was a silence while the Great Engineer finished winding his clocks. At last he said, "It does not matter, Jacopo. You cannot suppress an idea, as I long ago discovered. Once it is loosed on the world it acquires a life of its own, as in the Greek story of Pandora. Often it is enough for someone sufficiently skilled to know a thing is possible—I once amused myself by telling my pupils that I had done such and such a task in such and such a way, and having them attempt to duplicate my efforts. Most could, and although no one way was exactly the same as any other, there was, as it were, a familial resemblance. The model was not important, but the idea behind it was, and that is abroad."

The guard, Jacopo, said, "Well, perhaps we were unsuccessful in keeping the camera secret, but this is a more dangerous matter."

Pasquale said, "Salai believes the model important, master, which means he has found a buyer for it. I believe that he's taken it to the Venetian magician, Paolo Giustiniani, who will sell it on to the Spanish. The Spanish will use it against Florence. I helped frustrate his plans the first time, although entirely by accident. He was working through intermediaries last time, but now he has moved openly. I would try and stop him, if I could."

Jacopo said, "You mentioned this Giustiniani before. Did Salai tell you why he treated with him and not directly with Spain?"

Pasquale thought back on what Salai had said, and admitted, "Not in so many words, but the way in which the Savonarolistas were attacked on the river has Giustiniani's mark. Besides, the Savonarolistas are fanatics who would not pay for the device—or not as much as Giustiniani could no doubt promise."

Jacopo said, "But you've no evidence, eh? Well, whoever he has gone to, Salai won't be back this time, master. It's treason he's set on. Open treason."

The Great Engineer put his hands over his ears.

"That'll do no good," Jacopo said loudly. He was leaning at the join the window made with the wall, idly looking out at the city. He added, "You know he's really done it this time. You won't be able to buy him out of this kind of trouble. You'll have to rescue him from himself."

This Jacopo had a sly comfortable air, Pasquale thought, protective but self-serving, too, like the youngest son who humors his father's every whim in hope of a share of the inheritance. There was best Flemish lace at the neck and wrists of his armor, and his sword had a finger-guard of fretted gold, set with little rubies like flecks of blood.

The Great Engineer put down his hands and looked at them. "How did I get so old, Jacopo? And my beautiful boy?"

"I suppose it was the usual way, master."

"Salai trusts no one," the Great Engineer said, "for after all he knows in his own heart that he is not to be trusted, and so he thinks all men are the same as he. You were right, young man, to call him the prince of lies. I named him in punning reference to the name of the god of the Moorish peoples, for from the first he seemed a very limb of Satan. Such a pretty boy, but such manners and such sulks. And greedy too, of course, taking whatever he wanted. Like a little prince, in a way. So it has come to this. No doubt he will have you killed, by and by."

"We haven't rescued this young man to let him be killed by Salai's bullies, master," Jacopo said. "You know that very well, so stop trying to scare him."

"It's only the truth."

"Only if you let it be the truth," Jacopo said, and winked at Pasquale again.

"Yes, you'd like to see Salai's powers diminished," the Great Engineer said.

"He has altogether too much power over you, and his faction has too much power over the other artificers. A spot of humiliation will do us all good."

"And will do you good most especially," the Great Engineer said. "Don't think I don't know how you try and poison my mind against Salai."

"Hush," Jacopo said. "Not in front of the servants."

A page entered, bearing a tray of fruit and soft black bread and a sweating pitcher of water. He set it on the low table in front of the center of the lensed window and withdrew. Jacopo, still lounging by the window, told Pasquale, "Eat what you will."

"What about your master?"

"Oh," Jacopo said loudly, glancing over his shoulder to make sure the Great Engineer was listening, "he'll claim he's already eaten. He eats hardly enough for a mouse, and sleeps even less. In anticipation, he says, for the long sleep that is to come." More softly, Jacopo told Pasquale, "Eat, and let my master think matters over. He'll warm to the idea, sooner or later. He'll soon see that if Salai succeeds it can only reflect badly on him. And believe it or not, he still has a soft spot for Salai. He won't want him to come to harm."

Pasquale knocked the tray to the floor; focused by the curved glass of the window, it made a particularly satisfactory crash. The Great Engineer blinked at him, his eyes mistily magnified by the blue lenses of his spectacles. It was the first time he had looked directly at Pasquale.

Jacopo had drawn his sword. "You fool!" he said.

Pasquale sprang to his feet and said, "I must ask

you to let me go, master. It is not too late to stop
Salai. I will do it, if you will not."

"Sit down," Jacopo hissed. "You don't know what
he can be like. He still loves Salai."

"Peace, Jacopo," the Great Engineer said mildly,
"and put up your sword. Do you think this young
man will attack me with a plum, or a handful of figs?
As for you, young man, there's no need to get excited.
I have said that I will help you, as in fact I already
have. If it is in my power, you will leave the tower
before Salai returns, or as is more likely, before he
learns that you are free and sends the order that you
are to be locked up more securely."

"That's kind of you, master, but I would ask
more." Desperation had made Pasquale bold. Salai
had said that Niccolò was still alive, but what would
happen if Giustiniani had all he wanted? He said, "If
you let me go free that is one thing. Perhaps I can
stop Salai, perhaps not. What I do know is that I must
struggle against his plans while also evading the
plans of Signor Taddei, who would ransom me in
exchange for Raphael's body. I can try my best, master, but I am but a painter, and hardly more than a
pupil at that, while you can call upon so much that
for you it would be a simple matter to drag Salai from
his meeting-place."

"Keep your counsel," Jacopo said in a fierce whisper. "You'll scare him, and then nothing will
happen!"

"It is nothing but the truth," Pasquale insisted.

"You fool—I'm on your side!"

The Great Engineer said, "Salai has tried to poison
me twice, and a few years ago a soldier shot at me.
He missed and was killed at once, but I have my suspicions."

"More than suspicions," Jacopo said.

Pasquale asked, "And yet you could not have evicted him?"

"Not now. His influence is too great, and he has intimated that my mind is failing. Well, perhaps it is. Besides, where else would he go? Poor Salai has never known another home."

"You see how it is," Jacopo said, flinging up his hands in frustration.

"But I loved him, and forgave him," the Great Engineer said. "I still love him, or the wayward child from which he has grown, and which still in some measure lives in him. Besides, the tower is not mine, or at least, this part of it is not. So that I might build it I made a compact with the Signoria, that if they would pay for the construction and allow me to work as I would, the tower would house a university of artificers. They were great days, once! We would work for days on end in pursuit of an idea. I remember when Vannoccio Biringuccio first rediscovered the principle of Hero's engine—he sealed water in a copper sphere, which he heated, and was lucky to survive the explosion. We thought the tower was falling! Who would have believed where that would lead, in fifteen years? Who would have thought that our simple inquiries into Nature would so change the world? What do you see, Jacopo?"

"What, through the window? Why, the city of course. It's still there, if a little singed around the edges."

"Lately when I look out I see a city in flames. I see flying machines fluttering above defensive walls and dropping pots of fire on those places which will burn best. I see the populace fleeing, harried by the same flying machines. I see men turned into devils. It may yet come to pass. Pick up your breakfast, young man.

Eat, drink. Regular habits make a regular mind. We have a little time."

"It's all right," Jacopo said quietly. "He's thinking about it."

"It may soon be too late," Pasquale said.

"Hush. He moves at his own pace. You've already caused enough trouble."

"I hope it is enough," Pasquale said, and bit into a plum. The rich juice flooded his mouth and awoke his appetite. As he fell to, the Great Engineer finished winding his clocks, and Pasquale observed (taking great satisfaction in the way that Jacopo rolled his eyes) that there was indeed a great deal of time stored here.

"Measured, rather," the Great Engineer said. "I find it interesting that it can be measured in so many ways. Sometimes I would rather I had been a clockmaker than an artificer. Or perhaps an artist, as I set out to be. But I have little power in my right hand now, and so cannot steady my left, and besides, it is a trade to which one must devote one's life. I took a different path after Lorenzo was assassinated, and yet sometimes I think I can glimpse what might have been, as when a climber mounts a high peak, and finds he has not conquered the world after all, for beyond it lie others, dwindling into the mists. Time is a tricky thing, as painters well know. We see it as a river, moving always in one direction, but perhaps God sees it differently, and can return to different events and change them as an author might correct a draft. In another life . . . Well, but you smile at these notions."

"You reminded me of my teacher, Piero di Cosimo."

"I know him well enough to realize that his fabulations which at first seem only amusing are in fact profound, for they strike at the roots of what we accept only by custom or habit without questioning. In that respect Piero is like a child, to whom all is new. Indeed, it's my contention that all artificers should first see a thing anew if they would understand it."

"Then I would ask you to see things anew, master. To see that things are not as hopeless as you believe. The device itself does not matter: it is the importance that certain people have placed upon it that matters. It . . . it's like the angel, the angel of the Annunciation! It doesn't matter what message the angel bears, what form of words is used. It is enough that he bears God's radiance. That itself is the message. If we can take the device back, the advantage will be ours."

Pasquale would have spoken more on this, and more boldly, but a bell chimed softly and Jacopo said, "The guards are coming back. No doubt their captain has been informed that you are loose—I never did trust that page. Master, we'll have to go now. Do you understand?"

"Of course I understand. I'm old, but I'm not in my dotage."

They went through the door which the page had used, down a long corridor with a window as tall as a man at its end, overlooking the city. Jacopo swung this open, and it proved to be a mirror or screen that cleverly reflected a view from a lens, with a stair hidden behind it.

They descended a long way, passing through small rooms that opened out at intervals like beads on a rosary. Jacopo explained that within the tower was a kind of anti-tower, hidden places only a few knew about. Many builders had labored to construct the tower, but they had worked on one part or another and had not the whole sight of the Great Engineer, just as an ordinary man cannot properly see the city in which he lives unless he is raised far above it so that, like God, he can see all. Pasquale thought that this was taking analogies too far, but the Great Engineer showed him how true it was in the next room they passed through.

It was windowless like all the rest, but larger, and circular, and lit not by acetylene lamps but by sunlight, projected through an aperture in the ceiling, which fell on a small table with a dished white surface. At the Great Engineer's order, Jacopo reached up and moved a lever, and suddenly the dished table was filled with an image of the city, shown as if from the eye of a bird hovering above it. More trickery with lenses, prisms and mirrors, but none the less compelling.

"Show me the house of this Giustiniani," the Great Engineer said, and after a moment Pasquale was able to find the villa, a white speck on the hillside inside the city wall on the other side of the Arno. For a brief moment, the shadow of his finger erasing the image, he really could believe that this was how God saw the world, that if he could but sharpen his eyesight he would be able to see Salai riding toward the house, or see through the roof of the house and spy upon the magician, or find poor Niccolò in his prison.

"Light is my abiding interest now," the Great Engineer said. His deep-set sad eyes were pools of shadow, and shadow etched every line of his face. "Light . . . it is purer than idea."

Pasquale said, "Together we can defeat Salai's plot, master. There is still time. The Spanish are a day's ride away. Even if they get the message that Giustiniani has the model, they must collect it. Come with me!"

"Isn't that what I am doing? You have already persuaded me, young man. Jacopo, are you with us? Close your mouth, man. You might swallow a fly."

"I am amazed as usual, master, by the sudden turns of your mind. I have been trying to persuade you to move against Salai ever since he tried to have you assassinated, and suddenly you will do it."

The Great Engineer said to Pasquale, "It was the way you burst through the window, so like an angel. I knew then, but I only now know that I knew. We will rescue Salai from his folly."

"Your science against Giustiniani's magic, master," Pasquale said.

"Magic is only science which seeks to hide itself as something else. I suppose that we have only a little time. We must hurry. Where will you take me?"

"But I had thought—"

The Great Engineer groped for a chair, and sat with a weary sigh. "What, that I could raise an army? There is none, except for the guards, and they are Salai's. All I have is inside my own head. I have no pupils, even. I have not had a pupil for twenty years, only followers."

"Who glean your least idea like crows," Jacopo said.

Pasquale said, "There is only one man who can help us, but I do not know that he will."

"Never mind. Lead me to him! I have great faith in your powers of persuasion, young man. Together we will make him understand. But first, I must rest. There are times when I wish that I had not built the tower so high."

Jacopo took Pasquale's arm and steered him deeper

into the room. "He is an old man, and this enterprise will be dangerous for him."

"It is the only way to stop Salai."

"I see that we understand each other. Very well, then. Let me show you something—as a painter you are sure to be interested."

In the furthest reach of the room was a series of stone troughs lit by bloody light diffused through a red-tinted lens. A constant cold wind blew there. Jacopo said that this was where the Great Engineer painted with light. He showed Pasquale a rack of glass plates evenly coated with silver, and the lensed apparatus into which they fitted.

"Although first the silver must be made sensitive, by treatment with iodine vapor. Then, after exposure to light, the plate is held over a trough of hot mercury until the image forms, and is then plunged into hot salt water to fix it. Here is his latest. Be careful! The silver film is fragile, and although he tried a new varnish to preserve it, it is already flaking. Careful I say!"

For Pasquale had grabbed the plate and marched across the room to the table. Jacopo followed. "Be careful, be careful! You see it is a portrait of the feast for the Pope. There is the Pope himself, with the unfortunate Raphael beside him."

Pasquale was not looking at the dignitaries, but at the servants who waited behind them, ready to make the second serving of wine. In particular, the servant standing at Raphael's shoulder. He knew the pale face, that shock of hair, and finally understood all.

9

When Pasquale was delivered into Signor Taddei's presence, the merchant was playing chess with his astrologer, Girolamo Cardano, in front of the great stone fireplace. Documents were strewn about their feet; a mechanical tortoise, its ebony shell inlaid with a swirling pattern of tiny diamonds, was making its way across this drift of papers on six stumpy legs. Taddei's secretary was writing at a desk behind his master's high-backed chair, and an assistant was adding figures using an automatic abacus, fixing the settings and turning the handle and recording the result on a long sheet of paper with quick mechanical dexterity.

On the far side of the room, a trio of musicians was playing a sprightly piece, and the servant escorting Pasquale waited until they were done before marching him briskly down the length of the great hall. Cardano eyed him sardonically, while Taddei contemplated the board, a finger stroking his beard. The mechanical tortoise reached his feet: he turned it around and made his move before glancing up. They made an odd pair, the twitchy young black-clad aesthete and the comfortably expansive merchant, but such unlikely couplings were common, for often the master would recognize in a servant or employee an exaggeration of a trait lacking in his own character, and so would raise that man up to become a confidant and sounding-board for his own ideas.

"An unexpected pleasure," Signor Taddei said, and looked askance at the servant who escorted Pasquale.

Cardano moved a bishop across the board and then set the tortoise marching back toward Taddei.

The servant explained that Pasquale had marched up to the gate and demanded entry. Pasquale said boldly, "I came with a friend. I believe you should speak with him, rather than play at war."

"Is that so," Taddei said, and settled back in his chair and stared frankly at Pasquale. He was dressed in a red robe trimmed at neck and cuffs with dyed black fur, and a square hat was set on his balding pate.

"Beware tricks," Cardano murmured. His lower lip was swollen, and even as Pasquale watched he bit it so hard that tears stood in his eyes. The astrologer had had a lot to think about, it seemed. He added, "One man can do the work of many, in the right place."

Pasquale said, with a lightness he did not feel, "He is an old man, and no assassin."

"Appearances often deceive," Cardano said. "Be careful, master."

"In every way," Taddei said. The tortoise nudged his curl-toed slippers. Hardly glancing at the board, he moved a pawn forward one space and with his foot turned the little device around so that it started to march back toward Cardano.

Pasquale said, "I have only to glance at you, Signor Cardano, to remind myself of that."

The servant told Taddei, "There is an old man, master, and also a man escorting him, in armor."

"His bodyservant," Pasquale said. "He'll give up his sword if you ask him, and has no other weapon."

"Fetch this old man up," Taddei told the servant, and said to Pasquale, "You've caused me a great deal of trouble, boy. Tell me now that you are not in league with the Savonarolistas."

"You know that I am not," Pasquale said as steadily as he could. "It was the Savonarolistas who took me from your men at the Ponte Vecchio."

"I know nothing of the sort! Two of my men dead, and the third lingering with a bullet in his guts as likely to die as his companions. Perhaps the Savonarolistas took you, but now here you are, unharmed."

"Although not in the best odor," Cardano said.

"I had to resort to an unusual mode of transport."

"Unfortunately," Taddei said, "there is still no trace of Raphael's body. Did you see it, when the Savonarolistas held you?"

Pasquale said, "The Savonarolistas don't have Raphael's body."

"I always thought that you were poor enough ransom," Cardano said.

Pasquale said, "The Savonarolistas did not want me, but something I possessed—and I no longer have it. And in fact it was not they who set up the exchange, but another. They learnt of it because there is someone in your house, signor, who is in contact with them."

"If you were with the Savonarolistas, that is just what you would say," Cardano said. The tortoise was trying to clamber over his black boots, and he nudged it away impatiently.

"I'm not accusing you, signor. It will be one of the servants, perhaps the replacement for your signaler. In a way it does not even matter."

"If it is true," Taddei said, "it matters to me."

Cardano said, "We can't believe a word this boy says. How is it that he is standing here if he was taken by the Savonarolistas?"

"Hush," Taddei said. "It's your move, Girolamo."

"Oh, that." Cardano moved his queen so that it stood beside his bishop and leaned back, pinching the inside of his elbow with thumb and forefinger. "There. Checkmate."

"It is?" Taddei looked at the board distractedly, then pushed it away.

Pasquale said, "This is all you can do while armies march on Florence?"

Taddei regarded him with mild amusement. "I cannot send my goods out by road because the roads are closed by order of the Signoria, and I dare not send my goods by water, as the Spanish navy sits off the coast and like as not would sink any ship that dared try to pass. Meanwhile, citizens are calling for the resignation of the artificers' faction from the Signoria, the city is under martial law but is still threatened by mob rule, and my manufactories are closed because of a strike called by your Savonarolistas— but as for that, I wait only for my spies to identify the ringleaders so that they can be dealt with." He ground fist and palm together, to show what he meant. "You will tell me how you escaped from the Savonarolistas."

"They were taking me across the river, on a ferry they had captured, when they were attacked from the shore by what I believe were forces under the command of Paolo Giustiniani. I dived into the river, and swam to shore." There was no need to mention Rosso's role in this. The dead are dead, and there's no use speaking ill or good of them. Pasquale added, "If you need proof that I have nothing to do with the Savonarolistas, here it is."

He pulled out the plate, which he had carried from the Great Tower wrapped in a square of linen. He said, "I know who killed Raphael, now, for I recognize his man. This was taken at the feast after the entry of the Pope. You are there, Signor Taddei, at the end of the table, so you must remember it."

Taddei took the glass and peered at the smudged black and brown image. "I remember it being made," he said. "We had to sit still for two full minutes, and the glare of the lights was horrible on the eyes. Ah, there is poor Raphael!" The room fell silent as the merchant gazed at the picture. "Well," he said at last, "how does this advance your cause?"

"When was the picture taken?" Pasquale asked.

"Why, between courses. I cannot remember exactly when. No, of course, it was just before Raphael died. What is your meaning, boy?"

"Look in the background, signor. You will see the servants waiting to serve the wine for the new course. Fortunately, they too obeyed the instructions to stay still. You will see one at Raphael's shoulder. I know him. He is a servant of Paolo Giustiniani, the same man who tried to capture me in the Piazza della Signoria, and who later tried to break into Niccolò Machiavegli's room when I was there. Perhaps you remember him, Signor Taddei. He has red hair, and a skin as pale as milk."

Cardano said, "Even if you can show that you came by this representation legitimately, we have only your word that this servant is who you say he is."

Pasquale glanced over his shoulder, and to his relief saw the Great Engineer hobbling along beside Taddei's servant, with Jacopo in his glittering armor behind them. "As for how I came by this representation, my friend here can vouch for me. I think you know him, signor."

Signor Taddei followed Pasquale's glance, then jumped up in astonishment, sending the chessboard and the carved ivory pieces crashing to the tiles. With great and apparently genuine effusion, he took the Great Engineer's arm and escorted him to his own chair. Even Cardano seemed overcome by this apparition, and stood aside to watch with eagerness as Taddei settled in the chair opposite the Great Engineer and began to ply him with questions.

The Great Engineer answered with a nervous smile and a shake of his head, and indicated that Jacopo could speak for him. He was after all an old man in bad health, exhausted by the break in his reclusive habits and the short journey on foot from the Great Tower to the Palazzo Taddei. He slumped rather than sat in the chair which Taddei had given over to him, refused wine and, through Jacopo, asked instead for water. His eyes, behind the blue lenses of his spectacles, were half-closed.

Jacopo stood behind his master's chair, visibly amused by this turn of events, and said that his master would help as much as he could in the matter of Paolo Giustiniani. "He acquired something belonging to my master, a trinket which must be returned." He bent to listen to the Great Engineer, and added, "Or destroyed, my master says. In any event, it must not fall into the hands of the Spanish."

Pasquale explained as quickly as he could that it

was this device which Giulio Romano had originally stolen to the order of Paolo Giustiniani, who was acting as agent for the Spanish. That the Savonarolistas, who did not trust Giustiniani, had taken him because they wanted to capture the device and give it straight away to their masters. That this Paolo Giustiniani was not only acting as a go-between in the matter of the stolen device, but that he was also the instigator of the murder of Raphael, that it must be he who had stolen the painter's corpse. "This surely must have been either on the orders of Spain or simply to make money from its ransom. When Giustiniani learnt that I had the device, he decided that he would kill two birds with a single shot, and offered Raphael's body in exchange for myself and poor Niccolò Machiavegli, knowing that we knew where the device was. Instead, the Savonarolistas took us, although I cannot pretend to be grateful."

Cardano said, "Yet is it not interesting that this young fellow escaped when Signor Machiavegli did not? We still have no explanation of that."

Jacopo said, "You may believe him. My master considers him to be an honest lad."

While Pasquale had been speaking, the Great Engineer had picked up a sheet of paper from the litter on the floor and had started to doodle upon its reverse, quickly covering it with small diagrams. Now he held this up, and said, "With my help it is possible that we can quickly take this so-called magician by surprise. If he does not have the time to do anything beyond respond to the attack, then he will not have the time to destroy the body of Raphael. More importantly, he will not be able to take vengeance on my poor misguided Salai. I will have words for that wicked soul myself."

"We would wish that no one is hurt in this," Signor Taddei said, "but I would ask the cost of this expedition. I am not a poor man, it is true, but I would find it hard to furnish an expedition of this nature, most especially in these suddenly straitened times. Would you say that this device of yours is valuable?"

"It has already cost too much," the Great Engineer said.

Jacopo said, "My master means that we could come to some arrangement."

The Great Engineer grimaced at that, but said nothing.

Taddei said, "What do you think, Girolamo? Could it be developed?"

"I would have to see it," Cardano said with a shrug.

Pasquale said, angry and disbelieving, "You decide matters in the language of double-entry bookkeeping?"

"Peace, young man," Taddei said. "I am after all a business man. Perhaps you should look elsewhere if you desire unconsidered action, although I doubt that anyone else would listen to your wild tale. After all, that was why you came to me, was it not?"

"I came to you because you were instrumental in the attempt to regain Raphael's body."

Taddei gave Pasquale a shrewd look, and Pasquale blushed. After all, Cardinal Giulio de' Medici, the Pope's own cousin, had witnessed Pasquale's dispatch as ransom for the return of Raphael's body, and Pasquale could not even guess at what favors had been promised Taddei for that work, or what favors he had repaid by undertaking it. Nor of course could he ask. One did not speak of things like that directly, for it was too dangerous. Even knowledge has its own worth, and so its own dangers for the owner, as Pasquale now well knew. Unknowingly, he had been the possessor of the very knowledge which had cost the lives of poor Rosso and two of Raphael's disciples, and which now threatened to become the seed from which the destruction of Florence might spring.

Taddei was at base a kindly man, if brusque and practical. He said, "All of Florence's might and worth are founded on commerce, as I'm sure you realize. As for my own small worth, it springs from that most traditional of our enterprises, that of making textiles. Now, to secure advantage over our foreign competitors, we Florentines have used the banking system to our own great advantage, buying up the production of English flocks two or three years in advance. Thus, even before a lamb takes its first giddy steps on English soil, all the wool that will ever grow upon its back has already been bought. Yet that very advantage may now be our doom, for we must take in that wool and make good our promises of payment even if we cannot now use it to produce cloth. The Savonarolistas well know this, and so they would disrupt the manufactories. You understand then that this *is* a war fought as much on the pages of the double-entry system as it is on the battlefields, and while the war has already been openly declared on the former, the armies have yet even to begin maneuvreing around each other on the latter. So, signor, you see that even the smallest part I can play in this must be carefully scrutinized, for it would be to throw all to the winds should I win one part of the war only to lose the other."

The Great Engineer said, "Perhaps Signor Cardano might wish to scrutinize my plans on your behalf, Signor Taddei. I believe that he will find them reasonable. I have no wish to mount a bloody campaign and lose that which I care for, any more than you wish to ruin yourself for the benefit of others. With that in mind, I have devised a way in which the actions of a few will be seen as the actions of many, by use of devices which will cause confusion and panic in the heart and mind of the enemy while exposing those attacking to the smallest of risks. I have spent my life considering the experience of those men who claim to be skilled inventors of machines of war, and long ago I realized that those machines differ in no way from those commonly used in manufactories and elsewhere. So it is with the minimum expense and greatest haste that my devices may be put into effect, and any use that you believe you might find for them afterwards, well then, they are yours."

It was a long speech, and cost the old man a lot. He slumped in his chair, and it fell to Jacopo to acknowledge Taddei's effusive thanks.

Cardano bent eagerly over the sheet of plans, and almost at once fell to questioning the Great Engineer, who replied only with a smile or a shake of his head. Taddei called for wine, and put an arm around Pasquale's shoulder in a friendly although unwanted manner, and led him a little way down the room.

"You must tell me why you are in such a hurry, young man. I've always held that if a thing is worth doing at all, it is worth doing well, even though that means patience. You're as impatient as my astrologer there, and as young, the two things often going together."

"I would save my friend Niccolò Machiavegli. If he still lives, then he is in Giustiniani's hands: he was on the ferry when Giustiniani's men attacked the Savonarolistas, but was wounded and could not escape. The longer we delay, the less likely that he will remain alive. And once the Spanish take the device, then Giustiniani will have no further use for Niccolò or for the body of Raphael."

"He might still ransom them."

"More likely he would leave with the Spanish, if there is to be war. Besides, you might pay for the body, signor, but would you pay for the life of a journalist?"

"You're blunt," Taddei said, not without admiration.

"I find I must be."

"Then let me be blunt, too. I have it in mind that you will play a leading role in the engagement."

"Signor, I am a painter, not a soldier. If it was in my power to be otherwise—"

Taddei said implacably, "You'll go into the villa before the attack. If at all possible you will secure the safety of Raphael's body, and of your friend, and of this Salai. And above all, you will attempt to rescue this device. In that order. I was Raphael's good friend, and it is a matter of honor for me to ensure he has a decent burial. I hope you understand."

"But how will I do all this if I am to make myself a prisoner of Giustiniani?"

"You're a resourceful young man. If your balls are as big as your mouth, you'll find a way."

"You don't trust me, do you, signor?"

Taddei dismissed this with a wave of his hand. "It is not a matter of trust."

"I could go in and straight away betray your attack."

"Then I would know not to trust you, eh? I *do* trust you enough to think you will not. But what if you do? We will attack anyway, and if Giustiniani attacks first, then we will fight all the harder. And take no prisoners—you understand me, I hope?"

"Perfectly," Pasquale said, with ice in his spine.

"There is one favor I would ask. If I survive, I must leave the city. It will be too dangerous for me to stay, knowing what I know."

"Well, that's true," Taddei admitted. "Where would you go?"

Pasquale told him, and Taddei laughed. "I must admire your ambition. There's a ship leaving this night. If you can reach it in time, there'll be a place for you."

"Two places," Pasquale said. He was thinking of Pelashil.

"You ask a high price."

"The stake is my own life. Tell me, signor, do you think that this assault can work?"

"If it is possible, then let it be so."

"All things are possible to the Great Engineer."

"So they say." Taddei turned back and said, "Cardano, damn your skin, will it work?"

The black-clad astrologer came over. He pinched one pitted cheek between thumb and forefinger and said in a subdued voice, "I'm not fully conversant with the uses to which certain principles are put . . ."

"And will it cost me over-much?"

"The Great Engineer's man says that much of the apparatus can be taken from the workshops of the Great Tower . . . no, I don't think so. But the risk if even one part of this does not work . . ."

"Talk with my secretary, give me an exact figure. As to its working, we must trust to our genius." Taddei turned towards the Great Engineer, but the old man was asleep, his blue-tinted spectacles askew on his face, a half-completed portrait of Salai, young and idealized, fallen from his hand.

10

It rained a little just before sunset, enough to lay the dust and soften the ground. The night was cold and clear, and Pasquale shivered as he lay in long damp grass looking across the rutted road at the gate to Giustiniani's villa. If it kept up like this there would be a frost, the first of the year. In the vineyards on the hillsides around Fiesole, peasants would be sitting beside braziers loaded with tarred brushwood, to keep the frost from the last of the season's grapes.

Pasquale drew on his cigarette, cupping it in his hands to hide the coal. It was no more than a few twists of tobacco and marijuana seeds in coarse paper. The smoke tasted hot in his dry mouth. When the coal nipped his fingers he pinched it out and let it fall amongst the grass stems. It could be his last—a thought so morbid he must smile at it.

The walls around the garden of Giustiniani's villa glimmered in the light of the waning moon. When Pasquale had first been there with Niccolò Machiavegli, the moon had been red as it set beyond the shoulder of the wide valley. Setting now, it was a cold blue-white, for the manufactories along the Arno were shut down and their smokes dispersed. A doubly bad omen, then, this clear moon. Signor Taddei's men, under the instruction of Girolamo Cardano, had had a hard time of it, making their way through olive-groves that were a chiaroscuro of moonlight and shadow, every shadow potentially a servant or soldier of Giustiniani. Two had scouted ahead to make sure the way was safe before the others advanced, bent with heavy packs on their backs. Despite the caution of the scouts, Pasquale had jumped at every quiver of moon-drenched shadow, each scuttling mouse. He was not a brave man, merely foolish enough not to admit fear. Pelashil had said that he was a fool, and he believed it now, no matter how much he had protested then.

He had gone to see her that afternoon, while Cardano, armed with a warrant that Taddei had arranged through his connections, had gone to the workshops of the New University to requisition apparatus its custodians hardly suspected they possessed. Pasquale had given his word of honor to Taddei that he would return, and Taddei had acknowledged that promise by having him followed discreetly rather than escorted.

Pasquale had come into the bar to jeers and catcalls from his friends: one saying that he thought he saw a ghost; another that no ghost would look so bedraggled; a third that here was a notorious man indeed, with a summons to the magistrates upon his head. A fourth cradled a *viola da gamba* between his thighs, and called forth a plaintive melody from its warm wooden womanshape with dexterous use of a bow. To the percussive beat of his fellows' hands on their thighs—this kind of strong accompanying beat, borrowed from the chants of the New World Savages, was the latest musical fashion, its rude vigor sweeping away the traditional melodies—the viola player half sang the first verse of a popular love song, twisting the words to suit Pasquale's name so that his companions laughed and lost the beat in delighted applause.

Pasquale felt at once that he had returned home, but that while he had changed his home had not. He suddenly felt that he had nothing in common with these dandified youths, with their hair elaborately curled or sleeked to a lacquered shine with gum arabic, their fine clean clothes in carefully matched shades of rose and yellow and cornflower blue, their palms scented with fresh rose- and lavender-water, their languid drawls and knowing smiles, their petty intrigues and feigned passions for fine horses (which they could not afford) and fine women (likewise). The brown hose and doublet and black jerkin Pasquale had been given at Signor Taddei's were no more than serviceable, with a cut ten years out of fashion. He had not had time to wash his hair properly, let alone set it in its usual fringe of falling curls, and instead he'd caught it up in a net, like a soldier. He felt, all of a sudden, grown-up amongst boys. They urged him to sit with them, tell them what he'd been doing, tell them what he knew about Raphael's murder, to have a drink.

He said, "What's this about a summons?"

"You've been a bad boy," said the musician, setting aside his instrument and bow. "Did someone post an accusation in one of the *tamburi* against you?"

"Been banging someone's daughter, Pasqualino?" another said, and a third added, "More likely someone's son."

Pasquale remembered the monk and shrugged and

asked after Pelashil, and his friends started to laugh
again. The mercenary sitting beside the ashes of last
night's fire looked over at this noise, scowling. Pasquale met his gaze and looked away nervously.

"Where's Rosso?" someone said. "Come on, Pasquale, sit with us and tell us all about your wicked
ways."

Pasquale blushed with horrible shame. He could
not tell his friends that his master was dead, killed
by his own hand. Instead, he blurted that he must
see Pelashil, and roused the Swiss landlord, who was
dozing in a corner with his giant hound lying across
his bare feet. The man cursed sleepily and told him
she was out in the back, rinsing the pots.

"You take care," he added, "and be ready to duck
when you go through the door."

Pasquale soon found out what the Swiss meant.
Pelashil was washing plates in a bucket. Lunchtime
herring was cooking on a grill shoved onto the coals
of the stove, filling the air with a haze of smoke.
When Pasquale started to talk to her, she turned her
back on him; when he persisted she started splashing
grease-slicked water at him. He jumped back, mor-
tified. He said that he wanted only to say farewell,
in the very unlikely event that he didn't come back.

"That's done. So you go. Go now!" She was furious, rubbed at her eyes with raw red wrists, turned
her back and tried to shrug him off when he tried to
turn her to him.

He tried to make a joke of it. "Oh well, and I
thought you cared for me, and I see you are careless
of me instead."

"You men. So brave. So selfless. So you think,
playing your foolish games. Go kill yourself and
don't expect me to mourn you. Be a hero and enjoy

your grave. Your friends will give you a fine monument, I suppose."

"This talk of graves is making me nervous. I just came to ask you two favors. To look after the ape, just in case. You know . . ."

"It's no more trouble than the old man, and better company than you."

"Cleaner? Warmer? Come, I won't have it that you share your bed with such a monster."

She smiled, just for a moment, a flash of white in her lined brown face. "You think yourself such a fine gentleman."

"Well, am I not?"

"I've told you what you could be. You're a fool."

"Pelashil, I'm not sure if I want to be a magus. All I wanted a few days ago was to learn how to paint an angel in a way no one has painted an angel before."

"I showed you the way."

"I'm not sure what I saw, now." The polychrome bird, that was and yet was not Pelashil. Moments of time like bright beads on a string, vivid and fixed as stars. The creature he'd met in the weave of the cloth hanging.

"You can't learn from the híkuri until you are a mara'akame. Before that time your dreams are only . . . like plays."

"Entertainments?"

"Yes," Pelashil said, with a stubborn finality.

"It seems too a long road."

"Listen. When you first take híkuri, you look in the fire and see the play of colors, the many arrows with feathers full of color."

"Yes," Pasquale said, remembering.

"When a mara'akame looks in the fire, what does he see? He sees the fire-god, Tatewarí. And he sees the sun. He hears prayers venerating the fire where

Tatewarí dwells, and the prayers are like music. All this is necessary to understand: it is what you must do so that you can see what Tatewarí lets go from his heart for us. That is what you have taken the first step toward. That is what you are throwing away. There are two worlds, the world of things and the world of the names of things, where their essence lies. The mara'akame stands between them. Except for my master, you are the only one of this great and terrible city to begin to understand this, and you throw this understanding away for a fool's errand."

"It's hardly a fool's errand. Truly." Pasquale tried to explain about where he was going, the villa, the Great Engineer's devices. "If he can save all Florence, then he can certainly save me."

He was still making the mistake of joking about it.

Pelashil said, "I'll tell my master that there's going to be war. Perhaps we should travel on, so don't expect me to be here when you come back."

Pasquale tried to tell her what Signor Taddei had promised, that when it was over he would begin his journey, and she could be there with him, but she wouldn't listen, and turned away when he tried to calm her, then banged the dishes together in the tub of water when he tried to speak again, and wouldn't answer any of his appeals.

So in the end nothing had been settled. He'd gone out through the back alley rather than go in through the tavern again and face his friends. He had felt all of eight years old again.

Now, in the darkness, in the long grass by the road, Pasquale checked the time given by the mechanical timepiece strapped to his wrist. It was as thick as three ducats set one atop the other, with a single wedge which moved around a dial marked with the quarter divisions of the hour. Pasquale's fingers told him that the wedge was more than fifteen minutes from the hour, when according to the plan he would walk up to the gate and surrender to the guard. Cardano wore the twin of this timepiece, and at the end of the next hour he would set the attack in motion whether or not Pasquale had succeeded.

These synchronized timepieces were the least of the wonders culled from the workshops of the Great Engineer. Nor were they his only gift. When Pasquale had returned to the Palazzo Taddei from the tavern, with his tail between his legs, he found the old man awake again, picking at a bowl of heavily oiled fava beans flavored with rosemary. He had been filling page after page with diagrams, seeking, so Jacopo explained with a shrug, to work out a method whereby a square could be derived from a circle so that each shared the same area.

"In mathematics is truth," the Great Engineer said mildly. "Only in mathematics." Then he added, "Alas, I waste too much of my time on these problems."

Pasquale was becoming used to the old man's mood-shifts, whereby he raised something up only to dash it down. He remarked, "The Greek, Pythagoras, believed numbers embodied pure truth. As if they were the dust from God's robe."

"Many do believe so still. I receive many letters containing intricate calculations which claim to show how old the universe is, or how big, or how all laws which govern it may be subsumed into a single simple statement. Isn't that right, Jacopo?"

"How would you know, master? You make me read them for you, and very tedious they are, too. Like Pythagoras and his followers, and like hermetic scientists such as this Venetian, Giustiniani, the fools who write to you believe that the universe is a great puzzle, which may be solved by devising the right key. And they further believe that this hypothetical key will grant unlimited power and knowledge to those privy to it. They make offers to you, master, that you will have half the kingdom of Heaven if you help them solve their puzzles."

"And yet," the Great Engineer said, "I am reminded that Pythagoras and his followers, who saw numbers as the true essence of things, were confounded by the simple observation that the diagonal of a regular square one unit to a side is a number which is not a regular fraction, that is, the ratio of two whole numbers. This was so fundamental a flaw that one disciple, Hippasus, was ritually drowned for revealing it. Poor man. I have always sympathized with him. I fear the irrational deluge that can in one day destroy all of man's works."

Pasquale asked the old man's permission and picked up a sheet of paper to study. "These abstract designs are almost decorative."

"Oh, often I have picked out designs for architectural features from these doodlings, most especially for stained glass."

"I am sorry that I destroyed your window. I would have liked to see it."

The Great Engineer leaned forward, his eyes suddenly filled with fiery enthusiasm. "When you burst through it! It was the most marvelous sight I have seen for some time. I have been too long in the tower, away from the world . . . but the world is a confusing place, not well ordered. I need order to think, more and more. The strange thing about these mathematical fancies is not that they generate what we apprehend as beauty, but that one cannot predict which geometry is beautiful. There is no equation of beauty: it arises randomly, as a snatch of song may be apprehended above the buzz of a crowd, before sinking into the general noise again. Euclid proposed that geometry was a solid base for rational exposition of the universe, but even in Euclid's expositions there are puzzles to be found. I have long wrestled with this or that problem . . . perhaps I have wasted my time. Perhaps there are irrational properties in geometry which cannot be derived from Euclid's sand-drawn axioms. But if the absolute certainties of geometry are overthrown, then so too are all our architectures and our artistic endeavors, our navigation and our fixing of the stars."

Pasquale felt a giddy excitement—if the world was not fixed, then every man was surely free to determine his own fate. Nothing could be measured against one thing, but all was free, true only to its own self. Angels and men. The world of things, and the world of the senses. He said, "Yet Cristoforo Columbo found the New World."

Jacopo shrugged. "While aiming for something else."

"But others follow his navigation. Piero di Cosimo, for instance."

The Great Engineer crooked a finger, and Jacopo cleared his throat and said with a certain formality, "My master reminds me to tell you that Taddei is not to be trusted. Don't count on his sponsorship, Pasquale."

Pasquale said, "There is something I would ask you, Jacopo. When I am gone, I'd like you to call on a certain important household. I could never gain entry, but you are the personal servant of the Great Engineer, and I trust that you are well known in such circles."

Jacopo swelled with self-importance. He asked, "Who is this person?"

Pasquale told him, and gave him the message, and from Jacopo's look of glee at this intrigue knew that it would be delivered.

The Great Engineer said wistfully, "If I were younger then I might wish to sail with you."

"Don't be foolish," Jacopo said. "When you were a young man you would never have been allowed to set forth on such a dangerous voyage, for you were too valuable to the city."

Their talk turned, slowly, to painting. To Pasquale's angel.

The Great Engineer listened as Pasquale explained how he had wrestled with the problem of painting something new, an angel no one had seen before, but then a silence fell. Pasquale believed that the old man had fallen asleep, but suddenly he said, "He would not look stern or sorrowful, you know. That is what a man might feel, but not a creature of God. An angel would be ecstatic, for he would be doing God's work, and besides, he would also see the future. Your angel would know that the Fall would set man free, for before the Fall man was perfectly attuned to God's will, and since the Fall man must strive to regain the ability to hear the secret and solemn music by which the spheres of the universe are ordered. For having fallen, man has gained the chance to mount higher than angels."

"How high? Surely you don't mean—"

The Great Engineer smiled, and touched a finger to his lips. They were rose-red inside his silky white beard. Pasquale suspected that they were dyed. The old man's fingernail was long, yet quite clean, and painted with some substance that gave it a pearly sheen.

"Don't say it. It will get you into trouble even thinking it here."

Jacopo said, "Signor Taddei is a close friend of the Vatican."

The Great Engineer added, "He would say such pride filled Lucifer, and in that instant he rebelled and in the same instant was overthrown. But Lucifer Lightbringer was of Heaven, while we have nowhere to go but to mount higher. Your angel would see this, and so would be filled with joy."

"A stern kind of joy, it would seem. Perhaps I am not equal to the task."

"Doubting that you are able to do the work is the first step. When you know what you do not know, you can begin to gain knowledge. Otherwise, in ignorant bliss, you learn nothing. I have always wondered if angels are intelligent, or even rational, for if they are perfect servants of God's will, then they need know nothing, proceeding as they do from that which knows all."

The guard went past the gate again, the fifth time since Pasquale had settled down in the undergrowth. The lights of the villa could just be glimpsed beyond the walls, glimmering as cold and remote as the moon.

Mastering the science of light, the Great Engineer had told Pasquale that afternoon, would be the achievement of the age. The recording of light and the motion of light would revolutionize the way in which time was perceived. He foresaw a way in which the slow chemical process by which light freed silver from its iodine salt could be hastened, so that an exposure could be made each second, capturing the way in which men and animals moved. Such sequences passed before the eye imitated movement, falling one after the other just as in life.

Jacopo added with no little pride that his master had already essayed such a technique before the Pope, but that was simple trickery, as Pasquale would see. Amongst the devices to be used against Giustiniani was one which employed the same kind of trick.

"I hope we do not need to use it," Pasquale said. "I must treat with Giustiniani, on Taddei's request." He thought for a moment, and told the Great Engineer, "Seeing your drawing, master, has given me an idea of how to set about that task. If you would spare me a few moments, then perhaps there is a way in which I can seriously bargain for the life of my friend, and my own safe return."

There was the sound of a galloping horse, the creak of harness and the thud of wheels. A carriage swayed up the steep road, pulled by a sweating coal-black horse. The gate clashed open as two guards hurriedly stepped through. From where he lay, Pasquale was no more than a few *braccia* from the nearest, could see his white face under the shadow of his peaked steel helmet—a heavy-set man with a thick mustache that lapped a thick-lipped mouth, eyes blue as the mountains of the moon. A Swiss or Prussian mercenary, like the men Taddei had hired for this expedition. Pasquale had a brief vision of the hireling soldiers of both sides throwing down their arms and greeting each other as brothers: he really had no stomach for the fight.

The carriage was reined in. The guard closest to Pasquale caught at the traces of the sweating horse, which hung its head, blowing heavily through its nostrils, and spoke to the driver in guttural Prussian. The milk-faced driver laughed and swiped off his loose hat, letting curly red hair fall over his forehead. In that moment a sliver of ice seemed to pierce Pasquale's breast. The driver was the servant of Giustiniani, the man who had driven Giovanni Francesco all unknowing to his death, the man who had handed the poisoned goblet to Raphael, who had chased Pasquale in the Piazza della Signoria, whom Pasquale had glimpsed at the window of Niccolò's room.

The guard waved the carriage on. As it slowly rattled beneath the arch of the gate, Pasquale stood up and walked into the road.

The guard leveled his pistol in reflex, then relaxed a little when he saw that Pasquale was alone. His companion said in halting Tuscan, "No visitors. Go away like a good fellow."

Pasquale said, "I have business with Signor Giustiniani."

He made to pull the papers from inside his jerkin, and the first guard raised his pistol again. The second stepped up, knocked aside Pasquale's hands, and drew out the sheaf of papers.

"For Signor Giustiniani," Pasquale said.

"We take them. You go."

Pasquale hadn't foreseen that he would be turned away—but why would the guards recognize him? He said, "I want payment," and snatched at the papers.

The second guard pushed him over. Pasquale sprawled in soft rutted mud and for the first time since he had set off for the villa felt anger, fierce and hot. He sprang up and snatched at the papers which the guard waved overhead, out of reach. Both guards laughed at this crude Prussian bully-boy joke. See the spic jump, hear him cry out. How fine it is to be a good strong stupid Prussian!

"You'll be in trouble," Pasquale said breathlessly, quite beyond fear, "when Signor Giustiniani hears of this."

The carriage had halted on the white gravel beyond the gate. Now the driver jumped down and walked back. He recognized Pasquale at once and broke into a broad grin. "The party is complete. And just in time, too. Tomorrow, we would not be here."

"Then you have the Spanish envoy with you."

The red-headed man laid a finger alongside his prominent nose and winked. "He's in the coach. I admire your balls, signor."

Pasquale snatched the papers from the guard and held them up like a shield. "Your master will want to see these. Salai has not told you the whole story."

The red-headed man shrugged. "I'm not the person you want to convince. Climb up on the board, and I'll take you straightway to my master." He turned, and told the guard, "Close the gate. There'll be no more visitors this night."

II

As before, light blazed from all the windows of the villa. In every room, glass chandeliers were filled with luminous tapers, like so many burning bushes slung under high plaster ceilings where friezes of putti and cherubs frolicked in buttocky profusion. When Pasquale entered the villa through double doors which stood wide open, following the red-headed servant and the Spanish envoy, he heard a woman laughing somewhere. The echo of her laughter floated across the entrance hall, where white marble statues posed under a pale blue ceiling. The laughter soared, breaking toward hysteria, and then stopped as abruptly as if a door had slammed upon it.

Pasquale realized that he had been holding his breath. He glanced at the red-headed servant, who merely smiled and said, "This way, if it please you, signors."

Many of the rooms through which the servant led Pasquale and the Spanish envoy—a straight-backed, taciturn man in ordinary red and black hose and doublet, and a leather tunic cinched by a belt with a big silver buckle—were empty, and the rest held only a scattering of furniture. In one room soldiers played dice before a massive fireplace, so intent on their gambling that they scarcely looked up as the three passed through. A fortune in books, a hundred or more, was stacked along the wall of another.

The door on the far side of this room was shut. There was, incongruously, a kind of door-knocker, in the form of a mask of tragedy, set square on its planks. The red-headed servant touched the lips of this mask lightly and reverently before opening the door and ushering in his two charges.

Pasquale stopped, struck again by fear. It seemed there was no end to fear.

The room was the same room in which Giovanni Francesco had been murdered. There was the same grate in the fireplace, in which logs burned with a fierce spitting sound; there was the same throne-like chair, its dark wood modeled with intricate carvings picked out in gold-leaf. And in the chair, as before, sat the Venetian magician, Paolo Giustiniani.

He wore a square black hat, a black robe embroidered with silk thread and slit to the waist up both sides, his hairy muscular legs bare beneath it. His feet were cased in black slippers with upturned toes. He turned to the two other people in the room so that his spare hawkish face was in profile to Pasquale and said, "As you see, the sending was successful. Now we are ready."

One of the men was Salai, who simply shrugged. The other, sitting upright and composed on a stool, his wrists manacled and laid in his lap, was Niccolò Machiavegli. He turned his quiet ironic smile to Pasquale, and Pasquale smiled back, his heart turning over with hope.

"Ill met again," Niccolò said, "although I hope you may find this interesting, Pasquale."

"Do not hope," the magician told Pasquale. His Tuscan was flavored with a heavy Venetian accent, with spitting *x*'s instead of *ch*'s. "There is no hope here, especially not for you."

The red-headed servant shut the door and leaned against it carelessly, smiling quite without malice at Pasquale.

The Spanish envoy began to protest, in a slow sonorous voice, that he was here on serious business, and business that had been paid for.

"Oh, give him what he wants and let's be done with it," Salai said. He stuck a cigarette between his meaty lips and bent to light it, then blew out a riffle of smoke with an impatient florish. He still wore his red velvet tunic, with a slim sword at his side. He added, "All this bores me."

"I am not here for your entertainment," the envoy said, with affronted dignity.

Salai bowed mockingly. "Forgive me, signor. The way you are dressed I believed that you were here for a masque."

"Be silent," Giustiniani said. He cupped his hands together, the left on top of the right. When he parted them, the device stood on the palm of his right hand. "This is yours, signor," he told the envoy, and the red-haired servant stepped forward and handed the flying device to the envoy with a flourish.

Giustiniani said, "Now, let us hear what the painter has to say." He had a way of holding up a hand when he spoke, to command attention. Pasquale didn't think much of this: if he was any kind of leader, a man should be able to command respect without tricks.

"Surely you know what he will say," Salai said,

"having drawn him here. Or was the funny business
with a mirror and burnt hair a charade?"

"It is all in earnest, as you will see," the magician
said. He pressed his hands together at his chest in a
mockery of prayer and told Pasquale, "Lay on, boy.
You have brought me a gift. Show these people what
it is."

Pasquale drew out the crumpled sheet of paper.
"Here, magister. This, for the life of Niccolò Machiavegli. The rest of it when we are released with
the body of Raphael."

"There must indeed be much written there."

"Salai did not tell you the truth. When he lost the
plates he also lost important information. The model
is not enough. You will also need these calculations,
of which I have brought you the first half. The rest,
as I said, on my release, together with my friend, and
the corpse."

The magician took the paper, glanced at it, and
handed it to Salai. "This is your master's writing?"

"It is," Salai admitted.

The magician took the paper back, and passed it
to the envoy.

Salai burst out, "But there is so much writing. The
old man does nothing but scribble scribble scribble.
One damn fat book after another. This could be anything, anything at all."

"Look at the bottom," Pasquale said steadily.
"You will need a mirror to read it easily."

The red-headed servant produced one and handed
it to the envoy, who used it to examine the cramped
backward writing. There, as Pasquale and Jacopo had
conspired to compose, and had patiently dictated to
the old man, was written, *This is the record of the
true calculations by which a man may fly using a*

*vertical screw to draw himself through the air. I, Le-
onardo, do so depose this.*

The envoy read this out. Salai spluttered a cloud
of smoke and protested, "A trick. Anyone with any
training as an artificer can build the device from the
model. There's no need for anything else, no need to
pay any other price. No need to trade with that, that
creature."

"Be still," the magician said. His voice rang out in
the room, and Pasquale felt his heart pause for a moment, as if obedient to this command.

Niccolò said, with amusement, "An interesting
problem." His eyes were glittering, and he sat forward in his chair, bright and inquisitive as a bird. The
chain which linked the iron cuffs of his shackles was
coiled in his lap.

"I delivered all that was requested," Salai said.
"Nothing was said about any papers. In any case,
they may not be the old man's."

The envoy said, "You said that the handwriting
was his."

"So I was wrong."

"You change your mind?" the envoy said. "It is
indeed a conveniently malleable thing."

The magician said, "The document was written by
a mathematician. Anyone else in Florence would use
the Roman system—they use it in accounts," he told
the envoy, "because it cannot be falsified by adding
extra signifiers to the end of a number. That's a
measure of how much they trust each other in Florence. But mathematicians use the more sensible Indian system, which is far more flexible. So here."

The envoy said to Salai, "*You* said nothing about
the need for any papers, signor. That is the point
here."

"Oh, exactly," Niccolò Machiavegli said. "Right

to the heart of the matter. You will trust the Great Engineer, or you must put your faith in the opinion of his catamite."

Salai made to strike Niccolò, and the red-headed servant stepped forward and caught Salai's wrist. Salai strove against this grip for a moment before wrenching free and turning away.

The envoy said, "Let them go. What need do we have of these two?"

"Ah," the magician said, "but I do need the corpse, as an altar, and it is no coincidence that this number has gathered here." He was sweating—the air in the room was heavy, as if freighted with a portentous unspoken word.

Pasquale thought of the picture he had rescued from the fire, and felt a chill.

The envoy said, "The body must not be returned. That was also the agreement."

"And I will keep it," the magician said. "As soon as the ceremony is done, signor, it shall be destroyed. That is, if it is not taken by the one I shall call. And he will come, this time. The time is right. I can feel it."

Salai started to laugh, but almost immediately fell silent. Everyone in the room was watching the magician, whose face was possessed by a kind of sick eagerness.

Pasquale said, feeling as if he were treading air— as an angel might feel, for an angel could never touch base earth, "All or nothing. Release us without the body, and the rest of the calculations will not be given to you."

"I think not," the magician said. "After all, why should we release you now, with a great matter at hand?"

Pasquale surreptitiously felt the device at his

wrist, and was surprised to find that less than half an hour had passed since he had hailed the guard. He'd done that earlier than planned, and there was still almost an hour before the attack would begin. He tried to make himself relax. He had plenty of time to treat with the magician. Even if he rescued only Niccolò, it would be a victory. Raphael was already dead. Nothing worse could happen to him, because the worst had already happened. Not even being the altar for a black mass was worse than being dead.

The Spanish envoy said to Salai, "If more information is needed, then you can be sure that we will not pay you, signor. Our agreement was for the whole, or nothing."

Salai said furiously, "It will work! I have told you that the model is all you need, no more and no less. This young fool is bluffing, that's all. Oh, perhaps he is brave. I will give him that. Perhaps he is given to fine motives, even. But for whatever reason, he's simply trying to pull the wool over your eyes. Kill him and be done with it. Take the papers he has, if you like. What do I care? They are worthless, you have my word on that. And even if they aren't, why then I will personally guarantee that I will get the rest, even if I have to kill the old man. I swear this."

"As for assassination, that would be a new commission," the Spanish envoy said. "I cannot negotiate with you on that point."

The magician said, "If I wanted the Great Engineer dead, I could send an invisible spirit that would blacken the air of the chamber while he slept, and suffocate him."

The envoy said with obvious distaste, "I'll not hear of such matters."

"You'll do a good deal more than *hear*," Salai said gloatingly.

The envoy said, very much on his dignity, "All I know, signor, is that you promised much, but it appears you may not have delivered all you promised."

Niccolò said to the envoy, "It's like the angel and the devil and the two doors. Do you know the story?"

The magician said, "We all do. Peace."

The Spanish envoy said, "Well, I don't. If it has a bearing on the matter I should like to hear it."

Salai threw his hands in the air and turned away.

Niccolò smiled and explained, "Imagine you are in a room, with two doors leading out, one to death, and one to freedom, and nothing to show which is which. In the room with you are an angel and a devil, and you can ask only one of them a single question. The devil, naturally, is given over to telling only lies, while the angel tells only the truth. Oh, and of course both are invisible, so you will not know which has answered. Now, which one question do you ask to make sure that you will escape with your life?"

The magician said, "No more puzzles. The matter is plain. You," he said to the envoy, "shall take Signor Machiavegli with you, as well as the papers this young artist so kindly carried here. If it is true that they are valuable, then I will act, without commission, as courier for the rest, in return for Signor Machiavegli's release. If not, then you may dispose of him as you will. In any event, you shall pay us as you agreed, or none shall leave here except those I choose."

Pasquale said, "That changes nothing! You must free my friend, Niccolò Machiavegli, and return the body of Raphael."

"But things *are* changed," the magician told him. He was not smiling, but he was amused. He steepled his long fingers together and regarded his nails. "What has changed is that you are here, and that you may return freely. Bring the rest of the papers and your friend goes free. If not . . ."

The envoy said, "If you will lend me two men, Signor Giustiniani, then it shall be done as you said. It does not exceed my powers. Although I will say that Admiral Cortés will not be pleased at the delay."

"I appreciate that you are a far-sighted man, signor."

The envoy said, "It is foresight that will win us the world. He who holds the key to the future has the power to hold history to ransom."

Niccolò said cheerfully, "I would say that he who holds that key will find himself under siege by those who want it."

The magician told Niccolò to be silent. "As for power," he said to the envoy, "you will see now how little temporal power matters. I have gathered you all here on this, Saturn's day, to assist me. To begin with, you must be robed."

The envoy started forward. "I'll have no part in any devilment!"

The red-headed servant caught him and put an arm around his throat, and held a knife to his eye when he started to struggle. The magician held a candle to the envoy's face and moved it slowly back and forth, all the while speaking in a low monotonous voice. When the servant released the envoy, Pasquale saw that tears were banked in the man's wide unblinking eyes, and that he trembled like a young tree in a gale.

"Does anyone else have an objection?" the magician said. He turned his level gaze to Pasquale, and then to Niccolò.

"Steady, Pasquale," Niccolò said.

"What does he want of us?"

"I believe he will call up a spirit, if he can. He has boasted that he will gain much power this night, and

I understand now that it is not from the Spanish. Are you frightened?"

"No spirit," the magician said, "but an angel. One of the seven archangels, in fact."

Salai giggled, "This is my beloved son, with whom I am well pleased."

"Beware," the magician said quietly. "This is a serious business. I believe you have an interest in angels, painter. Tell me, would you like to see one?"

Pasquale said, as steadily as he could, "I do not yet know if my imagination has failed me."

"Do you believe angels exist?"

For a moment, Pasquale's mouth flooded with the bitter-sour taste of the wrinkled leather button of the híkuri which Pelashil had fed him. He said, "Oh yes. Yes."

The magician smiled. "And if you would paint one, surely you should not turn from the chance to see one? What other painter could boast as much?"

Pasquale, remembering his broken panel, said, "Once I thought of nothing else. But things have changed."

"They will change again," the magician said. "You will obey me, painter, and you, Signor Machiavegli, or I shall be forced to control you too. Do not think I would not do it!"

The red-headed servant released Niccolò from his chain and lifted white linen robes from a chest, and handed out paper hats, of the kind that stonemasons wore to keep dust and chips from their hair. Under his instruction, Pasquale and Niccolò pulled them on. The servant dressed the Spanish envoy, then closed the shackles around Niccolò's wrists again. Pasquale obeyed with a heartsick eagerness. He seemed to be split into two parts. One part wished that he might see an angel; the other knew that this was dark, dark business, and that his very soul was in peril. It was one thing to imagine the face of an angel, quite another to be on the threshold of gazing into that face.

"Courage, Pasquale," Niccolò said.

Pasquale whispered, "Can he really call upon an angel?"

"He believes it. But if men such as he have powers such as they claim, why are they not ruling the world?"

"How do we know that they are not?"

"In secret, you mean." Niccolò considered this for a moment. "No prince can rule in secret, for even with cabbalistic powers he must at some stage manifest his will so that it may be carried out. No, even I do not believe such a secret conspiracy could exist."

"It's good to talk with you again, Niccolò."

"I'm sorry I can bring no comfort. I fear for both of us, Pasquale."

"No more than I," Pasquale said, thinking of the devices that Cardano commanded. He did not trust Cardano.

The magician girdled a long broad-bladed sword around his waist and took off his black cap, revealing that he was tonsured like a monk. "Now we begin," he said. "No one is to speak unless I tell him, not even you, Signor Machiavegli, nor will any of you move from his station."

He led them into the adjoining room. Its marble floor was marked with a huge design. It was drawn in red chalk. A five-pointed star was framed inside a circle, with a second circle drawn outside the first. Lesser circles were drawn inside the five triangles of the star, and in its center was a square of red cloth a yard on each side, with an ordinary ironwork brazier standing at one corner. In the margin between the circles strange symbols, as if of some hermetic mathematics, were carefully drawn. Pasquale recognized Roman lettering mixed up with Greek and Hebrew characters, but there was not a word or a name he knew, except for the astrological sign for Saturn at the top or north of the five-pointed star. At each point of the star burned a single fat candle of white beeswax half the height of a man. More candles stood at each corner of a kind of altar which stood in a lesser circle to the northeast of the main diagram. On the altar—

Pasquale gasped. He could not help it. Laid on the altar was the naked dead body of Raphael. His skin had been washed and shaved and was covered in red and yellow writing drawn with a kind of greasepaint. His hands were crossed on his hairless chest, and his blue-nailed fingers were wrapped around an inverted cross. A crucible sat in his groin.

The magician looked at Pasquale and with an ironic smile touched a finger to his lips, then held up the little leather pouch that hung around his neck, muttered a few words, and kissed it. It was an evil moment.

The close rich scent of the candles in the shuttered room was dizzying. The red-headed servant showed each man where to stand: Pasquale and Niccolò in the circles in the eastern and western arms of the five-pointed star, Salai and the somnolent Spanish envoy in the two southern arms. The servant handed a flask of brandy to Pasquale, and another of camphor to Niccolò, and told them that when instructed they were to shake as much liquid as a man's cupped palm might hold onto the brazier.

Meanwhile, the magician had folded up the red cloth in the center of the diagram, revealing a triangle drawn in the same red chalk as the rest, and bordered with ivy. He draped the folded cloth over his left shoulder and plunged his sword into the charcoal heaped in the brazier. It kindled with a muted crackle and immediately sent up a dense pungent white smoke.

The servant took up his position in the circle at the top of the diagram, and the magician used the tip of his sword to score the flagstones and close up the diagram.

"No one is to move," he repeated, and crossed back to stand by the brazier.

The room was slowly filling with smoke. It was at once sweet and acrid, and as dense as an artificers' smog. Pasquale felt a curious light-headedness. His fingers and toes tingled. At the magician's command, he shook brandy onto the coals of the brazier, and Niccolò added camphor. The servant set down a crucible, and blue flames licked up inside it.

The magician intoned, in Latin, "Hear me, Uriel! From this valley of misery and the misery of this valley, from this realm of darkness and the darkness of this realm, to the Holy Mount Sion and the heavenly tabernacles, I conjure you by the authority of God the Father Almighty, by the virtue of Heaven and of the stars, by that of the elements, by that of the stones and herbs, and in like manner by the virtue of snowstorms, thunder and winds, that you perform the things requested of you in the perfection of which you move, the whole without trickery or falsehood or deception, by the command of God, Creator of Angels and Emperor of the Ages!

"In the name of Emmanuel, in the name of Tetragrammaton Jehovah, in the name of Adonai, King of Kings, demonstrate to me your terrible power and give to me of your immeasurable largess. To this, I dedicate my altar."

The magician kissed his sword and plunged its tip into the crucible at the feet of his servant. At once, blue flames licked up its length. Holding it in front of him, the magician crossed the circle and touched the tip of the burning sword to the crucible set upon the groin of Raphael's corpse. Sparks and smoke sputtered up, and continued to fly upward as the magician carefully paced backward to his triangle.

The smoke was now so thick that Pasquale could hardly see the others, except as featureless shadows looming through a general whiteness. The sparks which flew up from Raphael's corpse seemed to sketch fleeting faces, some near, some far. They were wistful and stern, gay and grave. Pasquale was so drowsy with fear and with the effects of the smoke that the magician had to speak twice before he remembered to cast brandy on the glowing coals of the brazier.

The magician set his naked sword, which no longer burned, across the toes of his slippers. "I command and adjure thee," he intoned as solemnly as a priest at mass, "Uriel, great minister, by the power of the pact I have sealed with thee, and by the power of the armies that thou dost command, to fulfill my work. I call on thee, Pamersiel, Anoyr, Madrisel, Ebrasothean, Abrulges, Itrasbiel, Nadres, Ormenu, Itules, Rablon, Hamorphiel, you who command the twelve angels of the twelve tribes which govern kings and governments, from the fire through the thirty abidings to the ninety-one parts of the Earth, arise, arise, arise!"

For a moment, nothing happened. Then the entire villa shivered under three quick, heavy blows. The air in the room seemed to compress as if great wings were beating it, and the flame of the candle burning in front of Pasquale shivered and then flared up.

White smoke writhed before him, as if trying to take shape. For a moment a wild expectation lived in him, as bright as the candle-flame. Then, behind the heavy drapes, glass fell out of the tall windows with a ringing sound. A great wind filled the room and all the candles went out.

12

Pasquale knew at once that no angel had tried to manifest itself. He had been betrayed: Cardano had started the attack earlier than agreed. At any moment Pasquale expected to hear the sound of more missiles. There had been six of them, carried in straw-insulated cradles on the backs of the men, already heated so that the water inside had turned to steam, vigorously pressing for an exit. All that was needed to launch them was to open a valve.

"Stand fast," the magician shouted, but Salai was already at the curtains, peering around one edge. "It would seem that someone has set fire to your house," he said.

The servant came back, carefully closing the door behind him. Pasquale had not even seen him leave. Plaster-dust calcined his bush of red hair. "Rockets," he reported, "although there's no sign of the launch-frames, and no one saw their fires. The men are panicking. I should see to them."

And he was gone again.

Standing at the center of his ruined ceremony, the

349

magician brushed lime-dust from his black robe and looked at Pasquale with a grave calm. The big candles flickered around him, throwing his shadow across the far wall; the brazier's smoke poured around his feet, a spreading sea roiled by the air that blew in through the broken windows. The crucible set in the groin of Raphael's body still burned and sent up sparks, making a small but distinct crackling sound. The envoy was blinking hard, staring at his hands as he flexed his fingers.

"You are the Judas goat," the magician said, and raised his hand. He was suddenly holding a staff made of black ivory.

"I'll kill them now!" Salai sprang to Niccolò's side, drew his sword and held it to Niccolò's throat. Niccolò stood quite still, looking calmly and levelly at the magician as if challenging him, for all that he was chained and a moment from death.

The magician said, "Leave off, until we know the size of the force ranged against us. We may well need them alive, to bargain."

Salai shook his head so violently that his ringlets fluttered around his fat choleric face like a bush in a storm. "No!"

The magician flung out his hand and his staff promptly transformed into a black snake. Continuing the same motion, he threw the snake at Salai. Wild with fear, Salai slashed at the serpent with his sword, missed, and screamed and ran from the room.

The magician stooped and picked up the writhing serpent, and ran his thumb down its back. It went rigid. The magician shot his sleeves and then he was holding a black ivory staff again. There was a noise growing outside, a wild drumming and a mad ear-splitting skirl of pipes, as if made by men with arms of iron and throats of brass. Pasquale remembered the drumming machine, its bellows and weights and clockwork arms.

The envoy said, in the dazed manner of one suddenly awakened from a dream, "Are we surrounded?"

The magician said, "My men will fight free, with my help. You will take charge of this prisoner, signor, and follow me." He bent over Niccolò and brought his hands together. Niccolò's chains fell away from his wrists, leaving his hands bound by a device which locked his thumbs together.

Niccolò said calmly, "He who moves first in a battle is generally the victor."

The magician struck him with the back of his hand, so hard that the sound echoed in the smoke-and dust-filled room. "If you will live, you will follow me," he said, in a conversational voice.

Niccolò brought his head back and met Giustiniani's stare, a half-smile playing on his thin lips. "It's never wise to admit to losing the game," he said.

The magician turned on his heel and grabbed Pasquale by the arm. "Come," he said, and marched Pasquale out of the room without looking to see if the envoy and Niccolò followed.

The villa was filled with dust and smoke. The magician marched Pasquale through a series of empty rooms, past mercenaries running to and fro with bound chests or weapons or stacks of books. Clearly, they were preparing to retreat. One half of the entrance hall was afire, a fire that clung to the walls and the frames of the broken windows. The ceiling was down, filling the floor with lath and plaster, and most of the statues had fallen from their plinths. The fire filled the space with a strong dry heat and a great roaring noise and a piercing sweet smell: it was the smell of Greek fire, with which the hollow heads of the missiles had been filled, spilling and catching alight upon impact.

Heat scorched Pasquale's skin as he followed the magician outside. The shouts of the magician's men were mixed with the cacophony of the drumming machine. Vast, vague lights flickered beyond the boundary of the garden, and shadows moved within the lights. Some of the mercenaries were taking pot-shots, their muskets sounding as frail and harmless as twigs snapping in a fire. And indeed they could do no harm, for the shadows at which they fired were no more than that: shadows made to resemble the silhouettes of an army advancing against a background of brilliant lights.

Two men were hard put to hold the stamping horse which was harnessed to the black carriage. They were in silhouette against the fierce light that beat across the lawn, the light of the reflector lamps, each with spinning blades, which Taddei's men had mounted in the olive-grove.

As the magician started to hustle Pasquale down the wide marble steps toward the carriage there were three muffled thumps beyond the wall and the arched gate. Pasquale flinched, but the magician kept him upright by main force, so that he saw the three vapor trails as the steam-powered missiles flung their arcs through the black air. One struck the crown of the gate with a dissonant clang and enveloped it in a ball of orange fire. The other two rose higher, and Pasquale glimpsed their fat shapes turning like fish in the black air as they came down. One burst harmlessly amongst trees, but the other smashed through the roof of the villa. A moment later a ball of fire shot into the air. The horse, maddened by this, reared and plunged. It broke its traces and galloped away around the corner of the villa, dragging its handler behind it.

Down the line of the road to the gate, the griffin stirred on its plinth. Perhaps someone had activated it, or perhaps the shock of the explosion had jarred its mechanism. It rose on stiff legs, eyes glaring red, then started shivering in a kind of mechanical palsy. Steam burst from its joints, from the ruff around its neck. Its beak spasmed, chattering like the teeth of an idiot. Jets of vapor spurted from hidden vents, raising a great cloud that was driven upward by the heat of the burning villa and the burning gate. This mist refracted the lights beyond the wall, so that things took on the aspect of a small grainy dawn suspended in the deep night.

The magician's men were firing in the direction from which the steam-driven missiles had come, running to and fro in the glare of the lights, their shadows thrown in overlapping confusion over the lawn. Some used muskets or crossbows; others whirled slingshots around their heads, hurling glass globes into the glaring lights. But Pasquale had warned of this tactic, and Taddei had equipped his mercenaries with charcoal masks. A stilt-man tottered across the lawn, gaining speed, and plunged into the shrubbery. A moment later there was an eruption of fire and a fountain of bits of burning bush.

Giustiniani drew Pasquale close. He suddenly had a knife in his hand. It had a twisted blade with red characters printed on it. The magician spoke directly in Pasquale's ear, his clove-scented breath feathering Pasquale's cheek. "How many men, and what disposition? Tell me now."

"No more than seven, magister."

The point of the knife pricked the soft skin just

beneath Pasquale's left eye. Pasquale could not help
but flinch.

The magician wound his hand in Pasquale's hair,
and pulled his head back so that he was looking up
at the black sky. "You will tell the truth, painter, or
first you will lose this eye, and then the other."

"A hundred at least! They surround the place,
magister!"

"Is this the city militia?"

The knife-point withdrew slightly. "No, magister.
They are the private army of the merchant Taddei."

"I know the name. A friend of Raphael."

"He wants the body, magister."

The magician said grimly, "He can have yours instead."

"He calls on demons, as you have seen."

"My magic will defeat his," Giustiniani said.

One of the cedar-trees at the edge of the firelit lawn
began to shake its lowest tier of branches. The magician turned just as a shadow flung itself from the
tree and shot across the lawn. Mercenaries scattered
in panic, unable to shoot at the apparition for fear of
wounding each other.

The magician flung Pasquale away and raised his
arms above his head. Gas suddenly whirled up from
a scattering of brief detonations in front of him. It
was yellow, acrid and choking. Pasquale reeled back
as the ape—it was Ferdinand—shot through this
cloud. It danced from side to side and beat the ground
with its fists. Its eyes redly reflected the fire behind
the magician.

The magician stepped back and, with a flourish,
produced his black ivory staff. Pasquale shouted a
warning just as the magician threw his arm forward.
The snake struck the ape in its throat, and it rolled
over and over, gripping the thrashing snake by its

head and tail. Pasquale ran to the ape just as it flung the broken-backed snake away. It kicked out and quivered, all its muscles in tetany. It could not breathe, and all Pasquale could do was hold its horny-palmed hand as it suffocated.

"Thus I destroy all demons," the magician screamed, and then he was running. He grabbed a passing mercenary, shouted something at him and pushed him on, ran to grab the next. He was trying to marshal his resources, running to and fro amongst his scattered troops, his white legs flashing through the slits in his black robe.

Pasquale closed Ferdinand's eyes, as if the ape had been a man, and turned away. His eyes filled with tears. Some great grief was threatening to wrench itself free inside him, if he would let it. Then hope returned, for the second time in as many minutes. A figure emerged from the burning villa, one arm flung up to shield his face. The man tottered down the steps and fell to his knees, and Pasquale ran toward him. It was Niccolò, soot-stained and scorched but otherwise unharmed.

Pasquale got him to his feet and they staggered a little way across the lawn. Its grass was withering in the heat. The mechanism that animated the griffin had jammed. It stood in a half-crouch with one paw raised, its mouth clacking emptily on wisps of vapor. Pasquale and Niccolò took shelter by its plinth, and Niccolò explained with a smile that the envoy had wisely decided to look after his own self.

"He has what he wants, after all. The device, and the papers you brought. That was a brave bit of trickery, Pasquale."

"You saw through it!" Pasquale had to shout to make himself heard over the drumming and the rifle-fire.

"Salai was forced to tell the truth, yet no one believed him. A pleasing irony."

"And the envoy really let you go free?"

"Let us say I slipped away in the confusion."

"And your shackles dissolved."

"Oh no. I took the key from Signor Giustiniani when he hit me. While it seemed that he released the chains by sleight of hand, he of course used a key. By my own sleight of hand, I took it from him, and then used it to open the device which locked my thumbs together." Niccolò looked about him. "I believe it is time to leave. What is the plan?"

Pasquale said, "Taddei would have us die, I think. This attack came far sooner than we agreed. Perhaps we should stay where we are."

"How many men out there?"

"Seven."

"No more than that?"

"The Great Engineer supplied certain devices."

"In that case we have little to fear from those attacking."

Pasquale saw movement in the flames that engulfed the broken arch of the gate. He said, "Don't be too sure."

The device emerged from the burning gate with patches of fire clinging to its burnished hide. It was the utilitarian cousin of Taddei's jeweled tortoise: a thing the size of a hunting-dog, with a dome of steel plates no more than a couple of *braccia* high. It marched forward on a dozen stumpy legs. Rifle-shot rang on its hide as the mercenaries turned their attention to it. Then it stopped. Pairs of spring-driven shafts shot out on either side and began to lift it above the gravel road.

Pasquale pulled at Niccolò's arm and told him to run for it. They had made the corner of the villa when the device exploded and sent discs of sharp-edged metal scything across the lawn. Wounded and dead mercenaries toppled even as another device marched through the burning gate and bumped into the remnants of its fellow and went off prematurely, discharging most of its explosion into the ground, vanishing in a burst of earth and broken metal.

Niccolò said, "I've always held that man will never rise to grace until his capacity for creation equals that for destruction!" He was dangerously exhilarated, his black eyes gleaming with more than firelight. "With just a handful of those devices a single man could destroy an army!"

"If we are not careful they may destroy us."

"There'll be a way out of here, you can depend upon it."

"How can you be so sure?"

Niccolò grinned. "Quite simply because Giustiniani would not live in a house with only one entrance and exit from its grounds. Look there! Come on, Pasquale! We have but one chance now!"

The red-headed servant was running in the opposite direction to the surviving mercenaries, who were fanning out across the lawn under the direction of the magician, advancing upon the shadow-play of forces beyond the wall. The magician was making war on demons, finally caught up in his own system of sleight of hand and illusion—for after all, had he not just defeated a demon which had attacked him? He brandished his ebony staff and it ran with blue flames. Pasquale knew then that the snake had been a snake all along, produced by a trick, although this brought no consolation. The real snake had been as deadly as if it had been magical—perhaps more so.

Niccolò gave chase to the red-headed servant and Pasquale picked himself up and followed. They ran past the mechanical griffin. Its head had been blown away by the explosion of the walking cannon, and the ragged stump of its neck erupted a jet of steam. Pasquale told Niccolò to circle to the right, and he himself ran off to the left. They closed on their quarry, who had stopped to kick at the plinth of a statue of a nude woman with the shaggy, horned head of a goat.

The statue abruptly rolled backward. The servant glanced behind him and saw that Pasquale and Niccolò were almost upon him. He drew a pistol but hesitated as to which man to shoot. That was enough for Pasquale to run straight at him and knock him to the ground. Niccolò snatched up the pistol and aimed it at the servant with shaking hands. "Bravely done, Pasquale," he said. "You see, we have our exit."

The plinth was hollow. The statue had moved back to reveal stone steps that descended down into the ground.

The servant grinned up at Niccolò. Blood ran from one corner of his mouth, but he paid it no mind. "If you're going to threaten me with that pistol, you'll need to cock it first," he said.

Niccolò eased the brass lever with his thumb. The pistol was the same pan-loading multiple-action type he had carried on the first expedition to the villa. He told the servant to stand up and move aside.

The man clasped his hands on his bush of red hair but stayed where he was. "If you were going to shoot me, why, you would have done so. Let me show you the way out. It is as tricky as the way in."

Niccolò said, a touch wildly, "I have shot at men before, and have no desire to shoot at you, but I will if pressed."

Pasquale said to the servant, "He means that you

should lead on, although why we should trust a man who is bent on betraying his master is beyond me."

"There's no more profit to be had here, that's for sure." A stray musket-ball cracked past overhead. Niccolò and Pasquale ducked reflexively, but the servant stood straight, hands still on his head. He added, "In fact, profit is about to become a loss. May I take my hands down? The passage is not particularly easy."

When the three men reached the bottom of the steps, the statue ground back over the opening. Little beads of blue flame sprang up in scattered niches. The passage was scarcely half Pasquale's height, dry, and lined with bricks. The servant led the way, and Pasquale brought up the rear, with Niccolò breathing hard between.

Halfway along, the passage made a U-shaped loop—to trap any besiegers who discovered it and tried to make use of it, the servant explained cheerfully. They had to wait there while something made giant footfalls overhead, shaking loose thin streams of dirt from the unmortared joints of the bricks.

The servant remarked, "A fine tomb this place would make."

"You may yet put that to the test," Niccolò said.

In the light of the blue pinpoint flames, scarcely brighter than starlight, Pasquale could just see the servant's white face over Niccolò's shoulder. The man was smiling, as cozy as a rat in its burrow. He said, "What was the answer to that riddle about the devil and the angel? I've been turning it over and can't see an answer to it. Make an end to my torture."

"Signor," Niccolò said, suddenly very much on his dignity, "it is but a pinprick to the humiliations and trials which your master has put me through this past day. Let it rattle your brains. I'll get little enough joy from the thought, but it's more than I expected."

The servant laughed. "You have me at pistol-point. I'm sure that's more satisfying. As for your hurts, I was following orders, as you well know."

It suddenly came to Pasquale in the sideways fashion that answers to puzzles often did. He said, "You ask what door the other spirit would recommend. It is the only question to which both will answer in the same way."

The servant laughed again. "Ah, then the devil will lie, and recommend the door of destruction, knowing the angel would lead you to safety. But the angel, the angel . . ."

"I'm not surprised that you cannot understand the minds of angels," Niccolò said. "Despite that your master would call one up, if he could."

Pasquale said, "The angel also points to the door to death, knowing that the devil would recommend it, and so both spirits will answer the question in the same way, and you may escape by taking the other door. I'm sorry, Niccolò, I only just now understood."

Niccolò said, "Listen."

"I don't hear anything," Pasquale said, after a moment.

"Precisely. The war has moved on. So should we."

After the tight bend, the roof of the passage was a little higher. It ended at another stair, rising up to a small square ceiling.

The servant put his fingers to his lips and winked. "My master that was would tell you that it's all done by incantations, and the binding of demons. In fact it's simple hydraulics, as I'll demonstrate."

He shifted half a dozen bricks from the wall. Reaching inside with both hands, he turned something with a deal of effort. There was a rushing noise underfoot, the noise of water evacuating a reservoir. The ceiling that stopped the stairs ground aside, and the servant took the steps three at a time. Pasquale gave chase after him, afraid that the man would escape, or turn at the top and seal them in. But when he clambered out, he discovered the servant sitting on the shelf of rock which had stopped the hole in the heathy ground, the ankle of one leg crossed on the knee of the other. He seemed quite at ease, as if being captured and forced to reveal the bolt-hole were part of his plans all along.

They had emerged about a hundred *braccia* from the verge of the road which ran along one side of the villa's wall. Inside the wall, fire made a welter of orange light and red shadow. The villa was ablaze from end to end, and those trees nearest it had caught fire too, tossing harvest after harvest of sparks into the black air. Near at hand, blue flames of Greek fire clung to the ruins of the gate. The lights of the Great Engineer's devices, on the far side of the burning villa, dimmed by the blaze, crossed and recrossed in the sky, while the noise of the automatic drumming came and went on the hot wind, mixed with the fainter shouts of the beleaguered mercenaries. Suddenly, a great red smoke rose within the walls. As it rose it grew into the shape of a leering demon, but then air rushing to feed the fires took it and tore it apart.

"Just about the last trick," the servant remarked. "You gentlemen may run along. I've one loose end to deal with, and for that I'd like my pistol back."

Niccolò said grimly, "I would be quite glad to let you go, signor, except that you were a witness to what happened. We shall need you as proof of the schemes of Giustiniani, and of the fate of Raphael's body. On that still hangs a war."

The red-headed servant stood. "Why, signor, that's hardly enough to hold me. The corpse is your concern, not mine. As for being a witness, you forget that I was responsible for Raphael's death. I'll not be a witness to my own execution warrant."

"All the more reason for you to be a witness," Niccolò said grimly. "You have been a willing accomplice to this devilry, signor. Hanging is the least of it. We burn witches in this city, and will burn you if you do not cooperate."

"I've already survived one attempt to burn me," the servant said, "so you'll excuse me if I do not tempt fate and put myself forward for a second go-round."

He stepped forward, and only smiled more widely when Niccolò raised the pistol. Then he reached out, and Niccolò snarled and pulled the trigger. There was only a dry click. The servant moved in a rush, turned Niccolò around and jerked his arm up behind his back so that he had to let go of the weapon.

Pasquale managed to land a blow on the servant's head that sent him staggering, but when he pressed his attack a swipe of the pistol clipped him on the corner of a cheek. Pasquale reeled back, and the servant sprang upon the flat rock. He flipped off the pistol's empty pan, jammed on a new one, and fired once into the air.

Pasquale and Niccolò exchanged a look. Pasquale's own warm blood coursed down the side of his jaw and dripped from his chin. The wound was just beginning to hurt.

Pasquale said, "The game's not worth our lives, Niccolò. Leave him."

The servant bowed mockingly, then raised a slim

whistle, the kind the municipal swineherds used to summon their charges from roaming the city cloaca. He blew a single piercing note. A man stepped from a clump of trees that stood on a rise off toward the olive-grove through which Pasquale and Taddei's men had approached the villa. He made his way toward them slowly, and before he was halfway there, Pasquale recognized the Spanish envoy.

"That's far enough I think," the servant called, and raised the pistol.

Pasquale saw the envoy's expression change to astonishment. He reached for something in the pouch at his belt and as he brought his hand up the servant shot him three times in rapid succession. The envoy sat down with a sudden rush. The servant took careful aim and fired again. The envoy's head snapped back and he fell over, and with his last moment of life he set free the thing he'd taken from his pouch.

It was the device. Pasquale saw it quite clearly as it rose into the night, even imagined he could hear the whir of its bands unwinding—but that was impossible, for the drums, the drums, the drums were still beating off in the distance and the fires were roaring, and the magician's mercenaries were shouting and shooting at the shadow-show.

The servant ran out across the heath, leaping and snatching at the device as it fluttered higher, suddenly not borne by its flexing wings but by the wind that fed the fires. It flew sideways, on a rising curve. For a moment it seemed that it would rise above the flames which clung to the ruined gateway, but then the gust of air failed, and the device dipped and instantly kindled. A burning scrap made lighter by its burning, it rose again, a feather on the breath of God whirling high above the destruction. And went out.

The servant had reached the margin of the road, and was staring up at where the device had vanished, as if it might suddenly reappear like the phoenix. As he turned toward Pasquale and Niccolò there was a flat crack and he stumbled and pitched forward.

At first Pasquale supposed he had tripped, but when he did not rise Pasquale knew that he had been shot. He tugged Niccolò's sleeve and made him crouch in the dubious cover of a clump of wiry grasses. A figure was making its way along the road to where the servant had fallen. Suddenly, Pasquale realized who it must be, for no one else would have brought the ape. He stood up and waved and shouted, for all that Niccolò cursed him as a fool, telling him that Taddei would as soon have both of them dead.

But the person on the road had already turned to them. Pasquale ran forward. It was a woman. It was Pelashil.

13

Pasquale, Pelashil and Niccolò Machiavegli made a long way of it back toward the river. They did not trust the road, for Pelashil said that men were waiting there for any who escaped—she had seen them take a fat man in red, which must be Salai, and force him into a carriage. Pasquale asked if one was a priest, or wore robes, and Pelashil said, "Yes, and a hood, and a big cross, here." She placed a hand between her small breasts.

"It's as I thought," Pasquale said. "Cardano is the Savonarolistas' man."

Niccolò said, "Then Fra Perlata escaped. I wasn't sure in the confusion, when the ferry struck the shore and Giustiniani's men swarmed aboard."

Pasquale dabbed at his bloody cheek with his sleeve. "Once they find that Salai doesn't have the device, they'll be looking for us. We can't stay here."

They stumbled across the heath with the burning villa at their backs and the tower of the church of Santo Spirito rising against the scattered lights of the city ahead of them. Pelashil went arm in arm with

Pasquale. The long hunting-rifle was slung over her shoulder, its octagonal barrel rising a full *braccio* above her head. She knew he would need help, she said: Piero had seen it in a dream, and so she had brought the ape, intending to break into the grounds and use him as a distraction. But when the ape had seen the lights and the fire, and heard the strange noises, he had broken his chain and jumped the wall.

"He found me anyway," Pasquale said, and told her how Ferdinand had died.

There was more to the story, Pelashil said. She had seen a broadsheet with Pasquale's likeness upon it, and Piero had told her what it meant. It seemed that Pasquale was wanted for the murder of his master, Giovanni Battista Rosso. "But that matters not in the least," Pelashil said cheerfully. "You are set on the right road at last."

Pasquale walked on in silence. He was numb. It didn't stop, was all he could think. It was not like the chivalric stories of heroes who slew monsters and brutes or sought the Grail, and after they succeeded there was an end to their labors, and a reward. A woman's hand and rightful ascension to the throne, the Grail found, and Heaven with it.

"Taddei will be behind it," Niccolò remarked. "The last of the scandal has been diverted upon your head, Pasquale. Of course, he did not expect you to survive this holocaust, and so you would not be an inconvenient witness at your own trial."

"So I thought," Pasquale said at last. He turned to Pelashil. "Perhaps you will come with me. I was trying to tell you before that there may be a way—"

"I already have a master—"

"After this? You are your own master, or mistress, it would seem. Pelashil, I can take you back to your home. Piero hardly knows you are there. He wants to be alone. That is his fear: fear of the other. Thunder, crowds, anything not inside his head. He is even frightened of me, and I would be his pupil if he would allow it."

"I have my life here," Pelashil said. "Piero took me in, and taught me when my own people would not. I look after him. He teaches me, so that I will be a mara'akame. Is that simple enough for you?"

"I wouldn't steal you from him. I ask only because I don't believe that you are his slave."

Pelashil let go of his hand and said angrily, "Why do men understand nothing? I stay with him because I want to. No one owns me. I am not his slave, nor his wife. I look after him because I want to. Yes, he's frightened of me, of many things, but he is a great and skilful mara'akame, and a better painter than you will ever be. There is a reason, if you need one."

"I'm frightened of you, too," Pasquale said.

"Good."

"I didn't even know you could shoot."

"The old man taught me. In my country, before I came here. Before he came back to this terrible city."

Pasquale discovered that he did not want to know, as he had often wanted to ask, whether she had ever slept with Piero. He said, "All I know has died in the city. What hold has it on me now? Rosso was right after all. If I had agreed to go to Spain with him he would be alive, and so many others too."

Niccolò had prudently walked a little way ahead of them while they argued, but now he stopped and they caught up with him. He said, "You may have your wish. Or rather, it may be that Spain will come to you."

They had reached the crest of the slope. A road ran downhill, gathering houses around it as it descended toward the docks. The city spread on either side, and in every part of the city green and red sparks were making small precise movements.

Pasquale asked Niccolò, "What are they saying?"

"If you're patient, perhaps I'll be able to tell you in a moment. They are all sending the same message, in plain talk . . . Well," Niccolò said flatly, "it is to be war. What a comedy of errors, eh, Pasquale?"

"So we did nothing in the end, except what we thought was right." It did not seem unexpected. Pasquale found that he felt nothing, not even disappointment.

Niccolò said kindly, "Perhaps we made a difference, although we should not know it. It would be gross egotism to imagine otherwise. Only princes affect the course of history, Pasquale, and with your pardon, I do not believe any of us are that."

"Except the Great Engineer."

"He was once a prince, perhaps. But even princes have their day, and I think he had his long ago, in the war against Rome. His devices won that, but someone else must win this."

Pasquale saw lights move on the river. The great ocean-going *maona* was preparing to warp out of its dock, a bank of lights looming beyond the prickly masts of the smaller vessels, supplemented by the small, luminous comma of the churning wake of a paddle-wheel tug.

"Come on," he said. "I only have this one chance," and started to run. And as he ran, gathering exhilaration lifted his heart. It didn't matter if his plea had been delivered by Jacopo or not, or even if it had been answered. All that mattered was the hope, the chase. He stopped at the bottom of the hill, breathing like a Hero's engine, and when Niccolò and Pelashil caught up he led them on down to the river, following a muddy path between the tall chandlers' shops and warehouses that looked out over the docks. People crowded the floating stage of the dock. The ship lay a little way beyond. The tug was laboriously turning it toward the lock that would let it gain the channel of the Grand Canal. As Pasquale fought his way through the crowd, he saw a flash of silver above the packed heads of the crowd. It was the polished armor of the Great Engineer's servant, Jacopo, who was standing on the roof of a carriage and looking this way and that.

When Pasquale, with Pelashil and Niccolò following, won through to the carriage, Jacopo jumped down from its roof and opened its door. "She would speak with you," he told Pasquale, smiling.

"And I hope with me," Niccolò said.

Lisa Giocondo was waiting inside, her face glimmering in the light of a scented taper—the only light in the carriage, for its window-shades were drawn. Pasquale and Niccolò sat opposite her on the plush bench, but Pelashil paused at the door, shook her head and turned away.

Niccolò said, "No doubt you would hear all that has fallen out since we last spoke."

Lisa Giocondo folded her long fingers together. Her heavy musk filled the little carriage; as before, she wore a net veil, lifted up from her face. She said, "No doubt you would enjoy telling me all, Signor Machiavegli, but there is little enough time for that now. All I would know is whether my husband was involved."

"It was the Venetian magician Paolo Giustiniani who killed Raphael," Pasquale said. "Signor Taddei has evidence that it was a servant of Giustiniani who administered the poison, and he will find the body of that servant by the gate of Giustiniani's villa."

Lisa Giocondo made a breathy sigh. She said, "Then I am in your debt."

"As to that," Niccolò said, smiling his slight, closed smile, "I would have words with your innocent husband, signora. I have seen the declaration of war made from every signal-tower in the city, and would seek to serve as I once served."

"I will do what I can, but you must understand that I have only a little influence with my husband. You must convince him of your worth."

"Readily," Niccolò said eagerly.

Lisa Giocondo pressed a docket into Pasquale's hands, telling him that two places had been reserved as promised. "Although it cost me dear. This may be the last ship to leave before war breaks out. Did I see a woman outside—your wife, perhaps?"

"Not yet," Pasquale said, blushing. "Perhaps never. She still has a duty here. Niccolò, unless you will come with me, I must make my farewell."

"You needn't worry about me," Niccolò said. "The broadsheets will all be closed, but the Signoria will need an experienced voice to calm the populace. War is a way of life, Pasquale. There has been war, there is war, there will be war again, as long as there are states which strive against each other. War is but another kind of politics, or perhaps its purest expression, for its springs fully armed from the cardinal vice of ambition. All states desire peace, but any state which renounces war will at once find itself besieged by its neighbors. So I do not fear it, just as I do not fear the weather."

"I'll miss you, Niccolò. You are comforted by the strangest things."

Niccolò laid a finger alongside his nose. "Florence is ready for war, and that is the first necessary thing on the road to victory. And unlike Spain, the citizens control the military, which is the second. The Republic will survive, and grow greater."

Lisa Giocondo smiled at this, and Pasquale told the journalist, "You're already writing the propaganda, Niccolò. Just say farewell."

Niccolò grasped Pasquale's shoulders and kissed him like a brother, and said with a quick smile, "We won't meet again, Pasquale, but I hope that I will hear of your adventures. Go now. You have a ship to catch."

Pelashil and Jacopo were waiting outside. Pasquale told Jacopo, "Your master will be pleased that the device is no more."

"I'll tell him. And Salai?"

"The Savonarolistas have him. Taddei's astrologer, Cardano, is one of their number, and turned the attack on Giustiniani to their advantage. It was only by a stroke of fortune that the flying device was destroyed before it could fall into their hands."

"The news will break my master's heart, but in my opinion he's well rid of the little shit." Jacopo looked past Pasquale's shoulder at Pelashil. "This is the woman you're taking?"

Pasquale blushed again. "She is staying."

Jacopo said, "I suppose I should be surprised that there are limits to your powers of persuasion. My master asks me to give this to you. You'll need to buy wine and provisions for the voyage. You can do that at Livorno, although you'll have to pay through the nose."

Pasquale weighed the small bag of coins. "I wish I could thank your master."

"He is safely in his tower, thinking of ways to deal with Salai. He is a fool for a pretty face, Pasquale. I'm glad you won't be around to abuse his notion that you are some kind of angel. This way now, quickly."

"But the ship—"

"What would you do, swim to it? Signora Giocondo has arranged a ferry for you, at no little expense. I won't ask what favor she is returning—it must be considerable."

A small landing-stage floated on the river's flood beyond the berths of the large ships, guarded by two men-at-arms. A small boat was tied up at its end. Its master sat with his back against a mooring-post that slanted above his head. He was an old man, whiskery and wrinkled, one eye white-capped and half-hidden by a drooping eyebrow. He was wrapped in a blanket against the chill of the water, and smoking a cigarette which he pinched between two fingers and stowed behind his ear before clambering aboard his craft.

Before he boarded this leaky shell, Pasquale dared to hug Pelashil, who after a moment unbent to return his embrace.

She said into his ear, "You know that my people are the Wixarika, that they live in the mountains to the north and west of the empire of the Mexica. It is difficult to reach, Pasquale, for there are many canyons and other deep places, but if you follow your path you will find small villages of round houses, each with a kalihue where the mara'akate dance, and fields of maize all around."

"Pelashil, I've heard Piero talk about this a hundred times."

"Yes, and how much do you believe?"

"I'll believe what I see."

"We say that one day all will be as we see it in Wirikuta, in the place we go to hunt the híkuri. The First People will come back and the sun will grow dimmer and the moon brighter, until there is no difference. All will be one. Until then, we stand between the world of the sun and the dreams of the moon. Remember that, Pasquale."

Jacopo said, "The boatman can't row faster than the ship. If you want to board it, you'll have to go now."

As the boat was pushed out, and the boatman unshipped his oars, Pelashil called out across the widening watery gap, "Send your first picture back, Pasquale, so that I know you are alive! Piero won't live forever!"

And then she turned away, Jacopo following, and Pasquale saw them no more. The ship was moving slowly into the lock at the entrance to the Grand Canal, and Pasquale saw that his was not the only boat going out to meet her. She had undocked hours early, it turned out, to make open sea before the Spanish blockaded the canal. Many had no dockets, and Pasquale had to hold his up and call out Lisa Giocondo's name over and over until at last a knotted rope was dropped and he climbed aboard.

It was morning, and the ship was already being towed through the wide channel beyond Livorno, amid a flotilla of small craft bearing merchants who were doing good business selling fresh fruit, clothing, mirrors, beads and other trinkets (for bargaining with the Savages), guns (which must at once be handed in to the armorer) and much else, when Pasquale was finally given a berth. It was no more than a chalked space two *braccia* by four, with a little locker at its head where Pasquale could stow away the necessaries he had bought from the floating merchants and from the quartermaster, a dour fat man who had his office in the black bowels of the ship. The passenger hold was marked out with half a hundred such spaces, but no one was asleep. Along with everyone else, Pasquale leaned at the rail of the ship's promenade, at her waist beneath the raised platform where the captain stood beside the steersman. Pasquale felt a strange thrilling excitement, looking amongst his fellow passengers and wondering which would be his friends, whether any enemies would be made, or lovers found amongst them on the long voyage to the New World.

The merchants' craft fell behind. The paddle-wheeled tug cast off its lines and slowed, so that the ship drew abreast of it, and then it too fell astern. Ahead was a widening line, the hard blue sea under a clear sky.

Pasquale carried under his arm a board with a cover of oiled cloth, and two bands to hold paper down against the wind. He had kept his silverpoint pen through all his adventures, and his little knife, and blocks of chalk. Paper and more chalk was to be had from the quartermaster at a price. But he was not ready. Not yet. He was sure that there was money to be made from sketching portraits of his fellow voyagers, but not yet. He was still filled with tumbling images from his adventures. There was the burning gate and the trees caught afire, the burning bridge and the luminous stained-glass window shivered to pieces around him, the puzzled fading gaze of the dying ape and Lisa Giocondo's smile, the wry wise face of his friend and Pelashil's fierce, scornful independence . . . And gathering form from all this, although he would not yet admit it, were the lineaments of something more than human and less, something that, poised between the world of thought and the world of things, between Word and Act, might possibly be (for how could he ever again be certain of anything?) the fierce luminous wondering face of his angel.

Also by Mary Morris

PICADOR USA   NEW YORK

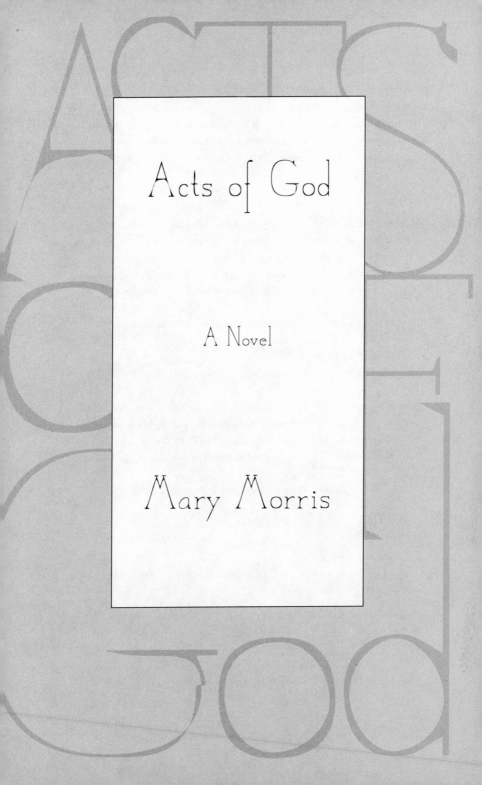

Acts of God

A Novel

Mary Morris

AUTHOR'S NOTE: This book is a work of fiction. Winonah is a made-up place and its inhabitants are characters from the author's imagination. Any resemblance to actual locales, events, or persons, living or dead, is entirely coincidental.

Picador® is a U.S. registered trademark and is used by St. Martin's Press under license from Pan Books Limited.

Book design by Victoria Kuskowski

Grateful acknowledgment is given to quote from "Small World" by Stephen Sondheim and Jule Styne. © 1959 Norbeth Productions Inc. and Stephen Sondheim. Copyright renewed. All rights administered by Chappell & Co. All rights reserved. Used by permission of Warner Bros. Publications U.S. Inc., Miami, Florida 33014.

Library of Congress Cataloging-in-Publication Data
Morris, Mary.
  Acts of God : a novel / Mary Morris.—1st ed.
    p. cm.
  ISBN 0-312-24663-3
    1. Family reunions—Fiction. 2. Suburban life—Fiction. 3. Friendship—Fiction.
  4. Women—Fiction. I. Title.

PS3563.O87445 A615 2000
813'.54—dc21

00-033986

First Edition: September 2000

10 9 8 7 6 5 4 3 2 1

This book is dedicated to the Elm Place Gang and Jane Supino

and Paige Simpson—Illinois girls all.

To D.R. for the memories, to Miss Dorsch for the lessons,

and Larry and Kate for the rest.

*In little towns, lives roll along
so close to one another;
loves and hates beat about,
their wings almost touching.*

—WILLA CATHER, *Lucy Gayheart*

1

My father used to say that sometimes you think you know a person, only to find out that you don't. That life, when it comes to people, is full of surprises. I've found this to be true. You think you understand someone, only to realize that you didn't. That you were wrong all along. Perhaps this is why I have chosen to live in such a remote place—a ramshackle house on a spit of land on the Pacific Coast.

Friends who live elsewhere tell me—and they may be right—that this California coast isn't a place where anyone can live. That it is meant to slide, collapse, or drift out to sea. But I'm not uncomfortable on the edge of disaster; I'm not uneasy being where it might all fall apart. My father, who sold insurance for a living, also had a sense of taking risks and this was one of the things he imparted to me.

For years I've led a straightforward life. No wild parties, no mad flings. Still, sometimes I drive too fast along the Coast Highway. And I run in the mountains where cougar roam. Cougar, my son, Ted, likes to remind me, are predatory animals and they will stalk you to your front door, knock it down, and eat you in your own kitchen. I know I shouldn't drive fast or run alone where cougar dwell, but I take these small chances—these little risks. They don't seem so bad and, after all, this is why I have chosen to be in this part of the world.

Otherwise my life has been stable. One marriage, one divorce, two kids. Until recently I didn't seem to want anything big to happen, having felt that enough had happened to last me a lifetime. What I needed now was peace and quiet. I was fairly close to this California version of Nirvana when the first invitation arrived. It was slipped under my door on a sun-drenched morning when I was out on my run. I must have stepped over it as I came in.

The air had a sweetness to it that day and I'd gone way up into the hills, then jogged down to the shore, where the yellow ice plant bloom. I followed the beach for a mile or so, the waves crashing at my feet. Then I climbed the dunes home. I have my routine. Walk in the door, grab a water bottle from the fridge and a towel from the drawer. Cool off, then shower.

I was taking gulps of cold water and wiping my face when I noticed the envelope lying on the floor. The envelope had a cat's face printed in the upper-right-hand corner and in blue lettering, "Home of the Winonah Wildcats." The mail doesn't come until after noon so I knew it must have gone to Betsy, my nearest neighbor. I hardly know Betsy except to wave, but often, for reasons neither of us can comprehend, we get each other's mail.

It was handwritten (a nice touch, I thought), addressed to me— Theadora Antonia Winterstone. A mouthful, I know. More name than a person like me needs but there you have it. When I was growing up, nobody called me by all those names. I was Theadora to my teachers, Tess to my acquaintances, Tessie to my friends, Squirrel to my family.

In my family we all had nicknames. We were, looking back until a certain moment, a happy family. When my father wasn't on the road, selling insurance or settling claims, we had our meals together. At night we were tucked into our beds. In the summer there were barbecues, a ball tossed around. Dogs, report cards, food fights. Normal things. I have no doubt when it all changed. But before, before that, Jeb was Trooper and Art was Squirt and I was Squirrel. "Trooper, Squirt, and Squirrel," our father called when he was back from his days on the road.

Why was I Squirrel—a name some family members still call me affectionately or if they want to tease me; why Squirrel? In part because I scurried about, and still do, dashing from here and there, but mainly because I collected things—hoarded them, wouldn't let anything go. My pockets were filled with feathers and bones, stones and coins, stamps, seed pods and bottle caps—whatever I found on my way home from school. Leaves I pressed between wax paper, doll parts, ribbons. Whatever I found in the Cracker Jack box. Grudges. And my share of secrets too. I've held on to these as well. Stuff, my mother called it. Squirrel and her stuff.

My mother, Lily, was always checking my pockets when I came home from a walk in the woods, trying to toss out whatever she could. For God's sake, she'd tell my father or my brothers, "Don't give her any more stuff." There was a certain dread when it came to cleaning my room. But my room was not a hodgepodge of these things. No, it was a carefully arranged place, museum quality, with everything neatly ordered, dusted, labeled on my shelf. Bird feathers, shells. Periwinkles, scallops, cockleshells. Souvenirs from outings we went on—a star key chain from Starlight Lake, a small wooden carved bear from the Dells.

Anything ever given to me, anything ever found, if anyone ever said, "Here, Squirrel, you can keep this," I kept it. It was mine. I kept things for a long, long time and when I outgrew something, I put it in a box, labeled and tucked away, until Lily, on one of her massive cleanups, would go into the basement and throw it away.

Because of this side of my character, there were many speculations about what I'd grow up to be—a rag picker at rummage sales or a researcher for the CIA were among my less flattering prospects, but my father was sure I'd become a great collector and classifier—a biologist who discovered new species like that tiny East Indian owl, believed until recently to be extinct. Or a curator of ancient objects, a lawyer with a genius for precedents. Chief librarian at the Library of Congress. My father had great dreams for me and it was a known fact among the members of the Winterstone family that I had an archival mind.

But in fact I did not become any of these things. Nor much else, for that matter. I suppose I've been a bit of a professional dilettante, dabbling here and there. Though many things in life have interested me, I never landed on anything that would really matter very much. Looking back, I know that there are reasons for this—moments I can pinpoint in time.

Nothing ever came of all the stuff I collected until now. It is the remnant of my archivist's nature. I know how to put things in order. Every fact, every date, who was where and when.

This is what enables me to tell this story now. I know where everything is.

I examined the folded sheet with its goalposts and letter sweater with a big "W" for Winonah emblazoned across the front. As I headed to the shower, I tossed it into the recycling bin. When I left home to go to college, I had my reasons—and they were good ones—for going away. I thought one day I might return to the Middle West to live, but I never did. Twice a year I flew to Chicago to see my parents, but I never drove up to Winonah. I kept my distance. I stayed away.

I moved as far as I could and still be within the continental United States. I went to college in Berkeley. Then I married Charlie and had two kids. After my marriage broke up, I moved down the coast just below Santa Cruz, where I now live. I bought a stone house, built by Francis Cantwell Eagger, the poet whose work has had a recent surge of renown. It is the second place I've ever called home, and I intended it to be the last.

I tossed away the next invitation, which arrived a few months later, as well. I didn't even have to think twice about it. I wasn't going and that was that. It was my daughter, Jade, who dug the third and final reminder out of the bin. Pack Rat Jade, we call her, always rummaging in the trash. The apple didn't fall far with this one. Snooping through my things. We are alike in this way, my daughter and I. Jade is great at flea markets and in musty basements. "Wow, Mom, look at this," she'll say, holding up an old doorknob, the cuffs of a long-gone fur coat. Jade can find a use for anything or can just sit for hours reading my old letters; nothing I'd ever meant for her to see.

It's pointless for me to buy lipstick because she'll snatch it, or have a private life because she'll uncover it as well. My daughter, the sleuth. So when she found this paper, she put it in front of me as if she'd just discovered evidence of some heinous crime. She pointed a bitten fingernail at the page.

"What's this?" Jade asked, hovering beside me, running her hand—another nervous habit of hers—through her close-cropped hair.

"It's an invitation to my thirtieth high school reunion," I said, snatching the paper from her.

"Wow," she said, "that's so cool," as if she thought it really was. She looked at me, defiant almost, as if it were a dare. "Well, you're going, aren't you?" It was inconceivable to her that I would not. But in fact I wasn't. Winonah, for me, wasn't a place to go back to.

"No," I said, "I'm not."

"Not going where?" Ted put in, walking out of his room. From the corner of my eye I could see his door open. On the door the words "Clato Verato Nictoo" appeared. I didn't know what these words meant and Ted wouldn't tell me. I tried dozens of times to unscramble them as if they were an anagram, to read them backward, to extricate their meaning. "If you have to ask . . ." Ted said whenever I wanted to know. Clato Verato Nictoo. Just one more thing that keeps me from my son.

"It's an invitation to Mom's thirtieth high school reunion." Jade snatched it back and held it up as if she were dangling a dead rodent by the tail.

"Oh, Mom, you've got to go," Ted said, swinging the peace medallion with the shark's tooth he wore over his surfer's shirt. His buzz-saw cut revealed the pink of his skull. "It will be fun."

"It will be boring and probably sad," I told them but they continued to protest.

"You might have a good time; you'll see everyone again. Besides," Jade said, giving me a wink, "you never know."

For years now they'd been trying to get me to go out, meet someone new. We live south of Santa Cruz, where a cool, winter mist makes this the artichoke capital of the world. It is true our house looks on to the sea and I can tell you a million things to do with an artichoke, but it's not as if I live in the Bay Area or even Marin or Sausalito, where I might get a chance to meet someone new. I've had a few relationships since my marriage ended, but nothing has really stuck.

I suppose the end of my marriage stunned me. Charlie sat across the table one evening while I was clearing the dishes away and said he wanted a divorce. It was a Thursday night in summer and the kids were playing outside. I could hear their voices, calling to friends in the yard. A ball bounced in the street. When I asked him why, he replied, "Because I don't really know you. You don't give anything away."

I looked around, thinking for a moment that he meant my stuff— the hats and jewelry and antique coffee grinders that cluttered our house. "We could have a garage sale," I said.

Charlie shook his head. "That's not what I mean at all."

We went back and forth, breaking up, staying together for several months, and then it was over. There have been a few others— briefly—since. I dated a psychologist from UC Santa Cruz the longest. When he drove off after our last date, a pebble hit me in the head. Since then, when the kids ask how a date was, I reply, "Pebble in the head." Now I can just point to my forehead and they know what I mean. I suppose Charlie was the one I really loved. At least, looking back, I recall it as a true passion. The kind where you think about this person all day long and when you lay down beside him at night you feel like you've been plugged into an electric socket. But in the end Charlie saw it more accurately than I. It was never quite right. There was something missing. There always seems to be.

I have no idea what has drawn me to one person and away from another. I've never been the most insightful person about myself, not like some people I know. Once or twice I've gone for counseling, but it never added up to much. It helped me get some new hobbies, though, that sort of thing. But it didn't enable me to understand what pulls me in one direction as opposed to another.

Probably what I do with my time doesn't help either. I always seem to be running around. First there's the kids, the house, and my plans, once the kids are out on their own, to turn it into a bed-and-breakfast.

A few days a week, to make ends meet, I work for my friend Shana, a real estate broker, where I show time-shares and seasonal rentals in Carmel. And in my spare time I volunteer for a wildlife rescue league.

I didn't go to school to learn how to do this, though I have studied on and off. Before I had a family, I worked for Fish and Game. They sent me to some remote locations where I counted salmon swimming upstream. I watched them shattering their bodies against the rocks to feed their young; this gave me lots of ideas. I even began to write a little book of aphorisms about this experience called *Reflections from the Salmon Counting Tower,* but nobody wanted to publish it.

After a while mammals became my focus. I seem to have become a kind of local expert on beached things—whales, dolphins, orphaned otter pups. They bring them all to me. The whales I can do little about, but I've been surrogate parent to a number of sea otters. I am convinced that what makes a creature beach itself isn't a suicidal tendency as some experts claim. I think it's a blip on the radar screen, a sonar misfiring that sends the wrong message.

Who knows why the message goes wrong—a virus, noise pollution, a genetic flaw—but the animals turn mysteriously in the direction of their ruin. I am left with the remains, with what has washed up on the shore.

I had no intention of going to the reunion or anywhere else, for that matter. Over the years I have tended to stay put, not to wander far from this coast. Besides, I didn't want to see people I hadn't seen in thirty years and would probably no longer recognize. Or open the proverbial can of worms. But the morning of the reunion Jade and Ted appeared at my room with my bags packed, a plane ticket which they'd charged on my Visa in hand. "Surprise," they said.

"I'm sick," I told them. I'd been fighting a cold. But they had the Tylenol ready. They looked to me as they once had when they were small on my birthday or Mother's Day, standing with a breakfast tray in hand, a pleased look on their faces.

"You're going," Jade told me. "We want you to." It was a fait accompli, they said.

2

As I flew home for the reunion, it was the summer of the great floods. The Missouri and the Mississippi had left their banks, burst their levees. So much for the Army Corps of Engineers, my father would have said. Below me, what had once been a great river appeared as a series of lakes with channels connecting one to the next.

From what I'd read in the newspapers I knew that people had drowned. A family went for a boating expedition as the waters rose; all were lost. Two boys had tried to go fishing; their bodies were found in a tree. Houses sat like little islands in the midst of these pools. As we flew over them, it was a clear day and on the roofs of some I could see the numbers of their insurance policies scrawled. This would have driven my father wild. He'd be racing from farmhouse to farmhouse, helping the farmers file their claims.

Before I was ten, I knew how to read a disaster, how to calculate the loss of life and limb. I understood what landfall meant, what an 8.2 on the Richter scale was; I knew the damage an F5 tornado (inconceivable) versus an F6 (unimaginable) could do. Debris paths, flood basins—none of this was news to me.

And I'd learned a few things about odds. "What are the chances?" my father used to say. "If it's three to one a tornado will blow through southern Illinois during the tornado season, then what're the odds it will blow through the Loop?" Actuarial statistics were the subject of family dinners. The death of a child wasn't worth a fraction of the death of a working spouse. Loss of income was greater than loss of consortium (the word my father used when he referred to companionship). Property costs more than grief. Dollar signs lurked behind every heartbreak. Over dinner I heard tales of farms foreclosed, policies lapsed.

From an early age I came to associate my father with bad weather. I developed a fear of oncoming storms—a phobic dread of wind and rain. I can't say I've ever gotten over it completely. When thick black clouds gather over the Pacific, I have to brace myself. When my father was on the road or even when he was home, I listened obsessively to weather reports, scanned the skies for that blue-gray sky that threatened snow, a yellow-green cast that foretold a tornado touchdown. It all meant claims. It meant that once again my father would be taken from me. I had no idea how much or how far, though in the end it wouldn't be the weather that took him away.

Now as I flew home, the flooded plain stretched below me. My father had always been opposed to the levees. He knew the rivers. He'd been born near them, grew up along their banks. He said when it came to rivers, and I suppose to anything else, for that matter, let them flow. Don't try to contain them.

A river will find its own shape and direction. There are two hundred sunken steamboats from the Missouri River that now lie at the bottom of plowed fields. This is because the river has chosen to go its own way. You can't trust the river; you never know when it will burst its banks and reroute itself.

My father knew better than to tell the farmers not to live on the silt-rich soil that lined the floodplain. Along the riverbanks you could reach your hand into the dirt and pull up the richest black earth in the world—fistfuls—and my father wasn't one to tell anyone to live elsewhere. But he did try to convince them to build on higher ground.

If my father were flying in this plane, looking down at this water-clogged land, if he were looking at what I saw from this height, he would have felt very sad and very vindicated. He would say, "They should've asked me. I would've told them."

I spy, what do I spy, something that is yellow. Is it a truck? I asked my brother Jeb. Is it my father's shirt or that yellow jacket that flew into the car? A freight train car, a street sign, that stripe down the center of the road? It's corn, Jeb shouted back at me. It was the summer I turned nine as I gazed at fields and fields, but I didn't see any yellow. All I saw were flowing carpets of pale green. But it's in the husk, I said, and Jeb just threw up his hands.

It didn't seem quite fair, the rules my brother played by, but still it was all around us. Miles and miles of corn. I'd never seen it before. For years I'd waited for this. My father was letting me go with him for the first time to the floodplain. Jeb was twelve and he'd been going with for the past two years. You had to be ten to go along, that was the rule. But since I was almost ten, my father made an exception for me. That was how he put it, "I'll make an exception for you, Squirrel," and even though I didn't know what an exception was at the time, I was happy to have one made for me.

Art cried because he was only six and had to stay home and Lily tried to explain to him that when he was bigger he'd go. In the end she had to pry his fingers from the car door. "Another year or two, Squirt," our father said, but Art just screamed that it wasn't fair and in the end our father had to agree with him. "You're right, son," he said. "Life isn't fair." Lily stood in the driveway, in an apron, holding Art back with one hand, blowing kisses with the other as we drove away. Her skirt caught in the wind and she pushed it down.

My father blew kisses back, a smile on his face, but the minute we turned north on Lincoln and drove under the railroad trestle, he put the radio on loud and started to croon. My father sang at home, but never loudly. Lily came from a big family and she didn't like noise. "But it's music, Lily," he'd argue with her, but she didn't agree. No shouting; no doors being banged. No music played loud. If you slammed a door behind her, my mother jumped in the air.

My father moved silently through our lives, but as soon as we were past the railroad tracks, heading west, he was tapping his fingers, humming along. We weren't half a mile from the house before we were all singing along to "You Ain't Nothing but a Hound Dog." We sang for miles at the top of our lungs.

When we stopped for gas, I slipped into the front seat, but Jeb complained. "Trooper," our father said, "you always get to sit there. Give Squirrel a chance."

It was hot even with the windows rolled down. The air smelled of pigs and fertilizer. The sun was boiling, heating up the vinyl seats of the car, but I didn't care. This was an adventure. Where we were going there had been a flood. Last year it was drought; this year it's flood, my father lectured us as we drove. Now the Everly Brothers were singing "Dream" and my father sang along. Though he was a little off-key, I was surprised he knew all the words.

My father had a deep baritone voice that would sound good on the radio, I thought. I could imagine him announcing things—the weather, the news, sports. Sometimes when I listened to the radio, I pretended it was my father's voice coming to me from far away. Now it almost made the car shake. I had only heard that voice at night when he sang to put me to bed, but it wasn't this big. It seemed to take up all the farmland that stretched before our eyes. For the first time I saw the land as he did—wide and empty and flat. Every Monday he drove out this way and every Thursday he came home. "Get a whiff of this, kids." He rolled down his window as we passed a pig farm. We held our noses, groaning, and our father laughed.

There were dozens of things my father could have done with his life besides sell insurance and settle claims. He had a keen sense for business and as he grew older, he constantly chastised himself for the mistakes he'd made. He was always kicking himself for not giving a few thousand bucks to the friend who came to him with a new invention—a little spray gadget you put on the top of bottles for hair spray and household cleaners. He and Lily had sat, watching the little demonstration. "No," she'd said afterward, "we can't take the risk." Aerosol cans. My father missed his opportunity to invest in aerosol cans. "I could've made millions," he muttered as he patched the roof or fixed the plumbing on Saturday afternoons.

His ambition once had been money—to make lots of it and get rich, then do what he wanted with his life. But he fell into the insurance line through a distant relative of my mother's, a man who said that insurance was a good, steady way to lay your foundation. In the end all the schemes for getting rich fell through and insurance was what he did. He learned to take pleasure in it as he took pleasure in most things.

Though he was a city boy by birth, he came to love the loamy smell of soil, the rich, earthy odor of dirt being overturned, of the freshly planted fields. Even the piquant odor of fertilizer or the stench of a pig farm was somehow pleasing to him. It was not what he ever expected to come to love, but then there were other things Victor Winterstone had not expected he would love. For example, our mother, Lily, the plain, freckle-faced girl who made a beautiful home and ran it like a tight ship.

He was a claims adjuster who adjusted. That's what he was, my father who chuckled to himself as he drove; that's how adjustable he'd become. He was happy as he drove, whistling, two of his children at his side. Head tossed back. He listened to the radio, tapping out the rhythms. Rolling down the window, he got a smell of the fetid earth. Compost. Dead things decaying out there in the fields. The promise of new life.

In the city he'd never felt the cycles of life. He'd felt the bars he frequented and the music and the parties and the girls who clung to him, but he didn't feel this. The way life moved on from one moment to the next. Seasonal change, things growing and dying. He wanted to reach out and grab it. Take what was left, hold it by the throat. And never let go.

I stuck my face out the window like a dog, breathing in the air my father breathed. In the backseat Jeb groaned, "Dad, I'm gonna be sick." He was mad that I'd displaced him.

"Jeb," my father said sternly, "cut it out." Jeb had a turkey feather he'd found in the gas station parking lot and he kept tickling my ear. I stuck my tongue out at him in the rearview mirror.

Illinois was flat. No one had ever told me this before but it was very flat. Sometimes there was a hill or two but then it was flat again. And green, but mostly it was corn and soy. Wheat. The wheat bent in the wind. I waved at farmers on their tractors. If they saw me, they waved back. Some kept waving until we were far away.

It took all day to get to where we were going and when we got there, it was all lakes. I'd expected rivers, running streams, but it was as if people were living in the middle of lakes. A cow floated on her back in one. Someone's bed was in the middle of another. "No one should live here," my father said under his breath and I knew we'd reached the floodplain.

My father had an office to go to in town that had the name of the company he worked for on it. Farmers Protection. He said he didn't just insure farmers, but that's how it began so they called it "Farmers." He insured all kinds of people for fire, theft, life. But in the office, people who looked like farmers were sitting, waiting for him. Men in overalls. A woman in a smock was in tears; a boy gripped her arm. Everyone looked weary.

My father was a practitioner of sleight of hand—small magic tricks he did to amuse children, mainly his own. He pulled quarters out of ears, turned a silver wand to gold. He could cut a rope in two, then make it whole. He made eggs disappear. Jeb told me on previous summers when he'd gone from farm to farm with my father that this was what he did to entertain people who'd lost everything they owned.

I kept expecting him to do one of his tricks—pluck a quarter from the ear of the boy who wouldn't let go of the woman in the smock. Instead my father sat at a desk. "Crop insurance," I heard him say, "that's what these farmers need." Then he told me and Jeb to go outside. He gave us money to buy a hamburger and a milk shake. "Now you watch out for her," my father told Jeb. The river had left its banks.

As we wandered out into the street, people started shouting at my father. The woman in tears cried harder. We found a drugstore and sat at the counter. We ordered cheeseburgers, fries, shakes, but I didn't eat that much. Afterward we walked around town. It was a small town, but we found a playground. Jeb and I got on swings and pumped our legs harder and harder until we were swinging way up, then came way back down again. We swung until our legs ached.

Then Jeb took me down to where the river had burst its banks. It was only four or five blocks from where we were, but even as we walked there, I could see the strange sight of streets filled with dark ooze. A rushing stream of roiling water pushed just ahead of us. Houses sat in the middle of it with water up to the first-floor windows. In one house a dog barked mournfully on the roof.

Jeb stood, staring at the water. At its dark, brown color, churning, angry as Jeb's face. Why should my brother look so angry? So responsible, as if he were the cause of this flood? He picked up a stick and hurled it in with all his might and we watched the stick being carried along with the current. Then he hurled another. Then he pretended to walk toward the water, to put his foot in and I screamed, holding him back. But he pushed me away and started to walk again toward the water's edge and this time I grabbed his shirt. Real tears came down my cheeks and when he saw my tears, he stopped. He laughed at me. "You didn't think I would, did you, Squirrel?"

I was still pulling on him, afraid to let go, until he stepped back from the river's edge. When we went back to my father's office, the people were gone. My father looked weary. We'd been thinking of driving straight back, but my father said he was too tired. He decided we should spend the night so we drove for an hour or so, which our father said was all right because it was on our way home.

When the air cooled and it began to grow dark, we stopped at a roadside motel that was mostly a parking lot. A big neon vacancy sign blinked on and off and the "V" was burned out so it read "acancy." I don't know why, but Jeb and I found this word very funny. Acancy. The motel was painted turquoise on the outside and had a TV in the room, and a small pool with lots of dead bugs in it.

The room was plaid and smelled of stale cigarettes, but we swam in the pool, though I was more tentative about water now than I'd been before I saw the flood, the water rising to the windows of houses. My father used a strainer to get the bugs out of the pool. Then he let us swim in our T-shirts and underwear. In the morning we had to put on wet clothes.

Then my father took us out for steaks and French fries. We ate in a restaurant that had green and pink Formica tables and a steer's head over the door. I got to eat my steak with a serrated knife and it cut smooth as butter. That night in the room we watched TV and Jeb and I jumped from bed to bed, pretending that below us there was a roiling sea. We had a pillow fight, something we could never have at home, while our father sat watching the news. We didn't go to sleep before we were tired.

When it was time to go to sleep, Jeb grabbed some covers and headed for the floor, but our father stopped him. "No way, young man. Only Indians or barbarians sleep on the floor." After some back-and-forth, they eventually shared the bed. I got the bed closest to the window, where the amber light from the parking lot shone in. It was a big bed but with scratchy sheets. It was also soft, not like my bed at home, which was harder. I found a cozy place to slip into. Jeb and my father both fell asleep right away, my father sputtering in his sleep, and I drifted off, listening to the heavy breathing of men.

In the morning we drove back to Winonah. It was a long, hot drive and the way back looked different from the way there. It was flat farmland, but as you got closer to Winonah and the lake it closed up on you. The trees made the landscape thicker. They broke the flatness, but I felt as if I couldn't breathe. I missed the open stretches of road.

When we got home, Lily was sitting on the front porch, crying. She looked like one of those farmer's wives from the floodplain.

When she saw us, she dashed off the porch. "Oh, I expected you last night. You should have called," she scolded my father, shaking a finger, but she was hugging us. I thought my mother was going to be angry. Instead she held us very tight.

That night as I was going to sleep, my mother came into my room. I had heard my parents arguing downstairs. Now she looked tired, but she didn't seem so upset anymore. She sat on the side of my bed. "So how was your trip?"

I told her I'd seen a cow floating on its back and a bed drifting down a stream. She seemed to like this so I told her more. I told her I'd seen a dining room set in the middle of a lake and a family picnicking on the roof of their house and when we'd driven by the waters had parted like the Red Sea.

Now she seemed a little annoyed with me. She ruffled my hair and rose from the bed. "No fibs, Squirrel," she said, pulling the covers to my chin. "Always tell the truth. Don't tell stories."

4

I never thought I'd be driving down this road again, but suddenly there I was, following the shore, on my way to Winonah. I followed the dips of the old Hiawatha trail that the Potawatomi had blazed a century ago when they traveled these bluffs. The steel-blue lake was to my right and I caught glimpses of it as I took each turn. I drove by the dome-shaped Bahai temple that my brother Jeb christened "God's orange juice squeezer" when we were kids, hot and bored in the backseat. After that we laughed whenever we passed it, making slurping noises until our father told us to pipe down.

I careened through the twisting section of road called the Hills, carved by Ice Age glaciers, and took the turns as if I were driving the bumper cars at Riverview. As a child, the Hills seemed to promise some kind of adventure. When I drive along the Coast Highway where I now live, I get this same surge—as if anything is possible. Above me loomed maples and oak, the sturdy trees I'd grown up with. I eased the car around each turn on the narrow road I knew like the back of my hand.

We used to take this road all the time when I was a girl and we'd visit our grandparents "in town." My father preferred the highway because it was faster, but my mother always said, "No, let's take the Drive." "The Drive" was slower with its winding turns, but there were things to see—stone houses where rich people lived tucked behind blooming shrubs. Famous houses designed by Frank Lloyd Wright. When we passed one of those, my mother pointed. "How'd you like to live here? He made everything small, like he was."

It had been almost three decades since I'd gotten on the Drive and headed north. But I wanted to go this way and not the highway. I wanted to come back slowly, to take my time. But still Winonah came upon me suddenly. When I crossed the town line and saw the sign, I felt a twinge as if I'd taken a wrong turn. But there was no wrong turn. It's the way Winonah is—a town where it seems as if you can't go wrong. But, of course, you can.

As I came into town, even in the dark I could see how Central Avenue had changed. A Gap was at the corner where we used to buy school supplies. Coffee bars with green awnings dotted the main drag. A fancy restaurant with curtains inhabited the spot that had once been Irv's Deli. Irv and his wife, who both had numbers tattooed on their arms, had shouted at each other day and night.

Some things hadn't changed. Crawford's Clothing was still there— the dresses in the window looked as if they were frozen circa 1970. The old drugstore was the same as it had been the last time I chained my bike to the rack and walked in to buy Prell shampoo. The big and brassy clock on the Bank of Illinois building told the time as it always had.

I'd arrived in Chicago that afternoon, stopped home to see my mother, Lily, who had a tunafish sandwich with chips on the side and a Coke waiting for me, as if I'd just walked in from school. Lily looked the same—her nose still turned up with freckles along the bridge, her hair streaked with gray, her green eyes watery. She was too thin, perhaps. Her hands felt cold, her skin was pale. I wanted to open the blinds, air out the place. I never liked being in my mother's apartment. It seemed as if she'd never unpacked, never quite settled in. The furniture from the old house was crammed into three rooms. My baby brother, Art, who lived nearby, tried to get her to sell some things, but she wanted to hold on to most of what she had.

The apartment was dark, slightly overheated, and smelled of cigarettes, though she swore she'd quit years ago. In each room was a copy of the *Comprehensive Crossword Dictionary* next to a pair of store-bought reading glasses. While my mother shuffled between the kitchen and the dining room with my sandwich and Coke, I opened to a random page: "*Continent.* 1) chaste 2) land mass as in Africa 3) legendary or lost as in Atlantis." She put the sandwich in front of me, removing its Saran Wrap cover, and watched as I ate it and sipped my Coke.

We talked for an hour or so about the kids, the weather in California. She listened as intently as Lily was able to before she began her list of complaints about her back, her sinuses, her cleaning woman, always prefacing her remarks with "Now, I don't want to complain" or "I don't want to pry, but . . ." and then she'd complain, bouncing from one subject to another.

When it was almost dark, I'd borrowed her car and headed north. I'd left later than I should have, but I didn't care. I wasn't in a hurry even though the party had begun without me hours ago. I knew how to get there, but I took my time. Now I drove slowly through Winonah, like a policeman on his evening rounds.

The streets lined with maples and elms shimmered in the heat and the air was hazy. Fireflies whose green lights flickered like fairies danced in the tended gardens and the song of cicadas filled the air.

Casting a ghostly light upon the houses, mist rose from the trimmed blue-green lawns. I could almost see my father coming out of that mist, pushing the mower up and down in even rows.

I steered past houses where friends once lived, looking into homes where I'd spent half my youth, though this gave me an eerie feeling, as if I could look inside the houses and still see their mothers stirring a pot on the stove; fathers, who had moved to Winonah to give their children a better life, reading in the den. But, of course, nobody I knew lived in those places anymore. They had not lived there for a long time.

Somewhere in the night a train whistle blew. I rolled down my window to listen to the *Milwaukee Road* making its last run. When I was growing up, we lived about a quarter mile east of the tracks. At night from my bed I could hear the trains—their horns and even the ringing of the gates as they went down. I knew that the whistle we heard on our side of town was the same whistle they heard on the other side of town and this has always been a humbling fact to me.

Winonah is a town that divides itself in every sense along its railroad tracks. The side closest to the lake is the right side and the side farthest away, heading out toward the farmland, the cornfields, and the highway, has always been the wrong side. A lot of people got rich on things you wouldn't think you could get rich on—gift cards, car parts, coffee cake—and they lived closer to the water. Many were Jews such as ourselves or wealthy Protestants. The Catholics—the Irish and the Italian—they lived on the other side. There were no blacks then in Winonah, though there are now.

We lived on the right side, but it was close enough by some standards to be considered the wrong side. We lived near the intersection of Dearborn and Lincoln. From my bedroom I could hear the sound of the cars driving across the wooden boards that lined the tracks, so different from the sound a car makes on pavement. That steady *thump-thud*. I must have heard it a million times when I was growing up. Even now in the night, though I live two thousand miles away, I wake up thinking I've heard that sound.

We barely made it, though we did; that was what mattered most to my parents, especially to my mother, who saw great value in such things. My mother who liked the table set just so, everything in its place. We had been secure enough to "keep the wolves from the door." This was an expression my father used, and when I was small I thought he meant real wolves. Many nights I drifted to sleep thinking I could hear them howling.

Actually what he meant was disaster. My father who sold insurance for a living in the floodplain of the Middle West had a clear sense of what disaster was. He'd seen lifetimes obliterated with the flash of a flood, a twist of wind. I was raised with the first law of insurance pounded into my head: You can't protect anything that really matters. You can't insure love or health. You can't guarantee peace of mind or your place in the world.

I hadn't thought much about my father's advice to me in a long time, but as I drove through Winonah, heading toward the railroad tracks, I began to think once more of what he was trying to tell me. Pausing at the tracks, I crossed into Prairie Vista. Here it was less pristine. Beer bottles and trash lined the tracks. Flashing neon signs lay ahead.

Prairie Vista was on the wrong side of the tracks, but that's where I was going that August night. We called it the land of a thousand bars—the only place where our parents could sip a little wine or go for a good time, and when we got older, it was where we went as well. For some reason, after Prohibition was repealed the towns along Chicago's north shore decided to remain dry. Winonah was famous for its music festival, for the invention of the hearing aid, and for the fact it was dry. But if we wanted a drink, we just drove across the tracks into Prairie Vista.

It was a hot night and the humidity made my spaghetti-strap dress stick to me. I drove with the skirt hiked up my thighs, the radio on an oldies station. It made sense that the reunion was being held at Paradise. Where else would they have it but in Patrick's bar?

It was as sweltering a night as any I can remember in Illinois. Sometimes on a night like that you can get a whiff of the alewives that coated the shore in late summer, their bodies sucked dry by lamprey eels. When I rolled down the window, things smelled rotten and dead.

5

Paradise was located on the strip of bars that lined the railroad tracks on the Prairie Vista side. I recognized it right away by the Christmas lights strung up and the hokey sign of heaven with little angels above the door. Dozens of cars were parked out front and a lot of them were cop cars. The music blared from the patio, which was also decorated with lights. Each light had a tin halo over it.

As I walked up, a Motown CD—Diana Ross and the Supremes—played, but a local band was warming up. They were very noisy and already the crowd was begging them to stop. The air smelled of ashes and beer. Polyester shirts clung to men's chests, revealing hairs. These men were ragged; their bellies, once taut and the color of bronze, rolled across their belts. They had elastic in their waistbands.

At first glance the women looked better. They smelled of almond soap and avocado cream. Hair concealed the lines of their face-lifts. Some had the fine-toned muscles of women who ride a treadmill all day, sipping mineral water through a straw. There was a well-preserved look to them; others did not look so well. But it didn't matter because I hardly recognized a soul.

In the entranceway someone took my ticket and stamped my hand with the letter "W" for Winonah High. Then she looked at me. "Tess," she said, "Tess Winterstone?"

Discreetly I glanced at her badge. "Penny, how are you?" She was Penny Wilcox, who'd been in my homeroom for four years, the one who married Gus Garcia. In high school she'd been a petite girl but now she'd puffed out (she'd puffed out in high school but there had been other reasons then). I reached for a name tag. It was clear I was going to need one. I looked around a room of strangers.

"Would you like the commemorative blanket?" Penny asked.

"The commemorative blanket?"

"Yes, from Winonah's centennial. It has all the historic sites on it. The proceeds go to the high school development fund. It will be mailed to you."

I was looking around to see if there was anyone I knew. "Sure, I'll take the blanket," I said, distracted, checking the box.

"Hey, Tess." A tall, middle-aged man hit me on the back. Who was he? The quarterback of the football team? The class president? Some people asked how my brother was. A woman I didn't know asked how my sister was doing. I replied fine, even though I don't have a sister.

Someone grabbed me from behind. "My God, Tess." It was Maureen Hetherford, whose hair had turned pure white since her divorce a decade ago. She looked like a very old woman with a very young face, like someone out of Shangri-la who would crumble once the spell was broken. "You're here."

"I am," I said.

"Hey, Tess, you made it," the Dworkin twins said in unison. I still couldn't tell them apart.

Most of the old gang was there. Though my father called us "the girls," to ourselves we were "the gang." There were ten of us and we moved like a herd of sheep in one smooth motion across a hill. We wore pleated skirts and bobby socks rolled down, cardigan sweaters buttoned up the back, saddle shoes. We bought our clothes in matching sets at Crawford's Clothing. After school we went to one another's houses and put on lipstick and danced to *American Bandstand*.

We knew all the dancers. We knew what it meant if Francis danced with Bobby, if Bobby danced with Charlene. Sometimes before we put on the lipstick, we practiced kissing, just to see what it felt like. We curled up in beds in each other's arms, lips touching. Never with our tongues.

Now Grace Cousins, who'd married a plastic surgeon and resembled Cher with her high cheekbones, was giving me air kisses. She wore a silver lamé strapless and told us to all come by for a swim in her checkerboard pool later. Samantha Crawford rushed over with her husband tagging along, the way he had since the day she married him, like a puppy dog. No one ever got to see her alone. Wendy Young gave me a hug. She looked the same as she had before she joined the itinerant religious sect.

"I think I want some pictures," I said. I had brought a new Olympus point-and-shoot with me and began snapping.

"Better take them fast," Lori Martin, who'd been head of the Winonah Wildcats cheering squad and president of the student council (no one had ever done both in the same year), said, mugging at the camera. "This is the last reunion we'll look good at."

"Oh, I wouldn't say that," Grace Cousins said, sucking in her cheeks. Suddenly Vicky was there, sweeping me into her arms. "I knew you'd make it."

"I didn't know myself until this morning," I told her.

"It's so good to see you. You look great, Tess." Vicky had been my best friend during high school. It was to her house I ran when I had to get out of mine and vice versa. We'd seen each other sporadically over the years, usually for lunch downtown.

"So do you." She clasped me with her long white fingers, those hands that opened aspirin bottles and tied ribbons on TV. Vicky had wanted to be an actress, but ended up as a fairly successful hand model. ("Well, at least part of me is acting," she liked to say.) For years her hands had been insured with Lloyd's, though she'd never disclose for how much.

"Well, what do you think of this?" Vicky asked, her seagreen eyes gazing around the room. Her strawberry-blond hair fell loosely across her face and she kept brushing it away. Her arms were bare in her thin rayon dress. Her gymnast's body was still firm and taut and she had freckles everywhere—like a farm girl, my mother, who also had her own share of freckles, used to say.

"I think I don't know anybody anymore."

"Oh, you know them. You just don't recognize them." She seemed to be making eye contact with someone. "But I see someone you'll recognize."

"Who?" I asked.

"Oh, you know who," she said.

I suppose Patrick had been staring at me for some time when I turned. Even before I saw him, I sensed that he'd seen me. Of course, it was his bar so naturally he'd be there. "I thought you'd come," Patrick said when he walked up to me. "I was sure you'd make it."

"Why is everyone so sure about what I'd do?" He looked the same. He was a little gray around the temples and maybe he'd put on a few pounds, but none the worse for wear.

"It made sense that you would. So how are you? How have you been?" I started to reply when the band struck up and it was impossible to talk.

"Let's go somewhere else," Patrick said, taking me by the arm. He walked with me over to a corner of the bar, looking at me askew, but that had to do with his bad eye. Basketball was supposed to be his way out. He would have gone to college on a sports scholarship and maybe even become a coach. He could sink anything from half court and slip in and out of guys twice as tall. Then someone put an elbow in his eye and he never went to college. He never left Prairie Vista.

"You look good, Tess, you really do," he said. He stared at me at an angle so he could get a look at me. I rarely gave much thought to how I looked, but as Patrick gazed at me, I suppose I did look good. I stayed out of the sun. I ran four times a week. We lived in the artichoke capital of the world and the mist that keeps the artichokes firm had also kept the wrinkles from my skin. My body had stayed small and compact. My hair had stayed dark auburn, thanks to a bottle, and I had let the curl go natural. Tonight I'd pulled those thick curls back with a silver scrunchie.

"Well, so do you," I told him, "you've hardly changed." It was true. He looked the same. Before Patrick and I ever dated, my parents went to a costume party at their club dressed as moving men. Patrick's father had a moving company and my parents borrowed Hennessey Moving and Storage overalls and cardboard boxes. I have a picture of them in overalls with strained looks on their faces as they pretended to move the giant boxes.

"Oh, but I have," he protested. "I'm not what I once was. But you look like you take good care of yourself."

"I run a lot and probably the place where I live is good for my health. And you?"

He was about to answer when I heard a laugh, sweet and smooth, except that it was too high pitched, almost shrill, like an opera singer's laugh. Only Margaret Blair had a laugh like that. It would have been one of the beautiful things about her, like her hair and her skin, except for its high pitch and the fact that it came too often.

Margaret stood just ahead of me, her black hair spilling down the back of a creamy satin dress. It was the color of pearls and hugged her breasts and her hips. It was as if thirty years had not happened to her. I dodged left, then to the right because she was the last person I wanted to run into now. "Come on," I told Patrick, "let's go over here." But when I turned, she was in front of me—her head tilted back, surrounded by a clutch of admirers, men I didn't recognize, though I'd probably once passed notes to them in study hall.

Patrick touched my elbow as he tried to steer me toward the bar, but it was too late. "Tess," she called. "Tess, is that you?"

Margaret came over, tottering slightly, holding a glass of wine. As she hugged me, her breasts pressed against mine. The chill of her wine-glass against my bare shoulder sent a shiver through me. Then she stood back and looked me up and down. "You look the same, Tessie, except for your lipstick." Patrick turned toward the bar, a quiet gaze settling over his features. I kept thinking he'd drift away, but he didn't.

"My lipstick?"

"You used to wear red. But this peach color suits you."

My hand instinctively went to my lips. I didn't remember wearing red. "Well, you look the same too." It wasn't what I wanted to say. Many times I'd rehearsed this meeting in my head. How I'd tell her what I really thought. But now that I actually stood before her, I found her still beautiful, but rather pathetic, and myself almost speechless.

"You never answer my letters. You never return my cards."

"Oh, but I think about you," I told her, which was true in its own way. "I'm bad about answering my mail." I thought about the seasonal letters Margaret sent each winter. Those cheery Xeroxed epistles that outlined her family's accomplishments and failures—Nick's rise in his father's real estate business, Danielle's knee surgery, from which she'd recovered brilliantly; Margaret's small decorating business flourishing. It was inscribed for all to read, copied on red paper and stuffed into green envelopes, where she'd put stickers of reindeer and Santa Claus.

At the bottom of each seasonal letter, Margaret drew a smiling face and wrote, "Why don't I hear from you anymore?" The fact was I didn't want to know anything about her. I didn't want to hear from her ever again.

"Well, I think of you all the time," she said with emphasis, as if she were accusing me of something. "You were always nice to me." A somber look crossed her face. "Not everyone was, but you were. That meant a lot, you know, when I was the new girl."

"Well, I'm glad if that's how you remember it."

"It is. It's how I remember it." She took a long sip of her white wine, then pressed the glass to her cheek. "So tell me. What have you been up to all these years? Are you still living on the Coast?"

"Oh, you know, same place. Divorced, a couple of kids." I laughed, but she gave me an odd look as if she was sorry for me, and that made me angry. I'd always felt sorry for her because of where she lived and because her father never came and took her back to Wisconsin, the way she said he would.

The wineglass teetered in her hand and she took another sip from it. Her face was flushed and I thought that she'd already had too much to drink. "Well, you must come by. Nick and I would love to have you over." She rested her hand on my shoulder. "Come by and see us." Then someone pulled her away and I was happy to move on.

Patrick was waiting for me and he told the bartender to give me a beer. "She used to be my girl," he said, patting my arm. The bartender said the beer was on the house and Patrick found us two stools off to the side. "I'm sorry if she upset you," he said after a while.

"Just because she took you away from me . . ." I teased him.

Patrick grimaced, staring down into his beer. "You know it wasn't just that, Tessie. Things happen when you're growing up, things you can't quite understand."

"It's all right," I told him. "I forgave everyone long ago."

"We were young."

"I wonder what my life would have been if I'd stayed here and married you," I said with a sigh.

"You'd be divorced with two kids and I'd be running a bar." Patrick and I spent much of high school driving around in his father's car. I'd rest my head on his knee and stare up at the passing trees as he rubbed my head, my neck. The trees in Winonah arch so gracefully over the roads. The wind off the lake keeps their branches rustling, and I'd watch the branches from the vantage point of Patrick's lap as we drove. Sometimes his hand slipped to the side of my breast and then I felt that sweet awakening, a kind of ache that is more memory than anything else now.

Often he came to my house and we watched television in the finished basement my father built or sat in the den. There was something about him—a kindness that I carried with me over the years. His touch was light, as if it fluttered over me, and I imagined I'd find that same gentle hesitancy everywhere I went in the world.

Patrick and I, heads bent together, talked about this and that. He was estranged from his wife, though they were trying to work it out. Basically for the kids. "You know, Tessie, whenever I don't have anything to do, I drive by your old house. I just look at it and think to myself, Tessie lived here."

"Do you? That's nice."

He nodded, sipping his beer. We were silent for a minute. Then the band came blasting back on and we could hardly hear ourselves think. "Let's get out of here," Patrick said. "Let's go somewhere where we can talk."

We were heading outside to get some air when we ran into Nick Schoenfield walking in with a younger crowd. He wore a Hawaiian shirt open to his chest, which revealed a slight paunch. He was wide, built like a safe, and boisterous. Giving a wave to his friends, telling them he'd see them inside, Nick looked at us with his dark blue eyes, and laughed as if he'd just heard a great joke. "Tessie," he said, recognizing me right away, "It's good to see you."

"Well, it's good to see you, too."

He and Patrick exchanged a series of male pleasantries—slaps, handshakes, and locker-room jabs. "Just like old times. You two back together?"

Patrick laughed with him as if I were somehow their private joke. "How ya been, Tessie?" Nick said.

"I've been good. I'm still living out West."

"Well, the Coast agrees with you." He nodded, looking me up and down. "I always think of you as the one who got away."

"Did I?" I asked.

"Well, you give the impression you did. I thought you'd end up a star out there. You know you were voted 'The girl the boys were most likely to be secretly in love with.' "

"I was? By whom?" Nick opened the reunion brochure, pointing. There it was. Tessie Winterstone. "I had no idea. When did all this voting take place?" I wiped the back of my neck with a cocktail napkin.

"The ballot was in one of the invitations." Patrick laughed. "You probably threw it away." Nick smiled, his blue eyes piercing as if they could see through steel doors. His grin was warm and he hadn't lost his looks. He had been a beautiful boy and the years had been kind to him.

For a time when they played varsity, my brother Jeb and Nick had been friends. When Jeb first started bringing Nick around, that was the way he smiled at me—the wide, confident grin of a boy who is sure of himself. His boldness unnerved me. I had a crush on him, but then all the girls did. I used to bring them tunafish sandwiches and Cokes on Sundays when they watched football games in the den. If I asked questions, they ignored me. Sometimes I stood in front of the television just to annoy them.

My last memory of Nick was when he intercepted a pass and scored the winning touchdown in a game that made the Winonah Wildcats first in the state, beating Evanston. Evanston had huge, black players. (The joke used to be "Why did Evanston get the blacks and Winonah get the Jews?" And the punchline: "Because Evanston got first pick.") It was a big deal for the white boys to win. Nick rode around town, waving from the back of a convertible while the town cheered.

Larger-than-life caricatures of him were painted on the picture windows of all the big stores. Though he never realized his athletic promise, everyone believed he'd grow up to be just like his father. Mr. S., as his father was called, had once been a star quarterback for the Chicago Bears. He was a beefy man with knees so bad he wobbled, but he'd given the Bears some of their finest victories. In local restaurants people asked for his autograph.

Nick was being groomed for something big. That much you could see from the start. His father rooted for him at every ballgame and chided him whenever he missed an easy pass, a basket, a pitch, depending on the season. He was always coaching his son from the sidelines. On Saturdays Mr. S. made Nick work at Prairie Visita Automotive, a business he owned a share of. Nick didn't like to go, but his father insisted because it built character. All through high school Nick had grease under his nails. Now I noticed that they were manicured and buffed.

Nick paused, his head cocked, a frown on his face. He seemed to be listening for something, like a distant train. "Lousy band," he said at last. Patrick shrugged and said they were local and he couldn't afford better.

"Well, tell them to get a new bass player." Nick ruffled my hair as if he was really glad to see me. He had that same wide grin he'd always had, though his features were puffy like those of someone who didn't sleep much or did his share of drinking.

"So is she there?" Nick asked Patrick, an almost pathetic but slightly bemused look on his face.

Patrick nodded. "She's there."

"Well," Nick said, "is she behaving herself? How drunk is she?"

"Drunk enough," Patrick said.

Nick dropped his head down and shook it, the way I'd seen him do when a pass wasn't received or his team had lost an easy point. Then his smile came back and he slapped me on the arm. "So, Tess, what do you hear from Jeb?"

"Oh, the usual. He's still making out like a bandit." My older brother had, in fact, done exceptionally well for himself. He worked on Wall Street, had three kids, an apartment on Park Avenue, a house in the Hamptons, an impenetrable wife. We rarely spoke, though he sent me money from time to time, with a note, saying it was a gift for the kids. But it was always too much for a gift and more than the kids needed. He and I knew that.

"And you?" he asked. I told him it had been going great.

"Oh, less of a bandit."

I laughed. I told him that I had two terrific kids, and I worked for a real estate broker near Monterey. I got divorced a few years back but it was all right because I liked my freedom.

Nick listened intently, taking this in. "Well," he paused, "you always did." I wasn't sure how he knew this or if it was even true, but he said it in such a way that it seemed to be so. It left me feeling strange, as if this person I hadn't seen in years and who hardly knew me then was aware of something about me that I didn't quite know myself.

Nick heard someone call his name and said he had to get going, but it was great running into me. He told me his business took him west from time to time, and I gave him my card from the real estate office, scribbling my home phone on the back. Then he ruffled my hair again, gave Patrick a fake punch, and walked inside.

The houses get bigger as you drive down to the lake. It wasn't anything I'd ever really noticed before, but I noticed it late that night as I drove down to the shore. I took Lake Road and watched as the small brick- and wood-frame split-levels near the railroad trestle turned into sprawling ranch houses, which we called prairie houses, and then as I got nearer to the lake those houses built close to the ground rose into the two- and three-story mansions made of stone where the rich people lived.

I passed the old Everett Log Cabin, which had been my favorite house when I was growing up and for which Mr. Everett himself had chopped and honed the big trees and where his son still cut his lawn with a scythe, which my mother for years considered to be an abberation. And the Frank Lloyd Wright house on the corner of Laurel. Then I came to the old fairy castle where a princess was said to live.

I paused here, gazing down the long driveway at the house with its huge castle-like structure with turrets, a round tower, a big circular drive, and a fountain that poured around an arched cupid. The gates were looming, black wrought iron, and the huge front door was made of glass and wrought iron. From the road you could look down the long drive and see into the marble entranceway.

My mother liked to walk me down to this house when I was little. She'd stand with me at the wrought-iron gates. Sometimes she'd wrap her fingers around the iron as if she were trying to get in. I didn't usually feel sorry for my mother, but I did when she brought me here because I could tell there was something she wanted that she'd never have. Everytime we came here she told me the same thing. That the family was reputed to come from an obscure branch of Hungarian aristocracy and a real princess lived inside. Years later when I grew up, I learned that she was not a real princess at all but the heiress to Princess Pat cosmetics, but my mother—who knew the truth—liked to pretend we had royalty living in our midst.

When I was a kid, I tried to imagine what it was like to live in this castle. I envisioned myself dancing on its marble floors, sleeping in a canopied bed. But no matter how often we came here we never saw anyone waltzing inside, and we never got a glimpse of the princess. Still I imagined for her a happy, wonderful life.

The road down to the lake was dark and winding, black really, but once I got beyond the twists and turns of the old Indian trail, the moon was out and the beach shimmered a hot bright blue. I pulled up so that the car faced the lake and sat with the windows rolled down. The moon sent a trail of gold out across the water. The water lapped the shore peacefully, though I have known Lake Michigan to be not so peaceful.

The thing about Lake Michigan—what makes it a dangerous lake—is that it has a pretty shallow shoreline, then it takes this big drop about a mile out, and it's about as a deep as a lake can be. In the middle nobody knows how deep it is. It's also true that there's as much magnetism on its shores as on the North Pole, so it is very difficult to navigate by compass when you're out in the lake. A lot of ships have gone down over the years, and almost everyone who goes down in them is lost. It's a dangerous place that looks nice and safe, which is what in part makes it so dangerous.

Tonight it looked peaceful. For a few moments I sat, enjoying the view. Other cars were parked nearby with their windows down. A pair of legs stuck out of the backseat of one. I used to come here with boys and kiss in the backseat of their cars. Now I was gazing out at the lake, alone. I sat for what seemed like a long time, half an hour or so, not wanting to leave. But then I forced myself to turn on the ignition, which seemed so loud in all that quiet, and drive back toward town.

In town I turned left instead of going straight to the highway. I knew I should be heading back, but there was one more thing I wanted to do. I took a detour down Dearborn to Sandburg, then crossed Lincoln, following the railroad tracks to the trestle. Driving under the trestle, I made a right and went a block or two until I came up to 137 Myrtle Lane.

I pulled over and got out of my car. It was still a hot night, but there was a breeze now coming off the lake. I stood under the sycamore and maples as the branches rustled. The house was dark, but in the moonlight it seemed to glow. I hadn't stood in front of this house since I'd left for college. It still had the white picket fence around it, but the old rose bushes had been taken out. There was a thick, unsightly hedge now. Heavy white wrought-iron furniture lined the front porch and a flagpole was spiked in the lawn.

Once I went with my parents to the house when it was being built. It smelled of fresh paint and sawdust. The toilets had no walls around them and the bowls were filled with cigarette butts. My father walked around with a set of blueprints in hand. My mother wanted a closet somewhere and my father stared at the blueprints, shaking his head.

When they weren't looking, I found a razor blade. I'd never seen a razor blade before and I drew it across the skin of my forearm, cutting a line. Blood flowed, soaking into the unfinished wood. It wasn't a very deep cut, but my parents screamed, horrified. It left a thin white scar. When I touch it, I think of home.

I used to imagine that I'd live in this house again one day and I was furious with my mother when she told me she'd sold it. "What do you want me to do," she shouted at me into the phone, "keep living in the past?" She moved into a condo in town and neither of us went back to Winonah again. There was no reason to, really.

But for years I used to dream of going inside the house once more. In the dreams there were doors I'd never seen before that opened into secret rooms. One room opened into the next until I found myself in a completely different house—a place I'd never been. Now I stood looking at the house in the moonlight. It made me feel odd to know that other people were sleeping inside. I'm sure if they'd seen me, they would have phoned the police.

I don't know how long I stood there before I got in my car. I decided to take the highway home. I put myself on automatic, turned the radio on high, and tore down the road like I was a kid again and my curfew was coming up fast.

6

Horse chestnuts come in hard shells with pointy thorns, looking like instruments of medieval torture. When they split open, out slips the smooth, dark seed, like polished stone. I didn't know what it was, this sharpness and this smoothness, but in the fall of the year they held infinite interest.

The best place to collect them was in front of the old Episcopal church, where the flowering chestnuts bent with bursting white flowers in late spring, cool shade in summer, and the chestnuts in their green, thorny pods in the fall. On my way home for lunch I paused there, scooping what I could, filling my pockets with prickly pods or, when I split them, with the wondrous polished seeds. I would spend my lunch hour collecting them.

If Jeb saw me, he'd shout, "Hey, Squirrel, last one home's a rotten egg." That's when they really started calling me Squirrel. When they'd find me under these trees.

I didn't care if he beat me home. I was always late, wolfing down the peanut butter and jelly sandwich with chips on the side and chocolate milk that waited for me in the breakfast nook. But during chestnut time it didn't matter to me if I got home for lunch or not. I couldn't get enough of these seeds, couldn't slip enough into my pocket. I was greedy for their touch. I never ate them or asked my mother to cook them, but I wanted to have them in my pockets, or on the shelves in my room.

Vicky and I and the rest of the gang found endless things to do on our way to and from school. We took this walk four times a day. Up and back, up and back. Sometimes we got a ride, if it was very cold or inclement, but mostly we traveled on foot, books strapped to our backs. We liked to kick leaf piles, taking care that no smoke came from them. If there was smoke, there was fire. We gathered gold and scarlet maple leaves, pressed them into our math books, and had our mothers iron them between sheets of wax paper. We put them in the windows of our rooms where the light shone through as if they were stained glass. And we collected horse chestnuts.

Now suddenly a new girl was there with a paper sack, digging under the leaves. She'd grab a pod, split it open with her bare fingers, hold up a shiny chestnut. "Look," she'd say, that wide grin on her face, "I got one." Her black hair tumbled over her shoulders and leaves got caught in its thickness. Her blue tweed coat was frayed. When she stooped down, I could see where the lining was torn.

I don't remember when anyone else came to town, but I remember when Margaret Blair did. Like magic, one Indian summer morning she suddenly appeared, sitting at the desk I coveted in Mrs. Grunsky's fifth-grade homeroom—the one in the sun, a little off to the side, not far from the turtle's bowl.

She didn't come at the beginning, but almost in the middle of the first term with her neat pile of pencils and books. Already the sugar maples were golden and there she was with her thick black hair and her rosy cheeks, her round body, her face that smiled as if she knew us already, as if she'd always been there.

Mrs. Grunsky said, "This morning we have a new girl." And that's what she'd be from then on. She'd always be the New Girl. What is she? we wondered. Spanish or Italian? Eastern European? Our parents spoke of Gypsy blood. The boys called her a spic or a wop. A dago or meatball or just the girl from the other side. She was trash or beautiful. Strange or mysterious. She'd be whatever we wanted her to be.

The year when Margaret appeared, I had the best homeroom in the world. Our gang formed a neat, little clique. Ginger Klein, who told great jokes, was there and Samantha Crawford, who lent me her clothes, and, of course, Vicky Walton, and we all sat near one another. Lori Martin was just down the row. The year Margaret Blair arrived was the one when we got to move from classroom to classroom and carried our books.

And now this new girl was here, walking between classes, waiting for us after school. Thinking she could just be one of us, but, of course, she couldn't. We wouldn't let her.

We called her Wishbone. Not to her face, though sometimes we did. We called her that because of the way her legs shaped themselves into those smooth, arching curves you felt you could just snap in two. Bow legs, my mother said, from a vitamin deficiency or from sitting on a horse.

Later we liked to taunt her. Make a wish, Wishbone, we'd shout, and we'll break you in two.

I'd never seen hair so long and thick, or the color, almost blue black. We weren't even sure it was real. During recess some of us placed candy bar bets, daring one another to go up and tug on that hair. Some of the boys raced behind her and tried to grab it, but I just went right up and asked. "Can I touch your hair?" I said. In the corner of my eye I saw the gang, huddled, giggling.

"Sure," Margaret said, giving me a wide smile, the way you do when you think someone's going to be your friend. I reached out and touched it. It felt like a horse's tail and was wavy as a snake. I thought it would turn itself into a serpent and wrap itself around my neck, but it didn't. It just lay there, compliant, agreeable in my hand. It was smooth as silk and, though I was only doing this on a dare, I kept on holding it like a rope you could use to slide down the castle walls. To escape with. "You can touch my hair whenever you want," Margaret said.

"It's like a horse's tail," I announced when I got back to the huddle of the gang. "It's real." Still nobody believed me.

She'd never catch up. How could she? She'd missed fractions and pioneer history. Half the social studies curriculum on petroleum. We'd already read three books for English, so we knew she couldn't catch up. But she did. The first question Mrs. Grunsky asked, her pale hand shot up.

She'd never be one of us. She'd never belong.

We didn't know anything about Margaret. Who she was or where she came from. We didn't know how she got to and from school. She just appeared out of nowhere on a street corner and walked with us before we even asked her. We assumed she lived with her family in a house on the Winonah side of town—our side. For in Winonah we all had our visible histories. We had our families, our brothers and sisters. People by whom we located ourselves in space and time. We knew who we were. We never had to ask. Until Margaret came to town, there were no question marks after our names.

Then one day my mother asked Elena, the Italian woman who ironed my father's shirts, if she knew anything about the new family and who they were. Because that little girl kept coming around. And Elena told my mother that they'd moved into an apartment above Santini's Liquor Store in Prairie Vista. Elena told my mother that there was just the mother, who dressed in short skirts that were too tight, and there was talk about her. Just that woman and her daughter. No man in sight.

My mother was shocked, not because there was no man or because Mrs. Blair wore short, tight skirts, but because it was so rare that a child from Prairie Vista crossed over to Winonah. The lowest place you could live was above one of those stores across the tracks in Prairie Vista. And my mother made it clear, though I don't remember how, that it would be better if I didn't have much to do with someone who came from that part of town.

On weekends we went to one another's houses. Vicky lived in a one-story ranch, like the one we first lived in before we built our two-story white Colonial. I didn't know what any of this meant, but I knew that's how our parents referred to our houses—ranch, prairie, Colonial. Colonial was best, I knew that. Vicky's father was a CPA and every morning he took the same train and came home on the same train like clockwork. Her mother had pure white hair even when we were small.

We cut pictures out of magazines and glued them onto paper, making collages. We could do this endlessly. Time had not occurred to us yet. It was amazing we ever got from A to B, as Vicky's mother liked to comment. Vicky's mother was a large woman with square bones. I was afraid of her. She never hit us or yelled at us, but she just looked at us in a way that was frightening.

Vicky was afraid of her as well. Vicky's mother had little china things all over the house. Bone-china plates and china statues—dogs and one statue that we always laughed at of two lovers in an embrace. You had to be very careful when you played in Vicky's house. Vicky had a big garden and once we got in trouble for eating green beans on the vine. We loved the taste of those green beans that we plucked, snappy and sweet. One day when we were eating beans, Vicky's mother came outside. We tried to hide in the vines near the corn, but she found us. She stood in front of us, shaking that big finger of hers, telling us never to eat beans out of the garden again.

Then Margaret showed up at Vicky's uninvited on a Saturday morning and broke a porcelain dog. "My mother will kill you," Vicky said, but Margaret just went calmly into the kitchen where Mrs. Walton was, the fragments of the porcelain dog in her hands. I'm not sure what we expected—screaming, Mrs. Walton's shouting. We hovered by the kitchen door and I heard Mrs. Walton say, "That's all right, dear. Accidents happen. You did the right thing by telling me." When we peered into the kitchen, we saw Margaret munching on fresh-baked cookies and drinking milk.

The next Saturday she showed up at my house. My father must have answered and let her in. He didn't even ask who she was. He just assumed she was one of the gang, which she wasn't. I don't know how she knew the others were at my house, but she did. The gang and I were in the upstairs playroom, eating chips and drinking tall glasses of chocolate milk.

The playroom was above the garage and in it there was the cedar closet. My mother was adamant about putting the summer clothes in the cedar closet during the winter, and winter clothes in the cedar closet during the summer. Inside it smelled like forests, the deepest parts of forests and ravines, the places you have to walk a long way to get to. There were shelves and cabinets inside the cedar closet and they made very good hiding places. When we played hide-and-seek, I always hid there.

It was one of the rules of the gang that we made ourselves at home in one another's houses. I could open a dozen refrigerator doors in Winonah and take anything I wanted and no one would think twice about it. Margaret wasn't one of the gang, but still she was eating chips, changing stations on the radio.

"Let's play hide-and-seek," Samantha Crawford said.

Lori Martin wanted to play too and said she'd be it. She started counting to ten, but when I went to my spot in the cedar closet, Margaret was already hiding there. I looked at her, shocked. "Who said you could hide there?" I spoke in an angry whisper.

She just shrugged. "It seemed like the best place," she said. Then I hid behind the sofa and was found right away.

When the gang went home, my sweaters lay on the bed; books had been taken down from the shelf. My collections so neatly arranged on the shelves were suddenly in disarray. Feathers were where the shells should be. I had a cardinal feather and a bluejay's which I couldn't find. None of the gang would do this. I yelled at Jeb and Art. "Did you guys go in my room? Did you mess up my stuff?"

"Take it easy, Squirrel," Jeb shouted back at me. "Who'd wanta mess with your things?"

Jade was waiting at the airport when I arrived. Her hair was cut short and she'd spiked it with goo. She wore ripped jeans that were much more expensive than jeans you just buy and rip yourself. She had four rings in each ear and a new one in her nose. The blue lipstick gave her face an eerie, spectral air and I tried not to look at this concoction that was my daughter as she told me that our house was slipping down the cliff.

It isn't anything noticeable, she assured me as she stood there, tugging at the crystal amulet around her neck. She informed me matter-of-factly that the insurance company had sent an appraiser by while I was away who noted that the northeast corner of our house needed to be shored up and that the foundation seemed to be giving way.

Under normal conditions I would have considered this news very bad, but Jade is such a warm, friendly girl and she greeted me with a great big hug and a no-big-deal smile on her face. Smacking her gum in my ear, she said, "Don't worry, Mom. Like you always say, there are only solutions. No problems. How's Grandma?"

"The same."

"How about that old boyfriend of yours? Did you see him?"

"Oh, we spent some time together. He's on his second divorce."

"So you have things in common." Jade gave me a big wink. I stared at my daughter with her close-cropped hair, her sharp, bony body.

On the way home we stopped at Half Moon Bay Diner, a little cappuccino and sandwich place I'd stop at for the name alone, perched up high on the edge of the road so you can look down at the Pacific. It's a place where I love to sit and Jade knew that, which is why she stopped there.

Since I first saw it, this part of Northern California has always been just right for me, with its dramatic vistas, its crashing sea. But now as I munched on an avocado and sprout sandwich on pita, I felt distracted the way you do when you think you've left home with the coffee pot on.

"So, Mom," Jade said, "did you see anyone? Did you do anything?"

"Of course, dear, I saw lots of people and we did lots of things." She sighed and I realized this wasn't the kind of answer she wanted to hear. She wanted to know that something exciting had happened in my life, that I would be a different person now that I'd been away for a few days. I was afraid that once more the ordinariness of my life was a disappointment to her. Jade was young enough to still believe that you can walk into a room and a sea change will occur; that the earth will move.

I'm the one who named her Jade. The Orient had once been a passing interest of mine, one of many passing interests, I might add. A place I wanted to visit. When I was younger, I'd sit for hours looking at pictures of those fine carvings out of stone. Rocks that contained an entire world. Swans, flowers, villagers going about their daily chores. Delicate, miniature universes imbedded in stone.

When I told Charlie that I wanted to name her Jade, he said, "Why don't you call her Sunset or Aurora? Give her a real California New Age name." I'd told him for years I really liked the name. Except that now all her friends called her Jaded. She got a kick out of the grimaces I made when a friend called and asked, "Is Jaded there?"

"Well, did you have any *fun?*"

"Yes and no," I said thoughtfully. Jade rolled her eyes as we munched our sandwiches. The sea crashed below. White spray blew up against the rocks. "It was interesting," I told her. "It was nice to see everyone."

"Mom," Jade leaned over, squeezing my hand, "aren't you ever excited about anything? Doesn't anything get you going?"

"Yes, dear, you do." I patted her cheek and she dropped my hand, determining me to be a hopeless case. With a sigh she handed me the keys to the car. "You drive," she said, and she slept the rest of the way home.

———

When I pulled up in front of the house, gawkers lined the driveway. There were ten or twenty cars. More than I've seen in a long time. "What're they doing here?" I asked her.

"I'm not sure," Jade said, "they've been staked out for days."

The house I live in was built by the poet Francis Cantwell Eagger on a plot of land where nothing would grow. A farmer sold it to him dirt cheap and Eagger spent half a century building his house. When he died, I bought it from his son, who had many debts of his father's to pay off. He told me I was doing him a favor, taking that wreck off his hands.

Of course it needed work, which it still does, but I couldn't believe my luck. To buy a poet's house, built stone by stone, at the edge of the sea. The son said he hated that house—resented it deeply—because when his father wasn't writing, he was piling stones. That is what his childhood was, he told me as he handed over the keys, a pile of rocks.

How was I to know that Eagger would get famous again? That some small press in Minnesota would reissue all of his books in special editions and pilgrims—true believers in his words—would come and stand on the road and stare at me and my children and the house for hours at a time. Still, I had been here over a decade and, despite the oglers and devotees, the constant knocks at the door from readers who want to see the vistas that inspired such poems as "Coastal Views" and "Water at My Window," I have never wanted to leave.

In my living room I have the complete works of Francis Cantwell Eagger. The books have nature titles like *Along the Rocky Shore* and *Rock Climbing in Yosemite*. Sometimes I take down the volumes and read verses such as "The sea pounds the shore/shattering my dreams/like the morning alarm/I wake, unsure of where I am/or ever have been."

It wasn't clear to me why his work was having such a resurgence but Jade told me it was because he wrote about darkness and mortality. I argued that every poet writes about that, but Jade said there was a drunken edge to his. Sometimes he wrote about drinking and Jade, who was contemplating writing a book about the poet (she wanted to call it *Living on the Edge with Francis Cantwell Eagger*), said he drank himself to death in our breakfast nook.

One of the gawkers—a young man who wore jeans and a tweed jacket and a pair of wire-rimmed glasses—who was standing dangerously close to the house (I had warned them that I'd get a court order to keep them off our property) approached me. "It's an anniversary," he said. "Eagger's centennial; he's a hundred years old this month." I'd seen this young man before, as he strode beside me, trying to take my bag with his fleshy palm and convince me to let him inside.

Sweat ran along the side of his brow and he looked as if he had just begun to shave. "Please, Mrs. Winterstone," he said, "couldn't I just see the views from the inside? It's for my doctoral dissertation."

"We'll have to charge admission," I said to Jade, shaking my head as I made my way to the house.

"Mom, why don't we let them in?" Jade pleaded. "They just want to look. Then they'll go away."

"Because it's my house," I said, grabbing my bag from the young man and heading toward the door.

When I walked in, I found everything much the same as I'd left it. Even the coffee mug I'd left as a little test for my children was still in the sink. Ted was sitting, bare chested, listening to ska music in the living room. When he rose and hugged me, I could feel the ring through his right nipple. Every time I saw this ring I cringed. When he was a baby, I used to rub that nipple to soothe him back to sleep. Now someone had pierced it with a staple gun. When he turned his back, I tried not to look at the wing tattooed on his shoulder blade either, the one he said proved he was an angel.

Though he had promised he wouldn't maim his lips, his nose, or his tongue, the rest of his body was off limits to me. Things could be worse, I told myself; he could have purple hair in spikes the way his friend Chuck had. On the other hand, Ted could have a job, as could

Jade, since they were both, at least for the summer, out of school. In Ted's case, I believed he was permanently out. They could help me make ends meet, which appeared to be the constant struggle for which I was placed on the planet Earth. But they preferred to be home, hang out at the beach, cruise the highway.

It wasn't that they hadn't tried to get summer jobs. Jade, a politics major at Berkeley, had landed one for a time at a fish-and-chips place near Santa Cruz, but then she told me jokingly one day that she had other fish to fry and had been home ever since. Before I left, I saw a copy of *What Color Is Your Parachute?* lying around, and the makings of a résumé, so I was hopeful. Ted, who for a short time had worked at a bungee-jumping tower where he'd put a halter around young girls and shout, "One, two, three, bungee," had larger ambitions (film, TV), and his father—his dear father—kept promising to set him up for a big one soon, but I had been married to his father and so I knew what I could and could not expect from that man.

"Hey, Mom," he said, picking up my bag. "Did you have a good time?"

"It was all right." A girl with beautiful cheekbones and green streaks through her hair sat on the couch. "This is Cherri."

Cherri smiled but made no effort to rise. She gave me a little wave, though. "Pleased to meet you, Mrs. Winterstone," she said, her tongue ring clicking against her teeth. She spoke in a voice so soft that I felt like a judge asking her how did she plead. When I took my things to my room, I had a feeling they'd been sleeping in my bed. A little while later when I came out, Cherri was gone and no mention of her was made, as if she hadn't even been there.

That night as the gawkers drove off and Ted and Jade sat in front of the TV, watching various evening specials, I rinsed out the coffee mug and other dishes that had been left in the sink. After the dishes were washed, dried, and put away, I wasn't sure what to do with myself. I thought I could go into the den, read, pay bills, but the television was too loud.

I made myself a cup of mint tea and settled into the breakfast nook with my mail. The breakfast nook has been my preferred place to sit since I bought the house. From here I can gaze down at some pine trees, and then at the drop into the Pacific. It's a pretty sheer drop and when the kids were small, I worried a lot about them falling off that cliff.

Now I sat in the breakfast nook, listening to the surf. Canned laughter came from the living room as I sifted through the pile of mail, bills that awaited me, the note from the insurance appraiser concerning the slippage on the northeast corner that needed to be shored up. I calculated how much this would cost and how long this would be my house. Month to month I was having trouble making ends meet and Charlie was already hinting, now that the kids were technically out of school, that his support would end soon.

Not that I lived off my ex, though I had gotten some things that I felt were owed me. I had seen him through two professional schools by working odd jobs. I'd raised our kids more or less without him so I'd felt some help was due to me, but now the kids were older and I knew that the time was coming soon when I'd have to find the way to really support myself. I couldn't do it just by handling seasonal rentals and time-shares.

I looked at the kids sitting there, the remote between them. When the phone rang, they both jumped. I picked up the phone and heard voices already speaking. A man said, "I just don't know what it is. I don't know what I should do."

"Well, maybe you should tell her," the woman replied. "I think that's always best." The voice of the woman was slightly familiar to me. I wanted her to talk more so I could place it.

The man paused, taking this in, then said, "Well, I know it's best. It's just that there's so much I still like about her. . . ."

"Like what?"

"Hello," I shouted into the phone, "excuse me. You're on my line." I shouted two or three times, but they couldn't hear me so I hung up.

The kids stared at me from the couch, both waiting to see if the call was for them. They had that eager, slightly sad look of pets thinking they might be fed. "It's a crossed line," I said and they settled back down.

Though Jade was basically just veging, Ted wasn't actually watching TV. He was studying it. His eyes stared into the tube and, if I didn't know better, I'd say he looked like a supplicant before an altar.

Of course, Ted, like just about everyone else we knew, wanted to be in the movies. It's the new immortality, he liked to explain to me; it used to be heaven, now it's celluloid. He was a good-looking boy and he believed he'd get his break. Or at least he believed his father would introduce him to the right people. Charlie made commercials and directed reenactments, so I wasn't sure who the right people would be that he knew. But, of course, once Charlie had his own dreams, so I wasn't too hard on him, except where my kids were concerned.

The phone rang again and this time the kids got it. I could hear them talking to Charlie in the somnambulant way they had when the TV was on between them. "Sure, Dad. Uh huh, Dad." Monosyllabic sentences.

"Mom, it's Dad," Jade called from the living room so I picked up the phone.

"Hi, there," Charlie said, his voice perky. "I had the hardest time getting through. Line was busy forever."

"That's funny," I said, "no one was on." But then I thought about that crossed line problem we were having. "Oh," I said, making a mental note, "I better call the phone company. I think there's a problem with my line."

"So how was your trip?" I chatted about the reunion and he chatted back. He had stuff to discuss with me. A trip he was thinking about taking with the kids. His concern, which I shared, that they weren't working. Then I heard someone calling him in the background, the woman he lived with, Luci, whom I'd never laid eyes on, and before I could ask for money, we were off the phone.

Basically Charlie and I had always been friends. When I met him in an art history class at Berkeley twenty-some years ago, I'd liked him right away. I liked his big bear body and his green eyes. He laughed about all kinds of things. We'd only known each other a few weeks when we drove up to Alaska—a long, tedious drive of landscapes moving past us. Yet I loved the sensation of just being beside him for miles and miles of road.

Charlie was writing a paper on outsider art. He drove around the country in search of the primitive, the folksy. We found people with giant bugs made out of wire on their lawns, others who'd turned their yards into a series of pulleys, homemade amusement parks. One man had a spaceship in his yard, the lights of which had caused the air force to make several impromptu inspections of his property.

Charlie loved this stuff and he could talk to anyone: a gas station attendant, a survivalist out in the woods, or some guy with a lot of money who wanted to make a movie. He had planned on writing a book about all of this, but got sidetracked with the costs of raising a family and the desire for money, which moved him into more commercial ventures. He'd had a fair amount of financial success setting up multimedia trade shows. His biggest success, though, had been in reenactments. For various centennials he'd done Washington crossing the Delaware, the arrival of Coronado into Santa Fe, the California gold rush.

In that trip up to Alaska we stayed in cabins that had what we called "outs" with no houses. We showered in ice water until we learned we could bathe at public showers in local Laundromats. In the morning we found bear scat around our cabin. Charlie thought all this was great. He made love to me three times a day and when we were finished, he cradled my face in his hands and told me how much he loved me.

It usually took me a moment after I spoke with Charlie to catch my breath, as if I'd been punched hard in the gut. When I married Charlie, there had seemed to be something that stood between us. I wish it hadn't been that way, but it had. For months after we separated, I thought about what he'd said. How I never gave anything away. I remembered when I was a kid there was a toothpaste that had this active ingredient, Gardol. In commercials on TV Gardol was an invisible shield. When it came down over your teeth, Mr. Tooth Decay, a hideous black creature with nasty jaws, couldn't get through.

For a long time I imagined Gardol protecting me as Mr. Tooth Decay—or whatever else I needed protection from—fought to get through. I imagined invisible shields everywhere and at some point it became clear to me that I couldn't shake them. I kept thinking somebody would come along and fight his way past, but he or she never had. I was always sorry after I talked to Charlie that he hadn't been the one.

I went to the door of the living room and called, "Hey, Teddy, Jade. Why don't we order a pizza? Or I'll make a noodle casserole. Would you guys like that?"

"No thanks, Mom," Ted shouted back. "Not hungry."

"Me either," Jade piped in. I poked around in the fridge, found some leftover casserole, which I dug into with a fork. When I was their age, I had things I wanted to do with my life. Now, night after night, they sat watching *Seinfeld* or listening to Loose Screw. Recently Jade had been saying she wanted to go to massage therapy school. Before that, she talked about being a flight attendant.

I gazed at the bills for a new roof, mortgage, car payments, the appraiser, setting aside the ones that would have to wait a month or so. There was also the set of keys I kept to all the houses I was responsible for. These were houses of fairly wealthy people who were away half the year, but wanted the income from a rental to cover their costs while they were in the Bahamas or back East. Maybe I *should* charge admission to my house, I thought. It seemed like a sensible thing to do.

I had been thinking about opening the bed-and-breakfast in earnest. In fact, ever since my little start-up company, Mind Your Own Business, failed, it'd been about the only thing I could think of. Mind Your Own Business was a company for people who wanted to start their own at-home small businesses, and the idea was that my company would get them set up. I had a partner—a friend from San Francisco—and we offered office design, computer setup and programming, file management, marketing surveys, mailing lists—whatever a client needed. The problem was most people in start-ups didn't have the money for my services. We lasted a year. I still thought it was a good idea.

But for now, turning the house into a bed-and-breakfast seemed the way to resolve everything. Though the house was small—just three bedrooms—it had two baths and I could convert the garage into a separate apartment, which would be good for families. I could even turn the den, which had a breathtaking view of the sea, into a small room. This would give me five spaces to rent out. I would be able to keep my house, which everyone wanted to see anyway. Lots of historic houses (like Lizzie Borden's, Ted reminded me when I brought up this idea) were being turned into B-and-Bs. It would pay for bills and provide a decent tax write-off. I could have guests whenever I wanted, but I wouldn't have to all the time.

Besides, I liked the idea of people from Stuttgart or Bogotá stopping for a night on their way down the coast. I could offer walking tours of this craggy shoreline, share my knowledge of marine life. Or provide the devotees of Eagger with a night within the walls of their beloved poet's home. I'd serve them cranberry scones with whipped butter and cream in ceramic jugs and gourmet coffee in the morning, and slip after-dinner mints onto their pillows at night as they sipped cinnamon tea downstairs by the fire.

And when they left, they would hand me their business cards or write their names in the leather-bound guestbook and tell me to look them up when next I was on the Continent or traveling through the Andes. I'd call it the Eagger House Bed and Breakfast, and I could envision the brochure. A picture taken out at sea, another of the view from the breakfast nook. A perfect place for a monastic rest.

If my father had been alive, he would have told me that the house was a fairly crazy place to live. I could only insure it for fire and theft. I had flood from above but not from below, which meant if it rained I was okay, but if a river of mud flowed down from the hills, I wasn't. I'd tried to get an act-of-God rider but my insurance agent, John

Martelli, said the house was going to roll off the cliff one day and I'd be left with zilch. There was no premium I could afford for that. I had to say he probably had a point.

I knew a little about what natural disasters could do because I traveled with my father to the floodplain and saw catastrophe up close. We traversed a town in a canoe. The cornfields were lakes. Cows waded up to their knees in muddy water as if they were the water buffalo of Thailand. A bed, still made, drifted by. A house stood without walls as a river flowing through it carried its pots and pans away. Trophies, photo albums, a wedding dress flowed past us in the debris.

My father had shaken his head. "Hold on to what's yours, Squirrel," he told me that day. "You never know when it will be taken away."

8

I was Daddy's girl. Everyone said it. All their friends. The Rosenmans, the Lauters. Whenever they came over, they said, She's Daddy's girl, all right. And I was. I clung to his chair when company was over, and when he let me, until I got too big, I'd sit in his lap. It was a firm, muscular lap with bony knees and I could sit there for hours, just rocking on his knees. When he left on Monday morning, I was always there to wave good-bye. And when he drove back in on Thursday after school, I was always there to greet him. "Where's my little Squirrel," he'd call, waving as he pulled in the drive.

When he got home, he liked to put a record on. He enjoyed old jazz like the Jimmy Dorsey Orchestra or show tunes. Once he put on *South Pacific*. When "Some Enchanted Evening" came on, he tried to get my mother to dance. "Come on, Lily," he said, waltzing into the kitchen with an invisible woman. "Dance with me." He caught her in his arms and tried to spin her into the living room, but she batted him away.

"Victor, I've got dinner on." She wiped her hands on her apron.

My mother always had a million things to do—clothes to hang up, newspapers to throw out, meals to prepare. "Now let me be."

Though my father was used to this, he pretended to pout, then turned to me and made a deep bow. "May I have this dance?" he said. He scooped me up and we waltzed, dipping with each glide, singing, my father gazing with pretend infatuation into my eyes.

When the school year ended and summer came, my father took me and Jeb back to the floodplain. I knew he wouldn't go without me. When Art saw we were leaving, he howled again, but our father told him he still wasn't old enough. He'd just turned seven. It was too long a drive for a seven-year-old. You had to be ten. "Next year, Squirt," he said.

My father rolled down the window to say good-bye. "Now, please call if you're going to stay away longer," our mother said.

"Don't worry." He kissed her on the lips. Art shrieked as we pulled away and I put my hand to the glass, gave him a little wave. As our mother held Art back, she gave us a little wave like a windshield wiper, back and forth.

Once he couldn't see them in the rearview mirror, our father clicked the radio on high and began to sing along. I hadn't heard his voice loud and booming like that in almost a year. He knew new songs now. "Pretty pretty pretty pretty Peggy Sue, oh Peggy, my Peggy Sue . . ." Dumb lyrics, but he followed along.

This year I knew the road. It was old hat, an expression Lily liked to use. Old hat. I anticipated the flatness, the yellow land, the smell of pigs and fertilizer. It was less amusing when Jeb and I had to hold our noses. We were too big for road games. That was old hat as well.

The flood was less spectacular. No floating cows, no bedroom sets. Jeb didn't try to fool me that he was going to dive in. Instead he seemed to pay more attention to some giggling girls in shorts by a picnic table. He tried to act cool and pretended he didn't know me.

We stayed in a motel but my father had called ahead this time. We had a reservation. When we arrived, the desk clerk said, "Good afternoon, Mr. Winterstone," even before my father said his name. I missed "acancy." I wanted to go back to that place where the clerk with the bloodshot eyes who smelled of smoke looked startled when we walked in the door. I wanted to surprise him again.

But here we were expected. My father had reserved two rooms. Adjoining rooms, they were called. "One for you, Tess. This year you get your own room." I didn't want my own room. I didn't know what to do in it. It had a connecting door and for most of the evening we kept the door open, moving freely between our rooms. My father wanted to read and rest, so Jeb and I watched television in my room. Then my father called Jeb when it was bedtime. My father gave me a hug, a peck on the cheek, then closed the door between our two rooms.

With the door closed I sat up in the big bed with the scratchy sheets (that was the only thing that was the same). I thought about opening the door, but I didn't. Almost all night I stared at it. I put my ear to it from time to time so I could hear them breathing on the other side.

Every night when he wasn't on the road, my father came and tucked me in. He sat at the edge of the bed, told me a story, sang me a song. Usually it was the Whiffenpoof song about how we're poor little lambs who've gone astray. I sang it to my kids when they were small. But not long after that trip to the floodplain, when I turned ten, everything changed.

He stopped walking into my room without knocking, and after a while he just gave me a peck on the cheek before I went to bed. I tried to get used to being alone in my room. I busied myself with rearranging my stuff on the shelves ("It looks like a museum in here," Lily always said when she came in my room) or trying to read, but basically I was waiting for him to tuck me in. My room had pink wallpaper shaped in squares. If I was tired, lying on my side, the wallpaper seemed to move in strips like film through a projector, like when you're sitting on the window of a train, watching the world go by.

I had two beds. I slept in the one near the window and my stuffed animals slept in the other, unless I had a sleepover, and then the stuffed animals got moved to the shelves. Mostly I used the extra bed for my clothes, which I tossed there on a daily basis and didn't hang up until my mother shouted at me to hang them up, which I did about once a week. There were often big piles of clothes because, God forbid, we wouldn't be caught dead wearing the same thing two days in a row.

I lay there one night watching the wallpaper move, thinking I'd heard footsteps. My father, having had a change of heart, coming to tuck me in. I couldn't seem to get used to it. The silence, the lack of footsteps coming toward my door. Four nights a week my father was on the road, but the other nights, the ones when he was home, I waited for that sound.

For hours I waited. The wallpaper moved miles and miles; dragons, maps, years passed before my eyes. But he didn't come. I tiptoed into their room hoping he'd change his mind. My father was sitting in the chaise longue, reading. My mother sat in bed with the TV on. I asked him if he wouldn't come and tuck me in.

"Why not, Victor?" my mother said. "She's still a little girl."

"No, she's not," my father said with a laugh as he gave me a peck on the cheek. "She's in the double digits now." Then he gently swatted my backside. "Off to bed now."

My mother got up and took me by the hand. "I'll tuck you in, dear," she said.

She brought me down the hall to my room, waited until I slipped under the covers. She kissed my forehead, smoothed my covers, and said good night. But it wasn't the same thing.

I wasn't sure why this double digits was such a magical threshold I didn't even remember passing, except we had a party just like every year (ten girls, swimming, box lunches with fried chicken). I wasn't even sure when my father stopped coming into my room without knocking and sitting at the side of my bed, telling me a story he'd made up while he was on the road driving around selling insurance— about a raccoon who lived in a hollow log or a snowflake that didn't want to fall to earth and leave its family behind. Or real stories about someone he might have met or a tornado he saw twirling in the horizon against the sky. It happened slowly, so I hadn't noticed it at first, but once that swimming party was over, I don't remember my father coming into my room at night again.

Some nights when my father was on the road, I woke up from disaster dreams—the earth splitting, a swirling wind carrying me away. A huge black wave rising above my head. I woke from these dreams breathless, my hands clawing at the air. I'd never had these dreams when he was home, tucking me in. Only when he was away. But now I seemed to have them all the time.

There was one dream I had over and over again. I am sitting in the yard playing when the sky turns yellow. I do not notice the color, but I notice the silence. There is no sound of wind. Everything is still. Two hands reach down and grab me just as the tornado whirls by.

9

John Martelli had his office at the Salinas Mall and he insured me for car, home, life, and theft. Somehow Charlie managed to keep me on his medical plan, but John took care of all my other insurance needs. His office was in a strip mall, beside a Starbucks and a Staples. He brokered for Allstate, but he also put together packages for difficult-to-insure clients such as myself.

I drove over there and parked next to John's car, a beige Volvo with a license plate that reads URCOVERD. John smiled as I walked in. The Beach Boys played on the Musak. "Hey, Tess, how you doing?"

His braided ponytail swung behind his back as he got up to greet me. His office smelled of deli sandwiches and coffee. John's hand was moist as he shook mine, squeezing the knuckles together until I felt the bones crunch. Behind him on the wall a framed imitation Whitman sampler read, "You Can't Be Too Careful."

"What can I do for you?" John Martelli had a big smile that never put me exactly at ease. He made you feel as if he were pulling one over on you and probably he was and I always thought he should be selling cars, not insurance.

He motioned for me to sit across from him. "I understand, John, that I have a slippage problem that needs to be taken care of."

"Yep." He nodded as if he didn't quite remember, shuffling through papers on his desk. "Just one moment now." Punching something into his screen he came up with what I believed was my policy. "Your foundation needs some basic maintenance, you've got to do some shoring . . . I'm afraid it's going to cost you."

I nodded, taking this in. I had just enough money to get me through each month, give or take. If Charlie withdrew his support of the kids, then I wouldn't have enough. I saw no way that I'd be able to repair the foundation of my house without a sizable loan, and I couldn't see who would give that to me. "Well, I've been thinking about turning my house into a bed-and-breakfast, so I was wondering what other improvements I needed to make."

"Good tax write-off," John put in, tapping a pencil on his teeth. But he was already shaking his head. "No can do. You need everything—all kinds of liability, earthquake, mud, brushfire. Who's going to give you brushfire?" John leaned back in his chair, hands over his head. "The premium will cost as much as the house. Can't get you into the Fair Plan now. I don't think there's any way you can get the inclusions you need." He began explaining something about rate adequacy, if this was worth x and that was worth y. I started to feel a surge of something I hadn't felt in a while. I didn't want to be told what I could not do.

"John, my father was in the insurance business." I'd never raised the specter of my father with John before, but now seemed like as good a time as any. "He used to say there are only solutions, never problems."

"Well, times have changed." John raised his arms, that grin on his face. His ponytail bobbed behind him. "He's not in the business anymore, is he?"

"No, John, he's dead." John paled, telling me he was sorry. "But if he were alive," I said as I walked out the door, "he'd find a way to help me."

My father's death seemed to be one more way he slid in and out of our lives, one more sleight of hand he'd perfected. His decline was barely noticeable and he was still a relatively young man, in his mid-sixties, when he died a decade ago. He had the usual complaints, especially about his legs. They refused to do what he wanted them to do, like put his foot on the gas or walk eighteen holes.

He collapsed on the golf course one Saturday, but then got up and insisted on driving himself home. My mother had tried to get him to the hospital, but he said he was all right. When I asked him that night on the phone how he was, he said, "I'm fine. I played the best golf game of my life." Hours later he died in his sleep.

There was a storm at sea that night, the kind of bad weather I'd once associated with my father, and I hadn't been sleeping all that well. Waves pounded the shore and I was lying there, listening, when the phone rang. My mother was calm, almost composed when she told me. "He died happy," she said.

They had met just after the war at a friend's wedding at the Blackstone Hotel in downtown Chicago. The way he liked to tell it, my father said to his brother, "Who is that girl?" She was a Russian Jew, as was my father, but with freckles and a turned-up nose. Nothing about her reminded him of the oily smells and grim corridors he was trying to escape from. On their first date they took off their shoes and waded through Buckingham Fountain. My father thought this was a girl he could have a good time with, and for a few years he did.

I flew in with the kids. Charlie, who had liked my father, joined us. Jeb and his family only stayed for the day, which enraged my brother Art. My father's funeral was well attended. I was surprised at how many people he knew, how many people told me he had helped them along the way. They had enjoyed his magic tricks and his boisterous laugh.

When I turned to look at who was there, I saw Clarice Blair, Margaret's mother, standing in the back of the funeral chapel. She was dressed in a short black dress, the kind she often wore, and a hat with a veil. I thought to myself, What is she doing here? But my mother, to her credit, went over and shook Clarice Blair's hand.

10

Prairie Vista Automotive was located across from Santini's Liquor, where Margaret and her mother lived. Every few weeks I went with my father to take the car into the shop. The Schoenfields had a part-interest in the repair shop, as they did in Santini's Liquor and in the other shabby buildings along the strip—the electronics store and the deli. In fact Cy Schoenfield had an interest in half of Prairie Vista. He'd had made a lot of money during his football years and as my father said, he put his money where it counted. In bricks and mortar.

The car often didn't need repairs when we went there, but still my father liked to go. He liked to schmooze with the boys at the garage. And the car was his livelihood after all, so he had to have it just so. Once in a while he had a fender bender or a scratch where the metal was revealed. Sometimes you couldn't even see the scratch, but it seemed as if he always had to go to that garage and have something done to that car. He told me a body can rust and you don't even know it.

It was our outing, those Saturdays. "Come on, Squirrel," he'd say, "let's get the car checked." I liked to go with him not only because it was something we did together, but also because once in a while I'd get a glimpse of Nick. I went out of my way to look nice, putting on a matching short set. Afterward my father and I stopped at Lindsey's Delicatessen for a corned beef sandwich and a black cow.

At about ten on Saturdays we drove down to the northside of town, then crossed the tracks to Prairie Vista. I waited outside because the smell of fumes—paint, oil, and grease—was so strong. Inside the repair shop was a dark world of mechanical parts, hubcaps, fenders, tires, rusted exhaust pipes, mufflers. I'd only go inside if Nick was there, learning the business from the ground up. If he saw me, he'd give me a wave. "Hey, Tessie," he'd call, smiling from beneath the hood of a car.

I went and stood beside him, peering with one of the mechanics at the twisted guts of the car. He leaned over me, pointing. "That's a spark plug and that's a distributor . . ." His greasy hands tugged at wires. There was a bang on the hood of the car and Cy Schoenfield, who liked to make the rounds on Saturdays and survey his domain, stood there, laughing. "Always flirting, aren't you, son? No wonder you don't get anything done." He pretended to close the hood of the car on his son's head. "Tessie, where's your old man?"

"He's in the front, Mr. Schoenfield," I said and watched Mr. S. wobble on his bad knees. My father and Mr. S. slapped hands. They talked sports, wondering if Winonah would take State and how the Cubs would do, and business until the work on my father's car was done.

The entrance to the repair shop was a narrow passage where your car got lifted up and carried in or where you just drove carefully through the thin opening into that dark circle surrounded by broken parts. It was a grease-stained world of men with blackened hands and faces who stank of fumes and could never light a match for fear of going up in smoke. When the fumes got bad, my father came outside and stood with me.

One day, when Nick was not there working on an engine, I went and stood outside with my father, waiting for a dent to be battered out of the car. My father was smoking a cigarette when Margaret Blair and her mother suddenly appeared across the street. Mrs. Blair wore tight skirts and had a cackle laugh not unlike Margaret's. But there was something buoyant and puffy about her that made me think of pointless things like cotton candy or yo-yos.

They were dressed up as if they were coming from somewhere. They both wore navy cloth coats, though Mrs. Blair's looked a little frayed, and gloves. Mrs. Blair had a red scarf around her neck which looked pretty with her dark hair and red lips. Margaret saw me first. "Tessie," she called, waving frantically, "Tessie," which only my best friends called me at the time.

I watched them coming toward us and my father tossed his cigarette into the gutter. Mrs. Blair's heels clicked on the sidewalk and I thought her navy skirt was too short and tight for a woman her age, just like our laundress, Elena, said. She had long sleek legs and a big friendly smile. She had clips in the side of her hair and shiny beige stockings with a seam up the back. They stopped and said hello. "So you're Tess," Mrs. Blair said. "I've heard so much about you." As she held out her hand to me, I could smell her perfume and her lipstick looked thick and red.

My father smiled, patting me on the head. "Who's this, Tessie?"

"It's Margaret Blair and her mother." I mumbled an introduction.

"How do you do, Mr. Winterstone," Margaret said in a sweet, syrupy voice I'd never heard her use before. She gave my father a big grin and he reached across and patted her on the head too.

Then Mrs. Blair extended her hand to my father and said, "Clarice Blair." I'd never seen him shake a woman's hand before, but she extended hers and he took it. When she smiled, you could see her teeth.

"Well, it's very nice to meet you," my father said.

"It's nice to meet you too," Clarice Blair replied, "and I'm so happy to finally meet Tess." Mrs. Blair paused, then gazed up at the sky. "You know, it's so beautiful this fall. Don't you agree, Mr. Winterstone? I think this is the most beautiful fall I've ever seen."

"Please call me Victor. This is your first fall here, isn't it?" Mrs. Blair nodded. "Well, every fall is beautiful in Winonah."

"You're right," she said, "I'm sure you're right about that." Then she laughed a big hearty laugh, and my father stared at her as if he'd never seen a woman laugh before. There was an awkward moment after that and no one knew what to say so it was good-bye and see you in school. Mrs. Blair called, "You should come over and play some time, Tess," and then she caught Margaret by the hand and walked away.

My father followed them with his eyes as they walked toward Santini's Liquor, where Mrs. Blair discretly slipped her key into the side door. The glass in the pane was broken and the stairs were dirty gray. Mrs. Blair glanced back at us once, smiled an embarrassed smile, then the two of them disappeared up the stairs. "Now, who did you say that was again?" my father asked after they were gone.

"Oh, Margaret. She's just the new girl. She lives with her mother above that store."

My father nodded, looking up, clicking his tongue. "Tough place to live," he said. With my eyes I followed his gaze to the window above the store. It was a grimy building with paint chipping from the front. The fumes from the repair shop reached over there.

"Nobody likes her," I added, as if this would somehow matter to my father.

"Why is that?"

I couldn't exactly think of a reason. "We just don't. She's stuck up and nosy."

"Oh, really?" My father nodded again. "Well, you should be generous to people, especially if they don't have all the advantages you've had. You don't know what her circumstances are."

Mr. S. came out just then and he stood with my father, shaking his head. He seemed to loom over us. He was so big and square and wobbly at the same time. He gazed in the direction of Santini's Liquor, as if he'd known what we were talking about. "They're tenants of mine," Mr. S. said. "My boys can't get much work done when she's around."

"I can imagine," my father replied, making a clucking sound with his tongue.

Afterward on our Saturdays my father went outside while the car was being looked at. He stood with me—the two of us gazing up at the windows with their drawn shades. Sometimes we heard the music from a violin. Once in a while we'd catch a glimpse of someone— even now I can't say who—drawing the curtain back, looking down at us.

11

I stopped at Starbucks for a tall iced skim "even keel" (half decaf, half regular) latte, then the post office. I'd received a notice that there was a package for me. There's always a long line at the post office. A woman ahead of me wanted the new rock-and-roll stamps, which the postmaster didn't have. A man had to report a lost registered package. At last the postmaster took my yellow slip and handed me a small, brown package. It was from Winonah and I had no idea what it was. Opening it on a side counter, I found a blue and white blanket with all the historic sites of Winonah woven into the fabric—the Winonah Wildcats, the train station, one of our Frank Lloyd Wright houses, the old Everett cabin. It was quaint, I thought, wondering what I'd do with it.

The blanket reminded me that I hadn't dropped off the film I'd taken at the reunion. I drove over to Photofax One-Hour Developing, where I left the film, said I'd be back, then sped over to the real estate office, where Shana had several calls for me to handle. "So how was the reunion?"

"You know, thirty years later . . ."

She ran her hand through her hair, which she'd let go gray (I dye mine the same color it was—auburn—when I was a girl, though Jade is always on my case to go natural).

"Time marches on," Shana said, staring into her computer screen. In her sleeveless dress I could see the scar that coursed up her crooked right arm. Shana and I have been friends since we both moved here and basically raised our kids together.

She was a grade-school teacher when I met her. She loved being in the classroom, but one morning during homeroom a little girl got up to ask her a question and Shana rose to answer it. Just then there was a loud, cracking sound, and Shana fell against the blackboard. Shana looked down at her arm and saw blood flowing from her elbow, fragments of white bone shining through.

A half mile away some hunters, having target practice in the hills, had shot a bullet against a rock. It ricocheted down the hills, through the classroom window, through the desk of the little girl who had risen to ask Shana a question, and entered Shana's elbow, finishing its trajectory into the blackboard, which splintered in two. The mother of the little girl, weeping, had called it a miracle, but Shana would never straighten her arm again. She'd never been able to go back into the classroom, either, though she'd tried for years, and finally she'd gotten her real estate broker's license.

Once while she was trying to win her lawsuit against the hunters, I sat with her in the courthouse waiting room and she said to me, "I used to believe that everyone made his or her own destiny. Now I just believe in fate."

"What's the difference?" I asked her.

"Big one," she said. "I know this man. He was walking down a street in Seattle. He had his whole life planned out. He was on his way to law school, engaged to a girl he'd known since college. They even had a house picked out on some island in Puget Sound. Then, suddenly, as he's walking down the street, a steel beam from a construction crew falls off a roof and lands right at his feet, just at the tip of his toes. Another half an inch and he would have been a dead man."

"So," I said.

"So he broke up with the girl, forgot about the house and law school. He's a rancher in Wyoming, married an Indian he met out there. He forgot about his so-called destiny and decided to just do whatever the hell he wanted."

That's what Shana told me she did. Never went back into the classroom; changed her life. She told me that now she preferred this line of work. She liked showing people in and out of houses where they might live, homes they might buy. She liked having the keys to so many homes, this entry into strangers' lives. She even hinted that she sometimes prowled in rooms, dug into drawers.

I must admit that I had come to enjoy it as well, since a year earlier her business was doing so well that she asked me to take over seasonal rentals and time-shares. I enjoyed the jingle of keys in my pocket, the access it provided. Though I can't say I did any prowling, I peered farther into a closet than I needed to, opened drawers I might just as well have left shut. But the fact is, such searches always disappointed. I never found the secrets, the hints of hidden lives I wanted to believe were there, and in recent months I'd stopped looking. Mostly things are what they are; that's the lesson having keys in my pocket taught me.

Now Shana gave me a few rentals to check out, make sure they were in good order before we took clients there.

"Okay, I'll do that, then I have some film to pick up and errands to do. Let's say I get back here at around three?"

Shana said that was all right with her and she handed me the lists of apartments to check on.

"Shana, can I ask you something?"

"Sure."

"You know, your house, it sits out over the ocean, right?"

"Yep, median tide is right under our living room."

"Well, is it insured?"

"Sort of. Under the Fair Plan. But the truth is, if it got washed out to sea, I'd never recover its value."

"That's what I thought," I said, giving Shana a little nod as I headed out the door and she waved back with her crooked arm.

My first stop was the seashell house, which was done entirely in seashell decor. Seashell pillows, cowrie shell artwork, abalone lamps, scallop curtains. It rented well to retirees who may or may not have discovered the porno the wife (the only interesting thing I'd ever uncovered in one of those houses) kept under her clam-shaped dressing table. It was spotless, as always, when I arrived, and I made a quick walk-through, rubbing my fingers along the mantel to see if we needed to send in the Polish cleaning crew.

I stopped at the tchotchke apartment which had knickknacks everywhere that could not be touched. It was the kind of place I loved; if I'd let my nature for collecting things run wild, I'd have lived in a house like that, with a million ceramic dogs and glass goats. Cruise-ship memorabilia was everywhere. An alleged life preserver from the *Titanic,* a crystal goblet from the *QE2.* On one shelf was a collection of cereal-box prizes. The people who lived here were control freaks and I had to be sure that every bear and cat was in its exact place. The husband had handed me a grid when I got this account, showing me where everything should go. Once, just to see if they noticed, I messed things up a bit—put some ceramic poodles where the *QE2* goblet was. They noticed right away.

My last stop was the Mitchell place. The Mitchells put away all their cotton sheets and terry-cloth towels and had polyester for the renters and slipcovers on everything. I didn't know why anyone rented that one, and almost everyone who did went out and bought their own linen. Invariably the renters complained.

Everything was in tiptop shape, ready for the new season. I called Shana to report in and told her I'd be back the next day to take care of some paperwork. On my way home I stopped for groceries at the food co-op, where Ted and I each put in three hours a month and got great prices on organic produce, and finally at Photofax for the film from the reunion I'd dropped off a few hours before. When I got into the photo place, I fumbled through my wallet but couldn't find my ticket.

"I'm sorry," I told the man behind the counter, who knew me since Photofax did all our film, "I can't find my ticket. It must be in my car. It's Winterstone."

He poked around in his box of film that had just been processed and handed me a thick envelope, thicker than I thought it would be. Then I drove home with the trunk full of groceries and the film.

When I pulled up in front of my house, the young man who had planted himself there a few days before was back. This time he had a notebook and pen in his hand as if he were waiting for his teacher. I shook my head when I saw him, but there was something rather sweet in his thin, sandy hair, his cheerless face.

He was probably close to Ted's age, but he looked so much like a boy as he stood there in his glasses and a red sweater, chinos and All-Star Converse monochrome sneakers. I couldn't help feeling he was trying to make a good impression.

I gave him a dirty look as I pulled up, but he rushed over to my car. "Mrs. Winterstone, please, may I speak with you?"

I got out, threw open the trunk, and he stared at the bags of groceries. "I've been away for a while." I stood back and stared at him. "What is your name?"

"I'm Bruno. Bruno Mercedes. I have a letter here that Francis Eagger wrote to my father. They carried on quite a correspondence over a number of years, yet they never met. My father, he was a minister, and he and Mr. Eagger exchanged letters about religion. You know, Mr. Eagger was a deeply religious man, as well as a nature poet."

"No, I didn't know that." So why did he drink himself to death in our kitchen? I wanted to ask Bruno Mercedes. Instead, as I scooped up the film and the blanket, I said, "Bruno, would you help me carry my groceries inside?"

I may as well have been asking him to carry pieces of the cross, the Holy Grail. Bruno reached into my trunk, clasping a brown bag of raw vegetables and rice cakes, another of cereals and paper products. These were not heavy bags, but the boy shook under their weight.

He followed me like a disciple toward the house. He knew, and I knew, that I wasn't asking him to carry these because I couldn't carry them myself. I was asking him to do this so I could invite him inside without actually asking him to come in. I wanted to know what it would be like to have someone like Bruno Mercedes, a devotee, a believer, and a potential boarder, inside my house. Or the former house of Francis Eagger.

With a hushed silence Bruno entered the living room. I heard him sigh and then he said, as if he would fall over, "Where should I put these?"

"In the kitchen," I said, pointing the way.

I paused in the den to toss the blanket over the chair near the hearth, then followed behind as Bruno made his way into the kitchen, where he put the bags down on the counter and then took a deep breath. "Can I see the rest of the house?"

I led him first down the narrow corridor into Jade's room, which faced the woods. It was a simple room and she'd hardly changed a thing since she was a girl. She still had dolls on the top shelf, a collection of shells, Sierra Club calendars, flip tops that she'd been stringing together since she was about five years old. A doll collection nailed to the wall. A large mural on the opposite wall she had painted in shades of gray and brown that had something to do with U.S. intervention in Central America. Little wizards holding crystal balls sat on her desk. A stained-glass rainbow hung from a string, casting rainbows around the room.

When Bruno nodded solemnly, we moved into my room, which was small, with just a double bed and dresser, but it looked out to the sea. There were no pictures on the wall, no photos on the dresser. There weren't even books on the bedstand. It was odd, seeing my room with a stranger standing beside me, and I thought how stoical and barren it looked, as if the person who lived here had moved away years ago.

We paused before Ted's door and the words inscribed on it, "Clato Verato Nictoo," which I gazed at each time I stopped by the door. Bruno paused, hesitating with me as well. He read the words carefully, then nodded. "Do you know what they mean?" I asked him.

"Not exactly," he said, "but I know what they come from."

"You do? What?"

"They are the instructions that needed to be repeated in *The Day the Earth Stood Still.* Clato Verato Nictoo is what you need to tell the robot to keep it from destroying the earth."

"Oh, and what happens?"

Bruno shrugged. "I don't remember, but I think no one tells this to the robot and the earth gets destroyed."

"So this wards off destruction?" Bruno nodded as we entered Ted's room. I hesitated to show him the room, which had a view of the mountains and was papered wall to wall—those precious stone walls that Francis Eagger had built—with James Dean, Bogart, grunge-rock groups (Loose Screw, Nervous Breakdown Number III). His father procured these posters for him—it was the one perk, as far as I could tell, that came from having Charlie as his father. On his dresser was a Kurt Cobain shrine. His bookshelves were lined with *Vampires of the Masquerade* books and assorted other volumes of horror. But the view into the hills was spectacular and it was not lost on Bruno.

In the living room Bruno's hands touched the cold stone walls. He ran his fingers over the exposed wooden beams. At the bookshelf he examined the feathers, pine cones, and shells, giving me a querulous look. "I collect things," I said. "It's a childhood habit."

When we completed the brief tour, Bruno followed me back into the kitchen. "Mrs. Winterstone, I can't thank you enough. I can't tell you what it means to me to see this view—this vista—where he wrote 'The gods rage against me and I can do no more but hope and be humbled by what crashes below, against this fragile shore.' "

"So, Mr. Eagger was a religious man?" I said, curious now to know more about him.

"Yes, he believed, well, not in organized religion, but he believed in a certain power. The power that made this landscape."

"I'm a realist, Mr. Mercedes. I believe that oxygen and various elements and our relation to the sun . . ."

Bruno Mercedes sat down in the breakfast nook and stared out to sea. "It doesn't matter what you believe, Mrs. Winterstone. It's what you feel. What you feel sitting right here. People spend too much time thinking about what they think. Francis Eagger invites us to feel. I like the feel of this place, just like I like the feel of walking on pine needles and looking at a great painting and hearing a piece of music I haven't heard before or seeing a rainbow or having a friend ask me for help. It means there's something bigger than me out there in this world. And yet I can still be a part of it. I can embrace it and it can embrace me. Do you understand what I am saying?"

I looked at this young man with thin, sandy hair and glasses, sitting in my breakfast nook. There was something slightly sad and lost about him. "Yes, I do understand."

"This place should be a temple. A sanctuary."

"It is my sanctuary, Mr. Mercedes."

"Please call me Bruno."

"Well, then, call me Tess."

He nodded. "Mrs. Winterstone . . . Tess, if I could just spend a little time absorbing this place, taking this in. You see, my dissertation is on the religious inspiration in his poems and I believe that the correspondence he carried on with my father—"

"Your father knew him?"

Bruno hesitated, as if he had gone farther than he intended. "Not exactly, but my father was a minister and they wrote letters over two decades. . . . It is a long story, but my parents and I did not speak for many years. We had, well, a falling-out. Eagger had a similar falling-out with his parents, only his lasted a lifetime."

"And yours?"

"In a sense Francis Eagger brought us back together. I became interested in him and then my father shared these letters with me. That was the beginning of our reconciliation." Bruno coughed, looking away. He didn't seem to want to tell me any of this, but had felt he had to. He sensed perhaps that it was his way into my house. I felt badly, as if somehow I had forced him.

"Bruno, make yourself at home. I'll just unpack the groceries, do a few things." I watched him as he sat in the breakfast nook, staring out to sea. Then he opened the small notebook he had brought with him and began taking notes, leafing through a tattered book of the collected poems he pulled from his knapsack. I put away groceries, tossed out dead lettuce. Bruno seemed content looking at the views, touching the stone walls, so I opened the package of photographs from the reunion.

There seemed to be more pictures than I remembered taking and as I opened it, I saw why. The first picture was of the side of a building. The second of an empty room. The third of a table and chair in that room. There was a picture of a refrigerator, a stove, a toilet. Then a suitcase in the room. There was a picture of a cot, more chairs. Chinese food on the table. Plates.

Then people began appearing slowly in the pictures. First one person—a college-age girl with straight, sandy hair—sat at the table, then another. A mother appeared, a father. They were fairly ordinary-looking with brown hair, dark eyes. More people entered the frame. An older woman wore braces. A man had his hair combed across a bald spot.

These were pictures of a family I'd never seen before. Older people, younger people gathering around laughing, eating. Toasting, glasses raised. These were pictures that could matter only to those whom they concerned—and clearly they were not mine. Since I had not had my ticket when I went to get my pictures and had just given the clerk my name, I reasoned that there must be another family named Winterstone who lived in the area. And they had recorded every moment of their move into a rather shabby, not very interesting apartment.

Quickly I put the photos away. When I had to return to work, I looked at Bruno, still sitting there in the breakfast nook. "Bruno," I said, "I have to go now, but if you would like to come here from time to time, if it will somehow help you to write your dissertation by sitting there, then please feel free." Even as I invited him, I wondered what I was doing. What had gotten into me, letting this boy into my house?

"Oh, Mrs. Winterstone . . . Tess, I can't tell you how much it helps. To experience what he experienced. To be here in his home. Listen to this unfinished poem. It is called 'Indigenous to Growing Up' and we only have fragments of it: 'Beneath one dark, soft covering of pine, the hunchback tree stands, its arms sloping like old-fashioned leaves . . . In spring when it rained we lay beneath those branches; touching the places where it curved.' Do you have any idea where that hunchback tree might be?"

"I'm afraid I don't. Bruno, this is fascinating. It really is very interesting, but I'm afraid I have to go back to work." In truth he was making me uncomfortable and I was annoyed that I had been given those photographs that belonged to someone else. I was anxious to leave. I was afraid that I'd already opened the door too much for him and that he would be here all the time.

I walked with him outside, taking a deep breath. Checking to make sure I had the keys to the seashell house because I had a couple who were very keen on seeing it, I waved good-bye to Bruno. "Come back soon," I said, fearing he would.

"I will," he said. "I definitely will."

On my way to the appointment I stopped at the photo store, where I explained to the clerk what had happened. He was grateful that I had returned because, he said, the other Winterstones had been looking for their film. They were very upset, he told me, that he had given someone else their film.

Now he gave me my pictures of the reunion, none of which came out very well. I leafed through them, but most were very dark and everyone had red eyes like rabbits when you catch them in your headlights late at night. In one I saw a person who was clearly Margaret, waving from the back of the crowd.

12

For months after he stopped coming into my room, I still stayed up at night, waiting for my father to tuck me in. I'd sit up, listening for the 9:47 to go through. It was the last train I'd hear before I had to go to sleep. But even after I heard its mournful whistle disappearing in the night, it was still difficult for me to sleep.

One night when it was raining, I heard the train whistle, but I stayed awake, listening to the rain on the roof outside my window. It sounded like small animals running across the shingles. I could hear the TV on in my parents' room and I thought of asking someone to tuck me in. Instead I lay awake, a Nancy Drew mystery open in my lap.

Then it seemed as if the storm had picked up. I heard what sounded like hail at my window. Maybe the storm had turned ugly, though I was pretty sure it couldn't be hail because it was April and it never hailed in April, except once that I could recall, and then Illinois was declared a disaster area because the hail did so much damage, keeping my father busy with claims for the next six months.

I was drifting off with the book open, when the sound of something fiercer than hail woke me. I was past believing in monsters trying to get in, but something was being hurled against my window. Opening the window, I gazed down below. The breeze blew hard. The branches of the maples beat against the side of the house. But in fact it was pebbles, stones from our driveway that were making the sound. I could barely make out a hand waving at me in the rain. "Tess," a voice called. "Come outside. It's me, Margaret."

I could just make her out down there in a wet T-shirt, hair drip-ping wet. "What are you doing?" I shouted, for even I knew that it was crazy for a ten-year-old girl who lived on the other side of the tracks to be at my house at this hour in bad weather.

"Come down," she called. "Slide down the drainpipe."

It had never occurred to me that I could do this, and now it came as a kind of revelation. My bedroom was just above the eaves to the kitchen, and in fact it wasn't much of a drop. But I refused. "Go home," I told her. "You'll get sick."

"Come down," she called again. She was spinning in circles on the lawn, her head tilted back, drinking in the rain. I tore the jumbo rollers out of my hair and took off my pajamas and put on a pair of shorts and a T-shirt. Then I slid down the drainpipe. I was stunned at how easy it was to slip out and escape from my life. Though up until then I hadn't felt the need to.

"Look," she said, holding out her arms. She began to spin again, her ponytail swinging around. She was laughing, head back, mouth open, the rain pouring off her face. I spun with her. I tilted my head back in the wind and the rain and just like Margaret, I spun. It was more fun than I imagined it would be.

Then she stopped suddenly. Taking my hand, she put it on my chest so I could feel my heart throb. "Feel that," she said. "When I was very little," she said, "my father told me I had a time bomb in my chest. He said I had to be careful or it would explode. For years I was afraid to run."

Weird girl. I thought that this was a funny thing for a father to tell his daughter. "Why would he tell you that?" I asked.

"Oh," she dropped my hand, "he always told me strange things like that. You know, my real name isn't even Blair."

"It isn't?" I asked, incredulous.

"No, it's De la Concha. Margarita de la Concha. My father is Spanish. Margaret of the Shell; that's my name. Beautiful, isn't it?" She tossed back her head of shimmering black hair, threw her hand over her head, and gave a little "olé." Then she laughed so that her white teeth shone. She made them clatter together like castanets. "Beautiful?"

I nodded, laughing with her, and we did a little flamenco dance in the driving rain. "Yes," I told her, "it is a beautiful name." And I thought it was. Certainly better than Theadora Antonia Winterstone.

We snuck onto the screened-in porch and I brought down some old beach towels that we hardly ever used so my mother wouldn't notice if they weren't in the linen closet. Margaret and I huddled in the towels. I suddenly felt bad that I hadn't invited her to my birthday party but my dad said I could only have ten kids, and of course the first ten I invited were the gang, so that was that. But now I thought for the first time that Margaret was nice. Strange, but nice. Though I didn't really want to, I found myself liking her.

Margaret said she was hungry so I went and got us something to eat. I tiptoed through the kitchen, carefully opening cabinets, and returned with Cokes, a bag of chips, some cookies. When I returned with the food, I found her cold, shivering, really, her teeth chattering away and her lips turning blue. So I went back inside and grabbed a blanket off my bed and my Chicago Cubs T-shirt. She wrapped herself in the blanket and dried her wet hair with one of the towels. Water flew off her head. Even in the dark her eyes were so white and black. As she peeled off her wet shirt, I saw that her breasts were small and dark. She slipped the Cubs shirt quickly over her head.

My mother hadn't taken the plastic covers off the summer furniture yet. As we sat on top of the plastic, our bare legs stuck to the covers and made farting noises when we moved. This sent us into such paroxysms of laughter we had to stuff the towel into our mouths so that my parents didn't hear us.

"This is a nice house," Margaret said after a while, looking around. "We used to live in a nice house, even nicer than this."

I was a little hurt by her saying she lived in a nicer house than we did and part of me didn't quite believe her, but I didn't think she'd make something up after we'd spun around in the rain and all. "Oh, really," I said. "Where?"

"In Wisconsin. It was a big white house by a lake like the one the Schoenfields live in. My father, he's a very successful businessman. He runs a valve factory."

"Valves?"

"Oh, yes, you know, pipes. They regulate the flow of things."

From science I knew that the heart had valves, but I couldn't quite envision manufacturing them. Still, it sounded plausible that Margaret had a father who did this for a living and did it well. "Your parents are divorced?"

Margaret ignored my question. "We've just hit a bad patch," she said. I remember her saying "bad patch" because it didn't sound like something a girl our age would say. In fact, nothing she said struck me as something a girl our age would say, and something about her seemed as if she were already grown up. "I'll live in a nice house again," she said. "You'll see. I'll live in a big white house by the lake." She said this in a way that made me think she would.

"Yes, Margaret," I said, "I believe you will."

"We're so much alike," Margaret said. "Let's be real friends. Friends for life." She said it in an insistent way that made me uneasy, as if I had no choice. "Here," she said, "You can have my locket." It was a small gold heart on a chain, the kind you can buy at Woolworth's for a few dollars. She slipped it off her neck and onto mine.

Then she asked if she could have something of mine, a keepsake, as if we were sealing a pact. "I won't keep it," she said. "Just let me have it for a little while." I offered her my Chicago Cubs T-shirt, which she was already wearing, but that wasn't a keepsake, she told me. "A keepsake is something you always want to keep with you."

I thought about this for a while, then offered her the scarlet rabbit's foot Jeb had given me the Christmas before. I took it with me everywhere—piano recitals, exams, football games. "Okay," I told her, "you can have this, but you have to promise to give it back." We made a thumb-touch-pinky-twist swear.

That night as we sat huddled on my porch, I felt good about giving her something that mattered to me. After we made our little exchange, I said I was getting sleepy and Margaret said she'd get going.

"Going where? How're you going to get home?" I wanted to wake my father to give her a ride, but she grew adamant.

"Oh, no," she said, "I know the way. It doesn't take that long."

"But it's at least two miles and it's raining." I thought of how far she had to go. Past the police station, the library, through the downtown, along Sheridan Road, under the railroad trestle, then into Prairie Vista. Maybe an hour on foot.

"No," she said, firmly, "I'll be fine."

The porch door banged and she disappeared into the night. I could only see her shadow receding as she walked down our driveway and vanished in the rain.

13

Fisherman's Wharf is my least favorite place to meet someone in San Francisco. I can't stand all the ticky-tacky shops selling T-shirts and caramel corn and the left-hand shop that sells all kinds of scissors and stuff for people who are left-handed. I can't stand the sea lions that live on the docks and have been turned into a tourist attraction.

I've been having this fight for years with the people at the wharf, who claim they don't feed the sea lions to make them stay, but how do you explain a few hundred sea lions hanging out right there on the docks? So when Nick Schoenfield called to say he was in town for business and asked me to meet him at Fisherman's Wharf at such-and-such a time the following Tuesday, I wanted to say no, but then I thought, Tourists, what do they know?

He said to meet him at that seafood restaurant that overlooks the bay and serves dishes like lobster Newburg. Nick was already sitting at a table by the window when I arrived and he waved at me as I came in. He wore an open shirt and jacket and had a breezy way about him I'd always liked. When he stood up to greet me, he was large, looming.

"Tessie," he said, opening his arms. Bending down, he gave me a hug. Then he laughed his big laugh as if my arrival came as a complete surprise. Nick was the kind of person you'd ask to open a jar or unlock a door because he made it seem as if he could do anything. Solve any problem you might have. He was such an easy-going person that he appeared to be almost shallow, as if he couldn't feel very much for very long. But I'd never thought that was the case. Though I'd heard his life had not been an easy one with his father and now his difficult wife, he seemed like someone capable of happiness.

"I'm glad you could meet me."

"Oh, I wanted to. It was no problem," I said, easing my way into the booth. In fact it was a long ride and I'd never been fond of the Wharf, but I didn't want him to know. On the piers sea lions honked. The waiter spilled water on the table as he filled our glasses. Nonchalantly Nick dabbed at it with his napkin.

"I love it here," Nick said. "You're lucky, living at the edge of America." He took a deep breath as if he couldn't get enough air. "I get landlocked back home." I found this a strange comment coming from him since he lived in his father's old house at the end of Laurel with a giant picture window that took in the entire lake.

"My house is on the ocean," I told him. "It's not much to look at, though I bought it from a famous poet's son. You'll have to come see it sometime."

He nodded, taking this all in. "I'm always interested in the sons of famous people," he quipped. "What's the poet's name?"

"Francis Cantwell Eagger," I told him as our drinks arrived.

"Well, I'll have to look for his work if you live in his house. I would like to see where you live," he said, "but not this trip."

"Oh, I didn't mean on this trip."

"Another time." He gazed out across the bay. "I think I'll be coming out here from time to time."

"Well, when you are, you should drive down. We can walk on the beach."

He picked up the oversize menu, which was so large I could no longer see his face. "I'd like that. If this deal goes through, I might be here quite a bit more." His voice came from the other side of his menu. When he couldn't see me, he put it down. He explained that he was trying to create a broader base for Schoenfield Enterprises and was talking with some local people about real estate speculation. He wanted to develop some resort property in Hawaii or the South Pacific.

I reminded him that I knew a little about the real estate business. "I rent time-shares."

"Well, maybe you'll help us. If we ever get this off the ground, it will be very big. I'm trying to interest some money people." He paused as if he'd forgotten something. "I never quite imagined you in real estate, Tessie. I always thought of you as going into nursing or some medical field."

He didn't seem to want to talk further about his business venture and looked away from me as he changed the subject. "Oh, really? Why is that? I can't see myself as a nurse," I said.

"I've always thought of you in the helping professions."

"I'm surprised you've thought of me at all."

"Well, I have." He stared at me with those steely-blue eyes, then glanced down at his menu. "What do you recommend?"

"Seafood. The mahimahi should be good."

As we waited for our drinks, we gazed across at the Golden Gate Bridge. I've loved that bridge since the first time I saw it. It gives me a fleeting sense of endless possibility. "You couldn't ask for a nicer view," Nick said. Our drinks arrived and we sat, looking out at the bridge, and Nick kept saying how it was the gateway to America and what a great bridge it was.

"There was this story in the paper the other day about a guy who left a note in his car that said 'I drove all the way from Iowa to jump off the Golden Gate Bridge.' But they found his car parked on the

Oakland Bridge. The guy didn't even know which bridge to jump off of. Can you imagine?" I told Nick, laughing. "He couldn't even get it right when he killed himself."

Nick started laughing too, but then he stopped. He shook his head as if this had happened to someone he knew. "Poor guy," Nick said. "That's a sad story."

I had the mahimahi with a baked potato and Nick ate a pasta with mixed seafood. He was quiet as he ate, asking me questions about my children. He showed me a picture of Danielle, a somber child with dark circles under her eyes. "She's a pistol," he said, though I didn't see it.

I told him I thought my kids had suffered from the divorce. "They're rather aimless. I worry about them."

"It's probably a phase. Didn't we all grow out of it?"

It was still early after dinner and Nick suggested we walk around. He had never been to San Francisco before and asked if I would give him the grand tour. We wandered up the hill toward Coit Tower, then down into North Beach. From there up through Chinatown and into Union Square where his hotel was. It was a nice leisurely walk to take on an October evening when it wasn't too chilly. I enjoyed pointing out the sights.

When we stopped back in his hotel, he invited me in for a drink. He didn't want to sit at the bar and suggested I join him in his room. It was a standard plaid hotel room with a king-size bed. In the bathroom he had a shaving kit, but nothing was hung up in the closet. It didn't seem as if he'd be staying very long. On the bedstand were a pile of magazines, newspapers, a paperback thriller.

"I like mysteries," Nick said, seeing me glance at the bedstand. "What'll it be?" He opened the minibar. I requested a brandy, which he poured, and we sat down at a small table with two chairs. "So, Tess," he said, "what's it like, living right by the sea? Do you get up feeling great every day?"

"You have the lake."

"It's not the same thing. Salt water, the wild seas."

I told him that in the morning I liked to run up in the hills, then down to the coast. That from my kitchen window I looked out on to the ocean. That sometimes I rescued wildlife stranded on the shore. He leaned forward with his hands folded across his knees as if he really wanted to hear what I had to say. I was beginning to talk more about my children and my divorce, about my stone house and how I wanted to turn it into a bed-and-breakfast, when the phone rang. Nick made a face and for a moment I thought he wasn't going to answer. He let it ring a few times, but then he got up and went to it. He walked stiffly, as if he'd suddenly become an old man or someone expecting bad news.

When he picked it up, I had a sense of what was going on at the other end. He had a deep, husky voice on the phone, different from when he talked to me. I heard him saying things like yes, of course I'm here, no, I'm alone. Don't be silly. Yes, I saw her, but now she's gone home. The kinds of things you say when you are trying to calm somebody down and are lying to her at the same time. His hand tightened around the receiver and his shoulders and back, which faced me, seemed firmly set, as if he were carved out of stone.

I knew it was Margaret and that she was in a flap. It didn't surprise me that they were having a difficult time. I was never quite sure how it was that Margaret Blair had come to marry Nick Schoenfield. They had dated briefly in high school, but it had never amounted to much. After high school, they had married other people, then divorced. Both moved back to Winonah from wherever they had gone. Vicky said they met again over a beer at Paradise.

The Schoenfields were more "our kind" of people—that's what my mother would have said. Prominent Jews with money and maybe some links to organized crime, though no one mentioned those. If I'd stayed in Winonah the way the rest of my friends had, I probably would have married someone like Nick. It was no secret in Winonah that Mr. S. was disappointed over Nick's marriage to Margaret Blair and that he had never quite forgiven his son for marrying her.

The conversation took a long time and I sipped my brandy slowly. It is always strange to be on one end of a conversation, but I could imagine what was being said on the other side. Nick kept saying, "No, that's not true. No, I didn't do that. You know I wouldn't." I had to drive home so I put the brandy aside, not wanting it to go to my head. Finally Nick put the receiver down and with a big sigh looked up at me. "I guess you know who that was."

"I guess I do," I said.

"Well, it just hasn't been easy. She's pretty impossible, you know."

"Actually, I don't know. I mean, I remember how she was when we were girls, but I don't know how she is now."

"You can't imagine. Sometimes she goes into the city and doesn't tell us where she's going. Oh, she's always home by bedtime, but it still drives Danielle crazy. She's nice, then she blows up for no reason. It's as if she doesn't care about me at all, then suddenly she has to have me." Nick shrugged. "I'm going to leave her. I haven't told her yet, but I'm not staying. It's like living with a time bomb."

I was surprised to hear that. It sent a chill through me because I remembered when Margaret told me she had a time bomb in her chest. I was also surprised that Nick would confide so much in me since we didn't know each other well and hadn't seen each other for many years. "But you've been together a long time."

"She's never really loved me," he said. "I loved her, but she never loved me. She just wanted things. That's what's been the worst of it for me, loving someone who doesn't love me."

"I'm sure she loved you."

"No, she didn't. She can't. She loves our daughter. That's the only person she loves. Even then, I wonder. There's a part of her that's just not here."

I nodded, wondering why he had married her in the first place. "There was always something strange about her, Nick."

"Yes, maybe that's what I liked about her." He said thoughtfully, "She was unpredictable, but she made things interesting. That counts for something, doesn't it?"

"It does," I agreed. I said I needed to head back and he walked me down to the lobby. "It was good to see you, Tess." He kissed me on the cheek. "You haven't changed." As I turned to leave, he pulled me to him. I wanted to burrow into his chest and stay there, but just as quickly as he held me, he let me go. "Drive safely," he said, helping me into my car.

As I drove, the highway twisted and turned before my eyes and I had trouble following the road. I'd driven this road a million times and now it was as if I'd never driven it before. But that happens to me sometimes. I'm somewhere I know very well and all of a sudden it's as if I'd never been there before.

When I got home, I went straight to bed. In the morning I went for a long run up in the hills. When I started out I was fine, but once I got up into the wilderness area I started to feel as if I wasn't alone. I felt as if there was something trailing me. Many times my children have begged me not to run up here without a buddy, but then, what's the point of going with a buddy if you want to be by yourself?

As I ran, I kept turning around, expecting to see something barreling down on me, but I never did. Still, I couldn't help but feel that there was something out there and it was watching me.

14

In the dog days of summer, when we could think of little else to do, Vicky and I formed the Firefighters of America. I'm not sure what it was about fires—the heat, the possibility of being trapped with no way out—but it seemed we wanted to stop them. Not that we had ever really seen a fire, except once when Lindsey's Delicatessen burned down, or had ever been in danger of a fire, but we spent hours thinking about how to prevent them and put them out.

We did some research at the fire department and learned that a "dead man's room" is a room with only one exit. We liked the way the firefighters smelled like burning leaves. We made a list of all the kinds of fires we wanted to put a stop to—fires made by foolish children playing with matches, by careless mothers who left hot oil on the stove, by too many plugs in one outlet. Brushfires started when a cigarette was tossed from a moving car or when lightning struck the ground in the woods. Wildfires. We wanted to put a stop to all of these.

We made little badges out of cardboard with FOA carefully inscribed. Small, contained flames leapt into the air on our badges. We colored them orange with a blue glow at the base. We wanted them to be just so, just right. I had no idea how we would protect anyone, but still we made up these little badges.

Then we went from door to door, canvassing the neighborhood. We rang doorbells, and the neighbors who knew us were very nice. I thought that this was what it must be like for my father as he traveled from town to town, talking to people about the disasters they could avert just by signing their names. The neighbors who opened their doors to us listened politely to what we had to say, accepted what we had to offer. We asked for small donations for being members of Fire-fighters of America. The most we ever got from anyone was a quarter and we bought candy with it.

After a few days we had done my neighborhood and hers and weeks of the summer still stretched before us. We thought about expanding, casting a wider net. We followed the road along the railroad tracks, stopping here and there. We cut over to the other side. In some of these houses people didn't come to the door.

People spoke with accents. Dark men, unshaven in T-shirts, answered the door. These men smelled of cigarettes and hair oil and something sour we couldn't quite place. In the background we could see broken furniture, sofas with their stuffing coming out. Often these doors were slammed in our faces.

We knew the houses along the railroad tracks weren't where we should be. It was different here, and we felt as if we had wandered into a foreign country, past the safe boundaries of our own. Old women sat not far from the doors as if they were expecting someone, but not us, to arrive. Strong cooking smells came from behind these doors—greasy meats, sauces, dead animals. Once or twice we passed Prairie Vista Automotive and, looking up, saw where Margaret lived.

"What do you think it's like up there?" Vicky asked.

I thought of Mrs. Blair in her short skirts, her heels clicking on the asphalt, and my father watching her laugh. "I know what it's like," I told her. "The woman who irons my father's shirts has been up there." It was a lie, but I thought of those Saturdays when my father and I stood peering up at the apartment above Santini's Liquor. I concocted dingy rooms that stank of onions and smoke, gray sheets, linoleum floors. I invented walls that were gray, red-striped wallpaper pulling away from them. In her spare time Margaret would peel it back some more. She had found trains in her room, boats in her mother's. The rest of the house was trees.

I found myself making up entire scenarios, full of misery and intrigue. Her mother tells her to stop peeling back the wallpaper. She says there's lead in it or something, and she says she's ruining the walls, but Margaret can't seem to stop wanting to see what's on the other side.

Clarice Blair cleans the place all the time. She gets on her knees and scrubs the floor. She scrubs the cabinets and the counters as if company is going to walk in at any moment, but they never do. Nobody ever goes there. Still, her mother never stops her scrubbing, then she yells at Margaret because she doesn't do anything to help. Margaret is a bastard, but Clarice has never told her. Clarice isn't even sure who the real father is.

Sometimes on purpose Margaret leaves dishes in the sink. She doesn't make her bed. Just to anger her mother. Or she'll make it, but not fluff the pillow just right. She does this just to drive her mother wild. Margaret is ashamed of who she is and where she lives. She doesn't want her friends to hear her mother speak with her cackly laugh or see her put on her uniform to go to work. When Clarice Blair goes to work for Dr. Reiss, the dentist in town, she dresses all in white—white stockings, white shoes, a white uniform.

Clarice Blair should not wear white, or yellow, or any of the pale colors. She should wear blue brocade, red taffeta. She should be presented at balls. Instead she lives with her daughter above a store. She never complains, though her daughter does. Still, this is a woman who once lived in a house surrounded by lilac trees and played the violin on a stage. Now she dresses in white and keeps a doctor's appointment book. She is paying for her many mistakes.

Vicky listened to all of this, aghast and enraptured as I described for her the strange and tragic life of Margaret Blair. "Elena told you all that?"

I was proud that Vicky had believed my fib. "That and more."

Vicky nodded. "Well, it makes perfect sense."

"I'm sworn to secrecy, so please don't tell anyone."

Vicky crossed her heart and hoped to die, promising she wouldn't tell a soul.

That was the summer when the alewives died. They died by the millions. Their stinking carcasses covered the beaches and carpeted the sea for half a mile or more. The stench made its way up from the waterfront and the bluffs to the houses, such as ours, that were blocks away. No one knew why the fish died, but we knew that we could not go down to the beach that summer.

Day after day Vicky and I canvassed the neighborhood, trying to interest people in the Firefighters of America. Our search took us farther and farther from home, deeper into Prairie Vista than we'd ever been. We had more doors slammed in our faces, people shouting at us to go away.

After days of discouragement, Vicky wanted to ring Margaret's door. What's the worst that could happen? Vicky said. I hesitated, knew that all I'd told Vicky was lies, but then it seemed to me that perhaps I hadn't lied. That probably things were much as I'd envisioned them. It was a hot July day and the air stank of garbage and dead fish and the fumes from the repair shop across the way as we rang the buzzer at Margaret Blair's door.

Standing on the hot asphalt we waited a few moments and then I said to Vicky, "See, no one's home. Let's go." We were starting to walk away when someone buzzed us in. We entered a dingy vestibule and Margaret called down to us, "Up here." We climbed a flight of stairs and there at the landing was Margaret, nicely dressed in blue Bermuda shorts and a matching top and smiling as if she had been expecting us all along.

To our surprise the rooms were cheery. The walls were painted bright colors—rose and aquamarine; there was no grayness. No peeling wallpaper. The apartment smelled of soap and potpourri—nothing of what I'd imagined. No bacon-and-eggs smell. Vicky gave me a "I thought you said . . ." look and I shrugged back at her "I guess Elena got it wrong."

"It's so nice to see you girls," Mrs. Blair said, an apron around her waist, a wide smile on her face. Her jet-black hair pulled back, red lipstick on as if she had someplace to go. She invited us to sit at the table and poured for us tall, cold glasses of lemonade. She placed a plate of cookies in front of us, cut into the shapes of diamonds and stars, so buttery they melted in your mouth. It was hot but a fan blew and we felt cool and comfortable inside.

"Margaret, give them the grand tour," Mrs. Blair said with her hearty laugh, so we got to see the rest of the apartment, which was four more rooms. Her mother's room was all white with big pillows on the four poster bed. The bed had a canopy and I'd never seen one before and Margaret let us sit under it for a few minutes. Then she showed us the living room, where there were pictures of horses chasing foxes on the wall, and the bathroom that had pink, fluffy towels. I asked if I could wash my hands so that I could touch one and it was very soft. When I asked Elena if she could make our towels that soft, she told me to shut up and mind my own business.

In Margaret's room the shelves were filled with blue-eyed dolls wearing lacy dresses. Stuffed bears and rabbits and dogs covered her bed. We played with Margaret's dolls and she introduced us to each one and they had names like Deirdre and Gruswalda. Strange, foreign names. Margaret wanted to know about the Firefighters of America and we explained to her what we'd learned about putting out fires. How you never throw water on a grease fire. How if a person is burning, throw a blanket on top. We told her about the "dead man's room" and she seemed very interested in this.

"You mean there's no way out."

"There's only one way out, but if there's a fire, then there's no way out."

"No way out," Margaret said, running her hands up and down her arms as if she had the shivers. "Explain it to me again."

Vicky and I sighed, thinking she was dumb. "You're trapped," I told her.

"Oh, I get it now." After that, Margaret said she wanted to volunteer for Firefighters of America. She wanted to help us the next time we went house to house. We said sure, though Vicky and I soon lost interest in our organization and never went house to house again.

We played until it was dark, when Clarice offered to drive us home. Margaret came along for the ride and she told her mother exactly where to turn. She knew the way to our houses as if she had been there dozens of times, not once or twice.

When she dropped me off, Clarice commented on how beautiful our houses were. "You live in a very pretty house," she said, holding my arm with her long red nails. "Oh, it must be so lovely to live here." As I opened the door, she said, "Say hello to your nice father for me." Then she begged me to come back again. She said it so many times that I found myself racing to the door.

15

Spices filled the air. Cardamom, cinnamon, cilantro. Jade was testing me to see if I could name them. She was cooking something, some kind of stew. "You have to try it, Mom," she said. I took sips, dipped into the savory broth. It was spicy, hot. Jade had become a vegan, announcing she wouldn't eat anything that moved. Nothing with arms or legs.

When Jade wasn't home, I sneaked ham sandwiches, cheese, but lately, since Ted now spent most of his time with Cherri up the coast, this cooking filled the house. Now my daughter brought these savory smells. "So I saw him again," Jade said as she stirred the pot. She said it slowly so I wouldn't think she was crazy.

"You saw whom again?"

She nodded slowly. "You know, the old sea captain. On the cliffs the night you were in town. He was holding his compass."

I wanted to take Jade into my arms, hold back the tide of her fears. Two or three times she had seen this old captain walking the bluff past our house. I'd always attributed this to Jade's wild imagination and to the fact that she's never liked to be alone.

Yet I had a sense, since I'd returned from Winonah, that things weren't quite as they'd been before. I am still, though not to the extent that I was as a girl, an orderly person with an archival sense of where things belong. So it surprised me when I found small objects out of place. A slip of paper was missing from a drawer, shoes were not on their shelves. I found sweaters draped over chairs. There was a scent of perfume. Once in the shower, I felt hands coursing my body. Hands that knew where they were going. For an instant, I couldn't catch my breath.

Jade served me her vegetable stew, which she poured over curried rice. I was taking my first bites as she warmed her hands over her food, said a prayer. She had explained to me something about how she was transferring the energy from the food into her body and how she was thanking the vegetables for sharing themselves with her, but I didn't quite understand it. "This is delicious," I told her, and it was.

"Thanks, Mom. I want to be healthy. I want to eat better food."

"Well, that's a good idea." We ate in silence for a while. "So do you have plans for this weekend?" I asked her.

"Maybe," she said, her head bowed over her steaming rice, "not sure."

"I was thinking we could do something. Drive up to San Francisco. You could see Dad."

She shrugged. "I don't know . . . Weren't you just in San Francisco the other day? Didn't you see one of your old pals?"

"Yes, I saw a man named Nick Schoenfield. His father was a famous quarterback."

"That's nice. You gonna see him again?"

"Maybe. When he comes back to town." I found that I wanted to talk about Nick and our time together, but I didn't think she'd understand. Could I tell her about his bad marriage? About the hopes he'd once had of being a great athlete like his father? Jade would find these things quaint, like old pictures she discovered in dusty frames that were charming but not quite relevant to her.

After dinner Jade took her dishes to the sink. "You cooked; I'll clean up," I told her, so without a protest, she left them there and headed to her room. After a little while I got up and rinsed them, washed the pots. Wiped the counters clean. Then I went and sat in the living room, thinking I'd read for a while.

The den felt chilly. A draft seemed to be coming from the stone fireplace. In some of the rooms of the house—the ones where the light never gets in and the walls are always dank—I kept blankets on the backs of chairs. The blanket from Winonah's centennial was one of these.

I didn't, in fact, like to sit in the den that much, even though, along with the kitchen, it has the best coastal views, because the chill never leaves these walls. There is a dankness to certain rooms and at times I have kept one or two locked. Still there is always a draft and the wind around the house is a relentless howl.

Wrapping the Winonah centennial blanket around me, I sat in the den, sipping my tea. On the coffee table was a volume of Francis Eagger's poems and I leafed through it until I came upon the poem Bruno had liked, entitled "Old Hat." I remembered how that was a favorite expression of Lily's. I read a few lines: "sleepers swathed in gauze; a young girl dashing naked through city streets; wild swans attack children who feed them, engulfing them in their wings. These are just bad dreams."

These lines surprised me. Once my brothers and I were attacked while feeding wild swans. They swooped down on us, battering us with their wings until our parents chased them away. And just recently I'd had a dream of me chasing Jade, who was running naked down a city street. It was as if the poet had read my own dreams, written them there.

I was shivering so I wrapped myself tightly into "Home of the Winonah Wildcats." The train station and Winonah Summer Festival graced my lap. Trying to get warm, I felt restless now and wished Jade would come and bother me. My visit with Nick was on my mind. Our talk over dinner, a sadness that seeped into his blue-gray eyes. I felt uneasy as I thought about Margaret. It seemed she was drinking too much and her marriage was on the rocks. She's not my problem, I told myself. She never was. Other things were my problem—like how I was going to make ends meet.

Money seemed tight and there were bills I had to put aside. I thought of calling Jeb and asking for a loan, but Jeb has a way of making me feel I have mismanaged my life and so I don't like to ask him for anything unless I have to. In the end he always tells me—as does Charlie—to sell my house, which is now actually worth something. It does no good to argue with either of them that this is my home. Instead of calling him, I sat curled up, making income and expense lists on pads of yellow paper. The sea pounded below my house in a way that was almost frightening and made me think about the reunion and what it had been like being back home. How it had felt, parking my car on the beach, being there once more. I felt a funny kind of longing that I can't quite remember ever feeling before though I'm sure I felt it a million times when there was someone I wanted. I sat there, thinking I missed something I didn't even know mattered.

The house felt lonely and cold with Jade in her room with the door shut, listening to music. There was no one I could talk to. I decided to call Shana and see if she'd meet me for dinner the next night. But when I picked up the phone, I heard the voices on the line. The same voices I'd heard a few weeks before. This time the woman, whose voice was still familiar to me, had a problem. A fight with her husband, who was jealous over her friendship with another man. "Excuse me," I said. I tried to shout at them that they were on my line, but once again they could not hear me.

"Well, does he have a reason to be jealous?"

"Oh, I don't know."

"Well, if there's no reason, then what's the point?"

Because the voice was familiar, I continued to listen as they went on to share a recipe for Moroccan chicken, which required lime pickle, purchased from a spice store in Saratoga. Then the conversation went back to some difficulty the woman was having.

As I listened, I suddenly placed the voice. It was my nearest neighbor, Betsy Bernhart, a person I hardly knew, except that she sometimes got my mail and now, it seemed, I got her phone calls. Once I had to return her cat to her and once or twice she'd complained when the kids played their music too loud. But now I listened as she told him that things hadn't been too good lately. That she had been having second thoughts about her childless marriage. "Don't let appearances fool you," she said to the man.

"Really," the man said, "I didn't know."

When I hung up, I decided that the next time I saw Betsy, I'd have to tell her that our wires were crossed. It was not long afterward that the phone rang again and I decided that if it was another crossed line I'd have to go and discuss the problem with her now.

Instead I heard a man's voice on the other end. "Can you talk?" Nick said.

I was surprised at how glad I was to hear his voice. "Yes, I can talk." I curled up with my legs under me, the blanket across my lap. His voice sounded distraught and far away.

"Listen," he said, "I know you don't live here anymore, but you did. You know what it's like. I can't really talk to anyone, but I thought I could talk to you. I felt as if you understood my situation the other night."

There was something warm and comforting in Nick's voice. We could be friends; we could be there for one another. Yet at the same time it seemed as if I were sinking into a dark hole, a place I wasn't sure I wanted to be. A strange, slightly scary place. I didn't know what I had or hadn't understood. "I'm not sure I can be helpful."

"Tessie, you know Margaret. You were once friends."

"I don't know if we were ever really friends."

"But you know things about her." He sighed. "I wish you were here. I wish we could sit and talk. I have so much I want to tell you. If we could sit across from one another and talk all night long, I think you'd understand."

Holding the phone tightly against my ear, I nodded. "Yes," I said, "I think we could tell each other lots of things."

"I'm going to leave her. She lies to me all the time. She's a drunk. We aren't a couple anymore. We haven't been for a long time. She threatens me with all kinds of things. . . ." He sounded very tired. "If it weren't for Danielle—"

"She threatens you?"

"Oh, she says she'll kill herself. Or she'll take Danielle away from me. But that's mainly when she's drunk."

"You have to do what you think is best."

"Best for me or best for everyone?"

I hesitated, not because I didn't want to answer, but because I suddenly thought about my neighbor, Betsy, and the crossed line. I wondered if she could overhear this conversation the way I could overhear hers. And what would she be making of it?

"I like you, Tessie. I feel as if we can be friends."

"We are friends," I said.

"Yes," he said, "we already are. But I want to know about you. I don't want to just talk about me. I want to learn about you. . . . Listen, can I call you from time to time? When I want company . . ."

His voice wasn't as bold, as sure of itself, as it had been. There was a slight tremor, a shaky edge that I hadn't heard before. I'd never thought of Nick as being weak when it came to emotions. He always struck me as a person who had the upper hand. But now he sounded almost afraid.

Wrapping the blanket more tightly around my legs, I found myself reassuring him. "Of course you can."

"That's great, thanks." He sounded relieved. "I'd really like to know you're out there if I need you. Look," he said, "I've got to go. I'll call you soon." Then he hung up quickly, as if someone had just walked in the room.

16

"We really should have them over, don't you think?" Lily said, running her hands through her hair. I was sitting at the dining room table, doing my homework while Lily perused some cookbooks. She entertained more than she used to, poring over recipes when our father was on the road. Sometimes she tried her recipes out on us, but mostly they were for guests. On counters lay open *The Joy of Cooking, The Secrets of the Italian Kitchen*. She made *canard l'orange* and *steak au poivre*. "At first I didn't want to, but now I just think we should."

"Have who over?" Victor replied, a Cincinnati—half beer, half cream soda—in his hand, standing in the kitchen doorway.

"You know," Lily went on, not really looking up at him, "the new family, the new people. The mother who lives with that girl over the liquor store. In Tess's class, the one she walks to school with now and then."

"I'm not sure which girl that is," Victor said.

"Oh, yes, you do, you know the people. I feel sorry for that girl. There's something about her. Something so sad. They are nice, actually. The mother—she has an odd name, Clarice—she works for Dr. Reiss. I've spoken with her from time to time when I call for appointments. She has the nicest things to say about Tessie. I think they're just, well, poor. Down on their luck."

Victor pondered this while Lily made her case. "Oh, yes, I met her, didn't I, Tessie? A few weeks ago. The mother and girl who live across from the repair shop."

"I don't think they live there anymore," I said, looking up from my homework. "They've moved to one of those houses just past the railroad trestle."

"Well, that's good," Lily said. "I'm sure it's better over there."

"And the father?" Victor asked. "Has anybody met him?"

Lily shrugged. "There doesn't seem to be a father."

"Margaret talks about him all the time, but I've never seen him," I offered.

"Well, I think we should invite the mother." Lily flipped through her cookbooks, scribbling down future menus.

"So then, yes, why not. Have them over." My father disappeared back into the kitchen with his Cincinnati.

"Don't you think we should have something small, something simple?"

"Sure," my father called, "whatever suits you." But something always came up and Lily never quite got around to making the phone call, inviting them over. She thought about it, the way my mother thought about everything, mulling it over, thinking it through, weighing the pros and cons, then forgot about the idea for a long, long time.

We lived a block or so from the railroad tracks on the south side of town. During the day when I wandered around, I liked to walk along the tracks, where I found the crushed remains of birds and squirrels. Once I found a cat cut right in two.

As soon as I crossed under the trestle, I found myself in the part of town where the houses were small and gray with front porches with broken screens, tricycles on the front lawns, laundry hung out to dry in the warmer months. The Skid Row of Winonah, my father called it.

There were smells I couldn't quite recognize but they left an oily taste in my mouth and there were garbage cans you could see, not hidden in a big bin like ours were. I don't even remember my parents ever taking out the garbage, though of course they must have, but here you could see it in cans that lined the sides of the houses, sometimes spilling over the tops. Often I saw men in uniforms coming in and out of these houses and they weren't coming to fix things, but actually lived here.

It was to this row of gray houses with battered front porches that Clarice Blair settled with Margaret a year or so after she'd arrived in Winonah. She'd taken a job as a receptionist for Dr. Reiss, a dentist who worked out west near Crestwood, and I guess she'd done well enough to move. It wasn't the house on the lake that Margaret said she'd once lived in, but it wasn't over Santini's Liquor Store either.

You could tell that Clarice had tried to fix the place up because the porch screens were repaired and she'd painted the house white. Though there wasn't any trash on her lawn and she had even planted a few pink and white flowers out front, there was plenty of trash on the lawns around hers so it seemed a little pointless. She'd tried to make the house look pretty, but it still looked shabby like the others around it, as if it were going to fall down.

Whenever Clarice or Margaret saw me walking by, they invited me inside. It seemed as if I couldn't walk down this road without being seen by one of them. I had a feeling after a while that they were waiting for me. Usually Margaret came onto the porch to greet me, then asked me to come inside and play.

The house was small and smelled like cats, but Mrs. Blair had tried to make it cozy. Pictures of dogs and flowers hung on the walls. There were toys in corners and a few potted plants by the windows and one plant I liked very much, with long, purplish-green tentacles, that hung in the kitchen and Mrs. Blair told me was called a Wandering

Jew, which I thought was a strange name for a plant. "Just like you, Tessie," Mrs. Blair said, "always wandering around."

Whenever I stopped by, or whenever they spotted me walking and called me in, Clarice Blair always gave us milk and a plate of cookies and then Margaret would ask me to go upstairs into her room. Margaret's room was done up nicely with pink bedspreads and white curtains. But Margaret never wanted to just sit in the sun and gossip about the boys the way the rest of the gang did. Margaret had elaborate scenes she liked to act out. Pioneer sisters was one of her favorites. I was a sick sister who had to be nursed back to health and only Margaret could do this, pressing poultices to my head. She liked to save me more than she liked having me save her. She wanted me to do dramatic things that went against my nature—stagger into the room, collapse breathlessly upon the bed so she could rush to my side and lament. Once real tears coursed down her cheeks, which I thought was taking the game too far.

When we played pioneer sisters, she had calico skirts and bonnets we had to put on. Or satin and tulle skirts if we were princesses. When we were princesses, we were sentenced to the Tower and only Margaret knew how we'd escape. These games were complete with informants, guards, and go-betweens, often played by Margaret as well, and we played them as if they were not games at all, but something very real.

Before I left, Clarice Blair always made a point of telling me how much she appreciated that I was friends with Margaret; how much that meant to her. She said that Margaret hadn't had an easy time because they had moved around so much and that sometimes little girls misunderstood her. I was ashamed when Clarice Blair said these things to me and I hoped when I left the house that none of the gang would ever know I went there.

To get from my house to Margaret's you had to walk a block or two, then pass under the railroad trestle. It was just a viaduct. The trestle itself led to a big turnabout where engines could be turned around. Before Margaret came to Winonah, I never walked on the trestle because it was a bridge and if a train were coming, there was nowhere to go. Some of the boys—the bad boys who hung out at the Idiot's Circle, that small circle of grass at the train station where boys with nothing better to do sat and smoked and drank beer after school—raced the trains across the trestle, but no girls did. My brother Jeb came home with stories about boys who almost didn't make it, boys who'd had to make a dive for the bushes. The most I ever did was put a nickel on the tracks and see how flat it came out after the train rode over it.

But Margaret, once she'd moved from Santini's to the house near the trestle, always dared us to go with her to play there. She taunted us. She stood in the middle of the trestle, waving her arms. "What is it with you guys? You so scared?" We got tired of her taunting and agreed to go along.

The first few times we crossed the railroad trestle, we dashed across. But Margaret stood in the middle, arms akimbo, laughing her high-pitched laugh. She stood there, her black hair blowing in the breeze, her olive skin looking so sleek and smooth, and you almost had the feeling that she could stop a locomotive if one came barreling down on her.

In October we had a burst of Indian summer and the knowledge that the warmth and freshness in the air were the last hint of summer we'd have before winter set in. We wanted to take the long way home, to meander through the ravines one last time before they were filled with ice and snow. I was the only one who knew the routes the way Margaret did and together we ambled through the ravines, soaking our shoes, but we didn't care. The air was warm and the sunlight shone through the maples that had already turned gold. Scanning the ground, we searched for arrowheads but found none.

We walked until we came to Lincoln, past the library, the police station, under the trestle to where the old turnabout was. We lingered here, tossing stones, and when we looked up, we heard Margaret calling to us. "Last one across the railroad bridge gets a free milk shake." That was always the dare, not to be the first, but the last.

Because I lived so close to the tracks, I knew the times of the trains. I could recite them in my sleep. The 8:05, the 9:32, the 10:27, and so on. I was used to the bell ringing, the gates going down. "The four twenty-four is due," I said, but Margaret laughed and raced up the grassy embankment to the trestle. We scrambled on with her and then started to run. But in the middle we paused because Margaret had some nickels and pennies she wanted to place on the tracks. She was meticulously lining up her coins when I heard the train whistle.

"Run, Tessie," Vicky, who was already across the railroad bridge, shouted. "Tessie, run!"

Behind me the 4:24 was barreling down. I ran as fast as I've ever run before or since. The train seemed to be gaining on me and I heard its whistle blow as if it were right inside my head. I ran perhaps only twenty yards or so before I dove for the bushes, breathless, my heart pounding.

Even as the train approached the trestle, its horn blaring, I heard that sharp, staccato laughter. That *ta-ta-ta,* almost like an opera singer during a mad scene. "Oh, Tessie," Margaret shouted from the middle of the railroad bridge, "you looked so funny and you had it beat by a mile."

When we turned, we saw Margaret standing there, arms outstretched, black hair waving in the breeze. Her eyes were shut tight and she seemed to be taking enormous pleasure in the moment. I shouted to her, "Margaret, run, *run!*"

When it already seemed too late, as if all were lost, she began to run. She dashed across the bridge and just as the train seemed about to run over her, its whistle blaring, she dove for the bushes. She lay there, still, and we thought she was unconscious or even dead. Blood trickled from scratches along the side of her face. Other cuts bled on her hands where she'd landed in the briars.

"Oh, my God," said Samantha Crawford, who was always a little afraid. "What're we going to do?"

"She's fine," I said, "she's just faking it." I shook and shook her, but she didn't move.

"We should go get help," Vicky said.

"I'll go," Lori Martin, with her take-charge attitude, said. Just as Lori dashed off, Margaret opened her eyes and laughed that high-pitched laugh. "Fooled you, didn't I?" she said, laughing as blood trickled down her cheek.

"It's not funny," I told her. "We thought you were hurt."

"Oh, Tessie," Margaret said, "you take things too seriously."

One night, just a few days later, Margaret came to my window and tossed pebbles until I came down. I was still angry with her for the trick she'd pulled on the tracks and I told her so. "I'm sorry, Tessie. It's just that you guys seemed so scared."

We sat down together on the grass and she picked a blade, made a whistle of it between her teeth. I plucked a blade and tried to whistle through it, but I couldn't get that high, piercing sound Margaret got with hers.

In the distance we heard the 8:35 rushing through, announcing my bedtime. "Have you ever had this sensation?" Margaret asked me. "You are sitting in a train in the station and the train next to you starts to move. You think you're the one who's moving when, in fact, you're standing still."

I told her I couldn't remember ever having had that sensation.

"Well, when you have it," she said, getting up to leave, "you'll know."

Those were the last warm days of fall and then winter was upon us. It seemed an especially hard winter that year. The snow drifts were six feet high and we had to wade through them to school. I stayed inside more than I wanted and found it confining, as did my brothers. So we were relieved in January when there was a thaw. An unusual warm spell, you could never predict. The temperature rose and the snow melted. Big soggy pools of it. There was mud on the lawns. Puddles to jump in, splash through. For days we frolicked. Went to school in our shirtsleeves with just windbreakers on. We played ball, skipped, and the air had the green freshness of spring, as if the flowers would pop out of the ground, and the woods behind our house were carpeted in jack-in-the-pulpits.

Then one night it began to rain. We were asleep so we hardly noticed the rain or the temperature falling. It dropped steadily in the night so that before dawn a freezing rain was falling and by morning it was a glazed-over world. Everything white and shiny, slippery to the touch.

The power lines were down. There was no heat. Our father built a fire in the fireplace in the middle of the day, and we toasted wieners, marshmallows, whatever could be toasted over the flame. We huddled by the fire while my father thought about what we should do because it was all slick outside and nowhere to go.

When I pressed my face to the glass, my steamy breath made little snowflakes, and when I wiped it away, there she was. Skating on our lawn, up and down our driveway. "Look at that," our father said.

I wiped the glass, pressed my face closer, and saw for myself. Margaret was skating across our lawn in long, even glides. When she saw us at the window, she beckoned for me to join her. "Well," my father said, laughing, "you've got to go out there."

At first I was reluctant, but then I put my skates on. Together we skated up and down on the lawn, then on the streets, my parents gazing at us through the frosty glass.

In the spring of that year when the air was fresh and there was a hint of leaves and grass—you could already feel things starting to grow—my mother told me that we were having company for dinner. She didn't say who, except that it was a surprise. She told me I should go upstairs and get cleaned up. Since we often had company for dinner on the weekends when my father was home, I wasn't particularly curious, though I always wanted to know what we were eating.

Soon the house was filled with the bustle of preparations. We had "help"—a grumpy older woman named Emma who came in a white uniform when there were parties—and my mother told her exactly what to do. My mother fluttered through the kitchen, her hands flying as she chopped something. She could whip up just about anything in half a second. She made creamed spinach I can still taste, buttery and smooth. She fried fish with almonds and brown butter so it came out so crunchy you'd never know it was fish. It wasn't like other houses, where you got meatloaf every night of the week. People loved to come to our house.

When I asked who was coming, Lily looked distracted. My mother always seemed to have a million things to do, but if people were coming over, she never stopped until the party was over. The freckles on her nose glistened with sweat as she pushed a strand of hair, which I noticed for the first time was turning gray, off her face. Her hands arched over whatever she was chopping. Nobody, she said, just a few friends.

I didn't bother asking how "nobody" could be friends, but I was surprised when I found Clarice Blair sitting in our living room with a cocktail napkin on her lap. She wore dark stockings and a short black cocktail dress. She had this funny hat on with a veil that looked ridiculous to me, as if she were coming to a funeral, not a dinner party. Her dress was straight and tight and she had difficulty keeping her legs together. She had great legs, legs Margaret would eventually inherit, and she kept swishing them back in forth in a single motion.

We had other people over as well—a golf partner of my father's and Mr. and Mrs. McKenzie from next door, who was blind as a bat, and Mr. and Mrs. Lerner, whose daughter was known for doing things with boys after basketball games, though these parents obviously didn't have a clue. While I was passing out a tray (my mother made me do stuff like this) with little cheese puffs, I heard Mr. Lerner say to Mr. McKenzie, "I can't tell you how many friends we have who don't even know they need an oil change." This was hardly my mother's A list of friends, not that she exactly had an A list, but my mother was a good hostess and she treated everybody, even the man who mowed the lawn, like equals, no matter what she thought about them or said behind their backs.

There were many stories circulating about Clarice Blair. Everyone wondered who she was and where she'd come from. It had never made sense that a white woman with a child would come to town and live above Santini's. People hinted that there'd never been any husband. I'd heard mothers talking over coffee: She acted like a lady, but she didn't live like one. Some said she was running away. That she was a tramp. I'd heard women say that they should be careful with someone like that in town.

But as my father sat next to her, playing host, I saw a thin, small woman with an oversized laugh who put Hershey's Kisses in her daughter's lunch and gave me fresh-baked cookies and cold milk when I walked by her rented house. She had eyes like someone asking a judge for mercy. You couldn't help but feel sorry for her and I guess my mother did since she had invited her.

My father could be a very good host, offering people drinks, making sure they had cheese puffs and cucumber sandwiches on their hors d'oeuvre plate. "Clarice, would you like another martini?" he asked. "Clarice, more cheese and crackers?" He passed her a tray. He made small talk with her about the kids and school and those kinds of safe things adults talk about when they don't know what else to talk about. "Oh, yes," I heard him say, "you really can't be too careful these days."

Careful about what? I wondered as I watched Mrs. Blair cross and uncross her legs awkwardly as she tried to maneuver a little hors d'oeuvre plate and a drink. My father was talking to her about his work. About the disasters he'd seen. When the tornado chased him down the road; the river that carried an entire living room set, one piece at a time, downstream. At each disaster she put her hand over her mouth and said, "Oh, and then what happened," over and over, still balancing her martini and plate on her lap.

My father went into great detail with each story as Clarice Blair listened intently, her eyes round as saucers. Then he paused and now he seemed to be watching her carefully, as if he expected her to topple over at any minute. From time to time she crossed and uncrossed her legs. Even from the other side of the room I could hear the sound of her silk stockings scraping together, a slick, whooshing sound like hockey skates turning on ice.

Later that night I sat on a chair in front of the mirror in my room. In the other room I heard my parents arguing through the walls. More and more common an occurrence, it seemed. My mother shouted something about how he had talked to that woman all night, telling her his lies.

I wasn't exactly listening as I tried crossing my legs the way she had, knees and shins tight together. First to the left, then to the right. Like a pendulum I moved my legs back and forth. Then I parted my legs and saw how dark it was. How you could hardly see what was inside.

17

Christmas is about the worst time to be in Illinois if you don't like winter. I actually do like winter, but I have a fear of being snowbound, trapped. A fear that I can't get out. But shortly after Thanksgiving my mother had declared that she didn't have long to live and asked me to come home. "This will be my last Christmas," she said. Of course, it wasn't, but since she hadn't asked me to come from California in a while and she often came to see me and the kids, I agreed to fly home.

Besides, Nick had been calling me almost every night and I thought this might be a good excuse to see him. I'd found myself waiting up for his late-night calls. I imagined him slipping out of bed, tiptoeing down to the kitchen in bare feet to the phone. He whispered into it when I picked up. I loved the way he said my name, with that silibant "s," the way people once said his father's. "Tessie," I'd hear.

Some nights if I couldn't sleep, I'd wrap myself up in an armchair in my Winonah centennial blanket, hoping the phone would ring. Some nights it did; some nights it didn't. When it didn't, I was surprised at how disappointed I felt.

Often our conversations revolved around him, around his marriage to Margaret. How she drank too much and seemed indifferent to everyone except Danielle. How it was hardly a real marriage anymore, though once it had been. But slowly the conversations began to turn to me. He wanted to know more and more about me so I spoke of my marriage, never quite able to pinpoint what had gone wrong. I told him that there seemed to be something that stood between me and the world.

I pondered these conversations as the plane flew. Though it was the holidays, perhaps I'd get a chance to see Nick while I was in town. From the window of the plane I looked down upon those long flat stretches; the green farmland; the wheat from what were probably now cooperative farms blowing in the wind, but that from above still looked like the wheat of the prairie I had always known. Even as I flew above the floodplain in winter, the Mississippi was swollen, its banks flooded, pockets of the river looking more like small lakes. Land laid to waste.

I have seen what water and wind and disaster can do. When I was a girl, I had to get away. I could not bear the open expanses. Everything was flat. I had a feeling even then that anything could happen. There was nothing to stop the water, the wind. It could all be swept away.

For a few days I slept on my mother's hideaway sofa and helped her with things around the apartment. I wanted to call Nick but resisted the urge. He knew where to find me. He knew I was at my mother's and where she lived. But still I found myself thinking about him, wondering if he was shopping for holiday gifts, if he would get something for me.

The first morning my mother and I ate cottage cheese and crackers and she talked about her will and who was getting what. In the last five years or so she always talked about her will and who was getting what, and it hadn't changed all that much. But it made her feel better to go over everything with me again.

As she was discussing her will, I kept waiting for the phone to ring. It did from time to time. Always a friend of hers. That evening I picked up the phone and called Nick. A child answered. It was the first time I'd heard Danielle's voice and she sounded older than her years. I hung up quickly.

My second day there my mother handed me a book of Santa Claus stickers, the kind you put on gifts, and she told me to put one on whatever possessions I wanted when she was gone. My mother sat watching CNN as I wandered through her apartment with my box of stickers. I paused at her silver, a pewter plate I'd always admired, a painting done by someone who was briefly famous in Chicago. I glanced at these objects, but I did not put a sticker on them.

My mother was slowly unencumbering herself of her belongings, she told me, shouting above CNN. "Art's gonna come and take whatever you don't want," she called. Silver trays, porcelain pitchers, antique tables. I could see them all in Art's collectibles shop on Walton. I moved from room to room.

I paused before a photograph on the wall of me and my brothers and my father and Lily. We are standing in front of a tepee and an Indian chief in full feather is doing a little dance. Jeb has a tomahawk in his hand, Art wears a silly grin, always the clown. I'm a bit crumpled, my long stringy hair falling in my face. But we are all smiling, mugging for the camera.

We are dressed like pioneers. Art and Jeb and I have on coonskin caps, my father is in a buckskin jacket, and my mother in a long skirt. I don't remember the trip we took to the Dells, where this picture was taken, except for one night.

We were sitting in a circle of bleachers around a campfire and the

Indians were dancing. I did not know that this was for tourists; I thought it was for me. They were dancing and as they danced they dropped colored sand onto the ground. Blue and red and green, and they made designs on the ground—a lake, an eagle, a cornstalk, the sun.

The music of the drums grew loud and the Indians moved in their moccasins, heads thrown back, and the colored sand was being tossed to the ground. An intricate pattern was emerging and I saw it illuminated by the light of the fire. Perhaps I was tired. I was cold and a chill ran through me. During the dancing, my mother reached for my father's hand. She touched him gently, but he pulled away. In the glistening light of the fire, tears formed in her eyes.

I took out a Santa Claus sticker and put it on this picture. It was the only object in her apartment that I put a sticker on.

18

Every Monday as soon as our father's car disappeared under the railroad trestle, Lily took over the house. She spread out into all the rooms. She slept wherever she wanted. Some nights we'd find her on the couch or on the chaise in front of the TV. Other nights she'd appear in one of our rooms, the cover pulled up to her chin, snoring slightly.

It frightened me to find my mother in my room as if she were a ghost, as if she were already dead, all white with the sheet up to her chin, but then I heard her breathing, and I knew that it was one of those nights when my mother roamed. In her own way it seemed as if she ached for him. Yet she seemed to do better when he wasn't around.

It was as if in his absence she had to fill a void. What was it about water—how it seeks its own level? How it displaces whatever has filled the space within. That's what she would do. Lily would expand, fill up the house. Some wives, when their husbands go away, fold up like a flower when the sun leaves the sky. I was this way with Charlie. But not Lily. She opened. She beamed and expanded. Projects suddenly presented themselves. Came out of the closets, where she'd tucked them. There were quilts to be sewn, family albums to fill. Bulbs she'd been saving suddenly got planted. Letters were written. Books she wanted to read piled up at her bedside.

And then on Thursday she started to pull it all in, put it away, as if the photo album or the quilt or the letters on her desk were some big dark secret, something she had to hide. Back in the closet they'd go. And then she cleaned up the house and did all the chores she'd been avoiding doing before Victor got home.

Then just as suddenly as he'd left, he'd be home—Victor Winterstone, the deli man, cutter of chubs, fine slicer of cheeses, full of stories from the road. No one could layer a corned beef sandwich like he could. He made us his favorite drinks—black cows, 7-Up floats. Then he would pour himself a Cincinnati.

We sat around the table and he'd say, "I want to hear everything. Everything you did all week." He listened to every word. Grades, friends, points we scored, what we lost. He wanted to hear it all. Then we begged him to tell us the things he saw. A house turned around in a tornado so that its front door was now its back. A cat, clawing the water, being carried downstream. Disasters, lives in disarray, those were the stories my father brought with him from his weekly trips on the road.

When our father came home, he was gentle at first. Subdued. He had the weary look of the traveler about him and on that first night he'd sleep a dozen hours. Never mind the chores, the home repairs that had to be done. He looked at Lily as if they'd just been introduced and it was beginning all over again.

Indeed, their children got to witness their parents' courtship begin all over again every Thursday. They locked their door on Thursday night and we could only imagine what might be taking place behind that closed door.

And then by Friday night they would forget they had just met. The shouting started from upstairs and downstairs. He called for his boys, his girl, his best girl, his Button, his Squirrel, his little men, and Lily, oh, Lily, never bothering to walk the flight or two to find us, but shouting for us just the same. His big, amplified voice carried through the house, past closed doors, and headed out toward the lake, out to the prairie, the plains, rattling through the Midwest, his voice like a sonic boom, bursting the limits. "Okay, guys, I'm home," he'd shout, and we'd make a pretend grab for the crystal.

Lily heard, but acted as if she hadn't. Hands over her ears, she walked around complaining of the noise, the disarray our father brought with him when he returned from the road. Soon our father grew subdued. It only took a day or two before Victor Winterstone became an intruder in his own home.

Every Monday like clockwork our father left and every Thursday, though sometimes it stretched itself into Friday, he returned. Those trips with him to the floodplain stopped, but we still begged our father to let us go. Art especially wouldn't let up because Art had never gone. To Art the cow floating on its back, the cars resting in trees were just stories we'd made up, something we lorded over him.

We asked in the summer on our vacations, "Can't we go, Dad?" and he'd say, "Come on, aren't you kids getting a little big for that sort of thing?" We'd kick and punch him in the arm, but the truth was we loved to go to those truck stops and eat pancakes stacked with butter and maple syrup. We loved the motel rooms with the TVs. I longed for "acancy" again.

But the trips dropped away and after a while we grew accustomed in the summer to the melancholy feel on the Monday mornings of our father's departures, the quiet that came over the house when he was gone, and the excitement that grew as the day approached when he came home.

We grew so accustomed to the way he eased himself in and out of our lives that after a while we didn't notice. After a while it seemed as if he hadn't really gone anywhere at all.

But obviously he had. The roof sprang leaks, paint peeled on the walls. He spent what little time he had at home fixing things, but still he seemed to leave earlier each week and come home later. Sometimes he didn't make it home on Thursdays at all. The Thursday night rituals, the platters of deli food, Victor and Lily acting as if they'd just met, none of this seemed to be happening anymore.

Though I can't say that I noticed. I was a busy girl. I was gone all the time to baton twirling and basketball, to student council and school paper. I had so many activities I couldn't think straight. On my wall there was a chart: "Where I Have to Be and When," it was called, and just about every box was filled in.

And Jeb. He was running wild, hanging out at the Idiot's Circle by the train station with the other bums. I'd see him smoking cigarettes, and he'd give me curt little waves. "You're going to get in trouble," I'd yell at him, but what did he care.

Jeb got straight A's. He never cracked a book. "How do you do it?" I'd shout at him in the evenings.

"I just listen and learn," he'd say, mocking me.

Lily walked around, cursing. Shouting at me to go get Jeb and bring him home. She'd say her children were running wild, all except Art, who still cried on Monday morning when our father left. Even though he was older we still had to pry his fingers off the car.

One Friday afternoon when my father returned, Lily gave him the silent treatment. Walking around in a huff, slamming doors. Then she stomped upstairs and he followed her. I heard them fighting in their bedroom. This was becoming a more common occurrence, but still I stopped to listen. Just like Jeb said. Listen and learn. I heard the voices rising.

"Why do you even bother?" Lily shouted. "Why do you even bother coming back here at all?"

"Because this is where I live," he shouted back.

"No, you don't. You're hardly ever here," she yelled at him. "We never see you. You don't really live here at all."

One night I woke to find my mother standing at the foot of my bed. She wore a white gown and at first I thought she was a ghost. She was weeping. It was a silent weeping, but I saw the tears that streaked her face. I closed my eyes and pretended to sleep.

19

Paradise was decorated for Christmas. Dozens of little angels were suspended everywhere. Colored lights were strung from one end of the room to the other. Stockings hung off the draft beer levers. Vicky was sitting at the bar, nursing a bottle of amber. I'd called her the day after Christmas and said I wanted to drive up. Jimmy and the kids were skiing in Wisconsin. She was glad for the company.

She looked a little older, as if she needed a vacation. Even she would admit how strange it was that she worked in a travel agency but never went anywhere. Vicky gave me a big hug as I looked around the place. "Forget it," she said, "he's not here."

Chills ran up and down my arm. I hadn't told her I'd been in touch with Nick. I wondered if somehow she knew. "Who's not here?"

"Oh, you know, Patrick. Seriously, did anything happen the night of the reunion? I'm dying to know."

"Things that slow around here?" I didn't want to talk about Patrick. I had other things I wanted to talk to her about. But I sensed that it was perhaps best not to talk about Nick. That it wasn't the right time to tell anyone, especially not in Winonah. It wasn't that I didn't trust Vicky. I didn't trust the town. It had a way of finding out what you didn't want it to know.

I ordered a rum and Coke and Vicky kept giving me the eye. "Okay," I said, "nothing happened."

"Nothing? You didn't make plans to see one another again?"

"Not at all. He walked me to my car. That was it."

"Oh, brother." She was still laughing when Patrick walked in. He didn't see us at first as he said hello to his bartender, to the cashier. The music was Del Shannon's "Runaway," and he turned it up as he walked by the stereo. He was going over the receipts, humming to himself, when he looked our way. Then he sauntered over in his jeans and flannel shirt. "You must be moving back."

"My mother's been sick," I said. "She asked me to come home for the holidays."

"I'm sorry to hear that." He looked genuinely concerned. He also looked tired and his bad eye started to wander.

"How've you been?"

"Oh, hanging in there." He laughed, slipping into the booth beside me. We chatted for a little while with his arm dangling across the back of my seat. Then he said he'd love to get caught up. "I don't want to intrude on your girls' time. I've got some things to take care of. Come back tomorrow and I'll take you someplace nice." He spoke to me, not to Vicky.

"I've gotta be back at my mom's tomorrow night."

"Well," he patted my arm, "next time then."

"Next time," I said.

When Patrick left, I was suddenly hungry so we ordered a pizza. I wanted a vegetarian but she wanted pepperoni and anchovies so we split the difference and got an anchovy and broccoli, which wasn't very good. "You know, I like that guy," Vicky said after Patrick disappeared somewhere back in the kitchen. "I don't know why, I just do."

"Well, I like him too."

"So how is life really treating you?" Vicky asked over another beer.

"Actually, it's not the easiest time for me. The kids can't seem to leave home and I want to get on with my life. I'm having trouble making ends meet and keep thinking about getting a real estate broker's license. What I really want to do is turn my place into a B-and-B."

"Good tax write-off."

"That's what everyone says, but I can't seem to get the insurance I need. I actually like the idea of people coming to stay. I love where I live. I don't want to have to move. We aren't getting any younger, you know—"

"You're telling me."

Vicky paused, staring at her hands. She turned them to the right and left in front of her. They were beautiful, with long, white, slim fingers, and she could hold them gracefully in front of her like a dancer. She had wanted to model her whole body, but only her hands had had any success. "You know, I used to be able to make real money with these hands. But it's not the same now. Ten years ago I did Pampers. Now I expect I'll be getting calls for Depends. I used to do Flintstone's aspirin. Last week I did Geritol. The producers are getting younger. They call me a 'tweenie,' somewhere between old and young. They look at me and say, 'Can we float her over a table? Can she stay awake for a two A.M. shoot?' In a few years, I'll just be doing the travel agency stuff. I don't mind it, but it's not what I think I was put on the planet to do. You know, we could get into something together. Start our own travel business or something. Specialize in spiritual journeys, some New Age thing that will make us rich. I've been looking to start my own business. You've always got the ideas, Tessie."

I tried to imagine what it would be like to go into business with Vicky and decided it wouldn't be so good. I loved to see her once or twice a year, talk about old times over a glass of wine. But a business was just something I knew I couldn't do. "Well, let's think about it." Resting her hands on the table, Vicky gave me a nod as if to say, sure, we'd think about it. Then she pulled them into her lap.

We had one more beer between us and I was pretty far gone by then. When we asked for our bill, we were told it had been taken care of, and we both started saying how nice that was of Patrick, how he shouldn't have. Then we staggered arm in arm across the parking lot. It was a freezing winter's night and the cold air stung our faces. When I breathed, my nostrils burned. We gazed up at the proliferation of stars. I'd forgotten how clear nights in Winonah can be. "Are you okay?" I asked. "Are you sure you can drive?"

"Oh, I can drive. . . . Can you?"

"If you stick to a straight line, I think I can follow you."

Vicky drove and somehow I stayed behind her on the way back to her house. Snowbanks were piled high along the road. My car slid a few times. I'd never been to her house before, but it was down Hazel, about a half a mile from the lake.

The room she put me in smelled fresh and clean, though the bedspread was some kind of polyester. The sheets were a little scratchy but, thinking how it was the first night I'd slept in Winonah since I'd left for college, I fell asleep as soon as my head hit the pillow.

20

Many nights I woke to the sound of pebbles tossed against my window. I tried to ignore it, but it would go on for a long time. When I opened the blinds, there she was. I didn't know how she got out, how she slipped away from her house. But she did. She motioned for me and I slid down the drainpipe and we huddled on my porch, eating Eskimo Pies and giggling over boys. I liked Patrick and Margaret was starting to hint—as many girls did—that she liked my brother Jeb.

Even I liked Jeb then. He had pale blue eyes, dark black curls, and he played basketball well. I thought Jeb liked her as well because sometimes he'd ask me why I didn't bring Margaret over on Saturdays to hang out.

She started following me home after school during the day. I didn't want her to, but she just seemed to appear on my corner, near my house, and what choice did I have but to ask her in?

Now she was below my window again, tossing pebbles. I slid down the drainpipe and she asked where my mother kept her sewing kit and I told her downstairs in the basement. We went down there and dug around until we found it. Then Margaret plucked a needle from the tomato-shaped pincushion. "Here," she said, "this is what we need."

"What are we going to do with that?"

"We're going to be blood sisters."

I didn't know if I wanted to exchange blood with her, but Margaret told me we should. "We're closer than you think; we're already like sisters, you know." I told her I didn't know. "Anyway, neither of us has a sister; now we'll be sisters for life." I didn't want to. I didn't want the feeling of Margaret sticking something into my flesh. I didn't want her to inflict pain on me.

But she reached for my hand, holding it tight. Slowly she opened my fingers. She massaged one finger, forcing the blood up to the tip as if she'd done this before. I pulled my hand away, but she grabbed it back.

"Don't do it," I said. "It's going to hurt."

"No, it won't. I'll do it very quickly."

"You won't and it *will* hurt."

"If I hurt you, you can stab me with the needle."

"Why would I want to do that?"

"You can do whatever you want."

"I don't want to do anything; I just don't want it to hurt."

"Look, let me see your hand." She unfolded my fingers once again, rubbed my hand with her finger, and then before I could pull away, she sank the needle in. It was quick and just a prick. Then my blood oozed.

"Okay, now you do me."

She opened her hand, which I saw was fraught with many lines jutting this way and that. I glanced at my palm and saw it was cut only by a few lines, clear highways. But hers was like some incomprehensible street map of an old European city, a city with twists and turns and secret alleyways you get lost in if you walk down, and years later when I traveled to some of those cities and saw their maps, I thought how they reminded me of Margaret's hands. "Do it," she said, staring at her finger.

I tried to sink the needle in, but I was surprised at the resistant flesh. I tried again and with a pop the needle sunk. Margaret jumped a little, bit her lip. The feeling of it going in made me cringe.

Then we pressed our fingers together, smeared blood to blood. And our blood became one. "Now we are friends for life," Margaret said, pressing her finger to mine. "From now on," she said, "when you cut yourself, I will bleed."

My stomach felt queasy and I thought I might retch. Out of all the friends I had, I wasn't sure that I wanted to be her friend for life. I didn't want to make this pact with her. I didn't even like her that much, but now she'd done this and I had joined in; she'd made us one.

Then she said she had to get going; she needed to head home. We went upstairs and Margaret walked outside. It was a warm, spring evening and I decided I'd walk her part way, until we came to the trestle. "Well, here we are, the great divide," Margaret said.

I knew what she meant, but I didn't say anything. Then Margaret turned to me as she was leaving. "You know, my father, he's going to come and get me soon. He wrote me just the other day and he was going to send for me in the next few weeks or so. I'm old enough to choose which parent I want to live with and I'd like to get away from my mom."

"She seems like a nice mother," I said, thinking how Clarice Blair seemed to try so hard.

"She drove him away. It was her fault," she said under her breath, as if speaking to herself. I was surprised by the bitterness in her voice.

"Well, it must be hard for her, being alone and all."

"Oh, she's not that alone. Anyway, it won't be that much longer. I'll be gone before summer's through."

I was slightly hurt that she said this. I didn't even want to be blood sisters with her and now I was and she said she was leaving. She must have read my thoughts because she tapped me on the chest. "My blood goes through you and yours goes through me. So even when I do go away, you'll be with me forever. From now on if I cut myself," Margaret said, "you'll bleed."

Shouldn't this be the other way around? I thought to myself. If *you* cut yourself—but no, she said it this way. *If I cut myself,* you'll *bleed.*

Margaret walked toward the trestle. She waved good-bye in long, arching waves. When she disappeared under the dark shadows, I turned and headed home.

21

When I woke in the morning, it was late and Vicky was gone. It took me a while before I could move my head and then the rest of me to get out of bed, so I'm not sure how long I lay there before I got up. Vicky had left me a pot of coffee, fresh-squeezed juice, and a jar of aspirin. She'd also written a note, saying she'd had to head off to work at the travel agency; she'd see me later in the day, and I should make myself at home.

Sitting in her kitchen, I sipped the juice. I ran my hand across her Formica tabletop, her pristine kitchen. A framed photo of her husband and kids was on the countertop, and on the icebox was a magnetic things-to-do pad, but other than that there wasn't the smallest trace of clutter, a crumb anywhere, and it made me sad to think of how I couldn't keep order in my own home, where Jade and Ted left their dishes in the sink, their sweatshirts draped across chairs.

I could envision the unpaid bills that lay tucked between newspapers and mail-order catalogs, the laundry that never quite got folded. The den I'd never gotten around to fixing up. But Vicky had somehow mastered her domestic tasks. Even her dog, Liberty, a big blond mutt she'd picked up at Orphans of the Storm, seemed somehow to eat neatly out of his bowl.

I was famished and made myself a breakfast of bacon and eggs, buttered toast, and more coffee. I ate slowly, looking out the window as I sat at her kitchen table. A blue jay and a few winter sparrows fluttered at the bird feeder. I took my time, savoring every bite of breakfast. It seemed as if this was how I started my day every day. When I was done, I let Liberty lick the yolk off my plate. Then I washed my dishes, the frying pan, cleaned every crumb off the kitchen counter. Next I took a long hot shower, using her lavender soap, her herbal shampoos.

I settled down to read some magazines—they were all lying in a big basket—after breakfast and the dog sat at my feet, staring at me. Every time I made a move, he followed me—upstairs, downstairs, into the bathroom.

I tried to read an article about a toxic-waste site near Crestwood, but the dog kept looking at me, reminding me that here I was back in Winonah with nothing to do. "Do you want to go out, boy, is that it?" Liberty leaped to his feet and began racing back and forth from my chair to the door. I wondered if he'd need a leash or if he'd just follow. I searched for the leash and couldn't find it. The dog was jumping circles in the air so I decided to let him follow me.

It was a freezing-cold morning, as cold as it was hot when I'd first come home last August. The weather of my childhood was a study in contrasts and extremes, and it was perhaps the one thing I'd missed since I had been living in California, the seasonal change. Out there I know it is winter when the fog settles in. Mud, earthquake, drought. Those have become the seasons of my adult years.

I wasn't sure which way I wanted to walk. At first I thought I'd stick to the road and just follow the houses, and Liberty trotted along, tail drooping. The wind was frigid off the lake and I decided I wanted to see Lake Michigan, to see if there were ice floes. I cut down Mulberry and over to the lake where the Indian trails were. The trails were old blazed paths. You could follow them through Winonah, then dip into the ravines and wind up just about anywhere. The spirit of Winonah was said to wander these ravines. The Potawatomi gave Winonah its name. Winonah was a princess ravished four times by a manitou god named Ae-pungishimook and she gave birth to four sons. Through her mating with a god, Winonah acquired fertility and long life. When I told Jade about the spirit of Winonah, she chortled, "So you come from a place named after a date-raped single mother with a lot on her plate."

There wasn't much trace of the Indians—except for the trails that wound their way down to the lake and the trees that they had bent and tied to mark those trails—because the Potawatomi were nomadic and lived in moveable lodges. It was less that they were wiped out than that they seemed to have just moved on, though some of their descendants live on a reservation in the Dells.

The wind was fierce off the lake and already I felt the cold seep into my lips, my cheeks. The dog walked with his head cast down, fighting the freezing wind. As we approached the first ravine, I thought we could get away from the wind if we climbed down into them. I often did this as a child, navigated my way home along the ravines. They wended their way through the town like trenches dug out at a time of war, cut by glaciers during the last Ice Age, and the Potawatomi used them for traveling. Gazing down, the ravine didn't seem that deep and its bottom was covered with snow. Liberty looked at me warily as I slipped down the embankment.

It was steeper than I recalled and I was surprised at how far down I went. The embankment was icy and slick and I lost my footing once or twice on my way down and slid partway on my rear. The dog refused to follow me, standing on the lip of the ravine, howling. He looked small up there, pathetic in his howls, and I had to call to him several times before he'd come. Then he just rested on his paws and slid down.

The bottom was icy with a layer of crusty snow, but at least we were shielded from the wind. In some places the snow had melted and I could see frozen leaves beneath the ice. It hadn't snowed in a while or else the bottom of the ravines would have had thicker snow. I was a little disappointed to be walking on ice, though perhaps it would be easier on my feet.

I hadn't been down in one of the ravines since I was a girl, when I liked to roam them on my way home, sometimes with a friend or two, but mostly alone. The ravines contained all the mysteries of the place to me. I loved the way they turned and wound their way into one another, and there seemed to be a million ways to go when you wandered in them, but no right way, exactly, and no way to get lost. They weren't that deep so you could always climb out, but they were deep enough so nobody could see you when you were inside. In this sense they were the perfect place to hide.

Sometimes in the spring, water ran heavily through them and I'd clomp along in boots, sloshing through mud. Though they have never overflowed, it is dangerous to go into the ravines when there is the rush of melting snow. But during the winter and fall they were dry, except for the piles of wet leaves or snow that collected, and I could make my way along them as if they were canyons.

As a girl, I'd found things down there. Arrowheads, or so I liked to believe of the polished stones I uncovered in the sandy slopes of the ravines beneath the underpasses, and bits of shard, which more likely than not were from broken beer bottles that boys flung down from their cars as they crossed the bridges on Saturday night. I pretended I was a pioneer girl or an Indian scout until I'd hear my father calling me to come home.

It didn't seem to matter which way we went so I let Liberty decide. He turned right and I followed him, taking the turns of the ravines. The air was fresh, but also freezing. My fingers and nose were already numb. Liberty lifted his leg by a pure white bank of snow. A yellow stream like a snake sizzled into the snow, leaving a yellow stain. I had to pee as well. I'd had too much coffee, but I couldn't bring myself to pee there. I kept going, my bladder aching.

I followed their twists and turns until we came to a small bridge with a culvert running under it. There were names graffitied to the walls of the bridge. There was also a condom and a crack vial. I never saw these when I was a girl and was wondering if it was a good idea to be down here when I heard the crunch of my boot on the ice. As soon as I stepped on the thin ice, my boot went through. It hadn't occurred to me that where the water flowed out of the culvert under the bridge, the ice might not hold. Cold water surged around my shoes as I stumbled past the soft spot, and the chill of the icy water seeped into my boots.

Liberty followed quickly behind me and he too stumbled into the shallow pool of freezing water. He yelped and jumped off to the side, licking his paws. Already my wet feet were starting to freeze. The dog whimpered and I decided we should climb out at the next place where the ravine was shallow. We walked on a little ways but in fact the ravine bed seemed to be deepening and I suspected we had turned northeast and were heading back along the lake. I remembered as a girl how this was the deepest part of the ravine, the part where the glaciers came off the lake.

Now the dog began to cry in earnest and my toes were turning numb. I tried to wiggle them in my boots, but they were stiff and aching. I figured I had about half an hour to get them warm before I was in trouble. Hadn't I grown up here? Didn't I know what the freezing cold and wetness could do? I was like a caged animal that had lost its instinct for the wild. I felt foolish and mad as I decided to climb out wherever we were, go to a nearby house, and call Vicky to come and get us.

The embankment was a sheet of ice. Icy and slick. It would be almost impossible for us to climb out. We wandered the ravine a little further until we came to a part where there was a clump of trees. I tried to claw my way up, holding on to the trunks of the saplings, and I got up a little ways before I realized that Liberty couldn't make it. He sat in the depth of the ravines, trying to scramble after me but slipping back down. I called to him, "Come on, boy, come on," two or three times but he just slipped back, howling at the bottom.

Somehow I would have to drag or carry the dog. I wasn't sure how I was going to do this since he must have weighed fifty or sixty pounds, but I knew that's what I had to do. Unless I left him there and went for help. But what if he wandered off and got lost? Or froze to death? I decided not to leave the dog but figure out a way to pull him out.

I slid back down the embankment and walked on a bit farther. Here the ravine evened out and I could see the tops of some houses. I knew we must be near the lake now and I thought I could hear its waves crashing against the icy shore. There were some clumps of trees I could hold on to. Once more I tried to coax the dog up the embankment, but he just sat back on his haunches and whimpered. Now I scooped my right arm beneath him. I would have to hold him in one arm as I pulled myself up the embankment with the other.

With my first step I slid back and the dog tumbled into the hard, crusty snow. I took off my gloves and found I could get a better grip, though my hands were freezing and already the tips of my fingers were turning white. Stuffing my gloves into my pockets, I reached for the dog again.

He was trembling now, shaking from head to toe and looked at me with pleading eyes. "I am so stupid," I told him, "bringing us down here." To think I had taken such a wrong turn, hadn't planned for this eventuality. Had forgotten the rules of this place that I'd known by heart as a girl.

Before my hands froze, I had to get us up that embankment. I looked for an easier place to climb and found one slightly ahead under another little bridge. It was less steep beneath the bridge and also there was some exposed ground. Sandy patches where I could get my footing. I called the dog to me, but he wouldn't come. Then reluctantly he limped over, the pads of his feet half frozen now.

"Come on, boy, give me a hand." Again I scooped him up and felt him trembling in my arms, a soft whimpering coming from his throat. "Not a very tough guy, are you?" I said. I used my free hand to brace me as I clawed my way up, first grabbing a branch, then digging into a patch of exposed earth. The dog started to shake harder, then struggle in my arms, and I almost lost my balance, slipping back down, but I scrambled, digging my heels in, pulling myself with my free hand wherever there was a branch or a sapling trunk.

The top was the most slippery because ice had formed a solid lip there that jutted out slightly and made it difficult to get over. As I felt along the ice, I knew that I would need two hands to get over the top. Bracing myself just below this icy lip, I tried to scoop the dog into both my hands and heave him over the edge. My feet slipped and I couldn't get any leverage.

Now I held him against my knees and shoved him up the side. He cried, then disappeared over the edge. A moment later he came back and peered down at me, a worried look in his eyes. "Stand back," I told him. I got as close as I could to the lip, then reached across it as far as I could and, finally, I hoisted myself over the top.

When we came up, I looked around. I knew I had to get to a house nearby and ask for help. At first I was disoriented, unsure of where the ravines had taken me, but as I looked around, I knew exactly where I was. I was on Laurel, and if I turned right it would take me to the bluffs and down to the lake.

That's where the Schoenfield house was. At the end of this street was where Nick and Margaret lived. Now I knew where I was going. I'd been going there all along.

22

"Let's have a sleepover," Margaret said. "Let's camp out in the woods." Some of the gang were hanging out in my playroom. The rec room was an idea of my father's; he built it himself with his own two hands. Grace Cousins, who had bad breath and never stopped talking, was there and so was Maureen Hetherford, whose hair would turn stark white when she divorced her first husband years from now. Vicky sat at the bar, sipping a Coke.

Lori Martin said, "That's a great idea." Lori was already set to organize things. "Let's go home, get sleeping bags. What about food?"

"Camp in the woods?" Grace Cousins, who was always chicken, said. "No way."

But the rest of us liked the idea. The best place to camp, and we knew it, was the small woodsy area behind my house. The rest of the Winonah woods were far from houses, but there were still a few acres behind my house, a small forest that sloped toward the bluffs. In the middle of it was a small clearing. It was close enough to my house that we could come back in if we got hungry or cold. Or scared.

Everybody called home, checked with her parents. My father said, "Whatever makes you happy, Tess." Lily told me to air out the sleeping bags because they'd been lying in a cold basement all winter long. Grace Cousins didn't bother to check with hers because she wouldn't be caught dead sleeping out of doors, and Vicky called Samantha Crawford because she was so nice and everyone liked her. It was a warm afternoon of early June and we agreed to meet back at my house at six o'clock.

With my father I went to the store. We bought hot dogs, potato chips, soda, marshmallows, graham crackers, Hershey bars for s'mores. My father said he'd help us build a small campfire, but we'd have to put it out before we went to sleep. I knew how to put out a fire—you kicked dirt on it; that's what you did. We could roast our hot dogs and marshmallows over it.

On the way into the woods we collected roasting sticks. I put a box of matches in my pocket and my father came with us, leading the way. In the clearing, with a small spade he brought, he dug a ditch. He'd brought some charcoal and he put it on the bottom. Then we piled on twigs and leaves. Some of us went and looked for logs. When my father had the fire going, he was ready to leave. I wanted him to leave so I could be with my friends. It was embarrassing that he was here at all. "Is there anything else you girls will need?" he asked and we told him no, but I saw in his eyes there was something uncertain, like a little bit of fear. He didn't want to leave us here.

"Well, if there is, just come back to the house. All right, Tess? If you girls need anything, you come home."

My father wandered off, clomping back the few hundred yards through the woods. His head was bent as if he was sad and thought he'd never see me again. Quickly we spread out our sleeping bags, everyone fighting for her space. Samantha wanted to be near Lori, but I wanted to be near Vicky and Lori did too. Nobody wanted to be near Margaret but somehow she wound up with her sleeping bag on one side of me. I made a face at Vicky, who shrugged, then moved her bag to the other side of mine.

With our roasting sticks we sat on logs and roasted hot dogs, marshmallows. We made s'mores with chocolate and graham crackers. We sat until it was dark, eating and telling jokes about boys. Everyone said who they liked and who they thought liked them. Then Lori Martin said, "Let's share secrets!" And Maureen, who always went along with Lori said, "Yes, let's share secrets."

We squealed and said we didn't want to, but Lori said it would be fun and we'd all get closer. We'd be better friends after that. Samantha Crawford told that she had borrowed some of her sister's clothes and worn them without telling her, which hardly seemed like a secret at all, especially since the Crawfords owned the only clothing store in town and Samantha was always loaning everybody her clothes anyway. Then Lori, who we'd always thought of as being the good citizen, told us that she'd stolen money from her mother's drawer and that seemed like a crime and something that should be kept a secret. It didn't seem like something Lori would do and we were quiet for a while, even after she added that later she confessed and paid her mother back.

Vicky said her mother kept this weird rubber disk in her drawer by her bed and Vicky and Ginger Klein got caught playing catch with it one day. Then Ginger told us that her parents made gross noises in their bed and she listened through the wall.

Margaret said she had one, but hers was such a big secret she couldn't tell, not to any of us, that's how big it was. We begged her, we pleaded, but she said no. Her secret was just that big. I didn't have a secret. I'd never had one and as hard as I tried, I couldn't come up with a single real secret. I couldn't even make one up. This bothered me a great deal that night as we sat around the campfire; that I had nothing I'd been holding on to, nothing I couldn't give away.

We were sitting, pondering our secrets or the lack of them, and suddenly Margaret jumped up and whipped off her shirt. "Let's be Indians," she said. "Let's dance around the fire." She began to whirl in a circle, her feet flying off the ground. With her hand over her mouth she whooped like an Indian. Her breasts were tiny buds, but by the light of the fire they bobbed up and down. In her underwear alone she twirled, her hair catching the light of the fire, its blue blackness like dark water reflecting the moon.

Her frenzied feet tapped as she reached for each of us, grabbing us by the hands. "Come on," she said. "Come on!" She pulled Samantha up and Samantha, who was always shy and cried at the slightest thing, whipped off her T-shirt. Her breasts weren't even formed. They were there flat on her chest, but she danced, pulling up Vicky. Then she reached for me. Now we were all whooping, whirling, bare-chested, circling our fading fire, our voices rising in the light of the moon.

I saw it only when I paused, looking at them. A shape or a shadow lurking in the trees. Now moving among them it was white, but barely. A specter moving among us, slipping in and out among the trees. "Look," I said, pointing, "what's that?" I'd heard about the ghost woman, bearer of Indian braves, whose heart was made of flint. She was there in white, darting, watching us from between the trees. We had disturbed her resting spirit with our brazen and disrespectful dance.

Now I saw the spectral form the ghost of Winonah peering at us from among the trees. "Stop," I told them. Their dancing ceased slowly, one at a time, as they paused and gazed where I was pointing. Suddenly hands went up to cover bare chests. They saw it too—the woman in white, watching us as we stood there frozen, naked, and scared.

Scrambling for our shirts, we dressed. We were screaming, shouting. Then we watched in silence for a moment as the apparition moved between the trees. "It's a person in a sheet," Lori said, but the rest of us trembled. Beside me Margaret cried, "I want my daddy; I want my daddy." There was a strange keen to her cry, a howl almost. I had never heard anything like it before.

"Shush," I told her. "Be quiet," I told them all.

I kicked dirt into the fire, putting it out. We hid our faces in our sleeping bags. When we looked up again, we saw that the spirit—whatever it was—was receding, disappearing in the direction of my house. A few days later Jeb would ask me what all that commotion was in the woods and if we'd slept all right.

Now as we lay in our sleeping bags, Margaret sidled up to me. "Tess," she whispered into my ear, "I can't sleep."

I always got stuck, I thought. I always got stuck with her. "Here," I said, unzipping my bag, "crawl in with me."

We zipped our bags together and I felt her long legs wrapping themselves around me, and her thick, unreal hair tumbling across my shoulders like a blanket.

"I want my daddy," she said again, trembling. Then she sobbed and sobbed. It was an otherworldly sob that came from deep inside of her and its desperation startled me. As she cried I realized that her father hadn't come and taken her away like she'd said he would. I stroked her cheek, told her that everything would be all right. Before I knew it, Margaret was asleep. I felt her warm breath on my neck as I peered into the woods, thinking that the specter would reveal itself again.

Step on a crack, you break your mother's back. Step on a dime, you break your mother's spine. It was that same June, just days later as I wandered through the town, playing the game I knew only too well. I avoided the cracks, fearing what would happen if I stepped on them.

I didn't see the storm clouds as I headed toward the tracks. Stop, Tess, I should have told myself. Don't go there. But I did not stop. I kept going, one foot at a time. I followed the street, across the road, under the trestle. I wanted to climb up on the tracks, go to the turn-about, but charcoal clouds gathered above me. The wind rose, dust devils spun at my heels. A storm had suddenly come upon me. The sky turned black as night and I couldn't see the cracks in the pavement anymore.

Lightning crashed overhead and I was frightened. I could run home, but I'd never make it. But if I dashed under the trestle, up the street, there, just ahead, not five minutes away, was Margaret's house. Not the one over the store but the one she moved into not so far from mine. Just under the trestle on the other side of the tracks. I would be safe there, I told myself. I raced the storm past houses with broken-down porches, automobile parts on the front lawns.

Then I reached the door. It was all like a nursery rhyme to me. *Knock, knock. Who's there? It's me. Tess.* Thunder cracked, lightning sliced through the sky.

Slowly Margaret opened the door. The smile on her face turned to a look of surprise. I heard voices, voices behind her, and one was a woman's laugh and the other the big, noisy laugh of a man. He had a big, boisterous voice that took up the whole room. Margaret stepped aside, making room for me to pass, and I walked in, shaking the rain from my hair.

My father was sitting in the living room. He had one arm draped across the sofa, feet resting on the coffee table as if he lived there. Suddenly he jumped to his feet. "Tessie," he said, "you're all wet. Did you get caught in the storm?" He was up, patting my hair. "Clarice wanted help with her insurance," he said, drying me off with his hand. "But I think we're about finished now, aren't we?"

Clarice nodded her head, smiling at me. "Would you like some cookies, Tess? Would you like a dry shirt?"

I was thinking about what day it was. How it was Thursday afternoon. It was early for him to be in Winonah. My father wasn't due home until suppertime. "Come on, Tessie," he said, putting his arm firmly around my shoulder, "I'll drive you home."

In the car my father tapped his fingers nervously on the wheel. He drove north toward the high school, taking the long way around. We drove in silence until he turned to me with his gray eyes and said, "Lis-

ten, no point mentioning this to your mother. You know how she is."
Actually, I didn't know how she was but then he reached across, patting
me on the arm. "Let's just keep it between you and me, okay, pal?"

"Sure, Dad, no problem."

"That's my Squirrel," he said, landing a fake punch on my jaw. As
we drove home, I felt a sour feeling in my stomach, as if I'd eaten
something that had gone bad. But it didn't bother me as much as it
should have because now I had something the other girls had. I had a
secret too.

23

I'm not sure what I looked like with a half-frozen dog in my arms as I
made my way into the small courtyard and rang the bell. I waited, but
no one came. I thought I would freeze on their doorstep when at last I
heard footsteps coming slowly to the door. The door was opened and
a girl stood there.

She was perhaps nine or ten and she looked as glum as any child I'd
ever seen. She had dark circles under her eyes, as she had in the picture Nick had showed me, and her hair was a stringy mess. At first I
thought she was ill or even disabled, but she spoke in a clear, distinct
voice, a little old for her years. "May I help you?"

"Yes, is your mother home?"

The girl hesitated. Then she shook her head. "No, she went to the
store."

"Well, could I use your bathroom and your phone? We've had a
small accident. The dog is very cold and so am I."

The child hesitated again but it didn't seem as if she was afraid to
let a stranger into the house. I felt more as if I was intruding on her,
imposing on her solitude. As if she was busy with something and
didn't want to be disturbed. But what solitude could a child need at
this age? I had no idea, but I asked once again. "I just have to make a

phone call. We've been trapped in the ravines. And if I could use the bathroom . . ."

Looking somewhat annoyed, she flung the door open. "Do you have a towel? So I can wrap the dog?" The girl left and came back with a red and blue beach towel with a giant bear on it. I took off my boots and my feet burned.

"Okay." I turned to the girl. "My name is Tess. I went to school with your parents and I need to use the phone." She looked at me as if I were from Mars and then pointed to a powder room in the hallway and into the kitchen for the phone. "Are you home alone?" She nodded, then disappeared into the back of the house.

I went into the bathroom first, where I thought I'd burst. It was all pink with a powdery smell, fluffy pink towels just for guests. I could barely get my fingers to work as I unzipped my pants. The toilet seat was cold and the hot stream of urine that seemed to go on forever burned my thighs. Then I ran my hands under hot water for a long time.

When I came out, the girl was nowhere to be seen so I made my way into the kitchen for the phone. The kitchen was messy, dishes piled in the sink, but there was lots of counter space. Shiny copper pots that hung overhead looked as if they'd never been used. I didn't have Vicky's work number with me and tried to remember the name of the travel agency she worked for, but couldn't. There were North Shore Yellow Pages tucked under the phone, so I looked under "Travel." Six were listed in the area. I phoned the first one but Vicky didn't work there. I tried another number and she didn't work there either. I was still shivering, my teeth chattering, and I decided to warm up before I tried again.

I walked in my stocking feet into the sunken living room. The house was a sprawling white ranch with lots of windows and wings jutting off. A small Japanese courtyard opened onto the living room. The large picture window of the living room looked over the lake.

The living room was furnished impeccably in whites and grays, but it was oddly devoid of personal possessions. There were no pictures, no mementos, except for one picture of Nick's father, a football he was about to hurl held in his hand, eyes set dead ahead. Except for that picture, the living room looked as if it were about to be photographed for *Architectural Digest*, not a place where people actually lived.

I couldn't help but think how far Margaret had come from that apartment above Santini's Liquor and that she had accomplished exactly what she'd set out to do. It's true I lived in a house by the sea, but it was on a spit of questionable terrain, badly in need of repairs, and I was barely making ends meet as it was. Part of me was filled with envy. And part of me was filled with surprise. I couldn't imagine how Margaret Blair had come this far.

I was standing in her living room in my stocking feet and Vicky's dog lying on a beach towel in the entranceway when Margaret came walking in. She was dressed in black stretch pants, a bulky red sweater, a small parcel in her arms. Her high black leather boots with stiletto heels clicked on the marble. Thick eyeliner rimmed her eyes. She moved stiffly, like a toy soldier, crossing the room. I wondered if she had been drinking.

She saw me before she was entirely in the door and, dropping her parcel, she ran to me. "Tess, my God, what are you doing here? And whose dog is this?" She looked at Liberty, curled up asleep on the beach towel.

"It's a long story. I had a little accident down in the ravines. Got down but I couldn't get up."

"The ravines? I haven't been down there in years." She gave me a look. "You did?" Her daughter stood in the doorway now and gave a little shrug. "It's okay, Danielle," her mother said. "This is an old friend."

"It's Vicky's dog," I said.

"Oh, Vicky's." Margaret took this all in, trying to understand what I was doing with someone else's dog. Suddenly I felt very tired and my head hurt. I was shivering, my teeth chattering.

"I'm staying with her. We took a walk. Look, I need to call Vicky and tell her where I am. Or maybe you could drive me back there."

Margaret took me by the hand, leading me to a chair in her sunken living room. "Tess, you're frozen. Why don't you have something hot? Or better yet, take a hot bath."

A hot bath did sound tempting, but I thought I should get going. "No, really—"

"Look, I'll call Vicky. You take a bath. I'll let her know you're here and she can pick you up after work." That sounded to me like a reasonable plan, not one to put anyone out, so I agreed. Margaret opened a closet and took out a fluffy white towel, a terry-cloth robe. She led me down to the master bedroom, a huge room with a giant, king-size bed and clothes scattered everywhere. "Oh, such a mess," Margaret said, picking up some dirty socks and looking at them as if she had no idea what to do with them. "The maid comes tomorrow."

"Oh, don't worry about it," I said.

"You did the right thing, coming here," she said.

She led me into a large, white-tiled bathroom that was the size of my kitchen. It was complete with Jacuzzi tub, bidet, glass shower, and heat lamp. Margaret started the tub, which I noticed had a ring around it. I thought Margaret might make an attempt to clean it out, but instead she just poured in a green liquid, made a thick bubbly foam. She sprayed the air with eucalyptus. "Here, you just relax. When you come out, I'll have some tea and something for us to eat. Then Vicky can come and get you."

When Margaret left, I slipped out of my robe and stood for a moment in front of her mirror. I wondered how often Margaret had stood in front of this mirror, admiring herself. Her long, lanky legs, her thick black hair. Now I gazed at my small but taut breasts, my firm thighs, my skin.

How many times had Nick stood in this bathroom watching her soak in this tub? Had they bathed together? Did he rub soap all over her body in here? I didn't want to think of this, not really, as I slipped in. The hot water stung my freezing feet. My body sank in, burning. Sweat broke out on my brow. I lay in the water, my eyes closed, and soaked for a long time in the steamy water. It seemed inevitable, somehow, that I was here.

Perhaps half an hour later I wrapped myself in the robe and made my way to the kitchen, where Margaret sat sipping tea. "All right," she said, "it's all set. Nick's on his way home. He's thrilled you're here. I talked to Vicky and you'll both have dinner with us."

"Oh, we don't want to impose. . . ."

She flicked her hair, waved her hand away. "Oh, please, you're not imposing. We want you to stay. Nick's going to pick up some wine and some food."

"Really, I should get going."

But Margaret waved away my protests. "Please just relax. Have dinner with us."

I thought perhaps she'd offer me something to drink, but she didn't. I sat down in my robe, moving an empty coffee cup out of the way. "Your place is beautiful."

"Oh, we've been lucky."

"This doesn't look like luck to me. It looks like hard work."

Margaret nodded, turning away. "Yes, I suppose it is. Nick's done all right, you know, with his father's business."

"Yes, I can see that he has."

"He's been able to do some development. He's got an idea for a resort somewhere. Fiji or something? I'm not sure. Ask him."

"Yes, I will." I was struck by how much I wanted to ask her. Over all these years I'd never really known. I thought to myself I should confront her. What about my father? I wanted to say. I'd always wanted to ask her, but never had. Was it really true and had she always known? Had she known even before we became blood sisters? Had she'd known but hadn't told? Was that her big secret? The one she'd kept from me all these years?

I was gathering up my nerve to ask her when a car pulled into the driveway. There was a screech of brakes that made Margaret wince. The car door slammed and moments later Nick walked in in a blue parka, arms loaded with groceries. He kicked the door open with his foot and a cold breeze swept into the room. "Tessie," he said, putting the groceries down on the counter, sweeping me up into his arms. "Are you all right? You aren't frostbitten anywhere, are you?"

"Yes, I'm fine. It was a stupid accident." He was examining my fingertips, my nose.

"But why did you go into the ravines? You could have been hurt. People have frozen—"

"Can't you see, Nick?" Margaret said flatly. "She's fine."

"Well, thank God for that." He hugged me and I found myself lost in the down of his parka, the tug of his arms, and the smell of chicken. I had to wrench myself away.

"Here," he said to Margaret, pointing to the bags, "I brought some things." When she opened the refrigerator to put the beer and soda away, I saw that it was almost empty. "Are you warm enough now?"

"I had a bath. Really, this is so embarrassing. . . ." I excused myself, slipped away to get dressed, thinking it odd that there seemed to be no food except for what Nick had brought in.

When I got dressed and returned to the kitchen, Vicky was there. She had arrived just as it started to snow. Not terribly big flakes, just a dusting, but it seemed to be coming harder and faster as the wind picked up off the lake. When she walked in the door, Liberty leaped from the corner where he'd been lying all afternoon and practically into her arms. "My God," she said, stomping in, covered in white snow dust. "Tess, what happened to you?"

"Oh, it was a dumb thing. I took a walk. It was cold, I went into the ravines. Then I couldn't get out."

Nick shook his head. "I'm so glad you're all right."

"I thought you were Miss Out-of-Doors," Vicky said.

"I haven't been in ice for a while."

"How about on ice?" Nick asked, holding up the bourbon.

"Sure," Vicky said. "Tess?"

"Why don't you just stay?" Margaret said, all bubbly now. "Why don't we have a good time? Can't we do that, Nicky? Have a good time. Let's make dinner. What did you bring? It's snowing; you may as well stay for a bite. Nick, you'll get them drinks, won't you?"

Nick was unpacking groceries. He put down the precooked chicken, a head of iceberg lettuce, a pound of spaghetti. "Of course. I've got some spaghetti sauce I made the other day."

"I didn't know you were a cook."

"There's lots you don't know about me," he said with a wink. "You'll be surprised. I'll make you a wonderful meal." Margaret disappeared inside the house, then returned, dressed in a blue silk shirt with black velvet stretch pants, gold earrings. Nick poured a good-sized bourbon for each of us. Large tumblers where the ice clinked. Margaret passed them around and we toasted. "To old friends," she said, taking a sip. "Oh, this is nice." She reached over for Nick, gave his arm a squeeze.

He pulled back, gazing around. "Where's Danielle? Where's my little Danielle?"

"Oh." Margaret took another sip. "In her room, somewhere. She's been a grumpy girl all day."

Nick frowned. "Well, don't you think we should ask her to join us?"

"I thought since we hadn't seen one another—the girls, I mean—in so long, it might be nice, just for once—"

"I know," Nick said with a laugh, "to have an adult evening."

"Well, yes, that's what I was thinking."

In the end Danielle came out of her room, looking sullen as she had when I first laid eyes on her. Obediently she helped her mother set the table. "Can I do anything? Can I give you a hand?" I asked.

"Oh, you can come talk to me," Margaret said. "I want to know everything. Let's get caught up."

I followed her into the kitchen while Vicky sat by the fire that Nick had built, legs up, reading a magazine. "It's so good to have you here."

"You seem to have done quite well for yourselves."

"We've done well enough, but not spectacular. Nothing spectacular, you know."

I looked out toward the window in the living room and saw that the snow was coming down hard. "Look at that," I said.

Nick, who had followed us into the kitchen, peered out toward the lake. The wind was howling around the house and a purple darkness fell around us. "Yes, it does look like a storm."

From the living room, Vicky glanced up as well. "What is it with those weathermen? They never get anything right."

"Maybe we should get going. I don't want to get stuck here."

"From the look of it," Nick said, taking a sip of his bourbon, "you already are. We may as well eat. Then see what's happening."

I was anxious and wanted to get going, but they all made me see that the blizzard was coming down from the north now and there wasn't really anywhere to go. But the thought of being trapped didn't appeal to me. I peered out at the blizzard and found myself wanting to be anywhere else but where I was. I longed for my ramshackle house and wondered what had conspired to bring me here. Margaret looked nervously outside. "It is coming down awfully hard." Then suddenly she seemed excited, as if this were a great adventure we were embarking on. "It won't be so bad."

"Really," I said to Margaret and Nick, "I should get going."

In the living room Vicky was peering out through the curtain at the swirling snow. "You can't see a thing," she said.

"But I just can't—"

"It's much too dangerous to go anywhere on a night like this. We have plenty of room," Margaret said. "I won't hear anything of it. You'll both sleep here. It will be fun. Just like when we were girls." She was still drinking bourbon, though I had switched to white wine.

Nick gave me an odd look, as if he was uncomfortable with this arrangement. I shrugged, mouthed, "Sorry." Then I glanced outside again. There was nothing but whiteness. "It's so strange," Margaret said. "We hardly see you for years, Tessie. Now you seem to be around all the time."

"Just twice," I told her. "I don't think I'll be back again in winter."

"But there's always spring and summer," Margaret said with an

almost angry voice now. "So perhaps we will see more of you?" Her
words slurred a little.

"Perhaps."

"Well, I'd like that," Nick said. Margaret shot a glance his way.

We sat down and ate the roast chicken, salad with Thousand
Island dressing from a jar, green beans, and a side dish of spaghetti
with meat sauce, all of which Nick had prepared. It was tasty and
Nick served a nice California Chardonnay that made me groggy and
homesick. Margaret only had a few pieces of lettuce and a chicken
wing on her plate. She didn't eat the wing, but she drank glass after
glass of wine.

Danielle again made a brief appearance during which her father
coaxed her to eat, but she disappeared soon afterward without saying
good-bye to either her mother or her father. Nick shook his head as if
to apologize. "Funny kid," he said. "She gets moody. She acts weird
when people she doesn't know are around." I found her a strange,
reclusive child, and seeing the way Nick watched over her made me
think that he did as well.

Afterward we cleaned the kitchen and decided to call it a night.
"We should get some rest," Nick said. In the unlikely eventuality that
the storm stopped, we'd have to dig ourselves out in the morning.

"Oh, let's stay up and play charades or Scrabble," Margaret said.
"Who wants to go to bed now?" Margaret began making charade
signs—three words, first word, sounds like.

I yawned. "I guess I'm tired from my adventure in the ravines."

Vicky said she wanted to turn in as well, but Margaret put her foot
down. "Nobody wants to have any fun. I don't understand it."

"They do want to have fun; they're just tired," Nick offered.

"Well, we could stay up and talk awhile," Vicky said. We agreed to
polish off a bottle of wine in the sunken living room, discussing old
times. What had happened to whom, what hadn't happened to so-and-
so. Margaret wanted to know who was married to whom, who had
children, who was divorced. She wanted to know about people who
seemed irrelevant to me, people she hardly knew. Margaret appeared

to be oddly out of touch, considering she lived in Winonah. Vicky told her about everyone she asked about. With almost every word we said, Margaret tossed her head back and laughed until it became annoying. Even when Vicky told her about someone who had died, she laughed. When she dropped her glass, it occurred to me that she was drunk.

Suddenly Margaret stood up and went to the window again. The light from the room reflected on the whirling snow. "I hate being trapped," Margaret said. She shuddered as if the wind that was blowing outside had come right into the room. "You know, when there's no way out."

"No one likes that," Nick said.

"You don't have to remind me," Margaret said, snapping at him. Then she turned to us. "What was that room in a house called when there's only one exit?" We looked at her, perplexed. "You remember, when you guys went door to door with the Firefighters of America?"

Vicky and I looked at each other, not quite remembering. Then I did. "It's a dead man's room," I said flatly.

"That's right; that's what this reminds me of. A dead man's room. There's no way out." Margaret kept staring out at the snow, still as a statue, as if she could not move. She let the curtain drop. "I'm tired." She covered her mouth as she yawned.

We agreed we were all tired. Margaret offered Vicky an extra bedroom on the floor where they slept and gave me a small guest room off a wing of the main floor. Then we went to bed.

I couldn't sleep that night as the storm settled in. From somewhere in the house I thought I heard shouting. It seemed as if loud voices had woken me, but perhaps it was the wind. I've never been very good at sleeping in unfamiliar places—I wake at the slightest creak of the walls, the sigh of an unknown bed—but now it was especially hard. The guest room was drafty, and no matter how deeply I huddled under the covers I couldn't get warm. Everywhere around me were noises of rattling, branches flailing about. First the wind seemed to come from the north and then from the west. I could hear Lake Michigan pounding the shore, and the force of its arctic gale sent shivers through me.

From time to time I gazed out the window by my bed and saw the blinding white. I thought how in blizzards like this cows freeze standing up. It brought back all the frigid winters of my youth and I knew that when the storm was over, we could be trapped for days.

I'm not sure what time it was when I got up, threw a robe over my shoulders, and made my way through the house. Besides the wind, the house was oddly quiet as I followed the long corridor that led toward the living room and the kitchen. I was suddenly hungry, though I didn't know what I wanted. Sometimes I wake up in the night with these unspecified needs. Hot fudge sundaes, granola, Stolichnaya.

Tiptoeing down the corridor I passed Danielle's bedroom with the door ajar. Peering in, I saw the child asleep. The light from the hallway illuminated her face, which wore a scowl. I wondered what could make a child look that angry. Her room barely seemed like that of a child. There were a few stuffed animals, a unicorn poster on the wall, but other than that the room seemed barren, not the kid's room overflowing with things I was used to.

I made my way to the kitchen, which was dark, the linoleum cold on my bare feet. Outside the wind howled like a crying child and something in it frightened me. Liberty was asleep in his makeshift bed in the corner and he looked up at me with sleepy eyes, yawned, and went back to sleep.

Though I wasn't comfortable snooping around someone else's kitchen, I wanted to eat something. I opened the refrigerator door. There were a few old pieces of orange cheese, two eggs, some milk. Celery stalks. If we were stuck here in the storm, I wondered how we'd survive.

I poked around in the dark, illuminated only by the whiteness of the snow. Outside the moon peeked through. The storm was breaking up. Liberty got up suddenly and pattered across the kitchen floor. "Well, look who's here." Nick laughed as I jumped, pulling my robe, which was too big, tightly around me.

"I got hungry," I said. "I couldn't sleep."

"Let's find something." He was still dressed in his jeans and sweatshirt and looked as if he hadn't been to bed.

Peering into the refrigerator, he shook his head sadly as if its emptiness reminded him of something he preferred to forget. "Why don't we have a drink instead." He began producing tea bags, honey, cinnamon sticks, and a bottle of bourbon. "I'll make toddies."

"Toddies?" I smiled and then I knew that that was what I wanted. Nick boiled the water, prepared the tea, put in the honey, a splash of bourbon, and capped it with a cinnamon stick. Handing me a mug, I warmed my fingers around it. I sniffed and took a sip. "This is good," I told him.

He nodded. "Just what you need on a night like this."

He sat across the Formica table from me, both of us with steaming cups in our hands. Liberty went back to his bed, satisfied that nothing was amiss. "So," Nick said, "isn't it strange? I've been thinking about you all the time, almost willing you back into my life, and here you are."

"Yes," I said, "here I am. It was just an accident really that I wound up here at all."

"Fate," he said, "Though Margaret doesn't seem to think so. She seems to think you came here on purpose and there's something going on between us."

"I thought I heard angry voices."

"She has a temper. So is there?"

"Is there what?"

"Something going on between us?"

I shook my head. "I don't know." The steam warmed my face. "And I don't think this is the time to talk about it."

He stared down into his cup. "You're right. It probably isn't."

I gazed around, changing the subject. "You've done well for yourself."

He made a face as if none of it mattered. "I haven't done much at all, to tell you the truth."

"But you have this. . . ." I waved my hand around the room.

He grinned bitterly. "I have nothing, in fact. I wanted to go to medical school. Do you remember that?"

I shook my head. "Is that why you thought I'd be a nurse?"

"Maybe. I wanted to make something of my life. Now I'm just running these businesses I inherited, living in this house I inherited. I've accomplished nothing."

"That's not how it appears from the outside. It looks as if you've accomplished a great deal."

"Not what I would have liked." Nick paused to listen to the wind. "You know what I remember about you once? You know what you did? We, me and Jeb, were playing ball and you wanted to play. We were maybe twelve or thirteen. We didn't want you to so we decided to play rough with you. We threw the ball hard into your stomach. You caught it and threw it back just as hard. I aimed one at your head. I know it wasn't very nice, but you caught it. Then you came right up to me, right in front of me. You threw the ball on the ground and walked away. It was like you just wanted to prove you could play with us. You wanted to show us. I always thought you were a pretty tough kid."

"It hurt like hell," I said. He gave me an odd look. "Catching those balls you threw. It hurt."

"But you had guts. I admired that. Will you accept my apology?"

I took a sip of my toddy. "I'll think about it."

Except for the wind swirling outside it was quiet in the house. Everything was still inside and raging outside. We sat in silence for a few moments, listening to the storm. Nick reached over and touched my hand. "Now you're here and I don't know what to do."

"Don't do anything," I said. Then I got up. "I'm going back to bed." Nick rose as well and walked toward me as if he were going to put his mug in the sink. Instead, he stopped right in front of me. "Tess," he said, then, "Tessie . . ."

"Go back to bed," I told him.

He hesitated. Then he gave me a pat on the head as if that was what he'd intended in the first place. "You too. Get some sleep." As he walked to his room, he gave me a backward wave. When he was gone, I went into the living room and watched an eerie purplish light spread across the sky.

24

My secret was growing inside me. I was surprised at how big it grew, at how much room it could occupy. Whenever I saw Margaret or thought about her, I thought about the pact I'd made with my father. It seemed as if it could take up all the space that was not filled with history dates or algebra or phone numbers.

When my mother came into my room and opened my shutters in the morning, I thought, There is something I know but I can't tell you. My mother always wanted the truth. "Don't tell stories," she told me once. "Don't tell fibs."

When she kissed me good night and I smelled her minty breath, I thought, There's something I know that you don't know.

It wasn't that I wanted to tell her. It was that not telling her was getting harder and harder. It wasn't anything, of course. It hardly mattered at all. The previous summer my father had stopped to sell insurance to Clarice on a Thursday afternoon before he headed home. It was nothing more than that, and it only mattered to my father and me. It was the thing we had between us now. That was what I told myself.

He'd never mentioned it again. It was never discussed. My father never said, "You know that thing I asked you not to tell . . ." It was as if he had forgotten about it. As if it was nothing to him. But it weighed on me like when you eat too much dough. I kept thinking that if I talked to him about it, he'd tell me it was all right. I could tell her now. I wanted to ask my father about it. About how long I had to keep this secret to myself. But he was hardly around anymore.

He came home on Friday afternoon, left Monday before we were up. When he was back, he was on the roof, fixing shingles, or playing golf. He hardly noticed that his children were running wild. When Jeb was not downstairs, hanging out in the rec room, he was at the Idiot's Circle. The Idiot's Circle was across from Mrs. Larsen's Stationery Store; Winslow Drugs and Faulkner's Hardware were also across the street from it, and those store owners had complained plenty of times about the kids hanging out there in black leather jackets, smoking cigarettes and doing God knows what else.

There were other rumors about my brother that came back to me, things that the gang whispered to me about. Trouble he got into, the fast crowd he hung out with. And talk about Jeb with girls—fast girls, girls who did things with boys behind trees, girls who boys lined up for. Things I didn't want to think about or imagine my brother doing.

My brother leading two lives. On weekends watching our father put drywall up in the basement, and during the week hanging out at the Idiot's Circle. That's where he spent his high school years, with a duck-ass haircut and tight black jeans, a black jacket, sunglasses, while Lily walked around the house moaning, "I don't know what to do. I don't know what's happened to my little boy."

When our father came home on Friday afternoon, she shouted at him, "The boy needs his father. The kids need their parents. Can't you stay home?"

Sometimes I heard her cry into the phone, "It's not about me. I can manage. It's about the children. Do you really have to keep doing whatever it is you're doing?"

Sometimes Lily went after Jeb, made him come home. Or she sent me, but God help me when I rode up on my bicycle. All those boys laughing so loud, hitting Jeb in the back. "Hey, Jebbie, Miss Goody Two-Shoes says you better come home."

That was the nicest shout I'd get. Miss Goody Two-Shoes. Little Miss Apple Polisher. Miss Straight A's. I was a good student, a straight-A student, because I worked. I studied hard. I worked ferociously, madly. Memorizing everything I could.

But Jeb was the one who knew all the answers. Mr. Smarty Pants, I called him. He knew it all in his head. Right up here, he'd say and point to the old bean. He went to school without a notebook or books, just a pencil tucked behind his ear, and he sat in class and just listened. I didn't know this because people told me. I knew it because I saw him, heading out to school; or when I was on hall patrol (which was a perk for honor roll students), I saw him sitting there, no paper or pencil in front of him, just taking in every word.

After school he hung out at the Idiot's Circle with the other bad boys. Jeb hung out there and got straight A's and all the teachers would remember him. Even as Art came up through high school, they'd say, "Oh, you're Jeb Winterstone's kid brother."

Like our father, my brother was hardly home. No matter what, Lily set a place for him. Sometimes after dinner on a summer night I had to go find my brother.

I didn't know quite how this was, but it seemed to me that my secret had something to do with what was happening to Jeb, though I didn't know how. But in my head I practiced saying what I wanted to say. I'd tell my mother while she was standing in the kitchen that I'd gone over to Margaret Blair's one afternoon because of a storm. My mother would understand this. She knew I was afraid of storms, afraid of what the weather might do. She even understood how this came from a deep-seated fear, from our dinner-table talks of tornados and floods. I would tell her that I'd gone to Margaret's because I was afraid of the storm. She would understand that. And I'd found my father there with his feet resting on the coffee table. And he'd asked me not to tell.

In my head, I rehearsed how I'd tell her, what I'd say. But whenever I saw Lily, ladling soup, testing a roast with a fork, the blood rushing into the pan, I couldn't. I'd see her, bent over, poking a chicken, and I'd want to tell her, but I didn't. I'm not a tattletale. I'm someone you can trust.

Baton-twirling practice had begun. We met in the mornings just before eight or on Saturdays at the football field. We worked on our figure eights, our hand-to-hands. We marched in formation. In unison we jumped in the air, released our batons, then caught them, still twirling, before they hit the ground.

One Saturday my mother came to pick me up. I was surprised to see her, but she said I needed new clothes and she wanted to take me shopping. We took the highway because it was the most direct way to get to the shopping center at Old Orchard. "Now let's see," Lily said. "What do you need?"

In the car as we drove we made a list. A pleated skirt with matching sweater, a dress for parties. Some corduroys. We went from store to store and she bought me whatever I wanted. Usually I had to decide between two things, but she said, "Just take whatever you want. Take everything."

I'd never seen her spend so much money at one time. I finally said to her, "Mom, it's all right, I don't need all this stuff."

"Who cares what you need? If you want it, it's yours."

When we finished shopping, we carried all our packages to the coffee shop that was in the shopping center. I ordered a hamburger and a chocolate soda. My mother ordered a Coke and a salad. She smoked a cigarette, which I rarely saw her do. She sat staring across at me, blowing smoke, and I thought she wanted me to tell her something. That this was why she'd brought me here and bought me all these clothes. So I would tell her what I knew. I was gathering up the nerve when I said, "Thanks for the clothes."

"I want you to be beautiful, Tessie," she said. "I want you to have everything you deserve." Tears came to her eyes. She fanned her hand in front of her face and said it was from the smoke. Then she crushed out her cigarette and asked for the check. Gathering up our bundles, we headed for the car and drove back the same way we came.

25

Ted believed in vampires. Not the kind you see in late-night movies or on TV, but real vampires. By day they go to school, hold normal jobs. At night they come out and suck your blood. He used to play Dungeons & Dragons. Now it was Vampires of the Masquerade. He told me it was a cult game, but I saw him leaving the house dressed in a red cape. "Why are you doing this?" I asked him and he shook his head.

"Vy not?"

Lily still spits in the air to keep away the evil eye. I do it from time to time myself. But garlic and crosses? Living on human blood? When I returned from Illinois, Ted informed me he was going to live with Sabe, a woman he had met at Vampires of the Masquerade in a role-playing session. Sabe had black fingernails, a thumbtack through her tongue. When she talked she rolled it around in her mouth and sounded like someone who'd just had a stroke.

I didn't say to him what my mother would have said to me: "Okay, it's your life. I did what I could."

I returned home to find my life in disarray, like the pieces of a jig-saw puzzle scattered on the ground. Pieces were missing and what I had didn't fit together anymore. Jade seemed to be avoiding me whenever I was in the house and Shana had left a message saying that business had slowed and she did not think she'd be needing me much over the next month.

When I arrived, Ted was literally moving, a big carton of CDs in his arms. "Honey," I said, "what are you doing?"

"I'm moving, Mom, I'm going to live with Sabe." In my mind I tried to remember who Sabe was. Blond, green eyes, small? Leggy, dark, tall? Nose ring, didn't get up to greet me from the couch? Then it came to me—black fingernails, pierced tongue. I frowned. I had given up having long talks with Ted about his future. About how smart he was and how he should be going back to school, but suddenly I couldn't bear the thought of my son just walking out the door.

"Ted, sit down; tell me about her."

With an impatient look, he put his box down. "She's a nurse practitioner."

Is she a vampire? I wanted to ask. "Oh, she looked so young."

"Naw, she's older than you think. She has a kid. Sonia is three."

"Oh, and the father, is he in the picture?"

Ted laughed as if this were a very funny joke. "He's definitely not in the picture. Anyway, Mom, I gotta go. We'll have you by for dinner in a week or so. I left her number on the fridge."

He gave me a hug. When I checked the phone number, it was for an area code in Oregon. A pile of mail sat on my desk, all of it, I felt certain, bills, and I had no idea how I was going to pay them. Charlie owed me a little money in back support payments and I had some income still from my father's estate. If I called Jeb, he'd send me whatever I needed, but I didn't like to ask. Night after night I poked the papers on my desk and listened to Jade come in and go out, sometimes hollering to me, "Be back later." Sometimes not. If I asked her what was going on, she said, "What will be will be."

One morning I pinned her down. "Jade, I want you to have dinner with me this evening. Can you be home by seven?" Reluctantly she gave me a nod and was out the door.

I was straightening up that morning when the phone rang. "Tess," a voice said, expecting me to know who he was, "How're you doing? Listen, I've got this idea for you. Isn't that house of yours famous for something—the guy who built it? The way he made it out of coastal stones?"

"Yes, it is." It took a moment for me to realize that I was speaking with John Martelli, my insurance agent.

"Well, I've got an idea for you."

Two hours later John Martelli's car with the URCOVERD license plate pulled into the driveway. From my living room I saw John fling his ponytail back, scoop up some files and head toward my house. I greeted him at the door. "Let's walk around it," he said.

In silence we walked around my stone house. John looked at the foundation. He shook his head at the distance between my house and the Pacific Ocean. "Well, it's going to be a tough one," he told me.

"John, what do you have in mind?"

"How famous is this poet, Tessie?"

I led John into my living room and sat him down in front of the complete works of Francis Cantwell Eagger. At the same time John handed me my new insurance policy with a premium I'd have to sell the house in order to pay. "John, I can't——"

He nodded. "I know, I know. That's what I'm here for. What did your father say? No problems, only solutions? Okay, I'm here with a solution."

He gazed around the stone walls, the ocean view. He opened one of the volumes and read the first few lines of "Coastal Views." "So he's a pretty important guy, I guess. Well, it's a long shot, like I said, but why don't you try to get your house on the National Registry of Historic Houses? Then it becomes like a national treasure. It has to be protected. Like I said, it's a long shot, but I'd give it a try." He handed me a brochure with their number, which was in Washington. "I've done a little research for you."

"Thanks, John," I said. "Can I offer you anything?"

"Well," he said slowly, his brown eyes turning dewy. "Maybe you could have dinner with me sometime."

I hadn't expected him to say that. I imagined that John was in his early thirties, closer to Ted's age than mine. "Well, I'm seeing someone right now," I replied, wondering if I really was.

John got up, slightly embarrassed. He flung his ponytail back again. "You know, sometime . . . in the future."

I thanked him for the brochure and his help. Pebble in the head, I told myself. After I heard the screech of his tires, I decided I needed some fresh air. I headed out along the cliffs, then wandered down to the shore, where I found a peach-colored shell I didn't have and a small animal skull, white and polished bone. I stuck these in my pocket. Then I gazed up at my house, which was going to fall down this cliff if I didn't do something about it. Looking at its stone walls, the way it fit so neatly into the hillside, I knew I wanted to stay here. I never wanted to leave.

When I got back up from the beach, I made a pot of coffee and phoned the National Registry of Historic Houses. The woman who answered seemed to be eating a sandwich as we spoke. She told me they'd need photographs, architectural drawings, documented historic information, and an on-site inspection. She also said that the chances were slim that my house would qualify and, off the record, they had hundreds of requests every week from people who wanted their houses taken off the registry so they could remodel. I said I wasn't planning on remodeling and I wanted it registered. The woman said she'd send me an application and wished me luck.

Then I made a veggie casserole and I put it down in front of Jade when she came home, but she looked like a cornered animal with nowhere to go. "I'm a little lonely around here," I told her. "Maybe we could eat together; just tonight."

"Sure, Mom," she said, but she got a look in her face I'd seen many times before. For a time when Jade was little, she went everywhere with a rock. She didn't want dolls or stuffed animals. She just wanted her rock. Charlie and I used to joke to each other that it was because of her name, but actually she didn't know that jade was a stone until she was older. It had to go everywhere with her—beside her in the car, to the dentist, to visit Charlie's family. If anyone tried to take it away from her, she got the look she had on her face now as she sat down to have dinner with me. Like I was going to take something away from her.

"Honey, we've hardly talked. I've scarcely seen you since I got home. You know, I have things I'd like to tell you about. I'm sure you have things as well." She sighed a deep sigh as she picked her way through brown rice and mushrooms. I reached across and touched her hand. "You can talk to me, you really can."

"Can I? I'm not sure." Her voice was barely audible.

"Yes, please, I want you to," wondering if I did want her to and dreading the worst. "You know, darling, I'm on your side. I'm in your camp."

"Which camp is that?" Her eyes got that cold, ironic look they sometimes had. A look I'd seen in her father's eyes as our marriage unraveled. "Summer, boot, or concentration?"

I smiled. "That's funny," I said. "It really is."

"Maybe I could do stand-up," she said in a way that made me think she was seriously pondering this option.

"Honey." I reached across for her hand. "Why don't you tell me what's wrong?"

Her face darkened. "Well, I'm just confused about some things right now. . . ."

"What are you confused about, dear?"

"Well, there's this person I like—"

"Person," I said.

She looked up at me, glaring. "Woman," she said.

"Okay, woman." The word slipped out of my mouth. I wasn't sure what to say. "Person. It's okay. It doesn't matter. I'm sorry," I blurted, "I didn't know."

"Well, now you know. But it's not what you think. Not really. Not quite. I still like men. Or I think I like them, but I'm also just not sure. I'm experimenting."

"Dear, you have to do whatever makes you happy."

"Do you really believe that?"

"I do. I think that's what you have to do."

Jade looked at me, tears coming to her eyes. "Is that what you did? Have you done what makes you happy?"

"I'm not sure," I said. "I've tried. I haven't always succeeded."

I reached up to touch Jade, who moved away from me now, her face shattered. "Don't touch me," she said, sobs rising in her throat. "I'm confused; I don't know what I want." Her fork clanged against her plate.

"Sweetheart, we don't always know——" but she shook my hand away. Jade, I thought, that soft green stone that is so easy and yet so difficult to carve. All those precious things sculpted there. But now I saw her hard, heavy gaze—stubborn and impenetrable. Why did you walk around carrying a rock? I wanted to ask her.

"Mom, I'm sorry, but I've gotta go. I have to figure this out for myself." She got up from the table and walked out, letting the door slam behind her. I listened to it slam and knew that I wanted someone I could talk to. I wanted Nick to be there. I wished I could call and tell him to come and be with me, but I couldn't. Still, I wanted him with me. It hadn't seemed that clear before.

I finished eating the casserole on my plate. Then I picked up the dishes, scraped the remains back into the casserole dish. I cleaned up the kitchen and put everything away.

26

You must be this tall to ride the Bobs," the painted face of the clown with the outstretched hand read. For a long time we weren't. We'd stand in line and the ticket taker would shake his head, nudging us away, but then suddenly we were. If we stood on tippy toes and stretched our legs, we were just above the thumb of the clown. That was the go-ahead.

In the summers on Friday nights or whenever we could coax one of our parents—some parent who wasn't drinking or too tired from commuting all week or working late or cavorting or had the lawn to mow or the taxes to figure out or the bills to pay or just wasn't too sick and tired of the kids—to drive us to Riverview, we'd go.

Often my father would be the one. He'd be back from his week of traveling, but right away he'd want to leave again. He'd drive us to Riverview, then wait in the car. He never went to movies or to the swim club or into Riverview. He just sat in the car. As I swam with my friends or watched monsters arrive from outerspace or kissed my first boy, I knew that my father was outside, waiting for me.

On the weekends before I turned sixteen and was old enough to drive, my father drove me everywhere. He drove me ice skating, to piano lessons. He drove me to the movies to see a show, to the circus when it was in town. But he never came inside. He never watched me skate or ride a horse. He never came and watched a show or ate popcorn at my side. Instead my father sat in the car, as if he were casing the joint. He could easily have been taken for an undercover cop, sipping his coffee, glancing at a newspaper but not really reading it.

Of course I pleaded with him. We all did, though Art least of all because he knew. He'd learned from all of us. I pleaded, "Daddy, please come and watch me skate." Or "Come see the show." But he never wanted to. He wanted quick departures, easy escapes.

I never saw a lion act or galloped through a field or kissed a boy without the thought that my father was sitting in the car, waiting for me. Even to this day I still have the sense that someone is out there, in a hurry for me to be done.

My father seemed to enjoy driving the gang to Riverview. It was as if he had to keep moving. Even though he'd just gotten home, he wanted to go out again. He seemed to like driving us to a big parking lot, then smoking cigarettes until we were done.

The girls were always grateful. "Thanks, Mr. Winterstone," Maureen would say, then Wendy Young, then Ginger, and then Margaret because somehow she always came along. She seemed to know when we were going and called just as we were leaving. If she didn't call, my father would ask, "Aren't you going to ask Margaret?" Even if we had a full car, we could always squeeze one more in.

So we all scrambled into the back of my mother's car, the station wagon that smelled of wet shoes and groceries and cigarettes. On the Bobs, Margaret and I shared a little car. We stared down the mountainous drops. We squeezed each other's hands. Afterward I was sick, thinking I'd retch, but Margaret looked stoically my way, that reckless look in her eyes. "Let's do the Roter," she said.

But I didn't do the Roter. I'd stood above it and watched as the floor dropped away. I'd seen faces arched in terror, arms and legs trying to crawl to a safe place. Others with their faces stretched back like a mask, arms out, crucified to the wall. I didn't do the Roter; I never had, but I pretended I did. "Oh, that Roter. It's nothing to me," I'd say, knowing that if you're chicken, they'd make fun of you. "That's a boring ride."

"I want to do it," Margaret said. "Do it with me."

"Let's do the Jet."

She started walking away. Although the Roter was not so far from the Bobs, Margaret took a weaving, circuitous route, through the arcades, the first of many circuitous routes she would take me on. She didn't turn around, but I was following. For a moment we lost the others, but Margaret, even as she weaved through the arcades—the Johnny Jump Up and the bean toss and the pie in the face—Margaret knew I was right behind her.

The Roter was a big round tub like a mixing bowl with a column up the middle. We went in through a little door. I was at the base of the bowl. We stood along the sides. Mostly boys rode this ride. One or two girls were wearing skirts, and we knew what was going to happen to them.

Even before it started to turn I felt sick. But I couldn't be sick because if I was, I was chicken. Margaret was across from me and I saw her face as they shut the door. It was a funny, laughing face at first, but then it wasn't. It was a different kind of face, a face like "I have to get out of here." But already the Roter was turning. It turned slowly at first, but I could tell it was picking up speed.

My face was pulled back as if someone had stuck tape on my mouth. My hands were pressed along the sides and now we were spinning. The skirts of the two girls near Margaret went up over their heads and their panties were revealed. They kept trying to push them down. One boy laughed, but then I saw him throw up. Vomit sprayed in the air. Everyone moaned and looked away.

Faster now. The bottom was starting to recede. Drop back. Down, down the floor fell away. It was a law of physics happening here, but which law? Centrifugal force, that was it. We were flung against the sides, pinned to the wall, glued, butterflies impaled. I looked across at Margaret. Her eyes were pressed back into her head, her face was plastered into a smile. Her hair slung around her as if she were Medusa, her arms were spread at her sides. And now the Roter spun faster and across from me Margaret was screaming, a loud cry coming out of her, and I saw her start to curl.

She folded first her arms, then her legs into her body, then turned on her side. All curled up, she started to crawl. Like a baby she moved her arms and legs, crawling as if she were trying to escape. "Don't do it, Margaret," I shouted, "stay still," but she was crawling away, heading toward the top of the ride and then, when she realized she couldn't, she just curled back up again, quivering like a baby, stuck to the wall.

She looked so frightened and small and I almost felt sorry for her. Then the ride slowed down. Skirts dropped, hands were released, Margaret straightened up. Her feet came down, her hands uncurled. The bottom came back and we planted our feet. The ride came to a halt and it was done. We staggered through the little door, down the wooden steps, and out to the arcade.

When we were outside, I put my hand on her shoulder. "Are you all right?"

She swatted my hand away. "Of course I am. Why wouldn't I be?"

Then we headed back to the car where my father waited, sitting as we'd left him. "Did you have a good time?" he said.

"We had a blast," we replied; no matter how sick we felt, our stomachs quivering, or how our hearts had stopped a hundred times, we'd say we had a blast, we'd had a wonderful time. Then my father put a hand on my back and another on Margaret's.

Shoving us gently into the car, he took us home. Margaret sat in front between my father and me. Everyone else rode in back. We had just gotten onto the highway when Margaret clutched my father's hand. "I'm going to be sick," she shouted. Quickly my father pulled over to the shoulder, hopped out, and yanked Margaret from the car. He kept his hand on her back as she vomited on the side of the road. Then gave her his handkerchief to wipe her mouth.

The rest of us made faces, grimaces. "Ugh," we said. When they got back in, my father was gentle with her. He made her sit by the window with the air blowing on her face. We dropped the gang off one by one until we came to Margaret's house. Then my father got out and helped Margaret to her front porch.

In the amber light above the doorway, I saw Clarice, dressed in only a housecoat, holding it at the waist. It was a peach-colored housecoat and the light of the porch seemed to shine through it, giving her an otherworldly glow. I assumed that my father was explaining to Clarice what had happened because I saw her put her hand over the little "O" her mouth shaped, the way it had when she'd first sat in our living room as my father related to her stories of disaster. Then Clarice ruffled Margaret's hair and with a pat pointed her into the house.

I thought my father would leave then, but instead he lingered. He said something and they both laughed. Clarice had that deep, gut cackle, the kind that betrayed her class. Or the lack of it. Then she reached out, touching my father's sleeve as if she were picking a thread off. And he paused the way he did when he was about to say something, then forgot what it was.

27

The Department of Coastal Studies is located in a shack just off Otter Point, a few miles below where we live. I'm on the list for wildlife rescue. The next morning after my dinner with Jade, Joe Pescari, who headed Coastal Studies, phoned to say that four young pilot whales had beached themselves five miles down the coast from my house near Gray Shark Cove, and could I help keep them wet until the tide came in. I put on a bathing suit and tossed my wetsuit into the car and drove down to the Gray Shark Cove.

From the ridge above the beach I could see four black whales, their thick bellies heaving on the sand. They breathed in heavy, asthmatic breaths and a crowd of volunteers had gathered around them, tossing water on their backs. I ran down to the beach, put on my wetsuit, and met Joe, who told me to splash as much water as I could on their backs. In two hours the tide would come in and we could ease them back into the water.

The whales lay passive, breathing. They were young and fairly small, but immobile and helpless where they lay. Their eyes were cloudy gray and their breathing sounded like sighs. With a bucket I heaved water on their backs. Slowly the water began to rise around them and by late afternoon we could begin to ease them off the beach. We pushed them. I got under the blubbery belly of one to get it off the sand.

As the tide flowed in, we guided the whales gently through the shallow waters, careful not to let them turn around and beach themselves again. They flopped, rolling from side to side, as if they could not navigate. We swam with the whales until they got their bearings. Often young mother whales, when they are giving birth, are followed up and down these coasts by older females, no longer of calf-bearing age. The old females swim with the young ones. When it is time for the young females to birth, the old ones shove against their the bellies, midwifing the birth. When the calf is born, the older whale will carry it to the surface until it begins to breathe.

Now we were like midwives to these whales. Coaxing them along. Keeping them on the surface, on a straight course. At last they began to breathe. Water spouted from their blowholes. The whales oriented themselves and when we were a few hundred yards from shore, they headed for open seas. We watched as they swam out past the point, and when we were sure they had gone in the right direction, we swam back to shore. From the shore we watched the whales turn north, heading up the coast, where they would beach themselves again—and die—the next morning.

When I got home, there were disturbing messages from Charlie on the phone. He wanted to know what was going on with Ted. Where he'd moved to. And with Jade. "What are these kids doing with their lives?"

I made myself a cup of tea and called him back, picking up where his messages left off.

"I don't know, Charlie. Ted has moved in with some woman I hardly know. Jade doesn't talk to me. It's too bad you don't live closer. Maybe they need their father more."

"Well, it's too bad you moved away."

"It was within the limits of our agreement."

"It's a fucking two-hour drive."

"I wanted to be down here."

"Jesus, Tess, you just wanted to be away. That's all you've ever wanted. I should've taken out a court order to stop you."

We've been in this one fight on and off for about a dozen years. Charlie decided he wanted joint custody after I bought this house. But it's his guilt that's got him. He doesn't come often to see them. When something goes wrong, he blames it on my living two hours south of the Bay Area.

When we were married, after Charlie and I made love, he used to cradle my face in his hands and say, right into my eyes, "I love you, Tess, I really do." Then I'd go to sleep right there in his arms. And I loved him too, or I wanted him. But there was always something I could never quite get past. This thing that had stood in my way.

A few days later Jade sat in the breakfast nook, writing in her diary. She was bent over, intent. A small satchel, like the overnight bags I used to pack for her when she was going off to camp, lay at her feet.

"Where're you going?" I asked as I walked in. She looked up, running a hand through her short, spiky hair.

She told me that that morning a seagull had landed on her windowsill and it had stayed there half the day. It just sat, looking in at her, its fat body pressed to the glass, as if it were beckoning to her, waiting for her to follow.

Jade puts her faith in miracles, omens. Everything is a sign. It's better than vampires, but still, as her father—a master of the understatement—would say, it's not perfect either. She believes that little signs, omens, will tell you which path to take. She leaves clippings on my desk about Ganesha, the Indian god, half elephant, half man, whose stone statues sip milk. About the anti-Christ coming to take the children of Bogotá away. When a tornado scattered Texas Christian University to the four winds, making atheists of several of the faculty, Jade said it should have made believers of them all.

Her friend Sigrid was in a car accident and when the first rescue worker on the scene fell in love with Sigrid, Jade said it was meant to be. She surrounds herself with crystals and amulets. Some of these she makes herself out of feathers she finds, and seed pods, dried flowers, and coffee beans.

Now she told me that all morning she watched the gull until she knew why it had come. When the gull flapped its wings and soared, Jade knew it meant that she was going away.

"Where are you going?" I asked her, thinking that suddenly I would have a house devoid of children, whereas just weeks ago it had been full. It was the oddest thing about being a mother, but I could still feel this child's mouth at my breast, smell the sweet smell of talc and her milky breath. I wanted to suckle them again, even Ted, though he had struggled against me. He had tried to get everything I had. When he didn't get enough, he had fought and turned away. But Jade had always been peaceful, lying there, content with what came her way. Suddenly I wanted to take her into my arms, tell her she could sleep there.

Now she looked at me as if she had never been close, as if she had never been content just falling asleep in my arms. She had that look like "I have no idea who you are."

"Oh, I don't know," she said coolly. "Maybe L.A. or Chicago."

"Chicago? To visit Grandma?" No, she told me, to volunteer for the Night Ministry bus that drove around after hours, offering prayer to the pimps and drug dealers. "I want to join something," she said to me, "I want to belong somewhere."

But you belong here, I wanted to tell her. You belong with me. Instead I said, "Honey, isn't there volunteer work you can do right here? Surely in San Francisco——"

She said she needed a change and she was leaving that night.

"Tonight?"

"Tonight I'm going to stay with a friend. Look, I waited until you got home to tell you. I could have just left you a note on the kitchen counter."

"Yes, that's true."

"It's just a friend, Mom. Don't be so judgmental."

I didn't think I was being judgmental. I thought I was just being a parent. "Honey, you're almost twenty-one. You can do whatever you want, but——"

"But what?"

"I don't want you to go."

Her face relaxed. She put her pen down. "Thanks, Mom. I understand that and I appreciate your saying it."

"And I can still be concerned about you, can't I? I mean, I am your mother."

She nodded, then put her pencil down. "May I say something?"

"Of course you may."

"You know, Mom, you should get in touch with your sadness."

"My sadness?" My hands fiddled with a piece of paper on the table. "What do you mean, my sadness?"

"There's this big dark cloud hanging over your head. I can see it wherever you go. It really holds you back." Gazing up, I pretended to look for my cloud. "I'm not kidding, Mom," Jade said.

"Just let me know where you're going to be so I can reach you."

"Okay, I'll try and do that." She kissed me good-bye. I realized I had no idea where she was going or when I'd see her again, but it seemed as if this was how she needed it to be. Still, I wanted to reach out and grab her, hold her to me. She was still a child in her own way, a floundering child, and, though this was the hardest part to admit, I didn't want her to go.

When she left, I got into the shower, scrubbing my flesh, my hair, my nails, but I couldn't get rid of the smell of dead fish and the sea. It permeated my hair, my hands. It reminded me of the stench in the air when I drove through Winonah on the night of the reunion. After the shower, I made myself a cup of peppermint tea. Jade was gone and an unfamiliar quiet settled over the house.

I wasn't sure what to do with myself so I decided to fill out the forms that had just arrived from the National Registry of Historic Houses. It was a huge packet, requiring all kinds of documentation and description. I began sifting through what needed to be done. I filled in the description of the house, the date it was built (which stretched over some twenty years), its materials, current owner information, and reasons for wanting it on the historic registry.

I spent perhaps an hour or two going over the materials, to which I would have to attach the deed to the house and other notarized documentation. When I was finished, I read over what I'd done. Everything seemed in good order. But then I noticed the address of the house. I hadn't written Box 406, Pacific Coast Highway. I'd written 137 Myrtle Lane—the address of a house I hadn't lived in for a long time.

28

I knew when it was February because the tapping began. The steady *tap, tap, tap*. Coming from the basement. It was always the same sound, like a woodpecker down there. My father lined up all the tools he needed—the hammers, the chisels, the screwdrivers. From my bedroom I could smell the shellac, the glue. The workbench had been dormant all winter, but now the house was alive with the sounds of hammers and saws.

He was building us a finished basement. Art had his Boy Scout troop now and I had the gang. It seemed kids were always tramping in and out. Though my father had stopped fixing things around the house, he got this idea in his head. Our father decided he needed to finish the basement so that we would have a place to play. A linoleum floor, bathroom, paneling, cabinets, even a bar.

As our father was downstairs, hammering away, Lily, hands pressed across her ears, walked around saying, "Oh, God, I can't stand this. I really can't stand this noise." Lily thought the upstairs playroom was good enough, but my father had his project and this occupied him for the better part of the spring.

But my father didn't seem to notice Lily's annoyance with the sawdust and din. He was downstairs, renovating the basement. It was a decision he'd made during the winter as he'd watched the gang stomp through the house in their wet shoes to the upstairs playroom. One day he said, "I'm going to finish the basement. Then the kids can play there." He drew up some preliminary plans, ordered some supplies. I have no idea how my father knew how to do this, but he did. Some afternoons he let me help him. He showed me how to hold a hammer, how to drive a nail. Straight on, keep your fingers away, hit the head, not your thumb. I held the paneling in place as he nailed it to the wall.

The new basement was to have a laundry room, a recreation room with a Ping-Pong table, a bar, and a TV room. There would be a bathroom off the laundry room. It was a fairly elaborate project, but my father hired no help. It seemed he could do this on his own. Some days he got Jeb and Art to pitch in. "Okay, now, Squirt, hold that board in place."

Art would put his shoulder against the board while our father hammered it in place. Often Lily came downstairs with grilled cheese sandwiches, potato chips, Cokes. She'd comment on our progress.

"Oh, that's going to be very nice." Or "I like the way there'll be storage cabinets in the rec room."

Then she'd go back upstairs. I'm not sure when I noticed, but my parents didn't seem to speak to each other during these brief visits she made into the construction area. My mother moved like a marionette when she came downstairs, as if someone else were pulling the strings.

One afternoon in the summer Margaret asked me over to play. She said Vicky and some of the gang would be over and did I want to come as well? I rode my bike, parked it on her lawn. I noticed that the porch looked painted and spruced up. Clarice Blair must be doing better in the world, I thought. When I walked in, something was different. "You've changed things around here," I said.

Margaret and the gang sat in the living room, eating chips and plates full of M&Ms. The Little Rascals were on. "Oh, just a few touches," Mrs. Blair said. She came around the corner with a plate of cookies that made my mouth water. The living room looked freshly painted and the small den off the living room seemed darker. It had nice wood paneling too.

"Our basement is paneled like this," I said.

And Clarice Blair, putting down the plate, smiled at me. "Yes. I've heard it is."

29

Traffic was heavy on 280 as I drove into the city through patchy fog. I didn't like this kind of weather or this kind of driving. It slowed me down, made me stop and start, think too much. And it was stop and start all the way to Chinatown. Nick had phoned and said he was coming West. He wanted to meet at Fisherman's Wharf again, but I balked. I told him to meet me at my favorite dim sum place.

He was sitting in a booth in the back, wearing a blue workshirt and jeans. He looked disheveled, his hair not quite combed, like someone who's had a bad night. He rose when he saw me, wrapped his arms around me, buried his face in my hair. "I'm so glad to see you," he muttered against my neck.

He smelled of aftershave and a smoky smell that was all his own. "I'm glad to see you too."

He had never had dim sum before so as the trays came by, I began to point at things I thought he might like. Soon our table was filled with shrimp dumplings, rice noodles, spring rolls, mushrooms with pork. Nick ate heaping portions. "This is so good. Can I have more?"

"Just point at what you want."

He pointed at me. "That easy, huh?"

I gave him a scolding look. "Not quite."

"You know how to show a guy a good time."

"Well, I'm glad you think so."

"I do." I sat back, watching him enjoy the dumplings and noddles. "Things haven't been going very well," he said softly.

"I'm sorry. I'm sorry to hear that."

"I've had a terrible time," he said. "My father was right about her."

"Your father?"

"He begged me not to marry her. He said she wasn't 'our kind.' I hated it when he said that. And sometimes I think I hated him. He was so big, so powerful. Everybody knew him. He was famous. I wanted to stand up to him. I think I wanted to do something he didn't want me to do. He was a hard man to stand up to, you know."

"I'm sure he was."

"I made a big mistake when I married her. I was infatuated. I thought she was beautiful. She was a free spirit. And perhaps I knew that it would gall my father. That he wouldn't be able to stand the fact that I'd married a girl of unknown origins whose mother had been our tenant. I don't know what I was thinking . . ."

"We've all made our mistakes." I put my hand across his. "God knows, I've made mine."

"You know," Nick said, "sometimes even now, and he's been dead awhile, I can hear my father say, 'Oh, you missed that easy shot,' or 'There was a hole in the center; you should've run for that.' Do you know what it was it was like all my life to hear my mistakes rattled back at me? It's as if he's still shouting from the sidelines and I'm never sure which way he wants me to go."

"Which way do *you* want to go?" I asked him.

Nick put his hands under my chin, lifting my face toward him. "Ever since we were kids, I've wanted to kiss you."

"You have? Well, maybe that's another mistake," I quipped. Even though it seemed inevitable, I wasn't comfortable with this turn in the conversation. "Anyway, if you've waited this long, you may as well wait a little longer." He gave me a hurt look. "I think we should wait . . . until things are resolved. Settled between the two of you." I was trying to be logical, but the fact was I wanted to kiss him. I hadn't wanted to kiss anybody in a long time, but now I did.

I knew I had to get out of there or I never would. "Look," I told him, "I'd love to see you. When you break up with Margaret, when you really leave her, why don't you give me a call?"

"I'm not going to be married much longer," he said thoughtfully, "and you don't have to live here."

"No," I said, "I don't, but for now I do. And this is my home. My children are here and I don't want to be responsible for breaking up someone else's family."

"You are not responsible," he said with a little laugh. "I absolve you."

We left the restaurant and as we walked down Grant toward Union Square, where I'd left my car, he kissed me. Not a gentle, tentative first kiss, but a hard one, his mouth pressed firmly against mine. I felt the strength of his arms, his tongue moving between my teeth. He kept his arms around me as we wandered back to his hotel. "Come up to my room. Have a drink with me."

In his hotel room, he poured two scotches from the minibar. He put on the radio to the best jazz station in San Francisco. Stretching out on the bed, he listened to the soft horn. I sat across the room until he said, "Why don't you come and sit here." Then I walked over and he pulled me against his chest.

I wanted to nestle there, to feel safe, but then I felt his mouth hot against my mouth, his tongue working its way between my lips. I was conscious of every moment, each gesture, and at the same time I was swept up in it. For all his bulk, he was gentle as he unbuttoned my blouse, slipped his hands on my breasts. Finally I found myself pulling away. "You know," I said, "I'm really not going to do this."

He sat up, his face flushed. "But what harm would it do?"

I didn't want to leave, but I knew I had to. "I've got to go," I said. "You're still living with her. It's not right."

"Tessie, please . . ."

"It's not just about her; it's about me. I'm already finding myself thinking about you. Wanting you. This isn't what I should be doing. Not now. Not yet. When you leave her, give me a call." Nick lay back, arms folded behind his head. He closed his eyes as if he were going to sleep as I opened the door.

I drove fast along the highway, taking turns faster than I should have. At any moment I could careen off the cliffs or have a head-on, but I still drove fast. I don't know what the rush was. I returned to an empty house. There was no message or note from Jade. There were several messages on the phone machine, including one from Charlie's lawyer, informing me that his client was ending his child support since neither child was in school. This didn't surprise me, but still it was another blow. But my thoughts were far from support payments and bills and how I was going to make ends meet. And then, there were several hang-ups, some of which lasted a long time.

When the phone rang, I was sure it was Nick and I rushed to answer it. "Hello," I said, "who's there?" but no one was. Wondering if it was another crossed wire, I listened for a long time to the breathing at the other end, as if somehow I would be able to recognize it.

———

In the morning I was awakened by the ringing again and once more no one was there. But this time the person was slower to hang up and I heard the breathing more clearly. "Who is this?" I asked insistently this time. "Is anybody there?"

And then I heard her speak. "Tess, it's me, Margaret. I need to talk to you about Nick."

"What about him?" I asked her.

"It's just that I know he's in San Francisco, but I haven't been able to reach him. He's not staying at the hotel where he said he'd be. Danielle is worried and so am I. I thought he might contact you. Do you know where he might be staying?"

"No, I don't. I haven't seen him." I wasn't sure why I felt the need to lie to her, but I did. Even as I lied, I wondered what Nick had said. Did she know if he'd seen me?

"Well, he was depressed when he left and I'm worried about him."

"He was depressed? Well, I'm sure he's all right."

There was a long pause. "Yes, he probably is. But if you hear from him, would you have him give me a call?"

Later when I phoned Nick at his hotel, he said she knew where he was. He'd spoken to her that afternoon. "She's just trying to trick you," he said.

"But why would she do that? Does she know anything?"

"It doesn't matter," he said. "It's just the way she is."

30

In eighth grade Margaret began to dress like me. It was fall, a bright September day. The first day of school. In just a few weeks Kennedy would be elected president and his Thousand Days would begin. The Cuban missile crisis would follow and Vicky and I would sit, spellbound, clasping hands in my finished basement, listening as the handsome young president told us we might be going to war. Soon I would know that there was a world that was not of my making. That the safety of our homes, the quiet little niches our parents had created, were just that—small corners tucked away from the real world.

But for the moment what mattered most was that I had my books in a bag and a new outfit. A red cardigan, a blue-and-red-plaid pleated skirt. A white shirt with a Peter Pan collar. New saddle shoes. I loved the first day of school. Number 2 pencils, sharpened to a fine point. Pads of paper, erasers, the sound of cracking book spines.

The halls smelled freshly painted, the floor slick and newly polished. Everything about the school and its smells and my new outfit was filled with promise. The gang gathered in the hall. Ginger was lamenting the fact that she got Mr. Green's homeroom and that Lori Martin, Maureen Hetherford, and I were all in Miss Olden's, who was known to be easy. Samantha told Ginger not to worry because she was in Mr. Mitchell's and there wasn't anybody she liked in that homeroom.

We were looking at our class lists, peering into our new books, when I saw Margaret. She too wore a red cardigan, a blue and red pleated skirt. A Peter Pan collar. I put my hand to my mouth, but Margaret smiled at me. I had planned for weeks to wear just what I was wearing. Now Margaret stood in front of me wearing the same thing.

"It's not possible," I shrieked.

Margaret laughed. "I can read your mind, Tess. I can read your mind."

Our teacher, Mrs. Chilford, gave us an assignment: Describe the person you'd most like to be. I wrote about Jackie Kennedy because I wanted to be married to the president and live in the White House. Vicky did Jane Addams and the rest of the girls did Eleanor Roosevelt, though a few did their mothers, not thinking it meant they'd be married to their fathers. A few days after the assignment, Mrs. Chilford stopped me in the hall. "What a nice tribute to you from Margaret, Tessie!"

"What's that, Mrs. Chilford?" I asked.

"Oh, don't you know? For some reason I thought you would.

Margaret said that out of all the people in the world, living or dead, she'd like to be you."

Samantha Crawford invited us to a party in her basement. There'd be Cokes and boys. It was one of our first parties like this, but now that we were thirteen, it would happen more and more. Samantha Crawford had some records. Bill Haley and the Comets, Del Shannon, Frankie Avalon. Motown was just getting going and one of the boys had brought a new record by the Miracles. Then the lights went dim and Johnny Mathis came on. "Funny you're a stranger who's come here; come from another town."

We chose partners and we were dancing. But there weren't enough boys to go around. The girls who were left began pairing up. "So dance with me," Margaret said.

"I will not."

"Dance with me."

She pulled me to her, swept me into her arms. I felt her breath against my ear, her hand on my back as we moved slowly through Samantha Crawford's basement. She pressed her hips into mine. In my ear she sang along, "I'm a stranger myself, dear, small world isn't it. . . ." I was relieved when Chubby Checker came on and we could do the twist.

A few days later we were sitting in Mr. Whitcomb's class. He taught math and was very strict. You had to sit straight in your chair. You had to have your paper and pencil neatly on the top of your desk. You could never be excused. No matter what.

Margaret raised her hand. She had to go to the bathroom. Mr. Whitcomb said he was sorry, but there would be no bathroom privileges. No one was allowed to go before the bell. "But Mr. Whitcomb," Margaret said, her voice pleading, "I really need to go."

"You'll have to wait like a big girl."

Margaret sat there staring straight ahead at him. As Mr. Whitcomb went on at the board about multiplication of fractions, she sat even as the mumbling began and someone pointed. "Look," I heard a voice behind me say. We turned and stared. A small puddle of blood like a crime scene had formed at the base of Margaret's desk. Blood ran down her legs, pooled on the floor. Even as Mr. Whitcomb, a shocked, flushed look to his face, told her she could now be excused, she just sat there, not moving, staring straight ahead.

Of course they wanted her. All the boys. How they wanted her. It didn't matter who they were or what side of the tracks they came from. They whistled when she walked by, they called to her. They touched that long black hair. They dreamed of touching her milky white skin. And the breasts. They didn't dare dream of those, but they did.

When she walked by, there was the smell of lilacs and cigarettes, of something moist and sweaty. They sang after her, "There she was justa walking down the street . . ."

We watched them want her. We watched and pretended we didn't see what it was all about. She was just the new girl, wasn't she? Even though she'd already been living in our midst for four years. She would never make it here. She'd never fit in.

I pretended not to notice the smooth curve of her hips, the shape of her arms. The way she walked, dressed like me. How was it that she was always dressed like me? And then in the summers stripped down, in two-pieces in the backyard. Margaret always called to see who was coming over. Who'd be there. One day we were all sun-bathing in the backyard, all of us in our two-pieces, Cokes in our hands, and when I went inside for a pitcher of something, Jeb came up to me and said, "Squirrel, which one is that one?"

He pointed out back and I squinted in the sun to see. I couldn't quite follow his finger as it pressed itself against the glass. "Who?"

"That one. I've never seen her before."

"Yes, you have. You know who that is."

But my brother looked at me dumbfounded and then I saw a look

I'd never seen in his face before, one I couldn't quite place, but I said to him more gently now, "You've seen her a million times. That's just Margaret. That's Margaret Blair."

One day on my way to tell my brother to come home from the Idiot's Circle, I ran into Margaret. "I have to tell my brother to come home."

Margaret laughed. "Oh, I'll come with you. Let me tag along."

It was summer and we were in shorts. I was wearing powder-blue shorts and Margaret wore black and pink stripes that showed off her long, bronzed legs, her black hair pulled back. We were thirteen years old. Jeb was fifteen. As I approached, all the boys in leather started hooting, calling out names. I said to Jeb, "Mom says you have to come home." I didn't have to describe for him Lily at home, tearing out her hair, slamming doors, muttering to herself about her kids running wild, her kids having gotten away from her.

He gave us a wink. "Sure, Tess," he said, docile as a lamb, "I'll come home." With a great flourish like I once saw Gene Kelly do before he was about to dance, Jeb took Margaret by the arm. "I'll come if you'll come too."

We all went home and down into the rec room, where Jeb put on a Sam Cooke record. I stood against the bar, clapping, tapping out a beat, watching Jeb and Margaret. They danced close during the slow dances. Only when the music was fast would they dance with me.

31

Nick wanted to see where I lived. He called to say he had some time. A meeting he'd been waiting for had been postponed and he could drive down. "I don't think it's a good idea," I said.

"I want to see the objects you have around you."

"Well, it's mostly feathers and shells. Stuff I find on the beach."

"Well, then, I want to see that. The beach, those vistas you told me about," he said. "Tessie, I want to see you." For some reason I imagined he would come out here and we'd still be friends. But there was something inevitable about all this. I couldn't stop it anymore than the driver of a runaway truck on a downhill grade could. We seemed to have been heading here for a long while. I knew it even as I told him, "Yes, I want to see you too."

I planned to have everything ready—table set, house cleaned—before I had to do my volunteer work at the aquarium. I was just finishing cleaning up the kitchen when there was a knock at the door. I was afraid it might be John Martelli. He had taken to stopping by. Once or twice he'd even dropped in. From time to time I thought I'd seen his car driving past my house.

I opened the door hesitantly, and instead I found Bruno Mercedes standing there. He'd come over to interview me about the house and to ask questions once or twice. But this was the first time he'd stopped by uninvited. He stood there, rocking on his heels in his navy slacks and tweed jacket. He had on glasses, which I didn't remember him wearing before. "Mrs. Winterstone . . ."

I gave him a little glare.

"Tess, I was wondering if we could talk."

"I'd love to talk, Bruno. But it's not such a good time." He stood there, looking so sad, almost begging. "Why don't you come in?"

He breathed a sigh of relief as I led him into the kitchen, where I poured both of us a cup of coffee. He took his light and sweet. "Lots of milk and sugar," he said.

I sat down across from him and we both gazed out the breakfast nook window through the grove of pines, the cliffs, to where the earth dropped away. "I've written something," he said. "I was going to mail it to you, but I decided to bring it myself."

He pushed across the table the envelope he carried, and the moisture of his fingers left an imprint. Slowly I opened it. It was a tattered manila envelope with coffee stains and assorted other stains on it, unspeakable things, I imagined. There was a neat title page and perhaps another thirty pages. The title page read: *Water and Rage: The Dark Vision of a Metaphysical Poet—Francis Cantwell Eagger.*

Bruno looked across at me, his eyes filled with anticipation. I turned to the next page, where I saw "This dissertation is for TW, who let me inside" and then the epigraph, which was a quote I remembered from one of the Eagger poems, "Dark winds batter all that I know. A tree crashes down the dunes, leaving a hole with which to view the sky."

"Bruno, is this for me?"

"Just read the preface," he said, his eyes never leaving my face. I felt awkward, as if something was expected of me that I did not have to give. Opening the manuscript, I read,

> *For many years I have tried to penetrate the dark vision of Francis Cantwell Eagger. I have tried to understand his work from what I could piece together of his life. Eagger left no journals, no unfinished poems, and only a few letters, several of which were exchanged with my father.*
>
> *The focal point of his work seemed to be the house where he lived, the one he built with his own two hands. After many months of waiting I was finally granted access to that house and it was only once I was inside that I felt I had found the way into the poet's spirit. Poetry does not arise from nowhere. We all know that the writer draws from what he or she knows. In building those dark, narrow walls of stone, Francis Cantwell Eagger perfected the dark poetic vision for which he is known.*

I turned the page, but that was all he had written. The rest was a bibliography and a list of poems. "Well, it is a very good start, Bruno. Very exciting for you."

"It's as far as I've gotten, but I found this fragment of a poem in a letter. It's a big discovery. I think it's from 'Desire Paths,' a poem he worked on for a long time, but it was never published and is believed lost." Bruno held the page in his hand, his fingers shaking. " 'Along the wind-racked bluffs/we have made our way/to the edge and back again/so many times/That we have made a path, worn down weeds and shrubs.' That's all that was in the letter."

"Well, you've got a good start. I think you should keep going."

"I want to," he said, "I really do, but I just need more. . . ."

I looked at his boyish face, his sandy hair that was already starting to thin, his tweed jacket. I wondered what my life would have been if I'd met a boy like this when I was a girl. "Is there something you want?"

He sat still, gazing off to the rooms of my house. "I was thinking you should turn this place into a museum."

I paused, wondering if I should say what I planned to say next. "Actually, I was thinking of turning it into a bed-and-breakfast."

His eyes widened in disbelief. His face turned pale.

"I need some income. Quite frankly, I'm broke and my alimony and support payments are running out. My plan is to turn the kids' rooms into guest rooms. It will give me a good tax break and provide a little income."

He looked at me, almost angry now. "You aren't serious, are you?"

"I'm very serious."

"The man who lived here was a holy man, almost a saint. . . ."

"Who drank himself to death and whose own son couldn't wait to get rid of this place because it reminded him of his terrible childhood."

"He drank to fill the void."

"We all have a void to fill."

Just then the back door opened and Jade walked in. Or dragged herself in. It had been days since I'd seen her and she looked dejected, miserable. As she ran her fingers through her cropped, purple-streaked hair, my arms ached to take her in. "Jade, darling," I said, my voice trembling, "how are you?"

"I'm okay," she said, though she didn't look or sound okay. She gave me a wave, Bruno a nod, went to the fridge, got out a Diet Coke, and flipped it open. "This is Bruno Mercedes," I said. "He's writing his doctoral dissertation on Francis Eagger."

Leaning on the wooden counter, Jade took a sip of her Coke. "Really?" She looked at him closely. "You used to stand in front of our house."

Bruno blushed a little, gazing down. "Yes, I've been working on his poems for a long time now. But I've just begun—"

" 'Where the sea falls, I fall. Where it rises, I rise . . . ' " my daughter said, looking out the window.

Bruno kept his gaze on her. " 'It is the place I come back to, the one I cannot leave, nor can I dwell in another land. . . . ' "

She looked up at him now, smiling. I hadn't seen a smile on my daughter's face in weeks, maybe months. " 'Coastal Views,' " she said. "That's my favorite poem."

"One of mine too," Bruno said. "It's about finding God."

"Oh." Jade gave him a funny look. "I didn't see it that way. I thought it was about love. But that makes sense. Well." She hit her hand on the Formica counter. "I've got a job." She gave me a look. "Back at the fish and chips. It was nice meeting you."

"It was nice meeting you too." Bruno got up and extended his hand. Jade looked at it as if she didn't know what she was supposed to do. Then she shook it and headed toward her room.

Bruno watched her leave. "Interesting girl."

"Yes, you could say that."

As I walked Bruno to the door, he said to me, "This is what I'd like to ask you. I'd like to come back here every now and then. I'd like to think in this house."

"Of course, Bruno," I told him. "Come back whenever you like."

That afternoon I sat at the edge of the tidal pool at the aquarium, where I volunteer from time to time. I was showing a starfish to a group of schoolchildren from Santa Cruz. They squealed as the starfish writhed, its tentacles sucking against their hands.

32

I wasn't sure whose car it was or where she got it, but in the spring of our junior year, Margaret showed up at my house in a red convertible with a stereo radio. I had no car. Or rather I had no use of a car. My father had taken that privilege away the week after I got my license. I had managed to have two minor accidents in a very short time span, including backing out of the garage into the car of a friend of my father's who'd stopped by to ask my father if he wanted to hit some balls. I knew that the car was there. I mean, I saw it as I backed out, but for some reason I drove smack into its front fender. My father apologized profusely to his friend, paid for the Prairie Vista Automotive job, and told me I could drive when I could see. He also made it clear to me that he did not anticipate this being in the near future.

The unspoken agreement between me and the gang was that on spring nights when the weather was warm and our homework was more or less done we'd show up at the bottom of Lake Road on the beach where the bonfire pit was. I could have walked. It wasn't that far and I knew how to slide down the drainpipe and how to sneak back in through the screened-in porch, which was never locked. But it just wasn't considered cool to walk. I may as well have come on a bicycle. You had to come in a car, preferably your own. But if not, anyone's would do.

One night I was hoping that Patrick would show or maybe Vicky or Samantha Crawford or the Dworkin twins. Anybody who had their license and wheels. I was as good as grounded without permission to drive and I had no idea when it would be granted. Miserable in my room, I went down to watch the stop sign on our corner for headlights. I told myself five cars and it would be for me. I got pretty good at seeing even the faintest glimmer of light in the stop sign and then I'd start my count. Sometimes there'd be a burst of them. Other times they would be few and far between. I could sit there in the dining room, looking down the driveway, and nobody knew what I was doing there. Nobody noticed, really.

One night nobody came for a long time and so I gave myself a few extra turns and then Margaret drove up. She had this neat red convertible with the hood down and her long black hair flapping in the breeze. I couldn't believe it when she drove up. I didn't particularly want to go with her, but on the other hand I wanted to get out of there. I dashed out the front door.

It was a warm spring night when the air felt fresh and green and everything was about ready to burst with buds and flowers. As I ran into the driveway, Margaret was waving at me. "Let's go," she said.

"Where'd you get this car?" I touched its shiny chrome, its red paint. The white leather inside smelled new. "Nice," I muttered, leaping in over the door without opening it.

"Oh, my dad," she said as she backed up quietly, then gunned it at the corner. "He promised me one when I got my license." She turned on the radio to a Beatles medley. They were very popular then and we turned it up high and sang, "I wanta hold your hand" and "Close your eyes and I'll kiss you." As we cruised toward the beach, Dion came on with "Runaway" and we shouted at the top of our lungs as we drove.

"Boy," I said, "you are so lucky." I thought about the family station wagon that sat idle in our garage. Even when my father gave me his permission, I'd never drive it again. I'd probably had those accidents because it was such a big lug of a car. "Your dad really gave you this?"

"Yes," she said with a strong voice of indignation. "He drove right down from Wisconsin and handed me the keys. Boy, did that piss my mom off." Then Margaret burned a little rubber as we zoomed into the beach parking lot, where big signs were posted everywhere that read NO PARKING AFTER DARK and BEACH PARKING ONLY DURING SEASON so that the police had some grounds for arresting us when we were going hot and heavy with our boyfriends in the middle of January.

Several cars were already assembled and I recognized most of them. Butch, Hawkeye, and JJ. The guys from Prairie Vista. They were there. Vicky's car was there and so were Lori's and Samantha's. I was a little pissed that no one but Margaret had picked me up. A bonfire was going and somebody had thought to bring beer. The cop cruiser usually came by every hour on the hour so we had a little while.

Patrick was lying in the sand, propped up on his elbow, a beer in hand. I was mad at him for not coming by for me so I played cool and ignored him. We'd already been going out for about a year or so. We'd gone to the sophomore hop the year before, which was the biggy, and we usually went to the movies on a weekend. Whenever there was something, it was just assumed we'd go together, though I'm not sure how it ever happened that we did. He never called me and I don't know that I called him. Now that we had cars we just showed up and then we'd go off together and neck in his car.

He saw me all right because I saw him perk up and laugh at something somebody said that wasn't so funny. He used to do that, laugh this big laugh when I was around so I'd notice him, but not really pay attention to me himself. I always had to go to him, it seemed, but I didn't care because it made him happy when I did. But tonight I didn't go.

"Hey," I said to Vicky, "what's the idea? Nobody came for me."

"We just figured Patrick would."

"Yeah, well, he didn't."

I turned to say something to him when I saw that Margaret had sidled up to where he was sitting. She stretched out beside him like a cat and Patrick grinned in the glow of the fire. When I went over to get a beer, he gave me a look like he couldn't help himself.

I stayed around for as long as I thought I could without all hell breaking loose when I got home. Margaret never moved but just stayed, joking with Patrick, and he kept sipping his beer, laughing at her jokes. Occasionally she tugged on his pants leg or tossed her pony-tail back as if she were swatting flies.

I sat down not far from them and Patrick kept giving me this dopey, hopeless look and I kept watching Margaret, who acted as if she didn't know who I was or that Patrick and I had been a thing for the better part of the past year. She just lay next to him as if this were her living room and she was stretched out on the sofa.

After about an hour I said I was going home. Patrick offered to drive me, but he made no move to get up. "Forget it," I said. Vicky said she'd take me, but she wasn't ready to go. I told them it was okay. I could walk. They'd all had a lot of beer, but they knew it was a fairly ridiculous thing I was suggesting I'd do, at that hour. They all told me to wait and someone would drive me home, but I was already heading toward the bluff.

They probably figured I'd take the road, which was the long way. I heard Patrick shout at me as I headed straight for the bluff. There seemed to be some discussion about whether or not to let me go because I heard an engine start, but I was already clawing my way up the bluff.

It was a steep incline of mud and rocks. I'd climbed up it before, but never at midnight, when I couldn't see. Still, it was the most direct route to my house and would shave half an hour off my walking time if I didn't kill myself. I reached for branches, found my footing in stones. Slowly I pulled myself up. Once I lost my footing and started a small landslide of pebbles, but in a few moments I was scaling the top without incident.

I took side roads to get home. I spotted a few cars I recognized on the main intersections, but I didn't want to see anybody. When I got home, the red car was sitting in my driveway. Patrick was with her and I suppose they were worried about me. I ducked around the rosebushes and sneaked in the back porch. I don't know how long they stayed there because whenever they pulled out, I was already asleep.

33

Outside tires screeched on the gravel and suddenly Nick was there in my driveway. He closed the car door, then just stood there for a long moment, taking in the view, smelling the coastal air. I opened the door, giving a wave. When he reached me, he held me to him, burying his head in my hair. Taking him by the hand, we walked around the house, stood at the bluff. "It's incredible, Tessie."

"If I sold this place, I'd be rich. The land alone is probably worth a million. But I'm never going to sell."

"Promise me you won't."

I crossed my heart.

Inside a fire blazed in the fireplace. I uncorked a bottle of good California Chardonnay as he wandered through the house. "I love this room," he said. "I love it here." He stood gazing at the view as I handed him a glass of wine.

"I knew I would."

He breathed a deep sigh as if he hadn't relaxed in a long time. Then we clicked our glasses together. "Can we take a walk? I feel like I've been cooped up. I could use the fresh air."

"Of course we can. We can do whatever you like." Putting our wineglasses on the coffee table, I took him by the arm and led him down the path of ice plants, through the grove of pines until we stood on the path the poet had carved through his own restless walks at the edge of the sea. Nick took a deep breath. "It's very dramatic, isn't it?"

Holding my hand, Nick followed the path. "I can see why you'd never want to leave."

I squeezed his hand, glad he could see that and wondering if it was still true. We made our way down the cliffs to the sea and walked the beach for a while, occasionally stopping to pick up a shell or a feather that struck our eye. We spoke very little, but I didn't mind the silence.

After we'd walked a ways, Nick paused and gazed up at my house. "Is it safe there?" he asked.

"Not particularly."

He laughed. "I didn't think so. It looks as if it could come tumbling down."

"It might," I said. "It could."

He put an arm tightly around my shoulder. "Be careful," he said. "I don't want anything bad to happen to you."

I took him by the hand, leading him up the path, back toward the house. "Nothing bad will."

When we got back to the house, I went to check on the bouillabaisse I'd made from whatever the local fishermen had caught that day. The kitchen was filled with the salty steam of fish and jazz was coming from my living room. Nick had put on a CD. Peter Duchin, Art Tatum? The music was dreamy, the way old jazz can be. It had been awhile since my house was filled with the smells of cooking and the sound of soft jazz. I peeked into the living room and saw Nick, sitting, glass of wine in hand, staring at the sea, a magazine open in his lap, as if he too belonged right there.

At dinner Nick ate a hearty bowl of bouillabaisse and drank down two glasses of Chardonnay. With a piece of bread he sopped up the juice on his plate. Then taking my hand, he led me into the living room, where the jazz played. It was Tatum, I decided. His head was tossed back. With one hand he tapped out the rhythm on my thigh.

Soon his fingers were moving up and down my leg. They were lifting my chin to his. His kiss was long and deep. "I've been wanting to do this for a long time," he said. His hands guided me down the hallway to my bedroom. He peeled off his shirt, his pants. He pulled my sweater over my head. Rising above me, he straddled my hips, hands on my nipples, eyes closed, body swaying. His hands were everywhere, his tongue coursed between my thighs. The hair on his back and shoulders was furry and thick as a beast's and I burrowed in. My fingers circled his nipples, reached down and held him. Everywhere his tongue went, he stayed for a long time. His body was firm yet soft at the same time.

When he entered me it was smooth and easy and he knew how to take his time. I felt as if I had taken a drug and was losing myself because I couldn't tell where his limbs ended and mine began. Suddenly I felt tired and I knew that I would sleep.

When I woke, it was just after midnight and the house smelled of fish and burning wood. The only sound was of waves crashing below. Moonlight shone in, splattering on the floor. Nick lay beside me, his eyes open, listening. When he saw I was awake, he reached up, stroking my face. "It's beautiful here." I rested my head on his belly. It had never seemed quite so beautiful to me before.

"I'm glad I'm here," he went on. "I've wanted to be with you for a long time. Maybe you've always been somewhere in my mind."

"I'm glad I'm with you too," I told him, rubbing my face on his chest. "You know almost everything about me."

"I'm with you because I want to be," he continued, still stroking my face, "but are you sure you know why you want me here? Are you sure you know why you're doing this?"

"Because I've grown fond of you," I teased, kissing his fingertips, his hands.

Nick turned over, resting his chin in his hands. The body that had seemed so large, almost overpowering to me just months ago now seemed gentle, tender. "I hope that's why. I hope that's so."

"Why else would it be?" I traced my finger along the line of his shoulder blade, down his spine in the moonlight.

"Because you want to get back at her?"

"Get back at her? Why? Why would I want that?"

"Oh, Tessie," he said with a sigh, "you know. You know why."

34

You never saw so many paper moons, all gold and cut out of cardboard, and roses, tissue-paper roses, perfumed, fluffed, tied with wire. We spent weeks making them, cutting the moons and twisting the roses until our thumbs got blisters. Painting the blue backdrop with the clouds. Boxes and boxes of them.

The gym, of course, would be transformed. It always was for junior prom. Not that I'd seen it before, but I'd heard. I'd heard how one day it smelled of sweat and basketballs, and the next of powder and eau de cologne. It was a vision we'd all conceived. We, the members of the junior prom committee. We'd eliminated Hawaiian theme (too much like the previous year, which was South Pacific). We'd thought about "Downtown," which was the big Petula Clark song that year, or "She Loves You."

Then somebody said why not "Moonlight and Roses." Yes, it was romantic, but then, we were romantic. We liked being romantic. We'd play songs like "Moon River" and "Paper Moon," silly romantic songs. The gym all decorated with paper roses and moons and the lights turned down low and the girls with their corsages and dresses, pumps and bags dyed to match.

It was, of course, what we dreamed of.

So we could just see it, the gang and me. And *of course,* we volunteered to decorate it. We who had practiced our pompon routines and our cheerleading and baton in this gym, yes, we would transform it into a different place. Another place altogether.

Of course I was going with Patrick. It was a fait accompli—an expression I didn't learn until college, but of course that was what was going to happen. No one doubted it, least of all me.

Still the phone didn't ring. I waited. It's not that it didn't ring, because it did. It rang all the time, off the hook, as Lily said. I had my own line now, not just for me, but for my brothers as well, but they'd make a phone call and it was "Meet me at the Idiot's Circle at five" or "See you at the field." Not like me, because I liked to talk and chatter and gab with the gang. If one of them didn't call every night or so, I was crushed, devastated.

But Patrick didn't call. I saw him at school and it wasn't like he was avoiding me. We chatted by my locker and walked up the hall and as far as I was concerned we were together. We were a couple, weren't we? Didn't we drive around in his car with his hand resting just below my breast? Didn't that count for something? So we were a couple; that's how I saw it. That's how everyone else saw it too.

Then Jim Richter called and asked me to the prom. Would you like to go with me to Moonlight and Roses? And of course I said no because I was going with Patrick.

"I don't think so" was Jim Richter's reply.

"What do you mean you don't think so?" I stammered.

"I think he's going with someone else."

Then I lost my cool because that couldn't be and I knew it was just an ugly rumor so I said, "Well, who might that be?" still trying to sound like I had a handle on exactly what was going on here.

And he said, "Well, I don't know . . . maybe I shouldn't say anything." And he hung up, just like that.

So I called Lori first and she hemmed and hawed, and then I called Maureen, and finally it was Vicky who told it to me straight because, she said, "Well, we just didn't know if you knew. We couldn't really tell what the story was because it seemed as if you didn't, but we thought maybe you were just trying—"

"Vicky, who is he going with?"

"Margaret."

"You're kidding. How could he? How could he do that to me?"

Vicky was silent. "I don't know. He just did. And she said yes."

"When did it happen?"

"Weeks ago."

I had my pride. I wasn't going to just lose it, not like that, not there on the phone. "Thank you for telling me. I appreciate it." Then I got off the phone. I shook, I cried, then I got my composure back and called Jim Richter.

"If you'd still like to take me, I'll go with you."

Jim Richter stood in the entranceway in his powder-blue suit, talking to my father. There was the dance to go to and then there was some late-night supper, and then a boat ride on the Chicago River, which my father hadn't known about, and I saw him blanch. "Oh, I don't know about that boat ride. How many in the boat, son?"

And Jim Richter said he didn't know, but that there were chaperons (which there weren't) and that I'd be home in the morning after a breakfast being held at some hotel, and it all seemed like so much and I wanted my father to say no to it all, but there I was in my rose-colored dress with pumps and bag dyed to match and I felt like a stupid flower and Jim stood there, a corsage in his hand because that was what the boys did, they brought the girls corsages, and I thought to myself, I don't want to do this, I don't want to go, not tonight, not to this prom. I want to put my feet up and read a good book or take a walk because I was sure to run into them and of course everyone knew.

We drove in silence, Jim Richter with his hand draped across the back of my seat, and I thought, Don't touch me, but of course he did. He let his moist hand graze my shoulder and I pulled away. All the cars were arriving as we pulled up. One after the other, cars pulled up with girls in satiny dresses—creamy blue and shiny pink, corsages that would leave elastic marks on their wrists, tied to their arms.

And the gym was transformed. Dark with evening-blue lights, the roses we'd made, the paper moons draped from overhead. On a platform the band played just like we knew it would—"Moon River." Dream maker, heartbreaker.

Jim Richter took my hand in his fleshy, sweaty palm and led me in and there they were, of course. I saw them. Margaret and Patrick, together, dancing. Close.

Drinks were being passed around. Boys had flasks under their coats and some had whiskey and some had gin and some had things I couldn't recall. Jim pressed me to him, made me dance with him, but every once in a while when a flask went around, I grabbed for it, took a long swig. I could see Patrick, his hand around hers. What happened? I wanted to ask him. Why did you do it?

But I knew why. Because for some reason she had to have what she didn't have. She had to have what was mine.

I drank from silvery flasks—scotch, gin. I didn't care. My mouth and tongue were warm, but my feet were numb, which was good because as we danced Jim Richter stepped on them.

And then we all piled into our cars and drove into town and had supper somewhere and then there was this boat, this boat on the river. By now we had all slipped out of our prom clothes into other things and I kept drinking from whatever flask and I saw the boat and I thought, I can't get on a boat on the river. So this is how it will end for me. Flailing arms, voices calling for help. But the boat moved easily from the dock and I drank from a bottle being passed around and the sky over the Chicago River was turning purplish, a lighter shade of purple, almost lavender and I felt Jim Richter slide his hand under my shirt, into my bra, pulling me to him, pulling me under him. I felt those hot, moist hands against my flesh and suddenly I knew I was going to be sick. I was going to throw up over the side, so I pushed his hands away and I shouted at him, shouted loud enough for everyone on the boat, all my classmates to hear, "How can you take advantage of a girl who's drunk?" I shouted it once, then twice, until Jim Richter shrank away and I turned and there was Patrick, his hand over my mouth to silence me, Patrick, leading me away to the side of the boat where I was sick.

"Tess," he said, "are you all right?"

"Get away from me," I told him. "I hate you. I hate all of you."

It was dawn when I walked in and my father was just getting up. "Squirrel," he called to me as I slipped in, "Squirrel, is that you?"

"It's me, Dad."

"Are you okay, sweetie?"

"I'm fine, Daddy. I'm just tired. I'm going to bed."

It was after the prom, just a couple of days or so later when Mom said, Take the car, Squirrel, take the car, and she handed me one of her lists, those long lists for the store. Sometimes she let me do the shopping for her and I liked to do it midweek when Dad was gone because I could buy a few extra things—things I knew he liked like root beer and popcorn we'd drink and pop the night when he got home. With the extra money she gave me I always picked up something special for my dad.

I liked the Indian Trail market with the giant Indian head on the front—a chief of some sort in full feathers, a tepee behind him (despite that fact that in Winonah there were no Indians who wore full feathers or lived in tepees. For tepees belonged to a nomadic tribe and the Potawatomi lived in lodges right in what is now downtown Winonah).

But still I liked the Indian Trail market with its wide aisles and everything you could imagine to eat, including lobsters in tanks and cereal from Switzerland, lemons from the South Pacific. All kinds of cheeses and peppers the color of the sky just before the sun goes down. All wrapped in plastic. Everything so orderly and neat that it just fit into my archival spirit, my love of objects and order. And I would almost always run into the mother of one of my friends, Mrs. Kahn or Mrs. LePoint, and she'd say to me, "Is that you? Tess, my God, you've gotten to be such a big girl. So pretty. I wouldn't have recognized you."

Some might comment that they never saw me since the swim club closed last summer. We belonged to the swim club and the synagogue. We were members of other things as well. My mother was active in the PTA and my father went to meetings of the Chamber of Commerce. We were citizens of the community we lived in and I loved that community. We belonged here. When I popped into Larsen's after school for gum, Mrs. Larsen knew my name. People knew who we were. That's how I'd define it best. People knew my name.

And my business. But in a good way, mostly. If you were sick, someone always brought you a casserole, a pot of soup. Neighbors were always stopping over to borrow things so that it was hard to know which cups belonged to whom or whose baseball bat we had in our garage or whose jacket had been left in the mud closet. It could be anyone's who lived within a ten-block radius or farther, just counting my friends and my brothers' friends who rode their bikes or cars to our house. A jacket could have been left by any one of a hundred people.

These were our friends, our neighbors, our community. The people we lived among, the people who knew us but didn't know our secrets. Or if they did, they didn't tell. At least no one told me.

The store was a mile, a mile and a half at most from the house, but I took my time driving. I still had that bad taste in my mouth from the prom and felt as if I had two heads. The car smelled of cigarettes and kids. I liked driving the car with the list in my hand, going to the store like a grown-up. I parked as I always did, got my cart, and slowly made my way through the wide, plentiful aisles. Aisles that smacked of the good fortune that had befallen the people of Winonah. We have done well, this store seemed to say. We are a success. I picked up coffee, broccoli, and potatoes quickly. I was on my way to cereal, then chicken breasts when I ran into Vicky's mom, Mrs. Walton.

"Tess, is that you? I don't recognize you anymore."

Mrs. Walton always embarrassed me, because she said it so loudly. I wanted to reply, But Mrs. Walton, I'm at your house every week, but I just said, "I've grown a lot this year."

"You all have. You girls are getting so big."

Perhaps it was then that I caught a glimpse of him out of the corner of my eye. Or perhaps not. Maybe I just remember it that way. But I slipped away from her, promised to be by to see Vicky soon. Already my hands gripped the cart too tightly, my list crumpled, sweaty in my palm. I made a right, then a left. Now the store was almost empty as I headed into its more remote wings—the bakery, the fish market.

Then I saw him, standing near aisle six, the dairy section. Right there on a Tuesday when he should have been no closer than Quincy. He had milk, juice, a package of hamburger in his hands. My father was shopping, picking up this and that at the store. But, of course, this made no sense since he wasn't due home till Thursday (he never got home before Thursday) and it was only Tuesday. And why was he shopping if I was the one doing the errands?

I stood there, motionless, watching my father select items from the shelf. He had no cart, but like a juggler was balancing them in his hands. It was odd to see my father picking cans off the shelf, reading labels. He took creamed corn. We never had creamed corn (or anything out of a can, for that matter) at home.

I didn't say hello. I backed up my cart and quickly slipped out of the store. When I got home, Lily yelled at me because I'd forgotten most of what I'd gone for. But I wouldn't go back to that store again.

35

All families have secrets, don't they? So why shouldn't mine have ours? Why shouldn't we keep things from one another? Even when you grow up within four walls with about as many people, you can't really know anyone for sure. Even families are built on fragments, the bits and pieces we show the world.

Still, it is a terrible thing to keep a secret inside. So far inside. Tucked deep like a tapeworm that works its way through you. Now I had to tell someone. And I knew who that would be. Once I knew I could hold on to it longer than before. Little Squirrel, guarding her nut.

I'm not sure when it was that my father became a man of alibis, of duplicity, a man who lived a double life. It never occurred to me that he was spending half the week with us as he always had and the other half across the railroad tracks, just a mile or so from where we lived. But it was a world away, really, where he went, a place where he could put his shoes on the coffee table and laugh out loud. Where he could sing as he put up drywall.

It has taken me a long time, but I can see it now. The disaster I feared had already happened. While I imagined him in the path of oncoming storms, racing tornados, dodging floods, the threat was in fact much closer and more real.

Sometimes I have these dreams in which my father is looming over my bed, larger than he was in life. He has come with a story or a song, something he has to tell me. I always wind up telling him the same thing. "It's all right, Dad. I already know."

"What're you going to do with your life, Trooper?" our father said to Jeb when he got home from Madison in June. Jeb was studying history and he unpacked his collection of books on the Crimean War, Central Asia, the Mongol empire.

"I'm going to figure out how the world works," Jeb replied without an ounce of irony, because that indeed was what he thought he would do—know how the world worked and then rule whatever corner of it that was allotted to him.

"He'll run for president, just like Abe Lincoln," Lily replied and Jeb nodded.

"I might. I just might."

That night Lily cooked Jeb's favorite dinner—a dish of juicy chicken and au gratin potatoes, green beans with almonds—and Jeb told us all about college. Art had a million questions. He wanted to know all about colleges. I waited a day or two. I waited for Jeb to unpack, unwind, settle back into being one of us again, part of the family. And I waited for Monday, when Dad set off on the road. I watched as Dad packed his car and we all waved good-bye. I was studying touch typing that summer and was working at the swim club. Jeb had a job with a law firm in town and Art was going to camp, but none of it had begun.

"Can we go somewhere today?" I asked Jeb.

"Like where?"

"McDonald's?"

We drove out along County Line and picked up a burger special and Jeb flirted a bit with this girl and that because he was now a very big man, strong, with nice skin, and our father's gray eyes. I sat silently, watching the girls come up, pat my brother on the arm. He turned to me and said, "You know, it's not bad, coming home."

I smiled and shrugged, but I felt shy, not like before when I always said what was on my mind and did what I wanted to do. Now it was as if there were a fence around me and somehow I was closed in. "You know, things have been a little strange since you left last spring."

"Oh, yeah?" Jeb took a bite from his burger. Some ketchup clung to his chin. "How so?"

He didn't seem to be listening to me or even wanting to be with me very much but I knew I had to go on. So I told him about prom and how Patrick went with Margaret and how I'd gotten drunk and this boy, well, nothing had happened, but this boy had tried to take advantage of me and I stood up on the boat and shouted at him, "How can you take advantage of a girl who's drunk?"

Jeb gave me a little punch in the arm and a "way to go," like brothers do, so I thought I could go on, I should go on, because he was the one person I could tell and I knew that Jeb more than anyone else would never, ever say a word. "But then a few days later this strange thing happened when I was at the market, you know, Indian Trail, Mom had given me a list of things to get. . . ."

Now he looked at me almost beady-eyed because he knew I was getting to the serious part, the real part, and something in his eyes told me that he wasn't going to be surprised with what I had to say, that whatever it was he already knew. And maybe he'd known for a long time, but I said it anyway. ". . . and Dad was there. He was buying things, but it was only a Tuesday and he shouldn't have been any closer than Quincy."

Jeb shook his head, then held up his hands as if warding off a blow. "I don't want to know about it," he said. "I don't want to hear about this, Tess."

"But what is it? What's going on with him?"

He finished his burger, crumpled up the paper. "Oh, Tess, don't make me be the one to tell you." He made a clean toss into the trash.

"But what about all his trips?"

Jeb shook his head. "Tessie, he hasn't been on the road for years."

I was silent for a moment. "Jeb, have you known for a long time?" My brother nodded his head ever so slightly. "Does Mom know?"

"Tessie." He looked me straight in the eye. "Everyone knows."

36

If a life is said to have a shape, then certain events form the structure of that shape. Francis Cantwell Eagger has come down to us as a man of contradictions—a gentle poet of letters who loved the rugged out-of-doors, a sensitive man known for his violent temper. What were the elements that shaped him? What made him the man he was? In the life of Francis Cantwell Eagger three factors can be viewed as defining. The first was a boyhood episode involving lightning, the second his flight to the West, and the third his parents' painful rejection when he turned to them for help.

Until he was thirteen, Eagger lived a life of privilege. His family was extremely wealthy (his mother was a Sutton and they lived on Sutton Place) and no advantage was denied him. He toured Europe, studied music, had his own horse. However, he was a lonely, introverted child and his parents were often away, leaving him and his younger brother with servants to fend for themselves. When he turned thirteen, he spent the summer at the family compound in Maine. One night he got up to go to the bathroom and a violent storm erupted. As Eagger returned to his bed, he heard a loud crash and saw a brilliant flash. Covering his ears with his hands, he crumpled to the floor. When he dared look, he saw that above his bed the wall was seared where lightning had struck and the impression of the lightning was branded into the wooden wall, making a letter "Z." (This episode is dealt with in his poem "Zorro," one of the few surviving poems from the lost manuscript that helps define his hero quest.)

Eagger was altered by this bolt of lightning. Life seemed unpredictable, random. Anything could happen at any moment. He lost interest in his studies and it was at this time in his life that he began to wander. He would walk all over Manhattan and once he walked to Westchester and back. His mother, who had never noticed him much when he was there, grew frantic when he would wander and this seemed to make him all the more determined to go further and further away from home. In the end he would flunk out of prep school after prep school and finally when he flunked out of Princeton, his parents sent him west. He was reluctant to go, but they gave him no choice. He either had to make good for himself or they would no longer pay his way. They set him up with a friend in the shipping business, but Eagger soon lost interest in it. Instead he attended classes at UCLA, where he met Jillian Palmer, the beautiful woman who would soon become his wife.

Eagger had fallen in love with the West as well and intended to make it his home. He would have even if he had not fallen in love with Jillian, for he had found his spiritual home in the rough, rocky Coast as had artists before him such as Robinson Jeffers, Henry Miller, and Ansel Adams. Jillian was brilliant, beautiful, ten years his senior, and divorced. He loved her passionate outbursts, her fitful intelligence. And he predicted, and he was correct, that his parents would disinherit him for marrying her.

The third and final formative event in Eagger's life (outside of the mysterious death of his eldest son, who died off the cliffs of the beloved seaside house Eagger had built for his family) was his parents' rejection of him. He tried for years to write them, to explain his love of Jillian, his marriage, his determination to be a writer on the West Coast. Finally when all else failed, and when little Thomas, their middle son, was stricken ill with tuberculosis, Eagger and Jillian drove across the country from San Francisco to beg his family for understanding and to help them in their financial woes.

Eagger writes in his poem "Dark Window" of what happened that day. He and Jillian returned to New York to the house on Sutton Place and as they walked up the front steps, he saw the curtains drawn, the house darkened to him. He and Jillian stoically got into their car and drove back to San Francisco. Francis Cantwell Eagger would mourn the loss of his family in his poems for the rest of his life, but he would never attempt to contact any of them again.

While Eagger was always an avid walker, he became obsessed with it upon returning from this journey. He walked for hours, sometimes days, with a pad and pencil. On his walks, he wrote down his impressions, jotted lines for poems, scribbled whatever popped into his head. Taking a walk with him was no pleasure because of these constant interruptions and in the end he walked alone. According to the letters of Francis Cantwell Eagger, a "desire path" is what hikers or walkers have worn thin through finding a better way, or a shortcut, to a desired place. From his poems we know that Eagger loved nature, that he was tormented in love, that he sought a better way. Once Eagger quipped in a letter to a friend that he preferred the dangers of nature to the threat of man and in his later years he grew more and more reclusive. In all of this, it is safe to say that he is the West Coast Robert Frost and indeed deserves his place in American literary history.

Bruno sat across from me at the kitchen table, pondering my slightest change in facial expression. "Bruno, this is fascinating. It really is very interesting." It seemed that Bruno had decided he could not write his doctoral dissertation without my help. So he brought to me page after page, note after note. Every word he wrote he ran by me.

He smiled at me, the smile of a child who has done something to please his parents. "Tell me. What do you like about it?"

"Oh, I don't know. I like the way it tells a story and that somehow the story it tells helps you understand the man." Bruno blinked, brushing his sandy hair out of his eyes. His hand trembled as it moved past his face. He seemed genuinely thrilled. I really didn't know what I liked about it until I said that to him. No one had asked me to read his doctoral dissertation before, and in a way it seemed rather boring, but interesting at the same time. "I like the way these events shaped this man's life. That's interesting."

He nodded, hanging on my every word.

I paused. "You must keep going," I told him. "I think it is very good."

"Oh, it means so much to me. That you like it. You know, Tess, I feel such an affinity for this man. In some ways our lives have been similar. I grew up in the East and didn't do very well in school—"

"And were you ever almost struck by lightning?" With a laugh Bruno shook his head no. "But you did have a falling-out with your family?" I asked a bit more gently for I could see where this conversation was heading.

Bruno nodded. "Yes, you know, my father was a minister and we didn't always see things eye to eye. I was seeing this girl, she was older. Anyway, my mother hated her and my father went along. When I moved in with the girl, we stopped talking. I felt they never approved of anything I did. We didn't talk for almost four years."

"How old are you now?"

"I'm twenty-six."

"So you must have been young when you had your falling-out."

"We only patched it up last year, but now we're good friends again."

"So are you writing this dissertation to find your father?"

Bruno thought about this for a moment, then shook his head. "To find myself," he said. "What about you, Tess? I don't know anything about you or your family."

"My mother lives in Chicago. My father died nine or ten years ago." Bruno gave me an odd look which I didn't understand at the time, but I know he was surprised that I couldn't recall the exact number of years. "He was an insurance salesman, on the road a fair amount. I have two brothers. We were an ordinary family. There was hardly anything unusual about us at all."

Nick phoned every day. It wasn't always easy with the time difference. Often he called collect from pay phones. He didn't want the calls to be on any of his accounts or on his calling card. But dutifully each week he sent me fifty dollars, which was what he assumed the calls were costing me. I was starting to think how we could live together, dividing our time between Illinois and the Coast, the best of both worlds. I started to have dreams of the future again.

Otherwise my life went as usual. Someone trashed the seashell house and Shana was beside herself. Vandals had gotten in during a few days when the house wasn't occupied and smashed the cowrie-shell mirror, shattered the scallop coffee table.

I had to deal with the owners, who threatened to sue us. I convinced them that it was an act of vandals and that the house was unoccupied at the time, but still there was much to do to straighten out the mess. During that time I became surrogate mother for a few weeks to two orphaned sea otter pups. And the National Registry of Historic Houses sent an inspector to look at the house.

I'd actually forgotten that I'd mailed in my application, but a very tall, thin woman knocked on my door one day and said she had come to inspect the house for the registry. She didn't say a word to me as she poked through rooms, stood across the street from the house, taking its picture. She wrote notes on a pad and after about an hour, she told me I'd receive a letter in a few months and that she thought it was a nice house, but she could not say if she would recommend it for the registry. I told her I wouldn't get my hopes up.

A few weeks later Ted returned with a story to tell—not a terribly pretty one. Sabe was into drugs and Ted had gotten out of there.

Soon both of my children became aware of the fact that I was accepting collect calls from gas stations and phone booths in the Midwest and they each asked me what I had going on. I told them what they had often told me. That it was my business and if and when I was ready to share it with them, I would.

Neither of them liked this answer. Jade asked me to go to lunch with her, where she pressed for details. She looked different than she had before going away. Her features were softer, her hair longer, no more purple spikes, though now she had a small gold nose ring. I confided in her as one might in a friend that I was seeing a man I'd known for almost my entire life, that his marriage was breaking up, and we hoped to find a way to be together.

Jade's jaw dropped when I told her this. "You aren't serious? That is so cool."

"I am serious," I said.

She gave me a little sock in the arm. "That's great, Mom."

They both got jobs. It was the law I laid down before I'd let either of them back in the house. Jade left her part-time position and went to work as a manager at a coffee-roasting factory. She came home smelling like the hills of Java. Ted got hooked up with an on-line company that sold space on the Web. He actually had a knack for this and began designing Web sites.

Then in the middle of the summer Nick called and said he could come out for a few days. He said to book us a room somewhere I liked to go and we'd have our first romantic getaway. I hesitated and he asked me what was wrong. "I can't do this," I told him. "Not while you're still living with her. Not while she doesn't know. I just can't do it behind her back."

"Tessie, I'm leaving her. Look, I was planning to tell her. I wanted her to know before I saw you, but she seems so fragile. Unstable, really. I don't know what it is, but it's as if she's transparent. She's not really there. She stares into space. Maybe she's on drugs. I feel as if I am living with a ghost, but I have to think of Danielle. I want to come and see you, and once I know what I'm going to do and when, then I'll tell her."

"It just doesn't seem right."

"Tess, she's going to know soon. Let me come and see you. I want to talk to you about it. Then we'll decide."

Along the coast the road dips and turns. Below Monterey the real cliffs begin. From the rocky points you can see terrifying vistas, the sea crashing against the shore. Nick had never seen this part of the coast and so I picked the Mermaid Inn down at Big Sur, though it was expensive. He said he didn't care what it cost. He just wanted to be with me. He flew into San Jose, where I picked him up, and we drove straight to the coast. He was stunned as the road curved and we followed the rocky coast down.

The Mermaid had a wooden mermaid over its entranceway. Our cabin had its own redwood hot tub with a special eucalyptus soap you could bathe in, a steambath, long paths lined with ice plants that led down to the ocean. First we took a long walk, climbing down the craggy pathways until we stood on a small, solitary beach. Seals and a pair of sea otters frolicked in the surf. Nick stood in the sand in his bare feet, just breathing in the air. "You're lucky, Tess," he told me, his arm firmly around my shoulder. "You got away."

"You've said that before. I know you think I did but I'm not really sure," I told him, "but, anyway, you could too."

"I'm going to." He squeezed my neck. "Just watch me."

When we got back to the room, Nick wanted to take a Jacuzzi bath. While the bath was getting ready, we ordered dinner in our room—seafood, salad, a bottle of California Chardonnay. Easing his way into the hot tub, Nick took a washcloth, dipped it in the eucalyptus suds, and began to wash me. He scrubbed the back of my neck and behind my ears. He let the washcloth dip under my arms, down my back. He brought it around in front of me, massaging beneath my breasts, along the ridges of my face. He covered me with suds and I lay back as the hot jets and the smell of eucalyptus and the motion of his hand on my skin made me drowsy.

I dropped my head against his chest as he reached down to my belly. I opened my thighs and he rubbed me between my legs. He moved his hand up and down, letting the washcloth reach farther and farther, coming back up slowly. Then he dipped back down again, rubbing me as I drifted, the air filled with the smell of redwood and eucalyptus.

Then we both got out, wrapped ourselves in the big terry-cloth robes, and made love slowly on the bed until we fell asleep. We woke when there was a knock at the door and a young waiter discreetly brought our dinner tray in, leaving it in the entranceway. Over dinner, we talked about Margaret and what we were going to do. "When are you going to tell her?" I asked.

"When I get back. We aren't even sleeping in the same room. We're hardly together."

"But still, I'd feel better—"

"It's not like you're taking me away from her. In most ways, except for Danielle, I'm already gone." I kissed him on the lips, and he kissed me back. "All right, if you'd feel better, I'll do it in a few weeks when the time seems right. Then we can be together."

"Yes, we can be together."

Then he lay back, staring at the ceiling. "You know, I've never done anything for myself. Everything has always been what other people—mainly my father—wanted me to do. Of course, he didn't want me to marry Margaret. He thought she was trash. Maybe I just did it to get back at him. Because I thought it was the way to have my own life. Anyway, it didn't work." He leaned over and pulled me to him. "I want something that's mine. My house, my work. Not what other people want me to have. Do you understand that, Tess?"

"Yes, I do understand."

"I know you do." He rested his face in my hair. "I know." In bed at night we made our plans. In October he would move out. He'd take a small apartment in town to be near Danielle. Then we'd decide what we were going to do. We'd figure out a way to divide our time. He'd help me refinance the Eagger house. I'd spend as much time in Illinois as I could. It all seemed fitting somehow. That after all these years I could finally go home.

"I've got this idea," he said. "We should plan to meet somewhere in town. At Starbucks or the bookstore. Run into one another as if we'd just met."

"Oh, we could do it in front of the Italian cookbooks."

"That's good," Nick said with a laugh, "I'll be working on my cooking anyway."

"People will see us; they'll think we've just met. So when we start to see one another, it won't be such a big deal."

"Yes, let's do that," he said. "Until then it will be our secret."

"Yes," I said, kissing him on the nose.

That night there was an angry storm at sea. Lightning forks shattered around us, thunder rolled like in some B-grade horror film. "I think a monster's going to walk in the door," I told him. Nick held me, stroking my hair. I told him about the little boy who got out of bed one night to go to the bathroom and lightning burned a "Z" over his bed. Like Zorro, I told him.

"What happened to the boy?" Nick wanted to know.

"He became a poet; I live in his house."

When we drove back up to my place the next day, the kids had made a dinner of spaghetti with broccoli and a green salad from our vegetable patch, which they'd neatly tended while I was away. They'd uncorked a wine bottle and set the table. I can't remember when they'd last done those things. Ted was dressed in a polo shirt and he shook Nick's hand. Jade did the same, looking him up and down the way she can do. But if I'd brought home a Martian, they would have approved. "Well, it's nice to meet you," Jade said so politely I almost didn't recognize her. "We've heard so much about you."

Over dinner Nick kept telling them how lucky they were to have me as their mother. He told them how in grammar school and high school I'd been such a popular girl. Their eyes widened in disbelief. I don't remember being that popular, but it was nice of him to tell the children that this was how he remembered me.

That night after we made love, I could just make out his face, those deep blue eyes. The house was quiet, only the katydids sang outside. They'd been brought out in the storm. From my bed we listened to the rise and fall of their song.

37

When early fall came, I was called back to Illinois in part because of my mother. Art told me she had left Post-its all over the apartment with our names, phone numbers, and birthdays written on them. But I was also drawn back, not only by Nick, but by something deeper in me than I can name. Even from California I could almost smell the crispness in the air, the scent of burning leaves. It had been so long since I'd seen the leaves turn, the seasons change.

If there is a place on the earth from where my life springs it is this place. This lake and this land, the golden light shining through the leaves as they turn, the hint of winter in the air, or the wetness of trails, the pull of the ground sucking down on your shoes and spitting you back again whole. I felt the pull of what I had known and what I had left behind. If longing has a tug, it is like that wet Illinois earth sucking on the soles of your feet.

I hopped into a cab at O'Hare and the driver, a West Indian man, asked me where I wanted to go. I hesitated because I wanted to go to Winonah, to find Nick and take him away with me. But we had both agreed that we had to be patient. We had to wait. He was sorting out what he needed to do with his marriage and Danielle. And I was still not about to rush into anything. Besides, my mother needed looking after.

The cab driver asked me again, but I gave him my mother's address on Astor Place in the city. As he drove along the expressway, giant murals of Chicago Bulls were everywhere. The faces of Michael Jordon, Scottie Pippin, Dennis Rodman covered the facades of giant buildings. The light was already waning and an orange sunset illuminated the buildings. I breathed in deeply as if a great adventure lay before me. On the dashboard the man had a photograph of four little girls with beaming faces. "Are those your daughters?" I asked him, thinking I could pass the time with idle talk.

"Yes," he muttered, "those are my little angels."

"They're beautiful," I said, looking at the four little girls staring at me with broad smiles.

"Yes." He nodded, not saying anything for a moment. "But they need their mother."

"She's not here?"

He shook his head and I noticed the heaviness in his shoulders. "She was killed. She went to work one day. Her girlfriends picked her up just like every day. And then they were all killed, just like that. Some guy ran right into them. He walked away with scratches." The man's voice was shaking and he seemed ready to burst into tears. "I don't know how we're going to make it without her. My little girls come to me and ask me to braid their hair. I don't know how to braid hair. How can you explain this? One day she is there. And then she is gone. Nothing will ever be the same. It makes me wonder. . . ."

He paused, unsure if he should go on.

"What does it make you wonder?"

"I don't know," he said. "I go to church and pray to God for strength and then my little girl comes in crying because there's no one to braid her hair and I just start to wonder." He shook his head, but didn't say another thing. We drove the rest of the way in the silence.

When he dropped me off, I gave him a big tip and he looked up at me with his watery eyes.

The smell off the lake was fishy and humid and it was already the start of Indian summer. Smelt fishermen lined the bicycle path along the beachfront. I didn't feel ready to go upstairs because I knew that once I went up, that's where I'd stay. Instead I dropped my bag off with my mother's doorman and ran through the underpass beneath the drive. I tried to shake off the image of those four little girls whose father did not know how to braid their hair. It sent a chill through me.

Along the shore the smelt fishermen sat with their pots, their sleeping bags, their small fires burning. Most would spend the night here. It was already growing dark and as I bent to look into the lake, I could see silver bodies, darting, rising to the surface, then racing back down again.

My mother's apartment stank of cigarettes and despair. Sour milk was in the fridge, along with too many cartons of leftover Chinese food. She sat in a housecoat in front of the television, remote in her hand. When I kissed her hello, she seemed bewildered, as if she didn't know why I was there. For two days I tidied up her apartment. I took her to the beauty parlor to get her hair washed and set, then to Bloomies for lunch. When she seemed better and her apartment was spic and span, I phoned Nick at his house. He picked up on the first ring as if he'd been expecting my call. I had already decided that if Margaret answered I'd hang up. "Thank God," he said, his voice sounding relieved. "I'm so glad to hear from you. How are you?"

"I'm fine, but I want to see you."

He told me he'd meet me the following night.

The next night Nick met me at a restaurant in the Loop. He wore a jacket and tie and swept me into his arms, held me to him. "God, Tessie, I've missed you." His hand slid to my back. We ate dinner slowly, talking about our plans. He had told Margaret he would be leaving.

"How did she take it?"

"She took it well. It hardly seemed to bother her at all."

"That's strange, isn't it?"

He shrugged. "Nothing surprises me."

After dinner Nick wanted to show me something. We got in his car, headed east, then south, past Buckingham Fountain, past the Field Museum until he came to Soldier Field. He drove around it once, twice. Soldier Field rose large and circular in the dark, right in the middle of the Outer Drive, like some Roman amphitheater.

Nick made the circle one more time, then pulled off into the parking lot. "Come on," he said, "I want to walk with you around here." We got out and stood in the empty lot, the huge round building looming before us. Nick stood, staring at the wall beyond, which was the field where the Chicago Bears played.

"I never saw my dad play here," he said. "But I'd always wanted to. I always wished I had."

"He wouldn't let you?"

"No." He laughed. "I wasn't born. I was born after his career was over. I saw videos and newsreels I saw him throw balls farther than anyone ever had, run faster, harder. Not bad for a Jewish boy. I went with him when he was inducted into the Hall of Fame. He cried like a baby. He used to tell me how people would shout his name, hissing over the s'es like a snake to cheer him on. He said how he loved the applause and he loved the crowds, but more than anything he loved the game. He would have played his whole life if his knees hadn't given out."

The thick, pale limestone of Soldier Field was illuminated by floodlights. Except for the whirr of traffic everything was quiet. "Sometimes I come here, just to try and imagine what it was like for him. The roar of the crowds, to be a hero like that. He did what he wanted to do and he did it well," Nick said. He pulled me to him and kissed me. "I'm going to do what I want to do as well." His hands groped under my shirt, touching the skin of my back, going up and down my ribs.

There was something monolithic, impenetrable about the walls of the stadium that rose before us. "My father never did what he wanted either. Something held him back," I said, wondering if this was the explanation for all that had transpired in my father's life. "It's good to do what you want."

Nick nodded silently. He led me to the car and we headed back past Buckingham Fountain, which was lit like a magic lantern, changing colors. He said, "My parents came here on their first date. They took off their shoes and jumped in the fountain." I tried to imagine my own parents barefoot and splashing in the ornate fountain. "You know," I said, "the lights and water are set from a computer in Atlanta."

"Really? How does that work?"

"I don't know. I just read it somewhere. I thought it was interesting that a fountain here would be controlled by something so far away."

"So, what's the point?" His lips were pursed and he had a scowl.

"There's no real point. I read it somewhere." I touched his arm. "What's wrong?"

"Nothing," he said. "I'm tired." But it seemed as if he was angry about something. As if he needed to tell somebody off. I watched the speedometer climb to 70, 75, 80 as he sped down the Outer Drive. His strength was focused on keeping the gas pedal down.

"Maybe we should slow down. We aren't in a hurry, are we?"

"I need to get home," he said. His face was filled with worry. "And I have things on my mind."

"What things?"

But he just shook his head. He turned off the Drive, cut through the side streets near where my mother lived. He was still driving too fast when we heard the thud. It had a dull, soft feel.

"What was that?" I asked.

He shook his head, sucked in his lip. He kept on driving. For a moment I thought he was leaving the scene of an accident, but he drove around the block. When we came around the corner, a small crowd had formed. I heard a woman crying. It's a child, I thought. He's killed a child.

Nick pulled over, got out of the car, and fell to his knees. A chocolate-colored cocker spaniel lay limp by the side of the road. Blood seeped from its mouth. The woman who cradled the dog was crying. "I am so sorry," he said, touching the dog, crying. "I am so sorry. . . . I thought it was a child. I thought I'd killed a child."

"Look what you've done," she said, shaking her dead dog. "You better be more careful," the woman screamed at him, "or next time it will be."

Tears streamed down her face. Her jacket was soaked in blood. Nick took out his wallet and tried to offer her money. "I don't want your money." She pushed him away. "You better watch out," the woman said, clutching her dog.

The Motel 6 by the highway just outside of Winonah had generic rooms—plaid bedspreads, scratchy sheets. The room smelled of smoke and stale air. When I pulled back the curtain, it had a view of the parking lot and the highway. Of course, I knew these rooms well. They were the motel rooms of my youth, the "acancy" I longed for. It was where I'd once felt the most at home, but as I opened the drawer the Bible was in, everything smelled tacky and sad.

When he had dropped me off the previous night, Nick and I had agreed to meet here. I wasn't sure I wanted to. The dead dog seemed like an omen; of what I did not know, but I thought that something bad was going to happen to me. Besides, this motel didn't seem like the place to consummate love. I wished there were a bed-and-breakfast in Winonah. Maybe I would open one.

I checked in early and had about two hours to kill until Nick left work. I phoned my mother to be sure she was all right and she was, though she kept asking when I'd be home. Then I called Vicky to say I was in town. I paced and wanted to smoke a cigarette, which I hadn't done in years. I didn't think Nick would show up before seven and I didn't want to sit in the room.

A bowling alley was next door so I went over and ordered a Diet Coke. I was nursing it at the bar, the sound of smashing pins around me, when Patrick walked in with a couple of guys and a bowling bag. He spotted me right away. "Tess!" He gave the boys a high sign and said he'd meet them in a few minutes. He sat down next to me and ordered a beer. "What're you doing here?" He gave me a peck on the cheek. "Oh, you don't have to tell me. I can guess."

"Can you?" I said.

"You know, it's a small town. Word gets around somehow."

"So what do you know?"

He paused, breathed into his beer, rubbed his hands up and down the stem. "I know you've been seeing Nick. I'm not saying this because I'm jealous or anything—though of course I am . . ." He gave his funny little laugh, the one I'd always liked.

"I thought it was our secret."

"This is Winonah, Tess. People talk. In fact, Margaret's said things. . . . Nick's a good guy, but I just don't see the two of you. I don't get it."

I was wishing I'd stayed in my room and started feeling annoyed. "There's nothing for you to get. It is what it is."

He raised his hands in surrender. "Okay, sure. Look, you can do whatever you want." He finished his beer, got up from the bar stool. "Of course, I wish it had been me, but it's not about that. I'd just be a little careful."

"Because I might get hurt?"

"Because someone might get hurt," he said. Then he picked up his bowling bag, making a face as if it were heavier than it really was, and walked toward the lane where his friends were waiting. I finished sipping my Coke, watching Patrick's lane. When he got up, he gave me a wink, hunched over the ball, and released it with a clear, even step, a good follow-through. Pins clattered as they tumbled down.

When I got back to the motel, Nick was leaning against my door. He had that pinched look he'd had on his face the night before when he was driving too fast. "Where have you been?" he asked, an impatient edge to his voice.

"You couldn't have been here that long. I got restless."

"I got here early."

"I'm sorry. I couldn't stand waiting."

Then he seemed to soften. "I've just had so much going on." He kissed me. He ran his hands up and down my body. "Let's go inside." I pulled him toward the bed, but he kept kissing me, standing where he was like a wooden Indian. "What's wrong?" I finally asked him.

Then he sat down on the bed. Picking at threads in the bedspread, he told me, "I think she knows about you . . . about us."

"How does she know?"

"Well, she's asked. She suspects it. She's threatening me, threatening to take Danielle away."

"But she can't do that."

"She seems to think she can," he said wearily.

"You have your rights."

"I know, but she can make it difficult."

He hugged me and we lay back on the bed. But his kisses were small, just light brushes, and his hands moved as if they had somewhere else to be. He seemed to be listening to something I couldn't hear, his head cocked, the way he had the night we met and he hadn't liked the band.

It was as if a different person inhabited his skin. We made love the way you do when you've got an early-morning meeting or there's a bill you don't know how you'll pay. Afterward he said he couldn't stay. He wanted to, but it was too complicated.

"I thought you were going to spend the night," I said.

"I'm going to be spending lots of nights with you, but it can't be this one. I need to sort some things out. I'll call you in the morning."

"Please don't go."

He put his arms around me and he was trembling.

"Are you cold?" I tried wrapping the blanket over his shoulders.

But he shook his head. "I'm frightened, that's what I am. I don't even know why but I'm just afraid." Then he kissed me hard and walked to the door. "I'll call you in the morning," he said. The door slammed behind him. After he left, I wasn't sure what to do with myself. I didn't quite know why I was here. I thought about driving back into the city, but it was late. Instead I watched a pay movie on the TV that didn't hold my interest. Then I slept fitfully and woke up when it was still dark out. For a long time I just sat, waiting for it to get light outside. Sitting there in that motel room, I realized how stripped down I felt. How vulnerable. I hadn't felt that way in a long time and it made me somehow afraid as well.

At seven I went down to the coffee shop for a breakfast of cereal and decaf, which I carried back to my room because I didn't want to miss his call, but Nick didn't phone. Lying down on the bed, I waited until ten o'clock, afraid to leave my room, thinking I would hear from him. But I didn't.

By eleven I needed to get out. I couldn't stand sitting in the room, waiting. I got in the car and drove. Once again I thought of heading back to Chicago, which I knew I should do, but instead, I drove into Winonah. I drove through the downtown and cruised past Prairie Vista Automotive. I wanted to see if Nick was in his office. I drove around the block once or twice, thinking about stopping in, but thought the better of it.

Instead I decided to drive the old route I used to take to get to school. First I cut over to Mulberry and down past my house. From my house, I headed over to Laurel. Though I wanted to go straight toward the school, instead I went in the direction of the lake. I drove all the way until I pulled up slowly in front of Nick's house.

There were no cars in the driveway. The house looked empty, as if it were on the market. I pulled over, parking on the street across from the house. Walking up the gravel path, I stood for a moment at the front door. I knocked, but there was no answer. I knocked again. Then I smelled the smoke. I had no idea where it was coming from, but the air around the house had taken on a slightly acrid, smoky smell. Something was burning.

I tried the door but it was locked. Then I went around to the side of the house where the smell was stronger and my eyes began to water. In the kitchen I could see gray smoke billowing from a pot. There was a side door and when I pushed it, it opened. I ran into the kitchen, covering my face against the thick, noxious air, grabbed a dishrag, and pulled the pot off the fire. The bottom of the pot was charred with burned milk that I assumed Margaret had forgotten on the stove.

I took the pot, carried it to the sink, let the cold water pour inside. The pot sizzled and steamed. When it quieted down I found myself standing there in Margaret and Nick's kitchen, unsure of what to do. I opened windows to let the smoke seep out and clear the air. I wondered if I should leave a note to explain the burned pot and what I was doing inside their house. But what if someone was home? What if Margaret was asleep or passed out, drunk?

Walking down the corridor, I stood alone in their vast living room. The smell of smoke still hung heavily in the air. I called out several times, "Hello, is anyone home?" I knew I should go. I had put out that small flame and now I had no business being here, but for some reason I couldn't bring myself to leave. My heart pounded in my chest as I stood still. I was going to turn around and walk out, but I decided to make certain everything was all right.

I headed down a corridor to the wing where the bedrooms were. Peering into each bedroom and bathroom, I made certain that no one was home, no one was hurt. I had wandered through people's houses like this dozens of times on the job, examining closet space, testing for the comfort of beds. I opened a closet in the hallway. The smell of cedar and mothballs wafted my way. Winter clothes hung in there—heavy woolens, parkas, lambskin coats. I closed it and continued down the corridor, pausing at Danielle's room.

I saw that the room was oddly devoid of a child's things, as Danielle seemed devoid of a child's spirit. The room even smelled old, as if someone no longer young lived here. The bed was a spartan cot with a gray comforter. A neat row of books, mainly mysteries—Nancy Drew, Boxcar Children—lined the bookshelf, but looked as if their spines had never been cracked. Two porcelain dolls and a stuffed horse stood like sentinels on a shelf. The only sign of childhood was a unicorn poster on her wall. If I could mother her, I thought, I'd buy Danielle silly things—a Slinky, bandannas, pop-bead necklaces. But of course she was their child, not mine, and I had managed my own mistakes with the two I had, though they were basically good kids. That much I knew.

I needed to get away from this room, feeling as if I could stifle here, as if someone had sucked the air out. I tiptoed down the hall, heading farther into the west wing. The door was open; I wandered in. I felt that pleasure Shana said she experienced having the keys to other people's houses, thinking about what might be revealed there.

In the room Nick and Margaret still shared, I opened drawers, rummaged through. I was looking for something, though I couldn't say what. Opening Nick's first, I found boxer shorts, neatly pressed and folded, T-shirts laundered a spotless white. The drawer smelled faintly of Nick's sweat and his Paco Rabanne cologne.

In the dresser on the opposite side of the room, I found her things. The top drawer contained blue silk underwear, a red teddy. The silk lingerie slipped through my fingers. I fondled black panties with a red trim. What could she possibly do in these? Nick had never mentioned this side of their life together. Had they played games behind these closed doors I didn't want to imagine? Was this the way she had enticed and held him all these years? I did not want to contemplate it.

I moved swiftly through T-shirts, athletic clothes, cotton pajamas. Then I came to a bottom drawer, different from the others in its disarray. It was filled with odds and ends—old receipts, a school ring, miniature soap and shampoo bottles taken from hotel rooms, sewing kits, odd buttons, a box of old letters. But I did not reach for any of these. Instead my hand reached around, looking for something but I didn't know what. I dug in the back and something soft brushed against my hand.

Reaching for it, I pulled out what looked like a small animal, soft and furry. I turned it, staring, because it was something I had seen before but couldn't quite remember when. I stood in their bedroom holding a scarlet rabbit's foot on a key chain in my fist.

On the plush carpet I didn't hear the footsteps. I missed the slamming of the car door, the walk across the entranceway. Now Margaret stood glaring at me in her stiletto heels and toreador pants, her black hair wild with thick curls, where I expected to see twigs and leaves as if she had just barreled through the woods to get here. Her eyes were red with rage. "What are you doing here?" she shouted at me. "What are you doing in my house?"

"There was smoke," I told her. Margaret sniffed the air. "I wanted to be sure everyone was all right."

"But what are you doing here?" If she'd had a gun, I believe she would have shot me. Instead she just stood there, hands on her hips. Defiantly I stood before her and now I opened my palm slowly, letting the rabbit's foot roll onto my fingertips. "I came back for this."

She stared at it, then back at me. Perhaps from her look she had forgotten it was there. Or when I'd given it to her. Or that she'd claimed to have lost it so many years ago.

Then she said, "If it's yours, take it. Take it and get out of here."

38

Two days later Margaret left a message with my mother, saying that she wanted to see me. I phoned Nick to ask him what he thought I should do. "Call her," he said, his voice sounding relieved. "Maybe she wants to make peace."

"What do you mean?"

"I'm moving out next week. She seems ready to accept it."

"All right, I'll see her."

We met at the coffee shop in the newly refurbished mall off Main Street. It was a trendy little place with lots of espresso machines and steamed milk and housewives in workout suits with strollers. Margaret came in, wearing a jacket with padded shoulders, tight black jeans, and boots. She looked ready for Los Angeles, not Winonah, and it seemed to me that she was a woman whose experiences had never quite lived up to her expectations, though she'd come close.

We ordered our coffee, then sat down at a table by the window. "This is a little awkward, I know," Margaret said.

"Yes, I guess it is."

"Well, all's fair in love and war, isn't it? Anyway, Nick and I were probably not going to make it. I want you to know this, Tess. I don't blame you. I want you to remember that."

"You don't blame me," I said. "Well, I blame you."

She looked at me oddly. "Because I went with Patrick to the prom?"

"You must be kidding. No. Because my father had an affair with your mother; because you knew about it for years and you never told me."

"I was supposed to tell you?" Margaret looked at me, stunned. "Your parents never broke up; they stayed together. You had your family intact."

"Everything was ruined."

"Not like it was for me," she said cryptically.

"What do you mean?"

"Oh, it doesn't matter what I mean. It's the truth, that's all."

I took a sip of my coffee, but it was too hot and I burned my tongue. In the background a child cried as its mother spoke in harsh tones. "I'm sorry I went into your house the other day. I'm sorry I went through your things."

"It doesn't matter, Tess. I don't blame you for seeing Nick. For wanting to get back at me."

"I don't think that's what I've been trying to do."

"Oh, who knows what we've been trying to do. . . . Anyway, none of it matters now." She got an odd, distant look in her eyes, as if she saw someone she knew crossing the street. I looked behind me, but no one was there. Then she laughed that high-pitched laugh, but I just shook my head. I didn't know what the real joke was.

"Anyway, I was going to give it back to you. Here. I was going to give everything back to you. I brought you a few things I wanted you to have."

She handed me a thick brown envelope and nodded for me to open it. Inside was my old dog tag with my name on it that I'd been missing for years. The cardinal and bluejay feathers that had once been in my room were wrapped in a piece of yellowed newspaper. The Chicago Cubs T-shirt I'd lent her that night when we spun around in the rain was folded neatly and pressed.

"I was planning on giving you back the rabbit's foot anyway," she said. "You didn't need to take it."

"You kept all these things?" I asked, stunned.

She nodded slowly. Some were stolen from me. Some I'd lent her. What surprised me most was how much at that moment Margaret seemed to resemble me. How she saved things just like I did.

"I know you never liked me that much," Margaret said. "I know you hold things that happened in your life against me. But remember, Tessie, no matter what, we're blood sisters. We're bound for life."

39

The day it happened was an October afternoon when the sugar maples turn a blazing gold, like treasure from a pirate's chest. It was the kind of Indian summer day we'd once walked home from school in, dragging our heels, leaves crunching beneath them, the smell of burning in the air. We'd stop in the Episcopal churchyard and scoop up horse chestnuts in their thorny shells, stuffing them into our pockets until the light began to fade. Then we'd race home before our mothers came looking for us.

I had always loved those days of Indian summer. I'd dallied in them, been late, faced my mother's reprimands, all for the crunch of leaves and a pocket of thorny pods and that smell of burning. But that has all changed. Now, something in that time of year has been irrevocably taken from me.

In the brilliance of that afternoon an ordinary blue car pulled over to the side of the railroad crossing. No one really noticed the car or that Margaret was waiting inside. Later the neighbors said that they hadn't paid attention to how long she waited at the intersection not far from the Potomie River. It is just a small commuter stop where you can't even buy a ticket and there's hardly ever a stationmaster there.

It's a convenience stop, really, just a few blocks from the site of the Havenhill Summer Festival, that music event that draws conductors and orchestras from all over the world, that for two months a year puts Winonah on the map. In the summer you can see people from Chicago and as far north as Madison walking with their picnic baskets and blankets from the station along Dearborn Road to the old Potomie park.

As a girl, I'd lain in the grass at Havenhill for a Joan Baez concert or Crosby, Stills and Nash. Or listened to the Chicago Symphony with Ozawa conducting Beethoven's Ninth on the Fourth of July. I'd eat fried chicken and potato salad and make out under a blanket with some boy I hardly knew, whose name I cannot recall, let alone his face. Once I came home with mosquito bites all up and down my arm.

But the music season was long over and it wasn't the busiest intersection anyway so no one noticed the blue car. Nor did anyone notice the woman inside or what she was doing. Many women in Winonah pull over by the side of the railroad tracks to wait for their husbands to get off the commuter trains that take them into the city. No one paid any attention that it was too early for husbands to be coming back or that the woman in the blue car was waiting on the Milwaukee side of the tracks.

But the people who lived nearby would always remember the sound of metal, the shatter of breaking glass. Some rushed out, thinking the train had derailed. Others would report hearing screams, but hardly anyone on the train was hurt, though a few were tossed about by the sudden stop.

I wasn't there. I only know what I read in the newspapers and what people told me, the people I have known all my life. I only know what happened because I read about it and I can imagine it. But I do know what kind of day it was. It was one of those brilliant, golden days—the kind of day when Margaret Blair came to live in Winonah in the first place.

It was in October that Nick phoned and told me he'd moved out. "Tessie, would you come and help me get settled?" Though I had only been back a few weeks, I didn't hesitate. I flew back as soon as I could. Nick was moving into an apartment in a building he owned—the same building where Margaret and her mother had first lived.

I rented a car at the airport and drove right to Prairie Vista. Nick had already unpacked the little he'd brought with him. Just enough dishes and silverware, sheets and towels to get him through the next few months. Yet there was something cheery and hopeful about the almost barren apartment, and Nick looked as happy as I'd ever seen him when I rang the buzzer. I walked up the dreary stairwell, and he greeted me at the top. "Come check out my new bachelor pad," he said. It was a convenience, he explained, just across the street from the office. "I'll just be here a month or two," he assured me.

Nick had decided he would sell the big house by the lake. He didn't need it, he said. "Besides," he told me, "it was never really mine. Not really."

He'd buy Margaret and Danielle a town house and he'd take an apartment for himself in the city. I noticed, I couldn't help but notice, that when he said this, he made no mention of our being together. But he was distracted and kept saying it was just a temporary move into the apartment across from the repair shop.

Besides, the neighborhood had changed over the years. It had changed so much that residents complained that the repair shop shouldn't be there anymore and if it wasn't the business of one of the town's most celebrated residents, they would have forced it out, though some of the newcomers didn't know who Cy Schoenfield, the great quarterback, was. Or if they did, they didn't care.

Nick had furnished the apartment with furniture loans from friends and a mattress from Dial-a-Bed. It was just for now, he kept saying. I helped him shove a dresser against the wall. Put the bed so that it faced the sunny windows. After we moved the bed, we made love, on top of the sheets, the sun pouring in. Afterward we just lay there. It was a warm, lazy afternoon and I thought we would stay there forever. I was pretty clear about what I was going to do and Nick and I had been lying in bed discussing it. If there had ever been a moment of decision in my life, it was now. In a month or so I would come home for an extended stay. If all went well, by next spring I'd put my house on the market. "I want you to be with me," Nick said, stroking my head. "We're going to make that happen. . . ."

"And I want to be with you," I said at last. Just then the phone rang. We both stared at it.

Nick hesitated to pick it up. Then he reasoned, "It could be Danielle." But it was Margaret, calling to say that Clarice had had some kind of an attack. "What kind of attack?" I heard Nick say.

Nothing too serious, Margaret said. They didn't know for sure. She just had a spell, a kind of fainting, but the doctors wanted to make certain it wasn't her heart, so she was in the hospital out in Crestwood and Margaret needed to get there. "Could you be sure to meet Danielle when she comes home from school?" Margaret said.

Nick said he would be there and wait until she came home. And then she added, "Say hi to Tess for me."

Nick looked at the phone oddly. When he hung up, he seemed perplexed. "She told me to say hello to you." Before he went home to meet Danielle after she got out of school, he told me to come with him. "She knows about you. I think she's all right about it."

When we got to the house, Danielle gave me that cold stare she'd given me the first time I'd come there, carrying Vicky's dog after we'd been stuck in the ravines. But she gave her father a hug. "Daddy, you're home." She said it in such a way that I knew she was thinking he'd come home to stay. "Where's Mummy?" she asked, looking around, almost looking through me, as if I weren't standing there. Nick told her that her mother had to go do something and she'd be back later. Danielle went and did her homework while Nick defrosted a pizza. I wanted to make them a proper dinner, but he said it would be too strange if I cooked in their kitchen.

"Yes, I suppose you're right."

We ate pepperoni and cheese pizza with a small salad and Cokes in front of the television. After dinner Danielle showed Nick her homework and he patted her on the shoulder because she had gotten all her math right, which was not her strongest subject, he told me. Danielle blushed and seemed to smile and that gave me the hope that she might warm up to me with time. Then he put on some Coltrane and asked Danielle what she wanted to do until bedtime. I could see that already he was getting anxious because Margaret was taking so long. He kept glancing at the clock over the mantel. "I wish your mother would call," he said at one point.

"Me too," Danielle said. "Let's play Scrabble until she gets here."

We played for a while. I had terrible letters. Useless consonants like "V" and "W" and two "O"s. There was little I could do on the board, though Danielle was very good and she had also drawn good letters. She put down "parrot" and "compass", but the best I could do was "who" and "vow." Nick was distracted as he played and he kept asking Danielle for help. He looked at the clock from time to time and Danielle kept asking when her mother was coming home.

Finally Nick got up and went into the kitchen to phone the hospital in Crestwood. I could see that he was concerned about Clarice. I followed him in, ostensibly to get something to drink, and saw his face turn pale, his hand tremble as he held the phone. He asked for patient information; Clarice Blair was not in the hospital. Nor had she been there that day. He asked over and over again, "Are you sure? Can you check again?"

Then he phoned Winonah General. Then he called Clarice at her house in Crestwood. When she answered, Nick told me later, he knew. "You aren't sick?" he said to her.

"No," she answered, "never felt better. Why?"

When he got off the phone, he called the police. Already Danielle was hollering from the living room for him to come and finish the game, but Nick just shook his head. He put his hand over the phone, shouting, "Tell her I'll be right there." When he told them that he thought his wife was missing, the police suggested he come down to the station.

When he asked why, the pitch of his voice rising, they told him there had been an incident on the railroad tracks. It was an express train, the police told him. There weren't many of those a day so she must have planned it well. Later a neighbor said that she thought she'd seen Margaret's car parked down the street, waiting until Nick arrived at the house. The last thing Margaret did was make sure that Danielle would not come home to an empty house.

I tried to hide how stunned I was. How was this possible? I found myself shaking as he told me and then went into the bathroom and sobbed, not wanting Danielle to see me. Before Nick went to identify the body, Danielle threw her arms around his neck, demanding to know where he was going.

"I'm going to get Mommy," he told her. Then he asked me to walk him to the car. "Would you stay here with Danielle," he said, "until I get home?"

"Of course I will," I said, leaning into the car.

Then he put his head on the steering wheel and began weeping, sobbing like a baby. I reached across, stroking his hair. Finally he composed himself. "How could she do this?" he said. "How could she leave a child behind?"

When he drove off, I turned and saw Danielle staring at me from the picture window of the house. When I came inside, she just stood there, glaring at me with her cold, dark eyes. "Do you want to read a book?" I asked her. "Would you like to play another game? We could play Monopoly," I said, "or Clue. I could make us some cocoa."

But she stood there in her little pink bathrobe, silent and morose, and I stared at this poor, motherless child who was just a decade old, the same age I'd been when I met her mother, and my heart went out to her. I could see how Margaret could do this to herself, but how could she do this to her child? When my children were small and my marriage was breaking up, I felt at times as if I could just jump off the bluffs, do myself in. But how could I leave my children behind? Now, gazing at Danielle, I thought I would raise her as my own. I could love her and my love would soften her, somehow take away her edges, make her want to curl up and read a book, listen to a story. Take the dolls down from her shelves. I'd bring her a pet, I thought. A puppy dog that she could love.

But Danielle kept looking at me in the oddest way. Then she said, "I'm not stupid, you know."

"Oh, I know you aren't stupid, Danielle."

"I know that something is wrong. My mother has never done this before. She has never not come home."

"You're right. Something is wrong. Your father has gone to find out what it is. Do you want to wait up for him? Do you want to play a game?" I just looked at her, not sure of what to say. I kept thinking she would burst out crying. I didn't expect she would rush into my arms, but I thought she might let me comfort her somehow. Instead she kept her icy stare on me. "We could do something," I told her, "to pass the time until your father gets back."

But she stood up abruptly. "I don't want you," she shouted at me. "I want my mother."

She stomped off to her room as I sat in the living room, folding my face into my hands where I wept silently. At the same time I was listening, ready to rush to her side, but I didn't hear a sound. After a few moments I went to check on her. Her light was off and she was turned to the wall. When I touched her, she was sobbing. "Danielle," I said.

"Get away from me," she cried.

"I'll be in the living room," I said, "if you want me."

I went back to the sofa where I stretched out, listening for her. I must have drifted off because when I awoke, there was a knock at the door. I thought it would be Nick, but instead there was a man I'd never seen before. A woman stood behind him in the shadows. Though her hair had turned gray and she seemed wraithlike in the shadows, I recognized her.

"Hello, Clarice," I said. "It's Tess. Tess Winterstone." I hadn't seen her since my father's funeral. I was surprised she'd had the nerve to show up, but she had. She'd stood at the back and hadn't gone to the graveside, though Art tells me fresh flowers come to my father's grave on the first of every month.

"I thought you might be here, Tess," Clarice said. "Nick told me to come and look after Danielle. He has things to tend to, arrangements to make."

"Well, I could stay," I offered, "and wait for him." Somehow I felt that if I went now, I wouldn't be coming back. I felt as if I had to hold on.

"He asked that we stay with Danielle. He said he'd call you in the morning."

I nodded. "All right, Clarice. I'll go."

"Well, Tess, I suppose you got what you wanted, didn't you? I suppose it's only fair. That we should both lose what matters most to us. That it should end this way." Clarice spoke in a bitter, unforgiving voice.

"I didn't have anything to do with this, Clarice, and I certainly didn't want it to happen."

Clarice was hidden in the shadows behind the light, where I could hardly see her. I couldn't make out her features. She was a thin, ghostly figure in the darkness. Deep, hiccuping sobs came from somewhere in her chest. She doubled over, as if she were in terrible pain, howling like an animal, and the man who'd come with her held her up. I went into the kitchen and wrote a note to Nick. I told him how sorry I was and that I would be at Vicky's.

I gave him her number and said I wanted to be there for him and for Danielle. Folding the note three times, I stuck it under the coffee-pot, where I was sure he'd see it in the morning. I told Clarice I was very sorry and she looked at me as if I were a stranger to her, not a girl she'd once begged to stay to play with her daughter.

When I left, they shut the door and pulled down all the blinds so that the house was cloaked in faint, shadowy light. I watched the house for a few moments. Then I got into my rental car and drove down the road toward the railroad trestle, made a left, and drove until I saw the police cars and the wreck.

She had killed herself just beyond the place where I liked to wander when I was a girl. At the place where the town divides itself in two, where the rich live on one side and the poor on the other. Just beyond the underpass where I used to say good-bye to her and she'd go her way and I'd go mine.

———

That night I waited at Vicky's for Nick to call, but he never did. Vicky had already heard, as had the rest of the town. "It's a very tragic thing" was all Vicky said, "especially for the child." There was something in her voice, I could tell, that was blaming me. Even though she didn't say it, even though she didn't even imply it, somehow it was my fault. Though I had never so much as shoplifted a candy bar as a kid, I felt like a criminal now. I had brought this on and even as Vicky poured me a drink, then said good night, I knew something about my friendship with her—and everyone else in this town—had been altered.

In the morning when I still hadn't heard from Nick, I called the house. Danielle answered the phone and surprised me by sounding so grown up that for a moment I took her to be her mother. "Could I speak with Nick, please?"

"He doesn't want to talk to anyone," she said.

"Danielle," I said softly, "I'm so sorry about your mom. It's me, Tess. Tell him I'm on the phone, tell him I need to talk to him."

But she'd already hung up.

After lunch I drove over to pay a condolence call. Cars lined the driveway. When I walked in, Nick saw me, but there was a blank look to his eyes.

"She didn't seem to even care when I told her I was moving out. She didn't blink an eye. I can't imagine what would have made her do that. I really can't," he said.

Then he told me what I hadn't known. Margaret left no letter, but she had a cryptic note in her bag when she died. He reached into his pocket, pulled it out. It read: *I waited as long as I could.* "Waited for what?" he asked me, tears in his eyes. "Waited for whom? What would make her do such a thing?" he said, now breaking down in sobs.

"I don't know." I shook my head. "I have no idea. I just know that I want to be there for you."

"Then leave me alone for now," he said. "Let me call you after the funeral."

The funeral was held the next day at Our Lady of the Meadows, a Catholic church in Prairie Vista. I bought a black dress and sat in the back. I was ashamed and tears rolled down my cheeks. This was all my fault. I'd brought ruin on all these people. At the funeral, Danielle stared straight ahead with cold, dark eyes. I kept thinking I'd see her break down and weep, but she just stared.

Once Danielle turned and looked at the crowd that stood behind her in the church and for a moment her eyes landed on me. But there was a blankness to her stare. Nick cried on the coffin. He wept and broke down and he had to be pulled away. I stood at a distance, watching him. In the end Margaret was buried in Winonah in the cemetery near the lake, the place where she'd always wanted to be.

That afternoon I joined the mourners back at his house and Nick took me aside. "I care for you, Tess. I really do. But I'm going to need some time. Go home and in a few weeks I'll come out and see you."

"But I don't want to go home. This town is my home too. I want to be with you."

He shook his head. "Not now."

When I returned to Vicky's that evening, she was waiting up for me, reading the *Winonah Weekly*. Her slender white fingers held the paper and I thought how she did have beautiful hands, how it was right that people should pay to admire them. She passed me the newspaper. "Here. It's all here."

The article gave the details of Margaret's death, said that Margaret Blair Schoenfield's car had stopped on the railroad tracks at a well-lit crossing. It was assumed to be a suicide and that she was despondent over her failed marriage to the son of a former football star. She was survived by one child, age ten, and her husband, from whom she was estranged. I read that the engineer said he saw her coming only at the very last moment, as if she'd appeared out of nowhere, and then it was too late. He wasn't even traveling fast because he was coming into the station, though it was not a scheduled stop. She just drove on the tracks and stayed there, he said. She didn't move.

"May I keep this?" I asked Vicky after I'd read it through.

"Of course you can." Vicky tore it out of the *Winonah Weekly* for me. "Still saving things. You haven't changed much, have you?" She handed me the clipping and I folded it neatly, then tucked it inside my wallet.

That night I went to Paradise and Patrick was there. He sat down beside me and had a beer. "I saw you at the funeral," he said.

I nodded, sipping my beer. "I feel terrible . . ." Patrick reached across, clutching my fingers. "But I saw Margaret just last week. She acted as if everything was fine. As if there were no bad feelings." Tears started to come to my eyes; in fact, I did not understand what had happened or why. I tried to reconstruct what had happened when I'd seen Margaret that day for coffee.

What had I missed? Some gesture, some word I hadn't quite gotten at the time? Of course it was strange that she'd given me those items that she'd saved over the years. But her manner was so natural, almost breezy. Now as I sat there, with Patrick's fingers wrapped around mine, I was certain there was something I'd overlooked, something I just hadn't seen.

"Tess, there was always something off about her. I don't know what it was. Maybe this doesn't have anything to do with you."

I just shook my head. "How could it not?"

"I don't know," Patrick said, "but maybe it doesn't."

Just then the door opened and Nick walked in with a crowd of friends. They were all quiet and subdued. When Nick saw me, he gave me a little nod, but he didn't come my way. "Just give him some time," Patrick said. "He'll come around. He doesn't know what hit him."

"Thanks." I patted Patrick on the hand. "That's good advice."

"Don't blame yourself, Tess," Patrick said.

When Patrick left, I stayed at the bar drinking my beer. I ordered another, but felt strange sitting there alone. I looked over at Nick, who sat with his friends, and gave him a little smile. At last he got up and came over to the bar and sat down beside me. His movements were wooden, like those of an actor uncomfortable in his role.

"Tess," Nick said at last. "I don't know how to say this, but I can't see you for a while. I feel sickened by everything. I don't know that I'll ever feel any differently."

"But it will pass," I told him. I hesitated, but then I said, "We can be together now if we want." I spoke softly, just loud enough for him to hear me. "There's nothing to keep us apart."

"Yes, there is," he said, shaking his head.

"Who? What?" I asked him, my voice quivering.

I was sure he was going to say Danielle, but instead he said, "Margaret will keep us apart. That's who."

40

Because I keep everything, and I always have, I knew just where I'd find the yearbooks. They were in the back of the old storage closet off the garage. When I got home, I dug them out and propped them up on the table in the breakfast nook. Then I went to the index and found where her name was listed.

I spent the next few days in my breakfast nook, where Francis Eagger drank himself to death, staring at the pictures of Margaret Blair. In fact she was not in many pictures. Though it wasn't easy in our high school to avoid being in the yearbook, she had managed fairly well. But in the few I found of her, Margaret seemed to be gazing down, the way she used to when she lived above Santini's Liquor in Prairie Vista. She stood in the back row, off to one side, her long black hair tumbling around her face. Was she hiding? Didn't she want to be seen?

In some she was just a blur, as if she had moved at the moment the picture was being snapped. This wouldn't surprise me at all. Because there was something about her even then that could never be pinned down, that was always trying to get away.

Margaret, frozen in time. She wouldn't wear reading glasses or see her hair turn gray. She wouldn't get those little wrinkles I was starting to get around the mouth, those furrows on the brow that Jade said came from frowning in your sleep. You look angry, Jade tells me, when you sleep. Margaret would just stay right there, the way she was.

Turning to the back of the yearbook I read what had been inscribed: "To Tess from Margaret, don't read what I've written in the corner." She had dog-eared a corner of the page. I opened this and read, "Only rats look in corners."

When the kids got home from work that night, Jade took one look at me. "What is it, Mom? What's wrong? You look terrible."

Then I told them about Margaret. It all poured out.

"What was it?" Ted asked. "What did it say?"

"It said that she'd waited as long as she could."

"What did she mean by that?"

"I don't know. Maybe she was waiting for Nick to come back to her. I don't know."

Jade was very upset. "Mom," she said, "what're you going to do?"

"I don't know," I told them, "be patient. Wait." A chill passed through me as I said that. Wait for how long? Wasn't that just what Margaret had tried to do?

"God," Ted said, "did she kill herself because of you?"

Jade motioned for him to be quiet, but that was the truth of it, wasn't it? She'd killed herself because of me. "Yes," I said, "I believe she did. And she left behind her child."

I stayed up that night, drinking. It wasn't something I normally did, but I could not sleep. I longed for Nick, but made a promise to myself that I would not call. I'd hear from him when he was ready. And with time I felt certain he would be.

But finally I couldn't stand it any longer. I had to hear his voice. In the morning when I picked up the phone to dial, my neighbor Betsy was on the line. She was talking to a doctor's office, setting up an appointment. I didn't want to listen, but I did. Infertility. She had tried everything to have a child.

The next day when I saw Betsy, I gave her a wave. I thought perhaps I'd have her over for coffee someday.

Later that night when I couldn't sleep, I poured myself a brandy. Then I picked up the phone and called Nick. I let it ring three, four times. Night after night I phoned, thinking he would be waiting by the phone, that he would know it was me.

But he never answered. I left messages, but he never called me back. I found I still could not sleep. I wondered where he was, what he was doing. I had dreams of him at night, of his hands on my body, of his body looming above mine. I found myself raw and exposed as I hadn't been since I was a child.

Once I phoned and Danielle answered. I heard her voice on the other end, insistent, almost in a rage. "Who's there," she shouted into the phone and I hung up.

In the paths in the hills above my house wildflowers grow. At certain times of the year after heavy rains the hills are carpeted in small blue and white flowers, thick patches of yellow, tiny shades of rose. It was that time of year now. I thought if I forced myself to get up early and go for a run, I'd be able to sleep at night. I began getting up before seven and heading into the hills. I'd run several miles, making a loop that brought me home. Each day I ran farther and farther, as if I had to get away. Morning after morning I would be gone an hour, then two. The path I took was paved, but it quickly turned to dirt. Wildflowers lined the path. Trees dropped back after the first mile or so. Higher up, the landscape turned to desert; scrub pine, thistle weed grew in abundance. I ran until I couldn't see the highway or any houses. Sometimes I thought I could just keep going and never stop.

One morning, the air was brisk, the ground firm beneath my feet. I ran for a mile or so, then higher. At the point where I should have turned back, I kept going, my body unwilling to return. I was soaring. I was flying and climbing as if I could just keep going. As if there was nothing to stop me.

In the hills the day was warmer and sweat dripped, evaporating as soon as it hit the air. So this was what it felt like to be free, to be a bird. My body flying through the air. My body flying like the wind. I went up higher into the hills, way above Salinas, behind my heels was a trail of dust. I kicked up the dirt as I climbed into the scrub pine, the desolate places where nothing will grow.

I was high above the ocean and I couldn't even tell it was an ocean anymore. It was as if the sky started just there at the shore, which was now the horizon. I didn't hear a thing except my heart and my feet pounding. My breathing was a steady pant and sweat poured down me, my T-shirt clung to my breasts. If someone wanted to rape me, I always told myself as I ran up here, he'd have to catch me first. So far no one had tried. I never saw anybody up here. There used to be a guy who trained in these hills but I hadn't seen him in a long time and anyway, we didn't run at the same time of the day. I was running on straight to a grove of pines, like nothing would stop me or could stop me, and then I saw her.

Those yellow eyes fixed on me. A dead stare. It took everything in me to stop. Stop cold. I thought my heart would burst. I'd die right there. It is a fitting end, I thought. Looking her in the eyes. Our eyes fixed on each other. She was in a branch, a low branch, and poised. Ten yards farther and she would have pounced on my neck. Now it's this standoff, I think, and if I move, I'm dinner. Or maybe I'm dinner no matter what I do. I'm a dead woman right here. I'm going to be eaten alive and they'll only know it's me from the dental records if they find my teeth. One of us has got to move and I know it won't be me.

Then I saw it. Her shoulder twitched. Just a tiny twitch but enough to tell me she was ready to make her move. She jumped down and all those yellow muscles rippled and her flesh moved like sound waves, like foam rubber. Muscles moving and with a thud and four rising waves of dust, she hit the ground, her yellow eyes never off me.

My heart pounded in my chest. Hairs bristled on my arms and I couldn't catch my breath. I stood there, staring straight at her as she stared at me. I vowed I would not be the first to move. Then suddenly, with all those powerful yellow muscles rippling, she turned and walked away.

I arrived home, panting, hot, dripping wet. Though I'd walked the last half mile home, my heart was still pounding, my hands shaking as I opened the mailbox. There was the usual assortment of junk mail, bills I couldn't pay, solicitations from organizations that I made nominal contributions to. Walking into the kitchen, I threw the mail down on the counter and poured myself a glass of herbal ice tea. I downed the tea, pressed an ice cube to my temple. Then I opened a drawer to look for some Tylenol.

There in the drawer where I kept recipes and over-the-counter drugs was the envelope Margaret had given me the last time I saw her—the one that contained my old dog tag, bird feathers, and the Chicago Cubs T-shirt. I sat down in the breakfast nook with my herbal tea and opened the envelope once more, spreading the items in front of me.

I kept the feathers in front of me, moved the dog tag and T-shirt to the side. The clipping the feathers were wrapped in was from an old Kenosha newspaper, dated some forty years ago. It was yellow and tattered, almost crumbling in my hands. I hadn't noticed it when Margaret first gave me the envelope, but now I unfolded and read it. On the back was an advertisement for soap. A notice about a missing dog. On the other side were obituaries. One was for a schoolteacher from Milwaukee who had been a believer in equal education. The other was for a Wisconsin man who had jumped or fallen to his death off a railroad bridge when he was forty-nine years old. Then it gave the funeral arrangements, and that was all.

I was puzzling over this clipping, wondering if there was any reason why it had been placed among my things, when there was a knock at the door. I stuffed everything back in the envelope and stuck it in the kitchen drawer by the sink, which was already filled with recipes and flyers for men who wanted to help me plant shrubs. Bruno stood in my doorway, staring at me, dripping wet. "Tess," he said, "are you all right?"

"I'm fine."

"Well, you look like you've seen a ghost."

"Just a cougar," I said.

"Are you sure you're all right?" He looked genuinely concerned.

"I'm fine," I told him. Suddenly I wanted to cradle him in my arms, hold him as if he were my child and not someone else's.

"Look," he said, waving a sheet of paper in my face, "I found it, I found it."

"Come in, Bruno. I really should shower." I reached for a kitchen towel and began wiping myself off.

"The poem, 'Desire Paths.' It was in some old papers, some drafts. I found it in the Santa Cruz library. Now I have the whole poem."

He handed it to me and I read it.

DESIRE PATHS
From the unfinished manuscript of Francis Cantwell Eagger

Along the wind-racked bluffs
We have made our way
To the edge and back again
So many times

That we have made a path,
Worn down weeds and shrubs.
We tried other routes
Through sharper rocks and
Steeper climbs
But this trail was the best by far
We forged the way
Of our longing.
Desire paths, these are called
Because this was the way we had to come
As if no other path presented itself
To the edge of this raw world
Where there is nothing left to do
But look down, then walk away.

"It's beautiful, Bruno," I said. "It's actually a very beautiful poem." And in truth it was the first poem by Francis Eagger that truly moved me. "It's great for your dissertation, isn't it?"

"Oh, yes," he said. "And I'm going to write some journal articles. This will help me get a job."

Holding the poem in my hands, I read it again. The way of our longing. Then I sat down in the breakfast nook and wept. I lay my head on the table and cried and cried. Bruno sat beside me, trying to comfort me.

"Tess, what is it? You can talk to me."

My body shook and I could not stop. "I think I've killed someone," I said. "I think I'm the reason that someone is dead."

"Are you sure . . ."

And then I told him about Margaret and Nick and how she had died. Then Bruno reached out for me and pulled me in. He held me tightly and I was amazed at the strength in his arms. It was the hug of a man, not a boy, but there was nothing improper in it. He held me for a very long time, then he pulled away, looking me square in the eyes. "Tess," he said, "you are also the reason someone is alive."

"I am?" I said, wiping my eyes.

"Yes," he said. "You saved me."

"I did?"

He nodded solemnly. "You don't even know it," he said, "but you did."

That night strange dreams overwhelmed me. I woke up shaking, feeling alone. I dreamed of sleepers in pods, wrapped in sheets, unable to extricate themselves. I dreamed of Jade as a little girl, going off to star in a Broadway show. I wanted to accompany her, but I was dressed in a nightgown and a robe. But the strangest dreams were always those of the two men. One was dark and clever, the other blond and simple. One was good and the other evil, but I was never sure which one it was. You'd think the clever one would be evil, the simple man good, but there was something in his simpleness that stifled me, something in the other's cleverness that uplifted me. I woke, knowing that I knew nothing of myself and never would.

After I had my coffee and sat in the breakfast nook for a while, it occurred to me that somehow these dreams were not my own. They belonged to someone else—to the troubled poet who lived here before me. Surely these haunted dreams were not mine.

Night after night I stayed up drinking. I couldn't sleep and the quiet of the house unsettled me. The children came and went but mostly they were gone. When they were away, I drank to try and sleep, then fell into a sleep that brought no rest. Nothing could save me. I tried to conjure Bruno's hug, but it too was slipping away. Nick wasn't returning my calls and Margaret was dead and I was lost as surely as if I'd wandered off into the wilderness alone.

I couldn't stand being alone in the house so I headed out into the pitch darkness along the cliffs where the poet who had drunk himself to death had lost his own son. I found the desire paths the poet had made and trudged along, finding my way. Branches cut against my

face. A razor-sharp thorn tore at my sleeve. I could feel blood trick-
ling down my arm, but I kept going. It was the blackest of nights and
all I could do was follow the roar of the sea.

I walked until I came to the edge with the sea crashing below me.
It was high tide and the beach was almost gone. It would be so easy to
slip, to fall. Everyone would think it was an accident. They would say
I had been despondent, but they'd never be sure, the way they had
never been sure with Francis Cantwell Eagger's son. Or with that
Wisconsin man in the clipping Margaret had given me. Not like with
Margaret. They were sure about her. If I slipped and fell here, no one
would know if it was what I'd intended. It would remain a big question, something people—my children, my brothers, Nick, the neighbors, even Betsy—would talk about for years to come.

My own thoughts frightened me. I'd never quite had these thoughts
before. I had to fight them, fight them back. I took a deep breath. The
air smelled fresh, almost lemony with the scent of eucalyptus. Then I
saw it, halfway down the bluff. The hunchback tree from Francis Eagger's poem, bent over, its arms offering protection. The tree bent back
in the wind. It was the one Bruno had been looking for. It had probably
fallen down the cliff due to erosion. Now I stepped away. I eased my
way back from the cliffs and, following the paths Francis Eagger had
shaped in his own despair, made my way home.

The next night the phone rang and it was Nick. He had some business to finish up in San Francisco and he wanted to talk to me. "Tess,"
he said, "I'll be there next week. I think I owe you an explanation."

41

The following Friday Nick drove down to meet me at Half Moon Bay.
We met at a Thai restaurant and sat in a corner booth on red vinyl seats
where it was dark and rather quiet. Large tropical fish swam in tanks

above our heads. No one bothered us. He looked tired and haggard. His face seemed jowly and he was not the same boisterous man I had known. In fact he slumped and seemed old. We ordered drinks, but Nick said he wasn't hungry. "I don't have much of an appetite these days."

I nodded. "I can imagine. How are things? How's Danielle?"

"Not so good. She's silent, then she blows up. I don't know what I'm going to do."

"She blows up? How?"

"She hits people. For no reason." Nick shook his head back and forth like a man who had reached the end of his rope.

"She needs a mother."

"She had a mother," Nick said, the bitterness unmistakable in his voice. "I will never understand this." He reached across the table for my hands. "Tessie, I wanted things to be different. I didn't want it to work out this way. I don't know why she did this. I don't know why it happened. I just know that at least for now we can't be together. I'm not going to be able to look at you and not think of her." He turned my hands in his. "I can't look at your face and not see Margaret's. Do you understand?"

"Yes, I understand. Maybe she wanted it that way. Maybe she did it on purpose." I was angry and wished I hadn't said what I just did.

"I don't know why she did it. She seemed to take it all in stride. She didn't want to stay married any more than I did. I don't know what it was. Honestly it's a mystery to us all. I never thought she'd leave Danielle; that's the part that makes no sense. But somehow I don't think it was about us. Not entirely anyway."

"Then what was it about?"

He shook his head again and he looked pathetic and small. "I keep thinking about the note. What was she waiting for or who? What did it mean? That she'd waited as long as she could?"

"Maybe it will be better in time," I said, wrapping my fingers more tightly around his.

"Maybe," he said, but he did not sound convinced.

"I was thinking I could move home, be near you and Danielle."

Nick raised his hands. "Oh, no, don't do that. Not on my account."

We were silent for a moment and I understood that it was no use. It was over. He planned to go on with his life and I was to go on with mine and that was how it was to be.

I signaled the waitress for the check. As we waited for it to come, I said, "Nick, may I ask you something?"

"Of course you can."

"Did Margaret ever talk to you about her father? She used to talk to me about him. She always seemed to be waiting for him to come and get her."

"She certainly wasn't waiting for him." Nick looked perplexed. "I was sure you knew. He died when she was a little girl."

"He did? She told me he was in Wisconsin." I couldn't bear to contemplate where all those gifts had come from. The clothes, the car.

"I don't think she was waiting. He was dead a long time before she ever moved to Winonah."

"But she told me . . ."

Nick downed his beer and kissed me lightly on the cheek. I couldn't let him go so easily. I reached up, my hands searching his face. My lips reached for his. If I could only, like some skilled fishermen, pull him in gently, bring him back to where we had been, but he was like someone with no memory of anything before. His eyes were red and watery. "I've got to go," he said. "I'll always care for you, Tess."

Standing up, he reached across, placing his hand on my cheek, and I let my face rest in it for a moment. Then when I looked up, he was gone.

Over the next few days, the mail built up, one letter after the next. I opened a few bills, then put them away. The creditors could take my house. I didn't care. I sat reading the complete works of Francis Cantwell Eagger. I felt I owed it to this house before I put it on the market to know the work of the man who lived here.

The children were away. Ted had gone back to Sabe. Jade was with her dad in San Francisco, looking for more substantial work. I found myself with nothing to do. Nowhere that I had to be. It was good because I seemed to be so tired. I had never felt so tired and thought this would be a good time to sleep. I slept perhaps for a day or so. I lost track of the time, just slipping in and out of bed to go to the bathroom, to get a bite to eat.

At first I had cereal, big bowls of it, until I ran out of milk. Then I ate carrots, small salads, crackers. Dishes piled up in the sink. The bed went unmade. I sat up in my pajamas in bed, reading. I read through and through the collected works of Francis Cantwell Eagger. Once in a while I'd check the refrigerator. I should eat something, I'd tell myself. I knew I should eat. I even had a memory of eating. Certain foods came to me, like fried chicken, olives, ice cream, but when I opened the refrigerator nothing appealed to me, nothing made sense. There were eggs, bread, beans, onions, jam, but I had no desire to combine these ingredients—to make a sandwich, a bowl of soup.

I had tea, cups of it, and when I ran out of tea, I sipped water with lemon. I stopped answering the phone or the door. There was no one I wanted to talk to, no one I wanted to see. I don't remember eating, though I do remember drinking at night, long sips of brandy. I drank until I was drowsy. Some nights I walked the cliffs, half inebriated. I am becoming the poet whose house I inhabit, I said to myself one night as I fell asleep in my chair, the Winonah centennial blanket draped over me. All day long and sometimes all night I read his work, one poem after the other, even the half-baked poems that somehow contained my own sorry dreams.

The days folded one into the next. Sometimes I slept when it was light out; often at night I read, then slept with my light on. I had lost track of time, the hours. I was sure there were things I was supposed to do, but I couldn't seem to remember what they were or why I had to do them. I was so tired. I couldn't seem to sleep enough, but I'd sleep, wake up tired, then sleep again.

One afternoon there was a knock at the door. I ignored it, went back to sleep. But the knocking kept coming. It was an insistent, almost angry knock. Betsy, my neighbor, stood there in blue jeans, a sweater, her dog on a leash. Betsy, infertile, in a second dead-end marriage, her pathetic life conveyed to me over crossed wires, held the door back and stared at me as if she'd expected to find someone else. I thought she was going to complain about the crossed wires or hand me a piece of my junk mail she had received. Instead she looked shocked to see me. "Your daughter phoned me," she said. "She's worried about you. She says you haven't been answering your phone." Then she looked me up and down again. "Are you all right?"

"I'm fine," I said, "I've just been very tired." But Betsy kept looking at me with concern.

"You don't look fine," she said.

"No, really, I am."

She tied the dog up. I noticed that it was an obedient dog. When she told it to sit, it just sat. Then she came inside. She saw the mess. "Are you ill?"

"I don't know. I don't think so."

I know a lot about you, I wanted to tell her. You can't have children, you give friends poor advice, your marriage is floundering. "You should eat something," she said. "I'm going to call your daughter and tell her to come. I'll stay here for a few hours while you rest."

"I'm not very hungry," I told her. "I think I want to go to bed."

"All right," Betsy said, "I'm going to help you to bed, then I'll wait until your daughter gets here." Betsy took me by the arm, led me back to my room. As I crawled into bed, I got a glimpse of myself in the mirror on the bathroom wall. I didn't quite recognize the person who stood there. I was dirty. My hair clung to my head. Dark circles like saucers lay beneath my eyes. I looked like a shell of my former self. How long had I been alone? Three or four days? A week? I couldn't recall.

Now as I crawled between the sheets, I was so tired. I couldn't remember ever being so tired. I was vaguely aware of time passing, the light moving across the wall of the room. Somewhere in the house, appliances whirred. It was a strange sleep, like on an airplane, when you are aware of everything around you, yet you are sleeping. I heard the sound of the dryer, clothes being tossed around. Somewhere a dog barked and I knew it was Betsy's dog.

When I woke again, it was dark and Jade was sitting in a chair beside me. She was staring at me in such a concerned way that I thought perhaps I was in a hospital until I heard the surf pounding below. "Mom," she said, "what's become of you?"

"I'm not really sure."

She put on the small light by the bed stand. It was just five in the morning, but she had me sit up. "When did you eat last?"

I shook my head. "I don't know, really. I was so tired."

Jade pulled the covers back and led me into the kitchen, where all the dishes had been washed, the counters wiped clean. She made me eat some soup that sat bubbling on the stove. Then Jade ran a hot bath with orange-scented bubbles. As the tub filled, I sat beside it. "Now, I'm going to help you take off your things." My daughter undressed me, dropping my pajamas into the hamper, helping me slip my panties off. When I stood naked in front of her, Jade took me by the arm, easing me into the tub. Then Jade sat at the side of the tub with a glass of ice water and a sponge.

The ice water she made me sip was so cold and the bath so hot. The blood coursed through my body again. As I lay there, I saw Jade go into my room, rip the sheets off the bed, bundle them up, put fresh ones on. I heard her fluffing pillows, shaking out comforters. Then she came back and knelt beside me. With a sponge she had me bend forward as she rubbed my back, my neck. She ran the sponge across my breasts, over my belly, down my thighs. She put shampoo on her hands, scrubbed my head. I was docile as a baby in her hands as my daughter made me sparkling clean.

"Now, let's get out of the bath," she said. I rose up naked, dripping wet, and Jade wrapped me in a towel, white and fluffy. The towel was warm and I knew she had just gotten it from the dryer. It felt so good to be wrapped in that warm towel. As I sat on the lid of the toilet, Jade combed and blew my hair dry. Then she helped me into fresh pajamas. "When did you have the time to do all this wash?"

"Betsy did it," Jade said.

"Betsy?" I asked.

"She cleaned your whole house, Mom."

When I was spruced up and dry, she put me back into the bed of fresh sheets and I slept again. When I woke, it was still dark and I was ravenous, ready for something to eat. Suddenly I wanted soup, a big pot of lentil soup, and I wanted to make it myself from scratch, never mind that it would take hours to cook. I had a good recipe somewhere in a drawer and I tiptoed into the kitchen to find it.

The kitchen floor was cold and I was barefoot as I stood rifling through the drawer where I kept all my recipes in a folder. I pulled out the folder and on top of it lay the envelope that contained the things Margaret gave me the last time I saw her. I took everything out, dumped it on the counter. Once again I gazed at the clipping of the man who had killed himself forty years before.

I stood in the breakfast nook staring at it, as I had several times before. Then for some reason I thought of the clipping of Margaret's death that I had taken from Vicky's copy of the *Winonah Weekly*. Digging into my errand bag, I found my wallet and inside was the article, still neatly folded where it had been since I put it there on the day of the funeral.

Now I was less hungry than I'd been. Forgetting my plans to make soup from scratch, I lay the two pieces of paper side by side. I looked from one clipping to the next. I knew that there was something in these two articles, written some forty years apart, some clue I'd over-looked. No names were the same, no details of the two suicides, yet I kept going from one article to the next.

It was a puzzle I was trying to solve and suddenly it became clear to me. I remember when the children had these activity books they did in the car—find the telephone in the tree, find the tiger in the closet. You scan the picture until you see, hidden in the intricate, leafy branches, the telephone, or in the clutter of an unkempt closet, a tiger. And of course once you've seen it you wonder what took you so long and you will always see it each time you look at that picture again.

I went over each detail in the two clippings. The places were different, as were the names. The years were different. Nothing appeared to be the same. There seemed to be no overlaps, but then I saw the dates of both deaths—October 12—and realized that Margaret had killed herself on the same day as this man, whose name I now noticed was Martin Burton. He had her initials and they had both died at the age of forty-nine. I sat thinking about what this meant.

I don't know why it had eluded me for so long, but at last I understood. The sun was rising as I gazed out across the Pacific, looking through my favorite grove of trees. Margaret wanted me to have this clipping. She knew I kept things. That was why she had given it to me.

It struck me with a clarity that stunned me and never would have occurred to me otherwise. She had planned it. She had planned it all along. And, the meaning of her note now made explicit, she had waited as long as she could. Margaret had known for years what she was going to do. And when and where.

I made my way back to bed, crawled into the sheets, and slept until late morning. When I woke the room was filled with light and Jade had a fresh pot of coffee brewing. She also had a pile of a week's worth of mail. Catalogs, junk, bills. On the machine, solicitations, messages from Shana, from Ted and Jade. I was tossing most of the mail away, but Jade retrieved the letter from the trash. Buried somewhere at the bottom of the pile of mail she found the letter from the National Registry of Historic Houses.

Jade opened the letter and informed me that my house had qualified, which meant I couldn't change the outside and that it had to have all the proper protections for historic houses under the law of the United States.

The first phone call I made with this news was to John Martelli. He was cool with me on the phone, but he said he'd look into the status of my policy, and a week later he wrote to say that all pertinent riders, including the act-of-God rider, had come through and that as a national monument my house, henceforth, would be fully insured.

"Thank you, John, thank you for all your help."

"It was my pleasure, Tess. I wanted to help you."

I hesitated, but then I said, "Perhaps you'd like to have coffee sometime?" It wasn't that I imagined anything would happen between me and John Martelli, but it seemed like a step back into the world.

"Yes," he said, "I'd like that."

I'd never expected they'd give it to me, but there it was. The premium was higher than I would have liked, but not beyond what I could afford, and I decided to open my bed-and-breakfast. I applied for a loan at the bank and, with Shana's underwriting, I got the money I needed to buy the fluffy green towels, the little bars of soap. I bought nightstands and fake little Tiffany lamps with green glass shades, cozy hassocks. I had the original poems of Francis Eagger, which Bruno had given me, framed. On the walls I hung photographs Francis Eagger had taken of the cliffs he loved so well.

In the library I made out a special place on the shelves for his work. I had a sign made that read THE EAGGER HOUSE BED-AND-BREAKFAST: GUESTS WELCOME. And a brochure printed up that Bruno helped me write:

Come stay in the home that the inspirational poet, Francis Cantwell Eagger, built stone by stone. Experience the house and read his poems. Walk the cliffs, enjoy the marine life below. Make this your weekend getaway or your stop as you head somewhere else.

Come walk with me and I will take you to the path we have carved for ourselves along the sea.—"Desire Paths"

Bruno, who understood now that this was the only way to keep my house, came and helped. I was surprised that he was good with his hands. He nailed up shelves, helped me repaper Jade's room. Jade was glum about all of this, but with a little work we fixed up the old woodshed and it became a perfect getaway room for her and she actually grew to like it. Ted helped convert the room over the garage into an extra bedroom and he said he'd live there when there were no guests.

Jade and Bruno would sit up late after a day spent working on the house. I'd hear their voices reading poems of the windswept shores, the rocky coasts, poems of trees and animals. Sometimes they'd whisper down below and I wondered what they were doing, but I stayed in my room. One night I heard Jade's door close and it did not open again.

In the morning Bruno was sitting at my spot in the breakfast nook, in his workshirt without his glasses, a sheepish grin on his face, poring over the morning paper. "Good morning, Tess," he said. "Would you like some coffee?"

Slipping into the breakfast nook, I said, "Yes, thank you, Bruno, I would."

In silence Bruno poured me a coffee. "How do you take it?"

"A little milk."

He poured a little milk for me. The coffee was strong but very good. A few moments later Jade came in, showered, her hair damp. She wore a baggy shirt, jeans, but there was a freshness to her face I hadn't seen in a long time. I wanted to reach out and hug her. They both looked hungry to me so I said, "Would you guys like me to scramble you some eggs?"

They nodded and I cracked into a bowl a half-dozen eggs, sprinkled in some cheese and herbs. Diced tomato and onion. I heated olive oil in the skillet and stir-fried the vegetables, poured in the eggs. I made a hearty omelette. I hadn't eaten an omelette like that in years. I watched them gobble it down, their intimacy barely hidden in their silence. "So why don't we all have dinner tonight?" I said. "Help me map out the future."

That night over dinner, Jade made the decision that she would bake for me. She found an interesting recipe for muffins with coconut and chocolate chips and cranberries that sounded terrible, but turned out quite delicious, and these we named Cantwell muffins; she baked scones and coffee cakes and we bought an espresso machine. The house was now filled with the smells of cooking and the sound of young people, but I was haunted by something I could not quite name.

I kept thinking Nick would call. That he would seek me out. How could he not want me when at last he could have me? Or perhaps that was just the point and I'd missed it all along. Perhaps that was what made him stay with Margaret all those years. The fact that he could not have her. No one could.

A few nights later I invited the children out to dinner. I felt there was a reason to celebrate, though I wasn't quite sure what it was. The end of something; the beginning of something else. We went to a trendy new place with lots of hanging plants and polyurethaned tables that was supposed to serve good burgers and vegetarian dishes. Bruno joined us and, just after we ordered, I noticed a family that came in.

They were a fairly large group, at least six or seven of them, and they were seated at the round table next to ours. They were rowdy, laughing, having a good time, but the odd part was I recognized them all. I knew them from somewhere. Even as we ordered and had our drinks, I couldn't help staring. I had seen them all somewhere before.

Even as the kids talked on and went up to the salad bar, I was still trying to decide who these people were. Were my kids friends with their kids? Had I rented them a house? Then I knew. I realized they were the other Winterstones. The family whose pictures I had inadvertently picked up when I went to get the photos of the reunion. I could still see the pictures of the empty room, the Formica table, the chairs, the open suitcase. Pictures of them moving into a simple apartment, laughing around a table with beers and Chinese food. And now here they were intact, eating dinner beside us, ordering hamburgers and onion rings.

I had to resist the urge to go up to them. To say, "I'm also a Winterstone. I'm the person who took your pictures once accidentally. I know something about you that you don't know. I know that you are happy; that you are whole."

But I didn't begrudge them a thing. Instead I joked with Ted about the company he was starting to form and listened as Bruno told Jade in detail about his discovery of the "Desire Paths" poem. As I sat there with Ted, Jade, and Bruno, his hand lightly resting on Jade's knee, surrounded by my children, I thought, This is my family, not the one I was born into, but they are what I have now. The family I have made.

42

It's an odd thing because I live so far away from where it all began and think there are a million things I could have done differently—we all could have done differently—and then maybe we could have saved somebody's life. But whose life would we have saved? That dour child who lives in a big house by the lake alone with her father now, or the child her mother once was who spun with me in the rain?

Or my father, who was a good storyteller and a charming man, but a liar all the same. I forgave him long ago. Or at least I've made my peace with him. I've come to pity Margaret because she waited all those years for a father who would never come. I wished she'd had another father; if only she hadn't wanted mine. I can still see him, dipping into those dark shadows under the railroad trestle and coming out into the sun. Then putting the radio on, singing out loud. His fingers tapping on the wheel.

I've stopped calling Nick. He doesn't return my calls. With time he might come around, but I'm not waiting. I'm going about my business. I'm going to open my B-and-B next season and the kids have agreed, all things being equal, it's probably the best thing. There'll be all kinds of people coming in and out, interesting people from other places. The place won't have this dank, empty feel much longer.

But then something frightens me and I'm not quite sure what it is. I feel it in the air around me. And then I know. I am afraid because Margaret could just show up again, right here. I think of how Margaret was always showing up at our houses, uninvited, searching for what she had lost long ago and would never replace. And though I know this is impossible, it feels as if I am expecting her.

Just the other day I rented the seashell house to a young couple from the Midwest who came highly recommended. They kept oohhing and aahhing and laughing over the accoutrements of the house—the mirror framed in cowrie shells, the shell-shaped sofa—and when I agreed with them that it was an eclectic place, they just started laughing again. Eclectic, they said, then started to laugh. Everything is funny when you are young and in love.

Afterward when I got home, things didn't seem quite where I'd left them. A sweater I hadn't remembered wearing was draped over a chair. A book I wasn't reading was off the shelf. But more than these small things (for Jade could easily go rummaging through my things), the house felt as if someone had been there.

I needed to be outside. I took my usual walk along the dunes, the Poet's Walk, I've come to call it (I've even made a little sign), the path he blazed with his grief, strolling among the ice plants, up and down the cliffs. I peered down at the hunchback tree that had inspired some of Francis Eagger's poems, still struggling to grow on the bluff it had slipped down, that same bluff that would eventually erode its way to my house. But hopefully that was years or decades from now.

I was glad to be outside, collecting pine cones and shells. The air was fresh and I roamed for a long time. The roar of the surf was soothing and I followed the paths along the cliffs. I found a red feather, which I kept. I wandered until the sun began to set. Then a chill came into the air as the wind from the ocean picked up. I was starting to shiver and I had no choice but to turn around and go home.

When I got back, it was just after dusk and I couldn't get warm. I sat up in an armchair in the living room near the hearth, though it had no fire. In a few months I'd rarely be alone in this house. Soon it would be filled with guests, strangers stopping on their way somewhere else. People with their own stories to tell about what has happened in their lives.

I was still cold so I grabbed the Winonah centennial blanket from the back of the chair and tossed it over my legs. The high school, "Home of the Winonah Wildcats," and the train station rested across my lap. Here I was, once more, ensconced in the past. It was time, I thought, to put it away. I took the blanket, folded it, placed it on the top of the linen closet.

Someday I would take it down again, but for now I tucked the blanket in the back of the closet and grabbed a plain down comforter—one that cats had slept on and children had napped in. I wrapped it around my legs until the chill was gone.

Acknowledgments

I want to thank Caroline Leavitt and Larry O'Connor for their excellent critical advice. I also want to thank Julie and Ruediger Flik and Sarah Lawrence College for travel grants that enabled me to do research in California and Illinois, and Mary Jane Roberts and Jerry Evans, who shared their home and their knowledge of California insurance law. I want to thank the friends of my youth for all we've shared, Ellen Levine and Diana Finch for their invaluable input and support, and my editor, Diane Higgins at Picador, for her focused attention. And my daughter, Kate, who traveled the road with me.